She was half woman, half child, and half wild, half tamed. The mystery of a man's body made her suspicious and wary of his touch, and he knew that he would have to curb his own impatient desire if he were to lure the passionate response from her that he wanted and that he knew she was capable of giving.

BURNING

"I fear you are deluding yourself, Captain," Rhea said, her voice shaking slightly with the onrush of confusing emotions she was experiencing, for he was standing so close that she could feel the rising heat of his body and see the pulse beating so strongly in his throat.

INESCAPABLE

"No, my dear, you are deluding yourself if you think that you have won this game, which you so foolishly started. You issued me a challenge, and now I am here to collect my winnings," he murmured as he slid his arms around her small waist.

Chance The Winds of Fortune

Laurie McBain

AVON
PUBLISHERS OF BARD, CAMELOT AND DISCUS BOOKS

CHANCE THE WINDS OF FORTUNE is an original publication of Avon Books. This work has never before appeared in book form.

AVON BOOKS
A division of
The Hearst Corporation
959 Eighth Avenue
New York, New York 10019

First Avon Printing, July, 1980

AVON TRADEMARK REG. U.S. PAT. OFF. AND IN
OTHER COUNTRIES, MARCA REGISTRADA, HECHO EN
U.S.A.

Printed in the U.S.A.

For my Mother and Father
with
love forevermore

*So my conscience chide me not, I am
ready for Fortune as she wills.*

Dante

West Indies—Spring, 1769

Chapter 1

SAILING out of the Serpent's Mouth, the narrow strait of water between the South American continent and Trinidad, the trade winds filled the square-rigged sails of the *Sea Dragon*. She was a Boston-built brigantine out of Charles Town,* in the Carolinas, and had seen action as an English privateer during the Seven Years' War. Many French merchantmen knew, to their misfortune, the figurehead of the grinning red dragon with the gilded tail and fins, whose lolling tongue seemed to mock their frantic efforts as the swiftly maneuvering brig bore down on their slower-moving cargo ships. Her intentions were never misunderstood as the first broadside fired from her guns ripped through rigging and sails, wreaking havoc and destruction in its wake. The *Sea Dragon*'s formidable reputation of seldom having failed to claim a captured ship or cargo as her prize had often preceded her, and

* Until the year 1783, Charleston, South Carolina, was known as Charles Town.

1

many a merchantman had struck her colors and surrendered without ever firing a return shot.

When the Treaty of Paris was signed by the major
European powers in 1763, the *Sea Dragon* had been left
to pursue a more private course of action, and, returning
to the warm waters of the Caribbean, she soon became an
enemy of her old ally. Now it was the British frigates and
sloops who faced the grinning dragon or, as happened
far too often for their peace of mind, watched her sails
disappear into some seemingly impenetrable mangrove
swamp, only to reappear weeks later docked innocently
in Charles Town. The *Sea Dragon* was a smuggler trading
in contraband; she slipped into secret coves along the
wild coasts of the Carolinas and unloaded her valuable
West Indian cargo of sugar and molasses there.

The *Sea Dragon* had sailed close to the wind many
times, but so far good fortune had steered her on a
smooth course away from what had always seemed, to
some of the more timorous hands on board, certain
destruction. She was sailing now, with the wind abeam,
through the murky waters of the Gulf of Paria, her sails
bellying out as they caught the easterly winds. She was
riding light, her hold half full as she began her return
voyage from her latest endeavor—a quest for sunken
treasure.

Standing on the quarterdeck, Dante Leighton, captain
and owner of the *Sea Dragon,* looked to starboard where
lay the Spanish island of Trinidad. Sparsely populated
since its cocoa plantations were abandoned years earlier,
thick evergreen forests now grew unrestrained up the
slopes of mountain ranges wreathed in wisps of cloud. On
this side of the island the low-lying coastline was clogged
with swampland and presented an inhospitable countenance to the sea-weary voyager. But on the windward
side there were stretches of narrow beach lined with
palms, where tropical rain forests crowded the slopes
above. It was there that the *Sea Dragon* had dropped
anchor, and her captain had gone ashore to search the
remains of an abandoned plantation house. In the overgrown ruins, which the jungle had reclaimed as her own,
Dante Leighton had cut a path into the inner structure

where once a courtyard had stood. With his dagger he'd pried loose a flat tile from the rough flooring and removed a rusty-hinged strongbox, its lock still intact. Back on board the *Sea Dragon* he'd knocked the padlock free and, with most of the crew crowding around, had opened it to disclose a small, neat pile of documents. Because his knowledge of Spanish was limited, Dante had inspected each document with careful thoroughness, without hurrying, despite the growing impatience of his men. But finally a loud cheer had gone up from the crew as he'd held up what was obviously a map, with the *X* clearly discernible to the treasure-hungry fortune hunters.

The *X* marked the spot of a sunken Spanish galleon, lost off the Florida Straits early in the eighteenth century. A convoy of heavily guarded merchant ships, loaded down with treasure chests full of gold and silver coins newly minted in Mexico City, had been bound for Madrid out of Havana when it had been hit by a hurricane and sunk. Any sailor who'd sailed for long in the West Indies had heard not only this particular tale of sunken Spanish treasure ships, but countless others as well. However, few, if indeed any, of these tall stories had ever resulted in the jingle of coins in anyone's pockets.

Dante Leighton had heard most of them, and had even given chase to a few of the myths floating around the Caribbean seas. Until now, though, he'd never really believed in them; never before had he felt a tingling of anticipation as he did now. Staring down at the treasure map held firmly in his grasp, he experienced the familiar stirrings of an old, but never forgotten dream.

Glancing to larboard, Dante watched the mountainous coastline of Venezuela slip by, as the *Sea Dragon* continued its starboard tack. Dante's gaze swung to the intricate rigging and towering masts above his head, where all hands aloft were busy trimming the sails as she came into the wind. The mainsails were drawing well as the *Sea Dragon* heeled slightly as she increased her speed.

"Come up a little, helmsman!" Dante ordered, his voice blending with the winds and flapping of canvas. "No nearer," Dante warned as he eyed the close-hauled sails. "Keep her so, Mr. Clarke."

"Captain, sir!" squeaked a high-pitched voice against the wind. "Here's your coffee, sir. Mister Kirby sent me up with it, sir," reported Conny Brady, the young cabin boy of not more than eleven years, as he tried to brace his legs and come to attention without spilling the captain's coffee.

"Thank you, Conny," Dante replied absentmindedly, his attention fixed between the *Sea Dragon*'s raking bowsprit, her stand of sail and the far distant promontory of land jutting out into their course. He took a swallow of the steaming coffee and smiled inwardly, for it was smooth and blacker than hell, the way no one but Houston Kirby, ship's steward and jack-of-all-trades, could brew it. Dante breathed deeply and tasted the salt spray thrown back at him by the wind. He felt at peace as the *Sea Dragon* rode the sea, her masts and yardarms creaking gently as the sails rapped fully and the deck canted alee.

"Captain, sir." It was Conny interrupting Dante's musings, daring to tug on the captain's sleeve as he tried impatiently to capture Captain Leighton's full attention. "Cap'n, sir, do you think we're really going to find sunken Spanish treasure? Longacres says each of our shares could be thousands of pieces of eight. We'll be richer'n King George himself. 'Tis true, isn't it, Cap'n, sir?" Conny pleaded hopefully, his large blue eyes beneath a recalcitrant curl of coal-black hair appearing far too innocent for the life he'd experienced at sea since signing aboard a slaver at the age of seven. He'd been a member of the *Sea Dragon*'s crew for three years now, and Dante had never failed to be amazed at the boy's understanding of the many moods of the sea. Nor had he kept himself from disapproving of Conny's knowledge of the sailor's way of life—especially while in port.

"I wish you would answer the boy, Captain. I'd be quite relieved myself to know that my pockets are going to be bulging with Spanish doubloons. 'Twould set my mind at rest, not to mention my creditors'," Alastair Marlowe, the supercargo aboard the *Sea Dragon*, commented dryly. Although he could have addressed the captain by his given name, he always chose to show him the respect he deserved as the master of a ship.

Dante Leighton glanced first at his round-eyed cabin boy and then at the supercargo, speculating with amusement about what other tall tales that old pirate Longacres, the ship's coxswain, had been spinning since they'd set sail with the treasure map.

"He is rather infamous for some of his more bloodthirsty yarns of piracy on the high seas," Alastair added with a slight grin, as he correctly interpreted his captain's thoughts and look of irritation. "Sometimes I think even I believe him," he admitted, causing Dante to raise a disbelieving eyebrow.

"You are one of the most level-headed men I know. That is why you happen to be the *Sea Dragon's* supercargo," Dante told him bluntly, eyeing the younger man who had, amongst the crew, a reputation for being far too serious and honest for his own good. Dante knew he hadn't even seen twenty and ten years yet, but at times he seemed a far wiser and older man. He was a quiet man, seldom sharing his innermost thoughts with others, but Dante knew that when the mood took him he could mimic any seaman on board with devastating skill, not to mention dignitaries and members of royalty, none of whom could stand up well to his brand of lampooning.

"I doubt whether you have ever been in debt, Alastair," Dante commented now as he sized up his supercargo, whose circumspect behavior gave him the benefit of any doubt.

Alastair smiled a trifle crookedly, looking slightly ashamed of what he was about to admit. "Well, I did, at one time, rather fancy myself a town toff. I associated with a disreputable bunch of young gentlemen in London, and I'm sure my family despaired of me ever turning respectable," he said. "I suppose they weren't at all grieved to have me sign on with you. Of course, if they could see me now," he added with a chuckle, shaking his head, "they would disown me completely, for they are quite proper folk."

Dante stared hard at his supercargo, thinking him, as always, uncommonly modest. If he did indeed have a vice, it was selling himself short, for he was not a man caught boasting of his own merit. And, if there were ever a man who Dante knew he could trust with his life, it was Alastair Marlowe.

Under this close scrutiny Alastair Marlowe began to feel uncomfortable. He wondered what Dante Leighton was thinking. Alastair ran an impatient hand through his sun-streaked, light brown curls, for although he'd known Dante Leighton for close to nine years, he was no nearer today to understanding the man than he had been that first day when Dante had rescued him from a very determined press gang. Even an English gentleman, which was what he'd thought himself to be long ago in 1761, had not been exempt from the long reach of the Royal Navy when it had been ordered to fill its ships with able-bodied men—whether willing or not. And *he* certainly had not been willing. Alastair could still feel the bos'n's cudgel catching him on his head, sending him crashing to his knees in the gutter, his fine silk stockings torn and his satin breeches stained with stinking mud. He could still remember his surprised panic as he'd struggled to his feet, weaving like a drunken sailor and clutching his aching head, only to find himself jerked back by a powerfully muscled forearm. He heard the cruel laughter of the press gang spinning around him as he'd been herded down the narrow, cobbled back streets of Portsmouth like a lamb being led to slaughter.

He wondered if he would be alive today if the *Sea Dragon* hadn't happened to dock in Portsmouth that very day, and if Dante Leighton hadn't loomed up before the startled press gang like the devil himself. Already blurred of vision from the blow he'd sustained, Alastair could remember blinking his eyes rapidly as he'd tried to focus on the tall figure barring their path. Under a flickering torch, held by one of the sailors, Dante's dark, caped figure had seemed almost supernatural, especially when a light drizzle began to fall and the torch started to sputter and the smoke swirled eerily around them. In Alastair's confused mind the ensuing events seemed like a scene out of Hades, with the flashing of swords and the loud explosion of a pistol shot, the smell of sulfur lingering even after the smoke had cleared. Out of Dante Leighton's wavering shadow a slight figure had emerged with a pistol primed and ready in his left hand. This apparition had been Houston Kirby, a strange little man Alastair would soon come to know.

"Well, gents?" Dante Leighton's deep, amused voice had questioned the press gang, who were now grumbling more to themselves than to the menacing, caped figure confronting them. "What's it to be? Is your captain to be one man short," he'd asked, first indicating a wide-eyed Alastair, then continuing with a nasty-looking smile, "or is he never to see his bos'n's mate and swabbers again?"

Alastair, to this day, had never forgotten the ugly glint in the eyes of the press gang's leader as he'd swung his cudgel in a harmless arc before him. "Juz doin' our duty, sir. Reckon this time ye've scuppered us but good, *m'lord.*" His manner of addressing Dante Leighton was contemptuous, but he little knew how accurate his description had been.

Then, mockingly doffing his cap, he'd signaled for the release of the prisoner. Now Alastair could smile at the haste with which his order was carried out, and how he had been thus deprived of the privilege of venting his anger and outrage at His Majesty's Navy. As he'd stood there swaying, the rain dripping down his face, he'd finally met the pale gray eyes of his rescuer, but instead of feeling reassured, the expression in their luminous depths had sent an uncontrollable shiver of premonition through him. There was a wildness in the dark-lashed eyes, a lawless quality that had made him wish to be back on his family's estate outside of Portsmouth. There, as an untitled, younger son, unlikely to inherit either estate or title, all he'd had to worry about was whether or not he should buy a commission in the cavalry or join the ministry. Either choice would have been acceptable to his family. He knew that as long as they no longer had to foot the bills, they cared naught what happened to him.

That was all he remembered of his first meeting with Dante Leighton, for the next moment he'd fainted, something he'd never done since. Then he'd awakened on board the *Sea Dragon,* the gentle rocking lulling him into a false sense of security until he'd realized where he was. But his fears had been groundless, for a gruff but solic-

itous Houston Kirby had dressed his head, fed him full of
steaming broth, helped him dress in clean breeches and
coat, and then admonished him against trying to move
around until he'd found his sea legs. The steward's
bossy familiarity had reminded Alastair of the older,
much trusted servants who'd been with his family since
before he'd been born.

"B-but where am I?" Alastair remembered demanding
with false bravado. "W-what's going to happen to me?
W-where is that man who rescued me?" He still cringed
with embarrassment as he recalled how he'd stammered
his fears.

The small steward had stopped his work and answered
him patiently. "Now you listen to me, young sir. You've
no need to fear the captain or anyone on board the *Sea
Dragon,* unless you go prying into things you shouldn't.
Captain Leighton don't like to be disappointed in a person," Houston Kirby had warned him. "His lordship
didn't need to take the responsibility of you. Could've
left you staggering around Portsmouth for another press
gang to snatch."

"His lordship? *He's* a titled gentleman?" Alastair could
still remember his surprise as he'd voiced his disbelief.
For the man who'd held up the press gang had been no
pampered gentleman of leisure.

"Aye, that he is, and don't you be doubtin' it, young
sir," was Houston Kirby's short reply to Alastair's comments. "Although there do be some who question the
gentleman part," Kirby had continued, his tone of voice
leaving little doubt what his opinion of his captain's detractors was. "But the captain ain't one for standing on
much ceremony, exceptin' when it comes to sailing his
ship; then he's the captain, and no one else. You do as
he says, and you'll be all right."

Alastair had taken heed of Houston Kirby's advice and
had never regretted the results. After close to an hour of
conversation with the enigmatic man called Dante Leighton, during which time he felt as if he'd bared his soul to
him, he had been asked to join the crew of the *Sea
Dragon.* Alastair still swore to this day that there had
been a twinkle in the captain's eye when he'd asked if

Alastair had ever thought about going to sea—voluntarily, of course—and then said that since the *Sea Dragon* was undermanned they could use a good hand. With the enticement the conversation had been concluded, leaving Alastair's aching head spinning with more than just the cudgel's bite. This condition was not lessened when the captain casually informed him that the *Sea Dragon* would be under sail by the end of the week. It had been no easy decision to make, and Alastair could still feel the sadness of standing on the quarterdeck and watching the familiar shores of England fade as the heavily armed brig caught the offshore breeze and sailed out into the English Channel toward what he'd thought at the time was an uncertain future. But then, *at that time,* he hadn't known Dante Leighton very well.

Now Alastair felt an insistent tugging on his sleeve and glanced down, blinking his eyes to clear them of the past as he stared into Conny Brady's young face. The cabin boy's eyes were as wide and blue as the sea. "Yes?" Alastair inquired, momentarily confused by the penetrating heat of the West Indian sun beating down on him instead of the cold drizzle of that winter's rain eight years ago in Portsmouth.

"The cap'n says for you to tell me, Mr. Marlowe, about how he found that treasure map," Conny repeated slowly, as if explaining to some dull-witted stowaway. "You know, Mr. Marlowe, sir, the clue to the map."

Alastair flushed slightly, wondering if the captain had been aware of his temporary lack of attention. " 'Twas in a card game on St. Eustatius. There was the captain, the Dutchman, I think," Alastair said, trying to remember the faces around the green baize table that night. "Bertie Mackay was there, I know that for certain, and a planter gent out of Barbados. But 'twas from the Danish slaver that the captain won the document. The captain had been having a good run of luck, and the Dane hadn't; and so the Dane hands this yellowed piece of parchment across the table to the captain."

"That was to cover his bet, Mr. Marlowe?" Conny interrupted, bright eyes aglow with the thought of the captain sitting at the card table with a winning hand.

"Aye, although 'tisn't looked upon with much favor anymore," Alastair continued dryly. "Too many forged treasure maps have been palmed off on too many gentlemen for them to take kindly to being hoodwinked. But to the other players' surprise, the captain, after looking it over, agrees to accept the paper in payment if he wins, which he did," Alastair concluded, as if there never had been any question that the captain would not.

"What was written on the parchment, Mr. Marlowe?" Conny demanded and waited breathlessly for the super-cargo's answer.

" 'Twas the last will and testament of some old Spanish foretopman. He'd been a member of the crew on one of those galleons that sunk in that hurricane off the straits. He managed to survive somehow when his ship went down. In fact, he was one of the only survivors, and he saw it as some kind of portent against returning to Spain, and his first wife and family. So he deserts the fleet and stays here in the Indies."

"And?" Conny said, hurrying Alastair along.

"And since he remembered where the galleon had gone down, he decided to put some of that gold to good use, and over the years he looted it. Had himself a private, undersea treasury to plunder for over a quarter of a century. But, like most guilty folk, he found his conscience when on his death bed and wanted forgiveness for his sins. Bared his soul, as well as the location of that strong-box with the map of the sunken treasure ship inside."

"Coooee! What a blackguard he was." Conny whistled between his teeth. "You think he found the gold under the bones of his old mates?" he asked, his mind lingering on the more gruesome aspects of the story. "But, Mr. Marlowe, sir, if this other cap'n had it, then how come our cap'n found the map? Wouldn't the slaver have found it first?"

"From what the captain said," Alastair explained, to set at rest young Conny's anxieties, "the Danish captain had just come across this will. The Spaniard was his wife's late father, and she'd kept the will hidden for many a year because of the disgrace of her father's perfidy, as well as the humiliating discovery of her own illegitimacy.

Over the years the Spaniard had become quite a respectable planter, and the daughter didn't want to sully the family's good name, or her own."

Conny frowned thoughtfully. "Why would the Danish captain risk losin' such a thing, Mr. Marlowe?" he asked, bewildered at such an incredible occurrence. "I'd sure have locked it up tight."

"When you've got the fever in a card game, you never think you're going to lose," Alastair explained. "Besides, maybe the Dane thought it was just another fool's dream. He probably thinks the captain's the bigger fool for accepting it. He won't give it a second thought, Conny," Alastair reassured him. "Those slavers always seem to have well-lined purses. He's making his fortune that way."

"They're not very nice ships, Mr. Marlowe," Conny said quietly, his blue eyes shadowed as he remembered his voyage on a slaver off the coast of Africa. "Them slavers are real bad people, Mr. Marlowe. Real bad," he muttered as if he were hearing the echoes of chained slaves groaning as they died below decks.

"I know, Conny," Alastair said awkwardly, knowing there was nothing he could say to help this boy, who had seen things far beyond his own experiences. "Sure hope that Spaniard didn't have too expensive tastes," he said now with an exaggerated look of concern. "I'd like to think he left some of them Spanish doubloons for us to be spendin'!"

"Aye, Mr. Marlowe," Conny agreed readily, his face lightening at the thought of that sunken treasure. " 'Tis ours now."

Alastair glanced over to where Dante Leighton was leaning negligently against the taffrail, his thoughts known only to himself as he stared toward the east, his gray eyes narrowed against the blinding glare on the water. Alastair didn't think the captain had changed much over the years, at least not physically, for his dark, chestnut hair was streaked by the sun, not by age, and he could still wear the same size breeches he had worn nine years ago. He was a remarkably handsome man, his features classical in their near perfection, yet there was an underlying strength and hardness to the deeply tanned face that

11

gave it its look of character. Dante Leighton was the type of man the ladies always found fascinating and irresistible, Alastair thought with a good-natured sigh. His own features were, he had to confess, unremarkable and, if truth be admitted, downright plain.

Alastair followed the captain's gaze, wondering what he was seeing beyond the brilliant blues and greens of the Caribbean sky and sea. Dante Leighton was a driven man, and Alastair knew that until the captain settled an old score and laid to rest the pale ghost who haunted him, he would never find peace. Even when he'd been rowed back to the *Sea Dragon,* the successfully retrieved strongbox held firmly on his lap, the captain's face had mirrored no excitement or pleasure at the find. There'd been only that same grim determination that was always there. Over the years Alastair had gleaned something of Dante Leighton's past, and knew what manner of man he was, so he suspected he knew what the captain would do with his share of the treasure. And it would take a king's fortune to put right the wrong done to the captain, and it would take that much as well to save Dante Leighton from the gallows if he carried out his revenge.

Alastair sighed, wondering what troubles awaited them with the recovery of this treasure. He smiled slightly as he gave in to the sweet seductiveness of his own daydreams. The bright scarlet and orange colors of the West Indian sunset faded and were replaced by the pale gray skies of an overcast English afternoon, cold rain dripping from the bare branches of an old oak, and in the distance . . . Alastair shook his head, clearing it of such foolishness, for they had yet even to find this treasure ship, and here he was already spending his share, as well as drumming up trouble for Dante Leighton.

No, the first duty of the day was to keep the winds filling the sails of the *Sea Dragon.* Once they reached the Florida Straits they would decide about the treasure, allowing, of course, that they sighted no Union Jacks fluttering at the jackstaffs of His Majesty's ships—as well as any other sea vermin. His Majesty's Navy had got real nasty of late, Alastair muttered, harboring no fond memories of the Royal Navy. A worried frown creased his brow at the thought of the increasing numbers of British men-of-war now patrolling the coasts, zealously enforcing the Acts of Trade. It seemed to him that the *Sea Dragon* hardly would have docked, the bow-fast not yet secured, before there would be some officious customs officer on board, prowling about from stem to stern, making a nuisance of himself until the memory of the unpleasant odor of burning tar sent him scuttling back to the safety of the customhouse. Not that the *Sea Dragon* had ever been caught with a hold full of contraband, thought Alastair, proud of her untarnished record. And even had the unforgiveable happened, and she'd had her cargo seized, the *Sea Dragon* had powerful friends in the Admiralty Court.

Squinting his eyes against the sun, Alastair scanned the far distant horizon, fervently hoping that they wouldn't sight another sail until safely docked in Charles Town. He particularly did not care to see H.M.S. *Portcullis,* an eighteen-gun sloop, under the command of Captain Sir Morgan Lloyd. It seemed to Alastair that the Welshman was always there, lying in wait to catch the *Sea Dragon* with her hold full of contraband. Aye, but that was wishful thinking on Captain Morgan Lloyd's part, Alastair thought with a smile of grim satisfaction, for the *Sea Dragon* had out-maneuvered and out-sailed H.M.S. *Portcullis* on too many occasions for it to sit easily in the Welshman's belly. And yet, despite their being on different sides of the law, there seemed to be no true enmity between the two captains. Apparently, they shared a mutual respect for each other's abilities and indeed carried on as if it were all a chess game, with their respective ships serving as queens. If he hadn't known Dante Leighton better, then he'd have said that the crew of the *Sea Dragon* was just a pawn in the game, but he knew the captain cared about his men and his ship. He still had much the same crew he'd had eight years ago. They had acquired a few new hands over the years, but most were the same faces that had been on board the *Sea Dragon* when he'd first set foot on her decks. There was Longacres, the coxswain, full of pirate tales and sea

lore; Cobbs, the bos'n, Norfolk born and bred; Mac-
Donald, the Scots sailmaker, who sported a curling blond
moustache and wielded his clay pipe as if it were a deadly
claymore; Trevelawny, the dour-faced Cornish carpenter,
who knew every plank, timber and beam in the *Sea
Dragon*'s hull; Clarke, the quartermaster and self-styled
dandy out of Antigua; and Seumus Fitzsimmons, the first
mate, who was a Boston-born colonial with revolutionary
sympathies and an Irishman's way of making eloquent,
inflammatory remarks. Alastair smiled as he thought of
Houston Kirby, who never left his captain's side; Conny
Brady, the cabin boy, who would most likely make a fine
captain himself one day; and Jamaica, the ship's cat, the
half-starved tom the captain had rescued in Port Royal
over five years ago.

No, the *Sea Dragon* was manned by a good crew, and
if Captain Sir Morgan Lloyd was determined on crossing
bows with her, then he would be sailing into more than
he could handle. Alastair could promise him that. And if
it ever came to trading broadsides with H.M.S. *Portcullis,* the Welshman could count on seeing the bottom.

Well, no sense in borrowing trouble, Alastair decided,
turning his thoughts to the more pressing matter of how
to put an end to the growling of his stomach when dinner
was still over an hour away. He shielded his eyes as he
watched the descent of the crimson sun burning its way
into the west. His eyes caught a flash of movement in the
darkening sky as a flock of scarlet ibises flew southward
seeking a landfall for the night. Their wide span of wing
caught the flame of sunset and caused Alastair a breathless moment when the sky looked as if it were igniting on
wings of fire. Streaks of scarlet slashed across the pur-
pling skies as the sun, in all its glory, sank into the sea,
leaving an almost awesome serenity in its wake. But
Alastair knew not to be deceived, for in the east there
was a thunderstorm brewing, the fall of darkness blending
with the blackness of its roiling insides. Aye, they were in
for some foul weather, he thought, grimacing unconsciously as he felt the freshening winds.

Alec MacDonald sucked in his cheeks again and again
as he struggled against the wind to get his pipe to draw.

Finally, when a thin trail of aromatic smoke floated up from the tobacco-filled bowl, MacDonald leaned against the foremast, his eyes trained aloft as he proudly surveyed his sails, every inch of the mended and patched canvas having at one time or another gone through his calloused hands.

"The cap'n has a gentle hand on the wheel," Cobbs commented, glancing aft to the quarterdeck, where Dante Leighton had taken over the helm. "Likes having her in his hands. Like a fine woman, she is. You can't beat that, a woman and a ship. They be the finest sights to a man's eyes, but both can bring a man to his knees."

"Aye, lad, ye've got to give both plenty o' respect," MacDonald agreed.

"To be sure, I was thinking that fancy widow in Charles Town was going to be catching the cap'n last time we was in port," Seumus Fitzsimmons said. He was mending a pair of rather well-worn breeches, his long, sloppy stitches causing Alec MacDonald to raise his bushy eyebrows in growing dismay as he imagined those stitches coming loose at an inopportune moment.

"That widow in question, Fitzsimmons," interjected Barnaby Clarke, joining his mates on the forecastle, the captain having relieved him from the helm, "happens to be a very genteel young woman and should be addressed with proper respect. 'Tis a pity she was widowed so young."

"Speakin' of showing proper respect, mate, tha's no way to speak to the first mate," reprimanded Cobbs. Clarke's fancy gent ways had never set too well with him anyway.

"Very well, *Mr.* Cobbs," Clarke responded, bowing deeply to the assembled hands, who chuckled. "I think *Mr.* Fitzsimmons should show the proper respect due the lady."

"And, to be sure," Seumus Fitzsimmons responded easily, "I am showing her all the respect she's deservin'. Heard tell she broke the captain's heart. Made him the laughing stock of Charles Town, she did. Reckon she got to thinkin' herself too fine for the likes of our captain. Reckon her be too good for the smuggler who puts

15

fancy brandy on her table. Hear she high-tailed it to London for a season of hunting." Seumus grinned. "Hear she was looking for a titled gentleman. Reckon 'tis sometimes better to do your looking closer to home, eh, mates?"

"Figure the cap'n's weathering it well enough. Perhaps he's better off'n you think," contributed the close-mouthed Trevelawny.

"Reckon she might start looking the cap'n's way fast enough when he's got that treasure fillin' his purse," Cobbs said, spitting a stream of brown tobacco juice over the bulwark. "Hope she don't come back empty-handed from her scalp-huntin' trip to London. The cap'n'll be in real danger then."

"What makes you think that?" Grimes, a seaman who worked the yards and masts, asked curiously, for Cobbs' words had been full of meaning.

"Something I heard said when Mr. Kirby was in his cups. Got a tongue runnin' on wheels. 'Tis amazing the things that little fellow knows," Cobbs said with a wide grin. "Could be, if that fancy widow don't get the cap'n, she might set her sails after Mr. Kirby, or, devil take her, one o' us!"

"Ye really thinks we'll be findin' treasure?" Sampson, another topman, inquired hesitantly. " 'Twouldn't hurt none to be rich. Could have three sheets in the wind every night if I wants. Ye thinks this Cap'n Leighton'll be sharin' fairly wi' us?"

"Reckon we'll not keel haul ye this time, matie, seein' how ye ain't been with the cap'n of the *Sea Dragon* long enough to be knowin' better," Longacres warned him, while several "ayes" sounded threateningly behind him.

"Here now, mates. I meant no disrespect to the cap'n," Sampson quickly apologized, noticing the expressions on the faces of the loyal crew of the *Sea Dragon*. "I was just wonderin', fer sure, mates."

"Aye, well it'd better have been just that, and now that we've set yer mind at rest, I'll not want to be hearin' anything more about it," Longacres said grudgingly, his big fingers moving deftly and delicately on the fragile piece of ivory he was carving.

16

" 'Cause we happen to be on the subject," Cobbs began importantly, then winked at Conny Brady, who was curled up at Longacres' feet, "I'm wonderin' what ya going to do with your share, ya old pirate?"

"Got meself some plans," Longacres admitted. "Maybe open up a tavern in St. Thomas, now that 'tis a freeport I'd be gettin' plenty of trade. And what about yeself?"

A wide grin split Cobbs' face. "I always fancied meself as Squire Cobbs, country gentleman, that I have."

"To be sure, Cobbs, they'll be callin' ye Squire *Nabobs*," Seumus Fitzsimmons chortled. "And if given a free hand in the designing of yer countryseat, 'twill most likely be called Cobbs' Folly."

Cobbs grinned appreciatively as he was engulfed by laughter. "And what will yew be doin' with yours, Mr. Fitzsimmons? Buying yeself the Blarney stone?"

Seumus Fitzsimmons returned his barb with a mocking glance. "No," he replied. Then for once he turned serious. "I'll be purchasin' meself a schooner, and outfittin' her as a privateer. I've got a feeling that it'll be coming to a raisin' of arms soon, what with them damned redcoats being sent over from the *mother* country, and, I might be addin', causing nothing but trouble."

"Here now, watch that tone of voice," someone growled. "I don't have much love for them redcoats, but I'll not 'ear nothin' bad said about England."

Alec MacDonald sent a cloud of bluish smoke over the group. "Aye, though, 'tis the truth, that. There's war coming. Reckon ye'll be needin' a good sailmaker tae make your sails strong, Mr. Fitzsimmons. Been thinkin' of late, I have, of opening myself a shipyard along the Chesapeake Bay. Thinkin' there'll be a need for good ships soon. Nothing in the Highlands for me since I fled after the '45," he said, his light blue eyes darkening with remembered anguish. "Aye, Culloden finished it for us. My home is in the colonies now."

Conny Brady stared with open-mouthed amazement at his fellow shipmates. "You'd abandon the cap'n?" he exclaimed. "Who'll man the *Sea Dragon?*"

"Well now, if I'm not mistaken," Seumus Fitzsimmons said thoughtfully, his dark eyes twinkling, "and I'm remembering me legends proper like, lad. Then, it seems to me that dragons have always had a soft spot for gold, and I'm thinkin' the *Sea Dragon* and her captain might be finding a safe harbor to be anchoring in with that treasure. Besides," the Irishman continued, "the cap'n's no colonial. He's a blue-blooded gentleman if there ever was one, not that I'm holdin' that against him," he added quickly. "He's a fine man. As good as any Irishman I'd care to be liftin' a glass with, but he *is* a gentleman born and bred, and despite his dislike of King George's edicts, I'm not seeing the cap'n raisin' arms against him. From what little Kirby has let slip, I'm thinkin' the cap'n has more titles to his name than captain."

"Aye, yer right there, but he's got more on his mind than that. Strange, a man like 'e bein' out here. Maybe with his fortune found 'e'll go home and settle his affairs," stated Trevelawny, to everyone's amazement, for the carpenter seldom offered an opinion.

"Could be. How about yeself, Trevelawny? Goin' home?" Fitzsimmons asked.

"Aye, I'm a Cornishman. I'll be with the *Sea Dragon* when she heads home. I'll be with the cap'n until he needs me no more. Got a brother workin' a copper mine near Truro. Might just invest in it."

"Well, to be sure, we've all got our shares invested in somethin'," Seumus Fitzsimmons said with a comical look toward the darkening skies. "Now let's just hope we can be findin' this treasure, and that storm coming ain't a warnin' to us to be leaving well enough alone, and the dead in peace."

"D'ye think the sunken treasure ship is haunted?" Conny Brady demanded, his eyes widening with fearful excitement.

"Aye, and they be after *your* blood, young Conny," one of the mates growled, "unless ye get yeself below. Mr. Kirby wants ye to help him with the cap'n's meal. So get!"

Conny Brady scrambled below, leaving the other hands to enjoy the last few peaceful minutes of the sunset while they smoked their pipes, did their mending chores and gossiped. Soon the new watch would be set, and with the oncoming storm now a certainty—a flash of lightning sliced through the black belly of a thundercloud looming to starboard—they knew it was just a matter of time before they would be swarming over the rigging and up the masts to furl the royals and top-gallant sails, reef the topsails and batten down the hatches before the deluge.

The blackness of night had fallen with a vengeance, cloaking the *Sea Dragon* in its shroud. Below decks, Dante Leighton, anticipating the lee lurch of the *Sea Dragon* as she rode the heavy seas, grasped his goblet of wine before it could tumble from the table. The worst of the storm had passed, but the sea was still rough as the snug brig slammed into a wall of water. A pale, flickering light gleamed against the rich mahogany paneling of the captain's cabin, the lantern's glow creating an island of warmth against the stormy darkness surrounding the *Sea Dragon*, whose bow was now pitching into the trough of a wave.

"Captain, ye've hardly touched that nice breast of chicken I sautéed especially for ye," Houston Kirby berated him as he began clearing the dishes from the captain's table. "Now look at Mister Marlowe's here, he cleaned his plate nearly through to the table top, that he did. Nicely brought up young gentleman he is. Always thought he was, ever since I laid me eyes on him. And despite what he's learned at your side, beggin' your pardon, m'lord, he still is a well-mannered gentleman," Kirby continued, barely pausing for breath. "Still thanks me proper for my trouble, even now as he was hurryin' topside. Don't suppose he's seasick, d'ye? Still suffers from that, he does." The steward sniffed as he scraped the contents of the captain's plate into a chipped china saucer. "Reckon ye purposely saved your share for him," he grumbled with a derisive snort as he glanced over at the orange and white tabby, who was lazily stretching on the captain's berth.

After giving his whiskers an efficient wash, the cat sniffed appreciatively, hopped silently off the berth, and unhurriedly made his way to the captain's table. There, he settled himself beside the captain's chair and watched unblinkingly, with celery-colored green eyes, the little steward's every move.

"Do hope 'tis cooked to your highness's taste," Houston Kirby said with sarcastic sweetness, his sandy brows hiked up to within a quarter of an inch of his hairline. "Looks like he's always ready for a meal. Never missed one yet, he hasn't," muttered Kirby beneath his breath, continuing the feud that had become an everyday ritual between himself and the big tomcat. Houston Kirby placed the saucer before the cat, whose white, furred chest looked as if a large, linen napkin had been tied around his neck in preparation for his meal.

Dante leaned back in his chair, holding the silver goblet of wine carelessly while he watched the two antagonists sparring with each other. "Well, what do you think?" he demanded suddenly.

His steward glanced up, the wet rag he'd been using to wash the table now dripping water onto his rolled-up sleeve. "Reckon he likes it well enough. Licked it clean, he did," he replied, eyeing the cat's empty plate.

Dante grinned and rubbed the soft fur of the cat, who was now curled up on his lap. "I was not speaking about Jamaica, or how much he enjoyed his dinner. You know what I'm asking," he continued relentlessly, despite the steward's obvious reluctance to answer his query. "Do you think we shall find treasure this time?"

Houston Kirby gave a final swish with the damp rag, then straightened up. "Maybe. Maybe not," he allowed finally, a frown of concentration on his face while he busied himself with stacking the tray.

"You don't sound overly enthusiastic about the prospect. You do realize what it might mean?" Dante asked softly, his gray eyes glowing strangely in the candlelight.

"Aye, m'lord," Kirby replied evenly, "I do realize what it will mean."

Dante smiled thoughtfully at this tactful reply. "Do you not trust me, Kirby?"

"I know ye well enough, m'lord," Kirby said, looking directly into the captain's eyes. "Aye, that's the problem. I know ye only too well. And don't ye be forgetting, m'lord, that I helped ye into your first pair of breeches.

Aye, I know ye well, cap'n. I know what ye're planning, m'lord, and it has me grievously worried, that it does."

"Now, Kirby, you know that I am a man of discretion. I am well used to biding my time," Dante answered, a grim tightness around his lips. "I shall be subtlety personified."

Houston Kirby cast the captain a doubtful glance. "Aye, ye might at that, *until* ye set eyes on the bastard's face. Then I'd not care to be in his shoes."

"Tch, tch, Kirby," Dante sighed, making light of the steward's doubts. "I must say I am disappointed in your lack of faith in me."

"And I'm afeared I'm not going to be disappointed by your actions," Kirby muttered as he stomped from the cabin, Dante's amused laughter following him even after he'd closed the door with exaggerated care.

"I think we shall not be disappointed this time, Jamaica, old boy," Dante whispered into the sleeping cat's ear. "This time we shall find our treasure."

Dante Leighton, captain of the *Sea Dragon* and Marquis of Jacqobi, smiled unpleasantly as he let his thoughts travel further. "Yes, you have reason not to trust me, Kirby," he told the empty room as he continued smoothing the cat's striped fur with a firm, yet at that moment, gentle hand.

A little over a week later the *Sea Dragon* was rounding Cape San Antonio, the prevailing winds carrying her along as she caught the Gulf Stream and the coast of Cuba fell astern. Dante Leighton was standing, legs braced slightly apart, on the lee side of the deck, his spyglass trained on the horizon as he swung it slowly in an arch from fore to aft. He knew he was the center of the crew's curious speculation, for only a crazed man, if given a choice, would dare to challenge the Florida Straits with nightfall closing around his ship and the treacherous passage hemmed in by reefs and sand banks.

"Captain, 'tis dangerous, this course you are about," Alastair said quietly as he moved up beside the captain.

Dante lowered the glass. "Aye, Mr. Marlowe, but you've got to take chances if you are to win."

"If you'll pardon my indiscretion, Captain," Alastair continued, "what urgent need is there to risk the reefs at night? The way the winds come up out of nowhere, we could easily run aground."

"Believe me, Alastair, the need is there," Dante replied, not in the least offended by his supercargo's questioning. "I suspect the lookout will spy a sail aft any moment now," he informed the startled Alastair, who spun around quickly and strained his narrowed eyes into the falling twilight.

"A sail? Where? I don't see one."

"Sail ho!" the lookout cried from aloft.

"Good God, how the devil did you know even before the lookout saw it?" Alastair exclaimed. "Can you make her?" he asked, standing by helplessly while Dante stared through the spyglass.

"She's no British ship-of-the-line," Dante replied. "But then I didn't expect her to be."

"She's maneuverin', Cap'n! Crowding on!" the lookout called as he watched the pursuing ship set all of her sails.

" 'Tis the *Annie Jeanne,*" Alec MacDonald said, as he came to stand beside the captain on the poop deck. "I recognize her rigging and sails. And the tartan flag as well."

"Bertie Mackay?" Alastair expostulated. "What the devil's he doin' out here? He was in St. Eustatius when we were. He said he had a cargo he had to deliver to Charles Town. I wonder what happened to it, 'cause unless he had wings, there is no way he could have made it there and back in this short time." Alastair was reasoning aloud, thinking of the portly captain of the *Annie Jeanne,* who happened to be one of the best smugglers in the Carolinas. Cuthbert 'Bertie' Mackay, who had a crew of cutthroats even a pirate would think twice about taking on board.

"The Cap'n's got mighty fine eyesight," MacDonald said casually. "I don't imagine the lookout would hae seen the sails unless he'd been told to look for them in that direction."

Dante smiled and glanced over at the shrewd Scotsman. "Right you are, Mr. MacDonald. I suspect that Bertie Mackay has been riding in our wake since St. Eustatius. I first caught sight of him two nights ago. I'd come up on deck during the graveyard watch, and was quite surprised to find someone signaling the *Sea Dragon*. However, I was even more surprised to find the *Sea Dragon* answering."

"Good God! A spy on board the *Sea Dragon*?" Alastair blurted, unable to contain his shocked dismay. "Who the devil is it?" he asked, glancing around as if the culprit might be lurking next to him.

"You will find out soon enough," Dante said, not in the least concerned. "Ah," he added then, as a scuffling of feet on the deck below and the sound of angry voices could be heard coming closer. "I believe our questions shall be answered very shortly."

Suddenly, however, pandemonium broke loose as a group of men scrambled from the companionway and set off across the deck in pursuit of the first man, who'd shot out as if he'd had the hounds of hell on his heels. This noisy group, some swinging boat hooks and others, belaying pins and mallets, cornered their quarry near the foremast.

"Mission accomplished, I see, Mr. Fitzsimmons," Dante remarked lazily, his gray eyes narrowed with displeasure as he watched the struggling seaman being held very much against his will between Cobbs and Trevelawny.

"Aye, he tried to cut and run, he did," Cobbs spat. "But he's got the devil to pay and no pitch hot now."

"To be sure, Cap'n, we caught ourselves a real fishy-smellin' vermin this time, that we did," Fitzsimmons added with a wide grin. "When he sees us comin' he tries to jump overboard. Only a guilty conscience could make a man do that, I'm thinkin', especially when he doesn't know how to swim."

Cobbs jerked his prisoner up closer to the railing. "Turned real nasty, he did," he said, rubbing his slightly swollen jaw.

"Do you indeed have a guilty conscience, Mr. Grimes?" Dante asked quietly.

"Dunno what yer talkin' about, Cap'n. What's this all

about anyway? I been mindin' me own business. At least I was until these lubbers come chargin' after me like a bunch of harpooned whales. What's it about, Cap'n?"

"That is what *I'm* asking you, Mr. Grimes," Dante responded with a smile, which should have warned the manhandled Mr. Grimes to tread lightly. "I'm sure that I, as well as the crew of the *Sea Dragon,* would be greatly interested in hearing about your clandestine communications with your *real* captain, Mr. Grimes. Now, come along, Mr. Grimes, this is no time for misplaced discretion. Your life may very well depend upon what you tell me and the crew of the *Sea Dragon.* I'm sure Bertie Mackay will understand the delicate predicament you now find yourself in."

At Dante's mention of the rival smuggler's name, a murmur of surprise and protest rumbled through the men gathered around the captive, whose own reaction was even more violent.

When Grimes continued to remain silent, Dante shrugged. "Very well, Mr. Grimes, as you wish. A pity, though. Well, enough said, 'tis your decision. I'm sure, however, that Captain Mackay is anxiously awaiting further communciation with you. I shouldn't like to disappoint him."

Alastair frowned in confusion. "I don't understand this, Captain. Grimes has only been with us for about four months or so. How did Bertie Mackay know we'd find a treasure map?"

"I suspect that our Mr. Grimes here was placed on board the *Sea Dragon* for other purposes. This treasure map is an added bonus for Bertie. Am I not correct, Mr. Grimes?" Dante asked conversationally. But when the topman remained silent, Dante smiled. "Odds-on that I am correct."

"What was he here to do, Cap'n?" Conny demanded as he peered at the prisoner from the safety of Longacres' side.

"To observe. To mark our secret coves where we unload our contraband. To cause mischief, and ultimately, to turn us in to His Majesty's Navy, I shouldn't wonder,"

Dante told the gathering. His words sounded like the death knell in Grimes' ears when he glanced around at the ugly faces staring at him.

"Lies! 'Tis all lies. Don't listen to him. He wants to cause trouble. Split us up so there's more treasure for himself," Grimes cried out, only to fall silent as a hand was shoved over his mouth.

"Found this map, marking our special coves, in his locker, Cap'n. Reckon we would ha' found one of His Majesty's cutters waitin' fer us one fine night," Longacres said angrily.

"Well, what are we going to do with the fellow?" Mr. Clarke asked. "We could certainly hold a trial right here on deck. Have a jury made up of his peers," he suggested, his guilty vote already cast.

"I think, Mr. Clarke, that we need to facilitate matters a bit, considering that Mr. Grimes is not his own man," Dante said, overriding his helmsman. He glanced at his coxswain. "Ah, Longacres. Just the man. Let's lower a boat, shall we? I think Mr. Grimes here will be far safer in the gig than he might be spending the night here on deck. Don't you agree, men? Oh, and so he won't get lonely in the dark," Dante continued smoothly, the tone of his voice silencing the grumbling from his crew, who were disappointed about losing their catch to the sea, "put a lantern on board. Make sure it will be seen from the stern, Mr. Cobbs. I do not want Bertie Mackay to lose his way in the channel, not after he's come this far with the help of the *Sea Dragon*."

Alec MacDonald chuckled as he caught the captain's drift. "Aye, but the devil himself couldn't hae come up with a better, more diabolical plan. My compliments, sir."

"Thank you, Mr. MacDonald."

"Bertie will follow the light from the gig, just as he's been guided by the light flashing from the *Sea Dragon*," Alastair said, thinking about the light gig drifting onto the reefs with the swiftly moving current, leading the *Annie Jeanne* into the shallows. "Blast it, but I'd like to see Bertie Mackay's face come sunrise, if he's still afloat, when he discovers we've given him the slip."

"Cap'n Leighton, sir! You can't be doin' this to me!" Grimes called out as he was hustled to the small boat. "Cap'n Mackay will cut me heart out for this! I'm beggin' ye, Cap'n, sir. Don't be a-doin' this to me. I—" His quivering voice was cut off abruptly as the darkness swallowed him up.

"Hit his head, 'spose," MacDonald commented as he puffed on his pipe. "Reckon he won't miss much. Morning will be soon enough for him to enjoy the scenery."

There was a splash of water, then silence as the *Sea Dragon* continued on her course through the Florida Straits. Above her tall masts and billowing sails a myriad of stars shimmered in the black skies, an encouraging sign that no storm was gathering to hinder their progress.

"When do you think we will come back to look for the treasure?" Alastair asked his captain as they stood in silence on the quarterdeck, the cooling breeze off the water dampening their faces.

"*If* there is a treasure to be found," Dante replied cautiously, "then we shall have to make some plans, Alastair. For unless I am sorely mistaken about Cuthbert Mackay, he will hound us within an inch of our lives. He's nobody's fool. He hasn't gotten where he is in life by ignoring his hunches, and I suspect he has the same one I do about this sunken Spanish galleon. Most likely, over a few bottles of rum, he had an interesting, and very informative, conversation with the Dane. He realizes there is a very good chance that we might discover a treasure ship, and he intends to be there when we do. Besides, he'll not easily forgive me for tonight's unfortunate contretemps. No, Bertie will keep close to our stern, and what we must try and figure out is how to sink him. For if indeed there is a treasure, I have no intention of sharing it with the captain and crew of the *Annie Jeanne*," Dante promised, glancing over at the dark, shapeless form of the Florida coastline.

It was a place of mangrove swamps and mosquitoes, of unforgiving reefs and shifting shoals. It would become a deadly adversary if it fought to keep its watery hold on the sunken Spanish galleon. But a fight it would have,

Dante promised, as he continued to stare challengingly at the untamed shore.

"Lay the course, Mr. Clarke. We're homeward bound. At least for now," Dante added to himself as the *Sea Dragon* sailed through the Florida Straits, her bowsprit swinging towards the Carolinas.

There is something in the wind.
Shakespeare

England—Summer, 1769

Chapter 2

THE great house of Camareigh had been built on a knoll with a commanding view of the surrounding English countryside. Constructed of honey-colored stone mined from a local quarry, its golden-hued walls gave off a soft radiance, like a lambent flame. Early in the seventeenth century, on the crumbling ruins of the medieval house that had stood there since the middle of the fourteenth century, the first stone of the foundation of Camareigh had been laid. Stately and proud in its grandeur, the main block of the house was flanked by wings running east and west, with two towers standing sentinel at both intersecting points. Two rows of tall, broad windows pierced both floors and opened the house to sunlight. The central portico was approached by a wide avenue lined with magnificent chestnuts and carefully planted groves of copper beech, maple, and birch. In the fall Camareigh was a study in autumnal glory, but now it was summer, and bluebells covered the parkland, which slopped gently down to the sylvan lake. On the far side, protected by ancient cedars, the medieval chapel still stood.

Wild irises and daffodils blossomed in the woodland, their petals dappled with raindrops from the sudden spring shower that had disturbed the pastoral quietness of the valley.

It was a peaceful valley, and Camareigh and the ancestral lands of the Dominicks had weathered well the passage of over six hundred years. Its history was not a gentle one, however, nor a bloodless one. The first Dominick to set foot on English soil had come in the eleventh century, with William the Bastard and his army of conquerors from Normandy. In payment for his service to Duke William, soon to be crowned king of all England, Roger Dominick de Camaré, a knight of chivalrous conduct, was awarded the lands of a defeated Saxon lord.

Through the centuries the fortunes of the Dominick heirs continued to prosper, culminating with Francis Dominick, the ninth Earl of Carylstone, being made Duke of Camareigh for his service to his king, Henry V, in the Hundred Years' War. But during the Wars of the Roses, when the great houses of York and Lancaster battled for the throne of England, the Dominick fortunes fluctuated while the warring factions jockeyed for power and position. But destruction was not to be the destiny of the Dominicks at this time, and, with peace reigning supreme in the kingdom under the House of Tudor, Camareigh soon flowered again in the Golden Age of Elizabeth I. But with light comes darkness, and when the Civil War bloodied the fields and meadowlands of the English countryside, the fifth Duke of Camareigh was captured in battle while he fought for his king, Charles I, against the followers of Oliver Cromwell. With the ancestral home and estates confiscated by the Roundheads and her husband beheaded for his crimes, the Duchess of Camareigh and her young son fled to Holland with other Royalist families. Soon, Charles I would be publicly beheaded outside Whitehall Palace, and his son and heir, Charles II, would be in exile in Europe after an abortive attempt to overthrow the Protectorate and its lord protector, Oliver Cromwell. For the Royalists, many of whom were fortunate to have escaped with their lives, the long, ensuing years of exile were spent grieving over their dead, their diminished wealth, and their trampled heritage.

By the time of the Restoration, when Parliament had restored the monarchy and Charles II had returned triumphant to his homeland, the young Duke of Camareigh had become a man. He now returned to England with his king, and a wealthy French wife, who helped restore the family coffers and regain Camareigh from its Roundhead usurper.

That had been over a century ago. A hundred years of peaceful existence, of the pains and joys of everyday living, had mellowed the stone walls of Camareigh. It was a house filled with happiness and the sounds of laughter. No echoes of its past tragedies haunted its halls, and certainly not on this day in 1769.

"Eeeeeaaah!" A terrible scream split the serenity of the rose garden, where yellow and gold blossoms scented the warm afternoon, and bees robbed nectar from the lilies bordering the stone path.

The couple engaged in earnest conversation beside the water-lily covered pond was startled into momentary silence by the blood-curdling sound. Only moments before, they had made an idyllic scene of young love. The soft brim of the girl's silk slouch hat had presented an enticing view to the young man of her flawless profile. He had also seen how one soft golden curl dangled on her ivory shoulder. Her gown of light blue silk damask was trimmed in Chantilly lace at the flounced sleeves and wide bodice, and was opened in front to reveal a pale rose petticoat, lavishly embroidered. The lovely picture she made was no less colorful than the woven basket of assorted cut flowers that she carried over her arm. Her young gentleman friend fit well into the scene as he stood tall beside her in his finely cut coat of Superfine, the cinnamon cloth edged in gold trim, his waistcoat and breeches embroidered with gold thread.

But beneath his neatly powdered wig, his handsome face mirrored only horror now as he stared at the lilac hedge, which was quivering violently. "Good God! What the devil is that?" he demanded incredulously, as a fat, piebald pony with a young boy astride plowed through the hedge in a flurry of flying hooves and branches.

"What th—! Watch out there! I sa—" he began, only to be abruptly halted in the middle of a word when the shaggy shoulder of the sturdy little Shetland pony struck him a blow, catapulting the gentleman aside as it sped past, with its laughing rider still clinging to its flowing mane.

Wesley Lawton, Earl of Rendale, staggered from the pond, his fine coat dripping cold water and a tenacious lily pad wrapped around his silk-stockinged calf. His expression was at first comically disbelieving, but his face quickly became suffused with anger as he heard the incredible sound of laughter coming from his companion.

Lady Rhea Claire Dominick stood safely back from the water, her shoulders shaking with unbridled mirth. She knew better than to insult him further by offering assistance. Poor Wesley, he was really quite livid, Rhea Claire thought, biting her lip to contain her laughter.

"Rhea Claire, how dare you laugh. If I could get my hands on that little devil, I-I'd wring his blasted neck!" the much-affronted Earl expostulated as he stepped carefully from the slippery lily pond. Then he stood facing her as he shook his leg, trying to free it from the clinging lily pad. "Damned impertinence, beggin' your pardon. A switch oughta be taken to that young man's breeches," he complained, then added with a tightening of his lips, "and I would appreciate it, Rhea Claire, if you would stop that infernal laughter."

"Oh, Wesley," Rhea Claire said breathlessly, her laughter almost escaping her, "you do look so ridiculous standing there shaking your leg like a drenched rabbit. Forgive me, but I can't help but laugh."

"I do not find this in the least bit amus—"

"Lord Robin! Lord Robin, ye get yeself back here this instant. Right this instant! I'm a-tellin' ye fer the first and last time, Lord Robin," yelled the head gardener, as he charged through the broken hedge, his fist raised impotently. Then he nearly tipped over, coming to a sudden standstill, his mouth gaping open as he stared around at the destruction of his glorious gardens. His eyes wid-

31

ened perceptibly when they finally caught sight of the muddied, bedraggled figure of the Earl of Rendale.

"Lord help us," he muttered, doffing his cap. Then his gaze traveled on to the young beauty standing next to the fuming Earl, and the grizzled gardener's lips quivered briefly when he heard her muffled laughter. "Pardon me, Lady Rhea, but did ye happen to see which way young Lord Robin was headed in?"

Rhea Claire pointed toward the trampled border of the path. "I'm sorry, Saunders, but I'm afraid it is only too evident."

Saunders nodded, a long-suffering look crossing his weathered features. "Aye, m'lady, I was afeared he was headed in the direction of me prized Gilly flowers, and Her Grace's favorite at that. Oh, Lordie, but there's going to be heads a-rollin' for this day's work," he prophesied as he started to take his leave. "I don't know what's to be happening, for I knows His Grace is going to be madder'n hell, and Her Grace, bless her, will most likely take the side of young Lord Robin. Lord help us," he repeated beneath his breath again and again as he made his way along the path of destruction like a hound on the scent.

"Impertinent fellow," Lord Rendale remarked. "I'd not have him speaking so disrespectfully of the Duke and Duchess in my presence if I were you, Rhea Claire. The man oughta be taught his proper place," he added peevishly, glancing down at his ruined breeches.

Lady Rhea Claire Dominick lifted a delicately arched eyebrow in a perfect imitation of her father. "Camareigh," she began in a tone of cold hauteur, "is his home, Wesley. He was gardener here thirty years before I was even born. His grandfather was head gardener here, and *his* grandfather before him, and I suspect he knows more about my family than I shall ever learn. He happens to be a wonderful man—and loyal," she added. "He would probably give his life for my mother, so I'll not have you stand here criticizing him."

"You are far too familiar with your servants," Wesley retorted, grimacing as he wrung out his dripping cravat. "And I have noticed on occasion that you are too lenient with them, not to mention that mischievous brother of yours. If he were my brother, I'd have—"

"But he is not your brother, Wesley," Rhea Claire interrupted him with growing impatience. "And thank goodness for that, for I dare say you'd crush him with your ponderous sense of humor."

"Just because I do not find falling into a lily pond overly amusing, you accuse me of having no sense of humor. There is a time and place for everything, m'dear, and you would do well to develop a more appropriate sense of decorum," Wesley advised stiffly, missing the glint in her eye as he squeezed water out of his sleeve.

"Indeed, sir," Rhea Claire said mockingly, "then I should advise you to go and change, for 'tisn't I who is standing here looking the fool."

Lord Rendale's lips thinned ominously under her sarcasm. "With no thanks to that brother of yours. And," he added with rising indignation as he directed his full wrath at Lord Robin Dominick's small head, "where on earth did he get that creature? It's one of them damned Scots ponies, isn't it? Barbaric place and people," he muttered contemptuously.

"That creature, Wesley," began Rhea Claire with a smile of anticipation for what she was about to say, "happens to be a gift from my Uncle Richard. You do remember him? He lives in Scotland, on the ancestral estate of my great-grandfather, who," she paused for effect, "happened to fall at Culloden while fighting for Bonnie Prince Charlie. We are part Scots, or had you forgotten that?" she asked sweetly, her eyes full of devilish amusement.

"Oh," Lord Rendale said weakly, a flush of painful embarrassment staining his cheeks as he realized he'd committed an unforgivable *faux pas*. "Lady Rhea Claire, please, do forgive me. I shouldn't have said what I did, i–it was truly unforgivable, but I had forgotten about your uncle, the Marquis, and that he lived in Scotland. Although why he should wish to live in such a godforsaken place is beyond me. The place is so deso—" He broke off, flushing an even brighter hue of red. "Lud, but my cursed tongue, I could cut it out."

"Yes, Wesley, I should advise you to do that before you dig your grave any deeper," Rhea Claire said with an indulgent smile, for she was not one to stay mad at anyone for long, and Wesley was, after all, a rather harmless, if at times stuffy, gentleman.

"Uh, yes, well," Lord Rendale began, his soggy spirits lifting when he caught the flash of a smile beneath the wide brim of her silk hat and knew he'd been forgiven. "No more shall be said of this unfortunate incident. I shall spare Lord Robin any further embarrassment, and," he continued magnanimously, "I shall forgive you, m'dear, for laughing."

"How very generous of you, Wesley," Rhea Claire declared, struggling to keep her mouth from twitching as she waved him toward the house. Her smile broke free as she watched him trudging along, his progress hampered repeatedly by his stockings refusing to stay rolled up and, instead, curling around his ankles.

"You may come out now, my Robin Goodfellow," Rhea Claire called softly into the shrubbery.

The branches in question trembled, then parted to reveal a curly black head and a heart-shaped face with huge, violet eyes framed by long, black lashes. The impish slant of those eyes belied the sweetly curving mouth, which had fooled many an unfortunate person incautious enough to have tweaked a cheek. But they had never fooled Rhea Claire, who was wise to her brother's ways.

Lord Robin Dominick, now at the advanced age of ten, threw caution to the wind and stepped from hiding. Leaves clung to his blue velvet breeches, and what looked suspiciously like blackberry juice stained his white shirt front.

"I see you have been more than busy today," Rhea Claire commented as she looked him over. "What happened to Saunders and Shoopiltee?" she asked while she rubbed a smudge of dirt from Robin's cheek. "He was after your hide."

Robin sighed. "Shoopiltee got hungry, and I couldn't get him to budge another step, and so Saunders caught up with us in the herb garden." Robin laughed suddenly, remembering Lord Wesley Rendale. "He sure looked funny stalking off with his stockings rolling down around his ankles. I wonder what Father will say when he sees stuffy ol' Rendale walk into the hall soaking wet?" he asked, giggling. "I bet Mason will be horrified at the sight of the Earl. Maybe he'll even make him enter by the servants' entrance," he speculated excitedly before dissolving into uncontrollable giggles.

Rhea Claire smothered her own laughter as she thought of Mason, their very proper butler. Robin was right, he would be horrified at the sight of the Earl leaving puddles in his spotlessly polished entrance hall.

"If I were you, Robin, I'd be worrying more about what Father will be saying to *you*," Rhea Claire warned him, thinking of the cold displeasure that could settle on the Duke's occasionally austere face. "He will be most displeased."

Robin shrugged his narrow shoulders, remaining unconcerned. "No, he won't. He doesn't even like the Earl. Heard him telling Mother the other day that the man was better suited to be the Earl of Duncedom than Rendale. Said he was a-a," Robin said, pausing and frowning as he tried to remember the exact words, "pompous dunderhead!"

"Robin!" Rhea Claire said indignantly. "How dare you repeat such a thing," she warned him, but they both knew it was a weak reprimand when a chuckle escaped from her tightly compressed lips. "You brat," she said fondly, and rumpled his curls. "I don't know why I put up with you. You are always in trouble of some kind, and those ears of yours, Master Jackanapes, will get you in over your head one of these fine days."

"You're not really going to marry the Earl, are you, Rhea?" Robin asked. "I don't think anyone really likes him. And I know that Father doesn't at all."

"Now that is enough, Robin," Rhea told him seriously. "I have not decided yet. Besides, just because others do not care for him, why should that matter to me? I make my own decisions, and I happen to think that the Earl needs a few friends. I suspect he is quite lonely." Now Rhea Claire was defending him against her own thoughts of late about accepting the proposal she knew would be forthcoming from him. "I really don't *dislike* Wesley. He's quite a gentleman, and far more likable than all of those aging roués I met in London. I could certainly do far worse."

"Or far better, I suspect. But you don't say love, and isn't that what should be important, Rhea?" asked Francis Dominick, eldest son and heir of the Duke of Camareigh, as he stepped through the gaping hedge. "Lord, what a mess! Saunders is still muttering about all of this, not to mention old Mason, who's in high dudgeon up at the house. What a ruckus. I don't think Lord Rendale will ever be the same, although it probably did him a wonder of good to get knocked down a notch or two. Far too serious a fellow, your Earl, Rhea," Francis said, succinctly summing up his sister's suitor.

"He is not *my* Earl," Rhea retorted, stung. Although she was a year older than her brother Francis, who was at sixteen, he stood a good foot taller than she did.

"Well, he would certainly like to be," Francis said, glancing around at the once peaceful garden.

"What happened up at the house, Francis?" Robin asked, unable to curb his curiosity any longer.

Francis turned a knowing blue-gray eye on his young brother. "I s'pose Father is out cutting a switch for your breeches, seeing how the Earl let slip how he came to fall into the lily pond."

"He told Father!" Robin squealed. "But he promised he would not tell, the tattler. I knew I was right in never having cared for the cut of his coat," he added audaciously, stamping his foot in indignation.

Francis grinned. "Well, what did you expect him to say when he met our father in the hall? The Earl looked as guilty as a common thief as he tried to sneak up the stairs. But much to his chagrin, Mason caught him, probably tipped off by one of the footmen. Father and I had been in the library, and were entering the hall when we stopped in amazement at the sight that greeted us on the Grand Staircase," Francis told them with a laugh. "The Earl was trying to escape a very solicitous Mason, who happened to have a tight hold on the Earl's arm and wasn't about to let go. The Earl was shooshing him quiet, while trying to shake him loose. The look on Lord Rendale's face was unbelievable. I think he'd rather have come face to face with the devil himself than see Father standing there watching him."

"Poor Wesley," Rhea said, feeling sorry for the bewildered Earl.

"I wonder if this means the picnic will be canceled," Robin said glumly, thinking of the tables that would have been spread across the lawn, groaning under the weight of his favorite dishes, not to mention desserts. And what of the games he would miss playing with his cousins? It was just too horrible to think about.

Francis watched in amusement while Robin tried to straighten his shirt and breeches in an attempt to bring some semblance of order to his disheveled appearance. Feeling sorry for the little fellow, he finally decided to set his mind at rest—at least about the picnic.

"I shouldn't worry about them canceling it. If Aunt Mary arrives tomorrow as planned, then they will certainly have it. You know how she and Mother like picnics," he said. "But right now, Father wants to see you in his study, Robin," he added, putting his arm across his brother's shoulders. He'd noticed them slump slightly at his mention of the upcoming interview with the Duke. "It'll be all right. Father really doesn't care much for the Earl, you know. But he will not stand for discourtesy of any kind in his home, especially toward a guest under his roof. So you'd better have a good explanation on your tongue," he advised.

Rhea Claire glanced between her two brothers, each so different, and not just in one being so fair, while the other was dark. Robin was a little devil, and Rhea Claire had heard her father say often that he was her mother all over again. Francis, on the other hand, was quieter, more deliberate in his actions; he was definitely the Duke's son, or so her mother often swore with a shake of her curly black hair.

"Well, all I've got to say on the matter," Rhea declared, taking each of her brothers' arms as they walked beside her through the gardens, "is that I hope I do not have to serve as your witness, Robin, for I'd have to swear that I saw you glance back and laugh when poor Rendale fell into the lily pond."

"I wasn't laughing near as hard as you were, Rhea," Robin reminded her, glancing up to catch her grin before they all started to laugh.

From the Private Drawing Room in the south wing, Sabrina, Duchess of Camareigh, watched her three eldest children approach and wondered what it was they found to be so amusing. She could see Robin's dark head bobbing up and down as he hurried alongside his fair-haired brother and sister. Robin would always seem her baby, even though she had given birth to the twins almost two years ago. Finding herself enceinte after eight barren years had come as a complete surprise, but not as great as the actual birth when she had brought two lives into the world, instead of the one she had been expecting. It had been a difficult time for her, and she knew that there would be no more children, but she accepted it, and indeed was rather relieved about it. Far too many women died in childbirth, and she intended to fully enjoy watching her children mature into adulthood, and to share with them the pains and joys of living.

The Duchess stared down at her eldest child, Rhea Claire, and found it hard to believe that her daughter was seventeen. What a beautiful girl she had grown into, the Duchess thought, filled with pride for her firstborn. At times she could be a stubborn and willful young beauty, but that arrogant streak was tempered by an incredible gentleness and compassion that had at times worried her, for Rhea Claire was inclined to let her heart, when it was troubled and touched, rule her head. How many times, the Duchess wondered with a sigh, had Rhea Claire brought a wounded bird or stray cat into the house to be protected? And how different were her feelings now, pondered the Duchess, thinking of the Earl of Rendale, whom she suspected had aroused nothing more than pity in her daughter's tender heart.

The Duchess smiled wryly, amazed at her thoughts, for it seemed only yesterday that she herself had come to Camareigh as a young bride. She hadn't been much older than Rhea Claire when she had first seen Camareigh. She could still feel her own awed panic when she'd caught sight of the magnificent house. The coach which had carried her away from her own home and familiar surroundings seemed to be approaching the grand house far too quickly, and the house had seemed to her, at that time, not to be very welcoming. But whether she resented it or not, she had become its mistress and duchess, and soon would give it its long-awaited heir.

Had she realized, in that moment of uncertainty and trepidation, just what exactly *was* behind those honey-colored walls, she might well have leaped from the carriage and taken to her heels, for nothing in her previous life had quite prepared her for the responsibilities of being the Duchess of Camareigh. Nor had she been prepared for the army of servants who had greeted her—rather suspiciously, she remembered—upon her arrival. Of course, she had not known them then, nor they her, and she could well understand their dubious opinion about this new mistress, who looked as if she should still be playing with dolls.

She had held her breath as she'd stared down the long line of unfriendly faces, their expressions striking terror into her already quivering heart. She could remember meeting the austere butler, Mason, his stern countenance seeming gentle compared with the tight-lipped and obviously resentful housekeeper, who she later discovered recognized no mistress other than the Dowager Duchess. Well, the *ex*-housekeeper had certainly misjudged this Duchess, Sabrina remembered with a chuckle, for she had sent the old harridan packing with a flea in her ear and a note to the Dowager Duchess that the woman's services would no longer be needed by *this* Duchess. It had also served warning to any other malcontents to beware, for this was no mealy-mouthed and cowed mistress they were dealing with. And from that day forward the new Duchess had a loyal staff eager to serve her, for no one had much minded that she'd fired the housekeeper. In fact, the housekeeper had been heartily disliked by everyone, because every misdemeanor or infraction of household rules, no matter how slight, even an incau-

tiously spoken word, had been parroted back to the Dowager Duchess by her overwrought and insanely loyal
lackey. Now that the old battle-ax had left, they could
get back to doing the work they'd been hired to do, which
had been woefully neglected during the reign of the previous housekeeper.

And indeed, the Duchess remembered, there had been
a lot of work to do before the great house once again
assumed its proud mantle of excellence. From the tireless
Mason, who oversaw every polished silver spoon and
dusted off every bottle of wine, to the new housekeeper,
who personally saw that every bed had been aired and
made up with freshly scented sheets, to the cook, who
saw that her kitchen was scrubbed down to the bare
wood and her scullery maids worked almost to the bone,
to the steward, under-butler, assistant housekeeper, footmen, maids, ostlers, master of music, secretary, chaplain,
stable boys, grooms, porters, coachmen, dairy maids,
and the head gardener and his staff—all worked together
to build the harmonious atmosphere that now existed at
Camareigh. They made it the great house that it was, and
a *great* house it was indeed.

There were two wings consisting of the Ducal apartments, family apartments, and State apartments, all of
which were comprised of various drawing rooms, dining
rooms, salons, bedchambers and dressing rooms, ante-
chambers and studies, the ever-expanding Library and
Grand Ballroom, the music room and Long Gallery, kitchens and servants' hall, and other rooms and backstairs'
cubbyholes too numerous to even know about. Outside,
there were the stables, greenhouses, and orangery to be
looked after, as well as the topiary gardens, rose gardens, kitchen gardens and natural gardens, and the extensive grounds of the estate itself.

Close to twenty years now, the Duchess thought with
a reminiscent smile, she had been mistress of Camareigh;
she'd borne her children under its bountiful roof, and
seen many a summer turn to autumn as she'd basked in
the glow of its honey-colored walls. This was her home
now, a home she'd come to love as much as her husband
Lucien did, and he'd been born and raised at Cama-

reigh, and had had pride for this great house drummed into him all of his life.

While he was still in the nursery, his indefatigable and imperiously proud grandmother, the Dowager Duchess, had instilled in him all of her own dreams and hopes for Camareigh, and she had not allowed death to take her until she'd been assured of Camareigh's survival through succession. The Duchess knew that the Dowager Duchess had been disappointed to find her first great-grandchild was a girl, but she had taken to Rhea Claire, and when Francis had come along a year later, she had been exultant and had presented her granddaughter-in-law with her most prized possession—a ruby and pearl pendant, suspended from a pearl necklace, which had been a wedding gift from Queen Elizabeth I to a Dominick bride. Lucien had gained his grandmother's undying devotion, and he had the satisfaction of knowing, when she died a few years later, that she'd been a very happy and smug old woman who had lived life to the fullest, and seen all of her dreams come true for the house she loved above all else. The Dowager Duchess may have been a tyrant, the present Duchess thought, but despite all of the old woman's scheming, she had liked her, for the old woman hadn't really been mean or horrible, just stubborn and determined to have her own way. Much like her grandson. The Duchess smiled, thinking how Lucien would have hated that comparison, for he'd been at odds with his grandmother for most of his life and had only got back in her good graces by siring a son and heir, so . . .

"And what are you daydreaming about, my love?" the Duke inquired softly, startling the Duchess, for he'd come up behind her without her having heard him. He pressed a light kiss on her nape, his warm breath tickling the sensitive spot beneath her uplifted curls. "Odd, is it not, that I should have never tired of your fragrance?" he questioned, breathing deeply of her lightly scented skin.

"Lucien," Sabrina whispered, never failing to find his touch exciting. "Odd, is it not, that I should never have tired of your touch?" she responded in the familiar banter they used with one another.

The Duke's arms tightened around his duchess's small

waist. "Not at all, my dear, for I have made it my life's work to please you, and I accept nothing less than your undying love and devotion," he warned, his mouth covering hers for a lingering moment. "Especially as you have mine. And as you well know, we Dominicks are a stubborn breed."

Sabrina stared up at him, all her love for him openly revealed in the dark depths of her violet eyes, eyes that had captivated the Duke since he'd first glanced into them. With a flash of sapphire and ruby rings, the Duchess ran a gentle finger along the scar that etched its way from his left cheek to the corner of his mouth. "My only love, my heart," she said simply.

Lucien pressed his lips to her soft palm before tucking her arm within the crook of his elbow. "Now, what were you daydreaming about? Perchance 'twas me, and your wish has been granted?"

Sabrina smiled indulgently. "You Dominick males are also very vain; however, you are partly correct. I was thinking how amazing it is that Rhea Claire could actually be seventeen. I was watching her come across the gardens with Francis and Robin, and I was feeling very proud of our children."

"What were they up to?" the Duke demanded, glancing out of the window. But the garden below was empty.

The Duchess raised a delicate eyebrow at his choice of words and his doubting tone of voice. "You sound suspicious of something, my dear, but you really needn't be," she told him confidently, feeling little cause for concern. "I shall set your mind at rest, for all they were doing was laughing. Now what else should they be doing but enjoying themselves on a warm afternoon?" the Duchess asked as she made herself comfortable on her favorite rose-colored silk sofa, which had been positioned near the fireplace for maximum warmth. The early morning fire had long since burned itself out, and the Duchess's embroidery lay long-forgotten on the carpet.

"Laughing? That is precisely why I am worried. And I suppose Robin was laughing harder than the others?" the Duke asked with a gleam in his sherry-colored eyes that boded ill for the Duchess's young son.

"And what is wrong with that?" she demanded with a laugh of her own. "And why have you singled out Robin for your displeasure?"

"I have singled him out, my love, because he should be soundly spanked."

"Whatever for?" the Duchess asked, a little less confidently this time, for she knew only too well what sort of mischief her son could get up to.

"For causing Rendale the dunking of his life," the Duke informed her as he sat down beside her. "That damned pony of Robin's knocked the Earl into the lily pond," he continued, waiting patiently for her laughter to stop before he continued. "I would imagine *that* is what your three children were just laughing about. Although I should think that Robin would find the situation less amusing since he has been ordered to my study."

"Don't be too hard on him, Lucien," Sabrina said softly, her eyes entreating on behalf of her precipitate son while her slender fingers caressed Lucien's hand.

"Have I ever denied you anything, Rina?" the Duke responded with a tolerant smile, his eyes lingering on her slightly parted lips.

"Yes, many times," the Duchess returned with a low laugh. "You can be a terrible tyrant at times, and I quite despair of coaxing a smile out of you."

"Liar," the Duke whispered, a tantalizing smile curving his lips. "I shudder to think what my life would have been like if you had not stormed into it that night," he speculated, smoothing a soft, unpowdered black curl from her temple. He pressed his lips against her hair, approving of her refusal to bow to convention and society by hiding the beauty of her hair under layers of white powder. "Do you remember that night, my sweet?"

"Remember?" the Duchess questioned with an impish grin identical to that of young Robin's. "How could I forget? You nearly killed me!"

"Ah, but I didn't, much to my delight and eternal thankfulness. Although now that I am reminded," he added with a mocking glance, "you certainly led me one fine chase. And here you sit now, smugly casting aspersions on my swordsmanship. Really, my dear, you do me a grave injustice."

The Duchess smiled provocatively, the slight dimple in her cheek entrancing the Duke as much today as it had the first time it had peeped out at him. She was more beautiful today, if that were indeed possible, than she had been when he'd made her his duchess. With Sabrina by his side he had found the love and happiness he had always been searching for, and until his fateful meeting with this black-haired, violet-eyed hellion, that elusive bird had always flown free of his grasp. But once he had captured her, he vowed he would never let her fly free, for Sabrina was his life. It was as simple as that.

His duchess blushed slightly under the warmth of his gaze, but she did not glance away and continued to meet the message of love in his eyes as she touched his mouth with hers. And it was upon this intimate scene that the door was opened to admit a liveried footman.

"Lady Sarah Wrainton, Your Grace," he said in stentorian tones, and stepped aside for an attractive young woman who, at the sight of the closely positioned couple on the sofa, nearly stumbled as she tried to halt her progress into the room.

"My dear Sarah, do come in," the Duchess said, beckoning and rising to greet their guest.

"Please, I do not wish to intrude, Your Grace," Lady Sarah said nervously, quite in awe of the Duchess, even though she was her sister-in-law. "I-I had not realized His Grace was in here," she added, completely in awe of the Duke also, whose scarred cheek gave him a sinister look that left her knees shaking. He was an undeniably handsome man, and the years had certainly been kind to him, for there was no excess weight to slow him down or to strain against the buttons of his waistcoat. Tall and lean, his face marred only by the scar, he exuded a sensuality that even she, a happily married wife and soon-to-be mother, could feel, and she wondered what he must have been like twenty years earlier when he'd been in his early to mid-thirties. Despite his obvious happiness and contentment in his marriage, his face was still stamped by a certain cynical hardness, or perhaps it was merely the scar which created such an impression. But still, Lady Sarah wondered how the Duchess had managed to handle such a man all of these years.

But as Lady Sarah stared at the Duchess, she realized that Her Grace's beauty alone could hold any man spellbound. It was difficult to believe that she could possibly be the mother of five children, for her figure was that of a young girl's, her tiny waist rivaling any that Sarah had seen on acclaimed London beauties. The passage of time had enhanced the beauty of the Duchess of Camareigh, not stolen it away, for there was a glowing warmth and happiness from within that was reflected on her face. And that was something that no artificial beauty aid could capture.

Lady Sarah remembered herself in time and started to curtsy, only to find herself being raised gently but firmly by the Duchess.

"Now you listen to me, Sarah," she warned her with a glint in her violet eyes. "I will not tolerate any subservience from you. You are the wife of my beloved Richard, and as sisters-in-law, we are family. I happen to be Sabrina to my family. Do I make myself clear?" she added, sounding more like the imperious duchess than ever.

"You'd be wise to do as she says, Sarah," the Duke commented lazily. "I learned years ago not to cross her."

"You circumvent me, that is all. Don't think I am not wise to your methods, my dear," the Duchess responded with an arch look at her husband, who was smiling complacently.

Lady Sarah looked from one to the other of them, amazed at their teasing words, and suddenly she knew she would be blessed if she had only half as good a marriage as the Duke's and Duchess's.

"Now please do sit down," the Duchess ordered with a smile that robbed her words of any sting. "I do not intend to be the cause of your losing Richard's heir. How are you feeling? Not nauseous, I hope? Good! Now, would you care for a cup of tea?" the Duchess politely inquired. But her casual reference to so private a female condition had caused Sarah to blush with painful embarrassment when she happened to catch the Duke's eye.

"Oh, don't mind Lucien," the Duchess told her, correctly interpreting her sister-in-law's blushes, "he's played the expectant father far too many times not to understand what we go through. In fact," the Duchess continued, her eyes exchanging a special, shared memory with the Duke, "Lucien helped to deliver Francis, so he knows better than most men what childbearing is all about. I was a bit headstrong in my youth," she explained, sending the Duke a quelling glance when he said something beneath his breath at her offhand remark. "I was not expecting Francis for another month, or so I'd thought. I had been visiting my sister, when on the journey home, in the middle of a thunderstorm, no less," the Duchess said, her eyes now sparkling with the memory, "Francis joined us. I'm not sure who was more surprised," she said with an engaging laugh, "Lucien, Francis, me, or the coachman when he heard Francis's lusty cry. I'm afraid poor Richard thought I was going to die."

Sarah's mouth dropped open. "Richard was there?" she asked in amazement, realizing there was far more to her rather intellectual husband than she had ever imagined. "I knew that he had lived with you here at Camareigh after your marriage, and that your parents are both dead," Sarah said. She knew now that she had never before quite suspected the deep bond between Richard and his sister, as well as the bond between Richard and the Duke.

"Our mother died a few days after Richard was born, and we were raised for many years in Scotland, by our mother's father. Our own father wanted nothing to do with us. When Grandfather died," the Duchess explained, "we came to England and lived at Verrick House, where, oddly enough, we had all been born. When I married Lucien, Richard came with me. I'm not sure Lucien had counted on that," the Duchess commented with a smile that only her husband understood.

"I would have had it no other way, for indeed," the Duke said conversationally, " 'twas Richard's actions that instigated a reconciliation between us. We have had our differences in the past, Sarah. And there was a time, long, long ago, when I thought I had lost Sabrina," the

Duke confided. "These Verricks are independent and stubborn people, Sarah. In fact, they are a bit eccentric, but I've never once regretted marrying into the family," he told her.

The Duke's casual use of her name warmed Sarah and began to make her feel accepted at Camareigh. She knew this was important if she was to make a success of her marriage, for Camareigh had been Richard's home, and he worshipped the Duke and Duchess. She had wanted so very badly to be accepted by his family, and indeed, had desperately feared being rejected by them. For she was only the daughter of an impecunious army officer, who had managed, despite himself, to die bravely in battle, and as a last, dying gesture, had left his only child a ward of his commanding officer, General Sir Terence Fletcher, brother-in-law to the Duchess of Camareigh.

It had been while living at Green Willows, the country estate of Sir Terence and Lady Mary, that Sarah Pargeter had met Richard Verrick, Marquis of Wrainton and younger brother of Lady Mary and the Duchess. With his thick red hair, he resembled Lady Mary rather than the dark-haired Duchess, and his quiet demeanor and gold-rimmed spectacles made the impression seem well founded—at least until Richard Verrick was moved by amusement, anger, or passion. Then he resembled the Duchess, his blue eyes flashing a fire and spirit equal to his sister's.

Lady Sarah Wrainton glanced around the very elegant private drawing room of the Dominick family, and she could not help but compare the fine, plaster ceiling with its birds in flight and scrolled corners, the blue and gold flock wallpaper and ornately framed pictures, the silk-covered sofas and chairs, crystal chandeliers and damask curtains, to the shabby rooms she had lived in while traveling the Continent with her father. Their hand-to-mouth existence fluctuated with his wins and losses in card games in every gaming hall, from Vienna to London to Paris. She had never thought to find herself having tea with a Duke and Duchess, and in a room such as this; nor had she thought that one day she herself would be a Marchioness.

Long ago, she had given up hope of making a successful marriage, for she knew she was no raving beauty, with her ordinary brown hair and brown eyes. And all she'd had as a dowry were her father's staggering debts—his legacy to her upon his death. Sarah sighed, for her father may not have been a good father by accepted standards, but he had loved her, that she knew, and he had tried to do his best for her. He could rest easy, she thought, for she had married well, far better, in fact, than either of them had ever hoped for, and also, she had married for love.

"And where is Richard?" the Duchess asked now, as she pulled the bell for the butler. "He did promise to be here for tea. No," she commanded suddenly, holding up a slender, bejeweled hand before Sarah could answer, "do not tell me. He is in the Library, yes?"

Sarah nodded. "How did you know?"

"Where else *would* he be? He swears that he comes here to visit me, but I honestly suspect it is to spend his time in Lucien's library. We've added a whole new wall since Richard was last here, so I shouldn't be surprised if we shan't see him for days, the ungrateful wretch," the Duchess said, allowing her voice to carry just as the door opened to admit a lanky young man, who strode purposefully into the room.

"I do not know how, or why, you put up with her," the Duchess's younger brother complained, overhearing her comments just as he had been intended to. "Such defamation of character, and before a man's wife," Richard Verrick complained, glancing mockingly at his sister before placing a kiss on his wife's flushed cheek. "I swear Rina's tongue gets sharper with age. I always understood people were supposed to mellow with age."

But when Richard saw the quick retort quivering on his sister's lips, he spread out his hands in a gesture of surrender. "Pax?" he asked coaxingly as he approached the Duchess and kissed her cheek. Then he dropped down on the opposite sofa beside his wife. "I suspect I've been outmaneuvered again, and she has me just where she wants me. I don't know how it is that I managed to marry Sarah without Her Grace's assistance."

"Do you actually think you did not?" the Duke inquired, a mocking look in his heavy-lidded eyes as they lingered on his wife. "If I remember correctly, Sabrina corresponded almost daily with Mary while you were visiting Green Willows," the Duke informed Richard and Sarah, to their astonishment. Then a grin of amused satisfaction warmed his lean face as he met Sabrina's startled gaze. "Now, if you will forgive me, I've a small errand to see to," he excused himself. "And do not despair, my sweet, for I promise I shall not be too hard on Robin. Indeed, how could I, when he looks just like you?"

The Duchess gave an audible sigh of relief, for Lucien could be quite a stern parent at times. "He will settle down, Lucien. He's just excited; after all, Mary and the children will be here tomorrow, and then Robin will have plenty of companions to play with," she said to reassure her doubtful-looking husband.

"That is precisely why I want a word with him now," Lucien replied, shaking his head as he walked to the door. It opened just as he reached it, and his elder son and daughter hurried in, followed almost immediately by a loaded down tea tray.

"Poor Rendale, he'll never escape their pranks now that Robin will have accomplices," he predicted as he paused in the doorway, his narrowed gaze resting briefly on his two children. "I trust you will help keep an eye on your brother, for if there is any trouble, you will bear the brunt of my displeasure," he warned, disregarding their groans of protest as he left the room.

"Father! That isn't fair!" Francis called after his retreating back. "If Robin knew we were supposed to keep him *out* of trouble, he'd just get *into* more," he complained, frowning with concentration as he selected a plate full of sweets from the tray.

"And what was that dire warning about?" Richard demanded of his niece and nephew, swiping the rich, cream-filled cake that Francis's hand had been hovering over. Then his chuckles of appreciation filled the room as Rhea Claire recounted the afternoon's incident, Francis's uncharitable remarks making the Earl look more ridiculous than ever.

"I did warn you, my dear," Richard told his wife, "about marrying into this madhouse. And I believe Lucien is well justified in his concern for the Earl's safety, for Mary, despite her gentle appearance and manner, is usually the center of the storm," he joked, selecting another sticky-looking confection.

The Duchess sipped her tea, her eyes traveling around the room and lingering every so often on a laughing face. She spied her forgotten embroidery and smiled thoughtfully; she knew that Mary would most likely be more than pleased to complete it, for she had inherited their late Aunt Margaret's expertise with needle and thread. Dear Aunt Margaret, who had never quite known where she was, or even what year it was, Sabrina remembered, her smile turning sad. Yet Aunt Margaret could sew a line of delicate stitches straighter and neater than any royal seamstress. Ah, well, it would be good to see Mary and her family again, the Duchess thought in anticipation while she poured fresh tea into the cups being held out to her expectantly.

Rhea Claire's bedchamber at Camareigh was decorated in shades of pale blue, yellow, and silver. The tall windows, overlooking the gardens along the south wing, were draped with hangings of pale blue and silver damask. A canopied bed with hangings in the same pattern sat snug in one corner, while a molded fireplace occupied the wall opposite. A small chaise longue, delicately curved and upholstered with soft down cushions of blue velvet, and several curved-back white armchairs, with pale yellow and silver-striped brocade cushions, filled in the space before the windows. A small writing table and chair were positioned at the end of the Aubusson carpet, but it was at the rosewood and gilt dressing table that Rhea Claire was sitting, the mirror reflecting burnished golden hair cascading down her back and over her shoulders as her mother's personal maid brushed it into thick waves.

"And what gown will ye be wearin' today, Lady Rhea Claire?" Canfield asked, expertly winding the long strands into heavy loops.

"I thought I'd wear my pale green brocade," Rhea replied, handing Canfield a long length of green velvet ribbon and a bunch of artificial flowers to weave into the nearly completed and stylish coiffure that the maid prided herself on knowing how to create.

"I'd be most grieved, m'lady, to see ye soil that pretty gown at the picnic," Canfield told her with a disapproving look on her thin face. Meanwhile, she eyed a stray curl which refused to stay in place.

"But that is not until tomorrow, Canfield," Rhea told her, slipping a delicate, bow-shaped ring, set with diamonds and sapphires, onto her slender finger. It had been a gift to her from her parents on her seventeenth birthday.

" 'Tis today," Canfield corrected her as she marched over to the wardrobe; when she opened it, the colorful selection within was revealed. "Sir Terence and Lady Mary arrived late last night. Most odd, if ye be askin' me, 'twas," Canfield remarked with a sniff, not caring for anything that upset her carefully scheduled days.

Rhea Claire shrugged. "I think it is wonderful that they have already arrived. And I shall still wear my green brocade, Canfield," Rhea informed her adamantly, for if given an inch Canfield would take a mile. "I am no child to be spilling cocoa down my dress."

"Very well, m'lady, but I'm sure I don't know what Her Grace will be sayin'," Canfield capitulated, noticing the set of her young mistress's delicately rounded chin. "This décolletage is far too low for a young lady your age. Told the seamstress, I did, but would she listen to me?" Canfield continued in a grievous tone, sniffing contemptuously at the likes of the London seamstress who'd been brought in to make Her Grace's wardrobe, as well as her daughter's. "No, she did not. Too busy rolling them bovine eyes of hers at His Grace and ogling Camareigh to sew a proper stitch, her. Hrrmph, told her, I did. But she soon found out, she did. . . ."

Rhea Claire closed her mind to what would no doubt become one of Canfield's never-ending monologues, for the woman seemed to have an opinion on everything that went on at Camareigh, or anywhere else for that matter. Rhea Claire hurried into her green brocade, breathing in deeply as Canfield tightened the laces on her corset before fastening the gown snugly around her waist. She frowned slightly as Canfield insisted, under threat of not letting her out of her room, on attaching a modesty piece to the top of the corset, which effectively hid any cleavage that might have attracted an appreciative male eye, or Her Grace's eye, heaven forbid, thought a worried Canfield. But finally, Rhea was able to escape Canfield's overzealous ministrations, leaving her contentedly tidying up the bedchamber.

In the Long Gallery, the narrow, corridorlike room that stretched nearly the length of the east front, Rhea Claire stopped before the family portrait completed just months ago. It hung last in the long line of family portraits commissioned by the Dominicks over the centuries, its ornate gold frame bright against the aged oak paneling of the walls. With a misty landscape in the background, the Dominick family was gathered around the base of a sturdy oak in the foreground. The Duke of Camareigh was leaning against the gnarled trunk, with his youngest son, Andrew, riding his upraised leg, which he was resting on a fallen log. Sitting farther down the makeshift bench, with Andrew's twin sister Arden on her lap, was the Duchess of Camareigh, her primrose-colored, quilted petticoat a spot of brightness against the dominant greens of the painting. Rhea Claire glanced at her own painted face staring expressionlessly back at her from where she sat at her mother's feet, her blue satin skirts spread out around her. Francis was positioned behind their mother's shoulder, while Robin was squatting down in front, a pair of frisky-looking King Charles spaniels romping at his feet.

Rhea Claire stayed before the painting a moment longer, then continued along the gallery, her steps slowing every so often as she paused before a familiar portrait. One of them was the painting of her great-grandmother, the late Dowager Duchess, who, according to her mother and father, had been a force to be reckoned with as she'd tried to manipulate all of those within her sphere of influence. Her Grace, Claire Lorraine Dominick, Duchess of Camareigh, and daughter of a French count, who had been born to rule the ducal estates with an imperious nod of an elegantly coiffed, regal head, had held the reins with a hand of iron. She had been quite a woman, Rhea Claire thought, leaning closer to get a better look at the three golden-haired children grouped around their grandmother's chair. It was her father and his twin cousins. Grinning as she thought of her father as a little boy, Rhea moved on down the gallery, stopping before her favorite portrait, which was of an ancestor dressed in doublet and hose, a stiff ruff tucked beneath his bearded chin. He was certainly a handsome devil, Rhea thought, her smile changing slightly as she speculated on his unsavory reputation. The rumor was that he had been a privateer in the service of Queen Elizabeth I, and had added looted Spanish gold to the Dominick fortunes. Rhea Claire stared dreamily up at him, wondering what kind of man this adventurer ancestor of hers truly had been.

With an admonitory shake of her flower-crowned head, she hurried on, checking her gold pendant watch and thinking of her breakfast growing cold. As she neared the end of the Long Gallery, a door burst open and several giggling children sped inside. They halted mid-stride when they caught sight of her figure, but when they recognized her they continued, quickening their steps as they neared her.

"Rhea! Rhea!" a chorus of high, excited voices greeted her.

" 'Mornin'," Rhea Claire responded, eyeing them curiously, for they had a decidedly guilty look about them, and she knew her cousins well enough to suspect something amiss. "And what do you have hidden behind your backs?" she demanded, trying to catch a quick glance.

"Secret!" cried out Margaret, the seven-year-old, then hid her mouth behind a grubby little hand.

"Maggie!" her brother warned, his gray eyes glinting beneath rusty-colored eyebrows.

"I'm not going to tell. You can't get me to tell," chanted John, the youngest.

"Come on," Rhea Claire cajoled, holding out her hand and smiling down at them, "do tell, now. You know I can keep a secret."

"She can, you know," nine-year-old Anna declared with a grin, her admiration for her beautiful cousin evident on her freckled face.

"Well," Stuart said, his expression comically serious as he hesitated, "I guess it will be all right, but you have to promise not to say a word. Promise?"

"Cross my heart," Rhea Claire said solemnly, her eyes widening in surprise as four hands, palms up, were presented for her inspection. A warm cherry tart sat squarely in the middle of each.

"They're for Robin," John whispered conspiratorially, before he was nudged quiet by Stuart's elbow.

"Lud! I don't believe it," Rhea Claire said with a laugh. "I should have known he would have a hand in this escapade. What is he up to, I wonder?" she speculated aloud.

"We each get a ride on Shoopiltee, in exchange for one cherry tart," Maggie answered, her eyes glowing in anticipation.

"Why, that little brat," Rhea said indignantly, knowing Robin had been forbidden any desserts yesterday in partial punishment for his misdeeds. "If Father finds out, Robin'll get the whipping of his short life. That little devil! Making you pay to ride his pony. How did you wheedle these out of Mrs. Peacham? Nothing leaves the kitchens without her approval, or didn't you receive it?" The foursome was now silent. "Hmmm, I thought as much. A diversion, no doubt, then a sleight of hand, was it?"

"You promised, Rhea, not to tattle," Stuart reminded his cousin, not caring for that glint in her eye.

"Very well, but you tell Robin that I'm on to him," Rhea warned as they started to dart past her. "And stay out of the garden if you know what's good for you," she called as they disappeared, feet flying, down the gallery. Then Rhea Claire wondered what mishaps would befall Camareigh before the picnic was over and the younger members of the household were safely between the covers of their respective beds.

Lady Mary Fletcher was sitting quietly beneath the cool shade of a fine old chestnut, its spreading branches protecting her from the bright sun shining down from a cloudless blue sky. Her fingers moved mechanically with needle and thread across the linen material she was embroidering, but her thoughts were elsewhere as she stared across the smooth lawns of Camareigh to the magnificent house in the distance. She knew she would never quite get over her first glimpse of the Duke of Camareigh's home. Its splendor and elegance, its great history, was enough to awe a person into silence. However, she had never envied her sister living in such a place, and in such a grand style. Her own home, Green Willows, was a comfortable house, with a modicum of servants, just enough to keep the estate running smoothly and to see to the family's needs. But Camareigh, thought Lady Mary with a disbelieving shake of her red head, was almost deserving of homage.

She had often wondered how Sabrina had managed so smoothly over the years the responsibilities of being the Duchess of Camareigh. No, Lady Mary smiled, retracting her thought, Sabrina was strong and very determined, and when she set her mind on something, she always succeeded. If it hadn't been for Sabrina all of those years ago . . . how many now? Twenty, no, closer to twenty-five it was, when they had fled Scotland and the bloodshed of Culloden and arrived at Verrick House, the small Elizabethan manor that was their birthplace. But at that time it had held no memories for the three children fresh from the Highlands. They'd had a difficult time even keeping food on the table then, Lady Mary remembered, glancing over at the tables set up on the smooth lawn, their linen-covered surfaces cluttered with succulent dishes of every description, while several wine coolers and crystal bowls of punch were filled to capacity to satisfy the thirsty. Mary could still remember another time when . . . no, she would not think of those days, for they were of the past, and should be long forgotten. But it was hard not to think about one's memories, and of late, because she had been troubled by her thoughts, it seemed to Mary that the past was more vivid than ever before.

The sound of laughter drew Lady Mary's gentle gray eyes toward a group of young men playing croquet in the distance. Ewan, her eldest son, and his two brothers, George and James, along with their cousin Francis, were all there. With their coats thrown into a disorderly pile on the grass, and their shirtsleeves rolled up around their elbows, the cousins, all of a similar age, were hard to distinguish from one another.

Lady Mary's gaze sought out her husband's familiar figure as he came across the gentle slope of lawn, his stride slow but even as he kept pace with the Duke. They were deeply engrossed in conversation, and Lady Mary could well imagine what it was about, for the rumor of war seemed to be constantly raising its ugly head nowadays. Lady Mary was relieved to see that Terence's old wound wasn't bothering him, but then on a warm day like this, it seldom did. It was only during the long winter months, when the cold penetrated deep, that his war wound painfully stiffened his leg, causing him a great deal of silent suffering. Terence was not one to complain or easily accept sympathy. But that had never stopped her from seeing that he'd been comfortable, Lady Mary remembered, the glint in her usually soft gray eyes reminiscent of the look the general had to face often.

Mary sighed, knowing she shouldn't let it upset her still, but she knew she had never quite gotten over Terence's rejoining his regiment. They had enjoyed so many peaceful and contented years at Green Willows that she'd never imagined in her wildest of dreams that Terence would agree, after he'd been asked by his friends and former fellow officers, to rejoin his troops fighting on the Continent. She supposed it had been at the back of his mind all along, but that out of love and consideration for her and the child she carried in her womb, he had not seriously contemplated it until a delegation of officers had landed on their doorstep and pleaded with him to come back to his men. She had thought she would never be able to forgive him for abandoning her and their children, even though she had realized that for Terence it would have been not only dishonorable, but cowardly as well to reject his men's desperate plea. Terence was not a bloodthirsty man; in fact, he was a very compassionate man, but he was a soldier, and had been for most of his adult life. He enjoyed playing the country squire, but when the call to arms was sounded, it was hard for him not to respond, especially when men he had known and served with were being slaughtered on the field of battle. But as soon as she'd seen him come limping home, his wound still raw, she'd forgotten all of her resentment and channeled all her efforts into nursing Terence back to health. He had been promoted to general, received numerous medals for valor, and had even been knighted for his service to king and country. But none of that had mattered to her, for all she had prayed for had been Terence's safe return to Green Willows. And if indeed there was to be another war, what with this talk of rebellion brewing in the colonies, then she was thankful that Terence was finally too old to rejoin his regiment this time.

Giggling voices, crying out to be pushed higher and higher, caught Lady Mary's attention. She glanced over to where the younger children were playing on swings tied to the heavier branches of the trees, their dangling legs sweeping high and low as they took turns pushing each other into the heavens.

"Lovely, isn't it?" the Duchess commented lazily, her eyes following Mary's around the lawns. "I wish we could spend every single afternoon out here under the trees," she added dreamily, smoothing a fair curl from the forehead of her sleeping daughter, who lay curled up on her lap.

Lady Mary smiled. "You always have wished for the impossible, and yet," she paused thoughtfully, "you do seem to have your wishes granted sooner or later." Lady Mary glanced down at Sabrina's sleepy-eyed son, whose golden head was dropping against the Duchess's lap as he finally dozed off. Mary grinned and touched his soft cheek. "These two must have come as quite a surprise to Lucien."

"It shouldn't have. 'Twas his doing," the Duchess replied with an impish twinkle in her eye that reminded her sister of that little rascal Robin.

"There was a time," Lady Mary continued, "when I thought Rhea Claire might be your only child. She certainly has grown into a lovely young woman. I always did think, and still do in fact, that she was the most exquisite baby I've ever seen. I see much of you in her, Rina, especially in her eyes. But with that gold hair she is Lucien's daughter."

"Lucien says he is relieved she did not inherit my quick temper. Although I do wonder," the Duchess added, "if it is not better, perhaps, to rid yourself of your anger quickly, rather than let it simmer and build until it boils over. That is what happens to Lucien, and then there is all hell to pay. Rhea is like Lucien. She seems very indolent, even docile, but her anger will be simmering underneath. She will have been carefully thinking out her revenge, or her cutting sarcasms, and then she will strike back, leaving you quite stunned by the experience."

"Are you and Lucien going to allow a match between Rhea Claire and the Earl of Rendale?" Lady Mary asked curiously, a shadow of something flickering across her face.

The Duchess smiled at the thought. "I know Rhea is of marrying age, but she still seems so young. And as far as we are concerned, there is no hurry for her to wed. Also, I am not sure we totally approve of the Earl."

Lady Mary smiled now. "I doubt whether *any* man will ever be totally acceptable to you and Lucien. Wesley Lawton, however, does seem to be a nice enough young man," she added, her gaze traveling to the young couple in question as they strolled along the lake shore with Richard and his wife. "Things have worked out nicely for Richard. I do like Sarah."

"Yes, so do I," the Duchess agreed. "I am pleased that he brought her home to Camareigh for the birth of their first child. We will make sure that nothing goes wrong. Indeed, nothing would dare to go wrong with

Rawley overseeing the birth. Sometimes I swear she knows more about healing than most doctors, and yet, except for a year in London, she has spent her whole life working at Camareigh as a maid, and claims, quite vehemently too, that she has no higher aspirations than living and dying right where she was born. She says she belongs here, and nowhere else. She's quite fond of Richard, especially that red hair. She'll see that nothing endangers the life of his wife or his firstborn."

"I do miss Richard," the Duchess confessed. "But he does seem to love living in Scotland, and it is, after all, his heritage. Grandfather would have been pleased, I think. Although I suspect he'd think Richard a bit too English now. But as to Rhea," the Duchess continued, changing the subject, her eyes narrowed in thought as she watched her daughter and the besotted Earl of Rendale, "there is still plenty of time. Actually, we have had numerous offers for her hand in marriage, but the gentlemen have either been dirt poor and hoping to acquire an easy fortune, or aging libertines finally wanting to settle down before it's too late, or genuinely lovestruck young bucks reciting poetry, which, believe me, can become quite tedious. So far we have had little trouble rejecting their proposals, for Rhea has wanted nothing to do with any of them. However, I do think that Lucien strikes terror into the hearts of most of them, for there is nothing worse than a reformed rake as a father."

"Yes, I can see how Lucien might seem a trifle intimidating, especially if one's conscience is not clear. When Maggie and Anna are of age," Lady Mary stated with certainty, "I'm sure Terence will play the general to the hilt. I'm certain he shall have half of their suitors signing up for duty just to please him, as well as to escape his eagle eye," she added with a good-natured laugh, her eyes lingering on her husband before they moved on to gaze at the rippling waters of the lake.

As quickly as a cloud passing across the sun, Lady Mary Fletcher's smile faded, and her eyes became darkened by unseen thoughts. Flashes of strange and familiar faces, bizarre surroundings and hazy incidents swirled through her mind with dizzying speed.

"What is wrong?" the Duchess asked in concern, noticing the strange expression on Mary's usually serene face. "What is amiss? Aren't you feeling well? Perhaps a sip of wine would . . ." But the Duchess never finished her suggestion. A sudden thought had struck her, and she felt a cold chill spread through her. "You've had a vision, haven't you, Mary? That is what brought you to Camareigh a day early, isn't it?" she demanded in a hollow-sounding voice.

Lady Mary Fletcher turned slowly to face her sister, for she had lived too long with the curse of second sight not to fully understand the implications of her visions. Nor could she, or would she, lie to Sabrina about it—Sabrina, of all people, had the right to know the truth.

"Yes, Rina," Mary answered quietly, confirming her sister's worst fears, "I've had a vision."

"God, it has been so long since you've experienced one. I'd almost forgotten about them," said the Duchess, more to herself than to Mary, her brow troubled with her thoughts.

"I know," Mary replied sadly, "I, too, had hoped to be spared any more of these damned visions." Her voice was uncommonly harsh.

A single teardrop was clinging to her lashes as her darkening gray eyes met her sister's anxious glance. "Life has been so idyllic. Too much so, I suspect. If only I could tell you, Rina, exactly what it is that I fear," she said almost apologetically, her hands clenched into tight fists. "I feel so helpless. I always have. This damned sight only gives me fears. I sometimes think I would rather have something terrible happen, without the prior knowledge, than to know it is coming, to sit here expecting it, but be unable to do anything to stop it." A sob caught in her throat. "Do you realize that a hundred years ago I would have been burned at the stake as a witch, because of the knowledge I possess?"

"Oh, Mary, dear, sweet Mary," Sabrina breathed. "If I could help you, I would. If I could blind you to this tormenting inner sight, I would burn it out of you, but you know it is beyond our control. 'Twas meant to be,

Mary," Sabrina said softly, trying to comfort her sister. "Think of the times you have helped us, Mary. Of the times you saved Richard, and me, from certain death. Perhaps, with this warning you will be able to avert something terrible from happening. Now please, dear," she coaxed, holding Mary's cold hand in hers, "tell me what you have seen. Share it with me."

" 'Tis water, Rina," Mary began, her voice husky with tears. "I can see deep water, no, dark water. Dark water rippling around me. I can almost smell the stench rising from it. I feel befouled by it, as if it is going to suck me under. It is so black, so horrible!" Mary cried, burying her face in her clasped hands. "It is so cold around me. And there is such unbridled terror, and yes, death," she said in a whisper. "I can see something gold, shining like a star in the depths below. And above," her voice was cracking under the strain, "I see dragons. Oh, God help me! You must think me crazed, Rina, to be seeing dragons. They're laughing and snarling, and they're dangerous. I keep seeing these horrible red and green dragons. They seem to be haunting me. And sometimes I feel like reaching out to them; at other times I feel myself drawing back in terror. I'm so confused, Rina!"

Mary raised a ravaged face and stared out on the warm summer afternoon, taking deep breaths as she gulped for air. "You should hate me. Despise me for bringing such evil premonitions to Camareigh, but Rina," Mary said, reaching out to grasp Sabrina's hand in a painful grip, " 'tis *your* face I see full of grief. 'Tis *your* eyes I see full of such terror. How could I not tell you, warn you?" she pleaded.

Sabrina, Duchess of Camareigh, swallowed something painful that had lodged in her throat, her arm tightening instinctively around the innocent child sleeping peacefully in her lap. Her eyes scanned the horizon as if searching—but for what? What was out there waiting to strike? And what danger did it present, and for whom? Sabrina watched Lucien walk toward her across the lawn, Terence at his side, and she wanted so desperately to reach out to Lucien for comfort, for strength, but she couldn't seem to move or even to cry out. Mary's vision of terror had wrapped itself around her, paralyzing her as she stared helplessly at her loved ones, knowing that some tragedy was going to strike at the heart of Camareigh—and that all she could do was sit and wait and watch as ultimately the terror unfolded.

> *The fire which seems extinguished often slumbers beneath the ashes.*
>
> Pierre Corneille

Venice—Fall, 1769

Chapter 3

BENEATH the Bridge of Sighs the dark waters of the Rio de Palazzo rippled in the wake of the black, shallow-hulled gondola sliding silently past. The lacy-patterned, rose and white marble arches and columns of the Doges' Palace climbed like a wall of light out of the depths, while on the opposite side of the canal, as vivid in contrast as black is to white, stood the crouching form of the pozzi, the forbidding prison block that housed the less fortunate of Venice. Its ominous presence gave reason for the name of the Bridge of Sighs, for few who crossed over that covered bridge into the damp prison cells ever crossed back again into the light of freedom.

Sitting in solitary silence in the gondola was a figure swathed in the black of mourning, for the long, slender craft had just crossed St. Mark's basin from the Church of San Giorgio Maggiore, where the grieving woman had said her last farewell to her loved one. With slow, even strokes of his oar the gondolier, perched high in the stern, sent the canalboat smoothly along the winding

63

miles of narrow, back canals, which twisted into the heart of the city that had once been the proud, shining jewel of the Adriatic. The great domes of St. Mark's Basilica still glowed golden in the Italian sun, and many of the marble palaces of the once-powerful merchant-princes were still blessed and inhabited by the gilded few who could afford the expensive pleasures of their leisure hours. But there was a rot eating away at the city and her people, an ever-growing decadence of mind and spirit that ate away at the flesh of the body and was as destructive as the foul water lapping around the crumbling foundations of the buildings of Venice.

Through this spreading illness and adding to its darkness moved La Rosa Triste, The Sad Rose, one of the most infamous and sought-after courtesans of Venice. So named by the Venetians because she dressed in black and wore a single red rose in her hair, she was a figure of mystery—for no one had ever seen her face. In a city where the wearing of masks was not unusual, where aristocrat and peasant, high-born lady and whore, duke and gigolo could mix freely, without fearing the disclosure of a reputable identity, La Rosa Triste stood apart, her face and true name a secret even to her most ardent, and paying, admirers. But she was beautiful—a madonna, some said—and all of Venice knew this to be true. For on one or two occasions, when attending a carnival or grand ball, La Rosa Triste had left behind her usual domino, the black mask that covered most of her face, and had instead donned an extraordinary mask. Half of her face, from forehead to chin, was covered by a black silk mask, while the other half of her face was left bare. Her classical features were said to be as innocently beautiful as those of an angel, and with her pale eyes and hair she stood out like a shining star in a midnight sky.

Why La Rosa Triste dressed in black and red roses, no one knew for certain, although some who were less kind and perhaps jealous of her popularity said that it was merely for show, to catch the eye. But others, who seemed to know, said it was because her family and true love had been murdered in a vendetta, and that now she was burying the last of her loved ones. Her grief, at least now, was very real, for her beloved brother, Le Principe Biondo, The Blond Prince, as he'd been fondly nicknamed by the wealthy, noble ladies he'd played the *cicisbéo* for, was dead. He had been found floating in the dirty waters of the canal, a stiletto embedded in his back.

With his princely airs and beautiful face he had enchanted the jaded ladies of Venice when he'd acted as escort for them while their husbands had purchased elsewhere their own private amusements. By a lady's side he had served as escort, maid, confidant and companion, court jester and lover—always at his lady's beck and call. Perhaps Le Principe Biondo had played the *cicisbéo* too well, and a jealous husband had ridded himself of a rival. Or had an enraged noblewoman and former protectress wanted her lover back—and had been scorned instead? Had Le Principe Biondo insulted the wrong person, perhaps cast his eyes at some churlish gentleman's wife or mistress? He'd had the reputation of being contemptuous and jeering of those he thought beneath his dignity, and of those he didn't need to toady up to. Too often, while intoxicated from imbibing too freely of port wine and punch, Le Principe Biondo had given rein to his tongue, which had, more often than not, been coated with disparaging remarks that were bitingly sarcastic. No one had been exempt from his virulence, except perhaps for La Rosa Triste, although no one was the wiser about their personal relationship, and what passed between them in the luxurious palace they rented just off the Grand Canal.

"Lui è morto! Le Principe Biondo è morto!" The shrill cry sliced through the dark shadows of the canal as the gondola carrying La Rosa Triste slid beneath a bridge crowded with onlookers, some of whom were mourners. Roses floated down around the gondola as it reappeared on the other side and slipped farther down the canal, with wails of grief followed in its wake.

Suddenly a low laugh escaped from the black-clad figure, and as the slim shoulders began to shake, the laughter built into a crescendo of uncontrolled mirth. The gondolier nervously crossed himself as the eerie laughter continued, until finally it broke down into deep sobs of despair that left the cloaked mourner gasping for breath.

With a shaking hand La Rosa Triste picked up the single rose that had fallen onto her lap, pressing her lips to it as she breathed in its sweet fragrance. He was dead. She had seen him buried this very day, and he had left her alone in their exile. How dare he do this to her? How dare he leave her to suffer alone? God, if she only could drag him up from the grave she would. Damn him anyway, he had no right to die!

The gondola nudged against the landing in front of an elegant and strangely dignified baroque palazzo. The broad marble steps leading down to the water's edge were crowded with liveried footmen waiting to assist their mistress from the gently swaying gondola the moment she placed a satin-slippered foot on the carpeted stair.

Never before had the steps seemed so hard to climb, La Rosa Triste thought as she stumbled slightly, recovering before an attentive footman could reach out. Determinedly, she climbed the last of the steps, sweeping regally into her home through the carved double doors. Across the cold marble flagstones she moved, her black skirts whispering. With a steadying hand placed on the balustrade, La Rosa Triste climbed the curving flight of stairs to her private apartment. Her veiled head was bowed slightly as she entered through the tall doors and her black figure was reflected and multiplied in the mirrored walls, as were the rococo furnishings of the room. Ornately carved and gilded tables and scarlet, silk-covered chairs and sofas filled the room with splashes of color. Sparkling chandeliers with painted flowers hung from the frescoed ceiling above La Rosa Triste, who was standing in silent contemplation of the quivering shadows reflected off the water of the canal below.

"Mi scusi, Signora," Sophia, La Rosa Triste's loyal maid and ever-present shadow, spoke softly, almost in a whisper so as not to disturb her beloved mistress. "I tell him, you wish not to see him, but he say you will," she said, wringing her hands. "I tell him you bury your

brother today. You much sad, and you no wish to see him."

"Who dares to disturb me?" La Rosa Triste demanded as she looked up, her thoughts broken by her maid's apologetic voice.

"I do," said Conte Niccolò Rasghieri, rising from his seat. The high velvet back of the chair had hidden him from La Rosa Triste's view. He now came forward as if he had every right to be here in La Rosa Triste's salon, his casually elegant air and arrogantly held head telling its own story of generations of aristocratic wealth and privilege. He was not a young man, and his years of debauchery and sybaritic indulgences had left their mark on his thin face, in deep grooves that ran from his aquiline nose to his sensual mouth. His lips seemed to have settled into a permanent sneer of contempt and there was a weariness in the slight droop of his shoulders. But it was the tired, jaded expression in his eyes that mirrored his true feelings.

"Nicki," La Rosa Triste breathed her friend and lover's name. Then, after a moment's hesitation, she threw herself into the familiar arms she had known for over fifteen years.

Looking over her veiled head at the vigilant Sophia, he motioned the maid from the room with an imperious hand, ignoring the old woman's jealous glare as he completely took over comforting her mistress.

"He is dead, Nicki," La Rosa Triste cried. "He has finally left me. What shall I do without him? He was my other half. I shall miss him so, Nicki," she sobbed, then looked up at the tall Conte who held her so securely in his arms. "But I still have you. Always you come when I need you most. Why is that, I wonder?" she asked him, her pale blue eyes glittering strangely through her mask.

The Conte smiled. "Because I do not *have* to come. Because it is *my* choice alone, and I do not owe you anything. We have no ties to one another. That is why we are still friends today. We understand one another, my dear. You do not set down rules for me to follow, nor do I for you. I do not sit in judgment on you. I accept you as you are, and you accept me as I am."

"Did you never wish that I was not a courtesan?" she asked him, voicing a question on which she'd held her silence for many years. "That I could walk with pride into your home, meet your wife without being shunned?"

The Conte laughed, his hold tightening painfully on La Rosa Triste as she tried to pull away from him, her shoulders stiffening with indignation at his laughter. "God forbid that ever happening. She would bore you stiff, my dear. Besides, *you* have nothing to be ashamed of, for I sometimes wonder if there is really any difference between the two of you. She calls herself a lady, and you are called a . . ." He allowed his words to drop off and shrugged his shoulders. "But she has her lovers, as do most *ladies* of this town. But you, my dear, are at least honest about yourself."

"Thank you," La Rosa Triste said a trifle sardonically. "I never knew I had inspired such admiration in you."

"Of course, I suspect that there is more to your past than you will ever let me know about," he continued smoothly, his tone almost rebuking her for her secrets. "You have many of the airs and graces of a lady bred to the part. But you do not mimic your betters; in fact, many a fine lady of Venice has taken to wearing black in imitation of you—but none do it so well as yourself, madam."

La Rosa Triste sighed deeply. "You are so good for me. Already I begin to forget some of my misery. I know you never cared much for my brother, but he was all that I had." As she spoke tears were shimmering in her eyes. "And now he is gone, and I have nothing. Nothing! Everything from the past has gone now. I am alone, and soon you will leave me too."

"No!" the Conte contradicted her, a glint in his eye as he pulled her against him. "I will make you forget, ma rosa triste. You will think of nothing but me. I shall be your every breath from now on. I will have you smiling again, have you crying out with love," he promised as his mouth descended on hers, forcing her to forget her grief under the onslaught of his rising passion. With a sudden movement of his lean body, he swept La Rosa Triste up into his arms and strode with her into the bedchamber that he knew as well as his own, and, with a gentleness unusual for him, laid her down on the fur-covered bed that he knew so well. With a practiced hand he began to undress her, baring the slim alabaster body that had been swathed in black silk.

"You are as lovely today as you were fifteen years ago when I first lay with you," the Conte whispered, removing his own clothing as he stood over the bed. He stared down at her smooth skin, so pale and translucent, her breasts as small and delicate as a young girl's, and he felt his passion as fiery as if he were again a young man of twenty experiencing his first woman. Her glorious silver-gold hair tumbled down around her hips, teasing him with glimpses of soft, secret places.

"You flatter me, Nicki, but I no longer care about the truth. I know I am not a young girl anymore," La Rosa Triste admitted, not grieving for her lost youth. "I have lost some of the satin from my skin, but I have gained across the years so much more in experience," she said, reaching up and pulling him down on top of her. "I can please you far more today than I ever could have at sixteen. That is a fair trade, I think," La Rosa Triste told him with a promise of pleasures to come before her words could be silenced by his searching mouth. "Now make me forget, Nicki. Make me forget the rest of the world except for us. The memory of no one else must intrude. Not now, Nicki. Not tonight."

And so La Rosa Triste forgot her grief. Through the next few weeks she was seen with Conte Niccolò Rasghieri at every ball, carnival, soirée, and amusement held in Venice. From the glittering magnificence of the palazzos lining the Grand Canal, to the squalid gaming hells crowding the narrow back alleys, La Rosa Triste sought her pleasures. Even after the Conte left Venice to see to his country estates on the mainland, La Rosa Triste still roamed, restless and searching, looking for someone or something to help her forget.

But La Rosa Triste's hell-bent path of self-destruction was to be crossed, and ultimately altered, by a chance encounter, a conversation overheard, which would set into motion a terrifying chain of events neither participant ever could have imagined in his wildest dreams. The repercussions of this encounter would spread far beyond the tranquil canals of Venice.

It happened at a masque at the Palazzo Chalzini. The Grand Ballroom was crowded with masked revelers from every walk of life, from priests hiding their vows of chastity behind beaked masks and black silk hoods, to impoverished aristocrats and beggars, their true identities and situations in life hidden behind dominoes, to the incredibly wealthy, who could afford to lose vast sums at the gaming tables, their fingers flashing with jewels while they mixed with impunity amongst the rabble.

La Rosa Triste, dressed in black velvet, with a blood-red rose folded into the silver-gold hair she left unpowdered, moved with graceful assurance from group to group, speaking French, Italian, or English with fluent carelessness, as she playfully teased a French count, lost money to an Italian boatman, or berated an English lord for being too bold, even though she knew she might well make an assignation with him before the night was over.

Like a black widow spider in a dark corner, La Rosa Triste held court with a bevy of admirers, each of whom hoped he might have the good fortune of an hour alone with her. After all, what better claim to make as proof of one's manhood than to have spent a night of love with La Rosa Triste, a courtesan whose favors even the most titled of gentlemen were sometimes denied? With a crystal goblet brimming with wine in one hand, and a black feather fan held indolently in the other, La Rosa Triste surveyed her kingdom with a cynical eye. The gaudy surroundings and noisy people almost bored her, for she had seen it all before.

A loud, slightly raucous laugh caught La Rosa Triste's attention, and she turned her contemptuously amused, pale blue eyes on the woman who had dared to disturb her contemplation. The laugh had emanated from a portly woman, who seemed well used to being the cynosure of all eyes; perhaps in the past she had attracted attention with her beauty, but she now relied upon her range of voice. A black oval mask hid part of her face, although it could not disguise the double chins quivering with her laughter. Her thick hair was powdered and piled high, and it was woven with a string of pearls caught in loops held by ruby and diamond fasteners. A crimson damask gown covered a tightly corseted figure that looked tortured almost beyond human sufferance, but it was not the grand dame's appearance that now held a spellbound La Rosa Triste's attention. Rather, it was the name she had just spoken so casually, as if she said it frequently.

The pale blue eyes pinpointed an indolent young man, who was twirling his discarded mask in obvious boredom as he stood in attendance beside the large woman. He was a handsome boy and could not be more than seventeen, if indeed he was that, but there was a sulky look about him, as if he'd been pampered and petted by his family until he had become a petulant young dandy hanging on to his mama's skirts. He was the center of attention now, which he obviously enjoyed, since he was visibly preening himself, a self-satisfied smile curving his mouth.

". . . . half-brother of the Duchess, he is," the Contessa was saying, her words carrying across the room to the attentively listening La Rosa Triste. "Unfortunately, there was a slight misunderstanding between the Duchess and my late husband, the Marquis, who happened to be her father. This is true," the Contessa said with growing emphasis, catching the doubtful look of one of her listeners and shaking a bejeweled hand at her. "I swear it on my own mother's grave. I was James' third wife, and he was my second husband, but you know he was much older than I," she added with a sniff. "The Duchess and her sister and brother, who are all English, are from his first marriage. Most unfortunate match, you know, but, she was wealthy. But I am afraid," the Contessa continued, eloquently shrugging her thick shoulders, "that the Marquis was a bit negligent in his paternal duties to the bambini. But who would have guessed that the little fiery one would some day wed a Duke? She was a handful, that one, and such a beauty, too. She looked much like my James, and he was quite the proud papa when he finally met her. But her, well," the Contessa said, sadly shaking her head, "she was not one to forget past grievances, or to forgive her papa for his neglect. But the Duke, now there is a man. He was far more understanding, you know, and gave James quite a handsome sum for the marriage settlement, let me tell you. But then a man of his great wealth and stature can well afford to see that his in-laws are well provided for. Imagine," she stated with a proud lifting of her regally coiffed head, "I am the step-mother-in-law of the Duke of Camareigh. A most important man in England. This is the truth."

La Rosa Triste stood like a column of black marble as she heard the name she had first sworn never to utter aloud over a decade ago. The very sound of it made her heart swell painfully in her breast, while her cheeks burned with the heat of her emotions.

"But now that my beloved James has passed away," the Contessa was saying, a delicate lace handkerchief held to her eyes to dab at nonexistent tears, "I thought that the Duchess should be informed of her father's death. And now that his presence has been removed as an obstacle, I thought she should have the opportunity of meeting her brother. It does seem the only decent thing to do, *n'è vero?*"

"I'm not sure I wish to go to London," the half-brother in question commented, his mouth settling into a pout of displeasure.

The Contessa reached out with her fan and sharply tapped her son on the wrist. His responding yelp of pain satisfied her. "You hold your tongue. You have not even been invited to London yet. And you would do well to count your blessings if you are, for I have heard that Camareigh, the ancestral home, is no less magnificent than Versailles."

"If I am not mistaken, Contessa," said a doubting dowager sitting next to the Contessa in overly polite tones, "has not the Marquis been dead for nearly two years now? Why have you not visited this Duchess you claim is your daughter-in-law before now?"

The Contessa turned an eye of dislike on the old woman. "I tell you this, Signora Perelli," she said, for

CHANCE THE WINDS OF FORTUNE

there was no mistaking this meddling Venetian, despite her mask, "and it is most extraordinary, so you may believe me or not." The Contessa shrugged, her simple gesture conveying her lack of interest in the other woman's opinion. "My step-daughter, *the Duchess,* and her husband, *the Duke,* a devil if ever there was one, made a remarkable love match. Amazing, for you know he has a scar running down his face. Oh, he looks, and is, most diabolical," she added, raising her hands as if in prayer. "But these Inglese, they are the strange ones. I should know, I lived with the Marquis for over fifteen years. So cold they are at times, not to mention that country of theirs. Well, as I was saying, it is most uncommon, for the Duchess, when I had written, had just given birth to twins. Twins! Can you imagine such a thing? The Duke and Duchess are not newlyweds; in fact, they have been married for close to twenty years now."

"Amazing!"

"Si, but who *is* the father?"

"The Duke," the Contessa replied most assuredly. "They say, and this I have heard from friends in London, and they would know, that twins have been born in the Dominick family for generations. It is not unusual. Also, they say that the twins, a boy and a girl, are both fair-haired like the Duke. So I think there is little doubt that they are his. That is why my trip was postponed," the Contessa explained. "The Duchess was quite ill from their birth, and I should think so. Twins! And at her age, why it is most . . ." The Contessa's words trailed off as a strange cry drifted to the silent group. *"Che cosa è quello?"* she demanded, glancing around before glaring up at her son. "Did you make that awful wail?"

Young Giulio opened his mouth in surprise, then took a safe step backward as he indignantly protested his innocence. "Of course not, Mama!"

"Well, I should certainly hope not. I pray I never hear such a screech as long as I live. It sent a shiver up my spine," the Contessa said, fanning herself. "Giulio, go fetch your Mama something to sip. I think I am growing faint. Now, where was I? Ah, yes . . ." the Contessa continued, her eyes following her son's figure as he passed the empty corner where only moments before La Rosa Triste had stood.

"Signora! Signora! Che cosa c'è?" Sophia cried out in alarm as her mistress stormed up the grand staircase, leaving the puffing maid far behind. By the time Sophia had reached the doors to her mistress's private apartment they were barred against her. She hesitated before the closed doors, her eyes round with fear as she listened to the ranting going on within, which was broken only by the sound of shattering glass.

"Dio Mio," Sophia whispered, still panting from her speedy climb up the stairs; then, as a thud hit the door, she jumped back and crossed herself for protection against whatever evil was driving her mistress into an uncontrollable frenzy.

Beyond the closed doors La Rosa Triste stared bemusedly at the ruins of her once elegant bedchamber, her breathing ragged as she fought for control. Then with her breath coming in short, uneven gasps, she collapsed on the edge of her bed. Through the opened doors she could see the destruction she had wrought in her salon, yet she had no real memory of doing it.

"Twins!" La Rosa Triste cried out in disbelief and outrage. "How dare him! Twins!" She rolled over on the bed, her screams muffled against the soft fur coverlet as she beat against it with clenched fists. "Damn him! Damn his rotten soul to hell! 'Tis his fault. It always has been. I hate him, hate him! Look what he has done to me. He's taken everything away, everything. I hate you, Lucien!"

With a deep sob of despair La Rosa Triste climbed from the bed, tripping over her cloak. In a savage motion she threw it off and stumbled to the cracked mirror hanging off center in one of the wall panels. With shaking hands she began to untie the cords that were always securely tied around her head to hold her mask immovable. Not once in almost eighteen years had she seen her own face revealed without its protective mask. She had sworn never to gaze upon it, but now . . .

Without stopping to think she pulled the mask free, leaving her face bared, her inhuman cry of pain echoing around the room as she stared at the jagged scar running from chin to temple that destroyed forever the perfection of her features. The cicatrix was an ugly, reddish purple color that moved in a puckered line along the length of her face. The base of the wound pulled down the corner of her mouth just slightly, but it was enough to give her a grotesque sneer. The more La Rosa Triste stared at her deformity, the more the scar began to take the shape of a sloppily executed L, marking her for eternity with the brand of Lucien.

La Rosa Triste gazed at her strange reflection in the mirror, almost unable to believe her disfigurement. How many of these fine Venetians, as well as others she had known, would have given their fortunes to have gazed beneath her mask? Once or twice an overly amorous and drunken lover (for he would not have dared unless he were drunk), had tried to snatch the mask from her face. But with her able-bodied footmen standing close by outside her apartment, prepared for just such an occurrence, the foolhardy gentlemen had been shown the door. Only once, long ago, when they had first come to Venice, had anyone seen her face. It had happened before she'd gained her notoriety and power, for no one would dare to offend her now; she had many powerful friends, some of whom were her lovers—and with a softly spoken word in the right ear, a man could disappear forever.

She could barely remember that night. She had been having a private dinner with a man, and before she knew what he was going to do, he had lifted her mask from her face. His look of shocked horror as he'd stared at her scarred face still caused her unbearable pain. She couldn't remember at all what had happened after that endless moment of discovery, except that Percy had come into the room and found her standing over the man, who had a dinner knife protruding from his chest.

Percy had helped her dispose of the body, and no one had ever been the wiser about the man's disappearance. But she had learned a valuable lesson, and never again had she been caught off guard. Even the Conte had never seen her face. He respected her privacy, and her reasons for wanting to keep it. Perhaps he even found it exciting to make love to a woman whose face he'd not know if he saw it unmasked. Many men felt that way. They enjoyed the mystery surrounding her, but only she knew the truth.

She was not La Rosa Triste. She was Kate! Lady Katherine Anders, granddaughter of the seventh Duke of Camareigh, and cousin to Lucien Dominick, ninth Duke of Camareigh. She and Percy were the ones who deserved Camareigh, not Lucien. She and Percy should have been living at Camareigh right now, not Lucien. Percy. Percy, *her* twin. And now Lucien had twins. *Twins*—just like she and Percy had been.

They all wondered why she wore black. Black. Black for mourning. Mourning for all that she had lost, for what she had been cheated of by dear cousin Lucien. Her mourning for Camareigh had never ended, and now she mourned for the loss of the one person she had ever truly loved. Percy. Dear, sweet Percy. And roses? Red roses? Why, in memory of England, of course. Her beloved England. Her home, the land from which she had been exiled by Lucien.

Lucien had stolen everything from her, Kate thought, looking dazedly at her hideously scarred face, her fingers rubbing against the roughly healed scar tissue. And now he was the cause of Percy's death. Percy was gone. Kate's eyes drifted over to a painting which had miraculously escaped destruction. It was draped in black crepe, and could almost have been a portrait of Kate, so identical was the likeness. But it was a portrait of a young man dressed in blue velvet, the style of his coat and stock dating it back almost twenty years. The delicately molded lips were curved in a sweet smile, while the sherry-colored eyes seemed to reflect some inner amusement. He had been so beautiful then, so perfect.

A male replica of herself. Percy's face blurred through her tears as Kate remembered all of the times they'd had together, especially the ones spent at Camareigh. A deep-seated anger and resentment began to smolder within her as she reflected on all the wonderful, carefree days they'd shared before being banished from Camareigh and England.

It always had been just the two of them, and that was the way it always should have been. Even her brief marriage to Lord Charles Anders had not altered her closeness to Percy, for even a husband could not come between that special quality unique to twins. Of course, she hadn't loved Charles, so he'd never been any competition for Percy. She'd married Charles solely for his wealth and title. One day he would have inherited a considerable estate from his father, the Earl of Grenborough, as well as that old gentleman's title. But as fortune would have it, the Earl had outlived his only son, and the title had passed to a cousin after the Earl had finally died the following year. So close she had come, and yet before she could even blink her eye, she'd found herself a well-to-do widow, cheated by death out of becoming a Countess.

On the other hand, the fine Lady Anne, Percy's wife, had thought she could replace Kate in Percy's affection. She had sought to turn Percy from Kate, but she had been wrong. He couldn't forsake his Kate, for they breathed as one—they were nothing without each other. Percy had only married Lady Anne for her money. Percy and Kate had long ago spent all of the legacy left to Kate from her late husband's estate, and they were desperate for funds. But the marriage had done little to help them, for Lady Anne's money had not lasted long after they'd settled in Venice. And when times had got hard, what had Percy's little mouse of a wife done? She'd run back to England and the safe bosom of her family, leaving Percy and Kate to fend for themselves. Actually, Kate had been glad to see the back of that English miss and her runny-nosed brats. Why Percy had ever fathered them, she would never understand. Kate smiled, thinking

of Lady Anne back in England, not realizing she was a
widow. And nor would she find it out for a long, long
time.

She and Percy had been strong, and they had survived
those first long winters in Venice. But it shouldn't have
to have been like that. Kate knew it should have been
different. If Lucien had never been born, if he'd never
walked the face of the earth, then she and Percy
would've been the rightful heirs to Camareigh. They
would have been the golden ones, the ones with the
money and influence. But no, they had been the poor
cousins, the ones to have pittance doled out to them. As
Kate stared at herself in the mirror, her pale eyes hypnotized by her distorted face, she remembered once
again the agonizing pain she had suffered that day in
the small English inn when the pistol, which Percy and
Lucien had been struggling to possess, had gone off accidentally. The ricocheting bullet had scored a deep
trough through her cheek, leaving her lying in a pool of
her own blood. The blood spilled that day should have
been Lucien's.

Nothing had gone as planned, but then it seldom had
when it concerned Lucien. He led a charmed life. Kate
laughed harshly, thinking of the many times she and
Percy had tried unsuccessfully to end their dear cousin's
life. But he had always managed to survive, like a cat
with nine lives. It had been seventeen, no, eighteen
years now since she had last seen Lucien, and he must
have used up most of those extra lives by now. In fact,
he must be down to about the last one.

Sighing, Kate moved slowly toward her bed, sinking
wearily into the soft fur. She was so tired, so sleepy.
And yet she could not sleep, must not sleep, not yet.
She had to think. Percy was dead; she had to keep re-
minding herself of that. Her sweet Percy was dead, and
Lucien was still alive. Her twin was gone, and yet
Lucien had fathered twins.

Kate rubbed her throbbing temples as she looked
around the shambles of her room, her eyes dulled with
unbearable pain. She would think of something. There
must be some way to make Lucien pay for his crimes

against them. She couldn't let Percy die unrevenged. Yes, Kate decided, yawning as she buried her scarred face in the silky fur, Lucien would pay, and pay dearly. She would find a way of seeking retribution, but for now . . . now she must sleep. There would be time enough tomorrow to plan her revenge against Lucien Dominick, Duke of Camareigh.

> *The bright day is done,*
> *And we are for the dark.*
> Shakespeare

Chapter 4

THE early twilight of late autumn lingered in the hazy skies over the sprawling metropolis of London. Dark, grayish smoke curled upward into the sky from a thousand chimneys of red and gray brick and Portland stone, as the city's inhabitants tried to fight off the damp chill creeping in from the Thames. The slight warmth of the day was fleeing quickly under the fall of darkness. Whether it was a struggling family lighting a few precious pieces of hoarded coal in a tenement on the industrial east side, or a genial landlord rubbing his hands before a crackling fire of sweet-smelling wood in an inn or tavern in the Whitechapel or Limehouse districts along the river, or a busy maid tending a hearth in an elegant salon in one of the mansions in the fashionable squares of Russell, Berkeley, or Hanover, they all contributed to the grimy layer of soot settling down over the city.

Vendors were still bustling in the streets, hawking their wares, ringing hand bells to attract the attention of passers-by. Both the pungent odors of fresh oysters being sold cheap from wheelbarrows and yesterday's prawns being peddled at a bargain on every corner mixed with the noisome smells of the offal collecting in the open sewers and gutters, which needed a good, hard rain to wash it into the Thames. The more savory scents wafting from the muffin-men and pie-women were enticement enough to draw the eye of the prospective customer from other itinerant vendors offering asses' milk, fresh fruits, and vegetables, whose trays were weighed down with goods as they jostled for position along the narrow, cobbled streets of London.

Crowding close along miles of wharves was a forest of stark masts swaying and bobbing with the rise and fall of the tide. Dotting the surface of the Thames as it curved through London were ships representing every great and small seafaring nation of the world that traded with the ever-expanding, far-reaching British empire. There were well-seasoned merchantmen flying foreign flags and riding low in the water, barques with cargo nets stretched wide, luggers laden in bulk, schooners that had already discharged their cargoes and were waiting to be loaded again for their return voyages, and coastal fishing boats and river barges that knew well the tides and currents of the Thames. Filling the busy wharves to capacity, until they creaked and trembled beneath the weight, were crates and bales, barrels and chests of every conceivable size and content. The aromatic and exotic fragrances of coffee and cacao beans, nutmeg, clove, molasses and cayenne from the Indies, tobacco from the colonies, as well as countless varieties of teas from the China trade, all blended with the odor of the honest sweat of dock workers and seamen, who were lifting bales of finely woven silks, Genoa velvets, and delicate laces from convents in France, soft furs from the Northwest Territory for milady's cloak, barrels of flour and stacks of timber from across the Atlantic, and casks of aged wines and brandies from cellars on the Continent.

The London docks were a hive of activity as heavily loaded drays, their harnesses straining, were pulled away by teams of short, thickset Welsh cobs or the larger Suffolk Punches. But now that the dank, swirling fog was rolling in off the water, all business was coming to

81

a halt. As the workers retreated to the warmth of a favorite tavern, the sudden silence shrouding the docks was as deafening as the clanging racket of only moments before had been. The only sounds to be heard now along the docks were the muffled voices and laughter coming from inside smoky, well-lit taverns, and the creaking of masts and gentle lapping of the river current against wooden hulls.

Out in the river, the *Stella Reale,* a merchantman out of Venice, had long since made fast her moorings, unloaded her cargo, and sent passengers ashore. However, an odd trio of travelers had been the last passengers on board to set foot on dry land. The heavily veiled woman dressed in black and her hulking footman, who had moved with unusual grace for a man of his size, had been strangely silent, while the ancient little woman hurrying after them had never ceased her agitated flow of foreign words.

A hackney coach had been hired, and now was rattling along the narrow, twisting cobblestone lanes in the oldest part of the city of London, the grumbling coachman cracking his whip over the flowing manes of his pair of grays. From beneath his beetle brows, the coachman cast a curious glance at the silent figure sitting beside him on the box, who seemed oblivious to the sights and sounds around him, not to mention the nip in the air.

"Yer mistress there," the coachman began, jerking his head back. "Her's a queer one, sure enough. Who'd 'av thought her be an Englishwoman? Tryin' to be polite, Oi was. Just welcomin' a stranger t'London," he said, his voice heavy with disgust as he spat over the side of the coach. "And what does 'er laidyship do—and not even sparin' me a glance, she didn't! Says to me, ever so hoity-toity like, 'I am not a fool, my good man, so you might as well speak properly, if indeed that is possible for you, which I seriously doubt. I happen to be English, and speak the language better than you shall ever have hope of doing. And don't try to pad the fare, for I know London better than you ever shall,'" said the coachman, mimicking his upper-class passenger, then snorting with ill-concealed derision. "So Oi'm askin' ye now, if'n her knows London better'n meself, why is it her wants a tour of the city? Crazy her be, that's it. Juz me luck to get a crackbrained female as a passenger on a foul night like this'un.

"Don't understand a bleedin' word Oi've said, d'ye? Well," he added with another appraising look at his silent companion, " 'tis just as well. Wouldn't care to tangle with ye, that's fer sure. But Oi'm goin' to be sayin' this anyhow, 'cause Oi'm an 'onest man, Oi am, and Oi'm not takin' kindly to bein' accused of cullyin' practices. and 'twouldn't 'av made no different if'n she 'ad been *I*talian. Would've charged the same, Oi would've. 'Ow was Oi to be knowin' any different with that old woman ajawin' away in some feurin tongue? And now," added the much aggrieved coachman, his heavy brows lifted heavenward for emphasis, "her 'as me stoppin' fer flowers! Be dark soon, 'twill, and 'ere we are hurry-scurrin' across town and—

" 'Ere, watch out ye son of a whoremonger! Aye! And the same t'ye, and t'ye grandmother as well!" the coach-man yelled, shaking his gloved fist at the sedan chair that had shot across their path, the cringing, liveried footmen carrying it away from the powerful forelegs of the pair of grays.

Inside the coach, Lady Katherine Anders was smiling behind her veil as she listened to the familiar voices of London. The offensive language and abuse heaped on the heads of the unfortunate footmen's families sounded like music in her ears, for the sights and sounds of London could not be duplicated anywhere else in the world. And how she had missed it all, Kate thought now, pushing aside the leather covering of the coach window and staring out with burning eyes, never seeing quite enough to fill the deep ache within her.

The congested streets were lined with neat rows of narrow, sash-windowed shops that had gaily painted signs swinging above glaze-windowed doors. From chemists, carpenters, and printsellers, to publishers, saddlers, and picture frame makers, all were hoping to hear the bells above their doors jingling with a steady stream of customers.

As the coach halted at a busy crossroads, Kate watched a splendid coach-and-six rumble past, its liveried attendants hanging on for dear life, while outriders rode on ahead to clear a passage through the crowded roadway. Kate recognized the crest painted on the door of the coach and wondered whether time had been kind to the occupants. As she leaned back against the leather-cushioned seat, she speculated about where her old acquaintances might be headed. Ranelagh and Vauxhall, the pleasure gardens, would be closed for the winter season, but had they been open, their customers could have enjoyed concerts of Handel in the Pavilion, midnight suppers in secluded alcoves, and brief assignations along dark paths.

Kate's head lolled against the seat as the coachman sent the coach across the road, the big wheels sliding sideways on the slippery cobblestones. She buried her face in the soft petals of the roses she had purchased from a thin, bedraggled flower girl near St. Paul's Cathedral. The dome of that magnificent church sat like a jeweled crown above the city. With a deep sigh of satisfaction, Kate breathed in the sweet scent of English roses—she was in England at last!

The coach continued along the Strand, the time-weary roadway connecting the carefully planned squares of the Georgian aristocrats to the old parts of the city, with its Tudor shops and twisting lanes. The hackney coach stopped, as had been ordered, across from a Queen Anne style house in a discreetly laid out square near a small park. Although this square was not as elegant as some of the larger, more prominent ones, it was no less exclusive.

Kate stared unblinkingly at the red brick house with its steep roof and double-tiering of sash windows. There was a single mahogany door centered in the severe facade. Behind that door had been a marble-floored entrance hall and a massive staircase with carved balustrades. At the end of the hall had been a door leading into the garden. It had been a garden full of roses—her garden. Most of the rooms in the comfortable house had been oak paneled, although her own bedchamber and dressing room had been hung with the finest chinoiserie silk wallpaper. She could remember seeing the small park from her bedchamber window—not that she had spared much time or thought for it then. She had been more interested in St. James's Park, where it had been of the utmost importance to be seen, for only the best sort of people mixed there. Or perhaps she and Percy would have gone to Hyde Park where Royalty hunted deer, and she would have had a few words with . . . no, that was wrong, Kate thought with a frown of concentration. They no longer hunted deer in Hyde Park, did they? No, she had heard somewhere that they no longer did. Kate pressed slender, shaking fingers against her pounding temple, for she didn't like to think that anything had changed since she had last been in London. She wanted it to appear exactly the same, and for the most part it seemed that not much had changed. The house that she and Percy, and his family, had lived in was still the same. There were a few new buildings, and some of the streets had been widened. And there was a different George ruling as king, but to her eye not much had changed over the years.

As Kate watched, a carriage pulled up before the red brick house; then the mahogany door opened as several footmen hurried to the carriage. A moment later the owners of the house, people she had never seen before, swept down to the waiting carriage and were whisked away. Most likely they were dining with friends, then attending a play in Drury Lane, then afterwards supping, dancing, and playing cards at a private party, their evening's entertainment just beginning.

With a sharp tap on the roof of the carriage, Kate sent the coachman whipping his horses on to their next destination, a far grander townhouse in Berkeley Square. It was the Dowager Duchess's house, and always would be, even if Lucien now resided there when he was in London. It hadn't changed either, Kate thought when the coach rumbled to a halt before the darkened house. What a harridan the Dowager Duchess had been, and how they had despised her. She and Percy could never make a move without the old Duchess hearing about it, criticizing them for it, thwarting them at every turn of the wheel. How she had loved playing the grand dame, interfering in the lives of her grandchildren. Even Lucien had not been exempt from their grandmother's meddlesome ways. But Lucien had never suffered as much as she and Percy had, for Lucien had been a *Dominick,* and they had only been Rathbournes. Only one who bore the proud Dominick name and title deserved any special favors. How many times, Kate wondered, had the Dowager Duchess given Lucien a second chance? Anyone else would have been banished from her royal presence, but no, not Lucien; he remained the fair-haired one.

Kate's lips parted in a slight smile as she remembered the one time she had ever truly got the best of dear cousin Lucien. As she conjured up his lean, hawkish face she saw once again the scar *she* had put there. They had been just children, she and Percy years younger than Lucien. But when they'd acted together, as they always had, they were more than a match for him despite his larger size. That was how she had managed to scar him, for Percy had jumped Lucien, keeping his attention centered on a pair of swinging fists while she, unbeknownst to Lucien, had picked up a shard of broken china, slashed deep into his cheek with the sharp-edged, makeshift weapon, and scarred him for life.

'Twas ironic, then, that he should be instrumental in causing her disfigurement and ruining her life. But dear cousin Lucien had managed well enough through the years; in fact, the scar on his cheek had created a certain air of mystery about his figure, and had enhanced an already disreputable reputation. Lucien, Duke of Camareigh, had never had to bear the agonies that she'd had to. Lucien, despite all of their efforts, had inherited Camareigh. Lucien had all of the wealth and power that she craved, and now Lucien had twins. Lucien had everything, and she, Kate, had nothing—she didn't even have Percy anymore.

"Well, don't dawdle, man, I haven't got all day to sit here while you ponder the ills of the world," Kate called out to the patiently waiting coachman, impatience with her own thoughts tinging her voice with shrewish sharpness. "Take me to the King's Messenger Inn. 'Tis near St. Martin-in-the-Fields. I trust you do know of it?"

"Aye, m'lady," the coachman answered shortly, swallowing a retort about it being his job to know every inn, tavern, and coffee house in London, and that he had indeed known them since he'd been knee-high to a coach wheel. With the purpose of ridding himself of his strange trio of passengers, the coachman sent his coach hurtling toward Piccadilly as night cloaked the city of London in darkness, and a thick, unfolding fog blinded him from seeing as far as his horses' heads.

The King's Messenger Inn was a small, well-kept inn sitting snug on a quiet side street off St. Martin's Lane. It was an inn frequented by travelers arriving in London. Its closeness to the festivities held at Covent Garden and Drury Lane and to the shopping that could be done on Oxford Street, as well as its proximity to the fashionable squares and parks of the West End, made it a convenient place to stay if one were trying to get around London. But, despite these advantages, the King's Messenger Inn was not one of the more exclusive inns, which was why Kate had chosen it, for it was unlikely that she would cross paths with any past acquaintances from her former life in London, or see any familiar faces from Venice. The King's Messenger Inn was where Niccolò, Conte Rasghieri preferred to stay when in London. She had heard him speak of it often when telling her of his trips to England; she'd treasured and remembered his every word about her beloved homeland. It oddly comforted her now to know that the Conte had been here, eating and sleeping under this very same roof, Kate realized, as she stepped inside the inn, and a surging tide of warmth and light spread out around her. Coming from within the large common dining room to the left of the entrance hall were the unmistakable sounds of mealtime, and it seemed to be a jovial one at that; laughter was drifting from the room along with the clinking of china and cutlery. A serving girl hurried by holding a heavy tray shoulder-high, which was loaded down with brimming mugs of ale. The tray was balanced precariously on one hand. Her expression was harried as she easily sidestepped the newcomers filling the small hall.

" 'Erself'll be 'ere sooner'n them thirsty blokes stuffin' their faces can be emptyin' these bleedin' mugs," the girl said over her shoulder as she disappeared inside the smoke-filled room. Her entrance prompted a chorus of cheers and rude remarks from the patrons.

"Ye'll be wantin' a room, I s'pose?" inquired a woman of incredible obesity matter-of-factly as she waddled toward them, her bulk just barely managing to squeeze through the narrow door at the back of the hall. A ruffled mob cap was perched on top of her powdered curls, the bands tied in a bow that had nearly disappeared between her double chins. A matching apron was stretched around her jiggling midriff, and on her small, pudgy fingers an amazingly fine collection of jewelry flashed when she fluttered her hands.

And they were hands that could deal a stinging blow, Kate thought, seeing the serving girl cringe instinctively when she returned with her tray full of empty mugs, as if she were expecting a blow to fall on her unprotected shoulders as she passed her mistress.

"Ye'll pay in advance, that's me rule. And I'll not be havin' any of them feurin-lookin' coins in payment," the proprietress warned, jabbing a thick finger into her palm where she held several English shillings. "English. Comprenez-moi?" she demanded, placing her hands on her ample hips as she stared contemptuously at the old woman who was jabbering away in a foreign tongue. Meanwhile, the giant towering over the two women continued to stare silently into space. "Feuriners," she muttered beneath her breath, "expectin' me to be understandin' *their* language right here in London."

"Oh, but I understand you perfectly, my good woman," Kate responded in her most haughty tone, ice dripping from each carefully enunciated word. "And I wouldn't dream of paying in anything but English currency."

"Oh," the proprietress mouthed silently, a look of chagrin staining her face an unbecoming red. "Beggin' yer pardon, m'lady," she responded quickly, for she was no fool, and this was a lady if ever there was one. "Yer maid, talkin' in all them funny words, well, naturally I thought ye was foreign. Most of me guests are from across the Channel, and if ye knew the devil of a time I'm having in gettin' them to pay in good English money, well, let me tell ye—"

"Please do not. Since that problem is unlikely to arise, your domestic situation is of little concern to me. I have just arrived from Venice, and I am quite fatigued," Kate drawled in a bored voice. With an imperiously raised hand she had abruptly halted the garrulous woman's confidences. "Do you or don't you have rooms that I may take?"

"Of course, m'lady. Please follow me. The King's Messenger has a good reputation for cleanliness," she boasted as she heaved herself up the steps, the stairs groaning and creaking under her weight. "Air our sheets and got warming pans for damp ones. Neat wines. And, if I do say so meself, I'm one of the best cooks in London. Even know how to prepare a few of them feurin dishes," she declared magnanimously, never pausing in her stride even when a striped cat shot down the stairs, a mouse trapped in his jaws. "Got his dinner, he does. A good mouser, him. Now, here's yer rooms. Me best suite, and overlooking the street. Too noisy on the courtyard side. Figure ye might be wantin' it nice and quiet like," she added, her sharp eyes not having missed the mourning black worn by her guest. "Come fer a funeral, have ye?" she asked, clucking her tongue in sympathy.

Kate smiled beneath her heavy veiling. "Yes, 'I come to bury Caesar, not to praise him,'" she quoted with a chuckle.

"Here, what's that? Caesar? Strange name for a bloke —oh, Italian, is he?" the proprietress asked. She'd cast Kate a strange look when she'd heard the chuckle; then she shrugged, for as long as Kate's money was good, she was welcome at the King's Messenger Inn. "I'll have a maid in here right soon. Light ye a nice cheery fire. Take the chill away. Will ye be dining in here or downstairs?" she asked, glancing around the room to make sure everything was in order.

Kate was standing before the small mullioned windows, her shoulders slumping tiredly. "I'll take all of my meals in here," she informed her. Then, turning around, she glanced about the room too, but was not overly impressed by its cozy atmosphere. "Oh, and I shall want something *very* English tonight for supper. It will be my homecoming dinner, so I want it to be something special."

"Aye, 'twill be as ye wish, m'lady," the proprietress of the King's Messenger Inn replied, smiling nervously as she eyed the lumbering footman pacing around the room like a caged beast. "Don't say overmuch, do he?" she asked, jerking her bonneted head toward the silent man.

Kate followed her look. "He isn't required to. He has a strong back; that is all that is needed. Do you know," Kate added in a very confidential tone, concealing her grin from the woman, "that he once became so angered with a farmer who was beating a poor defenseless donkey that with his own two bare hands, Rocco twisted the farmer's head off."

"No," the proprietress breathed in awed fascination, sucking in her breath in a whoosh while she stared at Rocco's big hands as if they were, at this very moment, strangling the life out of someone. "Lord help us. Who would've thought such a thing of him? Looks so gentle like, he does. Don't ye ever get a wee bit worried havin' a man of his sort around?" she asked, touching her head meaningfully.

"No, not at all. Rocco is quite devoted to me and, in fact, I am quite comforted by his presence," Kate responded matter-of-factly.

"Aye, well, to each his own, I'm always sayin'," she muttered, taking a careful step backward. "If'n ye've got any questions or needs, juz be askin fer Nell Farquhar, that be me. I'll have someone bring up yer dinner, real soon, I will," she promised, heading for the door with incredible speed for a woman of her bulk.

Kate was warming herself before the fire when two serving maids entered with her dinner, their glances darting nervously to where Rocco was sitting in the corner, his dark eyes staring dreamily into the fire. Then

Kate knew that Nell Farquhar had wasted little time in spreading the story of Rocco's incredible strength, which was exactly what Kate had hoped she would do. A healthy respect for another's unpredictable temper certainly kept people at a distance, and also kept them minding their own business. Kate eyed Rocco with the same affection she would have for a devoted dog, for Rocco seemed to know only one thing in life, which was to serve her. He'd been her most valued footman for years now, his size and unquestioning obedience serving her well, and that was why she'd brought him with her to England, for he would do as she told him—never questioning, never criticizing, just loyally obeying.

"Beggin' yer pardon, m'lady," said one of the serving girls timidly, her thin hands holding her empty tray against her chest like a shield. "Where will yer servants be eatin'? Ye wants us to bring them somethin'?"

Kate waved them away. "I shall not be able to eat all of this. They can have what is left over. Don't worry, Rocco will not be coming down to dine. Of course," Kate paused, pretending to give the thought some serious consideration, "if you do wish him to join you, I am sure it can be arranged," she told them, enjoying with sadistic pleasure their obvious discomfort.

"Oh, no, m'lady!" the serving girls squealed in unison, bumping into each other as they backed to the door. "We was just wonderin'. We really didn't mean for 'im to be joinin' us. I means we don't have a set time for supper. We just grabs whats we can. If'n ye knows what I means?"

"Yes, I know exactly what you do mean. Now go, I grow weary of conversing with you while my meal grows cold," Kate ordered, a look of irritation crossing her face beneath the veil. "It would seem, Rocco, that only your mistress can bear to be in your presence," she commented as the door closed on the shaking serving girls.

Kate sniffed appreciatively at the cut of rare roast beef soaking in its own gravy on her plate. The good proprietress had certainly taken her at her word, Kate thought, eyeing the very English meal of roast beef, pigeon pie, and puddings, one of which she knew was a savory blend of steak, kidney, lark, and oysters, accompanied by several vegetable dishes, and followed by custards, tarts, and jellies.

For the first time since leaving Venice she was hungry, Kate thought in surprise, and poured herself a goblet of wine from one of the several she had ordered. Tossing off her veil she glanced around her strange yet familiar surroundings, her mask hiding any flicker of emotion that might have crossed her face. 'Twas odd, Kate pondered, that when living in London so many years ago, all she could abide was French cuisine, and yet, while in Venice, she would have given a fortune for an English pudding, something she once would have scorned.

Kate was well into the second bottle of wine when Nell Farquhar knocked on the door, and receiving permission to enter, stood awkwardly before Kate, shifting her weight from one tired foot to the other. Her round mouth was open in amazement as she continued to stare at the masked woman sitting negligently before the roaring fire, a sable rug draped across her knees, and a half-empty glass of wine held indolently to catch the flickering light from the flames.

"Ye wanted to see me, m'lady?" Nell inquired, casting an uneasy glance at Rocco and the old woman, who were busily putting away the leftovers from Kate's meal. The only sound was the smacking of their lips as they every so often licked their fingers.

"Yes, *Mrs.* Farquhar, is it?" Kate inquired politely, her blue eyes glittering behind the mask.

"Aye, in fact, I've had three husbands, I have. Johnny Farquhar was me last. This was his place, it was. Outlived them all, I have," Nell Farquhar stated proudly.

"Have you indeed? How extraordinary, and how enterprising of you, Mrs. Farquhar," Kate complimented her, recognizing a fellow opportunist in the proprietress of the King's Messenger Inn. "What I would ask of you now, Mrs. Farquhar, is, perhaps, some advice," Kate began smoothly, flattering the woman.

"Well, don't know as how I can be givin' the likes of ye advice, but I don't see as how it can be hurtin' none,"

Nell Farquhar stated with a fine show of modesty as she settled herself into her favorite stance of hands on hips.

"Oh, my dear Mrs. Farquhar," Kate responded with an equal display of graciousness, "you are too kind for words. But, of course, I shall recompense you for any information or assistance that you are about to so generously offer me."

Nell Farquhar's round face was beaming. "Well, m'lady, in that case, of course I should be more than happy to help ye," she responded with a widening grin.

"Yes, I thought you might," Kate murmured beneath her breath. Then, for the other woman's ears, she said, "I think we shall deal quite famously with one another."

"Aye, m'lady," Nell agreed, "I'm beginnin' to see how we might be havin' a similar outlook on life."

"Yes, I believe we might at that. However, as to my needs at this time, I shall want a recommendation from you. I need the name of someone upon whom I may rely, and upon whom I should expect the utmost discretion," Kate told her in an almost conversational tone. "Oh, and he needn't be . . ." Kate paused, sighing delicately before continuing, ". . . now how shall I put this so you do not misunderstand me?"

"Of too sterling a character or reputation, m'lady?" Nell Farquhar finished for her.

Kate laughed shortly, not amused at having been so obvious. "Yes, exactly my sentiments, Mrs. Farquhar. 'Tis a personal matter that I need some assistance with, in fact, my dear," she said in a very confidential tone. "I shall be absolutely honest with you. 'Tis a practical joke I have in mind to play on someone, and I will need help, but should the man have too much of a conscience, well, it would absolutely ruin all of the fun!"

Nell Farquhar stared hard at the strange lady in her black mask and mourning clothes, and even though she was a woman with years of experience in the cruelties of the world, she felt a shiver of apprehension shoot through her. There was something queer going on here, and Nell Farquhar hadn't been born yesterday to be taken in by this lady in black's fancy airs and games. Aye, this one meant bad news to some poor devil, and she'd just as soon keep her own nose clean of it. However, since they did have their slow days at the inn, and a decent woman like herself did have to make a living . . .

The sound of a pouch full of coins hitting the table brought Nell Farquhar's wandering attention to a sudden standstill.

"A name, Mrs. Farquhar," Kate urged her gently but firmly.

Nell Farquhar hesitated for only a moment before reaching out and grasping the small pouch of coins with a greedy hand. "Edward Waltham. Most likely be leavin' his own mum to the gallows if'n the price was right. Aye, Teddie Waltham's yer man, and a more slippery devil I've not had the pleasure of meetin'. Fancies himself a gentleman of sorts, although we all knows he was born of a bastard's brat over by Billingsgate. Says he's got royal blood in him from King Charles II himself, and that his father is a Duke," she snorted, sniggering behind her hand. "If'n that's true, then I'm Nell Gwyn! More'n likely his father was a fishmonger, but that Teddie Waltham, he can talk ye into believin' anything. Even sweet-talked his way out of Newgate, he did. Probably had the turnkey holdin' the gates open fer him as he sauntered past."

"Sounds a most remarkable man, your Teddie Waltham," Kate said softly. "And where might I find this honey-tongued exquisite?"

"Why, downstairs, m'lady." Nell Farquhar's deep laugh rumbled across the room. "But I'm not knowin' how exquisite he might be tonight, seein' how he's been tryin' to drink up all me best rum and cheapest gin, he has."

"Well, then, Mrs. Farquhar, so as not to disappoint the gentleman, have a bottle of your finest sent up, and then inform Mr. Waltham that I should like a word with him."

"Aye, m'lady," Nell readily agreed, not averse to making a few extra shillings for her night's work. "Oh! And who am I supposed to say wants to see him?" she demanded suddenly, realizing she'd never caught her guest's name.

"Just tell him a prospective employer," Kate informed her, which did not satisfy the proprietress's avid curiosity. "And one who is willing to pay quite generously for services rendered."

"Aye," Nell Farquhar remarked, a shrewd look in her eyes, "I reckon ye would be at that." And with that oblique comment she sauntered from the room, the leather bag full of coins held firmly in one fat palm.

The chimes had struck nine times, and at half past the hour Edward Waltham knocked upon the door. He nearly fell backward in surprised fright when the silent mass of the footman filled the doorway, and he very nearly came to running again when he saw the masked woman sitting before the fire, her black clothing striking him as an omen of ill luck about to befall him. But because his pockets were empty, and he could see the awesome shadow of debtors' prison looming before him, he reckoned he really had nothing to lose in listening to the woman. And, perhaps, he'd have everything to gain.

"Rocco, do let the gentleman pass, for if this is Mr. Edward Waltham, and he is as lacking in character as I have been led to believe, then we most definitely shall have something to talk about," Kate said as she invited a rather subdued-looking Edward Waltham into the room.

"Aye, I'm Edward Waltham. Ol' Nell said ye wanted to hire a man for a job," he informed her, fighting to clear his fuddled brain of rum, for he knew he'd need his wits about him tonight. "Reckon I might be your man, and then again, I might not be. 'Twill depend on what's in it for me," he told her bluntly, keeping a watchful eye on this fellow named Rocco, whose shadow seemed to be steadily growing until it had stretched across the whole length of the room.

"Marvelous, Mr. Waltham!" Kate exclaimed. "You have not disappointed me. No questions asked concerning the job, or what might be entailed, just what is in it for you. I can see we shall get along splendidly," Kate told him, gesturing for him to take the chair opposite her and to pour himself a drink from the rum bottle sitting close at hand.

Through the slits in her mask, Kate's pale blue eyes watched the man called Edward Waltham walk closer, his darting eyes searching the room for exits, weapons, or hidden third parties. He was a wily character, she decided, and just what she'd had in mind as an accomplice. His age would be hard to pin down, even if he could have told her, which she doubted, for he was one of those people of medium height and weight, with medium-colored hair and eyes, and with no outstanding features. Which was certainly in his favor, for no one would remember the innocuous stranger, and certainly no one would suspect him of any jewel theft or black-mailing scheme.

He was dressed now in imitation of a dandy, his claret-colored, velvet coat having seen better days and his lacy stock looking sadly yellowed from where it hung limply around his neck. His buff breeches had felt the darning needle many times, and his wig could have stood a good brushing. Yes, Kate thought with a satisfied smile curving her lips, Mr. Edward Waltham was exactly the kind of scoundrel she'd had in mind.

"How would you like to take a trip into the country, Mr. Waltham? I hear the air does wonders for the lungs," she began. Then a log fell in a shower of sparks and drowned out the rest of her softly spoken words.

The gently sloping meadows stretching away from the terraced gardens of Camareigh were brown, and the copses beyond the sylvan lake had shed the last of their autumn leaves. Now the trees stood etched against the gray skies of oncoming winter. There was more than a hint of rain in the air as a few drops fell from overhead, the clouds darkening with each passing second. A distant rumble of thunder was growing louder, drowning out the sound of a voice raised in fear.

"Rhea! Rhea Claire! Are you all right?" Francis called as, helplessly, he watched his sister tumble from her horse when the dainty mare balked at jumping over the privet hedge. The sound of thunder had frightened her, and she was now running free as she danced skittishly across the meadow, her reins hanging loose.

Rhea sighed, pushing her dark blue velvet tricorn out of her eyes as she pulled her skirts aside and stumbled ungracefully to her feet. She was straightening her waistcoat and jacket when Francis and Ewan rode up, the bolted mare in tow.

"Are you hurt, Rhea?" Ewan asked in concern as he caught sight of her torn and muddied skirt.

"No, I'm fine, but I fear I shall be in for a scolding when Canfield catches sight of my riding habit. Hello, sweetheart," Rhea said softly, placing a soothing hand on the little mare's velvety nose. "Give me a hand up, will you?" Rhea asked, rubbing her bruised elbow and wincing slightly.

James was off his mount before either of his brothers or cousin could make a move to assist Rhea. He gallantly presented his linked hands to Rhea, holding them firm as she placed her booted foot in them; then he boosted her onto the mare's back, holding her steady while Rhea hooked her knees over the horn.

"Thank you, James," Rhea said with a special smile for him. She knew her young cousin was experiencing the first pangs of puppy love as he stared up at her. Bemusement clouded his gray eyes as he eagerly returned her smile with a wide grin.

"Are you sure you feel like riding, Rhea? You could ride with me," he offered shyly, sending his older brother, George, a threatening glance when he heard a hastily smothered guffaw. "You took quite a fall. If we hurry, we can make the stables before it rains."

"No," Rhea contradicted him gently, her mouth set firmly. "We shall continue as before. I don't think 'tis going to rain just yet, and I do not intend to be the reason for depriving you and Ewan and George of a ride. You were cooped up in that carriage all of yesterday and the day before, and now that you've a chance to get out, I will not be the cause of ruining it. Besides," Rhea added with a glint in her eye as she glanced at the hedge, "I haven't cleared that hedge yet."

"You're not still going to jump it, are you, Rhea?"

Ewan demanded, even though he knew she was, and that there was nothing he could say to deter her.

"Father says not to let your fear set in. I'll do better, not to mention Skylark here, to take this hedge today. By tomorrow or the next day I would have had time to go over the jump in my head a thousand times, as well as my fall," Rhea reasoned. "I would be a thousand times more nervous than I am now."

"But, Rhea—" George began, only to be interrupted by a wise Francis.

"Better not to argue with her," he stated calmly, knowing his sister well enough not to waste his breath arguing with her.

"There, you see, Ewan," Rhea declared with a triumphant laugh, "haven't I always said that Francis had a good head on his shoulders?"

Another loud clap of thunder sounded across the hills as the storm rolled closer. Rhea stared up at the angry clouds and kept a tight rein on Skylark as she shied nervously. "I'm afraid that you are going to end up spending most of your visit inside Camareigh this time," Rhea predicted with a glum look. "No more picnics on the lawn."

"I'm afraid so," Ewan agreed, following her glance to the blackening clouds above.

"I'm pleased to see you," Rhea began, a perplexed look on her face, "but why did you arrive so early? The ball isn't until next week."

"You know Mother. When she gets her mind set on something, she can be as stubborn as a mule," George explained. "She said she had to be here right now. She wouldn't say why."

"One of her feelings?" Francis asked casually. He had started to follow Rhea and Skylark as they trotted some distance away from the hedge.

"One of her feelings," Ewan confirmed, repeating the phrase that he'd heard used all of his life to describe his mother's strange visions. His tone, however, was not disrespectful but full of reverence for her gift. He had seen too many strange things happen after his mother

98

had predicted them to scoff either at her or at any of her feelings.

"Maybe she's seen your engagement to the Earl of Rendale, Rhea," Francis guessed, a sly grin on his innocent-looking face.

"What!" James cried out, startled by the news.

"Francis is just trying to be amusing and failing miserably at it," Rhea retorted. Then, changing the subject, she said, " 'Twill be quicker if we ride along the lane rather than go back across the hills." She patted the mare's beautifully arched neck. "Come on, Skylark," she whispered. "Shall we show them how to jump?"

This time Skylark did not balk, nor did her hooves even touch the privet hedge when she cleared it with plenty of room to spare. A moment later four other horses cleared it as Francis and his cousins followed Rhea's lead. She was already well down the lane, her mare's white-stockinged legs flying and kicking up mud, when she suddenly pulled up.

"What is wrong now, Rhea?" Francis asked, looking at her as if she might be ill.

"I've lost my hat!" Rhea exclaimed, her eyes searching the roadside. "Demme! I've had it now. How can I face Canfield without a proper hat on my head!"

"Well, if you ask me—" George had started to advise his cousin, but his red eyebrows shot up in amazement when she rudely shushed him quiet.

"Don't you hear it?" she asked, holding a warning finger to her lips.

"Hear what? Don't tell me you have a talking hat?" Francis demanded mockingly, holding up his hands in entreaty when Rhea shot him a murderous look.

"I hear it!" James cried out, glancing around at the hedges bordering the lane.

"What did it say to you, James?" George asked with a serious expression, but a muffled snicker escaped as he tried to keep a straight face. "Did it tell you it'd rather be a bonnet than a tricorn?"

"Well, whatever it is," Ewan stated practically, " 'tis coming from that ditch over there."

"Shall we have a look?" Rhea suggested. Then, when

they all remained seated on their horses she dropped to the ground before anyone could assist her. "Not afraid, are we?" she dared them, her mare's reins looped over her arm as she walked to the edge of the narrow lane. "Lud, there's something down here!" she said excitedly.

"Wait a minute, Rhea. Hold on!" Francis warned her as he jumped down from his frisky chestnut. "Stay, El Cid," he ordered the young stallion before hurrying after Rhea, but she had already disappeared into the ditch, leaving James complacently holding Skylark's reins. "Rhea, don't go any nearer! It could be a mad dog!" Francis cried out—too late. Now he heard the sound that had drawn her.

"No, 'tis a sack of some kind, and 'tis moving!" Rhea called back as she slid down the muddy bank. She looked over her shoulder in relief when she heard Ewan slip down beside her, and she stepped aside to let him wade into the dirty ditch water. His boots protected him as he grasped hold of the squirming sack that was, every so often, letting out a series of squeals.

"Bring it up here on the lane, Ewan," Rhea told him as she struggled up the embankment, gratefully accepting assistance from Francis, who held out his arm and pulled her the rest of the way up. "Come on, Ewan. Hurry," she urged him, impatient as she watched him suspiciously eyeing his find.

"I have a feeling I should have left it where it was," he predicted as he climbed back toward the lane, his mud-coated boots slipping and sliding while he tried to make his way up the steep bank. George held out a hand as his brother neared the top and with a hefty tug, landed him on the hard-packed road.

Before Ewan could drop the burlap bag, Rhea was inspecting it, her gloved hands touching the sack here and there as she sought an answer. "I don't suppose you have a knife or something we can cut this string with?"

Ewan dropped the bag in the center of the quiet lane and stood back to admire his handiwork. Rhea was on her knees beside it in an instant, sawing away at the tight string with a sharp stone James had found. She grinned up at him when he dropped down beside her with his own crudely improvised knife and began to cut through the rough twine. Soon the string gave way with a snap and, glancing around at the expectant faces, Rhea rolled back the edges of the burlap bag to reveal six half-drowned, half-starved puppies shivering together in the bottom.

"Oh, the poor babies," Rhea murmured, impulsively scooping one of the sorry-looking little creatures onto her lap. "How could anyone abandon these puppies like this? 'Tis so cruel the way they have suffered."

"Well, the blackguard is long gone by now, Rhea, and *we've* found his puppies," Francis said as he squatted down beside his sister, unable to resist a closer look at the whimpering pups. "Demmed shame, but it happens all of the time. I wonder what breed they are."

"Mixed, most likely," Ewan commented. "What are we going to—" But he was interrupted by the unmistakable sounds of an approaching carriage. The jingling of harness and rattling of wheels was steadily growing louder, but they hadn't yet caught sight of the carriage, because the gentle bend in the lane hindered their view.

"Coming a damned sight too fast, I should think," Ewan remarked, a frown creasing his forehead as he glanced around at the narrow lane, and their position in the center of it. "Better move aside, Rhea," he warned just as the carriage appeared, the team of horses looking wild as they galloped down the road, straight toward the party of riders.

Ewan grabbed Rhea's arm as she scrambled to her feet, the bag of puppies cradled awkwardly in her arms. Francis whistled for El Cid; the chestnut followed him to the side of the lane as he and George led the other horses out of the way, although even at that it was going to be a dangerously tight squeeze unless the coachman could slow his carriage down. Francis eyed the muddy water in the ditch behind him, not fancying being tumbled into it. Amazingly enough, though, the coachman brought his team under control with a powerful pull on the reins, when he spied the riders ahead. The coach, rocking violently, halted just feet away.

As imprecations were called down on the coachman's head from the passenger in the coach, Francis hurried over to the window, ready to offer any assistance should the lady be injured, for despite the language being used, the voice was very definitely feminine.

"What in blazes is the matter with you! I'll have your—" The voice halted abruptly as the woman inside the coach looked out the window, her eyes catching sight of the young gentleman standing quietly beside her coach, a look of sardonic amusement curving his lips.

But when Francis heard the veiled woman's sudden indrawn breath, his smile faded and he leaned closer, peering into the shadowy darkness of the coach.

"Are you ill, madam?" he inquired in growing concern as he saw her press a shaking hand to her breast.

"No, I'm quite all right," the woman replied jerkily, her words hardly more than a whisper. " 'Twas a twinge, nothing more. Perhaps 'twas something I supped on at luncheon. You know what the food can be like in some of those ghastly inns," she said, her voice growing stronger with each word.

"If you are quite certain, madam," Francis said politely. He doubted her words, though, since she was obviously still agitated.

Kate returned the young gentleman's stare from the safe anonymity of her veil and mask, her pale blue eyes feasting on Lucien Dominick's son. For this boy could only be a Dominick, Kate thought, swallowing painfully as she gazed into a face that reminded her not only of Lucien but of Percy as well. The eyes were different, not sherry colored like Percy's and Lucien's, nor as pale a blue as her own, but there was no mistaking the hawkish features that branded him a Dominick.

Kate glanced out of the coach window to where the other riders were standing, her eyes narrowing as she caught sight of a rather bedraggled young girl holding a strange-looking package. Kate's knuckles whitened inside her gloves, for she could swear that the girl was yet another Dominick. Oddly enough, the girl's incredible loveliness seemed enhanced by her dishevelment, for her unbound hair fell to her hips in glorious golden waves and framed a face that could rival the painted sweetness of a Renaissance angel. Kate sighed, for many years ago she had possessed a beauty as untouched and ethereal as that young girl's. Kate's glance moved on to the other three riders, noting the red hair on two of them and the dark brown curls of the older boy. They were *not* Dominicks; she instinctively sensed this in her own Dominick blood—of course, as far as she knew, no Dominick had *ever* been born with red hair. Kate's pale eyes returned to Francis, the Fletcher cousins dismissed from her mind as insignificant. And for Kate, in that instant, they ceased to exist. The only people that filled her world were named Dominick. And here were two of them.

"Are you, perhaps, having some difficulties?" Kate asked now, her tone politely curious as she gestured toward the dismounted riders. "The young girl seems to have taken a fall. She isn't injured, is she? Rocco," Kate said. And before Francis could explain the situation, or put in a word to contradict her, she said something in Italian to her footman.

"Please, there is no need, madam," Francis said hurriedly when he caught sight of the hulking figure heading toward his sister and cousins. "My sister Rhea did fall," he began, trying to explain her extraordinary appearance, "but that was a while back. The reason we are blocking the road, and I am afraid I must apologize for the inconvenience, is that Rhea found some half-drowned puppies and came to their rescue." Francis grinned wryly and reminded Kate so much of Percy that she almost reached out and caressed Francis Dominick's cheek.

"I see. How very noble of her," Kate replied. "You must live hereabouts to be out riding in such inclement weather," she remarked casually, making a concerted effort to control the excitement she could feel pulsing through her veins. "Since there is only one estate near here that I have knowledge of, and that is Camareigh, you therefore must be . . ." Kate allowed her voice to trail away questioningly, leaving the young gentleman no other choice but to properly introduce himself.

"I am Francis Dominick, and that is my sister Rhea

103

Claire, and those fellows are my cousins Ewan, George, and James Fletcher," Francis said very modestly, never mentioning titles.

"Of course," Kate murmured, "you are the Marquis of Chardinall, and heir to Camareigh."

Francis Dominick raised a surprised brow. "You have knowledge, madam, of our family?" he inquired in a cool tone of voice. "You are, perhaps, a friend of my parents?"

"A friend?" When Kate tried the word, it sounded strange on her tongue. "No, I am more of an old acquaintance. Yes," she repeated, liking the sound of it, "I am an acquaintance from long, long ago."

"I see," Francis said. "Will you be visiting Camareigh? Perhaps you've come for the ball?"

Kate gave a negative shake of her head. "No, I'm just passing through the valley, but I have enjoyed meeting Lucien's son," she replied graciously, her thoughts racing ahead. "Now where is that Rocco? Sometimes he can be most tiresome," she complained, leaning out of the coach window and seeing her footman grinning like some kind of country bumpkin over a litter of pups.

Rhea Claire Dominick was smiling up encouragingly at the hesitant footman. She had been slightly startled at first, for when she'd heard the approaching footsteps she had glanced up to see a pair of sad, dark eyes staring down at her almost beseechingly. But she hadn't drawn back as had so many people when suddenly confronted with the large, slow-witted footman. Instead she had smiled, and she thought she had seen a flicker of response, or perhaps surprise, in the big man's broad-featured face.

"Surprisingly enough," Rhea was now saying softly to the footman as he hovered over her, "they are still alive."

Rocco continued to stare in fascination at Rhea's heart-shaped face and the golden hair tumbling over her shoulders. Something sluggish moved in his mind as he felt the genuine warmth of her smile reaching out to him. His dark, almost childishly innocent-looking eyes followed to where her outstretched hand was pointing, and he saw the furry puppies, whose pink tongues were licking Rhea's hand ecstatically as she cuddled them. Rocco slowly held out his hand, stopping midway to look to Rhea for permission, or denial, which was the usual response. Instead, though, she reached out, her small hand clasping his as she drew it toward the puppies and placed one of the squirming pups in his palm.

" 'Tis all right," Rhea said gently, patting his arm when she saw with surprised wonder the tears in his eyes as he held the puppy with almost breathless reverence. "I'm going to take them to someone who will take care of them," she tried to explain. "He loves dogs, and has the healing touch."

But all that penetrated Rocco's mind was that here was this golden-haired creature being kind to him, to Rocco, the slow one, the one who had been spurned and ridiculed by the villagers, and even by his own family. Rocco frowned, for the vague memories of a past dream were stirring in his mind, and he was once again seeing a gentle face such as this surrounded by flowing hair. The sweetly sad smile had beckoned to him, while her open arms had reached out to him as he'd knelt below her in supplication. He could remember shaking in terror and fear of the unknown when his mother had taken him into the big stone house. It had been so cold inside, and the walls had been so high that they had seemed to touch the heavens. He had been bad, he knew that, although he didn't understand how, and now he was to be punished, his mother had said. She had taken him away from his home and the village and left him there all alone in the cold darkness of the cathedral.

He was supposed to ask for forgiveness, but the silent robed figures swaying in and out of the shadows had frightened him, and he had looked up toward the light. Instead, he had seen only hideous, tortured faces gazing down on him. How could he ask forgiveness from faces that were so unforgiving, that damned him with their sightless eyes? He had cowered away from the stone faces, whimpering like a beaten dog until his eyes had met the eyes of the Madonna and angels. She had smiled down at him, welcomed him into her world and touched his heart with a warmth that was lacking in the cathedral's awesome chambers. But then it all had been snatched away from him, and he'd been driven out into the cold, the warmth of the Madonna's smile fading into the blackness of night as the doors of the great church were closed against him. He had never seen his Madonna again—at least, not until this day in the English countryside.

"Rocco! Answer me, you fool!" Rocco heard the strident voice shattering the peace that he'd once again found in a smile. "What are you doing? Is he bothering you, my dear?" Kate demanded as she tried in vain to attract her footman's attention.

"No, he isn't bothering me at all," Rhea reassured the woman. "In fact, he is being very helpful," she stated firmly, not caring for the tone of voice the woman had used on her footman.

"What are we going to do with them, Rhea?" James asked, wondering how they could possibly manage the puppies while on horseback.

"I thought we could take them to the elder Mr. Taber at Stone House-on-the-Hill," Rhea suggested, thinking of the old man and the barn full of sick animals that he cared for. "Since his son took over the farm, he hasn't that much to do except care for strays and sick animals people have brought him. Mother says 'tis a gift, his way with animals. She's always sending Butterick for advice when we've a sick animal in the stables."

"We'd better hurry, then," Ewan advised, glancing up and feeling raindrops falling on his face.

"Stone House-on-the-Hill is on the way to the inn where I am staying," Kate said, opening the door of the coach as she spoke. "Why don't you ride with me, my dear? I understand you have already fallen once today, so 'twould be much easier on you, and the puppies, not to get a soaking, which I fear the others shall," she added solicitously.

"Oh, I really couldn't," Rhea protested. "I'm not decent to sit with you in your carriage," she added, wrinkling her nose. "I'm afraid the puppies are a bit worse for wear and are not too fragrant right now."

"Nonsense, I insist you ride with me." Quickly, Kate

overrode Rhea's objections. "Believe me, I have smelled far worse odors rising out of the canals in Venice to be offended by anything now."

"Well . . ." Rhea began hesitantly, her muscles and bruised flesh already beginning to ache from her fall.

"Go on, Rhea," Francis urged, thinking it'd save them a lot of precious time if she carried the puppies in the carriage. It would, as well, keep her from a soaking and him from a scolding if their father caught sight of her, for although he was a year younger than his sister, he always felt responsible for her well-being.

"Thank you then, madam," Rhea responded gratefully. "I will accept your kind offer." She hurried to the coach, with Rocco just a step behind, his dark eyes never leaving her small figure.

"I'll bring Skylark," Francis called out to her. "We'll be right alongside the carriage."

"No, you mustn't delay your own progress," Kate told them, pulling her skirts out of the way as Rocco slammed the carriage door shut on Rhea's figure. "You will get soaked, for it is already beginning to rain. Please, go on ahead, and we'll meet you at Stone House-on-the-Hill. It isn't far, but far enough for you to catch your death of cold if you delay," she said persuasively.

The rain was falling steadily now, running in rivulets down Francis's face and seeping uncomfortably beneath his coat. "Very well, madam, we shall meet you there," he agreed. But his words fell as silently as the rain, for the carriage had already started to roll down the road. The footman had hardly climbed aboard and settled himself beside the coachman before the man had cracked his whip.

Francis stared after the disappearing coach with a slight frown of puzzlement on his usually smooth brow.

"Well? Come on, Francis," George urged his cousin as he mounted his horse and trotted across the road to where Francis was standing in what seemed to be a dazed state. "They'll be there before us at this rate."

Francis gave a shrill whistle and El Cid came trotting across. He vaulted quickly onto the chestnut's back and sent him, hooves pounding, down the road after the carriage. The rain was falling in earnest now, blowing against them in cold, wet sheets as they raced up the road toward Stone House-on-the-Hill.

"What's troubling you, Francis?" Ewan asked as he rode beside his cousin, sensing something was amiss.

Francis laughed shortly. Even though he felt a trifle embarrassed, he answered honestly, "I really don't know, Ewan. It is just a feeling I have, nothing substantial about it at all. But there *is* something strange about that woman."

"Hey, if anyone should be having feelings," Ewan complained good-naturedly, "then it should be me. After all, 'tis *my* mother with the gift of second sight, not yours."

" 'Tisn't that kind of feeling I have, Ewan. 'Tis silly, I suppose, but I feel uneasy, and I don't know why I should. Although it does seem rather strange that she should know as much as she does about my family. She knew my title, and I never even mentioned it."

Ewan seemed unimpressed. "The Dominick family is quite well known around these parts. And maybe she has a daughter she's heading in your direction," Ewan added with a grin. "Titles can make for strange bedfellows."

"Thank you for warning me, as if I weren't already treading very carefully. Those matchmaking mamas are already onto my scent, and I'm hardly out of swaddling," Francis joked.

"Well, I'm more fortunate than you in that respect," Ewan commented, thinking about his own situation in life, "for I've no titles, nor great estates to inherit someday. So when I choose a wife she'll be choosing me, not my fortune."

"Thanks a lot for your faith in my charm and good looks," Francis retorted, slightly miffed that his cousin thought his inheritance was all he had to offer a woman.

"You know I didn't mean it that way, Francis," Ewan protested, then adroitly changed the subject. "Did I hear that woman say that she was an old friend of your family?"

"So she said," Francis told him, still feeling uneasy about the whole incident. "I wonder how she knew about Stone House-on-the-Hill? Not many people would know it was not far from here."

Ewan remained silent for a moment, then shrugged. "Well, it isn't exactly a common name for a farm. She may well have heard the tale about the two brothers who fought over their land, one building a stone house on the hill, the other building a stone house in the dale. It makes for interesting gossip that they didn't speak for the rest of their lives, nor their children for generations afterwards. The Tabers of today are the first to speak to one another, aren't they?"

"Yes, that's true, I suppose," Francis agreed, not sounding totally convinced.

"Maybe she's having one of those secret assignations," George contributed, riding up beside them and overhearing their conversation.

"Could be," Ewan agreed. "We've got the setting, that's for sure: a mysterious veiled woman, a hulking foreign footman, and a damsel in distress. It all adds up to certain death on a lonely country lane," he said, holding his hand dramatically to his chest as if he'd just been wounded in a duel. "This could turn out to be quite exciting."

"As long as it isn't my demise we're talking about," Francis said with a wry grin. Then, giving El Cid a gentle nudge, he sent the big chestnut ahead of his cousin's mount. "Let's hope Rhea can find some clues to our mystery lady. Race you to the bend!" he called out challengingly as he lengthened the distance between them.

"Lady Rhea Claire Dominick," Kate was saying softly, savoring the girl's name while she stared at Lucien's daughter sitting not more than an arm's length from her. " 'Tis an uncommon name," she commented.

"Yes, I suppose so, although I was named Claire after my great-grandmother. She was French," Rhea explained, her hand comforting the puppies in her lap.

"Oh, I see. It is a very lovely name," Kate complimented her, dabbing a rose-scented handkerchief delicately against her nose.

Rhea bit her lip in growing embarrassment. "I'm afraid I must apologize for the odor."

"No, 'tisn't that. I just happen to like the scent of roses. It somehow comforts me, especially when I'm in strange surroundings. Roses have always brought me fond memories of my home." Kate spoke dreamily, a sad note in her voice.

"You are English, madam?" Rhea asked, curious about the woman who seemed to fit into two worlds, for although she spoke English without an accent, her clothes and mannerisms bespoke another country.

Kate nodded. "Yes, I am English, but I can see you are puzzled. I have not lived in England for many years. In fact, this is my first visit home in over fifteen years. I have been away for a long time, too long, I fear. But now I have returned, and I shall set things right. We should have come back a long time ago, Percy and I, but we were frightened of him, and of his power. But no longer are we afraid," Kate whispered, her words barely audible beneath her heavy veiling.

Rhea stared through the gloom of the carriage at this strange woman and felt a sudden pity for her. She seemed so utterly alone and bereft not only of friends but of hope as well. Rhea could sense the great loss in her. And the woman's grief seemed to go beyond the grave and the loved one buried there—as if she were long accustomed to wearing the black of mourning. Rhea's eyes narrowed as she sought to see beneath the veiling, but the fine gauze was so thick that she could see only an indistinct shape. Her heart gave a sudden jerk as her eyes met those of the woman, the pale blue orbs shining strangely bright behind the black shading of the veil.

For an instant Kate's teeth showed white as she smiled. She knew the girl was trying to see her face, and she knew she had fooled her. In Venice she would not have attracted notice by wearing her mask, but here in the English countryside it would have caused a sensation. And for once in her life, Kate wanted to move about in complete anonymity, which was why she had devised a new disguise. She had wrapped a pale piece of fine gauze over her face; the eyes, nose, and mouth were cunningly cut to appear almost without seam, and through the opaqueness of her veil, her face looked petal smooth and gloriously unmarred. Even she—in an instant of lost time while she'd stared into her looking glass—had been fooled into forgetting that . . .

"Madam?" Rhea asked softly, noticing with concern Kate's tightly clenched hands. "Are you quite all right?"

"Yes. Yes, I am just fine, now," Kate said thickly, her eyes wandering with glazed intensity to the countryside rolling past the coach windows. "We should be there any minute now," she commented vaguely. "I remember how long it used to seem to climb to the top of this hill. Yet now, why, we're here in no time," she exclaimed as the old stone house came into view.

Rocco had jumped down from the box and was opening the coach door before they had even come to a complete standstill. His eyes searched out Rhea and her foundling pups, and she handed the bundle to him. She didn't seem the least worried that he might drop them as he cradled them against his heart with one large, encompassing arm, while he helped her climb down with his other arm.

Stone House-on-the-Hill had always stood on top of the hill, or so it seemed to each generation of villagers. It had dug its roots in deep, long before the first golden stone of Camareigh had been carved. And the Tabers of Stone House-on-the-Hill had farmed the land around Camareigh for a hundred years before the first Dominick had sailed across the Channel from Normandy. Through the centuries the allegiances of people had shifted, crowned heads had come and gone as thrones were won and lost, and the blood of countless Englishmen had been shed on the field of battle. But two things always remained the same—the Tabers farmed the lands of Stone House-on-the-Hill and remained loyal to the Dukes of Camareigh.

The elder Mr. Taber, a wizened old gentleman with a shock of white hair, was standing in the shelter of the wide stone archway, his shriveled body hunched against the winds that were beginning to howl around the corner of the house. Even though his tired eyes were failing, he had seen the carriage climbing up the hill and had come out to greet his unexpected guests. His once spry gait had slowed considerably, but his family and the villagers claimed he was nearing ninety, and he was fortunate to be alive at all. No one had ever heard the old man complain about the aches and pains which must constantly plague him, and now, as he shuffled with painful slowness across the seemingly endless stretch of land between house and barn, he looked every year of his ninety and some years. He seemed as fragile as fine bone china, but his son and daughter-in-law, grandchildren, and great-children could attest to just the opposite: the old man still rambled around the farmlands and Stone House-on-the-Hill, rapping authoritatively with his knobby cane when he saw something he disapproved of and, more often than not, the family paid attention to him, for his mind was just as sharp, and his advice just as sensible as it always had been. With the great distinction of having outlived almost everyone in the village, including three of his own sons and grandsons, the elder Mr. Taber was much sought after for his near-century-old store of tales and gossip. Seldom did he forget a face or name and, with his colorful reminiscences of times past, he could conjure up the dead and their deeds, or misdeeds, as the case might be. Always, there was a chair held vacant for him before the hearth in the local tavern and a glass of ale kept brimming at his elbow, courtesy of his avid listeners.

Francis and his cousins had arrived at the old stone farmhouse hardly a horse's breath before the carriage pulled into the yard. The elder Mr. Taber knew good horseflesh when he saw it, and he'd reckoned these were no common travelers. However, upon recognizing the spirited chestnut of Lord Francis and the white-stockinged mare of his sister, Lady Rhea Claire, his weathered face split wide with a welcoming smile, for he'd always had a soft spot in his heart for the present Duke's children, especially young Lord Robin.

"And a good noontime t'ye, Lord Francis," he greeted the young lord as Francis jumped down from his mount's back and hurried over to pay his respects to the old man.

"Mr. Taber, sir, 'tis a pleasure to see you up and around again," Francis replied, for the old man had been laid up for a fortnight with an attack of rheumatism and looked none too well today. "How are you faring?"

"Can't complain, Lord Francis, can't complain," Mr. Taber responded in a quavering voice, his toothless grin widening. "Now where is that young Lord Robin? Don't see him there with t'others," he said, his faded eyes searching the Fletcher brothers for a curly, black head.

"He's at Camareigh, and probably up to no good," Francis said matter-of-factly, well used to his young brother's penchant for mischief. "And when he finds out what we've brought to you, without his assistance, he'll be so put out that I'll have to watch my step around him for at least a month."

Old Mr. Taber chuckled in appreciation, then glanced around expectantly. "Since I'm seein' Lady Rhea Claire's mare, and ye've brought me a surprise," he reasoned aloud, "I'm wonderin' what 'tis yer sister's found that's in need of mendin' and fixin' up good and proper."

Francis grinned and pointed toward the coach from which Rhea was being helped by a solicitous Rocco. The Fletcher brothers were grouped around her, but they were giving the large footman plenty of room as he continued to stand like a grotesque shadow at her shoulder.

"Lady Rhea Claire!" Mr. Taber called out, hobbling over to the coach, his blinking eyes not missing anything as they settled on the bundle she was holding protectively in her arms. As the old man neared her, Rocco moved forward almost menacingly, his dark eyes shifting between the old man, the puppies, and the fair-haired girl.

The elder Mr. Taber halted abruptly as he instinctively felt the mistrust and confusion in the enormous footman who was standing guard over Lady Rhea and the puppies. His rheumy eyes met Rocco's eyes and, with the same gift he had for gentling wild beasts and quieting those which were abandoned, the old man slowly reached out a gnarled hand and patted the big footman's tensed arm. His touch had an extraordinary effect on Rocco, who seemed to shrink inside himself as he felt his own hostilities fade.

"Oh, these are wee ones to be on their own, Lady Rhea," Mr. Taber said, making clucking noises with his

113

tongue as he handled the squirming pups. "And where did ye find them?"

"Someone had put them in this bag, then dumped them in a ditch along the High Road," Rhea told him, relinquishing her hold on them and giving them over to his loving care.

"A little bit of warm milk will do wonders, so don't ye be worrying that pretty little head of yours, Lady Rhea Claire, for old man Taber won't be letting ye down," he reassured her. Then, glancing up, he became aware of the carriage and its occupant. "Oh, good gracious me," he groaned as he shuffled closer and peered up at the indistinct figure watching from the opened door. "My apologies, Your Grace," he said in a deeply mortified tone of voice. "I don't know where my manners have run off to."

"I'm sorry, Mr. Taber," Rhea broke in quickly, "but this isn't the Duchess. This woman very kindly gave me a ride to Stone House-on-the-Hill."

"Oh, well, I thought I hadn't recognized Her Grace's carriage," he said, not in the least embarrassed by his mistake; in fact, had it indeed been Her Grace he would have been far more embarrassed. "But am I knowing ye, then? 'Tis a kindness ye did in giving the young lady a ride to Stone House-on-the-Hill. I hope 'twasn't out of your way."

"No," Kate replied shortly. " 'Twasn't out of my way, and I do not believe we have ever met. I am merely passing through the valley and chanced upon these riders in the lane. As you can see, the young lady suffered a fall, injuring herself slightly, and so I did the only proper thing and offered her a ride in my carriage."

"Ah," Mr. Taber murmured, continuing to stare with fascination into the coach, his weathered brow furrowed in puzzlement. "Are ye sure we've never met? I may be an old man, and my eyesight isn't what it once was, but I've never forgotten a body once I've made their acquaintance, and by that I'll swear. I'm sure I've heard your voice before. But where?" he persisted.

Kate glared down at the nosy old goat in disbelief. How could he still be alive after all of these years? He'd been ancient even when she'd been a girl living at Camareigh.

He must be pushing a hundred, she thought in amazement, and yet here he was poking his busybody nose into affairs that did not concern him.

"Aye, well, I'll remember soon enough," he was saying very matter-of-factly. "Pride myself on never forgetting a thing that's happened in this valley. Remember ye soon enough, I will," he promised.

"How very nice," Kate muttered. "I hope you will not be too disappointed when you fail."

He chuckled, somehow finding her remark amusing. "Aye, with each word ye say, I'm coming closer to remembering ye, that I am. But now," he added, turning back to Rhea Claire, "I'm going to take these wee ones inside. 'Tis too damp and cold out here for them any longer. By tomorrow, or perhaps the next day, ye won't even be recognizing them, Lady Rhea Claire," the old man said, clucking to the pups as he stumbled off.

"I'll be back to see them, Mr. Taber," Rhea called after him, and the old man nodded absent-mindedly as his bent figure disappeared around the corner of the house.

"There's a break in the storm," Ewan said, drawing their attention to the pale light filtering through the clouds. "If we hurry, we can make Camareigh before it opens up again."

"I'm so wet now, it doesn't much matter," George grumbled, shivering in his soaked coat. "But I'd sure like to get warm."

"Francis?" Ewan inquired, but Francis was unusually quiet as he stared at the woman in the coach. "Shall we go, Francis? Rhea isn't soaked yet, and we can probably just make it to the stables before it rains again."

"I think you would do well to follow his suggestion," Kate quietly advised as she gestured for Rocco to slam shut the coach door. "Personally, I'm beginning to feel the damp. But I would be more than happy to offer you a ride, my dear, if you are not feeling well," she offered politely.

"No, but thank you anyway," Rhea said.

"Very well," Kate said. Then she bid them a good afternoon and sat back against the cushions, disappearing from view as the coach pulled away from the farm. But

Rocco turned around on the box to catch one last glimpse of the golden-haired creature who had smiled at him.

"You've made a conquest there," Francis commented as he helped his sister to mount. "Strange pair, those two."

"I felt rather sorry for both of them," Rhea said as they rode away in the opposite direction from the carriage. "They seemed to be so unhappy."

"You wouldn't expect a woman in mourning to be full of mirth," Ewan said, as he rode alongside them, his horse's hooves splashing more mud onto Rhea's skirts.

"No, I would not, Ewan," Rhea agreed. "But it seemed to me to go deeper than the present. There was such a feeling of melancholy about them. 'Tis hard to explain, but there it is. Oh," she added, suddenly remembering something, "do you know, there was the strangest fragrance of roses about the woman."

"What's strange in that?" Ewan demanded. "Women always wear scent."

"Yes, but hopefully not *that* much. I felt I was going to suffocate under the fragrance. It was so cloying in that carriage that . . ." Rhea paused, looking uncomfortable.

"That?" Francis urged her, curious to hear her feelings about the woman whom he too had found strange.

"Well, it might sound crazed to you," Rhea continued, "but I felt almost as if I were in a coffin draped in roses. Now, you may laugh," she told them defensively, already feeling silly now that she'd voiced her thoughts.

"I'm not laughing, Rhea," Francis replied with equal seriousness.

"I must admit, it does seem odd," Ewan contributed. "Camareigh isn't exactly sitting in the middle of Charing Cross. This is a quiet valley, so what the devil is she doing here?"

"Well, *I* for one don't like the looks of that big fellow acting as footman for her," James piped in, feeling his first stirrings of jealousy as he remembered the spoony looks the large footman had cast at Rhea.

"*Well*, since we're all airing our grievances," said George, the ever-practical, "I'm for home. I've just about ruined my best riding coat, and I don't look forward to explaining any of this to Father!"

With that disagreeable reminder, the five cousins quickened their pace, arriving at the gates of Camareigh some twenty minutes later, just as the heavens opened up above their heads. The centuries-old gatekeeper's cottage looked snug against the blowing gusts of rain that spattered against its leaded windows. It had witnessed many a visitor to the stately halls of Camareigh, but perhaps none so cold and bedraggled as the five hurrying past at that moment.

The chestnut-lined drive had never seemed so endless as they rode against the wind and rain toward the great house. The low stone buildings of the stables were a welcome sight, the doors swinging wide as the group of riders were spotted entering through the stone-arched gates of the stable yard. The long straight rows of stalls, accommodations for the Duke's prized stock, were redolent of sweet meadow hay, molasses and oats, saddle soap and leathers, linseed oil, newly made poultices, and the everpresent horse droppings.

The stable block was the dominion of Butterick, a man in whose capable hands the Duke of Camareigh had entrusted the welfare and breeding of his thoroughbreds, as well as the maintenance of Camareigh's fleet of carriages. Butterick took his job very seriously and performed his duties as regally as any sovereign in his kingdom. Because he used so much pomp and ceremony as accompaniment to the everyday routine of the stables he was fondly and respectfully known as His Highness. Some, however, who were mostly stable hands and lesser menials, referred to him, beyond his hearing, less respectfully, as Old King Butt. Since their jobs were mostly concerned with the shoveling of manure and daily scrubbing down of floors, and since Butterick was considered a tyrant when it came to the spotlessness of his stables, their resentment could be well understood. Not that Butterick was a man who demanded of others what he was not willing to do himself. He had not always been the master of the stables and, in fact, had started out in the Camareigh stables as a lowly stable boy who spent many an arduous hour on hands and knees.

He was proud of his stables and honored to be in the

service of so fine a gentleman as the Duke of Camareigh. In Butterick's book there could be no finer man than one who knew his horses, and if ever there were a man who knew his horses, it was His Grace. He had never been fooled yet by a horse, and it was because of His Grace's eyes that they had a stable full of fine-blooded animals that had made them the envy of every groom, ostler, coachman, and lord in England.

But His Grace's eye hadn't been limited solely to horseflesh, for he'd picked himself a mighty fine little Duchess, who had more than proven herself to be of good stock. Butterick had to admit that he had misjudged her when His Grace had first brought her to Camareigh as its new mistress. He'd forgotten that size wasn't necessarily indicative of spirit or intelligence—both of which Her Grace had in plentiful supply. He'd also thought she wouldn't breed well, and then she up and gave His Grace twins! He oughta have his head examined, Butterick thought, disgusted with his own temporary disloyalty to Her Grace, or he should keep his nose out of affairs that were no concern of his.

But even as he silently voiced that thought, he was watching with an almost fatherly eye the five riders who'd raced the wind and rain into the dry warmth of the stables. Despite their shivering wetness they found something to joke about as they dismounted, their young voices filling the cavernous room with a brief breath of spring.

Young Lord Francis had turned into a fine horseman and would do His Grace proud one day. It was fortunate for Camareigh that Lord Francis was the elder, and heir to the title, for Lord Robin, bless his heart, was a mischievous little imp who could always be found in the center of a ruckus. Now on the other hand, there could be no finer a young lady than the Lady Rhea Claire. In his prejudiced eye there could be no little filly to match her, although now she looked hardly better than a milkmaid who'd just had a tussle with a cantankerous cow, and lost.

With a quick professional eye, Butterick looked over the horses, sighing in satisfaction when he found that none of his beauties had sustained an injury. With that discovery he allowed a slight smile to sneak across his florid features.

"Ye took a fall, did ye, Lady Rhea Claire?" Butterick greeted her, while he ordered in almost the same breath that the horses be led away, unsaddled, brushed, fed, and watered. His booming voice carried to the far end of the stables, reaching any laggards idling away a few minutes in a quiet corner. "'Twas the privet hedge, was it," he said, making it more of a statement than a question.

Rhea and Francis smiled, knowing Butterick's eagle eye well enough by now not to be surprised. James didn't know the man, though, and whistled in amazed admiration at this apparent magician's trick.

"How did you ever know that, Mr. Butterick?" he demanded.

"'Twas simple, lad, if you use your eyes," Butterick told him, enjoying his little joke as the youngster glanced over at Rhea's mount. A puzzled frown was on his brow as he stared stupidly at the mud-splashed flank and thigh.

Butterick marched over to the horse and patted the little mare on the rump; then he carefully and gently removed a small branch of hedge that had been stuck in her tail. "Privet," Butterick said, eyeing Skylark's chest and forelegs for a serious moment. "Been to Stone House-on-the-Hill, have ye? And how is the elder Mr. Taber?"

Even Francis was impressed by this piece of knowledge and stared open-mouthed at the man. "How did you know that?" he demanded, running his own eye over the mare's form as he searched for clues.

Butterick's barrel-chested laugh filled the stables. "One of the footmen was coming back from the village and saw ye headed up the hill," he replied, his shoulders still shaking with mirth.

"And what were we doing up at Stone House-on-the-Hill?" Rhea questioned, a challenging look in her eye.

"Why, Lady Rhea Claire," Butterick replied with an innocent look on his face, "I'm no gypsy fortuneteller. However," he paused, a twinkle in his eye, "if I was to be guessin', then I'd be sayin' ye might have found something abandoned and hurt and taken it to the elder Mr.

Taber, seein' as how he's got the healin' gift. 'Tis no magic in that guess. What did ye rescue?"

"Puppies," James told him. "Rhea found them."

"Aye, I thought 'twould be something like that. Abandoned, were they? The old gent will take care of them right and proper. Now ye'd best be gettin' inside," he told them, "or I'll be havin' to answer to His Grace if'n ye get the fever. Ye should've sent a groom back for the pups. I'm sure I don't know what Her Grace will be sayin' when she catches sight of ye," he added with a worried shake of his head.

"Rhea's more concerned about what Canfield will say," Francis answered.

"I have no regrets for what I did," Rhea said as they hurried toward the great house.

"Well, I really don't see how any harm can come from it," Ewan agreed. "You did a good deed, and I should think that one day you shall be justly rewarded for your act of unselfish kindness. How can that possibly bode ill for you?" he demanded as they entered beneath the noble coat of arms bearing the heraldic design of the Dominick family, which proudly proclaimed to all who entered the halls of Camareigh: "Yield Not Truth, Valor, Or Purpose."

"I think Rhea's reward has just arrived, although I wonder how just it is," Francis whispered loudly as they all glanced upward to see the Earl of Rendale descending the Grand Staircase in royal blue splendor, his appearance immaculate, his silk stockings without a wrinkle, his shoe buckles shining, his wig without a stray hair and powdered to perfection. This magnificence of dress was reflected in his rather complacent expression; then he happened to lower his nose as he stepped down and saw the rough-looking group staring up at him in silent fascination.

The expressions on four of the faces were less than pleased at the sight of that impeccable gentleman. The fifth face, that of Francis, showed a sudden purpose as he eyed the Earl with an almost predatory glance, which certainly boded ill for one Wesley Lawton.

"Good God!"

"Leave it to the Earl to never be at a loss for words," Francis said with an amused grimace as he felt a puddle of water beginning to form around his booted feet. His damp breeches were beginning to become damned uncomfortable, and he didn't relish the thought of standing here while the Earl lectured them on proper decorum.

"What has happened?" the Earl demanded, quickly descending the last few steps.

"We got caught in the downpour. So if you will kindly let us pass?" Francis requested with unusual politeness.

But the Earl wasn't sensitive enough to notice, and he stood his ground, his tall form blocking the tired riders' access to the stairs and to dry clothing. His haughty expression changed to one of growing concern as he took in Rhea's disheveled appearance.

"Lady Rhea Claire!" he exclaimed, ever proper of address despite how surprised he might find himself. "What has happened to you? Your hair? Your riding habit?" he questioned as he inspected the mud clinging to her skirts and the rent in her sleeve where it had been joined to the shoulder.

"I took a slight tumble, that is all," Rhea declared. Her impatience at being kept in her wet clothes in her own home while a guest conducted a private inquisition was beginning to show in the telltale tapping of her small, booted foot.

The Earl's aristocratic nostrils twitched ever so slightly. "But *where* did you fall?" he couldn't resist asking, despite his good manners and better judgment. Chagrined though he was, he could not control the look of distaste that passed across his features when he received an even stronger whiff of wet wool, dirty puppies, foul mud, and horses.

" 'Tis of little import, Wesley," Rhea replied, reluctant to divulge their afternoon's activities.

But Francis was not so reticent and cheerily informed the Earl, "Actually, we rescued a litter of half-drowned pups from a ditch. Or," he added, with a slightly malicious look in his blue gray eyes, "I should be more precise and say that Rhea did the rescuing."

"Rescued them?" the Earl expostulated with an incredulous look that Francis could have predicted. "Good God, whatever for?"

Francis hid his satisfied grin as he glanced between their faces: the Earl's was mystified and Rhea's was flushed.

"If you need to ask that, then 'tis only too obvious you'd not understand the reason why," Rhea told him frigidly, her voice going well with the cold shivers she was feeling as she stood conversing in wet clothes.

With a glance far surpassing in haughtiness anything the Earl could have produced, Rhea looked him up and down with lazy indifference. "Seems to me you've arrived a few days before we were expecting you?" she inquired softly, yet there was no mistaking the slight note of censure in her voice.

The Earl of Rendale turned a dull, painful-looking red, for he knew he'd committed a serious breach of etiquette, and if there was anything that the Earl of Rendale deplored, it was bad manners—especially in himself. "I arrived with Sir Jeremy and Caroline," he explained rather stiffly, feeling very ill at ease. Not that Wesley Lawton truly regretted his decision, for he had hoped to have a few private talks with Lady Rhea Claire, and since Sir Jeremy was His Grace's good friend, and Caroline was Sir Jeremy's daughter and Lady Rhea Claire's friend, and both Sir Jeremy and Caroline were related to him by marriage, why, what better kindness than to have offered them the use of his carriages? He stayed often at Winterhall, the country estate of Sir Jeremy, and this time he'd carefully planned his arrival to coincide with their departure for Camareigh. He had made up his mind to have Lady Rhea Claire as his wife, and if there was one thing a Lawton was, it was determined.

"Caroline is here?" Francis and Ewan spoke simultaneously and exchanged less than pleased glances.

"We weren't certain that Sir Jeremy and Caroline were going to come at all after we heard that he'd had another attack of the gout. You know how Sir Jeremy suffers with it," Rhea said, thinking how grumpy the usually jovial Sir Jeremy became when his joints began to swell and throb.

"I remember last time he was here and he had an attack," George contributed with a grimace. "He nearly bit my head off! Told me to shut the demmed window because the breeze was buffeting his big toe."

"I just hope the carriage didn't jostle him around too much on those bumpy roads and aggravate the condition," Rhea declared, thinking of all concerned. "Even at the best of times Sir Jeremy and Caroline are not very good traveling companions," she added, sidestepping the Earl and hurrying up the stairs, leaving him in an awkward silence with Francis and the Fletcher brothers.

The Earl coughed, clearing his throat as if about to resume his lecture, but before he could utter a word, George began to sneeze violently, causing the Earl to take a precautionary step aside, thereby clearing the stairway. Francis and the Fletcher brothers wasted no time in vaulting past the open-mouthed Earl, who now found himself standing alone, except for several smug-faced footmen, in the grand entrance hall of Camareigh.

"Well timed, George," Francis complimented his cousin, knowing well that lad's accomplishments in artful deceptions, for they'd pulled that same expedient ploy on many an unsuspecting person when they'd found themselves in difficult situations.

"Thank you, Francis," George replied seriously.

"Why did you mention the pups, Francis?" Ewan now asked his cousin as they wended their way through the long halls of the great house toward Francis's wing. Ewan eyed him speculatively, waiting patiently for an answer, for past experience of his cousin's ways had taught him, partly for his own self-preservation, to always suspect Francis's motives.

"Why not?" Francis answered innocently. "The Earl wanted an answer."

"Why not indeed, when I suspect you knew all along what the Earl's response would be to your explanation," Ewan said persistently.

Francis returned his look unrepentantly. "Let me put it as bluntly as I can," he said suddenly. "I do not fancy

123

the Earl as a brother-in-law. I've nothing against the man. I just don't want him in the family. Let's face the cold undeniable facts of the matter," he continued, sounding so serious and stern that he had his cousins' rapt attention, "and that is that the Earl of Rendale is a strutting peacock and an unbearable snob. If he raises that nose of his any higher and gets caught out in the rain, he'll most likely drown," he stated, much to the appreciation of his guffawing cousins. "Can you imagine the pall his pomposity would cast over our picnics?" he added with a look of such exaggerated horror that it should have been enough in their eyes to damn the man for life.

"And so you thought to show the Earl up in a rather petty light," Ewan said. "You knew how Rhea would react to his words."

"Naturally, and 'twas his own words and actions that tightened the noose, Ewan," Francis defended himself, thinking privately that Ewan was beginning to sound more and more like his father the general, whose voice still sounded at times as if he were ordering his troops into formation.

"But 'twas you, Francis, who put that noose around his neck, and very carefully and skillfully tightened it with the Earl's own hand," Ewan said, a grin curving his mouth, for he didn't care for the Earl any more than Francis did.

"I must plead guilty to the devilish deed," Francis admitted proudly. "But I truly do have Rhea's best interests at heart," he confided in a more serious tone. "She's far too kindhearted for her own good, and I'm afraid the Earl is not above using that to advance his cause. Well, enough of that for now. I think I've successfully spiked his guns for the moment," he added with a satisfied grin. "We'd better hurry. I'm starved for tea, and the Earl will have had a good half hour's start on us, and you know what an appetite he has for Mrs. Peacham's gooseberry tarts."

"Well, I just hope Caroline doesn't go on and on about this ball and that one, my lord this and my lord that, what dress she wore, and when, and how awful you-know-who looked," James said with a deep sigh of soon-to-be martyrdom. "She said something snide to me the last time she was here when I wanted another piece of cake," he reminded them, still smarting from her rebuke.

"Well, it was your fifth piece," George reminded *him*.

"Well, if we don't hurry, none of us will get any cake," Francis pointed out, suiting his actions to his words as he ran the rest of the way down the silent corridor.

Rhea was quickening her step along the corridor, too, but it was in the opposite direction, toward her own bedchamber. Her thoughts were centered on Caroline Winters as well, but not in speculation, for she knew with no uncertainty what she would find in her bedchamber. The door was partly opened, and Rhea's expression was one of familiar annoyance as she quietly stepped inside and found Caroline Winters prowling through her gowns with an almost feverish curiosity.

In that moment Rhea felt more pity toward Caroline Winters than she felt anger, for although Caroline had everything she could possibly want or need, she was never satisfied and never would be, because she always wanted more. It was not in Sir Jeremy's nature, nor had it ever been, to deny his only child's heart's desires. With the best of intentions he had unsparingly lavished love, devotion, and riches on his motherless daughter's fair head, thinking mistakenly that this overindulgence could make up for the loss of her mother. The results had been less than successful, for Caroline Winters had grown into a selfish and petulant young woman who wheedled and threatened tantrums, whined and connived whenever she was faced with opposition to her wishes. Poor Sir Jeremy had long ago given up trying to placate her, or even to rebuke her for her misbehavior, turning a slightly deaf ear to her ranting and raving as she tyrannized over him.

"Hello, Caroline," Rhea greeted her now. "Have you lost something?"

"Oh, Rhea!" Caroline gave a frightened squeal and spun around at the sound of Rhea's slightly mocking voice. "You did startle me so. I do wish you wouldn't sneak up on a person that way. Lud, but I feared one of those savages from the colonies was going to scalp me," she complained, seemingly not in the least embarrassed at being caught snooping through another's possessions. "I did knock, but you weren't here, so I came on in. I knew you wouldn't mind. I just had to find out if you had the same divine silk that Papa got for me in Paris. You do always seem to have something finer than me, so I was just making certain that I had the only gown fashioned out of that silk," she explained with a smug glance at Rhea. But as she became aware of Rhea's bedraggled appearance, her eyes grew wide and an incredulous look settled on her pretty features. "Lud! What the devil happened to you? You look horrible!"

Rhea smiled a trifle crookedly. "Thank you for your concern. I took a fall, that is all. I'm quite all right," Rhea said, moving toward the warmth of the fire that had been lighted by a diligent maid.

Caroline eyed Rhea up and down, a look of delicate distaste turning down the corners of her mouth. "You've absolutely ruined that divine riding habit. 'Tis a pity."

"I've another one exactly like it, so you needn't worry," Rhea reassured her. "Mother liked the material so much, and knew how often I would be wearing it, that she had the foresight to order two identical ones made."

"How extraordinary," Caroline breathed, thinking the Duchess quite ingenious. " 'Tis, or I should say 'twas, a beautiful shade of blue. It really would go better with my coloring than yours. We are of a similar size, aren't we?" she asked entreatingly, her eyes straying to the wardrobe where the second riding habit must be concealed.

Rhea glanced over at the other girl, recognizing well that tone of voice. "No, Caroline," Rhea told her firmly, refusing to give in to her and wishing the maids would arrive with her bath so that she could gracefully have Caroline ejected from her bedchamber. "This is my favorite riding habit, and now that I've ruined this one, I shall wish to wear the other one. I am sorry, but I'm sure you understand. Haven't you a favorite gown or hat?" Rhea was trying, unsuccessfully, to reason with Caroline; already, a small pout was beginning to form on the other girl's lips.

"Very well, but I'm sure *I* wouldn't be so selfish if I

had something you wanted to wear," Caroline said, frustrated anger trembling in her voice. She drifted over to Rhea's dressing table and began to sniff each of the various perfumes collected there in porcelain, clear cut glass, and silver bottles. Her jeweled hand lingered over an amethyst glass bottle with a millefiori pattern.

"I'm completely out of this scent, and I do love it so," she sighed with a melancholy look at the delicate bottle of scent.

"Please take it, Caroline," Rhea told her, hoping she would take her treasured prize and leave. "It has never been a favorite of mine."

"Oh, it hasn't?" Caroline asked, sounding a bit disappointed by the remark. Still, her greedy fingers wasted no time in grasping Rhea's possession to her breast. She glanced in the mirror at her reflection, her pleased smile fading from her lips, for although she was similar in size and coloring to Rhea Claire, her eyes were a lackluster blue and her hair a paler gold. It was a never-ending source of irritation to her that Rhea's eyes were an incredible violet and her hair a dark, fiery gold.

Caroline fingered an elaborately engraved, silver brush and comb set before moving on to touch a silver patch box inlaid with precious stones. With a bored expression she flicked open the top of a small music box sitting next to a delicate porcelain pastille burner, and the tinkling notes filled the room with a soft, sweet melody that blended well with the fragrance of honeysuckle and roses that scented the room.

The colorful assortment of toiletries crowded on Rhea Claire's dressing table were most of the necessary aides a young beauty of fashion might find useful, and they differed little from the articles that would be found on Caroline's dressing table at Winterhall. But still, to Caroline's jealous eye, Rhea's seemed more elegant and far more expensive than her own. *Lady* Rhea Claire Dominick had so much more than she did, Caroline thought now, including a duke as a father. Her own father was merely a baron, and hardly anyone of consequence at that, and Winterhall seemed positively shabby compared to the magnificence of Camareigh. Rhea would be much sought after by all of the eligible beaus in London, and certainly far more sought after than a mere *Miss* like herself.

Caroline stared across Rhea Claire's lovely bedchamber, dislike for the beautiful girl filling her with a growing bitterness. It just was not fair. Rhea Claire had everything. And even though she, Caroline, was three years older than Rhea, it would most likely be Rhea Claire who wed first. And unless she did something about it it might very well be the Earl of Rendale who Rhea Claire would wed. Caroline's small, square jaw tightened at the thought, for there were three things that she was determined to have—unlimited wealth, a title, and the Earl of Rendale. She had thought it all out carefully, and it was really quite simple. If she married the Earl of Rendale, she achieved, with little or no effort at all, her other two goals. Wesley not only had a great fortune, but his family name and title were almost as ancient and noble as that of the Dominicks'. And even though there was no dukedom to show for it, the Earls of Rendale had seldom not been on an equal footing with the most powerful and titled of England.

"Wesley rode with us from Winterhall," Caroline informed Rhea, a smile of smug self-satisfaction curving up the corners of her pouty mouth. "He was quite insistent upon offering us the use of his carriages. He really is so thoughtful," she continued, preening before the mirror as she straightened the lace on her sleeve. "He knows how delicate my health is, and how I do so hate to travel, especially in that old, evil-sprung carriage of Papa's. He absolutely refuses to buy another one, even though I've been begging him to for over a year now. But he just won't hear of it. Says he's fond of the carriage," she told a half-attentive Rhea. Then she cast her a sly glance and added thoughtfully, "I truly do think, Rhea Claire, that Wesley may have a penchant for me. I shouldn't be at all surprised to have him asking Papa for my hand," she said in a most confidential tone of voice, half convincing herself that it was true. "Of course, I should have to consider his proposal very carefully. After all, can you imagine how I would feel if after accepting Wesley, a duke offered for me? I had at one time," Caroline confided, "thought about marrying your Uncle Richard."

Rhea nearly choked. She turned from the warmth of the fire and stared in amazement across the room at the serious, straight-faced Caroline Winters. Rhea's lips quirked as she suppressed a sudden urge to laugh, for Caroline really had been seriously considering Uncle Richard as a possible husband.

"Of course, he is rather old for me, and forgive me but I just can't abide those spectacles he wears. And . . . red hair . . ." Caroline said, shaking her perfectly coiffed head. "And I would never have accompanied him to that castle of his in Scotland. Such a godforsaken place, don't you think so?"

"I am quite certain that Uncle Richard took all of those considerations into account when he chose his bride. Naturally, knowing your delicate sensibilities, he would not have dreamed of risking your health by proposing to you when he knew he'd be taking his bride back up to Scotland with him," Rhea said very seriously. But there was a teasing light already lurking in her eye when she thought about telling Uncle Richard how close a call he'd unknowingly had where Miss Caroline Winters was concerned.

Caroline silently considered Rhea's words. "Yes, I do believe you are quite right. I always had wondered why he'd never asked for my hand. I was most surprised when he up and married that little nobody."

Rhea's amusement faded, and she said coldly, "That nobody, as you call her, happens to be somebody very important to my family and much loved by us all."

Caroline shrugged. "I only meant that she hardly seemed the type of person a marquis should select to marry. She has no fortune, no title, and certainly no position or friends in society. What on earth made your uncle choose a penniless orphan?"

"He was in love with her," Rhea said simply.

"She's not even pretty, so how can he be in love with her?" Caroline demanded. "And it is disgusting how big she is now."

"She *is* going to have a baby any day," Rhea reminded her.

"Well, I know that," Caroline retorted snappishly. "That is why it is so disgusting. 'Tis quite outrageous of her to appear in public in her condition. Has she no modesty?" Caroline asked, her cheeks blushing with the thought of exactly how Sarah Verrick came to be with child. " 'Tis indecent for Lady Sarah to be displaying herself while so obviously enceinte."

"Would you have her lock herself up in her room for nine months?" Rhea asked, a smile of relief crossing her face as the door opened and two maids came bustling into the room, one carrying an armful of soft blankets. The other hurried immediately to the fire to add another log to the hungry flames.

Rhea had removed her outer garmets and had been standing before the fire in her petticoats and thin chemisette. Her wet and muddied riding clothes looked little better than a pile of rags. Wrapped now in the enfolding warmth of one of the blankets, she settled down before the fire and began to comb through the wet tangles in her hair. As she gave a small grimace of pain, another, older maid entered the room with a tray and two steaming cups of a dark-looking brew that Rhea knew well from past experience. "Mrs. Taylor's Special Treat," Rhea muttered, her grimace widening as she remembered the brew's unusual flavor.

"Her Grace's orders," the maid told her before Rhea could voice her objections. "Now the both of ye drink up!" she ordered gruffly, her sour puss face masking a generous, warm-hearted nature that she did her best to hide.

"Very well." Rhea capitulated and wrapped her cold hands around the hot mug. "But I swear sometimes that I become sick *because* of this concoction of Mrs. Taylor's. Drink up, Caroline," Rhea told the now silent girl, her smile mocking as she saw how suspiciously Caroline was eyeing the brew.

"Me?" Caroline cried, her face puckering into a comical mask as she sniffed the evil-smelling potion. "Lud! Why, this smells horrible. What is it? Poison?" She pushed the mug away, but the work-roughened hand holding it out to her moved ever closer.

"Her Grace gives me orders that Miss Caroline is to drink Mrs. Taylor's Special Treat, too, seein' how she was complainin' about the long, tiring carriage ride from Winterhall. Her Grace knows how delicate your health is, Miss," Rawley said, her face full of understanding as she moved the foul-smelling brew still closer to the young lady's turned-up nose. "Her Grace won't have no one gettin' sick at Camareigh, not if she can help it. You don't want to be displeasin' Her Grace, now d'ye?" Rawley added persuasively. "Be a good miss and drink up Mrs. Taylor's Special Treat."

Caroline's lips trembled slightly as she finally accepted the mug. "Who the devil is this Mrs. Taylor?" she demanded, making a horrible face and swallowing half the contents of the mug, tears rolling down her face as she choked and sputtered at the taste.

Rhea smiled in appreciation. "Mrs. Taylor is an old friend of my mother's who lives near my mother's old home, Verrick House. Mother says she makes the best mead between London and Land's End. I haven't seen her in a couple of years, but I remember her as being a robust and jolly woman. She has two sons, Will and John, who must be the size of mountains, or at least they seemed that big to me. They own a tavern."

"And Her Grace allowed you to associate with that type of rabble?" Caroline squeaked in amazement, her ill humor still sitting high in her stomach along with this Mrs. Taylor's brew.

"Mother is very fond of her, and especially of the Taylor brothers. She is godmother to all of their children, and between them, well . . ." Rhea paused as she tried to count up the sons and daughters of the two brothers. "I'm not sure how many there are, but there are enough little Taylors around to keep Mrs. Taylor a very busy and happy grandmother."

"What about His Grace?" Caroline asked. "Surely he can't approve of such familiarity with . . . with common tavern keepers?"

Caroline heard Rhea's laughter, but she couldn't see

her face. The maids were preparing a bath for her and had poured hot and cold water into a tub set up before the warmth of the fire, and the steam rising up around it masked Rhea's scantily clad form.

"Actually, Father is quite fond of the Taylors. He threatens in that sardonic way of his to take them out behind the orchard and thrash the both of them with one arm tied behind his back. They all end up laughing, although I've never quite seen the humor in it."

"Now you'd best be getting down for your tea, Miss Caroline," Rawley told her, holding the door open for the hoity-toity young miss who never could take a hint. "You don't want it gettin' as cold as Lady Rhea's bath water, now d'ye?"

"Very well," Caroline muttered as she sashayed to the door. "I s'pose Wesley will be wondering where I am. I hope he hasn't been too concerned," she added fretfully as she quickened her step and waved carelessly over her shoulder. "Wesley and I shall see you later, I s'pose. Lud, but 'tis going to take a whole pot of tea to wash that foul taste from my mouth," she said, sending an unrepentant Rawley a baleful glare before she left the room in a swaggering swish of silk skirts.

Rawley snorted in derision as she shut the door firmly on Caroline's smug, plump figure. "Like to wash that young missy's mouth out with soap, I would. And, more than likely, Lord Rendale hasn't even given her nibs another thought, especially after settin' eyes on Mrs. Peacham's gooseberry tarts. Reckon Mrs. Taylor would've gotten a chuckle out of seein' her Special Treat poured down that young missy's gullet. Only way to shut the girl up. Met Mrs. Taylor once, when I accompanied Her Grace to Verrick House. 'Twas for the buryin' of her dear Aunt Margaret, and Mrs. Taylor and me got together for some comparin' of recipes for mead. Reckon hers is better'n mine, but mine packs quite a wallop, that it does. Now, what gown will ye be wantin' set out fer ye, Lady Rhea Claire? The dark blue silk is mighty fine, reckon ye could wear it and the . . ."

Rhea sighed and let the warm, lightly scented waters of her bath soothe away all her aches and pains as she drifted off into a daydream. Rawley's voice droned on and on, her words growing hazy and indistinct. The heady scent of roses suddenly intruded into Rhea's thoughts, and she could not help but think of the mysterious woman in the carriage and wonder if she had reached her destination at last.

Arriving at her lodgings, the half-timbered Tudor building known to the locals as The Merry Green Dragon, Kate found her fine Billingsgate gentleman-for-hire nursing a bottle of the inn's finest brandy, his much-darned, stockinged feet stretched out to the warmth of a blazing fire, a very mellow look of contentment on his features.

"Enjoy your ride, m'lady?" he inquired without much curiosity, his speech slightly slurred. However, he still managed, much to Kate's annoyance, to inject a wealth of meaning into the title "m'lady."

"Yes, 'twas most edifying," Kate replied tightly, not caring one bit for his disrespectful attitude. "And you? Did you have an interesting exploration of your brandy bottle?"

"Aye, 'twas most enlightening, m'lady," he responded with a loud belch.

"A pity, 'twould be, if you had to pay for it yourself. Then you would most likely find it to be most expensive," Kate responded sarcastically as she held out her frozen hands to the heat of the fire. The flickering light danced on her veil as she stared, hypnotized, into the flames eating away at the logs.

"I am quite famished," she said suddenly, feeling oddly pleased with her day's activities. "I see you have already supped," she commented then, as she noticed the table laden with its layer of greasy plates and empty wine glasses.

"Aye, enjoyed it well enough," was Teddie Waltham's compliment to their host. "But then, most anything tastes good if washed down with enough spirits," he said calmly. At the same time he noticed his benefactress's growing lack of composure as she paced the floor of the private dining room, her black veil floating out around her and her high heels clicking a regular beat across the wooden planking. She could not disguise her nervousness as she slapped her leather gloves continuously against her palm. "Ye seem to be a might upset, m'lady. How about a snort?" Teddie Waltham generously offered her his half-empty bottle of brandy.

"Upset?" Kate retorted incredulously. "Not in the least. I just have to think, that is all," she said shortly, her mind spinning with the innocently beautiful faces of Lucien's children. "Go order yourself another bottle, and get me a bottle of wine. Oh, and while you are out there, send in the landlord," she commanded, beginning to nurture the germ of an idea. "Well?" she demanded, staring down arrogantly at the still-seated Edward Waltham. "Don't just sit there, man. I'm not paying you to warm your ass before the fire."

Edward Waltham rose slowly and gracefully to his stockinged feet; then he pretended to sway slightly, for he had a feeling it would be better as well as safer to be underestimated by milady. She would make a dangerous enemy if she were to become mistrustful and suspicious, but a buffoon would be beneath her notice, and acting like one would give him some space to maneuver should the occasion warrant a change of plans. "M'lady's wish is my command," Teddie Waltham said now as he bowed gallantly, then padded from the room obviously attempting to maintain his dignity.

With a satisfied sigh, Kate assumed Edward Waltham's place before the fire, her thin hands beginning to tingle as the blood rushed back into them with the warmth. Rocco had assumed his usual protective stance beside the door, but Kate sensed a new strangeness about him, and for a brief, absurd moment she felt frightened of the big man with the child's mind. Kate shook off her imaginary fears, ridding herself of her doubts as easily as she had her cloak only moments before.

She was contentedly sitting before the fire when Teddie Waltham returned with their genial host in tow, who had the requested refreshments riding on a tray carried before him. Teddie Waltham quickly snatched the bottle of brandy and a clean glass and sequestered himself in the window seat, where he had an unobstructed view of the proceedings.

"Ah, Mr. Higgleton, how very kind of you," Kate said to her host in her most cordial tone. "But then the service in The Merry Green Dragon has been exceptional, and please, my compliments to your cook. The food has been unquestionably the finest I have had since arriving in England."

Mr. Higgleton puffed out his thin chest in obvious pleasure at this fine lady's compliments to his service. " 'Tis an honor, m'lady," he responded graciously, "to serve so fine a gentlewoman as yerself."

"How very kind, Mr. Higgleton," Kate replied with a humbleness that nearly made her nauseous. Her eyes glittered up at the fool of a landlord as he simpered and preened before her.

Teddie Waltham took a deep swallow of fiery brandy, shaking his head in disgust, for he'd seldom heard such mealy-mouthed and toadying goings on, even from himself, and he had very little pride left. Even his best fawning ways fell short of her ladyship. Aye, she was something to behold, for he'd seldom come across an oilier character than m'lady here.

"And for tonight's repast, m'lady," Mr. Higgleton continued, spreading out his hands as if waiting for applause, "we have spitch-cocked eels and a fresh loin of pork, as well as me wife's famous jellies. No one makes them quite like her, bless her little heart. Reckon ye'll be wantin' that, eh?" he chuckled, thinking her ladyship wasn't near as haughty as he'd orginally suspected. "Give ye an extra big helping of the spitch-cocked eels, I will."

Kate smiled tightly. "How wonderful."

"Aye, thought ye'd like that. Says to the wife, I did, now there be a woman who enjoys a well-prepared meal. Never been wrong about people and their stomachs."

"Quite amazing," Kate murmured as she sipped her wine, her attitude suddenly one of dismissal as she contemplated the fire.

"Well," Mr. Higgleton said awkwardly, "s'pose I'll get the wife to work in the kitchen preparing that eel for ye."

He was halfway to the door when Kate suddenly spoke. "I came across several young people this afternoon while out for a ride. They were named Dominick. Do you happen to know them?" she asked casually.

"Why, they be His 'Grace, the Duke of Camareigh's children. Fine young 'uns, them," Mr. Higgleton said knowledgeably. "Spirited they be, like the young should, but never up to no malicious mischief. Just a spot of fun now and again. Especially young Lord Robin. Little devil, he is," the innkeeper said with an indulgent look.

"I don't believe I had the pleasure of meeting him," Kate commented lazily, as if the whole conversation were a bit of a bore. "However, I did meet Lord Francis and his sister, Lady Rhea Claire."

"Oh, aye," Mr. Higgleton said with a nod. "Lord Francis is a fine young gentleman. Does His Grace proud, he does. And Lady Rhea Claire," he sighed. "Ah, there is a true beauty, and with a heart just as pure. Takes after Her Grace, she does. A fine lady, Her Grace."

"A close family, are they?" Kate inquired softly.

"Oh, aye, that they are. And until the little 'uns was born a while back, young Lady Rhea Claire was His Grace's only daughter, as well as being the eldest. Reckon there's always something special about firstborns," Mr. Higgleton confided, not above enjoying a bit of gossip. "His Grace treats the young lady like a princess, he does. But then, I reckon she might as well be one, seein' how she's so pretty. Never heard a word spoken against the young lady."

"So, Lady Rhea Claire is much beloved by His Grace, is she?" Kate murmured thoughtfully, a half-smile curving her lips beneath her mask and veil. "How very interesting. Now, please, I've kept you long enough. Please forgive me," she said. "Oh, I also met an ancient gentleman by the name of Taber, I believe."

"Aye, ye be speakin' of the elder Mr. Taber of Stone House-on-the-Hill. Been around forever he has. Most people around here think he helped to lay the first stone of The Merry Green Dragon, and it's been here for nigh on to three hundred years now."

"A remarkably agile and sharp-witted old man." Kate said now, a slight worried frown crossing her brow. "Does he indeed remember everything and every person he has ever met?"

"Aye, he's a sly old fox. Never heard tell of him not remembering a face, or a happening hereabouts," Mr. Higgleton replied with a chuckle. "Always got a mug of ale for him and a place by the fire," he added, for he was proud to have as a fixture in his inn one of the oldest men in these parts. And it certainly didn't hurt trade to have an old gent like Mr. Taber spinning yarns every afternoon with a crowd of thirsty listeners gathering close around the fire.

" 'Twas quiet at Stone House-on-the-Hill when I was there today," Kate said. "Does he live there alone?"

"Oh, no, he's got his son and daughter-in-law," Mr. Higgleton confided. "And plenty of grandchildren."

"I see," Kate said as she held her hands out to the blaze.

"But they be gone to visit her mother over toward Bath. Didn't marry no local lass," Mr. Higgleton said with a disapproving shake of his neatly bewigged head. "Knew she'd be trouble the minute I set me eyes on her pretty face and seen her fancy airs. 'Tis no good for a farmer's wife."

"So, Mr. Taber *is* there alone," Kate remarked.

"Well, not exactly," Mr. Higgleton explained. "He has his young granddaughter there with him to do the cookin' and milkin'. See to his needs. But usually the house is packed full of bodies," he told his guest, who was obviously concerned about the old man's welfare. "Old man Taber will live another one hundred years, or my name ain't Horatio Higgleton!" he laughed. "Now, I'll be seein' about that dinner you're waitin' fer."

For what seemed an endless minute, there was silence in the room after the door had closed on the busy figure of Mr. Horatio Higgleton. But when a log fell with a loud thud, Teddie Waltham found his tongue. His consumption of spirits had not yet rendered him insensible, and he could still voice his suspicions.

"What's this about some high-and-mighty duke?" he demanded with a belligerent tilt to his chin. "And what are all of these questions about *His Grace's* children and some old man? Back in London there was never no mention of a duke," he told the veiled woman accusingly, whose continued silence irked him even further. "Playing tricks on a duke, of all people, was never mentioned to Teddie Waltham," he repeated.

"Did I really neglect to inform you of that small detail?" Kate remarked casually, while her fingers tapped out a melody of growing irritation on the table top. "Are you quite sure I didn't? I'm sure I must have. Perhaps you were a bit fuddled that evening, as indeed you are most nights."

"Never heard nothing about no duke," Teddie Waltham repeated firmly. "Ye never said nothing about it 'cause ye knew I'd have nothing to do with fooling around with one of them dukes. They got powerful friends, m'lady," Teddie Waltham said, trying to reason with his employer. "I'd take me chances in the colonies before crossing one of them fellows."

Kate snorted in disgust at this lily-livered cur sniveling in his bottle. "A good dose of courage is what you need, Mr. Waltham, not more brandy. But you needn't work yourself up into a sweat, for I've everything planned out. Nothing shall go wrong, that I promise you."

Teddie Waltham rolled his bloodshot eyes heavenward. "Aye, I've heard that before, and mostly from men one step short of the gallows. I went along with ye only 'cause I never thought ye'd be foolish enough to tangle with a duke, but, m'lady, ye be daft. And Teddie Waltham values his neck enough not to be sticking it out too close to the block. I've enjoyed me stay in the country, but I'm growing homesick for the soot and grime of London, so . . ." Teddie Waltham allowed his words to trail off as he shrugged. "I'm thinkin' of headin' back to familiar surroundings."

Kate said something in a sharp voice, and even though Teddie Waltham couldn't understand the foreign words, he was smart enough to know he was the object of them.

A moment later he found himself being held a foot off the floor by a giant hand that had snaked into his collar.

"Let me down, ye big lumbering ox!" he choked out, his face turning red as his collar tightened painfully around his stretched out, very vulnerable neck.

"Rocco responds only to me, Mr. Waltham," Kate told him as she relaxed in the chair, enjoying the predicament Mr. Edward Waltham now found himself in. She allowed a small chuckle to escape. "My dear, dear Mr. Waltham, you are not only a coward but a fool as well. You are in this thing with me, and there is no going back to London until I say so. I've hired you to do a job for me, and I expect you to do it or," she paused thoughtfully, a sad note entering her voice as she continued, "you might not care for the way I would exact punishment for your failure to please me."

Teddie Waltham was kicking aimlessly, trying to connect with the big man's shin, but it was to no avail. He coughed, struggling to answer as he felt the world spinning around him. "Aye, aye. Let me down! I'll do as ye wish. Let me down before ye've got a dead body hanging up here. Then nothing will get done."

Kate signaled Rocco, who dropped the squirming Waltham into a gasping heap on the hardwood floor. A couple of shiny coins fell with a jingle, one rolling unnervingly close to the big man's feet. Teddie Waltham sniffed, wiping a hand beneath his nose as he risked a glance upward.

"That should sweeten your stay a bit," Kate told him in a cold voice that sent shivers up Waltham's spine. "However, as I'm not one to overstay my welcome," she continued in a more conversational tone, "I have made plans to leave and return to London by no later than tomorrow afternoon. Does that suit you, Mr. Waltham?"

Teddie Waltham nodded, his hands soothing his sore neck where the rough material of his coat had rubbed painfully against the tender skin. Aye, he thought, it suited him just fine, and as soon as he saw the familiar cobbled streets of London, he would seek his freedom from this madwoman. He could only hope it wouldn't be too late to save his skin.

A pale crescent moon was slicing through a layer of silvered clouds as two riders entered the farmyard of Stone House-on-the-Hill. It was late. Far too late, in fact, for visitors. But these were uninvited guests, and they weren't there for a friendly visit.

Kate slid off her horse's back, her knees buckling slightly as her booted feet touched the ground. God, but she was getting old, she thought, swearing beneath her breath as she flexed her stiff fingers. She could feel in the aching of her joints every bone-jarring step that nag had taken between The Merry Green Dragon and Stone House-on-the-Hill.

Kate glanced around at the deserted yard, her eyes drawn to the pool of light pouring from a small mullioned window set deep in the stone wall of the farmhouse.

"Silenzio!" Kate hissed as Rocco came trudging up behind her, his feet scraping noisily against the loose stones of the path. She sighed in exasperation, wondering if this night would ever come to an end. She would gladly have left Rocco back at the inn had she thought she could do without him, but if there were difficulties, his strength would be useful. But he was certainly no horseman, and he had trailed behind her and slowed her down ever since they'd left the stables nearly an hour before. Nor had it added to the evening's success when he had been knocked from his horse's back by a low-hanging branch, leaving her to chase after his runaway mount.

Kate took a firm hold on his big arm as she made her way toward the lighted window; she preferred to know exactly where Rocco was. The gusting wind blew coldly against Kate's caped figure as she peered into the house, her veiled face looking like the disturbed shadow of a tree branch being blown by the storm.

She stepped back into the darkness and leaned against the side of the house as she stared thoughtfully around her. Inside, sitting in the warm light from the fire in the kitchen hearth, a young girl was sound asleep. In her lap, equally dead to the world, was a curled-up pup, while on the flagstone floor at her feet was a large basket holding the rest of the pups that had been rescued that afternoon. Also positioned around the girl's chair were several dogs, all of them lazily snoring away. They were obviously watchdogs that the soft-hearted old fool kept in on a cold night. The girl must be Mr. Taber's granddaughter, Kate guessed, then wondered where the old man was. She really would prefer not to disturb the granddaughter, but if she got in the way . . .

As Kate stood silently contemplating her next move, she suddenly became aware of a tuneless whistle drifting to her on the wind. She gazed toward the darker bulk of the barn on the far side of the yard; then a slow smile curved her lips as she caught sight of a sliver of light shining out beneath a poorly fitted door. With a new purposefulness in her step, Kate quickly crossed the yard, following the beam of light. A curse directed against the old man, whose meddlesome ways had forced her into taking this action, trembled on her lips as she carefully pulled open the door. Everything would be ruined if he remembered who she was and then blabbed the news to half of the valley. And talk he would, especially with a pint of ale in his hand and an inn full of gossips gathered around, and then it wouldn't be long before the news reached the attention of the Duke of Camareigh.

All would be lost if he found out too soon that she was back! She must, at all costs, protect her anonymity, she told herself as she slid into the barn, her black figure merging with the deep shadows filling the cavernous room. She paused, her eyes pinpointing the bent figure illumined by the glow of a single lantern.

"Aye, aye, I'll be along shortly, Janey," the old man spoke over his shoulder when he felt the cold draught of air that blew in from outside. "Ye git yerself back t'house, now. 'Tis too cold fer ye out here," he told her, his gnarled hands never stopping their careful, assured measuring of various liquids into a dark amber bottle. "I'll have this liniment for Haverstoke's prize bull finished before ye can get back to that warm fire."

When the silence continued, with no sound of anyone leaving, Mr. Taber glanced up, peering into the shadowy darkness. A frown formed on his wrinkled face as he stared hard at the indistinct figure moving closer.

"Janey? T'ain't ye, is it now? Who be ye?" he demanded as he corked the concoction he'd been preparing for Haverstoke's prize bull. Then, wiping his hands on an oily rag, he straightened up. "Who be ye, I'm askin'?" he repeated, his hand reaching out for his knobby cane.

" 'Tis only I, Mr. Taber," Kate replied softly.

"Ah," the old man sighed, relaxing his grip on the cane. "The Lady Kate."

Kate sucked in her breath in amazement, never having really believed he would remember her—but he had! Damn him, she fumed silently.

"Aye," the old man chuckled. "Ye didn't think I'd be rememberin' ye, did ye now? I told ye. I never forget a person. Remembered ye at supper, I did," he told her proudly. "So *ye* be the strange woman stayin' at the Dragon? Heard about ye, I have."

"Have you indeed," Kate commented, moving closer.

"Aye, a bit odd, that. Might be wonderin' why ye wasn't stayin' at Camareigh, except that I know there be bad blood between ye and His Grace, and that brother of yours," the old man said matter-of-factly. He strained his eyes past Kate, to where Rocco was standing silently by the door. "Now, tha's not young Lord Percy, unless he's gone and growed a couple of feet. Is he here with ye, then?"

Kate's clenched hands tightened as she answered shortly, "He's dead."

"Is he now?" the old man said, voicing little regret at the gentleman's passing. "Come t'bad end, did he? Always suspected he would."

An uncontrollable hiss escaped Kate's lips as she glared at the complacent old man who had, in a carelessly spoken comment, dismissed her beloved Percy like so much garbage.

"I won't be lyin' t'ye, Lady Kate," the old man continued. "I never cared much for ye, or tha' brother of yours. Ye've a mean streak in ye, both of ye had it, and I'll never be forgettin' the way ye put the whip to tha' sweet little mare of yours. Dove was her name," he said with a reminiscent look on his face.

Kate gave a strangled laugh of incredulity. "You actually remember the name of my mare. Lud, but I don't even remember that!"

"Oh, I remember her, right enough," Mr. Taber said, now with a grim look as he eyed the veiled woman. "Treated her poor bruised flesh time and time again, I did. But ye never learned ye lesson, did ye? Stubborn and hard-headed, you was, until finally ye took little Dove out and broke her leg. 'Twasn't necessary, that. No sir, t'wasn't neccasary a'tall. Said so at the time to the old Duke."

"Yes, you did, didn't you?" Kate recalled. "Since we're indulging in old memories, I recall you carrying tales and lies to my grandfather. Because of you I was forbidden the stables. You caused me a lot of trouble, old man. You always were an interfering busybody."

Old Mr. Taber nodded his white head. "Ye never did care to be crossed. Always wanted ye own way, you and Lord Percy. I always did think 'twas ye who put him up to most of the mischief. Remember, too, when ye and that brother of yours ganged up on young Lord Lucien. Scarred him good, didn't ye? Never thought 'twas an accident like ye said to the old Duke. 'Twas cruel of ye to do that."

"He got his revenge, old man," Kate told him grimly, her skirts rustling around her as she moved ever closer.

"Aye, been a long time since ye was here in the valley. Strange, ye comin' back now. His Grace never mentions ye. And ye say ye're not stayin' at Camareigh. Right strange, that."

A deep, throaty laugh came from Kate. "Poor Mr. Busybody. You don't know everything, do you? There are still a few secrets that haven't been ferreted out by you and that long nose of yours. You've lived so long, old man, you think you've seen it all, don't you?"

"I've seen enough to satisfy me, m'lady. Ye be right. I have lived a long time, and I know I've not much longer left," the old man replied, and even though he was bent over because his spine had curved under the weight of age, and his features were wizened, he possessed a simple and undeniable dignity that Kate knew she herself could never aspire to. "I don't want to know about you, m'lady. Your kind is bad. Ye be rotten to the core, and I don't want my last days to be tainted by ye. I'm goin' to die soon, I can feel it in me bones, so I don't care what I say to ye, m'lady. And I'll warn ye now," he added harshly, his voice trembling. "If ye be up to mischief, then ye'll be comin' to grief. His Grace is a fine gentleman, and much loved around Camareigh, as is his family. And the Tabers of Stone House-on-the-Hill have served the Dukes of Camareigh for centuries, so ye'll not be findin' any allies around here for your mischief-makin'."

Kate smiled unpleasantly. "I do believe you are prophetic, old man. Although I suspect you will die sooner than you counted on," she murmured, her gloved hand reaching out to fondle the short handle of a mallet lying on a shelf beside her.

"Now I'll be askin' ye kindly to leave, m'lady," Mr. Taber told Kate as he turned his back to her and began, with shaking hands, to put up his special blends and potions for mixing up liniments and poultices.

Mr. Taber of Stone House-on-the-Hill never saw the blow that felled him, nor heard the satisfied sigh that followed. He would have been touched, though, by the despairing moan that came from Rocco when he saw the old man fall to his knees against the wooden bench.

Kate felt nothing, however, as she stared dispassionately at the sprawled figure. "You've lived far too long, old man. You should have died years ago. You really should have."

Kate glanced up in surprise when she felt Rocco come to stand beside her. "What the devil are you blubbering about?" she demanded as she heard his sniffing and caught the glisten of tears in his eyes. "God help us! You're a fool to waste your tears on him. Don't you know the old goat would've seen us swinging from the gallows just as easily as he'd have said good morning. Now come on," Kate told the weeping footman, "we've got to get back to the inn before our fine Mr.

Edward Waltham discovers we are gone. I don't want him slinking off just when I may need him the most. And do try and stay on your horse this time," she warned him in irritable impatience, her mind already on her next move. "We have quite a lot of work to do in preparation for the morrow, which promises to be a very fine day," she predicted as she carelessly tossed the bloodied mallet into a thick pile of straw.

Thursday morn dawned bright over Camareigh, with an exuberant cock crowing the hour, despite the hint of rain threatening in dark gray clouds hung low over the horizon. The sounds of awakening spread with increasing volume across the estate as servants and guests alike stirred from sleep and began the preparations for the day's work, or play, as fortune might have it.

From the stables drifted the sounds of barking dogs greeting the stable hands, who were yawning and rubbing cold hands together while counting off the minutes until breakfast. Their chores of watering and feeding the horses, as well as mucking up the stalls, seemed endless in the chill morning hours. But in Butterick's book, the horses always came first.

From the kitchen wing of Camareigh the clang and clatter of pots and pans rose to a deafening din as Mrs. Peacham organized her sleepy staff of assistants. The scullery maids scurried about under the threat of a large wooden spoon that was being brandished like a sword by the diminutive cook, who took no less pride in her kitchens than Butterick took in his stables. Fires were stoked in the large fireplaces of the kitchens, bringing the contents of several black pots hanging low over the flames to a fragrant bubbling. A couple of kettles were letting off steam as they bided their time over the heat. Copper and brass saucepans of varying sizes with hardwood handles, pottage pots, fish kettles and pudding pans, as well as frying pans with half-hoop handles, were being selected for breakfast duty, while the slow-burning charcoal braziers were being made ready to keep the prepared food warm for the table.

Soon the aromatic odors of roasting coffee beans, fried

sausages, and eggs blended with the appetizing smells of freshly baked turnovers, tarts, and buns. A quarter of veal was already being basted as it turned on a spit over the coals, and a plump ham was baking in the oven— both were destined for luncheon. Across a wide table sitting squarely in the center of the kitchen, fresh vegetables were being scrubbed and peeled, pared and sliced, to accompany the meat as side dishes.

The delicate tinkling of fragile china and glass was added to the clamor of the kitchens as trays were prepared for their journey upstairs. Most of the guests who stayed at Camareigh enjoyed a light breakfast in their rooms as they dressed for the day's activities, many completing their toilette just in time for luncheon. The family, however, breakfasted together: Her Grace liked to see her children before they disappeared on the various pursuits and entertainments, which always kept her wondering what they were up to next.

". . . you should have waited for me," Lord Robin was saying between mouthfuls of egg. "I wish I could have seen that footman. Was he really eight feet tall? Even bigger than Will and John Taylor?"

"Robin, don't speak with your mouth full," the Duchess cautioned her son as she fed another spoonful of soft-boiled egg to Arden.

"Sorry, Mama. I can't believe anybody would be that big," he continued after completely swallowing his mouthful of sausage.

"Honestly, he was," James swore, crossing his heart.

"Well, I don't think he was *quite* that large a fellow," Ewan corrected his brother. "Although he was uncommonly big."

"Where did you say you thought he was from?" Richard asked curiously. At times he almost wished he were still young enough to gallivant across the countryside, but as an expectant father he was required to show more circumspect behavior. However, that didn't necessarily mean curbing his curiosity.

"Italy," Francis told him.

"France," George piped in at the same time.

"I'm sure it was Italian they were speaking," Francis said with assurance. "She was certainly a queer one."

"Francis! That is not a polite way to speak," the Duchess reprimanded him.

"Well, she was," Francis maintained, standing firm. "She was dressed totally in black and wore this heavy veil. I didn't even see her face."

"There really isn't much strange in that, Francis," the Duke commented, slowly sipping his coffee as he enjoyed these few peaceful moments with his family. "She is obviously in mourning. People can act strangely when suffering the loss of a loved one."

"She said she was an old acquaintance of *yours*, Father," Francis told him, a curious expression on his face as he eyed his slightly startled father.

"Indeed," the Duke said thoughtfully and exchanged an amused look with his wife. "And what was this woman's name?"

"She didn't say. But she certainly knew a lot about us. She seemed pretty sad, so I guess she was in mourning for somebody she loved," Francis said.

"Hmmm," the Duchess remarked, a twinkle in her eye, "just as I always suspected. I knew one of your old lady loves would show her face around here one day. Grieving for the loss of your very well-lined purse, most likely. Your past, my dear, is finally beginning to catch up with you."

"My dear, Sabrina, 'tis *your* past which I fear catching up with us," the Duke responded easily as he met the general's eye.

"Please, I'm too old for these games. I've retired from all active duty at last. I wish for no more worries than any well-bred gentleman spending a contented rainy afternoon with his family," Terence Fletcher complained good-naturedly as he finished off his breakfast.

"You're not too old, Uncle Terence," Rhea Claire said, disabusing her uncle of that idea as she entered the room and placed a kiss on his weathered brow. As she took her vacant seat at the table, Rhea sent an apologetic glance at her parents. "I am sorry for being so late, but I could not find my riding habit. It seems to

147

have vanished," she informed them unconcernedly, sure that it would turn up eventually.

"I'll ask Canfield about it. Perhaps she is making some alterations on it now that you will be wearing it," the Duchess suggested.

"Where are you going so early, Rhea?" Robin asked curiously.

"I'm paying a visit on Mr. Taber and my foundling pups. He sent me a note asking that I might come by, if I had the time, and see how they were faring."

"I'll come too," Robin volunteered quickly, for he always enjoyed a visit to Stone House-on-the-Hill and the menagerie of homeless strays that came close to overrunning the place.

"Me too," Stuart added loudly, his voice drowning out Maggie's and Anna's.

"And what about all of Mr. Ormsbee's tireless preparations for your Shakespearean play?" the Duchess demanded, glancing around at the expectant faces. "You each have a role in it, and Mr. Ormsbee has worked so hard with each of you in helping you to remember your lines," she reminded them, thinking of how the tutor had been almost obsessed these last few weeks as he coordinated the costumes, stage props, and sound effects, which involved the blowing of trumpets and beating of drums. Single-handedly, Mr. Ormsbee was managing to direct the energies of both the Dominick and Fletcher clans. And although the tutor would never have admitted it, his production of *Twelfth Night* wouldn't have proceeded further than a dull reading in class, if it had not been for Richard's calm, skillful handling of his nieces and nephews.

"I hope you've all learned your lines properly," Richard was saying now as he eyed each of the participants in turn. But their faces showed only innocent expectation.

"Father made sure *we* did," George admitted glumly. "He drilled us all the way from Green Willows. Thought I'd joined his old regiment for a while there," he added, pretending to fire off a cannon at James across the table.

"Mr. Ormsbee will be eternally grateful to you, Terence," Richard told him with mock seriousness.

"God forbid," the general declared with a deep laugh as he thought of the mild-mannered Mr. Ormsbee, whose whole world revolved around the schoolroom at Camareigh. "Now, if I'd had your Mr. Ormsbee in my regiment . . ." the general added, a speculative look in his eye that would have boded ill for the meek Mr. Ormsbee had he been there.

"I fear it would have been the death of the poor man," the Duke said with an appreciative smile. "He's a good enough fellow, though. I think he can barely wait until Andrew is old enough to enter the schoolroom. I do believe the man feels it is his duty and purpose in life to educate my offspring."

"Well, I just wish I didn't have to play the clown in this play," James said, his newly discovered manly pride woefully affected by the ridiculousness of the role he'd been assigned.

"You think you are upset," Francis stated with a grimace. "He has me playing that fat knight Sir Toby Belch!" Francis puffed out his cheeks and tried to create a double chin as he quoted his carefully memorized lines: " 'Welcome, ass. Now let's have a catch.' Or, a couple of my finer moments. 'Fire and brimstone!', 'Bolts and shackles!', and 'Why, how now my bawcock? How dost thou, chuck?' " Francis laughed. "Mr. Ormsbee has even gotten me wearing a pillow for padding!"

"I wish we didn't have to rehearse this morning," Robin said, his eyes straying to the sunshine pouring through the window. "This is the first sunny day we've had in a week. It's not fair that Rhea gets to go out riding and I can't. Why isn't she rehearsing too?" he demanded, not liking the idea of his sister going off without him.

"Because this morning we are being fitted for our costumes," Francis explained. "Rhea's already been fitted for hers."

"I think it's wonderful!" Anna said dreamily, missing the disgusted glances that were shot her way by cousins and brothers alike. "Do you think Mother will be feeling well enough to watch us, Papa?" she asked worriedly.

"She is fine, dear," Terence Fletcher reassured his daughter. "She had a rather restless night and is sleeping a little later this morning, that is all. She'll be up and around by noon."

The Duchess stared down at her hands, feeling troubled as she speculated about her sister's failure to appear this morning. Sabrina was worried, and she knew Lucien was aware of her uneasiness, but what could she have told him? What could she possibly have said except that Mary was having strange visions that made little, if indeed any, sense at all? Finally Sabrina glanced up, knowing she would find a puzzled, yet tender, look in Lucien's eyes if she chose to meet them. She knew he couldn't completely understand what she was going through while she waited, worrying about the inevitable happening. It had been such a long summer and now fall was upon them. Yet nothing had happened. But she knew it would. It was just a matter of time—and that was something both she and Mary knew. And nothing could change that.

Lady Mary Fletcher rolled about restlessly on her bed, the silken sheets sliding off her as she turned on her side. Her long red hair cascaded around her shoulders in wild abandon as she jerked her head from side to side as if fighting off an invisible attacker.

Small drops of perspiration beaded her brow and ran down her temples as she shivered with some inner turmoil. It was the sound of her own scream that woke her. She raised a shaking hand to her cheek in an oddly protective manner when she stared with deeply shadowed eyes into the mirror and saw her tormented face reflected there.

"Oh, dear God," Mary whispered brokenly, feeling nearly out of her mind with fear of the unknown.

She lay back down against the plumped-up pillows, her breathing shallow as she tried to compose herself. But the fleeting images of her dream kept intruding into her thoughts, causing her breath to quicken again as she remembered. I am so cold, she thought, pulling the quilted coverlet around her shoulders. She could feel death all about her.

"An old, old man . . ." Mary murmured dazedly. "Water . . . water . . . so deep . . . deep and dark . . . I can't swim!" she cried out, tears flooding her eyes. "Blood from so many . . . so many lives that have touched . . . then there is blue . . . so many shades of blue . . . blue eyes . . . a blue ocean . . . a blue sky . . . a blue riding habit . . . so many shades . . ." she muttered, drifting off into an uneasy and fitful doze.

Caroline Winters stared at her reflection in the mirror. The blue riding habit fitted a bit snugly; in fact, it was painfully tight, but wear it she would, she vowed, struggling to catch her breath.

"Yer goin' to be ripping out the seams any second now, Miss Caroline," her maid told her, shaking her capped head in disapproval.

" 'Tis a perfect fit," Caroline contradicted her, unwilling to admit that Lady Rhea Claire Dominick had a far slimmer figure than she did. "Fits like a glove, 'tis the way a riding habit should."

"A glove a couple o' sizes too small, if ye asks me," the maid grumbled out of earshot of her mistress, who, when she was in a tantrum, wasn't above throwing a hairbrush across the room in her direction. The well-trained maid eyed her young mistress thoughtfully, a grim tightness to her mouth as she took in the blue riding habit "borrowed" from the young Lady Rhea Claire. The maid would have bet a year's wages that her ladyship knew nothing about it, for the truth of the matter was that Miss Caroline had light fingers. It was strange, how other people's thing always managed to turn up in Miss Caroline's possession. And yet, never once had her mistress got into trouble for her pilfering. She always seemed to have some excuse or explanation when she sweet-talked her way out of responsibility for the act. But this time, the maid thought with an inner smile of satisfaction, Miss Caroline may have gone too far and gotten in over her head.

"Are you sure you heard the footman say that Rhea

Claire was planning to go riding this morning?" Caroline asked her maid as she adjusted one of the too-short sleeves of Rhea Claire's riding habit.

"Aye, heard him say so meself. She's planning on going out right after breakfast," the maid told her again. "And, while I was listening, so was Lord Rendale's valet. He rushed off right after hearing it. Most likely to tell his master, seein' how he's sweet on her," the maid said with a deliberate smirk.

Caroline spun around, the position of the feather in her hat forgotten for the moment as she glared at her maid. "Lud! What rubbish you do talk, woman. Now get me my gloves," she ordered, her face flushing red with irritation. "I don't want to miss my ride with *Lady* Rhea Claire," she stated with a purposeful tilt to her slightly pugnacious jaw. Then, giving her blue-clad figure one last glance in the mirror, she stalked from the room, mischief on her mind.

"Here she is, Lady Rhea Claire." Butterick was personally presenting Rhea's mount for her inspection. "Just as pretty and perky as a fine morning like this demands."

"Wonderful," Rhea said, patting Skylark on the neck as she slipped her a piece of apple.

"Now, Lady Rhea Claire," reproved Butterick, half-seriously, "ye don't want to be spoilin' the little darlin'. I've strict meals planned for her and—" Butterick was then interrupted by an imperious summoning by none other than the Earl of Rendale demanding his horse. Close on his heels was Miss Caroline Winters, her long feather bobbing up and down as she hurried to keep up.

Rhea sighed. "I won't need Bobby to accompany me now. I shall have plenty of company. Hello, Wesley, Caroline," Rhea greeted them, a welcoming smile on her face that successfully hid her disappointment, for her quiet ride was now best forgotten.

Butterick gritted his teeth as he walked forward to assist his lordship, for even though the Earl of Rendale could sit a horse as well as anybody Butterick had seen, he still didn't care for the man. And the little miss, well . . . as far as he was concerned she could bide her time behind the tea table, for never had he met a female with so little feeling for horses. It was almost criminal to him to put her on the back of one of His Grace's fine horses.

"I heard you were going for a ride, Lady Rhea Claire," the Earl of Rendale greeted Rhea, a broad grin spreading across his face. "So, as I had planned on a ride today, I thought, if you didn't mind, that I would accompany you. Where are you headed?" he asked politely. "The far side of the lake, perhaps? The Temple of the Sun is still quite lovely even with winter coming on."

"Actually I'm bound for Stone House-on-the-Hill. I'm paying a visit to six pups," Rhea informed him with a mocking look. "Are you quite sure you still wish to accompany me? 'Tis a fair distance off."

The Earl of Rendale hid his disappointment well as he nodded. "Of course, Lady Rhea Claire. Wherever you go, I go," he said lightly, but it sounded almost like a statement of intent.

"Well, I'm coming too," Caroline contributed, drawing Rhea's attention from Wesley. The Earl's attention, however, was now centered on his horse as he gave strict instructions for its saddling.

"Since you are here, naturally, I wouldn't think of not—" Rhea's words faded away as she became aware of Caroline's riding habit. So that was what had happened to her missing riding habit, she realized, anger flashing briefly in her violet eyes as she took in the other girl's appearance.

She said nothing for the moment, but the flash of anger, brief though it was, was enough to warn Caroline Winters that she may have presumed far too much this time. Taking an unconscious defensive step backward, she stood awkwardly before Rhea, waiting in a nervous silence for whatever might befall her.

"It isn't too tight, is it?" Rhea inquired softly. Then, with a look of disgust on her face, she turned away from the embarrassed girl and climbed onto Skylark's back, the rest of her angry words silenced. It would not have served any purpose to lose her temper with the girl, for

153

she was to be pitied not ridiculed. It would have been easy for Rhea to ridicule her—too easy, in fact, for it to have been fair. And Rhea's silent disapproval was far harder for Caroline to bear than if Rhea had angrily confronted her. She felt far more insulted and chagrined by the other's polite contempt than she would have by a public humiliation.

"Let's be off, then," Rhea said, waving farewell to Butterick, who stood between the opened doors of the stable and watched the three riders disappear among the trees lining the drive.

The crisp autumn air smelled sweetly of rain and wood smoke, and it kissed her hot cheeks with a cooling balm. Rhea could feel her anger toward Caroline evaporating as she sent Skylark galloping along the narrow lane, the wild hedges and brambles creeping close as they left the carefully maintained lands of Camareigh. As they rounded the blindman's bend in the lane, they saw a carriage moving slowly along the road in front of them, and Rhea was suddenly reminded of the day before when she and Francis and their cousins had nearly been run down by another carriage on this stretch of lane.

They slowed their pace to accommodate the slower-moving coach, but even as they fell into a trot behind it, it came suddenly to a standstill, halting at a slight angle across the narrow lane and effectively blocking it.

"What the devil?" the Earl of Rendale said loudly as he pulled up sharply on his reins, his horse pawing the air nervously. "Damned foolish thing to do!" he complained, glaring up at the coachman. But as he opened his mouth, ready to give a scathing setdown to the impudent fellow, the Earl's attention was distracted by two startling events that happened almost simultaneously. The door of the carriage was flung open and two men jumped out. And Caroline screamed with fear as she fell from her horse's back, unable to keep her seat as her mount shied away from the carriage.

The Earl of Rendale didn't know quite what to expect, but certainly not the pistol he found pointed at his chest by some surly-looking individual in a soiled, red velvet coat that had seen better days. But the Earl was no fool, nor a coward, and he sensed danger here. With hardly a second's thought, he reached inside his own immaculate coat for his pistol, which he always carried with him when traveling, for the roads were rife with footpads, highwaymen, and other malcontents up to no good, and a gentleman needed to be armed if he wanted to protect himself. The familiar feel of the butt of the pistol gave him an added surge of confidence as his hand closed around it. He began to pull it from his coat pocket, intending to wing the blackguard. Then his intention was to pull his sword on the other swine lurking behind, but the Earl of Rendale never had that pleasure.

Before he could even draw his pistol, the loud report of another pistol sounded across the still countryside. An expression of disbelief appeared on the Earl's face, no greater than that which crossed Rhea Claire's as she glanced up from the fallen Caroline to see the Earl tumble from his saddle. He landed with a dull thud in the mud at his horse's hoofs.

"Damn!" muttered the man who'd fired the pistol as he stared down at his mud-splashed stockings and breeches, for the Earl was a big man and had landed in the mud with quite a splash.

But with hardly a pause the man continued across the road, making his way purposefully toward the two young women, his expression grim as he contemplated them.

Rhea stood up on shaking legs and stumbled across the unconscious Caroline, standing protectively between her and the approaching man. Her eyes widened with terror as she watched Wesley's murderer coming closer. While she stood dumbfounded by what was happening, the man drew a small bottle from his coat, then a handkerchief, and as he took another step, soaked the cloth with the contents.

There was nothing she could do for Caroline or Wesley now, Rhea realized. Their only hope was if she could get away and bring back help. Before the man could anticipate what she was going to do, Rhea had jumped over Caroline's prostrate form and fled. But her progress was hampered by her long, heavy skirts, as well as the slippery mud in which she had to find a footing.

A hand grabbed her from behind and spun her around, her booted feet sliding her off balance. Her scream died as the handkerchief was pressed with suffocating intent over her nose and mouth, the nauseating odor sending a wave of blackness to engulf her.

Teddie Waltham picked up the unconscious girl with little effort. She was so light. She was also a beauty, he thought with an instant's regret, staring down at her golden hair and sweetly innocent face. As he carried her back toward the coach, he thought about how easy it had all gone, although he hadn't cared for the shooting of the gent. That bothered him—for he must have been somebody of importance to be in the company of a duke's daughter. Well, it was done, and there was nothing Teddie Waltham could do to bring the gent back to life again. No, sir, he hadn't counted on the girl having with her a gent well able to take care of himself—but then her ladyship was full of surprises, wasn't she, he thought, with a curse on his lips for that fine lady. Had it all planned, did she? Nothing could go wrong, she'd said. Well . . .

Teddie Waltham came to an abrupt halt as he became aware of the other girl lying senseless in the muddy lane, her hair golden, her face pretty. Carefully, he placed the girl in his arms down beside the girl in the road, then stood back to admire the results. He laughed, his head thrown back.

"What the devil do you find so amusing?" a strident voice called out from the carriage. "Certainly not a troop of redcoats, should they happen along to find you standing over an unconscious girl."

"Over *two* girls," Teddie Waltham replied with a humorless chuckle. "M'lady?" he called to her, his voice raised so she would be sure to hear. "If you please, m'lady."

"Well, what the devil is it now? Can't you do anything right?" the voice demanded.

"I think you'd better come here, m'lady," Teddie Waltham repeated, leaving her to wonder what was amiss.

"Oh, very well, but it'd better be good," Kate told him

as she climbed down from the comfort of her carriage and stomped across the muddy lane.

Teddie Waltham would have gladly given up his gold for just one glimpse of her face when she caught sight of the two unconscious girls. She was actually speechless, he thought, delighting in her predicament.

"Damn!" she swore.

"Ah, is there a problem, then?" Teddie Waltham couldn't resist asking, sarcasm dripping from his voice.

"You know damn well there is," Kate spat back, her gloved hands clenched before her as she continued to stare down in bemusement at the two girls who looked so much alike. She'd only seen the chit that once, so how was she to know which one was Lucien's brat? "Lud, but they're almost identical."

"Which one, m'lady?" Teddie Waltham asked. But Kate remained silent. "Hmmm. Pity they're unconscious," he commented with a wry smile, "or we could've asked which one was the girl we were going to kidnap. Makes it tough, this does. Well?" he asked his benefactress again.

"Well what, damn it? I don't have all of the answers," she swore in growing frustration. "I suppose we could take both of them. It doesn't really matter which is the real one."

But Teddie Waltham shook his head. "No."

"No!" Kate screamed in disbelief, her nerves stretched tight.

"I contracted for one female, not two. And one it shall be, or none. I'm not taking on two hysterical females. Which one?" he repeated stubbornly, hoping against hope that she might back down and forget this harebrained scheme of hers.

Kate sighed in exasperation; then suddenly a laugh broke from behind her veil. "Of course. That one!" she cried in triumph, pointing at Caroline Winters. "I remember the blue riding habit. I must admit, however, that I would have selected the other one. She seems more familiar to me for some reason, but I'm not sure. I am sure, though, about that blue riding habit. She's the one I want. Get rid of the other one. I don't want anyone becoming suspicious until we are out of the valley."

"The first sensible thing I've heard you say," Teddie Waltham said in relief, for he was not at all pleased with the morning's work—especially the body in the ditch.

As Waltham started to pick up the limp form of Caroline Winters, he became aware of the big footman trudging back across the lane, his shirt front smeared with the Earl of Rendale's blood. Teddie Waltham looked past him toward the ditch where he knew the footman had been ordered to throw the body. Hadn't taken the bloke long, he thought with a shiver of revulsion that turned quickly to fear when the footman continued toward him, his pace quickening. Teddie Waltham swallowed his fear, wishing he'd taken the precaution to reload his pistol, but his fears were unfounded as Rocco dropped to his knees at Teddie Waltham's feet.

"Here, be a good lad, and carry this one to the coach," Waltham told him. He considered that he'd had a very near brush with death, and his relief at being spared caused his voice to come out in little better than a squeak.

"Angel, hurt," Rocco said in bewilderment.

"I'm going to put this one," Teddie Waltham said, indicating the girl in the green riding habit, "on the side of the road. It will be a while before she wakes up, and even then she'll be so groggy she'll find it hard to even stand up. We should be long gone by then."

"Good," Kate remarked. Already, her mind was lingering with pleasure on the scene that would destroy the peace at Camareigh when Lucien discovered his daughter was missing.

"No, Rocco," Teddie Waltham said. "This one. Take this girl to the coach, not that one," he tried to tell the footman, who persisted in hovering over the girl in the green riding habit.

"Hurt. Angel hurt. Rocco help Angel get better," he muttered, turning a malevolent eye on the noisy Teddie Waltham, who took a quick step out of reach of the footman's long arm. His expression one of surprised dismay.

"She's all right, Rocco. She's just sleeping," he tried to reason with the man. "What's wrong with him, anyway?" he demanded of Kate.

Kate had been watching her footman's strange behavior with interest, and now a note of doubt entered her voice as she said softly, "I wonder."

"You wonder what?" Teddie Waltham demanded, trying to regain her attention as she spoke quickly, and unintelligibly, to his ears, to her overgrown footman. Rocco nodded, saying something back to her in a guttural voice before he picked up the girl in the green riding habit, his hands showing unusual gentleness as he cradled her against his chest.

"Get rid of *this* one," Kate now told Teddie Waltham, who was staring in amazement at the footman as he carried the wrong girl to the carriage.

"He's got the wrong one!"

"I think not," Kate replied easily, watching as Rocco carefully placed the unconscious girl inside the coach.

"I thought you said she was wearing a blue riding habit," Teddie Waltham persisted, thinking this whole business was crazy. But then, what did he expect, getting mixed up with a madwoman?

"Rocco fancies the one in green," Kate said matter-of-factly as she lifted her skirts and began carefully making her way back to the carriage.

"And you're going to follow *his* advice?" he asked in disbelief. "God, I knew I should've headed right back down those stairs the minute I saw him open the door," he added sourly.

"Rocco was quite smitten with the chit yesterday. I've never seen him act so strange before," Kate explained as she paused at the door of the carriage, glancing back at the bemused Teddie Waltham. "So I'm willing to believe that he knows which one is which, especially since I couldn't swear to it. I'll take the chance, Mr. Waltham."

"Aye, you do that, m'lady," Teddie Waltham agreed,

anxious to get the whole affair over with, and the sooner the better.

And so, muttering beneath his breath, Teddie Waltham scooped up Miss Caroline Winters and dropped her into the ditch on the opposite side of the road from where Rocco had dumped the gentleman. Only one of the riders' horses was still standing in the road, the others having galloped off when the shot had been fired. Teddie Waltham waved his hands and yelled, frightening the horse on down the road, its mane and tail flying as it raced out of sight around the bend. As he approached the carriage he signaled to the coachman, a man he'd known for years in London, who was willing to do a job, keep his mouth shut, and forget he'd ever seen you.

Teddie Waltham hopped inside as the coach pulled away, and swinging the door closed, settled down in one of the corners and tried to make himself comfortable. Surreptitiously, he eyed the silent giant in the opposite corner, not caring for the expression in the dark, usually black eyes when they swung in his direction.

"Hope the girl doesn't die," Teddie Waltham muttered worriedly when he noticed her labored breathing. Hypnotized, he watched the big hand smoothing back a stray curl from the girl's forehead.

"Why the devil should you care?" Kate asked, unconcerned.

"Because, m'lady, if she does, then I wouldn't bet on either of us leaving this carriage in one piece. That mooning footman of yours will more than likely strangle the life out of both of us if he loses his 'angel,'" Teddie warned her.

Kate brought her thoughts back from wherever she'd had them and became aware of the almost obsessed attention Rocco was lavishing on the senseless girl he was holding so protectively in his arms. "Lud! If 'tisn't Beauty and the Beast," she said, laughing harshly.

"I wouldn't be so quick to laugh if I was you, m'lady," Teddie Waltham advised, for the skin on his back was crawling, and he'd been too close to danger too often not to recognize it when it was staring him in the face. The sensation was so strong he could almost smell it, and Teddie Waltham was a man who liked to survive.

"Why, you pigeon-hearted milksop. I don't think I've ever run across such a poor-spirited individual before," Kate sneered at him.

"I just put a hole through a man, m'lady," Teddie Waltham retorted, stung by her contemptuous snort of derision. "But I noticed you stayed safely in the carriage until all the excitement was over. Well, you can be Madame Spunk for all I care, but Teddie Waltham doesn't have to put on a bold face for no one. That's why I'm alive today to be talkin' about letting sleeping dogs lie," he concluded with a meaningful glance at Rocco.

"Rocco is devoted to me. He obeys my commands better than a dog would. But I'm not as craven as you, so you may rest easy," Kate said, to bait Waltham. "I shan't let him strangle you while you sleep."

Teddie Waltham managed a tight smile. "I'm sure I'll be havin' sweet dreams with that assurance. Of course, I'd be dozin' even easier had I your assurance, m'lady, that *you'll* not be slittin' me gullet while I'm asleep."

"Oh, you do have my word on that, Mr. Waltham," Kate assured him. "For you see, I'm not through with your unique services just yet."

Feeling satisfied that she had dealt effectively with Mr. Teddie Waltham, Kate now turned her attention to the girl in Rocco's arms. She reached out a curious hand and touched the girl's smooth cheek. It was so smooth and soft, so untouched. This was dear cousin Lucien's daughter.

"Spawn of his seed," she spat, her viciously spoken words drawing an uneasy glance from a nervous Teddie Waltham.

"Well, I have you now, my sweet thing," she continued. "Oh, to see Lucien's damned face when he learns of your disappearance. What agonies of mind it will cause him, but no greater than mine when I lost Percy. He will suffer and writhe with the torments of a living hell as he wonders what has happened to his precious daughter, knowing he can do nothing but sit and wait and hurt inside."

Through the veil and slitted mask, Kate's pale eyes glowed with insane pleasure. "Dear Dowager Duchess, how you must be turning in your grave, for one of your prized heirs is about to join you in your cold sleep. You should really have let me and Percy have Camareigh, Grandmama," Kate said sadly, speaking aloud her most private thoughts. "The proud Duke of Camareigh will rue the day he banished Percy and me from our rightful home. May I burn in hell if I don't destroy him and his precious family. I'll bring Camareigh down around his arrogant head. I swear by all that is holy that I'll have him begging me for mercy before I'm through with the Dominick family," she promised, her eyes searching the face of the girl who might be related to her by blood, but whose death warrant she would sign as easily as any common criminal's. "I want Lucien to know that somebody has his daughter. That her life, or death, is in that person's hands."

Kate's eyes caught the flash of a jewel on the girl's dangling hand, and she reached out to grab hold of the small, slender finger. It was a delicate diamond and sapphire ring that had caught her eye. Quite a distinctive ring, in fact, and one that Lucien would surely recognize as having belonged to his daughter. With an ungentle hand, Kate pulled the ring from Rhea's finger. She continued to stare at the girl in thoughtful silence, realizing that the ring wouldn't be enough to torture Lucien with. No, she must find something more personal of his daughter's to send to him.

Kate's low gleeful chuckle sent a shiver of unease up Teddie Waltham's spine, especially when she pulled a slim, deadly-looking dagger from its jeweled holder at her waist. With a caressing hand, Kate touched a long curl that had escaped from Rhea's bound hair, and with slow, methodical strokes, sheared the long strands of hair in two. The golden hair curled around her hand like a living thing as Kate gazed at the girl's face, which was as pale and peaceful as a death mask. "Kill her, Rocco," she said quietly, and in so casual a tone that Teddie Waltham had no idea of what the footman had been ordered to do until the big man stirred violently, his unleashed power quivering like a taut bow string.

"Kill her, I say," Kate repeated shrilly to her loyal footman, who continued to ignore her as he stared down into Rhea's sleeping face. "Damn you! Do as I say, or I'll see you burning in hell, Rocco, so help me I will! It shouldn't be so hard to do. You have killed before, haven't you, Rocco? Kill her!" Kate ordered him again, almost snarling in rage when he looked up at her with his habitual dumb expression.

Teddie Waltham watched and listened in silence to the tirade that fell on the footman's head, and even though he couldn't understand a word of it, he could well imagine what was being said. He pressed closer into the corner, wishing he could disappear, and wondered how in the world a Billingsgate boy like himself could have got mixed up with the likes of these two miscreants. But whatever it was being said now, Teddie thought with a nauseating feeling rising in his belly, it wasn't setting well with her ladyship, for she was about to have a fit of apoplexy over the reply. Teddie eyed the hulking footman with new respect. Maybe he wasn't as slow-witted as he looked. Teddie swallowed the tight knot in his throat, anticipating her ladyship's next move and preparing to face her wrath.

"Very well, you may rot in hell for all I care, and believe me, I shall see that you do one day," Kate spat across the carriage at the footman, who had continued throughout her tirade only to shake his head in the negative.

Turning to her English hireling, she gestured arrogantly. "Kill the girl and dump her from the carriage. No one will find her body for weeks, maybe months, if at all. Now that I have proof of her capture, we don't need her alive."

"No," Teddie Waltham replied evenly.

"No?" Kate repeated incredulously, stunned by this growing mutiny among her menials. "You refuse me? How dare you! What do you think you are getting paid to do? For all the help you've been, I should've hired that fat innkeeper. I curse the day she ever recommended you to me," Kate ground out, her hands clenched before her. "If you think you shall be getting paid in full, then think again, Mr. Teddie Waltham."

"But, m'lady, that is just what I have been doing," Teddie responded in a quiet, confident voice. "The way I see it is that I'd never be paid in full if I tried to take the girl away from friend giant there. All I'd get for my efforts would be a broken neck. If you so badly want to see her dead, then you're going to have to do it yourself," Teddie Waltham dared her, shaking his head in regret. "And that Rocco fellow, well, he sure seems to have taken a liking to the little golden-haired lass. I'd watch myself if I were you. Of course, there is an alternative," he added. "If you would take my advice, seein' as how I'm an old hand at avoiding the hangman's noose, I'd say don't kill her. Bodies have a nasty way of popping up at the damnedest times. It can be devilishly awkward. My motto has always been, 'If you can avoid havin' a dead body around in the first place, then why take a step closer to the gallows?'"

Kate was fuming silently, for she had rather looked forward to shedding a little Dominick blood, even though Lucien's would be far sweeter to taste than his daughter's.

"Oh, very well," she capitulated. "Do what you wish with the brat, but make sure that she isn't around to complicate matters, or you *will* be feeling the hangman's noose tightening around that scrawny neck of yours."

Teddie Waltham breathed a shade easier, although he knew they weren't completely out of the woods just yet. But at least he hadn't killed a duke's daughter, or had to face Rocco. He could do without either situation, since he valued his admittedly disreputable skin. Aristocrats, especially dukes, could make for deadly enemies, seeing how they answered to no one in the land except themselves. And this Duke of Camareigh sounded like a ruthless fellow. Any man who could get the best of her ladyship here, which this duke seemed to have done time and time again, was a man who got Teddie Waltham's respect. But only from a safe distance, for he didn't want to meet the gentleman up close. Teddie shook his head wearily, for he had the feeling that even if he managed to squirm out of this mess without a scratch, he would probably spend the rest of his life looking over his shoulder for a vengeful duke's hand to grab him out of a comfortable tavern in Limehouse and toss him into a rotting cell in Newgate. Eventually, if the Duke of Camareigh were powerful enough, he might find his head the first one in years to be stuck on Temple Bar for all of London to gawk at.

"Well, what do you have planned?" Kate's raspy voice broke into Teddie Waltham's unpleasant speculation about his none-too-rosy future.

"Planned?" Teddie asked dumbly.

"About the chit, damn it!"

"We're headed back to London, I gather?"

"Yes," Kate admitted, reluctant to divulge any of her plans to this ruffian, about whom she was beginning to have serious doubts.

"Then I propose, m'lady, that we waste very little time in getting there," he advised. "I would even suggest stopping only to change teams and sup, but not to stay overnight. A few eyebrows might be raised at sight of Rocco and the girl. Besides," he added with an instinctive glance over his shoulder, "who knows what's on the road behind us?"

Kate nodded. "For once, Mr. Waltham, we are in complete agreement, for I had not thought to linger in the vicinity. I must own to being slightly curious," she continued in a sarcastically conversational tone, "about what you have planned for our little friend. You are not contemplating taking her all of the way to London, are you?"

Teddie Waltham glanced over at the still form being held so lovingly in Rocco's big arms. "I've got a lot of friends in London, m'lady, and I can count at least a dozen who'd be more than happy to take the little lady off our hands," he informed her, not really satisfying her curiosity. "In fact, we might even manage to profit by the transaction, if handled properly. Aye, London, 'twould seem, is the place for us, m'lady."

"Indeed, Mr. Waltham," Kate remarked as she settled

herself more comfortably in the corner of the coach. Sophia, who'd maintained a discreet silence, turning a blind eye and deaf ear to the goings on, now arranged, with solicitous care, a fur rug across her mistress's knees. Her only concern in life was her mistress's comfort. "I can see that I have been hasty in my judgment of your abilities, and indeed, may have sorely underestimated you," Kate now told Waltham.

But I haven't underestimated you, m'lady, Teddie Waltham thought as he leaned his head against the soft leather of the seat. But prudence advised him against slumbering in the watchful silence of the coach.

"It isn't the *horse's* blood, Your Grace," Butterick pronounced gravely, his words carrying like a death knell through the breathless silence of the stables. Butterick met the Duke's eyes squarely, his big capable hands hanging helplessly at his sides. If only he hadn't had to tell this to the Duke, Butterick thought with a feeling of rising despair, for it was beginning to look bad, real bad, and they didn't even have any idea of what had happened—except that Lady Rhea Claire and the Earl of Rendale were missing.

The Duke of Camareigh sighed, but he was not surprised, for he had suspected as much. But what could have happened? The dreaded thought of foul play hung heavy in his mind; but it just didn't make any sense. No one in their right mind from Camareigh, or the surrounding countryside, would dare to lay a finger on Rhea. She was far too well known as his daughter. So what had happened to her? Had some accident befallen her? Was she lying unconscious somewhere? And where was the Earl of Rendale? What had happened to him?

"If only the young miss could tell us what happened, Your Grace," Butterick said, glancing impatiently toward the big house where the unconscious Caroline Winters had been taken. After the three horses had found their way back to Camareigh, he'd sent out a carriage and several footmen and stableboys to find the horseless riders. At that time his fears had not yet been unduly aroused, although he'd felt the beginnings of concern, for both

Lady Rhea Claire and the Earl were fine riders. For either of them, and certainly for both, to have fallen from their mounts, well . . . it was a thought he hadn't liked thinking about. He'd sent a boy up to the house to inform His Grace of the incident and had been waiting for his orders when one of the riders had returned with rather startling news. He hadn't been prepared for the sight that met his eyes when he'd opened the carriage door to see a delirious Miss Caroline Winters, her blue riding habit muddied and torn.

The Duke himself had carried the stricken girl up to the house, and not a word had been heard from her since she'd been found wandering dazedly along the lane, a dark bruise beginning to swell over her eye. How long she'd been staggering on the road, or from where she had come, they didn't know. Only Caroline Winters knew the answers to so many puzzling questions, and she was temporarily lost to the world. The doctor had been sent for, but hadn't as yet arrived, so all they could do was wait.

"They were bound for Stone House-on-the-Hill," the Duke said, a speculative look in his eye. "I wonder if they ever got there."

"I reckon they went to see the elder Mr. Taber about the pups," Butterick mused.

"Rhea received a note from the old man requesting her to come. Naturally she went," the Duke told him, a gentle expression softening his face for a moment while he thought of his daughter's overly generous nature. And it was this act of kindness that may have cost her . . .

" 'Twas a note from the old man himself, ye say?" Butterick asked.

"I'm not really certain. Although, now that I think about it," the Duke said thoughtfully, "it does seem strange that the note should be delivered so early."

"Aye, that it does, but what has me interested, Your Grace," Butterick confided, "is that the elder Mr. Taber never learned how to read or write."

"Perhaps one of his family wrote it for him," the Duke speculated, not quite seeing the reason for Butterick's worried expression. But then Butterick was famous for his penchant for mysteries.

"He's there by himself, except for a granddaughter," Butterick explained. "And she's just a girl. She wouldn't be knowin' how to read and write. Most Tabers don't see any need for it anyway."

"Saddle my horse, Butterick," the Duke ordered. "And one for the general."

"Aye, Your Grace," Butterick said, sending the gawking stableboys into immediate action, "we'll get to the bottom of this, or my name ain't Old King Butt!"

"Oh," the Duke added, pausing in the doorway, "and saddle a horse for yourself."

A grin split Butterick's face wide. "Aye, Your Grace, 'twill be my pleasure, that it will."

A silence so heavy that it seemed deafening pervaded the guest bedchamber where Caroline Winters lay sleeping just beyond the reach of those standing vigil at her bedside. Although both the Duchess of Camareigh and Lady Mary Fletcher showed an outward calm that did them credit, their fears extended far deeper than their present concern for the girl lying unconscious on the bed. They were both remembering words spoken in early summer. Words that were now, perhaps, beginning to come true. Neither the Duchess or Lady Mary had voiced the troubled thoughts that were uppermost in their minds, nor did they need to, for each knew what the other was thinking.

The Duchess watched thoughtfully as Mary touched the soiled blue riding habit that Caroline had been wearing. It was Rhea's, of that she was certain, although why Caroline should have been wearing it was a puzzle. For an instant, when they had carried Caroline into the house, she had thought it was Rhea, forgetting that her daughter had worn her green riding habit. But then her heart had, God forgive her, leapt with joy when she'd seen it was Caroline. She had been so grateful that it had not been her daughter that lay injured, and she had looked toward the door expecting to see Rhea come striding in. But she hadn't entered, and no one knew where she was. She and the Earl of Rendale had vanished without a trace.

Her shadowed violet eyes strayed back to the girl who bore such a close resemblance to her daughter. If only she would awaken and tell them what had happened. The Duchess swallowed the lump lodged in her throat as a thousand different thoughts raced through her mind. No, she would not think of the bad things. Everything would be all right. It had to be.

A low moan drifted from the bed, and both the Duchess and Lady Mary held their breath as they waited anxiously for some sign of consciousness. But the pale eyelids remained closed, and the lips sealed.

Sir Jeremy fell back onto the seat of the chair as if his legs had been knocked out from under him. He was taking it hard, and the Duchess knew he was suffering, but there was nothing she could say to relieve his mind as he sat staring with red-rimmed eyes at his only child.

"We shall do all we can to help her, Jeremy," the Duchess told him, trying to reassure him. "The doctor will be here shortly, and of course, we do have Rawley," she added, gesturing to the sad-faced maid waiting quietly at the foot of the bed. "She is well versed in these matters. We trust her implicity. You can imagine. Jeremy," the Duchess continued, forcing a small, amused chuckle to her lips, "how many bumps, cuts, and tummy aches she has had to deal with, and not only with my children, but with Mary's as well."

"Aye, right ye are, Your Grace," Rawley agreed, following Her Grace's lead. "Why, I even remember once when young Lord Robin took a tumble down the whole flight of stairs, banging his head wide open. Didn't hear a sound out of him for nearly two days, we didn't. And then the very next day, while I was dozing, the young Lord Robin just up and gets out of bed and wanders down to the kitchens in his nightshirt. And there I found him, just as bold as brass, sitting there eating a piece of peach cobbler. Aye," Rawley said with a firm shake of her head, "there's no better cure for a good bump on the head than sleep, and plenty of it."

Sir Jeremy looked brighter as he peered closer at his

daughter's sleeping face. "Do you really think so? I do believe she seems to be breathing easier, Rawley. She's not nearly so flushed."

"There, didn't I tell ye so. Now we're going to keep her nice and warm. And as soon as she's awake, I'll give her a good dose of Mrs. Taylor's Special Treat," Rawley said, warming to her favorite subject, which was the art of healing. "That'll put her on her feet faster than sitting on a hat pin. I remember once, Sir Jeremy," she began, nodding to Her Grace before turning back to the slightly bemused but attentive listener, "when I was working as a maid in a London bawdy house . . ."

The Duchess and Lady Mary let themselves quietly out of the room, leaving Sir Jeremy and his daughter in Rawley's very capable hands. They had walked a considerable distance down the hall in a companionable silence, linking their elbows together the way they'd done as children when they'd run together laughing across sweet meadows of newly mown grass. The Duchess could feel the tenseness in her sister's rigid arm, and giving it a gentle squeeze, she met Mary's soft, gray eyes.

"I know it does no good to tell you this, Mary," the Duchess began, "but you mustn't blame yourself for what has happened."

"Or is going to happen, Rina?" Mary said miserably. "I always tell myself that I should not be so surprised when something from my dreams comes true, and yet I am left stunned by it every time," she said tiredly.

"You had another vision last night, didn't you?" the Duchess asked.

Mary nodded. "Brief images, nothing more. But this morning it was far more terrifying. I saw in my dream that blue riding habit. If only I had known that Caroline would be wearing it."

"She could not have been wearing it, Mary. That was Rhea's riding habit," she told her, watching Mary's reaction carefully.

Mary's breath caught in her throat. "I have never foreseen something happening to anyone but our family. Why should I have seen this happening to Caroline?"

"Because she was wearing Rhea's clothing, I imagine," the Duchess reasoned.

Mary bit a trembling lip. "Then . . ."

"Then the danger was meant for Rhea, not Caroline," said the Duchess, putting Mary's fear into words. "Caroline just happened to get in the way. But that does not tell us what happened to my daughter," the Duchess said, her voice taut with anger and fear. "I must know what has happened. I have to be able to help her. Now tell me, what else have you seen?"

Mary sighed. "The usual confused images. An old man. Water. The ocean, I think. A pair of blue eyes. What can that tell you?" Mary demanded, angry at herself for being so unhelpful. "Oh, and one last thing. I thought I was drowning. It was a horrible feeling, all of that water around me."

"Well, we can be thankful for one thing at least." The Duchess laughed shortly.

Mary frowned in perplexity. "What on earth could that be?"

"Rhea can swim. When we used to visit Verrick House, I would take Rhea and Francis to a forest pool I frequented often when we lived there," the Duchess explained, a reminiscent smile curving her lips. "Both Rhea and Francis took to the water like fish. They used to love it there. So, my dear, it is not Rhea you see drowning. And that, Mary, is some comfort to me, and I thank you for it."

"I only wish that I could give you more than that."

"For now it shall have to do," she replied vaguely, as they entered the salon where the rest of the family was anxiously awaiting news of Caroline's condition, and whether or not Rhea had been found.

All conversation was halted abruptly at their entrance, and all eyes unblinkingly stared at the two silent women. "Caroline is sleeping peacefully, I believe," the Duchess informed them, refusing the cup of tea being proffered by a serious-faced Anna Fletcher playing the hostess in the absence of her aunt and mother.

"No thank you, dear," the Duchess told her, smiling encouragingly at her family. But when her eyes met a pair of troubled brown ones, her expression changed. "Sarah! What are you doing out of bed? You shouldn't be exerting yourself," the Duchess told her sheepish-looking sister-in-law, who had risen with the awkward slowness of a woman heavy with child.

"Sabrina, I know you are concerned about me," Sarah replied apologetically, but with a firmness to her tone, "but I cannot sit quietly alone in my room, not knowing what is going on. Please do not ask that of me. Truly, I shall be far better off sitting in here with the rest of you than I would worrying myself to death in my room. I'm quite comfortable, Sabrina," Sarah reassured her.

"That I cannot believe," the Duchess replied with an understanding smile as she took in Sarah's well-rounded stomach. "But to please me, and to set poor Richard's mind at ease, do sit down," she pleaded, as she herself sank wearily onto the sofa and held her chilled hands out to the warmth of the fire.

"Caroline has not regained consciousness?" the general asked, shifting his stiff leg to a more comfortable position near the fire.

"No, Terence. I tried my best to reassure Sir Jeremy, but he is taking this hard. He's lavished so much attention on Caroline that I do not think he would know what to do if she were gone," the Duchess commented.

"You don't think she will die, do you?" Richard asked, his spectacles catching the light from the fire.

"No, I don't, but one never knows quite the extent of a head wound," the Duchess said. There was a helpless note in her voice. "You've seen wounds in battle, Terence. What do you think?"

Unconsciously rubbing the old wound in his thigh, where he could still feel a twinge of pain from the sharp thrust of the enemy's blade, Terence thought of all the young men, some hardly more than boys, who'd suffered and died in battle. "She has definitely sustained quite a bump on her head, but I suspect much of her problem— since you have led me to believe that Caroline is a highly excitable young woman—is caused by hysteria. I can, of course, only speculate on what occurred, but I would hazard a guess that she was knocked unconscious, then awoke to find herself stranded in a desolate country lane. Having to walk back to Camareigh, with a head injury, especially for a girl of Caroline's tender sensibilities, must have been quite traumatic for her."

"Whatever it was happened out there, *she* wouldn't have been of any help," James declared morosely, a look of confused anger in his eyes while he thought of his missing cousin.

"James!" the general reprimanded him sharply. "That was a contemptible thing to say. I am ashamed of you."

James swallowed his tears and dropped his head in shame. "I'm sorry, Father," he said in a choked voice.

Ewan and Francis exchanged glances, for although it was not proper for James to have said what he did, they all knew it was the truth. Francis made a grimace as he stared down at his belly: the wide sword belt holding the pillow against his body was beginning to sag alarmingly. Shaking his head, he glanced first at Robin, who was staring bemusedly into the flames, and then at his cousins. Their attire, and his own costume, would have been laughable had not the situation been so serious. They had been in the midst of a dress rehearsal. Mr. Ormsbee had been bustling around, fussing and fidgeting like a hen over a chick, when Robin had spotted the unusual activities down in the stables. And that had been the last Mr. Ormsbee had seen of his amateur actors.

Mary had persuaded her sister into accepting a cup of tea and was offering refills to the others when the doors to the salon were flung wide and the Duke entered, his expression grim. The expectant faces turned toward him did not make his request any easier, especially when he looked into his wife's violet eyes, for he could never hide anything from her.

"I am riding over to Stone House-on-the-Hill. That was where Rhea was headed—perhaps the old man can tell us something. Has Caroline said anything?" he asked.

"No, she's still sleeping," Mary answered while the Duchess stared at Lucien, a puzzled expression on her face.

"I'd like to accompany you, Lucien," the general offered, getting to his feet, his stiff leg forgotten as he contemplated getting into action.

The Duke smiled. "I thought you might, so I've had Butterick saddle your horse." Then he tried to forestall what he knew was coming when he saw his wife rise hurriedly. "No, Sabrina. I don't want you coming with us."

"Damn it, Lucien, I am," Sabrina contradicted him. "Rhea is my daughter, too, and I'll not be left behind. I have a right to be with you," she told him, looking at him squarely, a determined glint in her eyes.

The Duke grasped her shaking hands and held them against his chest for a moment. "I only wished to spare you, my dear. I do not know what we shall discover."

"I know, Lucien," Sabrina answered softly, "but we have always shared everything. Don't shut me out now."

"I want to go too, Father," Francis said boldly.

"Me too, sir," Ewan volunteered. His offer was then echoed by both George and James.

Richard had already stepped forward to stand just behind the Duchess. He didn't need to offer; they all knew he would not stay at Camareigh while the rest were out hunting for Rhea and the Earl of Rendale.

Before any further offers could be made, the Duke held up a silencing hand, which effectively halted the mass exodus. "I will not have the whole household racing around the countryside like madmen. I am touched by your willingness to help, but I think we should try and carry out this search in some kind of orderly fashion. If you agree, Terence," the Duke said, nodding deferentially to the general, "I think you are the best man to organize the search party."

"Thank you, Lucien. I shall try my damnedest to find her," he said quietly. "What I suggest," he began, his voice assuming the tone of one accustomed to command, "is that Francis and Ewan lead two search parties in different areas. Ewan, you take the east side of the lane: Francis, you take the west. That way we shall cover more ground. Also, I want you both to start at a designated point, then work north toward Stone House-on-the-Hill. That way we will know precisely what ground has been effectively searched, and we'll have closed a circle around the area in which Rhea was traveling. Does that meet with your approval, Lucien?" the general asked, unwilling to usurp the Duke's authority in his own home.

"It will be as you wish," the Duke replied, his eyes lingering on his wife. "If you insist upon accompanying us, Sabrina, then I want you to ride with me," he told her, his voice leaving her no choice. "Richard?"

Richard slipped his arm around his sister's waist. "I'll ride with you, thanks. Sarah?" he added, turning to look at his wife. "You will be all right?"

"I would have it no other way, Richard. And don't worry," she said with an encouraging smile, "I shan't have your heir while you are gone."

"What about me—us?" Robin amended as Stuart nudged him, eagerly pressing closer. "I want to help look for Rhea."

"I would prefer that you stayed here at Camareigh, son," the Duke replied, his tone of voice telling Robin that his request had been denied.

"But—"

"No buts about it, Robin. Someone should be here with Aunt Mary and Sarah. What if we received news about Rhea? Who would be here to send word to us?" As the Duke reasoned with his disappointed son, he noted with sympathy the trembling lip that Robin was fighting to control. He placed a gentle hand beneath his son's chin, and raising his face upward, looked him directly in the eye. "I shall be counting on you, son, to see that all is well here at Camareigh."

"Yes, sir," Robin replied huskily. "I'll watch out for Aunt Mary and Sarah. You can trust me, Father."

"I have no doubt about that, Robin," he said, ruffling his son's dark curls. Then he glanced around at the determined faces surrounding him. "Very well, then, let us delay no longer."

When the group of riders from Camareigh entered the yard of Stone House-on-the-Hill, all was quiet. From the chimney on the east side of the farmhouse a trail of blue smoke was rising slowly into the chill autumn air. There seemed to be nothing amiss in the farmyard. The big double doors to the barn were wide open, and fresh droppings of cow manure were strewn across the yard, giving evidence that someone had just recently led the cows out to pasture. In the distance they could hear distinctive lowing sounds from the grazing cows.

Butterick quickly dismounted and assisted the Duchess from her mount before either His Grace or Lord Richard could lend a hand. Her horse was a big chestnut stallion that he'd always thought unsuitable for a woman, especially the petite Duchess; she'd hear nothing against the horse, though, and to this day she'd yet to suffer a fall. Butterick sometimes had the feeling that the Duchess would far prefer riding astride the brute rather than side-saddle, but that, of course, was ridiculous and completely unheard of.

"Everything seems normal enough," Richard commented, glancing around.

"What seems to be, and what is, Lord Richard," Butterick stated knowledgeably, "are often two different things altogether. Always look beneath the surface, I do. That's where the truth is hiding."

For a second Richard gazed at the horse trainer in amazed silence. "Incredible," he murmured. "Shall I see if anyone's at home?"

"Most likely 'twill have gone with the cows—" Butterick paused, a smile lighting his face. "Aye, there I told ye so."

As they stood silent in the farmyard, the clear notes of a young girl's voice raised in song could be heard coming ever closer from the near pasture:

> It was in and about the Martinmas time,
> When the green leaves weer a falling,
> That Sir John Graeme, in the West Country,
> Fell in love with Barbara Allan.

> He sent his man down through the town,
> To the place where she was dwelling:

"O haste and come to my master dear,
Gin ye be Barbara Allan."

O hooly, hoo—

"—ooh!" The girl's voice rose into a squeal of fright as she rounded the house and came face to face with the five riders and horses crowding close in the yard. Another squeal followed close on the heels of the first one, but this time it was one of awed surprise as she recognized the Duke and Duchess of Camareigh. She quickly bobbed a curtsy, then remembered her skirts, which she'd tied up round her waist for trudging through muddy fields. And her pattens were indeed coated with thick, black mud. Blushing with embarrassment, she hurriedly brushed down her skirts and hid her petticoats from curious view, thereby maintaining her modesty.

"Yer Graces," she gulped, her eyes round with wonder.

"This is young Janey Taber, the elder Mr. Taber's great-great-granddaughter." Butterick introduced her, recognizing the young girl who could not have been more than thirteen. "That's right, ain't it, young Janey?"

"No, sir, Mr. Butterick," she answered shyly. "I'm his great-great-great-granddaughter. He's mighty old, Mr. Taber is," she reminded him.

"Janey," the Duchess said with a warm smile, "we are here to see your great-grandfather. Is he hereabouts? Perhaps inside?"

But Janey shook her mop of tousled, tow-colored curls. "Oh, no, Yer Grace, he was out of t'house early this morn. He's a ramblin' sort of fellow. Never sits still, he doesn't."

"Do you know where he has gone? We would like to speak with him. He was supposed to meet Lady Rhea Claire, the daughter of the Duke and Duchess, Janey," Butterick tried to explain.

"Don't know nothin' about that, sir. And I haven't even seen the old man this morn. He left the house afore I was even up. Didn't see him none last night, either," she admitted sheepishly. "Fell asleep by t'fire, I did. Takin' care of them pups he had in the kitchen. Lady Rhea Claire

177

brought them to me grandfather, didn't she? Oh, but she's a pretty one, her," she added dreamily.

Butterick coughed, a look of irritation flashing across his face. "Now, Janey, we haven't time for that kind of non—"

But the Duke held up a hand to silence him. "Janey, we'd like to speak to your grandfather. It is very important. Do you have any idea where he might have gone?" he asked her gently.

"No-no," she answered faintly, mesmerized by the scar cutting across the Duke's cheek. "He's most likely to wander halfway t'other side of the valley, if the feeling takes him."

The Duke sighed, not wanting to meet his wife's questioning glance. "Have you, perchance, seen Lady Rhea Claire this morning? Or the Earl of Rendale?"

"No, sir, that I haven't. I've been busy, I have though," she explained, sensing that her answer had disappointed these important people. "Milked the cows and herded them out to pasture. The three of them took their own sweet time, the stubborn beasties. I've still got me baking and churning t'do. Worse still, the hens been off their layin'. Reckon 'tis all of this rain we been havin' and—"

"Lucien! Richard!" called Terence Fletcher from the barn. While they were talking with Janey Taber, the general had wandered off and searched the yard for any recent sign of activity—horses' hoofs, footsteps, or whatever might seem out of the ordinary.

The Duchess eyed her brother-in-law with growing concern as she hurried to his side, for his expression, which often seemed grim, was grimmer now than any she had seen in years.

"What is amiss, Terence?" she demanded as she halted beside him, her eyes already straining to see past him into the dark barn.

"Keep the girl out here," he advised, meeting Lucien's eyes meaningfully. "Sabrina, I'd stay out here, if I were you," he added. But his request was futile. She sidestepped him and marched inside, then waited impatiently for him to follow.

Lucien shrugged his shoulders, for he was well used to

his wife's stubbornness, and followed her. The general and a curious Butterick came close behind him, and an open-mouthed Janey was left standing by herself in the doorway.

"Over here," Terence directed them, pointing to a dark corner of the barn. "It's the old man. He's dead," he told them, moving aside for them to view the scene.

The elder Mr. Taber was lying stiffly in the straw, his arms outstretched as if he'd tried to catch himself as he'd fallen. On the back of his silvery head was a dark patch of congealed blood.

"The poor man," Sabrina murmured sadly.

"It looks as if he tripped and hit his head against the corner of the table," Terence commented, noticing the blood smeared against the wood.

" 'Tis a pity. He was a good man, Lucien," Sabrina said, thinking of his many kindnesses to unfortunate animals, and how he'd unselfishly shared his healing gifts. "He had gotten rather enfeebled of late, though."

"He was an old man, Sabrina," Lucien said softly. He had been fond of the old gent, and for as long as he could remember the elder Mr. Taber had been a living legend around Camareigh. "We shall miss him."

"Aye, Your Grace," Butterick said sharply, his face flushed with growing anger. "He was a good man, a fine old gentleman, and there was no cause on this earth for him to die like this."

Terence Fletcher looked with surprise at the grumbling Butterick. "What are you talking about, man?"

" 'Tisn't a natural death, this. The old man was murdered, that's what I mean," Butterick replied firmly, setting his jaw as if preparing for battle.

"Good God, man! Do you know what you're saying?" roared the general.

"Aye," Butterick replied calmly, refusing to be intimidated by the general's military demeanor. "And I'll tell ye somethin' else, although I reckon you'd have noticed it soon enough, General, if you'd been of a suspicious nature like meself."

"What's that?"

"The elder Mr. Taber, here, has been dead since last

night." He spoke this startling news quietly. "So I'm thinkin' that them stiff fingers didn't write no note to Lady Rhea Claire," he said, and this horrifying conclusion sliced through the heavy silence like the blade of an ax.

The Duchess continued to stare with fascinated horror at the harmless old man's body. "I-I don't understand. Why should anyone wish to murder him? My God, Lucien!" she cried out. "He was close to a hundred years old! What harm could a gentle old man like Mr. Taber do to someone?"

"What I do not understand," Terence said worriedly, "is what the connection is between the old man's death and whatever has happened to Rhea Claire and the Earl of Rendale. And who, for God's sake, wrote that damned note?"

Butterick glanced up from where he was kneeling beside the body. "He's scrawled something here in the dirt," he said. He looked satisfied that he'd ferreted out a clue, even if it were indecipherable.

"A bird?" Terence Fletcher exclaimed in disbelief, staring over Butterick's shoulder at the scratchings in the hard-packed dirt.

Sabrina leaned closer as she squatted down beside the body. "It looks like a pigeon," she said wonderingly.

"Aye, right ye are, Your Grace," Butterick agreed. "But why the old man should draw a pigeon in his last breath of life, well," Butterick said with a frustrated shake of his head, "I'm sure I don't know."

The Duchess rose on shaky legs and stumbled away from the body. She closed her eyes for a moment as she leaned her forehead against the wooden support of the stall. Then she felt Lucien's arms close around her, and she allowed herself to be pressed against the familiar, comforting warmth of his chest.

"Oh, Lucien," she whispered, tears choking her voice. "What are we going to do? What has happened to our daughter?"

Lucien turned her around in his arms and stared down into her wet eyes, feeling more helpless than he'd ever before felt in his life. "I promise you, Rina, by all that I hold dear, that I will find our daughter. This I swear to you with my life," he vowed.

" 'Ere, what d'ye mean ye saw me Tommy with some saucy wench in Cheapside?" a shrill voice demanded. "Lies, that's what it is. Ye be sea green with jealousy 'cuz I got meself a man, and ye ain't! Wish ye had Tommy yeself, ye do. Aye, that's the trouble wif ye—what! 'Ere, there's no call fer sayin' such a thing, and about the dead, too. Me mother was as fine a . . ." But the rest of the denial went unheard, the voices drifting away as the two women in conversation moved briskly along the slippery cobblestones, hurrying to reach their destination before the light, cold drizzle turned into a downpour.

The man who'd been watching them was standing silently in the shadows and was wishing for a warm hearth and a mug of ale to take the chill away, but he knew almost for a certainty that that would be a long time coming *this* evening. Teddie Waltham hunched his shoulders, waiting for a group of boisterous sailors to pass; he knew that in their unrestrained mood anything or anyone unfortunate enough to cross their path was destined to end up in the gutter.

Teddie Waltham glanced around very surreptitiously, shivering slightly as he moved from the safety of the shadows and made his way with easy assurance through the back alleys and twisting lanes of London. He figured that he and her ladyship had made London in record time, and 'twas only a pity that they could never make it public, for it'd be a tough time to beat. Aye, but it'd given him a good feeling to once again see and smell the city in which he'd been born and raised. They'd returned to the King's Messenger, for 'twas a well-known place to certain people, and most of them knew they could find Teddie Waltham on the premises. Then he'd spent the better part of a cold, rainy day going about London, searching out old friends, leaving word here and there, getting suspicious looks from friends of friends who wanted to know why he was looking for so-and-so. . . . Well, now he wanted to make sure he received any messages coming back to him. And that was why he now found himself out in this inhospitable weather, for he had arranged to meet an acquaintance in about an hour's time. His steps faltered briefly as he thought of his next interview, which was with a certain unfriendly party, but the jingle of coins in his pocket kept his steps heading in the right direction.

He would have liked to stop off for a wee one at a coffee house he knew of just around the corner, but he thought better of it, for he needed a clear head to deal with her ladyship. He saw the dark bulk of her coach before he heard the snuffling of the horses, but he refused to allow himself to be intimidated by the upcoming confrontation and continued to shorten the distance between himself and the door that was already beginning to open for him.

Teddie Waltham vaulted inside, the darkness swallowing him up as the door closed behind him.

"Well?" Kate asked impatiently. The damp cold had seeped through her velvet cloak, bodice, skirts, and petticoats, and she was having a hard time controlling the chattering of her teeth, which she did not find at all amusing.

"In an hour, m'lady," Teddie Waltham told her uncommunicatively as he huddled in the corner. He sniffed the stuffy air curiously, his mouth tightening ominously. "Gave her another dose, did you?"

"Astute, aren't you?" Kate said sarcastically from her corner of the coach. "She was waking up. Or did you want a screaming, hysterical female bringing the watchman poking his nose in here, or, even worse, a couple of them damned Bow Street Runners?" she asked him, leaving him little choice but to agree with her decision.

"I just don't want her dead, that's all, m'lady," Teddie Waltham replied, eyeing the heavily drugged form wrapped in a cloak and held protectively against Rocco's chest.

"Well, I just hope this deal doesn't fall through like the last one you set up," Kate told him, her tone leaving him in little doubt of her opinion of his abilities. "My God, I could scarcely believe my ears when I heard that fool fall down the stairs. I did tell you to be discreet, but what do you do?" Kate said, warming to her grievance like a cat settling herself on a hearth. "You invite some drunken clown to meet you in *my* rooms! That biddy, Farquhar, is already getting suspicious about the chit. I'm not sure she even believes my story that the brat is my niece. And I'm sure she didn't believe me when I told her she was suffering migraine, and that that was why I had to keep the room quiet and dark. I think she suspects us of smuggling in the pox. I caught her snooping outside my door last night, so I'd just as soon not have to take the girl back there," she warned her accomplice.

"Aye, 'tis tonight or never for her," he agreed. "But you needn't worry that soft heart of yours about doin' her in, 'cause I've already talked to my friend, and he's very interested in the merchandise. There will be no problems this time."

"There had better not be, my good man," Kate remarked, unimpressed by Teddie Waltham's reassurances. "Who is this fellow?"

"He's a supercargo on board a merchantman sailing between London and Charles Town in the colonies. His cargo ain't always dry goods. Seems there's quite a profit in the trafficking of indentured servants. He figures he can take on one more passenger this trip. And they're weighing anchor with the tide. Just to whet his appetite for the deal, I also didn't neglect to describe our little beauty very enticingly. He is already counting his profit when he sells her in the colonies."

Kate startled him by clapping her hands. "The colonies!" she crooned, her harsh, unbridled laughter filling the coach. "Lud, but that's rich! The grand Duke of Camareigh's daughter being sold as a servant. Ha!" she chuckled, her shoulders shaking with mirth. "Oh, you have surely surpassed yourself, Mr. Edward Waltham. You and Percy really should have met. He would have loved this."

Teddie Waltham frowned, thinking that if this Percy fellow were anything like her ladyship, then he would just as soon prefer not to cross paths with him. "We're to meet my friend near a place I know along the river," he told her.

"Very good, Mr. Waltham," Kate said, tapping on the

roof of the carriage. "Give the coachman the directions."

"Oh," Teddie Waltham added, pretending that something had slipped his mind. "I take it that you, personally, shall be handing the girl over to my friend?" he asked with a meaningful glance at Rocco. "After all, you do have a way with him, don't you?"

"Indeed, Mr. Waltham," Kate replied, unworried. "There will be no difficulties, that I can promise you."

"Good," he replied with an equal show of unconcern. But he didn't at all care for the tone of her ladyship's voice.

They left the coach some distance down the lane where it would draw little attention from passers-by and proceeded on foot up the cobbled street. Then they turned into a narrow, garbage-strewn alley.

Teddie Waltham could almost hear her ladyship fuming as she carefully picked her way through the stinking refuse thrown down from the windows above.

"A fine place, indeed," she muttered as she felt her satin shoe slide into something indescribable.

"You said you wanted me to be discreet," Teddie Waltham reminded her, with great pleasure. Blowing on his cupped hands, his breath vaporizing, he tried to keep warm, but he could feel the drizzle and mists that were drifting in off the river seeping into his clothing. The sound of approaching footsteps caught his attention and he walked toward the end of the alley, leaving her ladyship behind with Rocco and his armful.

But as he neared the end of the alley, the footsteps continued on past without hesitation. Sighing, he started back. Then he heard the low murmur of voices and recognized her ladyship's impatient tones. He smiled slightly, for it looked as if her ladyship wasn't finding it as easy as she'd thought to convince Rocco to part with the girl. With a slight chuckle, he bent down to straighten his damp stocking as it began to sag; then he jumped a foot when the loud report of a pistol rang out, the echoes growing louder and louder in his ears as the seconds passed. He stared in amazed silence as the big footman suddenly toppled over like a fallen tree. Teddie Waltham sucked in his breath. Then he somehow managed to recover, and hurried toward the frozen figure of the veiled woman.

"Damn you, woman!" he hissed, glancing up and around nervously. But no windows had been flung open, or curious heads stuck out, and he suddenly realized that the loud singing and laughing coming from a tavern across the lane had successfully hidden the sound of the pistol shot. Either that, or everyone around here was dead to the world, as indeed was Rocco. With horror, Teddie contemplated the dead footman; then he looked up again to the silent woman who had fired the pistol that had put a hole in the man's broad back.

"What the devil did you do that for?" he demanded.

"He refused to give me the girl. He had turned his back on me and was walking away," she said incredulously. "I had to stop him, and you don't think *you* could have done any better, do you? Besides," Kate added indifferently, "he had served his purpose and he was no longer dependable. He had betrayed me—the woman who gave him a home and food and put fine clothes on his back to replace the rags. And so how does he repay my kindnesses?" Kate demanded, her voice rising with wrathful indignation. "He betrays me for that angelic-faced miss who has never done a damned thing for him—except get him killed. Some sacrifice, eh, Mr. Waltham?" Kate asked sneeringly, as she stared down at her late footman, who, even in death, was still cradling the girl in his arms.

Teddie Waltham swallowed the bile rising in his throat. God, but she was a cold bitch, he thought, keeping an eye on the pistol that was still in her hand. And knowing her ladyship, she'd probably have another warming in her bodice. If she could so cold-bloodedly murder a man who had faithfully and loyally served her for God-only-knew-how-many years, what would she do when Teddie Waltham had served his purpose and was no longer needed?

"Teddie Waltham? Teddie Waltham, is that ye back in there?" a voice called through the darkness. "If 'tis, then ye better be answerin'!" the voice warned. Whether this were friend or foe, only Teddie Waltham knew for sure.

"Aye, 'tis me, ye old sea dog," Teddie replied, letting his breath out slowly as he recognized his friend's voice.

He stepped over the dead footman and hurried to meet his friend, who had already entered the alley. He ignored Kate's hissed question of what they were to do with the body. Let her worry about it, seeing how her ladyship had got them into that fix, he thought maliciously, as he glanced back and saw her struggling to pull the girl from Rocco's deathhold.

"Daniel!" Waltham greeted his acquaintance like a long-lost friend. "Been a long time, it has. Figure you just got to have salt in your blood to go to sea. Me," he laughed, turning his friend around by flinging an arm across his shoulders, "well, I get seasick just crossing over the Thames!"

" 'Tisn't a bad life, Teddie," his friend replied. "And it certainly beats rotting away in debtors' prison. Ye'd be knowing about that, though. Reckon ye been in there enough that ye know the best and worst cells," he chuckled.

"They're all bad, friend," Teddie Waltham replied seriously, vowing to himself that he'd never let himself get locked up behind bars again as long as he lived.

"Aye, right ye are, Teddie," Daniel agreed, swinging away from Teddie Waltham's restraining arm and taking a good look down the alley. "Wha's the matter wif him? Gawd, but he's a big'un. Glad he's not on his feet in this dark alley, fer he's the one gent I'd not care to be meetin' up wif anytime, and come to think about it, I'm not too comfortable even wif him stretched out like he is," Daniel added, eyeing the footman suspiciously.

"Dead drunk, he is," Teddie Waltham proclaimed in a loud whisper that carried to Kate. "He won't bother us for a long time to come."

"Ummm, guess that sets me mind at rest," Daniel said, moving a bit closer. "Who's that female? Not the one going t'colonies, is it?"

" 'Tis a pity that all of our prayers can't be answered," Teddie Waltham murmured beneath his breath, thinking of an ocean between himself and her ladyship. "No, 'tis the one on the ground. Drugged, so she won't be giving you any trouble, Daniel," Teddie explained as he knelt down beside the still figure.

"Be wantin' t'see what I'm buyin'. Won't pay for some pig-faced chit, nor some prune-skinned hag," Daniel warned, keeping a curious eye on the caped figure standing quietly to the side.

"Never fear. Has Teddie Waltham ever let down a friend of his?" Teddie demanded, as he pulled out his tinderbox and struck flint against steel to ignite the tinder. When the light flared, Teddie lit a stubby piece of candle that he'd pulled from his coat pocket and held it over the still figure, revealing the innocently sleeping face of Lady Rhea Claire Dominick, daughter of the Duke and Duchess of Camareigh.

Daniel Lewis nearly choked on his own breath. His surprise was quite evident in his prolonged silence. "God, but she's a beauty. How did ye ever get ye hands on a sweet thing like this?" he demanded incredulously of Teddie Waltham.

Waltham ignored his friend's question. "So, like I said, Teddie Waltham never lets a friend down. Does she go to the colonies, or do we find another buyer for her?"

Daniel Lewis got to his feet and thrust his hands deep into the pockets of his coat. He rolled back and forth on his heels, as if unsure of the value of the product being offered.

"Come on, we haven't all night." Kate spoke for the first time, her patience running out with this senseless bargaining. They all knew the fool would take the girl.

Teddie Waltham shot her a damning glance, but Daniel Lewis was cold too, and he didn't care for the unnaturally silent shape of the big man lying on the ground at his feet. Seemed a bit too quiet for his peace of mind, since there was no snorting or snoring to show the man was even alive. But then, Daniel Lewis speculated, it must have taken a powerful lot of gin or rum—maybe both— to put that giant bloke under.

"Reckon 'tis a deal, Teddie. How much?" he demanded abruptly, growing suddenly fearful of the dark alley and the huddling shapes closing in around him. He bit his tongue before he could demand a lower sum than Waltham's offer, for he knew he could double it three times over in the colonies with a girl as pretty as this one.

So bargaining be damned. He accepted Teddie Waltham's first offer.

The coach seemed oddly empty as Kate and Teddie returned to the King's Messenger Inn. They had concluded their business in almost record time, because their customer had bought as soon as he'd set eyes on the goods for sale. The silence in the coach was oppressive as they sat in their respective corners, not saying a word, each acting as if the other one did not exist.

Suddenly Kate's voice penetrated the silence. "I think we did rather well tonight, Teddie," she stated smugly, and Teddie Waltham could almost see her expression beneath the concealing veil.

But he didn't waste time thinking about that, for her using "Teddie" had him concerned. "Aye, 'twas a good enough deal," he commented uncommunicatively.

Kate laughed with pure enjoyment. "I must admit, and against my better judgment, that I am beginning to have a fondness for you, Teddie Waltham," She said, much to Waltham's dismay. "Yes, indeed, I truly do think we shall deal quite famously together."

Teddie Waltham felt an uncomfortable tightness in his throat. "Well, m'lady, the way I see it, I've pretty well done my job. Don't see that there is much more for me to do."

"Oh, Teddie," Kate laughed, "we have hardly begun our fun."

Teddie Waltham nodded his head in the dark, not really understanding. "Might be a bit difficult for you, now that you've lost your footman. 'Spose he was pretty handy to have around. Maybe, since you've succeeded in getting your revenge on this duke fellow, you could justly feel that you had cleared off old scores?" Teddie Waltham suggested hopefully.

"Oh, Teddie, you are so wrong," Kate said softly, already thinking about and planning her next move against the Duke of Camareigh. "I feel quite wonderful! I have no fears, no doubts, for although I have lost Rocco, I now have you, Teddie."

Teddie Waltham seemed to shrink into the corner of the coach when he heard her words. To be tied up with this madwoman was the last thing he desired; she was destined to come to an untimely end, and although it wouldn't be undeserved, he didn't want to be with her when it happened.

"Ah, Teddie," Kate was saying now with a deep, satisfied sigh. "I do believe I feel like quite a feast this evening. What say we order some of Farquhar's famous pigeon pie? And I shall make sure that you have plenty of rum to wash it down. Yes, indeed, tonight is certainly cause for celebration," Kate chuckled. "Although I doubt they are celebrating at Camareigh. Don't you think, Teddie, that they would have received my little surprise package by now?" she asked, not waiting for a reply before she started humming the song "Greensleeves" beneath her breath. Teddie Waltham didn't have to see her face to know that she was smiling.

"I cannot bear the thought of yet another tasteless meal," the Duchess said as she contemplated the butler who was announcing luncheon. "And yet I must proceed as if nothing has happened, even though whenever I happen to glance up, I catch a half-a-dozen pairs of hopeful, frightened eyes watching my least little move. At times I feel so helpless I could cry, but I'll not do that to them. I'll not destroy the children's belief that everything will turn out for the best. Soon enough I shall have that unpleasant duty, but not now, not yet," she said vehemently. "I will not concede defeat, Mary. I will not bow down to an enemy whose face I do not even know."

Mary smiled sadly. Her eyes were shadowed, for the last couple of days had taken their toll on her as well as on her sister. "That is why I have always admired you so, Rina. You never give up. You keep on struggling, no matter what the odds. It was years and years ago, but I can still remember praying for just a little of your strength of mind and spirit. I used to think, and indeed still do, that they were indomitable."

The Duchess reached out and lightly touched her sister's hand. "Sweet Mary," she murmured, her voice full of love. "You have always known just what to say when I needed it most. You shame me with your words, for I feel such a coward inside," the Duchess confided. It was to very few people that she would admit such a thing.

"Only a fool knows no fear, Rina."

"Then I am certainly no fool," the Duchess proclaimed with a wry smile as she took a sip of her sherry. "If only I did not have to sit here doing nothing. I wish I were with Lucien right now," she added impatiently.

"Perhaps they will discover something," Mary said, daring to voice her silent prayers.

"I think not," the Duchess said flatly. "You have heard of a wild goose chase?"

"You don't believe Caroline's story, do you?"

"No, not one lying word of it," the Duchess admitted, an angry glint in her violet eyes. "Gyspies!" she spat scornfully. But her scorn was not for the much-maligned gypsies. It was reserved for the person responsible for such a tale, and a Canterbury tale it was in the Duchess's mind. "We haven't had gypsies at Camareigh in over a fortnight. I doubt whether there are any in the valley at all, and hardly any who would kidnap a young English girl. They don't care to have anything to do with anyone outside their tribe. Besides, Lucien, as well as his grand-father before him, has always let the gypsies camp on Camareigh land. He says it brings good luck. There has never been much trouble with them; in fact, we seem to have more trouble with the locals, especially the younger farmers, who go out to the gypsy camp just looking for trouble. The gypsies know Rhea, and they would never betray Lucien or me by kidnapping her. *That* is why I do not believe this fairy tale of Miss Caroline Winters," the Duchess said sharply.

Mary sighed. "Then why should Caroline lie about what happened? It is absolutely wicked. I cannot under-stand how anyone could be cruel enough to do such a thing," she said, the stitches she was taking in her em-broidery became uneven with her worry. "Oh, dear," she murmured, rattled by the disorder she had created, "Aunt Margaret would be so ashamed of this."

"You always look for the goodness in a person, Mary. You are seldom suspicious of them like I am. But you ask me why Caroline should lie about what happened. I suspect," the Duchess continued thoughtfully, "that Caroline rather enjoys being the center of attention. And for the last few days she has been showered with constant care and solicitude. And since she awoke, poor Jeremy has been at her beck and call night and day. I think it despicable the way she abuses his genuine love and affection for her. So what happens? She hears that Rhea Claire and the Earl of Rendale are missing, which puts them in a far more perilous situation than she now finds herself in. Especially if she can shed little light on their disappearance. What could be better than to fabricate a story about gypsies? So, because Caroline must satisfy her own greed for attention, I am now in more doubt than ever about what happened to my daughter. Can you doubt that I must restrain myself from strangling the life out of the girl whenever I see her?" the Duchess asked, and whether or not she were serious, even Mary, her own dear sister, could not be certain.

"I wonder when Lucien and Terence will return?" Mary asked, wondering how far they would have to ride to find the gypsy encampment.

"Well, whatever the distance," the Duchess commented, "it will take them away from this area. I still think they should keep looking around Camareigh. They have searched for two days now and found nothing. I realize that they have just about exhausted all areas around here to search, but still. . . ." The Duchess's voice trailed away in doubt. "I just have this feeling they should keep looking. That is why I resent so much this damned tale of Caroline's. It is such a waste of valuable time."

"When is the funeral for Mr. Taber?" Mary asked, adroitly changing the subject.

"Tomorrow. They wanted to wait for his son to return from Bath. Lucien and I shall attend. He was a fine old gentleman, and it isn't right that he should die this way. He never hurt a living soul."

The door to the salon opened, and Sir Jeremy, with a fatigued-looking Caroline leaning heavily on his arm, entered the room. Sir Jeremy greeted the Duchess and Lady Mary, while Caroline managed to smile valiantly, missing, in her self-absorption, the glances exchanged between the two sisters. She allowed her father to assist her in settling on the sofa, making an elaborate production out of getting comfortable and placing a fur rug across her lap.

"Comfy, my dear?" Sir Jeremy inquired solicitously as he refolded the fur rug for her. "I shall be right over here, my dear. I thought I would just rest my foot for a minute," he told her, sounding almost apologetic as he limped across the room to a large, well-used Queen Anne chair and convenient footstool. He sank down with a deep sigh of relief as he eased his weight off the painful big toe of his left foot.

"You'll not doze off, will you, Papa?" Caroline reminded him as she watched him rest his head against the soft cushion of the chair. She knew from past experience that he would most likely be asleep within minutes.

"Nonsense, my dear," he mumbled, perking up as two footmen, in attendance to the butler, entered with a tea tray and a decanter of brandy. "Ah, Mason, you truly are a man in a thousand," he stated approvingly, as he eyed the crystal decanter.

"I took the liberty, Your Grace," Mason explained deferentially, "of bringing some refreshment for Sir Jeremy and Miss Caroline, as well as a pot of fresh coffee for Your Grace and fresh tea for Lady Mary. I thought, perhaps a presumption, Your Grace, but that since His Grace is not returned, that Your Grace might wish to postpone luncheon, and, well . . ."

"A very good suggestion, Mason," the Duchess agreed. "And I think you should start with Sir Jeremy; he looks quite thirsty."

"I always said that Lucien had the devil's own luck when he found you, Sabrina," Sir Jeremy stated sincerely, beaming approval as his snifter was filled with a good quantity of brandy.

Caroline selected from an assortment of cakes, tarts, and other sweets offered to her by a liveried footman, her attention diverted for the moment from her own problems while she satisfied an appetite undiminished by her brush with death.

The Duchess signaled the butler away from Sarah, who

was dozing peacefully in another wing chair near the fire, her lashes fluttering against her cheeks as she fought off sleep. Then, as if sensing the Duchess's eyes upon her, Sarah awoke with a start, glancing around her in confusion.

"Oh, dear. I beg your pardon," she apologized, flustered and blushing as she realized she had been sleeping in their presence. "I just cannot seem to stay awake. I seem to be constantly tired nowadays," she said, looking stricken. Then she suddenly became aware that Sir Jeremy was in the other chair, gently snoring away the afternoon, oblivious to everything but his own private dreams.

"There, you see," the Duchess remarked with an affectionate smile for both Sarah and the sleeping Sir Jeremy, "you needn't be in the least bit embarrassed."

Sarah eased herself one way, then the other, trying unsuccessfully to make herself comfortable. She glanced up, catching Caroline's unsympathetic eye, and forced herself to sit still, folding her arms almost protectively across her rounded middle.

Caroline loudly sniffed her disapproval of such a blatant display of so delicate a condition, then returned her attention to a further, rather prolonged inspection of a plate of dainty sweets.

"Do tell me again, Caroline," the Duchess began, her voice coldly impersonal, "about the gypsies you *claim* accosted you."

Caroline choked on the sip of tea she'd just taken. Licking a dab of cream from the corner of her mouth, she glanced over at the imperious-looking Duchess and began to feel definitely ill-at-ease under the penetrating violet stare.

"Oh, Your Grace, I do so hate to think about it," she protested, her hands fluttering nervously. "I can actually feel myself growing faint."

"To please me, Caroline, do think about it," the Duchess requested politely. To Caroline's guilty conscience, however, it sounded more like an order for a confession, especially when coming in a voice that seemed suddenly tinged with steel.

Caroline coughed and sent a beseeching glance to her father, but Sir Jeremy continued to snore away peacefully.

"Well . . . it was quite awful, actually," Caroline began, her eyes glued to the lace ruffle she was fiddling with. "They . . . they were vicious looking . . . and . . . talked in a strange tongue. Oh, and their clothes, well," Caroline said, laughing uncomfortably as she met the Duchess's doubting glance, "well, they were almost beyond description."

"Yes, I can imagine that might be hard to describe," the Duchess murmured. "Please, continue."

Caroline bit her lip. "They . . . they . . . yes! They had a dancing bear! It was quite horrible! I thought for certain they would turn it loose on me. In fact, I wouldn't be at all surprised if it didn't attack poor Wesley. He was so brave in defending me, oh, and Rhea Claire, too. It growled so horribly. I should think it hadn't been fed in days and days. You know how they mistreat animals. Yes," Caroline continued, her tongue beginning to loosen as she embroidered her story, "I'm sure it was starved. Quite mad, in fact, with a blood lust. Oh, 'twas horrible, just horrible, Your Grace!" she cried, tears rolling down her face, for she was doing a good job of frightening herself with her own make-believe. "Oh, poor, poor Wesley," Caroline wailed, sniffing noisily, "if only I could see his dear face again. I would—" At that moment there was a commotion outside the doors to the salon, and Caroline glanced up as they opened. Then she let out a bloodcurdling scream that brought Sir Jeremy out of his chair like a bolt of lightning, his brandy splashing down his breeches as he stared incredulously at his daughter, who was beginning to keel forward in a dead faint.

"Good God! What the devil is going on here?" he demanded, turning to see who had had such a startling effect on his daughter. "Lud! I don't . . . it cannot be . . . Good God!" he said, his voice coming out as little better than a squeak as he stared with fascinated horror at the unbelievable sight of the Earl of Rendale swaying dizzily in the doorway of the gold and white drawing room, with a group of flustered footmen hovering just behind him.

Not many people would have recognized the Earl of

Rendale, who had always prided himself on his immaculate and impeccable appearance and deportment. He stood there now, looking like a man who has been to hell and back: how he could possibly still be alive was a tale yet to be told. Wesley Lawton's coat and breeches were torn and ripped beyond repair; they were also stained with a mixture of mud and blood. One of his white stockings was hanging in shreds around his bootless foot, while the other boot was so scuffed and splattered with grime that it would take a week of hard elbow grease to make it presentable again. The Earl's handsome face was bruised and scratched and caked with dried blood. He'd long ago lost his wig, and his own brownish locks were hanging limply around his face and neck.

"Wesley?" the Duchess said softly as she moved silently toward the dazed Earl. "Wesley, 'tis Sabrina, Duchess of Camareigh."

Wesley Lawton's glazed eyes moved sluggishly toward the approaching figure, but he couldn't make it out through his blurred vision. He could make out several other figures in the room, as well as hear a scuffling of feet behind him. Well, he thought with a grim smile, he would soon take care of these malcontents.

"Damn impertinence!" he yelled, his words echoing that terrible day when he had faced the barrel of a pistol. Now, before anyone could anticipate his move, the Earl of Rendale pulled his pistol from his coat pocket and waved it wildly about.

"Sabrina! Don't move!" Sir Jeremy warned, unable to make a move himself as he held his daughter's slumped body, and purposely placed himself in front of Lady Sarah's chair, keeping her out of the line of fire.

"Rina, don't, please!" Mary was echoing Sir Jeremy's request, as the Duchess continued to move slowly closer to the crazed, weaving Earl of Rendale. "He is out of his mind. He doesn't know you! Rina!" she screamed as the pistol was aimed at her sister.

"Wesley. Wesley, 'tis Rhea Claire. Please don't point the pistol at me, Wesley," the Duchess said entreatingly, her gentle voice soothing him and cooling his flushed skin. It reminded him of a summer's day, when they'd been in the garden and Rhea Claire had looked so beautiful. . . .

"Catch him!" the Duchess cried as the Earl began to fall unconscious to the floor. Then the footman had him, breaking his fall before he could injure himself further. "Oh, my God," the Duchess said, noticing for the first time the size of the bloodstain on the Earl's shirt front. She knelt beside him and felt his feverish cheek. "Send someone for the doctor and tell Rawley we shall need her immediately to see to the Earl, for I fear that he may be dying," the Duchess said urgently. Immediately, the staff went into action, lifting the bloodied and barely breathing form of the Earl of Rendale. Carefully they carried him toward what might very well be his deathbed.

The Earl of Rendale's life hung in the balance that night, and once or twice perhaps, Wesley Lawton took one step beyond the door of death. At the same time, though, he had the pride and tenaciousness of all the Lawtons, and the Earl remained planted firmly in the world of the living, refusing to be done in by some common and coarse individual in a well-worn red velvet coat. Lawtons didn't die at the hands of thieves and robbers, and thus the Earl of Rendale hung on, fighting for his life with a valiant effort that may not have been possible in a man less concerned with his own importance.

The Duchess of Camareigh awoke slowly from her troubled sleep. She had refused to go to bed until nearly dawn, when a rosy blush had tinted the eastern skies. Finally, though, she had succumbed to her tiredness and found a few hours of rest. But she was not rested, and now as she lay back against the plumped-up pillows of her bed, she reflected on the stunning arrival of the Earl of Rendale yesterday.

Lucien and Terence, along with Francis, Ewan, and Richard, had returned to Camareigh less than an hour after the Earl's dramatic appearance. It had not been surprising to her that they had found no trace of the gypsies Caroline had claimed to have seen. It had been a long and tiring ride through the cold rain, and since it had been completely unnecessary, the ride had been cruel indeed for the riders. Caroline Winters had confessed, during a fit of hysteria upon reviving from her faint, that she had lied about the gypsies. The sight of the half-dead Earl had sobered the spoiled young miss who realized, perhaps for the first time, how harmful and contemptible it had been for her to mislead them about the events of that afternoon. But about what actually had happened, she knew little.

Sir Jeremy was a deeply hurt and mortified man. For the first time in his life he'd been rudely awakened to his daughter's shortcomings. As soon as it was light, he was going to take a chagrined, subdued Caroline back to Winterhall, and the Duchess would bet that Miss Caroline Winters would have a far more difficult parent to deal with in the future.

The Duchess rested her head against the lacy-edged pillow, her black hair tumbling around her and spilling onto the silk coverlet. With her hair unbound and her shoulders slumped in defeat, there was a sad, vulnerable quality to her, which was what the Duke saw when he entered the room, already dressed for whatever the day might bring.

"Rina," he said softly. He placed the tray with the silver pot of hot chocolate and delicate china cups on the chest at the foot of the bed, then forgot it as he sat down next to her and took her into his arms.

"What are we going to do, Lucien?" she asked pathetically, her husky voice barely more than a whisper. "We've lost our daughter, and I am so afraid that we shall not get her back."

"Don't ever say that, Rina," Lucien told her, shaking her slightly to force her to look up at him. "I promised you we would get her back, and we shall. Where I feel most helpless, my love, is in trying to ease your suffering," he told her, pressing her face against his chest.

Sabrina smiled, rubbing her soft cheek against him. "You are here with me, and that is all that I need," she said simply.

"I swear, Rina," said Lucien against her fragrant hair, "that we will have our daughter back. I will not rest until I have the truth and Rhea Claire within my grasp," he promised, sounding so convincing that Sabrina almost found herself believing his words.

It was past noon when the Duke paused outside the nursery door, hesitating to enter as he heard laughing voices and giggling screams coming from inside. For just an instant, he thought about keeping this secret from Sabrina, but he knew that had he done so, she would never have forgiven him. Over the years they had shared their love, and now they must share their grief.

With a grim tightness around his lips and his scar whitening across his cheek, the Duke turned the knob and entered the room. He stood silent for a moment and watched, as his wife scrambled across the floor with the twins. Her slim, silk-covered calves slid out from under ruffled petticoats as she tumbled to a halt, a fair-haired child under each arm.

Gradually, the Duchess became aware of her husband standing so quietly just within the door. She grinned up at him, but when she saw his expression, her face lost its animation. As she met his eyes, she knew without a word having been spoken that something had happened.

"The Earl—he's dead?" she asked. It would not come as a surprise to her, since he had looked so feverish the last time she had sat with him. Then, when Lucien shook his head, she asked, "Sarah? Is she having her baby?"

"No," he replied, wishing more than anything else in the world that he didn't have to do what he was about to do. "A messenger arrived."

"Rhea! You've received news about Rhea!" Sabrina cried, struggling to her feet, tugging impatiently at her skirts.

"Rina, my dear," Lucien began, then didn't know how to continue as he met her searching violet eyes. "I received a package. It was sent by persons unknown."

At Lucien's words, Sabrina hurried across the room, the twins following behind her on their chubby, unsteady legs. "Lucien! What is it? Tell me!"

Lucien led Sabrina to the window seat, and there, making no pretense at hiding the contents, he revealed what lay inside the small box.

Sabrina gave a choked cry as she slowly reached out and touched the long, golden curl, recognizing at once its distinctive shade. After all, how many times over the years had she admired the matching color of her own husband's hair? How pleased she had been when Rhea Claire had been born with Lucien's golden hair, she remembered now. With trembling fingers, she picked up the delicate ring shaped like a bow and encrusted with diamonds and sapphires.

"Do you remember how happy Rhea was when we gave her this ring for her birthday this year?" Sabrina said softly, her voice thick with tears. "She loves this ring so. Oh, dear God, what does this mean, Lucien? Why has someone taken our Rhea? Why are they tormenting us this way? Why? Why?" She cried, not hearing the door open as Robin and Francis entered the room. The boys paused uncertainly when they saw their weeping mother.

"There is more, my dearest," Lucien told her, despising himself for having to hurt her even more deeply. "Perhaps it is meant as some kind of explanation, or, damn them, as a puzzle to be solved. But 'tis madness to me."

Sabrina glanced up, her eyes full of luminous tears as she sniffed and tried to focus on the thin piece of parchment being held out in front of her. "Damn! I can't see it, Lucien. You read it," she pleaded, picking up Andrew and cuddling him to her breast.

Lucien stared at the paper for a moment before solemnly reciting the words scrawled untidily across the page:

> *Roses have thorns, and silver fountains mud;*
> *Clouds and eclipses stain both moon and sun,*
> *And loathsome canker lives in sweetest bud.*
> *All men make faults.*

"What is that supposed to mean?" Sabrina demanded in tearful incredulity. "What the hell is someone sending us poetry for?"

Lucien shook his head; his thumb moved along his scarred cheek while he continued to stare thoughtfully at the puzzling note. "I am not sure what it means. But then does anyone ever understand the mind of a madman?"

Sabrina looked stricken at his choice of words. "Oh, no. No, Lucien, not that. Please, please don't let me believe that our daughter is in the hands of a lunatic!"

Lucien could have bitten off his tongue, but what else could he have said or done? Could he lie to Sabrina now that there was proof that someone had kidnapped their daughter? Would it not be hurting her far more cruelly to allow her to build up her hopes, only to have them crushed later on? But perhaps this was all part of the game that someone was playing with them.

Lucien's eyes narrowed, masking the bright flare of hate and lust for revenge that was now burning steadily with his realization that they were being carefully manipulated by some unseen hand. He understood that their worries and fears, tears and hopes for their daughter were being stoked and fanned as if someone were adding fuel to a fire, perhaps with the hope that these violent emotions would consume and destroy them.

"What is it they want from us, Lucien?" Sabrina demanded.

Lucien bent down and picked up his daughter who was crawling around his booted legs. With gentle fingers he smoothed her golden curls into place, then placed a loving kiss on her small, retroussé nose. As her tiny hands played with his watch fob, Lucien looked across his daughter's head and met Sabrina's questioning eyes.

"I suspect that we shall next receive a demand for money. What other reason could there be for kidnapping our daughter? We shall have to ransom her back, Rina. And you know I would forfeit Camareigh to have her safely returned to us," Lucien said softly. But the glow in his eyes remained as he contemplated his revenge against those who had dared to take what was his. And anyone who knew the Duke of Camareigh would know he would make no idle threats. Someday he would savor his revenge, and even if it were not tomorrow or even next week, the day of reckoning would come.

Lucien became aware of his two sons standing quietly in front of the door. Robin's face was wet with tears, and he was trying to muffle his sobs by burying his head in Francis's shoulder. Holding his arm comfortingly over his brother's narrow shoulders, Francis met his father's eyes, and the Duke made the startling discovery that his son had grown into a man. They did not have to exchange a word without both of them knowing that they were promising each other to retrieve that which had been stolen from them.

Sabrina, Duchess of Camareigh, stared out on the drenched landscape that stretched off into distant gardens and meadowlands. This was Camareigh, her home. She glanced back into the room, her gaze lingering on Lucien and her children. These were her loved ones, her family. And yet, out there, somewhere beyond her reach and the comfort of her arms, was her daughter. Out there was her sweet and gentle Rhea Claire, who was, perhaps at this very moment, feeling terror and despair. She was probably cold and hungry, bewildered and alone, while she, the Duchess thought with growing self-disgust, sat here in safety before a warm fire, with her family around her. With an agonized groan at her own helplessness, Sabrina buried her face against Andrew's soft, golden head, not daring to speculate further on the fate of her firstborn, Rhea Claire.

Under the fall of darkness, the merchantman *London Lady* received her last passenger before preparing to cast off her mooring lines and set sail for the colonies. There was no one standing on the docks to see this lone passenger on board, or to wish that person a safe journey and a quick return. The passenger was bundled aboard with as much fanfare as a cask of wine, the only accompaniment to this rather clandestine activity being the indistinct sounds of voices raised in song and laughter drifting from a nearby tavern. The accommodation for the last passenger to board the *London Lady* was a dark, damp corner in steerage that reeked of an incredible array of odors, the most predominant of which was a blend of bilge water, tar, and paint. But there was another scent that permeated the ship. It was one that was far stronger, and one that could almost be felt. It was the smell of fear.

Times go by turns, and chances change by course.
From foul to fair, from better hap to worse.
                                        Robert Southwell

Chapter 5

DANCING against the white plasterwork ceiling and Pompeian red walls of the library was the shadowy reflection of golden flames. A long-case clock, its cherry wood glowing warmly, ticked away the minutes with brass hands that inched across its expressionless face with monotonous regularity. An Oriental carpet spilled across the highly waxed surface of the hardwood floor; its splash of color was echoed in the sapphire-blue velvet hangings of the tall windows and in the rich crimson damask of a William and Mary easy chair placed before the hearth.

A branch, bare of leaf, scratched against the windowpanes with a shower of raindrops. It drew the attention of the man who was sitting in the chair before the fireplace, with his booted feet propped against a brass andiron. A big orange tabby slept peacefully in his lap. The man shifted to a more comfortable position, wincing slightly as he disturbed the painful mending of his cracked ribs.

Dante Leighton's pale gray eyes narrowed as they sought out the gauge in the barometer hanging on the wall in its elaborate mahogany and tulipwood case. But he didn't need to see that the pressure had fallen to know that a storm was unleashing itself over Charles Town. He could see the flash of lightning in the prematurely dark afternoon sky, and he heard the rumble of thunder, to which the crystal chandelier above his head tinkled in sympathy.

Dante took a deep swallow of brandy, hoping it would help ease the dull ache in his ribs, as well as hasten the endless hours of inactivity he'd been forced to endure since his accident. He glanced over at the walnut gaming table with its four silver candlesticks positioned in each corner, the tall candles standing ready to be lighted as soon as darkness enfolded the room. By the time the last card was dealt, the candles burned down and replaced many times over, Kirby would long since have drawn back the heavy hangings and allowed the first light of dawn to steal in. It was certainly one way of making the most of his convalescence, Dante thought with a slight smile, remembering how well his luck at cards had been of late, much to the disgruntled mutterings of his guests.

Dante rested his head against the soft cushion, thinking of another run of luck that had turned disastrous and imperiled the *Sea Dragon* and her crew. It had been one of those chance occurrences, for he'd sailed the *Sea Dragon* countless times between Charles Town and the Indies with never so much as a broken hogshead of molasses or a split goblet of wine. And yet this time out, just south of Savannah, a squall had caught the *Sea Dragon* while under press of canvas and nearly laid her on her beam ends. With her rigging snapped and sails split and one of her masts gone by the board, the *Sea Dragon* had managed to make port just ahead of another storm blowing out of the straits. Dante remembered the last leg of the journey as one full of pain, for when the mast had broken off, the wild swing of a luff tackle had caught him broadside and sent him flying to the quarterdeck like so much flotsam. Actually, he had been quite fortunate in suffering only a few cracked ribs and a twisted ankle, since the hook on the end of the tackle could well have taken his head off.

Several of the crew as well had received injuries, including a broken arm suffered by Barnaby Clark, the

203

quartermaster, who'd been on duty at the wheel when the squall had struck. The sudden spinning of the wheel had slammed one of the handles against his arm, snapping the bone cleanly in two. Seumus Fitzsimmons had been knocked unconscious by a broken-off piece of spar falling to the deck, although his mates swore that the spar had broken *after* it'd hit that thick-skulled head of his. And much to his embarrassment, in light of the other more serious injuries, Alastair Marlowe had sustained a broken little finger.

While they were recuperating, the *Sea Dragon* had been lying in dock, where she was refitted with a new mast, rigging, and spars. Within the month she would once again be seaworthy; then the captain and crew of the *Sea Dragon* would be Indies-bound with a fair wind filling her sails.

Dante thought of the ill-fated wind that had chanced across his path, and wondered if it portended a change in his fortunes. In his own mind, his injuries had been something of a mixed blessing, since his convalescence gave him a legitimate excuse for declining most of the invitations he had been inundated with of late. In fact, this surge in his popularity had coincided with the return from London of a certain young woman, whose unbridled tongue had regaled half of Charles Town with her adventures abroad, as well as the information she'd ferreted out about Captain Dante Leighton, better known to past acquaintances in London as the Marquis of Jacqobi. Strange it was, *or was it,* how a title could enhance one's image in the eyes of others. And yet, Dante thought with a cynical twist to his lips, he was still the same man, who only months earlier had been considered slightly disreputable by the good townspeople. Certainly, he had not been considered respectable enough even to nod good afternoon to the chaste daughters of those fine folk of Charles Town.

He far preferred his former reputation, since much to his displeasure he now found himself prey to every husband-hunting wench in Charles Town, not to mention their aspiring and less-than-subtle mamas. He was beginning to feel that it would be far safer for him to walk unarmed into a pirates' den than into a drawing room full of prospective in-laws all competing for him. Never before had he heard so many libelous remarks about supposedly upstanding members of society. It seemed to him that he was always hearing someone's good name being sneered upon and blackened. And it was not only the steely-eyed glances from the would-be-mothers-in-law that caused him qualms; Dante could also see the proud papas sizing him up as they speculated about how much influence he had at Court and just how profitable and beneficial a son-in-law he might make.

And despite his polite refusals to the invitations that continued to arrive—he was trying to lead people to believe that his recovery necessitated peace and quiet—he now found himself under siege by oversolicitous, gift-bearing hopefuls, who were determined not to be out-maneuvered. But Dante swore that if he had to sample one more homemade remedy and sure-cure, or one more sticky sweet baked especially for him, he would not be held accountable for his actions. And a short, bandy-legged steward would be one of the first to feel the brunt of his anger for having allowed those simpering misses past the front door in the first place.

There were some, momentarily maddened, who envied him his unique position, for if he wished to do so, Dante knew he could have taken to wife any available, or perhaps unavailable, woman in Charles Town. His speculations were tinged with amusement, not vanity, since he realized, more so than anyone else did, that had the Marquis of Jacqobi been Alastair Marlowe, Houston Kirby, or even Longacres, the *Sea Dragon*'s coxswain, the situation would not have altered. For it was the title that had sent a fluttering into the hearts of the unmarried ladies of Charles Town.

There were others, however, who thought that Dante Leighton's fortunes had suffered more than just the ill-luck of the *Sea Dragon*'s last voyage. For, as rumor had it, the *Sea Dragon* had been after sunken treasure. Apparently, or so certain people said, Dante Leighton had won a treasure map in a card game in St. Eustatius that showed the location of a sunken galleon. It had to be authentic, since the captain of the *Sea Dragon* was as steady as his ship, and some even said he was as cold-blooded as that mythical beast in whose honor he'd named his brigantine. Aye, if Captain Dante Leighton was after treasure, then the odds were that it was no wild goose chase. But this time the last laugh had been on the captain and crew of the *Sea Dragon*: The sunken treasure they'd hoped for had turned out to be no more than a few pieces of corroded silverware and some broken porcelain plates, a rusty astrolabe and a compass in a rotting box, as well as the abandoned cargo of the ship, which were the skeletonized remains of crates and barrels, their precious contents of exotic spices now claimed by the sea. Instead of finding a sunken treasure ship, with a cargo of pieces of eight, the crew of the *Sea Dragon* had discovered the wreck of a Dutch merchantman—and there was certainly no treasure to be found in her hold.

The *Sea Dragon* had swaggered her bow at the fates once too often, said the old sailors sitting around on the docks. These were men who'd seen the sea, in all of her beauty and fury, snap a proud ship in two like a frail twig, and send her arrogant captain and irreverent crew to the bottom, where they were never heard from again.

Dante Leighton smiled strangely as he recalled the rumors, repeated to him by Kirby and Alastair, which were floating around Charles Town concerning the fateful voyage of the *Sea Dragon*. Dante stared into the flames, a reflected light dancing in his pale gray eyes as he wondered what those sea dogs would say if they could read his mind now. Most likely, they would suspect the captain of the *Sea Dragon* of making a pact with the devil, Dante Leighton thought, with a smile of devilish satisfaction.

"M'lord?" said the steward, Houston Kirby, who was standing beside his captain's big chair. "We've a guest, m'lord," he informed the preoccupied Leighton, and his contemptuous tone left Dante in little doubt that the person in question was not in Houston Kirby's good graces.

"Ah, m'lord," Kirby said before Dante could ask his visitor's name. "That cat's going to have hair all over your fine breeches. 'Tis the devil to get off, that it is," Kirby scolded, glaring at the complacent tabby, whose single green eye stared back at him lazily.

"Our guest, Kirby?" Dante reminded the little steward. "I think you should show this—" But Dante got no further, for the doors of the study were flung wide as a jovial-looking man stormed the portals.

"Captain Leighton! 'Tis good to see you up and about again. Caught sight of you riding that big stallion of yours along Tradd Street, and I says to meself, 'You oughta pay Captain Leighton a visit.' Not that you'll be findin' me astride one of them beasts. No sir! Not Bertie Mackay. He's no fool. Never catch him on horseback. Don't see how you can do it," commented the rival smuggler, his eyes narrowed thoughtfully as he stared at Dante Leighton. "But then, I says to meself, 'Bertie, that Captain Leighton, he's full of little surprises. More to that gent than meets the eye, there is. He's a fine sea captain, I'll give him that, for Bertie Mackay's not a man to sell another man short. Now, not only is he a fine sailor, but he's a fine horseman as well. And I've heard tell he's a deadly shot, as well as being a daring swordsman. Reckon you've survived a few duels, eh, Captain?"

"Ah, my pardon," Bertie Mackay apologized with exaggerated concern. "'Tisn't proper, is it, to just be calling you captain? Aye, should be *m'lord,* eh?" he corrected himself, with a chuckle growing into a deep belly laugh that rolled across the room in his wake. "Bless me, but you certainly knocked ol' Bertie Mackay on his beam ends, you did. Fancy that, the captain of the *Sea Dragon* being a marquis. Nearly put me off spirits, it did. But," he added, wagging his finger, "not quite, and since I've a mighty thirst right now and a bit of talking to be doing . . ." hinted the smuggler-captain of the *Annie Jeanne* none too subtly, while he eyed the snifter of brandy being held negligently in his host's hand.

"By all means, Captain Mackay," Dante invited, gesturing casually to a chair beyond the warmth of the fire. "Please join me in a brandy. Kirby, a drink for the captain of the *Annie Jeanne,*" he ordered, ignoring the small steward's rude snort.

"Mighty hospitable of you, Captain," Bertie Mackay

said with a broad grin. Then he easily hauled the spindle-legged chair closer to the fire and lowered his considerable bulk into it. As he did so, the chair's delicate frame gave a protesting squeak.

With a pleased expression on his rotund face, Bertie Mackay glanced at Dante Leighton, only to have his smile fade slightly when he heard the low growling noises coming from the big tomcat curled in Dante's lap. "Surly-looking creature. Don't think he cares for me, eh?" said Bertie Mackay, laughing uneasily. Even though he could well have knocked the cat clean out of the room with one easy sweep of his powerful arm, the feline made him nervous. Damn cats always had and always would, he thought with a shiver.

"I imagine that he senses you've no love for his kind, Captain," Dante commented dryly, his hand smoothing Jamaica's slightly ruffled fur.

"Aye, that's it. Never could stand the sly-looking beasties. Always got the feeling they know something I don't, and I'm not liking the way they sneak up on a man from behind. Too quiet, they are. Like to hear an animal or a man coming at me; then I know what to expect, and where to aim my shot," Bertie Mackay said with a smile that had caused many a faint heart to sink sickeningly. Seldom did that smile bode well for the unfortunate individual under scrutiny.

"Ah," Bertie Mackay sighed with pleasure. Already, he had swallowed half the contents of the snifter handed to him by a less-than-obsequious Houston Kirby. "Now that takes the chill off these old bones better than any roaring fire. Mite nippy out," he said conversationally, while his large fingers tapped out a tuneless beat on the arm of the chair. "Just about got the *Sea Dragon* refitted, I hear. You wouldn't be thinking of parting with her, would you?" he asked curiously, meanwhile shaking his head, since he knew what Dante Leighton's reply would be without having to hear it. "No. Thought not. Pity, though, for I've always had a fancy for the *Sea Dragon*. Trim little vessel, she is," he muttered, his voice trailing off into the silence of the room.

"Thank you, Captain Mackay, although I doubt you

came calling merely to compliment me on my ship,"
Dante said, deciding to put an end to the informalities
and bring Captain Cuthbert Mackay's real reason for
visiting him out into the open.

Bertie Mackay's grin widened in appreciation. "Aye,
right you are, Captain. But please, call me Bertie. I insist
all of my friends do," he said to the man who'd been a
less-than-friendly rival for many years. "Now I'm a man
for plain speaking, and I've never thought of myself as
being a fool. And," he added, a warning glint in his eyes,
which wiped all geniality from his somewhat florid features, "I don't like to be thought one by others."

"I am sure no one in their right mind would assume
such a thing, Captain," Dante murmured softly, his fingers
never stopping their soothing motions through Jamaica's
fur.

"Glad to hear you say that. Yes, sir, that I am, for it
seems to me that we could become very good friends,"
Bertie Mackay suggested with a sly twinkle in his eyes.

Dante Leighton stared across the warmly lit space between them, his pale gray eyes narrowed speculatively
while he studied this disturbingly affable Bertie Mackay.
He knew that it was when the captain of the *Annie
Jeanne* was smiling widest that he was usually up to no
good. It had come as a great shock to many an unsuspecting person, lulled into a false sense of security by an
ingratiating grin and infectious laugh, to discover that
the fatherly Bertie Mackay could just as easily cut your
heart out as shake your hand. His appearance was completely misleading, since no one would suspect such a
jolly and apple-cheeked individual of acts bordering on
piracy, and indeed, if the truth be known, of murder most
foul. But most good townspeople, especially those receiving contraband from the genial smuggler, refused to believe that Bertie Mackay, loving husband and fond father
of five little Mackays, could be a murderer. They believed that if the captain of the *Annie Jeanne* had put a
man in the grave, then it had surely been in self-defense.

While in Charles Town, Captain Cuthbert Mackay was
a pillar of the community, a fine example of hard-
working, middle-class values. He escorted his family to

church on the Sabbath, was known to give generously to
the poor, and had never been caught carousing in any of
the numerous taverns about town. It was a well-known
fact that he was devoted and ever-faithful to his Annie
Jeanne, his Scottish wife. The two of them had been
young sweethearts setting out to make their fortune in the
new colonies in the wilderness. He was often heard to say
that there were none like his Annie Jeanne, and if the
listener chanced a glance at this paragon of virtue and
recipient of such undying devotion, he might well have
agreed, for Annie Jeanne Mackay was fair of face and
figure, with a bonny disposition and Scottish burr that
made her instantly beloved.

If there were any vice that Cuthbert "Bertie" Mackay
was guilty of, then it would have to be his inordinate
fondness for fine clothes. His coats and breeches were
made in London by the best tailors, and twice a year he
visited London to get fitted out in the latest styles. The
coat he was wearing now had been cut by a master hand,
the cuff appropriately wide and revealing the proper
amount of lace. His silk waistcoat was trimmed with gold,
and complemented the gold buttons adorning his coat. His
black velvet breeches were perhaps a bit out of place, but
Bertie Mackay had a fondness for velvet. His linen neck-
cloth, however, could not be faulted, nor could his neatly
gartered stockings or his shoes with the baroque buckles.

"Now what could possibly occur that might instigate
such an alliance between two so dedicated rivals, Captain?" Dante inquired lazily.

"Aye, you're quick, Captain, that you are," wheezed
Bertie Mackay with approval, for there was nothing better to put you on your mettle than a quick-witted opponent. "Well now, seeing how we are past rivals, I'm
willing to let bygones be bygones and forget any grievances I might have held against you, Captain Leighton,"
Bertie Mackay offered generously. "I'm a God-fearing,
forgiving man, and I'm not one to be holding unnecessary
grudges, Captain. You remember that."

Dante Leighton smiled slightly. "Yes, I shall, and I had
no idea I was so fortunate to find myself in your good
graces, Captain Mackay. But I am curious, Captain,"

Dante added, his lips twisting cynically, "about exactly what it is that I must forfeit in return."

Bertie Mackay threw up his hands, his expression showing that his sensibilities had been abused. "Ah, Captain Leighton, you struck me down unfairly then, that you did. To think you'd have such a low opinion of my genuine offer of friendship and be so suspicious of my motives, well," he said, shaking his bewigged head, "you hurt me, sir, yes indeed."

Dante's gray eyes narrowed as he continued to sit silently, waiting for what would surely be more dramatics, with, perhaps, a few revelations.

"Actually, Captain, 'tis more of a service that *I* can render for you, than the other way around," Bertie Mackay told him smugly, a pleased look replacing the calculating expression that usually lurked within the seemingly gentle blue depths of his eyes.

"You have me intrigued, Captain," Dante remarked, showing little curiosity about the means now being offered by Mackay to end their hostilities.

"Did you never hear the fable of the dog and the bone? No? Well, Captain, there is a lesson to be learned in its telling," Bertie Mackay advised, settling his bulk into a more comfortable position on the creaking chair. Then he took a tongue-loosening swallow of his brandy.

"You see, there was this dog. Fair to starvin' he was. Indeed, 'twas a pitiable sight to see him skulking along the lane, his tail between his legs as he dodged booted feet aimed at his backside. Reckon he thought he'd come close to his last days of breathing; then the fates smiled on him and he hears about a butcher who's going to be getting rid of scraps. And among these scraps is a bone that could feed him for the rest of his days. Never have to go hungry again, no sir. Ah, excited he was, that be for sure. But, as only too often happens, a rumor got started about this magic bone, and before the poor dog knew it, every flea-bitten mongrel in town was after that bone. Ah, the poor wee dog had not a moment's peace, Captain. Can you imagine how the wretched dog was hounded? Why, he couldn't even lift his leg without some growling cur snapping at his heels. Well, the day was drawing close, and this dog knew, for he wasn't without brains, that he'd never be able to steal his bone with that pack of mad dogs on his scent. The only thing in our dog's favor was that he was the only one who knew *which* butcher 'twas that was throwing out the scraps. Well, with a cunning seldom seen, he leads all of the other dogs on a wild goose chase as he noses about the offscourings of all of the butcher shops in town. Then, when most of the dogs had tired of the chase, for naught was found of a magic bone, he trots along home, quite pleased with himself, I might say. However," Bertie Mackay continued, the light tone in his voice disappearing, "there was this *other* dog."

Dante Leighton raised an interested eyebrow, a spark of amusement twinkling in his eyes. "Another dog, Captain? No doubt a Highland terrier?"

Bertie Mackay grinned widely with appreciation. "Ah, Captain, you're one of the brightest lads I've had the pleasure of dealing with in a long time. Never disappoint me, no sir! You're quick-witted, that you are, Captain Leighton," he chuckled, slapping his knee with his palm. "You see, this *other* dog was suspicious and figured that the first dog was not to be trusted, because the thought of misleading this pack of dogs had crossed his own mind several times. And so he decides to follow this dog, and what do you think he finds?" Bertie Mackay asked innocently.

"He sees this other dog," he continued, not waiting for an answer, "waiting patiently outside a butcher shop, which had been beneath the pack's notice earlier in the day. Now I wonder what it was this dog was waiting for. Could it be the bone? But every dog in town thought that there was no bone, for they'd followed this dog around and come away with empty stomachs, as well as the idea that this dog was a bit of a fool for wasting his time on so foolhardy an adventure.

"Now this other dog has two options, Captain, and which one he decides to use, well, 'tis up to the first dog to decide." Bertie Mackay grinned at his long-time rival.

"Is it really?" Dante commented politely. "How do you figure that, Captain Mackay?"

"Well, the way this other dog sees it, the first dog can

either join with him in purloining this bone, or," he paused, his words holding a wealth of meaning, "he can expect to lose possession of it. Because this other dog will call down the pack of wild dogs on him, and then he will be left with nothing. Maybe not even his life," Bertie Mackay said in conclusion, leaving an expectant silence hanging in the air between the two adventurers.

Dante Leighton smiled, but there was a dangerous glint in his eye. "And what did this cur do?" he asked.

Bertie Mackay was all smiles. "Why, he joined with the other dog in retrieving the bone. I told you he was a smart dog, didn't I? Better to share the bone than to have nought of it. Right, Captain?"

"Perhaps," Dante replied noncommittally. "But then," he added with a smile calculated to puzzle, "it all depends on the prize, doesn't it, Captain?"

Bertie Mackay's genial expression faded like the stars at dawn. "Aye, Captain, that it does."

"A very interesting little fable, Captain," Dante said with a slightly bored sigh. "But I do not see its purpose, nor its relevance to a lessening of hostilities between us. Ah," he added then, as if he'd just remembered something important, "you have not told me the moral to the tale, have you, Captain? And I am quite certain there is a moral to be told, is there not?" Dante invited the captain of the *Annie Jeanne*. His smile, however, was anything but encouraging.

"Aye, Captain Leighton, a moral there is," Bertie Mackay responded, his lips quivering tightly. " 'Tis far better to share with a friend, who can become an ally, than to make a pack of enemies and risk losing all."

The firelight glowed softly on Dante Leighton's chestnut curls as he gazed in absorbed contemplation at the fire that was consuming the logs in the grate. "An admirable philosophy, Captain. But, unfortunately, I am not a man who cares to share, nor do I know of many men I can call friend, or men whom I can trust implicitly. Granted," said Dante, so softly that Bertie Mackay had to lean forward to catch his words, "a pack of wolves can bring down a larger prey than a single wolf, but a lone wolf can move undetected where a pack would only draw attention. The lone wolf can move swiftly and silently, Captain. He strikes at will; then he is gone, with almost no one the wiser, except perhaps the victim," Dante said. His voice had slipped into such a conversational tone that Bertie was hardly aware of the threat in his rival's words, but one glance into Dante's icy gray eyes convinced him.

"Of course, this is mere speculation," Dante continued, "for I have nothing of value that you might wish to share with me. I do not share my women, but then you are happily married, aren't you, Captain? It can't be my stallion or other horseflesh, for you do not ride, do you, Captain?" Dante gazed speculatively at the other man. "And although you have professed a `wish to own the *Sea Dragon*, we both know that there can be only one captain on board, and I happen to be her master, so . . ." Dante allowed his words to fall into the heavy silence.

Bertie Mackay's deep roar of laughter was unexpected, startling Jamaica from his captain's lap. With a spitting protest, the cat skidded across the waxed floor, his claws making a scratching noise as he shot between Houston Kirby's legs and upended the startled little steward with his tray and its decanter of brandy. Although Kirby managed to catch the crystal decanter, its contents spilled forth onto his clean breeches and shirt front.

"Reckon I won't be sharin' any more brandy with you, Captain," said Bertie Mackay, with a hearty laugh for the steward's comical predicament.

With a baleful glare aimed at the captain of the *Annie Jeanne*, a fuming Houston Kirby picked himself up from the floor, his sparkling blue eyes searching out the miserable creature that had precipitated his humiliation before so despised a rival. But hard as he searched, he could not locate one vulnerable inch of orange fur; the dark shadows beneath the secretaire against the wall effectively obscured Jamaica's hiding place. So, with a muttering beneath his breath, Houston Kirby, his dignity riding low, stomped from the room.

"Ah, Captain Leighton, once again you haven't disappointed me, for I suspected you might be of a stubborn

214

frame of mind. Aye, 'tis a pity though, for I've enjoyed our little rivalries in the past, that I have."

"You sound as though I've already departed this earth, Captain," Dante remarked, his expression revealing nothing to Bertie Mackay of what was going on in his mind.

"Not at all, not at all," Bertie Mackay protested. "Of course, one can never be quite certain if one will return from a voyage or not. 'Tis a wide ocean out there. Many things can happen—unexpected things. A man's got to be mighty careful how he sets his sails. Could sail into a galeful of trouble, yes sir, that he could. I'd be real careful if I was you, Captain Leighton, especially now that the *Sea Dragon*'s sailing by her lonesome. She's got no friends here in Charles Town. At least none she can trust," advised Bertie Mackay. "Well, I must be off. I'm meeting with several captains here in port. We thought we might get together, form a company whereby we pool our resources. We are all ambitious men, but growing tired of smuggling. To be quite frank, the risk is becoming too great," he confided. "We thought we'd work together this one time—we could fill our purses for years to come. Kind of reminds one of that fable, don't it, Captain? Well, I must take my leave of you, Captain. Look forward to seeing the *Sea Dragon*'s sails unfurled again and rapping full. Good afternoon to you, then." Thus did Bertie Mackay, grinning captain of the *Annie Jeanne*, bid farewell to the sardonically amused captain of the *Sea Dragon*.

Dante Leighton continued to sit before the fire long after Bertie Mackay had left, frowning slightly while he pondered his guest's words. He knew the gauntlet had been thrown down, and he also knew that the captain of the *Annie Jeanne* was seldom carried off the field of contest.

"Somethin's amiss. I can smell it a mile off," Houston Kirby remarked glumly as he approached his captain.

Dante glanced over at his steward; his lips twitched when he noticed the hastily sponged breeches and shirt. "I suspect you are downwind of yourself," Dante commented wryly, his nostrils flaring slightly as he sniffed the brandy fumes emanating from Houston Kirby. "I wouldn't breathe too deeply, Kirby, for you could get drunk standing right where you are."

"Reckon I'm sober enough to catch me an orange tom-cat," Kirby said, glancing quickly about the room in the hope of sighting his prey.

"I'd think you and Jamaica would get along better than you do, since you both have an instinctive dislike for the captain of the *Annie Jeanne*," Dante remarked to the bristling little steward. "In fact, Jamaica growled at the jolly captain, not to mention hissing at him."

"Hissed at Bertie Mackay, did he?" Houston Kirby said, his stance a little less aggressive. "Hmmmm, well, I always did say the cat wasn't stupid. Aye, he can smell a rat the same as I can."

"Yes, I believe you are correct, Kirby," Dante agreed. "Bertie Mackay is not to be trusted. I do believe I've just been warned not to try to get the *Sea Dragon*'s treasure."

Houston Kirby sucked in his breath. "He didn't believe the story about the Dutch merchantman?"

"No, but then I didn't think he would. In his place, I wouldn't have either. He saw through our little ploy, but it was not solely for his benefit that I used it. I wanted to get the rest of that pack of dogs off our trail, which we did succeed in doing," Dante said reflectively. He was remembering how he'd hated having to lie to the crew of the *Sea Dragon*, but there had been no other way to keep secret the true location of the Spanish galleon. Since there were so many men on board who were given to loose tongues when drunk and carousing in port, Dante had recognized that the only way to assure their uncontested search for the sunken ship—as well as an unaccosted retrieval of its treasure, should there be one, and a safe voyage home for the *Sea Dragon*—was to deceive the crew. If they thought they had failed in their quest for the treasure, then other prospective fortune-hunters would believe the falsehood as well. As it was, it had been no easy feat to outsail the flotilla of cutthroats, jackals, and desperate men that had followed the *Sea Dragon* with the overly optimistic hope that an accommodating Dante Leighton would lead them to the treasure. Had they known the captain of the *Sea Dragon*'s thoughts, they could have relaxed, for Dante Leighton had every intention of allowing some of those hearties to arrive on the scene—but not until the *Sea Dragon* intended them to.

Dante suspected that Longacres knew the truth, for the coxswain had caught a good glimpse of the treasure map while the *Sea Dragon* was at anchor off Trinidad. Longacres had sailed the Caribbean since he'd been a lad younger than Conny Brady, and as a cabin boy he'd crewed aboard a pirate ship. He'd already seen far too many maps of sunken treasure to have his reasoning blinded by uncontrollable excitement, and he'd carefully studied the map in that brief glance he'd had of it. Since then, Dante had caught the weathered old sailor sending him speculative glances every so often. He seemed to be biding his time patiently, while keeping a watchful eye on his captain.

Alastair Marlowe, on the other hand, had been in on the truth since the beginning, for the supercargo had known about the sunken Dutch merchantman for many years now. In fact, they had discovered it together, quite by accident, while searching for safe, convenient coves in the Bahamas where the *Sea Dragon* could lie at anchor and make repairs should a sudden storm cause them damage—or if there were too many Union Jacks coloring the horizon.

The *Sea Dragon* had been anchored in a lagoon of clear turquoise water on the leeward side of a small, uninhabited island. After exploring the palmetto-studded islet for fresh water, he and Alastair had been rowing back toward the *Sea Dragon* when, just around a small headland, they spied beneath the gig's bow a faded figurehead nestled among the coral. Looking deeper into the watery depths, they had seen the wreck of a ship resting on the sandy bottom.

Alastair had stripped down to his breeches and dived overboard. Deep in the tranquil waters below, his pale figure had wavered strangely as he explored the wreck. Even from his position in the stern of the gig, Dante could see that the ship lying on the bottom was a seventeenth-century vessel, with much of her imposing sterncastle still intact. Several bronze cannons, half-buried in the shifting sands of the ocean floor, were scattered about the ship's rotted hull.

Gasping for air, Alastair had surfaced and tossed several discolored items into the gig; then he'd climbed aboard with an assisting hand from Dante. Barely taking the time to fill his lungs, he retrieved his treasure from the floor of the boat, grinning widely, held it out for Dante's inspection. The West Indian sun beat down relentlessly on the handful of corroded, silver *dubbelstuivers* and a rusty sword hilt—the only booty the wreck of the Dutch merchantman had been willing to part with.

The useless sword hilt had been returned to its watery grave, while the Dutch coins, at Dante's insistence, found their way into Alastair's pocket, as his just reward for making the find. No more was said or thought about the Dutch merchantman—at least until recently, when the merchantman had proven to be the answer to their difficulties.

Dante smiled now, remembering how he and Alastair had been put to the test when they'd had to draw another, duplicate map of the one in his possession. On it, they made a slight change in the location of the *X*. A small detail, but one that would lead the *Sea Dragon* a little southeast of the original location, directly into that cove where the Dutch merchantman was peacefully sleeping. Had they been caught out in their deception, Dante knew that he and Alastair would have been hard pressed to explain —if, indeed, they were given time to.

At first, upon finding the sunken ship, the crew of the *Sea Dragon* was ecstatic; then, after sending several men who could swim into the water, they had become downcast with the news that the ship was no treasure galleon. They hadn't had much time to commiserate, though, because around the headland had come several rival smugglers, their purpose clear as they fired several warning shots from their guns.

But Dante, unlike most of the crew, had not been caught off guard. His orders were given, the hemp anchor cable was severed, which freed the *Sea Dragon* from her mooring, and the lightly furled sails were cut loose to catch the wind. The *Sea Dragon* made her escape safely, leaving the Dutch merchantman and its unprofitable cargo to be fought over by the duped, would-be-pirates.

As the *Sea Dragon* had sailed away, they'd heard the roar of several more rounds of cannon-fire. Dante had wondered which of the scavengers would be unlucky enough to join the Dutch merchantman on the bottom of the cove.

As far as most people in Charles Town were concerned, that had been the end of the *Sea Dragon*'s quest for sunken treasure; yet, just northwest of the Bahamas, somewhere in a scattering of small islands, sandbars, and jagged coral, there might be a sunken Spanish galleon with a cargo of treasure chests filled with enough pieces of eight to make a thousand fortunes.

"Wanted in on our treasure, did he?" Houston Kirby's harshly uttered words cut through Dante Leighton's reflections.

Dante's lips quirked slightly, for there had never been any point in trying to keep a secret from the little steward. As far as Houston Kirby was concerned, there was no such thing as a secret. With little or no trouble at all, he could root out the secret of a matronly widow's age, a feat few could lay claim to accomplishing.

"Either Bertie Mackay is to become a partner, or," Dante paused meaningfully, "the captain and crew of the *Sea Dragon* will never get a chance to spend any of that treasure."

"Why, the blackguard," Kirby muttered, still embarrassed for having looked the fool in front of that swine Bertie Mackay. "Who does he think he is, anyway?" the little steward demanded belligerently.

"He happens to be a man who does not make idle threats. Nor is he a man who takes kindly to another man getting the better of him," Dante stated, knowing the captain of the *Annie Jeanne* as well as any man could.

"What's he planning on doin'?" Kirby asked, some of his anger fading after he heard the seriousness in his captain's voice.

Dante remained silent for a moment as he puzzled over Kirby's question, the flickering light in the fireplace playing across his unreadable features. "The captain of the *Annie Jeanne* is planning to join ranks in a rather uneasy alliance with several other captains who, most likely, harbor some grudge against me and would not mind settling a few old scores."

"Aye, Captain, we've made our share of enemies over the years, that we have," Houston Kirby agreed with a sinking of spirits, for he knew that his captain's extraordinary good fortunes, as well as his ruthless pursuit of them, had encouraged little besides jealousy and resentment in less fortunate men.

Dante Leighton was not a man to be crossed, for he could be a cruel and pitiless enemy, a man he would not care to be on the wrong side of, Houston Kirby thought, remembering men foolish enough to have betrayed the captain of the *Sea Dragon*. As a privateer and smuggler, Dante Leighton had more than proven himself a match for any man. His rivals knew this and accorded him the proper respect, for none of them, no matter how fearless, was reckless enough to want to cross bows with him. However, if several of them joined ranks like the captain said, well . . . he didn't even want to speculate on that, because they just might have the chance to catch the *Sea Dragon* after everybody else had failed.

Houston Kirby frowned thoughtfully as he stared at his captain; concern for the *Sea Dragon*'s master was uppermost in his mind as he thought about the dangerous predicament they would surely find themselves in if they went searching for that sunken Spanish galleon. Kirby gnawed at his lower lip, wondering if he dared to voice his thoughts. Even though he knew that he could get away with far more than most men could where Dante Leighton was concerned, there was still, even for him, a point beyond which it was wisest not to step. He had served Dante Leighton loyally throughout the years, watching, sometimes helplessly, as the young Marquis of Jacqobi grew into a hardened, vengeful man, who had only one goal in life—which was to seek retribution against the man who had destroyed his family.

Kirby shook his head, for he could well understand the captain's feelings. Dante Leighton's mother, the Lady

Elayne, had been a fine, beautiful woman, which perhaps was where the tragedy lay, for she had been so exquisite that everybody had loved her, some unwisely so.

Aye, he too hated the bastard who had contributed to the Lady Elayne's tragic death, for he had served the Leighton family before the captain's mother had married into it; he'd even had the privilege of being born at Merdraco Castle, so his loyalties to the family, and to its only heir, ran deep. A longing for Merdraco was as much in his blood as it was in the captain's, and he wanted to spill the blood of that bastard as much as the captain did. But the blood lust hadn't completely clouded his vision, as it had Dante Leighton's, and he knew that he might be the only one who could restrain the murderous intentions of the last Marquis of Jacqobi.

"Cap'n," began Houston Kirby awkwardly. "M'Lord," he tried again, liking the sound of that better, "I was just wondering if perhaps it might not be wiser to let the treasure, if indeed there is one, which I doubt, rest in peace in the deep. 'Tisn't worth gettin' ourselves killed for, m'lord. Reckon the odds be a bit high this time," Kirby concluded, on what he hoped was a persuasive note. He was quickly disabused of that idea, however, as he caught the sardonic gleam in the captain's eye.

"Do you indeed, Kirby?" Dante inquired softly, his steely-eyed glance reminding the little steward more than ever of the captain's grandfather, an implacable old man who'd ruled Merdraco with an iron hand for close to half a century. He could still recall, too vividly for his peace of mind, standing with shaking knees before the old Marquis, while those same pale gray eyes as his grandson's burned a hole through him.

"I suspect, Kirby," Dante Leighton continued, a slight smile curving his lips, "that you actually fear that there *will* be a treasure to be found. I do not think you have truly lost faith in my abilities to sail the *Sea Dragon* out of danger, but fear more," he paused as his eyes met the steward's, "what shall happen afterwards."

Houston Kirby lowered his bushy eyebrows, effectively hiding the expression in his eyes. Pursing his lips, he said,

221

"Reckon we can only wait and see what happens. Might not be as either of us expect it to."

"But whatever it comes to, I can count on you," Dante Leighton stated, knowing full well he had Houston Kirby's loyalty, even if his steward sometimes disapproved of his actions.

"Aye, you know you can, Captain," Kirby replied. "For you and Merdraco, and for the Lady Elayne, I'd follow you into hell, m'lord. Which is where I expect we're headed. Besides," Kirby added with a wry grin, looking over his shoulder as if someone might be standing behind him, "the old Marquis wouldn't let me rest in peace if I let you get into trouble."

Dante smiled, his eyes softening briefly and reflecting the genuine warmth he felt for the small man who'd always stood bravely at his side. He knew he could count himself lucky that he had Houston Kirby's loyalty and affection. He was a funny little man, taken to instant likes and dislikes. Opinionated and bossy, he preferred to appear irascible, while in reality he was little better than a mother hen in his concerns for the captain and crew of the *Sea Dragon*.

"What are we having for dinner, Kirby?" Dante asked. "I suddenly find that I am quite ravenous."

"Aye, thought as much when I saw Bertie Mackay come swaggering in. Went ahead and started that loin of veal turning over the fire and got a couple of ducks roasting nicely, not to mention an apple pie browning in the oven," Kirby informed him matter-of-factly. "You've always had a keen appetite when you've been planning mischief, only in the old days 'twas just your backside that was at stake. Now . . ." Kirby said with a shake of his grizzled head, ". . . well, I don't fancy having my neck stretched out like a turkey's. Of course, with a wind filling her sails, the *Sea Dragon* can—" He broke off, cocking his head toward the street as he heard the jingling of a harness and the sound of carriage wheels rolling to a halt against the cobblestones.

"Guests, Cap'n," Kirby muttered, thinking of the china cups piled high in the kitchen from the last visit, which would surely have to be rinsed out if the visitors were female, in order for tea to be served.

Kirby peered carefully around the edge of the velvet hangings, then gave an audible sniff of disdain which left Dante in little doubt about the sex of his visitors.

"'Tis Mistress Helene Jordane and her aunt, the old biddy," Kirby mumbled to the captain, as he stepped back from the window. "Better be washing a couple of cups, for the two of them will be staying for tea. Hate cutting into my freshly baked trifle, that I do," the little steward said, thinking about that lovely spongecake soaked in wine and covered with cream and almonds.

"Last time the two of them came to call they stayed past what was proper, and that aunt of hers ate a whole plateful of damson tarts," Kirby grumbled as he made his way to the door. The heady scent of brandy lingered in the room behind him. "Uppity females, the two of them. Actin' like they be royalty just because that old biddy's husband is a well-heeled merchant. Think they be blue bloods, they do. Humph! Not likely," Houston Kirby snorted. "That young widow actin' like she was some fine high-bred lady, when she's no better'n some wh—" Houston Kirby's unfinished word hung in the silence of the room like the blade of an ax, which he now could feel edging closer to his own neck. "Beggin' your pardon, m'lord; I had no cause to be saying that," he apologized nicely, although privately he was of the opinion that Helene Jordane was not good enough for the captain. That young woman had plenty of smiles when she wanted something, but as soon as a fellow's back was turned she could be a vicious little guttersnipe. She hadn't been so sweet and ladylike when the captain had been out of hearing. In fact, she'd tried to give Kirby orders in his own kitchen, which still made him smart with indignation when he thought of it.

Aye, she had acted the fine lady, and now she was ruing the day she'd thought herself too good for the likes of Captain Dante Leighton. Kirby chuckled quietly. Aye, 'twas stuck good and tight in her craw, 'twas, finding out that her smuggler captain was really a marquis. Ah, pity 'twas he'd missed seeing young madam's face when she'd found that out. She could've had the captain, at one time, that she could've. But young madam thought to do better for herself in London town, yes sir. Well, 'twas the way of fortune, that it was. Kirby smiled inwardly, thinking that Mistress Helene Jordane deserved whatever she got out of life, but that her life would not include becoming the Marchioness of Jacqobi.

"You needn't worry about your trifle, Kirby," said Dante Leighton, stopping the little steward in his tracks, "for I shan't be receiving any more guests today. I've suddenly grown quite fatigued."

A wide grin of devilish amusement settled on Houston Kirby's face, for he'd been a wee bit afraid the captain might be falling into young madam's outstretched arms again, which was something he'd hate to see happen, yes sir. "Aye, Captain. I'll tell the ladies you're not receiving visitors," Kirby repeated with relish. "Of course, the ladies are rather determined, especially that aunt of hers. S'pose I could say you're not feeling well?"

"Say whatever you like, Kirby," Dante told him. "But keep them out of here," he ordered emphatically. "Tell them I'm in the tub. I really don't give a damn, so long as they leave."

"Aye, Cap'n, that I will. You may leave it to my lack of discretion," Kirby promised, his eyes twinkling with the anticipated pleasure at turning young madam away from the door.

Dante sat for a moment in continued contemplation of the fire; then, when he heard the carriage pull away, he stirred himself. He thought of that excuse of a bath and decided that a soak in a tub of hot water might not be so bad an idea after all.

In less than half an hour, Dante was soaping the sweat from the wiry hairs covering his chest. While he was soaking in the hot water, his aching ribs seemed to ease and some of their tightness around his chest disappeared. Kirby had just poured another bucket of hot water into the tub and placed several towels before the fire to warm, before he'd disappeared to continue the preparations for dinner. But, as always, Houston Kirby was the ever-efficient, perfect valet; not only had he laid out breeches and shirt, but on a tea table within convenient reach of Dante's outstretched arm, he had placed a glass of brandy.

Dante sighed in satisfaction after he'd dipped his head beneath the surface of soapy water and rubbed his curls into a fragrant lather. Ducking under again, he rinsed them clean, shaking the dripping water from his face. When he heard the door open, then close, he held out an imperative hand.

"Kirby, hand me that towel. I've got some of this damned soap in my eyes," he said, squinting against the suds stinging his eyes.

A soft towel, warmed by the fire, was placed in his outstretched hand. With a muffled thank you, Dante dried his face.

"What the devil!" he swore, jerking upright when he felt a soft kiss pressed against his brow; then the soapy water slopped out of the tub as he abruptly sank back down. "Helene," he said without surprise, as he gazed up at the now-startled woman who, only moments before, had been smiling in smug satisfaction at having outmaneuvered Dante's officious little steward.

"Dante! Now look what you've done!" she cried out with growing dismay, as she stared down at her soap-stained gown. "I had this gown created especially for me in London. There isn't another one like it in all of the colonies. And now 'tis ruined. I wore it just for you, my love," she added, as she ineffectually shook out the red satin material.

"If you sneak up on a man while he is bathing," Dante replied unsympathetically, "you are liable to get more than you bargained for."

"Is that a promise?" Helene asked with a seductive smile that Dante knew only too well.

He eyed her thoughtfully, noticing not for the first time the new hairstyle she had affected since returning from London. Her naturally black hair was now hidden under a cascade of artificial, powdered curls that were styled in one of the highest coiffures he had ever had the misfortune of witnessing. He truly wondered how she managed to keep that haughty tilt to her chin under so much unaccustomed weight. Helene Jordane was of Huguenot ancestry; her grandparents had fled the religious persecution of Protestants in France during the late seventeenth century. She was a beautiful woman with ebony eyes and ivory-tinted skin. Her beauty was exotic and had served her well in this subtropical colony, where the summer's heat made less colorful beauties wilt into insignificance beside her more flamboyant figure.

Helene Jordane had blossomed like a dusky rose in this uniquely European-flavored city in the colonies. And, as a young widow, she was far removed from all of the reputation-saving restrictions placed on most unmarried young women of Charles Town. For if they desired a change in their status as single women, their reputations had to remain unsullied. Helene Jordane, however, could pursue her pleasures as she wished, as long as she went about her liaisons discreetly. She was not completely above reproach, and indeed, there were many in Charles Town who would have enjoyed seeing the arrogant Helene besmirched by scandal.

"Well? How do you like it?" Helene inquired coyly as she spun around for Dante's inspection, her satin skirt and petticoats billowing out to reveal slender, silk-clad calves. On her feet were red satin slippers, with diamond buckles on them that winked expensively at the man sitting in the tub.

"Very nice," Dante commented.

"That is all?" Helene asked with a tight laugh. "Do you know what this gown cost me? The prices in London are extortionate. I could have had my own seamstress here in Charles Town make me a hundred gowns for what this one cost me."

Dante smiled. "Yes, that may well be true, but none of those would have been made in London, which is what you are paying for, is it not? You want your friends to know that you are wearing a fashionable London gown. To see their envy makes it well worth the expense, does it not, my dear?"

"How well you know me, Dante, my love," Helene responded warily, not caring overmuch for the heavy sarcasm in his voice.

"How did you get in? I'll wager it wasn't with Kirby's assistance," Dante said.

"I came in through the garden gate. The latch is broken, but then you haven't forgotten that I *have* used it before. That little busybody steward of yours never even saw me. Not that it would have mattered, for I hardly thought to find the doors barred to me. You *were* expecting me, were you not?" Helene laughingly demanded, her tone implying that there had never been any question in her mind about her welcome. "However, 'twas a good excuse to get rid of Tante Marguerite. If you hadn't had the foresight to beg off, we'd still be sitting downstairs with Tante Marguerite acting as chaperone. This is far nicer, is it not, *mon cher?*" Helene asked, leaning closer to the tub. Her lace-edged décolletage gaped wide and revealed her pink breasts to Dante's leisurely perusal.

Staring deeply into his pale gray eyes, while her own eyes glittered with a variety of emotions, Helene whispered against his cool lips, "Why don't you have that steward of yours bring our dinner up here where we shan't be disturbed? You can't know how much I've missed you, Dante," she said huskily, her lips caressing his hard cheek, then lingering against his ear while her tongue tickled the sensitive skin. Her palms moved across his shoulders as she sought to draw him closer to her breast, but Dante was not aroused by her sudden display of passion. With little warning, he rose from the cooling water, forcing her arms to fall away from him.

Helene bit her lip in vexation, for things were not going as she had hoped they would. But given time, she thought as she stared boldly at his beautifully proportioned body and noticed how his muscles rippled like silk across his chest and shoulders when he reached out for another towel, Dante Leighton would once again belong to her. If a man could be described as beautiful, then he was, Helene thought. With a sigh, she watched him wrap the towel around his narrow hips, hiding from her ardent gaze that portion of his body which had the power to send her into an ecstasy she had seldom experienced. Certainly, she had not experienced it with her late husband, who had been a wealthy merchant, an old crony of her uncle's, and almost forty years older than her sixteen years when they'd wed. He had been a good husband to her, lavishing gifts and affection on her, but when he'd made love to her it had been solely to satisfy his own lusts, certainly not to give her pleasure. He had always left her feeling unfulfilled, and with a dangerous desire to seek further pleasures elsewhere.

But never had she felt that emptiness when she was with Dante. He knew how to love a woman, how to satisfy all of her needs. And she ached now with an insatiable need for him. It had been far too long since he'd held her in his arms and caressed her until she'd begged him to take her.

As she stood there, stunned by her own feelings, she watched as Dante began to walk away from her. Then, as if this were a sudden foreshadowing of her own future, she hurried after him, an almost uncontrollable lust for both the man and his title making her feel faint.

"Dante!" she groaned, her voice barely audible. But he had heard her, and he turned, his pale gray eyes halting her headlong flight.

"Yes?" he inquired politely, as if he were greeting a casual acquaintance on the street, rather than his former fiancée and lover.

"We have to talk, Dante. *Mon cher,* please, there is so much I have to say, to explain," she pleaded, her voice wobbling tearfully.

"We have no more to say to one another, Helene," Dante said, unmoved by her imminent tears. "As you can plainly see, my dear, I am hardly dressed for an extended tête-à-tête," he reminded her, drawing her attention to the scrap of toweling draped around his waist.

"Dante," she breathed, unwilling to accept defeat now that she'd finally gotten a few moments alone with him. Ever since he'd returned from the Indies, and she from England, he'd been blatantly avoiding her. If only they could spend an hour or two together, alone, with no one interrupting them, she knew she could convince Dante of her devotion.

"It's no good, Helene," Dante said harshly, as if he'd read her mind. "You made your decision when you traveled to London in search of that title that seems to mean so much to you. But while you were there, you discovered some very disquieting news that sent you scurrying home in hopes of retrieving something you had carelessly thrown away. Well, my dear," Dante said shortly, his words chilling and implacable, "it's too late."

"No! Dante, no, 'tisn't!" she cried. And rushing forward, she tried to fling herself against his warm body, wanting the touch of his bare skin against hers. Dante held her off easily, however.

"You came to me and told me that you were carrying my child. You were desperate and you were frightened, but you needn't have been, for I would not have abandoned you, Helene. I offered you my name. A name that I have always been proud of, and one that I thought you would not be ashamed to bear." Dante was speaking quietly now, but his words cut deep.

"I remember thinking at the time that you did not seem overjoyed at the prospect, but I allowed for the fact that you had naturally been suffering a great deal of uncertainty as to your future, and the future of the child you were carrying. But you accepted my offer, did you not, my dear? And so, with your future and your reputation secure, you returned to your uncle's home and began the heady preparations for our marriage. I even accompanied you, as a good fiancé should, to countless affairs held in our honor, and you must admit, my dear," Dante said with a mocking look, "that I was most accommodating."

"Dante, please, I—" Helene began, a worried look settling on her flawless features as she anticipated his next words.

"No, please, my dear," Dante interrupted, "allow me to finish, for it promises to become most interesting and enlightening. For, unbeknownst to you, your uncle had been planning—partly as a surprise for you—a trip to London. But now that you were marrying, you would not be able to accompany him as he'd originally intended. He was also going to tour Paris, a city you had longed to visit. My, my," Dante said, his voice full of mock sympathy, "that must have stunned you, my dear."

"Well, of course I was disappointed," Helene agreed. "But more so for Uncle than myself, for he's always been like a father to me. After all, he and Tante Marguerite practically raised me. He was so looking forward to showing me London, and he does have quite a few connections over there. I'd only been once before, and that was with my husband, and he spent all of his time in warehouses and down on the docks, while I was cooped up in an inn for most of my visit. Besides, he didn't know anyone of importance," Helene said petulantly, still smarting with the memory of that first visit to London.

"Precisely, my dear, for now you had the chance to return to London under very different circumstances. As a young, attractive widow with an important uncle, you would see a very different side of London than before. You must have had several sleepless nights full of indecision, for the lure of London must have been great. But you did have one, very big problem, didn't you? For how could you possibly arrive in London to dazzle and beguile those lords when you were well-rounded with child? You would never ensnare a rich and titled husband while carrying another man's child. So you decided to take drastic measures, did you not, for you were determined to have that trip to London."

"W-whatever do you mean, Dante?" Helene gasped, her heartbeat pounding deafeningly in her ears.

"Was it some caustic herb that you dissolved in a cup of tea? Was it bitter to the taste? You must indeed have been desperate to take so strong a drug, knowing that it would cause you to miscarry, and perhaps do irreparable damage to your own health," Dante said curiously.

"No! Dante, no! Why, where on earth did you get such an idea?" Helene demanded with a fine show of scorn. "How could you think such a thing of me? I couldn't do something like that to you after you had offered me your name. After I recovered from my initial surprise, I wanted your child, Dante. More than anything else in this world I desired it. Oh, how can you be so cruel? After all, *I* am the one who suffered the loss."

"You did not wish for *my* child to grow within you, my dear, no more than you ever wished for my name.

At least," Dante paused twisting his lips grimly, "you desired no flowering seed from our coupling until you discovered you would have been the Marchioness of Jacqobi if you had taken my name. But, at that time, I was merely a smuggler and an adventurer in your eyes. And you, my dear, had much higher aspirations, although while searching for that title, you were more than willing to make use of my services in bed. And when you thought all was lost, then and only then did you think my name good enough to take as your own. However, when you saw another way out, and one that might further your ambitions, you very conveniently forgot your sea captain lover and his child."

"No, 'tisn't true, Dante!" Helene cried out beseechingly, hot tears of frustration coursing down her face. "You have it all confused. Oh, love, you wrong me, truly you do. I lost our child naturally. I swear that I did. You may ask my doctor if it is not the truth. I-I was dreadfully ill. Why, I nearly died. Oh, Dante, I was so happy when I discovered I was going to have your child. 'Tis what I have truly wanted for so long, but in secret. I know that you always thought I was not interested in marrying you, but I only let you think that because I knew that you did not wish to take a wife. I tried not to let it matter to me because I wanted to be with you regardless of what it cost me personally. I disregarded my own feelings for so long, but when I discovered that I was carrying your child, well," Helene paused in her confession, as if at a loss for words, "I could no longer accept the difficult situation I found myself in, and I had to come to you. And you, like the gentleman you are, offered me your name. I was so ecstatic, so full of love for you."

Helene stared into the fire, as if lost in her thoughts. And troubled thoughts they were, for a slight frown creased her brow. "But then I lost the child, and I knew in my heart that I couldn't force you into marrying me. There was no longer any need for it, even though it was what I wished for more than anything else in this world," she admitted, tears muffling her voice.

"There was no longer any need for your gallantry. I

spared you, Dante," she continued. " 'Twas a great sacrifice for me to give you back your freedom. I only did it because I *did* love you so dearly. I was suffering so much that it seemed the perfect solution to accompany my uncle to London. I couldn't bear to be here with you any longer, knowing that I had lost you," Helene whispered, glancing up from lowered eyes to assess Dante's expression.

Dante was smiling, unpleasantly so. "Quite a performance, my dear. You should really have stayed in Drury Lane and gone onto the stage, for I'm sure most people, could they have heard you just now, would have been brought to tears. There is, however, one small detail that you neglected to mention," he informed her, his gray eyes paling into icy hardness.

"What do you mean?" Helene asked curiously, for he couldn't possibly know anything. Only one person besides herself knew the truth.

"People say that fortune smiles upon me, for I seem to have uncommonly good luck at times. And, in this instance, I am inclined to agree with them, for I had something happen to me by chance," Dante told an oddly silent Helene. In her mind, his contemptuous expression was a premonition of something worse to come.

" 'Twas on the Tuesday before you broke off our engagement. I happened to be coming back from the docks, when I spied your beautiful face in the window of a carriage rumbling into a part of town I was rather surprised to think you had business in. And so, being a concerned fiancé, I followed you, my dear," Dante said quietly.

Helene could feel herself blanch. "You followed me? How very considerate of you. I'm sorry I didn't know."

"Yes, I imagine you are," Dante agreed. "However, I discovered that I had worried needlessly, for you are a very resourceful woman, Helene. In fact, I am constantly amazed at the knowledge young women of fashion possess, for who would have thought that a decently brought-up young lady like yourself could possibly know about Madame Lasomier? I suspect that her past would really be best left alone, for I've heard quite a few strange tales about Madame Lasomier and her activities in the islands. I must say, my dear, that you were either remarkably brave or in ignorance of her unsavory reputation, for you walked without hesitation into her shop," Dante said, with a glance of mock admiration at the flushed Helene. "I was so concerned for your safety, as well as being a bit curious, that I followed you almost to the door.

"You would have found it quite amusing, my dear, for there I stood in the shadows of the courtyard, guarding you, or so I mistakenly thought, when to my disbelief I saw you drink down a potion that Madame Lasomier had brewed especially for you. I was about to rush in when you very calmly handed over a pouch of coins, saying quite distinctly, 'This had better work, old woman, or I'll see that you're run out of the Carolinas, and the wilderness won't even be a safe place for you to hide from me.' But you needn't have worried, for she assured you, did she not, that it had worked on countless women before you. And, indeed, she was correct, was she not, my dear?" Dante demanded coldly. "Several days later, I received your curt little note informing me that there would now be no need for a marriage between us, and that you would be departing for London within the week. You also said that there would be no further need for communication between us. You got your money's worth, did you not, for there was no longer any troublesome pregnancy for you to have to worry about."

"No! Dante, you are wrong! Yes, I did go to see Madame Lasomier, but not for the reasons you think I did. I went there because I had heard that Marie Lasomier could assure an easy birth and healthy baby. I wanted our child to be born strong. 'Tis the only reason I went there, Dante," Helene tried to convince him. "Everything I have ever done has been for you."

"I wonder how much you paid Madame Lasomier," Dante said speculatively. "Whatever the amount was, I paid her substantially more, my dear. And she was only too willing to tell me the truth of your visit. What you must remember, my dear, when dealing with people like Madame Lasomier," Dante said in soft-spoken tones, "is that they have no loyalties, and information is sold to the highest bidder. And in this case, I was the highest bidder."

"The old woman lied! She only told you what she thought you wanted to hear. She wanted your money, Dante. Oh, please, *mon cher,* all of this bitterness is quite unnecessary. You've misconstrued everything, although I must shoulder some of the blame for it, for I led you to believe that I did not wish to marry you when I lost the child. But now that I've explained the situation to you," Helene said with a trembling smile intended to soften him, "and declared my love, I don't see why we are standing here arguing. 'Tis just your injured pride that is keeping us apart."

Dante shook his head. "No, my dear, 'twas your greed."

Helene seemed momentarily stricken by his words. "Dante, please, listen to me. When I was in London I missed you so much that I ached for you. I discovered that I couldn't go on being noble, and that I had to return to try and patch things up between us. I would have come sooner, but my uncle had business to conclude; otherwise, I would have returned on the first ship sailing to the colonies."

"You returned, to put it quite bluntly, my dear, because as a mere colonial, you came off second best in London. You had gone there with very high expectations, but you were in for quite an unpleasant surprise. I imagine that there were not too many dukes and earls begging for your hand in marriage, no matter how refreshingly beautiful you might have seemed to their jaded tastes. And then, much to your horror, you discovered that you had let slip through your fingers the one titled gentleman who had offered you marriage. That must have cut you to the quick, my dear. I honestly can feel some pity for you. 'Twas a grave miscalculation on your part, Helene, my sweet," Dante told her, his pity now humiliatingly evident.

This was almost too much for her to bear. Already, much to her ever-growing humiliation, Helene had found herself the object of carelessly smothered titters from townspeople for having spurned the attentions of Dante Leighton, a man whom everyone had assumed was merely a smuggler of contraband. Who would ever had thought that he was actually a marquis? When she thought of what she had learned in London about him, she wanted to scream with rage at having been such a fool. She could have had everything. If she had married Dante Leighton, then today she would be the Marchioness of Jacqobi. She could have escaped this colonial backwater and gone to live in unsurpassed elegance and splendor in the heart of civilization. As a titled lady, nothing would have been denied her, Helene thought. Damn! What a fool she'd been! For not only was Dante Leighton rich and titled, but he was also one of the most handsome men she'd ever met. She had to get him back again, she just had to!

She had to admit that it was partly her own vanity and lack of discretion that had caused this predicament. Never had she imagined that she could not win Dante back. She had been stunned by his cold reception upon her return, even though she had been prepared for a slight coolness. She knew she had left him alone to face all of the curious stares and snickering remarks. But she'd had her explanations so carefully planned, almost believing the lies herself, that she'd never anticipated failure.

Of course, who would have thought that Dante would follow her to that horrible old woman's shop? But it was still her word against that ancient crone's, and, as Dante had said, Madame Lasomier had a bad reputation. Eventually, under the proper circumstances, she would have Dante begging her to marry him, Helene thought, her seeming self-confidence born from a desperation that she refused to recognize.

"I do not understand why you persist in being so difficult, Dante, for nothing has changed between us. Why can't we just forget about these little unpleasantries?"

Dante eyed Helene in disbelief, amazed that she could be so thick-skinned. As he stood silently contemplating his former mistress, he felt a slight draught, and glancing toward the door, could have sworn he saw it pulled quietly shut.

"The difficulty, my dear, lies in the fact that *you* seem to think that I am different. Well, the unpleasant truth for you, madam, is that I am still the same Dante Leighton, captain of the *Sea Dragon,* as I was when you sailed off to London. That has not changed, nor will it for quite some time. You seem to be laboring under the misguided assumption that my being a marquis in some way changes our relationship. But it does not, madam. We are finished," Dante said emphatically, a cruel light entering his eyes as he added, "and 'twas you who took measures to insure that."

Anguished anger began filling Helene's dark eyes as she realized that Dante Leighton was not going to forgive her, at least not tonight, and that unless she acted, her coveted title would slip out of reach forever.

"Dante, don't say that. I-I-I—" Helene began, only to have her words cut short by a sneeze. Reaching into her bodice, she produced a delicate lace handkerchief, which she held to her nose while she sneezed several more times. "As I was saying, I think we both need time to think more clearly about our feelings for each other. In fact, since we are being honest with one another, how do you think I felt to discover you were the Marquis of Jacqobi? I felt quite the fool, let me tell you. I think, under the circumstances, considering you had asked me to marry you, that you owed me the courtesy of confiding such information to me." Now Helene was berating him, putting herself in the role of the injured party. After all, how different her situation would be today had she known the truth about Dante Leighton.

"You don't know what it means to a woman to know that she has a secure fortune. To know that her children will be well provided for is something she longs for, but seldom succeeds in attaining. You say that you are still a sea captain. Well, that is hardly a comforting thought for your wife to live with, never knowing if you will return from one of your journeys. You lead a very dangerous life, Dante; in fact, at times I've thought you thrive on danger. But it is quite a different story when you have to sit here and wait for someone to come home. I've had to take many things into consideration when planning my future. After all, Dante, my late husband's estate is not going to last forever. And I'm afraid Uncle Edward is going to live another fifty years. I've never seen a man of his age so disgustingly hearty. I have to think of myself. You do understand my reasoning?"

"Indeed I do, my dear. But if, as you claim, you love me so desperately, then shouldn't that love conquer all obstacles? I'm afraid yours is a bit faint-hearted. That is why I suggest you look elsewhere for your future husband, for I shall not change my ways, nor do I suspect that you shall, either. We are too much alike, my dear," Dante told her as he spread out his palms to the warmth of the fire. The flickering light danced across his chiseled features, which were, at this moment, expressionless as a statue's.

"I've been accused of being an opportunistic, fortune-hunting bastard, as well as a few less flattering descriptions," Dante admitted. A sardonic gleam entered his eye as he added without hesitation, "and you, my dear, are a cold-hearted bitch. We make quite a handsome pair, but hardly an honorable one. We have enjoyed the pleasure of each other's company in the past, but I fear we now know each other too well for either of us to be comfortable with the other, and certainly too well for further lies and pretenses. And since there is no longer any need for a marriage between us," Dante told her indifferently, "I think it would be wisest for us to pursue our pleasures elsewhere."

Nervously, Helene moistened her dry lips, her frustration showing itself in the tapping of her red satin slipper as she stared at an apparently inaccessible Dante Leighton. But Helene Jordane was not one to give up, or to admit defeat when she wanted something, and she wanted Dante Leighton.

"Your detractors are right, for you are a bastard at times," she told him mockingly, making a concerted effort to appear unconcerned by his rejection. Hiding her fear and dismay, she continued almost conversationally. "I shan't even try and reason with you when you are in one of these stubborn moods of yours. 'Tis only your pride which is smarting, my love," she accused him, with

a short laugh that hung in the frigid air between them.
"And, Dante, *mon cher,* you've lain in my bed far too
long for you to find satisfaction with another," she
warned, a look of remembered passion flashing in her
dark eyes as she tried to fan the flames of his memory as
well. "You'll soon tire of playing the gentleman with
these quivering Charles Town virgins, and since you are
quite fastidious, I doubt you'll spend much time in the
local bawdy houses. You'll come back to me, Dante,"
Helene told him, her smile confidently provocative. " 'Tis
just a matter of time, and I have all the time in the
world. In fact," she added, her chin raised challengingly,
"I shall be accompanying m-my uncle t-to the country.
I-I'll be g-gone," she tried to say as she fought off a
sneeze. But she was unsuccessful and fell into a fit of
sneezing.

" 'Tis that damned cat! He's in here, isn't he? You
know I can't abide those dirty creatures. Whenever
they're around, I-I-I," she said and sneezed again, "I go
into a fit of sneezing. Oh, damn! I'll be breaking out into
blotches soon," she complained, worriedly examining her
pale shoulders for a disfiguring rash.

"I would suggest then, my dear Helene, that you'd best
leave," Dante suggested with solicitous concern. "Is your
carriage nearby? If not, 'twill be my pleasure to provide
mine," he offered generously, his dark lashes masking
the laughter in his eyes, as he caught sight of Jamaica
slinking through the shadows, seeking the warmth of the
fire.

"Yes, I must l-leave at once, o-or 'twill take me days
to get rid of these damned blotches," Helene agreed
readily, willing to end their conversation for the time
being. "I'll wait in the courtyard for your coachman. I-I
must g-get some fresh air," she said huskily, on the verge
of another fit of sneezing. Quickly, she retrieved her
cloak from Dante's bed, and with a swishing of skirts,
approached the man standing indolently in front of the
fire. Although wearing only a brief towel slung carelessly
about his hips, he seemed completely at his ease, an
amused smile curving his lips as he watched her come
toward him.

Helene halted before him, her eyes reflecting the burning flames of the fire as she stared at him longingly. Standing on tiptoe, she pressed her half-parted lips against his, and even when his lips remained unresponsive to her, she continued to kiss him, until finally she drew back with a look of heart's-ease. She alone knew how much effort it took to display that look. "Something to remember me by, my love," she whispered. Then, with a scornful laugh, she sauntered from the room.

Dante was fastening his breeches when Houston Kirby quietly opened the door and entered the room. The steward had a rather self-satisfied expression on his face as he hurried to place the captain's slippers close at hand.

"Jamaica's arrival was well timed, Kirby," Dante commented as he slipped his stockinged feet into the leather mules.

"Thank you, m'lord," Kirby replied. "I thought he might expedite young madam's departure from the house. My apologies, but I never saw her enter, and I'm afraid I forgot about the broken latch."

Dante glanced over at the tabby lazily grooming himself in front of the fire. Then he glanced back at the little steward. "I'm not sure which of you is the more pleased with himself."

"Most likely Jamaica, m'lord," Houston Kirby responded knowledgeably. "He's just polished off a plate of giblets. And speaking of dinner, where would you like me to serve yours this evening, m'lord?" he asked, while he began collecting the damp towels, folding them neatly across his arm as he awaited his captain's pleasure.

"I'll have it in my study, Kirby. I have some charts I want to refresh my memory about."

"You'll be dining alone then, m'lord?" Kirby questioned out of habit, even though he'd already set out the service for one.

"Yes, I'll be dining alone this evening, Kirby," Dante answered absently, thinking back to his conversation with Bertie Mackay earlier in the evening. Already, the image of Helene Jordane was fading from his mind.

"You'll not be canceling the card game this evening then, m'lord?" Kirby asked.

"No, I am still expecting the gentlemen at the regular time. Oh, you might have an extra bottle or two of port on hand. Pomeroy complained that I took unfair advantage of him last time. Claimed we ran out of his favorite spirit on purpose, and that he was forced to switch to several bottles of claret instead. I swear the man is bottomless. Never seen him tipsy yet," Dante complained, as he brushed his curls dry and plaited the hair into a queue, which he then secured with a black riband.

Dante took the poker and pushed an unburned section of log closer to the blaze. When the hungry flames began to eat into the log, a surge of warmth was sent into the room. Dante stared unseeingly at the rivulets of rain water running down the windowpanes, his mind drifting several hundred leagues south of the Carolinas.

"It will be good to be at sea again, Kirby," Dante said longingly, almost feeling the movement of the sea beneath the decks of the *Sea Dragon*. "I long to sail her home, Kirby. Home to Merdraco."

"Aye, Captain," Kirby replied. But whether or not he agreed with his captain was known only to himself.

Dante turned away from the cold draught seeping in through the window frame and held his chilled hands out to the bright flames licking at the half-consumed log, a smile of anticipation gently curving the corners of his mouth.

"Aye, Kirby," he said softly, unconsciously mimicking the little steward, "within the month the *Sea Dragon* will once again be sailing the seas."

Rhea Claire Dominick awoke to blackness. With a determined effort she lifted her heavy-lidded eyes, but still there was no light. She perceived only a cold, dark dampness surrounding her. Shivering uncontrollably, she huddled inside the cloak wrapped loosely around her body. Still dazed from the numbing effects of the drugging, she hugged the soft velvet cape closer, rubbing her icy cheek against the warmth of the fur lining. A hazy memory came drifting back to her as she buried her face against the thick pile and breathed in the scent of roses clinging to the fur.

A sudden lurch of the ship to port sent Rhea tumbling against a bulkhead, her cry of pain echoed over and over again by faceless voices in the dark. As she continued to lie sprawled against the partition, an unnatural stillness about her told her that she was not alone. She stared with wide, sightless eyes into the enveloping blackness, sensing the fear and desperation of the people crowded with her below deck as an almost tangible presence.

When she realized where she was, Rhea began to feel the terror rising like bile in her throat. The pungent odor of brine and bilge water, mingling with the souring remnants of seasickness, began to fill her senses, cutting through the grogginess of her mind, which had been the last barrier against the unpleasant reality. Overhead, she could hear the heavy creaking of the masts as they withstood the slapping and filling of the sails against a freshening wind.

Rhea tried to right herself, crawling onto her knees in an attempt to stand, but she was knocked off her feet by the heaving of the ship as it struggled through the roughening seas. Favoring her wrenched knee, Rhea withdrew into the protection of her cloak, retreating from the Cimmerian atmosphere in the bowels of the ship. Her teeth chattering from the combined effects of shock and cold, she crouched in stunned disbelief, suffering an agony of both mind and body.

Suddenly, she became aware of warmth on her skin, and when she raised a shaking hand, her stiff fingers encountered the wetness of hot tears falling down her cheeks. With her chin trembling, she held back the deep groan of despair she could feel filling the numb void of her mind. A small whimper was all that escaped her tightly compressed lips, as she began remembering fragmented, nightmarish scenes.

She had been out riding with Francis and her cousins . . . . No, she thought in confusion, that had been the day before. She had gone riding with Wesley and Caroline. Yes! That was it! She remembered now, for they had been on their way to Stone House-on-the-Hill. She was going to look at the pups she'd rescued, only . . . only they had never reached Stone House-on-the-Hill.

241

Rhea pressed her cold fingertips against her throbbing temples as she recalled the carriage blocking the lane.

An involuntary cry of fear escaped her lips when she remembered seeing Wesley tumbling from his mount. She'd been kneeling beside an unconscious Caroline. Yes, she could remember all of that, but then what had happened? Rhea's breath caught in her throat as she saw again the man in the red coat coming purposefully toward her. She had tried to escape him, but she had fallen, and then . . . she could remember nothing but the suffocating blackness that had swept over her as a cloth soaked in something enervating had been held forcefully over her face.

When a thundering crack sounded overhead, Rhea was reminded of the loud report of the pistol that had felled Wesley. He was dead. She was almost certain of that, for she would never forget that look of disbelief and pain that had flashed across the Earl of Rendale's face as he fell into the mud at his horse's feet. Suddenly, Rhea wondered about the fate of Caroline Winters. Perhaps she had been kidnapped as well, and was on board ship at this very moment. It was with mixed emotions that Rhea blindly searched the darkness, for if Caroline were indeed on board, was her friend any better off than she was?

"Caroline?" Rhea whispered, her hopes of hearing a familiar voice winning out over her reluctance to discover Caroline in the same predicament as herself. "Caroline?"

"Are you all right?" a female voice asked from the gloom.

Rhea sucked in her breath, surprised, for she hadn't really been expecting a response. "Caroline? Is that you?" she asked, her voice husky from disuse.

"No." The timid denial crushed Rhea's hopes. "My name is Alys. Alys Meredith," the disembodied voice confided. "I was hopin' ye'd be wakin' up real soon. I was afeared ye was dead," the young girl's voice informed her rather matter-of-factly.

Suddenly Rhea laughed, but the sound jarred strangely against her ears, as if she were listening to a person who was losing her mind. "No!" Rhea cried out, as she heard a shuffling on the floor beside her. "Please, don't leave me. I'm not crazed, truly I'm not."

"I'm not leavin'," said the voice that had identified itself as Alys Meredith. "I was just movin' closer. 'Tis so dark and cold down here. 'Tis like bein' in a grave, I s'pose, but not near so comfortable," she said, and Rhea could plainly hear the fear in the girl's voice.

Rhea reached out a hesitant hand, unsure of what she would encounter. She struck a bony shoulder shaking with cold; the thin cloth of the cape the girl was wearing offered little comfort against the biting chill of the ship's hold. "Would you like to share my cape with me? 'Tis lined in fur and very full. There is plenty of room for us both," Rhea invited, feeling genuinely sorry for the young girl, but also anxious not to lose contact with that human voice. The moans of the suffering passengers, combined with the eerie whistling of the wind through the sails, created an inhuman wailing that assaulted the senses relentlessly.

"I never could stand bein' in the dark. I've always been afeared of it," Alys Meredith said suddenly. "Me father, he was a fine man, he was. He always let me have a candle burning until I'd fallen asleep. Sometimes there was hardly enough money to keep food on the table, but still he'd let me have me candle. He was like that, always doin' a kindness fer someone and deprivin' himself of things he should've had. The only things he ever bought fer himself was books. Loved books, he did. Should've bought himself a greatcoat, I told him that. But he never listened to sensible advice. He caught a chill, then got feverish, and then he was gone," Alys said, so softly that Rhea could barely catch her words over the roar of the ship and the sea and the suffering.

"He was all that you had?" Rhea asked.

"Aye, 'twas just me father and me. Me mum died years ago. We lived over the shop. 'Twas nice and cozy, 'twas. He was a tobacconist. We sold all types of fine tobacco and snuff to the best gentlemen in London. We had the prettiest boxes for their tobacco and delicate silver ones for the snuff. And we had pipes and lighting spills and all sorts of wonderful things. The shop smelled so good.

I used to just stand there and sniff. But, 'twas a problem gettin' them fancy gents to pay, and me father, well, he wasn't a man to be pounding on another man's door demanding payment. Reckon he should've though," Alys said sadly, thinking of the new owner of her father's shop.

"Father had powerful debts, he did. Took all the money for the sale of the shop to pay them off, and then the solicitor said that I still owed him fer handling me father's affairs, as well as a few outstanding debts. He said I'd better sign, or I could end up in debtors' prison," Alys said, her voice quivering with unhappiness.

"What was it you signed?" Rhea demanded, her own problems temporarily forgotten while she listened in dismay to this girl's tale of misfortune.

"The indenture papers," Alys answered. "I-I didn't want to be signin' it, but what was I to do? He had been one of father's best customers. Always paid his bills, he did. He took me up before the magistrate to sign it proper, and I-I was so scared," she cried, sniffing with the memory of the bewigged gentleman in black, whose harsh voice had asked her if she were willing to journey to the colonies. With uncompromising sternness, he'd told her she'd be giving up her freedom for four years and that she must serve her master uncomplainingly.

"Said 'twas a legal and binding contract that I'd signed, and 'twas no way out of it unless I bought me freedom from the master. Mr. Phelps told me 'twas the only thing to do, and so I signed. Then the captain signed, 'cause he's the one who bought me. Agreed to pay me fare to the colonies, and to feed and clothe me. They tore the paper in two, and I got half, and the captain t'other half. Got it tucked away safe right here," she confided as she thumped her chest. "When we get to the colonies, I s'pose the captain'll sell me to someone else. Maybe it'll be a merchant, since I've worked in trade, or maybe to a family who needs a good scullery. Although," she added wistfully, " 'twould be nice to be takin' care of the wee ones. Always wanted brothers and sisters, I did, but 'twasn't meant to be. Reckon it can't be no worse than in London. The captain'll find a nice place fer me," she said, her hopeful words lingering in the silence.

"And make a fine profit, no doubt," Rhea muttered beneath her breath, for she had often heard her parents speak of this system of indenture, which was at times little better than slavery. Unfortunately, not every indentured servant found a generous and kind master, and ofttimes found himself worse off than before.

Rhea frowned, thinking about what Alys had just told her. She had intended to confront the captain of this ship with her predicament; however, if the captain were in league with the man who'd kidnapped her, which meant he was involved in the illegal trafficking of bonded servants, then she could hardly expect to receive sympathy from him. In fact, she might very well find herself in grave danger, for he wouldn't care to face the criminal charges levied against him by the powerful Duke of Camareigh. And while at sea, Rhea suddenly realized, she was in his power, and safely out of reach of her father's great influence. She could very easily come to grief, and no one would be the wiser about her disappearance. She had no idea how many of the crew were implicated in her kidnapping. Also, the man in the red coat could very easily be on board right now.

No, Rhea decided, guided by an instinct for survival, she would not reveal her true identity to these kidnappers until she reached her destination, wherever that might be; then she would have the great satisfaction of seeing them beg for mercy. But none would be forthcoming. They had murdered Wesley Lawton, and she would see that they paid for that crime. His life had been so needlessly forfeited by these greedy men.

The profit in this trade must be enormous and the risks apparently minimal, since there were always the hopefuls and dreamers searching for a better life, who would temporarily sell their freedom for that chance. As well, there were the cells in Newgate Prison, overflowing with petty thieves and debtors who might be given a second chance in the colonies. But this time, those who had been greedy enough to go to Camareigh had made a terrible mistake, for surely no sane man would have dared to take the Duke of Camareigh's daughter.

Yes, Rhea thought with a slight smile, she would enjoy

seeing their faces when they discovered their gallows-destined mistake. But right now, all she could wonder about was where her own destination was to be.

"Where are we bound for?" Rhea asked.

"A city called Charles Town. They say 'tis a lot like London," Alys informed her, as if trying to convince herself that it was not a wilderness full of savages. "How long did ye sign yer indenture for?"

"I didn't sign anything," Rhea told her bluntly. "I am here against my will."

Alys was silent for a moment. "Ooh, I thought there was something a mite strange about the way ye was brought on board. But I thought ye might be sufferin' some illness."

"I was drugged," Rhea enlightened her. Then, as she glanced around at the blackness engulfing her and felt the unrestrained fury of the sea throwing its might against the frail hull of the ship, she knew a sudden pessimism of spirit. "I want you to know my story, Alys," she said quietly, as if she'd accepted the fact that this ship might become her tomb. "I want you to know who I am. And, if for some reason I do not survive this journey, I want you to be able to tell my family someday what happened to me."

"Happened to ye?" Alys repeated nervously, sensing the fatalism in her new-found friend's voice. "Nothin' is goin' to be happenin' to ye. Please, don't be sayin' such things," she pleaded tearfully, her fingers digging into Rhea's shoulder with a death grip.

"I am not saying that anything *will* happen, but I would feel better if someone at least knew who I was and what had happened to me." Rhea was trying to convince the girl, but her teeth were chattering so much that she could barely speak. "Listen, Alys. I want to go home as much as you do. I don't wish to die. I was kidnapped from my home, and I have a family that I love very much, and I know that they must be dying inside wondering where I am and whether or not I am even alive."

"I don't even know ye name," Alys mumbled, stricken by the anguish in the other girl's voice. "I want to hear ye story. Please."

"My name is Rhea. Lady Rhea Claire Dominick," she told her, oddly comforted by the familiar sound of her own name on her lips.

"*Lady?*" Alys squeaked in disbelieving awe. "Coooeee! 'Tis the truth? Ye be a real ladyship? I never met any of them before, although I did meet a lord in the shop one day. Yer father, he be a lord, then?" Alys asked breathlessly.

"Yes, he is that. He is also the Duke of Camareigh," Rhea told her, not quite prepared for Alys's squeal of excitement.

"Oh," Alys breathed, momentarily silenced by the grandness of the title. "Yer mum, she be a duchess, then? And I bet ye've plenty of brothers and sisters, too? And I reckon ye live in a grand mansion, maybe even a castle? And ye've servants, and fine silk drapes hanging from all of the windows," she said dreamily, her terrified mind escaping from the miseries of her forced confinement and her uncertain future in the colonies. "Ye must have fine clothes, m'lady, and a room all of yer own. And d'ye—" But her daydreaming words were cut off abruptly as the ship heeled sharply, threatening to upend them across the slanting deck.

Alys's screams of terror were lost in the deafening roar of the sea and the splintering of cargo, as it broke loose from its moorings and smashed against the ship, leaving a path of debris-scattered destruction. Rhea gasped in horror as she was thrown across the floor, sliding on top of a moaning Alys. They ended in a jumbled heap against the bulkhead, with other tumbling bodies careening into them.

"Ooooh, that fair cracked me head wide open, it did," Alys groaned, feeling around in the darkness for Rhea. "Hey, where are ye? Are ye all right?"

Rhea sat slumped against the bulkhead, her head in her hands as she tried to keep from fainting. She could feel the bump on her forehead beginning to swell as she fought off the nausea.

"If only I could get some air," Rhea cried. Futilely, she tried to rise, but staggered against Alys, who had found her friend and was trying to place the fur-lined cape around the two of them.

"W-where are ye goin'?" she demanded. "Ye're not leavin' me? Oh, m'lady, please. W-what are ye goin' to do? No, please, sit down," Alys beseeched Rhea. "Ye can't be goin' anywhere, m'lady."

"Up on deck," Rhea murmured. "Fresh air."

"Ye can't get up there, m'lady. They seal the hatches. No one will be allowed up there until the storm is over. And I heard tell that this time of year, the Atlantic is stormy all of the way across," Alys said. Her knowledge-able words held no comfort for Rhea, who thought of the endless days and weeks that she might have to spend be-low decks, never knowing if the icy waters of the ocean might start pouring in, never knowing whether or not their ship would make the crossing safely.

Had Rhea known then how accurate her fears were, she might well have given up all hope, for the pattern of their journey was set that day. Soon she lost count of the days spent confined in the raw cold of the damp hold, and began to wonder if she would ever again see the light of day.

It was just as well that she had decided against con-fronting the captain of the *London Lady*, for of that man she saw nothing, nor did she see much of the crew, who were kept busy aloft, climbing the masts and yards. They were always shortening and trimming the sails while the ship labored through the heavy seas, her timbers straining under the pounding of the gale-fed waves. A rum-sodden ship's doctor, who doubled as the ship's cook, paid the prisoners of the hold a visit every so often, but he seldom stayed longer than it took to make certain the sick were still breathing.

Feasting on weak tea, noisome herring, potatoes, and oatmeal did nothing to assuage the wretched condition of the passengers in steerage; in fact, it worsened with each passing day. When a dark day dragged into night, the suffering would-be-colonials knew no difference, for their eyes knew no light, nor their flesh warmth, and the hours continued to tick away with unvarying sameness.

But the blackest day of all for Rhea Claire Dominick

had been the day when she'd discovered her ring missing. She had been rubbing her hands together, trying to restore the circulation to her stiff fingers, when she had felt the bareness of her finger. The loss of so treasured a personal possession, the ring that had been given to her by her parents on her seventeenth birthday, had been almost too much for her to bear. She had borne up well enough against the freezing cold that struck deep into her bones, against the unpalatable provisions she'd been forced to consume in order to survive, and even against her worst enemy—her own fears. But this final loss nearly doused that small spark, which was all that had remained of her spirit.

Day after day she sat listless and bleary-eyed, her limbs suffering with spasms of ague. Her riding habit fit her loosely now, the waist gaping wide, while the jacket hung baglike from her shoulders. Her long golden hair fell in untidy strands to her waist, where it curled limply.

It was strange that it should be young Alys Meredith, with her fanciful dreams of grand houses and silk curtains draping every window, who should be the one to draw Rhea Claire Dominick back into the realm of the living.

At first Rhea ignored her persistent requests for stories about life at Camareigh. She had resented the never-ending questions that kept her from slipping into a welcome apathy. But Alys was not to be denied, and finally Rhea had relented and begun to satisfy Alys Meredith's insatiable desire to hear about the Duke and Duchess of Camareigh, about Francis and Robin and the twins. Rhea told her about her cousins and her aunt with the gift of second sight, about her uncle who lived in a castle in Scotland, and about Butterick, Mrs. Peacham, and old Mason. As she described the grand house of Camareigh to her awed audience of one, Rhea revisited every room in her own mind. And never had there been a more responsive, spellbound listener than Alys Meredith.

Canfield, with her pernickety ways, Rawley and her special knowledge of herbs and potions, Robin's pony Shoopiltee, and Mr. Ormsbee and his Shakespearean plays all came to life with Rhea's vivid recollections of them. And from then on she fought off the seductive sleep of death, for she no longer felt alone when her memories could keep her company.

A bond of friendship had been forged between these two girls of such disparate backgrounds, and because it was nurtured under adverse conditions, it grew strong and inviolable. And yet, because of the darkness of their confinement, if they had met on the street, they would have walked past one another without a flicker of recognition.

It came, therefore, as somewhat ·of a surprise when standing on deck together for the first time to finally look into each other's faces, although, if Rhea had seen the reflection of her own visage, she would not have known herself, for the months of deprivation had taken their toll. Her once softly rounded, heart-shaped face now had chiseled, sharply defined cheekbones and chin, while her feverishly bright violet eyes seemed far too large for her delicate-featured face. Her rose-tinted complexion now looked translucent, the skin stretched taut across the bones of her face.

She could not compensate for her loss of weight, but she had made an effort to comb her hair into some semblance of order. Even though she might feel as if she had been through the private hell of an inmate in an asylum, she had no intention of looking like a madwoman with her hair tumbling in unkempt tangles around her shoulders. She had borrowed Alys's brush and comb, which her friend had produced from the small bundle of possessions she had brought with her for her new life in the colonies, and had then braided her hair into a thick rope which hung down below her hips.

Now Rhea stared into the soft blue eyes of Alys Meredith and felt a sense of recognition, as Alys smiled at her shyly. Alys Meredith was a tall, thin girl, who would not be described as pretty by any standards, and certainly not now with her straw-colored hair hanging dankly around her gaunt face. But under normal circumstances Rhea imagined that Alys's lightly freckled face would project a good-natured wholesomeness. A childish pug nose made her look younger than her fifteen years.

"Coooeee! Did ye ever see so much water, m'lady?"

Alys exclaimed, her eyes wide with wonder as she stared around at the endless expanse of whitecapped sea surrounding the *London Lady*. "Never did believe there could be this much, that I didn't. Reckon I was better off not knowin' all of this was out here," she said nervously. Then she began to turn a sickly green as she stared up at the tall masts swaying dizzily with the motion of the ship in the choppy sea.

A tangy spindrift caressed Rhea's face as she raised it heavenward. The sun was a pale shadow of its summer self, and it was hoarding its warmth like a miser. But the silvery gray skies were better than darkness, and the bleak winds were at least fresh; the stench below finally had become overpowering and unhealthy for those too sick to climb on deck.

Rhea could feel her heart pounding with excitement, for land had been sighted, which meant this interminable voyage soon would be over. She had long ago lost count of the days, but that no longer mattered. As she stared at the hazy outline of distant land, Rhea felt a surge of triumph when she realized that she had survived the voyage, and that soon she would be homeward bound. But that was not a voyage she feared.

Suddenly someone tapped her on the shoulder, and Rhea turned to see a stranger assessing her thin face. He stood no taller than she did, and he had reddish hair swirling around his sharp-featured face. His pale brown eyes darted about in a calculating manner that reminded Rhea of a fox sniffing out its territory.

"Ye haven't fared too well this journey, but then I s'pose most folks in steerage suffer a bit. Pity, though, fer ye was a real beauty when I brought ye on board," Daniel Lewis remarked. He knew by eyeing the goods that his asking price would have to drop, and his disappointment was evident. "Of course, ye still are a pretty little thing. A mite thin, ye are, but we'll fatten ye up and git ye into some clean clothes. Yes sir, we might fetch a goodly sum fer ye yet," he chuckled, pleased by the sight of the Carolinas sitting off the *London Lady*'s bow, and anticipating with pleasure the profits he would reap when they docked.

He eyed the young girl thoughtfully, thinking it always did these kidnapped ones a might of good to suffer some on the voyage across; after all, if they were left to their misery, they were usually quite subdued and agreeable by the journey's end. The only difficulty, which was easy to overcome, was their reluctance to sign the indenture papers that made everything nice and legal. Daniel Lewis grinned, for this little chit wouldn't give him any trouble at all. It was usually the strong young men, brought on board drunk after being escorted from a tavern, who gave him the most problems. By this time the liquor had long ago worn off, and it was about now, when they smelled their freedom, that they turned mean.

"Now, I know ye'd like to git off this ship real soon, but before ye can, ye've got to sign papers," Daniel Lewis began, his smile friendly, his words persuasive. " 'Twill be the easiest way to go about gittin' ashore. So," he said with a wide grin, his hands outspread, "I know ye won't be givin' me any trouble now, will ye?"

"You had better think again, for I am not signing anything," Rhea told him with an angry glint darkening her eyes.

"Aye, well, I can understand that ye might not know how to sign yer name," he replied agreeably, misunderstanding her reason for refusing to comply with his wishes. "I'll read the document to ye, I will. 'Tis me job."

"I am afraid that you have misunderstood me, Mister Whomever-you-are," Rhea responded, her confidence growing now that she was finally facing one of her kidnappers, "for I have no intention of signing anything, nor do I intend using your good offices to get ashore. You have committed a grave error in judgment this time, Mister Fox," Rhea informed him, a smile of her own curving her lips.

Daniel Lewis seemed momentarily stunned by this young girl's elegant speech and haughty manner. A doubtful look began to grow in his eyes as he stared at this proud creature, whose disdain for him was only too obvious. Despite her pitiful appearance, she possessed a certain dignity that put him to shame, reminding him uneasily of a certain select segment of London society that dressed in silks and satins, and could, with an indolent flick of a fan, have him gallows-hanged for his misdeeds.

"I dunno who this Mister Fox is that ye be talkin' about, but 'tisn't me. Ye got the wrong man," he said quickly. "Me name's Dan'l Lewis, and I'm the supercargo on board the *London Lady*. Now, what I'm wantin' to know, is who be ye?" he demanded aggressively, knowing before she spoke that his worst fears were most likely going to be realized.

"I am Lady Rhea Claire Dominick, daughter of the Duke and Duchess of Camareigh. And you, Mister Fox," Rhea said, satisfied by the spasm of fear that crossed his foxlike face, "are implicated in kidnapping and murder."

Daniel Lewis's mouth gaped open in surprise when he heard her words passing sentence on him. "Murder!" he choked. "I don't know nothin' about no murder," he said, lowering his voice as he glanced around nervously. "I'm innocent of any wrongdoing, honest I am, and I take exception at bein' so unjustly accused of so-so-so," he stuttered, searching for the proper word.

"So malicious an act," Rhea supplied kindly.

"Aye, m'lady, if indeed ye be who ye say ye are," Daniel Lewis agreed. "I don't know nothin' beyond me duties as supercargo on board the *London Lady.*"

"He was the man who brought ye on board," Alys contributed helpfully. "Ye was carried on board senseless, so he must know somethin'," she added, taking a step backward as Daniel Lewis eyed her with a look of growing dislike.

"Yes, it might be interesting to learn who the gentleman was who shot down the Earl of Rendale, then kidnapped me from my home," Rhea remarked, watching the different emotions fleeing across Daniel Lewis's paling face.

Although it was close to freezing on deck, Daniel Lewis was sweating profusely and silently cursing the name of Edward Waltham for getting him involved in kidnapping and murder—and not just the murder of any bloke, but an earl. Lord help him, but this was turning nasty, and he wasn't sure how he was going to get out of it. If it meant saving his own neck, then he would with great pleasure inform the authorities about Teddie Waltham. As for himself, well, all he was guilty of was illegally transporting a bonded servant. A man couldn't be hanged for that, could he?

He glanced back at the young girl. Her thin face looked pinched as the cold winds blew against her, making her cape billow out around her. The daughter of the Duke of Camareigh, eh? Aye, that was bad.

"Reckon the best thing to do is to have a word with the captain," Daniel Lewis suggested. "Now I'm not sayin' I believe ye, but just in case ye be tellin' the truth, I don't want no duke thinkin' I mistreated his daughter," Daniel Lewis said with a sickly grin. Then he looked around for the familiar figure of his captain.

"Ye best wait here while I have a word with him," Daniel Lewis suggested, but Rhea caught his arm just as he was about to walk away.

"I would like to have a word with this captain of yours myself," Rhea told him firmly, not trusting the man out of her sight. Even though he wasn't the man who had shot Wesley and drugged her, she knew he might very well be mixed up in this business far deeper than he was willing to admit.

"As ye wish, *m'lady*," he said sarcastically, bowing low before her. "This way, if ye please."

"Come along, Alys," Rhea said, tugging the bemused girl with her.

"Just ye, and no one else," Daniel Lewis said, then added with a malicious look at the plain-faced girl, "unless she be the queen? Which is just as likely a story as ye bein' the daughter of a duke. Reckon ye both just got scared about comin' to the colonies. I'm willin' to forget this conversation; all ye have to do is say the word and sign this paper of indenture. There'll be no hard feelings about it a'tall," he tried one last time in a conciliatory tone. But he could tell by the set of the young girl's shoulders that she was having nothing to do with it.

"Alys comes with me," Rhea told him, unimpressed by his attempt at peacemaking. "Take me to the captain, or I'll scream the rigging down around your head."

"Aye, thought ye might be of that mind. So be it." Daniel Lewis had finally capitulated. "Come along, then."

"Where are we going?" Rhea demanded, surprised when the supercargo began heading toward the companionway.

"The captain's not on deck. Reckon he's in his cabin. So, d'ye want to speak with him or not?" Daniel Lewis asked impatiently, shrugging his shoulders as if what she did mattered little to him.

Rhea gritted her teeth as she descended once again into the darkness of the ship, her mind rebelling against ever having to return to that hellhole called steerage. With an effort she quickened her steps and followed Daniel Lewis to a closed door, waiting patiently while he knocked. As a voice bid them enter, she steeled herself to face this man who might or might not be an enemy.

Captain Benjamin Haskell eyed the intruders with an unfriendly eye, and when he recognized his supercargo standing before him, his expression became even less friendly.

"Well?" he demanded harshly. "What do you want, Mr. Lewis? I do not like to be disturbed while I am resting in my cabin. You know that, Mr. Lewis. So why have you brought these people in here to disturb my peace and quiet?" he asked, his acrimonious manner unchanged when his supercargo began his whining explanation.

"You wanted to see me, girl? Why? Answer me quickly before I lose my patience with you, girl," he ordered Rhea, his dark eyes burning into her soul. But as she stared back unflinchingly, she sensed a deep anguish in his hollow-eyed face.

As if he were now sensing her perceptive scrutiny, he stood up, towering over the three intruders. He was a giant of a man, black-browed and barrel-chested, and even though his long arms dangled loosely at his sides, Rhea could well imagine them squeezing the life out of someone.

"Well? Are you deaf and dumb?" he asked, his voice raised in something just less than a roar.

Rhea had to keep a close rein on her temper, for she had never before been spoken to so rudely. "No, sir, I

255

am not deaf nor dumb, and I can hear you perfectly well without your yelling at me. I am not accustomed to being treated in so discourteous a manner. But then," she continued, her glance resting significantly on Daniel Lewis's short figure, "I have never been kidnapped before, nor witnessed a murder, nor been sent across the sea in little better than a prison ship. No, sir, captain, you will forgive me if at times I find myself slightly speechless about what I have been subjected to."

Captain Haskell's bellowing rage was silenced by her quiet rebuttal and her refusal to be cowed. "My pardon," he said simply. "You have me at a disadvantage. May I inquire what your name is?"

Rhea swallowed her fear, for she hadn't known how this mighty man, who growled as fiercely as a bear, would react to her denouncement. "I am Lady Rhea Claire Dominick, daughter of the Duke and Duchess of Camareigh. And if, sir, you are an honorable man, you will provide me with protection from this *thing* that calls itself a man," Rhea told him, her words so full of contempt for Daniel Lewis that they hung in the air like a bad odor.

Captain Haskell raised his heavy brow, a gleam of malicious humor brightening his dark eyes as he stared at an uncomfortable-looking Lewis. "Aye, aptly put, m'lady, for I believe you can even smell the stench of his rot. Well, Mr. Lewis, what do you have to say to her ladyship's charges? For unless I'm mighty thick-skulled, she's just accused you of kidnapping her."

"Ain't so, Captain. Had nothin' to do with no kidnappin'. Don't even know where she be from, that I don't. Man come up to me on the docks with her and wants ten pounds fer me to take her off his hands. Well, now I'm a man who doesn't look for trouble, but then I'm not a man to turn down a few extra pounds, either. I reckoned she would be a lot safer on board the *London Lady* than floatin' in the Thames. Ye should be thankin' me, ye should," he protested. "Besides, I'm thinkin' she's lyin' about who she be. Lord love us, but who in his right senses would snatch a duke's daughter? Coooeee! I ain't that stupid," he said with a weak laugh. "Reckon ye might be some man's discarded mistress, eh?"

"Enough, Mr. Lewis!" the captain bellowed. "It is true, then, that Lady Rhea Claire Dominick has signed no indenture papers? She is on board my ship against her free will? You certainly don't value that yellow-streaked skin of yours very much, do you, Mr. Lewis?" Captain Haskell inquired with a grin that sent a shiver up Rhea's spine. Apparently, the captain wasn't having any of Daniel Lewis's facile excuses, although, Rhea had to admit, they sounded almost believable to her.

"I have been watching you very carefully, Mr. Lewis," the captain informed him with an undue amount of pleasure derived from the other man's obvious discomfiture. "I have documented several very interesting transactions of yours, and I have quite a complete and extensive dossier on you, Mr. Lewis. But now," he added, looking triumphantly at Rhea, "now I have a witness. And if she is truly the daughter of the Duke of Camareigh, a man I have heard stories about, then, Mr. Lewis, you are as good as hanged."

Daniel Lewis stared at his captain with an almost comical look of disbelief. He had certainly underestimated the old sea dog, he thought, glancing worriedly around the cabin, wondering where the documents about him were stashed. "I dunno what yer talkin' about," he bluffed.

"Ah, but I think you do, Mr. Lewis," the captain replied, his dark eyes burning with an inner fire. "You're so scared you can hardly stand up straight. Well, let me tell you, Mr. Lewis, just to set your mind at rest. I know about that young girl you brought on board against her will, whom you then raped and tried to force into signing indenture papers. But you didn't count on her strength of spirit, just like this young woman's, did you, Mr. Lewis? But she was not so lucky, for she did not reach me, like Lady Rhea Claire did. She took another way out, didn't she? She jumped overboard in mid-Atlantic. You killed her, Mr. Lewis, and I'll see you swinging from the gallows before I rest," Captain Benjamin Haskell promised his supercargo.

Rhea glanced apprehensively between the two dueling men, realizing that she was not the focal point of their deep-seated enmity, that it stretched back further in time, and that she was merely the catalyst for the present airing of grievances.

Alys could feel the unnatural tension in the air as well, and she moved closer to Rhea while she stared at the two glaring men. Her fingers closed around Rhea's elbow for reassurance.

"I'll see ye in hell first, Cap'n Benjamin Haskell," Daniel Lewis spat. "And I reckon ye'll be there first, so mark a place next to ye fer me, eh? Reckon all I'm guilty of is bein' a mite greedy. Brought her on board, I did, but then she was unconscious, so 'twasn't exactly against her will, was it? All I been doin' is tryin' to make a decent livin'. Nothing wrong in that, is there? Could've gotten over a hundred pounds fer her, I could've. Not too many pretty faces in the colonies. Know a lot of gents who would've liked to have her warming their beds. Yes, sir, wouldn't have minded that meself," he said with a lascivious grin at Rhea's flushed face.

"Get out of here, Lewis!" Captain Haskell ordered, his face black with anger. "I'm still captain of this ship, and you'd better remember that, for I'm still man enough to take that cobbing board to your arse. And believe me, that would give me no end of pleasure," Captain Haskell promised his supercargo.

"Aye, *Cap'n*," Daniel Lewis sneered, as he sauntered with amazing casualness to the door. "We'll see who gets beaten this time," he added. Then, glancing at Rhea and Alys, he gave a mocking bow and said, "Ladies."

"My apologies for that swine," Captain Haskell said, a deep-seated anger and hatred for the man still burning in his eyes. "I think it would be wisest if you stayed here in my cabin, Lady Rhea Claire. Once we are docked, then I will personally see you ashore, and to the proper authorities. I suppose you have no fear of repeating your story to them, and that this is not just a ploy to escape from your past indiscretions? Granted, you may well have been kidnapped," Captain Haskell told her, "and forgive me my bluntness, but if you are a whore off the streets of London, then you will find little sympathy with the court magistrates. They will be inclined to think that you got your just deserts, and in the process you will have me looking quite the fool. I warn you now, girl, if you are lying about who you really are, then I will be a deadly enemy to you."

"You may rest assured, Captain, that I am indeed whom I claim to be, and I shall have no hesitancy in speaking so to the magistrates," Rhea told him, her direct gaze convincing him of her sincerity.

Captain Haskell nodded, his unforgiving gaze moving to Alys, who was standing meekly beside Rhea. "Who's that? Not another unwilling passenger on board the *London Lady*?"

"No," Rhea responded quickly, feeling the trembling in Alys's fingers as they closed even more tightly about her arm. "She signed an indenture paper, but I would like to buy her freedom from you, for I know that she is in debt to you for her fare to the colonies. She befriended me, and I will not abandon her to the mercy of some unknown master."

Bejamin Haskell rubbed his big hand across his bloodshot eyes; he looked almost resentful as he eyed Rhea. "I had forgotten there could be such gentleness of spirit. You bring back painful memories to me, Lady Rhea Claire, and that I will not forgive you for doing. I only want to forget that fine, gentle woman, much like you. But no, you stand here on my ship and bring me face to face with my soul," he said angrily. Then, in a sudden movement, he kicked the chair aside in a show of violence that startled Rhea and Alys, who both moved quickly out of his way.

A sad expression filled Benjamin Haskell's dark eyes when he noticed them shying away from him. "I would never hurt you, little ones. Don't you know that? So long since I've shown tenderness. So long . . ." he muttered, gazing at his big, powerful hands. "Stay in my cabin," he said harshly, a black scowl replacing the expression of softness, which had flickered only briefly across his heavy face. Then he moved to the door of the cabin.

"Captain!" Rhea called out, suddenly nervous about him leaving them in the quiet emptiness of the cabin. "You will see that we get safely ashore? You'll not let him come after us?"

Captain Haskell smiled strangely. "I promise, little one. I'll be here to protect you. You've my word." Then he was gone.

"Lord, but they be strange 'uns," said Alys, succinctly summing up the captain and his supercargo. "They nearly scared me out of me stockings."

Rhea bit her lip nervously, looking much the way her mother did when the Duchess was pondering a serious question or decision. Then she said, "I feel something is dreadfully wrong here, but I'm not sure what."

"Wish we had yer Aunt Mary here," Alys said wistfully, thinking she'd sure like to meet that lady one day. And with that thought, another one suddenly hit her, and she said very humbly, "Ye didn't have to say what ye did about buyin' me freedom from the captain, m'lady. I wasn't expectin' that, fer sure, I wasn't."

"I know you weren't, Alys, but I would have it no other way," Rhea told her with genuine affection.

"T-then ye really will take me back to Camareigh with ye?" she asked hesitantly, lest it be a cruel joke.

"Yes, I meant every word I said," Rhea said reassuringly, and the girl let out a deep sigh of relief. "I'll have to borrow the money from someone, but I won't sail for England without you," Rhea promised as she pulled up a chair and sat down weakly, her shaking legs no longer able to support her.

How many hours they spent quietly waiting, Rhea didn't know, but soon her eyes grew heavy and she fell into a deep, dreamless sleep. She awoke startled, and glancing around, saw the door opening with an unnatural slowness. She staggered to her feet, her eyes still bleary with sleep, and it was then that she saw the captain, whose head was buried in his folded arms as he sat at the table, an empty bottle of whiskey tipped over at his elbow. But there was no stain spilled across the table and onto the floor, for the bottle had been empty when it had been knocked over, and Rhea could smell the whiskey fumes rising from the heavily breathing captain of the *London Lady*.

Rhea spun around, catching sight simultaneously of

Alys curled up on the captain's bunk and Daniel Lewis's rusty-colored head sticking inside the door.

"Captain! Captain, please! Wake up!" Rhea cried out as Daniel Lewis and another man entered the cabin.

"He won't hear ye, m'lady," the supercargo commented with obvious pleasure. "He's dead to the world with all of that whiskey in him."

Rhea turned to face him, her heart fluttering as she stared into his amused face. But it was the pistol he held in his hand that caused her the most concern.

"Aye, I'd be lookin' a mite concerned meself if I was ye," Daniel Lewis agreed as he stepped closer. "The poor captain," he said unsympathetically. "He can't seem to leave the bottle alone, that he can't. He's fine enough while at sea, but once we've docked, he's got a powerful hunger fer it. Never been the same, he hasn't, since his wife and daughter died of the pox while he was away at sea. Real fine gentleman 'til then, he was. Been eatin' away at him fer years now. Promised them he'd be there with them, what with his wife carryin' their second child, but he didn't make it back in time," Daniel Lewis told her, as he poked the captain's shoulder with the barrel of the pistol. "Nope, he won't be any trouble. Probably won't even remember yer pretty little face, m'lady," he said with an ugly grin. "But me and me friend, here, will."

"What are you going to do?" Rhea demanded, knowing it would be useless to plead with the man, for there was a look of deadly intent in his eyes as they lingered on her flushed face.

"First things first," he said, gesturing toward the sleeping Alys.

"What are you going to do with her? She's harmed no one," Rhea protested, hurrying to Alys's side just as the other man reached the girl and dragged her to her feet.

"M'lady!" Alys screamed, her face full of fear and confusion.

"Let her go!"

"Ow!" the man groaned, as Rhea's booted foot connected sharply with his shin.

Alys struggled free from his loosened grasp and flung

herself against Rhea, clinging to her as if Rhea would, in some miraculous manner, be able to save her.

"Lady Rhea Claire! What are they doin' here? Where's the captain?" she cried as ungentle hands grabbed her from behind, seeking to pry her loose from the other girl. "Don't let him take me, please!" she screamed, her hands holding desperately onto Rhea's neck as she struggled.

Then suddenly she was flung away from Rhea and raised screaming and kicking into the air. Rhea tried to run after her, but Daniel Lewis was holding her tightly against him, and her struggles were to no avail.

"Alys! Alys!" she called out. Her expression of terror was a reflection of Alys's as the other girl was bundled out the door.

"Lady Rhea Claire! Lady Rhea Claire, please don't let them take me!"

Rhea slumped against the arms that held her as she heard Alys's last frantic cry for help. With a little sob she stared over at the captain, her eyes accusatory. "You promised," she whispered brokenly. "You promised."

Daniel Lewis pulled her across the room, his hand like a vice around her wrist. Hurriedly, he searched through cabinets and drawers and beneath the captain's mattress and bedding, dumping ledgers and charts onto the floor in his haste.

"What are you going to do with Alys? Is she back in the hold?" Rhea demanded of her captor when he paused for a moment to look around the room for some place he hadn't rifled.

"She's gettin' ready to be sold, m'lady," Daniel Lewis chuckled. "She's in Charles Town."

Rhea suddenly realized that something was different about the ship: The wind was no longer howling through the masts and flapping the sails with loud claps of thunder, nor was there the sound of the ocean slapping against the hull in a fury. There was only a gentle lapping of water against its sides as the ship nudged the dock with the tide.

The *London Lady* had docked while she'd slept. They had reached Charles Town, and if the captain hadn't gotten drunk, she would now be free. Rhea looked into

Daniel Lewis's eyes and shuddered at the callous indifference she read in them while he was contemplating her demise.

"What are you going to do?" she asked again, preferring to know what her fate was to be.

"Anxious, ain't ye?" he laughed, his hand tightening excruciatingly around her wrist. "Well, the way I see it, the captain brought ye in here to his private cabin to have his pleasure of ye, and bein' full of whiskey, he gets kind of mean. He's got a well-founded reputation for it too. He nearly destroyed a tavern single-handed one night. Aye, won't come as no surprise to anyone to hear about the tragedy," Daniel Lewis predicted, his sly grin turning smug. "Ye see, ye grabs this pistol to protect yeself, but he won't listen to reason, and ye have to shoot him dead. Reckon ye be so scared of the consequences of shootin' the captain, that ye jump overboard," concluded Lewis with a wide, satisfied grin.

"No!" Rhea said, and tried to twist free from his grasp. With a vicious yank he pulled her closer to the table, where the captain still sat in his whiskey-induced stupor.

"I've been waitin' a long time to pull the trigger on you," he said, his eyes narrowing in contemplation of his act as he lowered the barrel of the pistol closer to the captain's vulnerable temple. But it never reached its destination, for the captain's hand snaked out and wrapped itself around Daniel Lewis's wrist in a death grip. Lewis cried out in surprise, as did Rhea, who stared into the dark eyes of the captain; their look of entreaty scorched her and she took a step backward. At that moment she felt her wrist released from Daniel Lewis's grasp.

"Run, little one. Run!" Benjamin Haskell yelled at her, his lips pulled into snarl as he staggered to his feet, lifting the astonished Daniel Lewis with him as he rose. The pistol dropped between them to the floor.

Rhea stood mesmerized by the struggle to the death being waged before her eyes. Had the captain not been drunk, the outcome would have been decided without delay, but he was slow on his feet, his wits still sluggish, and Daniel Lewis knew he was fighting for his very life with the big man, and that one mistake could cost him that ultimate penalty.

Rhea finally found her senses and fled to the door, turning for one last glimpse of the captain. Then she saw the unbelievable happening as the captain stumbled, his large form unwieldy. As for Mr. Fox, he was squirming around the larger man and managed to grasp hold of the pistol before Benjamin Haskell could catch him in another bone-crushing bear hug. Knowing he had only seconds, Daniel Lewis rolled over and pulled the trigger, firing the pistol directly into the big man's chest.

Rhea desired to witness no more than this, and she rushed up the companionway, knocking the tray out of the doctor's hands as he stumbled down, his steps already none too steady. But Rhea stopped for no one, ignoring the curious gazes sent her way by some of the loitering sailors still on board. Some voices called out to her, their words lost in the laughter that accompanied them, but she paid little heed until she heard the one she feared calling after her. With the cries of murderess ringing in her ears, Rhea fled along the dock, hearing the pounding of feet behind her as Daniel Lewis's shrill voice inflamed his mates.

"Murderess! Murderess! She's shot our captain dead, mates! A hundred pounds to the man who brings her to me!"

Rhea tripped over a coil of rope and fell against several heavy casks. She was on her feet before she could feel the pain of her skinned knees. Then, without pausing to think of anything beyond where her next hiding place would be, she moved stealthily along a line of overturned boats. When she heard the sound of approaching feet, she crawled beneath the propped-up bow of one and huddled in the concealing darkness, her mind reeling with the murder of Captain Benjamin Haskell that had heralded her arrival in Charles Town.

Dante Leighton glanced across the crowded taproom of the White Horses Tavern, his pale gray eyes narrowing thoughtfully as they lingered on the rotund figure in claret velvet. Bertie Mackay's rich belly laugh spread like ripples in a pond, as he slapped his dinner companion across the back in appreciation of a joke.

It had been almost two months since they'd had their heart-to-heart talk in his study, and Bertie Mackay was a man of his word, for since then everywhere Dante had ventured, he had felt the presence of the jovial captain of the *Annie Jeanne*.

Sometimes there was an elongated shadow at his heels, sometimes a significantly shorter one, or a rounder one, or a thinner one, but there was always the shadow of someone. It seemed as if spies were as plentiful as rats along the waterfront, if indeed the rats were not outnumbered by them. Now Dante noticed (and not for the first time) the familiar figure of the man he had seen that very afternoon lurking outside his house. This man was now deep in conversation with a grinning Bertie Mackay.

"He seems well pleased with himself," Alastair Marlowe remarked as he watched Bertie Mackay out of the corner of his eye. The rhythmic motion of his jaws never faltered on the tough piece of beef he'd been trying to swallow for the past few minutes.

"I imagine he has been just as impatient to get to sea as we have," Dante commented. "Most likely, his man there has just told him the heartening news that the *Sea Dragon* is taking on fresh water and supplies, and will be sailing by the end of the week. Kirby was on board most of the day pottering about. You know how particular he is about his personal supplies."

Alastair Marlowe lifted his eyes heavenward. "Lord help the fool who tampers with anything in the captain's cabin, or dares to mention that he put too much seasoning in the stew."

Dante grinned. "Jamaica never complains, nor has he ever turned up his nose at any of Kirby's leftovers, which secretly pleases him, I suspect. I'm afraid Kirby won't be pleased with me, however, for when I left him on board this afternoon, he was expecting me back to dine." Dante glanced down at his half-cleared plate of beef and overcooked vegetables drowning in a grease-laden sauce. "I would have done better to have complied," he decided then, grinning wryly and pushing the unappetizing platter away.

"Captain Leighton?" The polite inquiry sounded beside Dante's chair.

Dante hardly needed to glance up to know what name to call the speaker. "Captain Lloyd," Dante murmured, even before he met the other man's eyes. With a slight smile on his lips, he indicated the third chair standing empty at their table. "Will you join us in a drink?"

"Thank you, Captain," Sir Morgan Lloyd responded easily. "I had begun to despair of finding an unoccupied chair in here," he commented, placing his cocked hat on the table and taking his place. "Strange 'tis, how every chair seems to be taken when an officer of the Crown makes a move toward it. One sees fewer and fewer solitary redcoats about town anymore. They seem to think it safer to carouse in groups," he said with a curious smile, as he accepted a mug of rum punch.

Lifting it in salute to his host, he said, "Here's to a successful voyage, Captain Leighton."

Dante raised his mug and drank to the toast. "I trust it will be, what with most of the town showing an interest in my affairs."

"Ah, well, Captain," Sir Morgan said with a lopsided grin, "secrets, as you well know, are impossible to keep along the docks. Of course," he added with a glint in his smiling blue eyes, " 'tis my business to know the whereabouts of the captains and ships of Charles Town."

"I had not forgotten that, Captain," Dante reminded him.

"Heard that Bertie Mackay nearly ran aground in the straits," Sir Morgan said casually, a smile tugging at the corner of his well-shaped lips.

"Did he?" Dante asked curiously. "That surprises me, for I had thought him a far better master than that. Of course, we all become misdirected at times," Dante added, his eyes meeting Alastair's for a brief moment.

Sir Morgan Lloyd hadn't missed the exchange between the two men, and Dante Leighton knew that he hadn't. To Alastair Marlowe, this sparring between the two men was nerve-racking, and he lived in fear of saying the

wrong thing. Alastair eyed the British officer, thinking, as
always, that he was no fool. He was certainly a likeable
enough fellow, but not one who could be trusted. He was,
after all, the enemy. It was his sworn duty, no matter how
friendly he was while he drank with them now, to try and
apprehend them, sink them if necessary, should he catch
the *Sea Dragon* smuggling.

"And you, Sir Morgan?" Dante inquired politely. "You
will be sailing now that the worst of the storm has
cleared?"

"With the tide on the morrow," Sir Morgan informed
him. "I imagine there will be quite a few ships weighing
anchor."

"You will be busy, Sir Morgan," Dante remarked casually, as he glanced around the taproom at the cluttered
tables. The captains and crews were all gathered round,
swilling down mugs and goblets of ale and rum, French
wines and Madeira. Overhead, hanging from the low,
smoke-blackened beams, were several ship's lanterns,
their golden light spilling onto the gleaming pewter below.
A cheering fire added its warmth to the room, helping to
fight the chill seeping in from outside along with the
frequent traffic entering and leaving. A black pot bubbled
with something savory, which blended with fragrant odors
wafting in from the kitchen. The tavern keeper was kept
busy at the bar, filling mug after mug to brimming from a
large oaken cask. The sounds of laughter and voices
raised in song filled the room, drowning out the private
conversations between certain closely grouped individuals,
whose angry glares and hushed words showed they were
most likely discussing politics.

"Another one, Cap'n?" asked the well-endowed serving
wench, winking saucily at Alastair Marlowe as she caught
his eyes lingering on her full breasts. Their voluptuous
contours were barely covered by her lacy-edged bodice.

"Not for me, thank you, Cap'n," declined Sir Morgan
Lloyd when Dante glanced at him. "But allow me to buy
you and Mr. Marlowe another one," he offered in return.
"I have to see that my ship is properly fitted out. Perhaps
we shall be able to lift a glass or two together when you
return to Charles Town, for I would be most interested in

hearing about the outcome of your voyage, Captain. Scuttlebutt has it," he said lightly, as he stared down at an indolent Dante Leighton, "that you are going to have quite a dog fight on your hands."

Dante smiled, then laughed. "I only have a ship's cat, Captain."

"That's why I'd wager you and your *Sea Dragon* come out on top," Sir Morgan returned, a speculative gleam hardening his blue eyes. "Cats always seem to squirm out of tight spots with a couple of lives to spare. Besides, I like a good adventure yarn, and this one promises to be quite interesting, so don't let me down," he warned, picking up his cocked hat and taking his leave of them. But he'd only taken a step or two when he turned and added challengingly, "I'd hate to have the *Sea Dragon* go to the bottom without ever having crossed bows with her."

Dante smiled mockingly. "You needn't worry that I shall disappoint you, Captain. For I have every intention of returning from the Indies. However, my concern is more for H.M.S. *Portcullis* should we indeed cross bows. I hate costing the Crown good money."

"I look forward to the contest, Captain." Sir Morgan Lloyd grinned and walked away, his tall figure in its blue coat cutting a widening path through the congested room. His expression remained unreadable even though he must have overheard the rude remarks being muttered about his person. However, the sword swinging at his side was warning enough against anything more than defamatory utterances.

"Not much he misses," Alastair grumbled, watching the cocked hat disappearing out the door.

"That's why he's still alive today to challenge me," Dante replied. "However, I am not sure whether or not I'd enjoy crossing bows with H.M.S. *Portcullis*."

"You admire him, don't you?" Alastair asked, gazing at the captain, the man he himself admired.

"Yes, I do. He does his job to the best of his ability. He's a good captain and an honest one. But it is not my suspicion that we would sink him that has me concerned," Dante added with a strange glint in his eye. " 'Tis the thought that we *both* might end up on the bottom. We think too much alike for it to be anything but a draw, unless one of us has incredible good luck, or bad luck."

"Now let's have that brandy Captain Lloyd so generously bought for us," Dante said, his smile sending the tavern wench's heart plummeting into her clogs.

"Here's to our Spanish foretopman," said Dante, toasting their late benefactor. A devilish grin settled on his face as he lifted his glass to Bertie Mackay sitting at the table across the room. "And to what the future may hold."

Rhea Claire Dominick peered cautiously along the dock; her head and shoulders were revealed from her hiding place while she eyed the warehouses and wharves. Crates and barrels were stacked high, offering safety for anyone who might like to remain unseen.

She glanced up at the tall masts, bare of sail, that lined the waterfront. Countless ships were docked along its rambling length, some being loaded with supplies and cargo, others having their holds emptied. Rhea glanced around nervously, but no one had noticed her crawling beneath the boat. Nor did anyone seem overly interested in the group of men searching the docks for the runaway indentured servant who had shot down their captain. They were too busy hurrying to finish their jobs and get inside before a warm fire to concern themselves with other people's troubles.

Rhea tucked her hands into her cape, warming them against the fur as the cold sea air began filling her hiding place. When she heard footsteps approaching she quickly ducked back inside. The boat trembled slightly as someone kicked it in frustration.

"Damn! She's got to be around here somewhere! She couldn't just vanish into thin air," swore a voice she recognized as Daniel Lewis's.

"Maybe she slipped and fell into the river. Would make it easier fer us," offered another voice.

"That wouldn't help unless I knew fer sure she had," Daniel Lewis complained. "Until she's breathed her last breath, I'll be feeling a tightness around me neck. She saw me shoot Captain Haskell, and if she is really who she says she is, then she'll be able to get plenty of powerful folk to listen to her little story," he predicted. "I don't intend to have her talkin' her head off to no one. If it's the last thing I do, I'll strangle the life out of her," he promised, and Rhea could almost see the look of hatred on his foxlike face.

"Come on, let's look over there," he said. The voices faded as the men moved away. Rhea risked a glance over the top of the boat and saw the two of them stop a bandy-legged little man who'd been hurrying lickety-split along the dock.

"Ye seen a fair-haired little chit running this way? She killed our captain, and we be mighty anxious to find her. She's a runaway indentured servant, killed her master, she did. Can't have that, no sir." Daniel Lewis's voice drifted back to Rhea's hiding place.

"Ain't got no time to waste on huntin' down runaway females," the little man replied irritably. "Enough of them around to fill an ocean anyway. A lot of trouble they are, if ye ask me," he said, quickening his steps, his grouchy mutterings audible to Rhea when he passed her hiding place.

"Yeah! Well, no one was askin' ye, ye little bas—" hollered Daniel Lewis's companion after the fleeing figure. "There's some of the crew. Wonder if they've seen anything?" he asked as they moved further along the dock, gradually increasing the distance between themselves and Rhea's place.

As Rhea watched, the groups of men searching for her disappeared around the side of one of the warehouses. Then, knowing it was now or never, for they were certain to come back, Rhea emerged from her hiding place. She was making her way through a stack of barrels that towered high over her head, when a dog came shooting through the narrow space, with another one just behind him. Rhea stepped aside, suddenly finding herself in the open, and at that instant there was a horrible ruckus on the other side of the barrels.

Without stopping to think, Rhea bolted up the gangway directly in front of her. Her steps carried her to the deck, where she dropped quickly out of sight.

And just in time, too, for voices were raised in alarm, several of which she recognized.

"Damn, 'tis molasses, and all over me shoes!" someone cursed loudly.

"On mine, too. Hell, we're never goin' to find her. She could be hiding anywhere. I gotta git this off me shoes, the sticky mess."

"Come on, 'twas just a dog," Daniel Lewis told his men. "We haven't looked over there where those boats are."

"Yes we did, don't ye remember?" his friend corrected him. "We were just there."

"Aye, that we were," Daniel Lewis agreed sarcastically, "but did I see ye lookin' beneath them? Aye, 'twould be a good hiding place, I'm thinkin', and I'm beginnin' to think I'm the only one around here doin' any. Now, come on, all of ye," he ordered.

"Be with ye shortly," said one of the men who'd stepped in the spilt molasses. "Can't go nowhere with this on me shoes."

As the others moved along the dock, Rhea risked a glance down the gangway, only to draw back in surprise when she saw the two men who'd been left behind sitting there quietly smoking their pipes.

Rhea sat back on her haunches, a sigh of tired desperation quivering on her lips. As the cold wind blew off the water, her shoulders began to shake. Overhead, gray clouds were beginning to group together with a promise of rain.

Glancing around, Rhea stared curiously at the apparently deserted ship. Perhaps she could go below and get out of this wind. The ship would certainly offer her a safe refuge until the gossiping men on the dock moved on, she thought. Her teeth were beginning to chatter.

She was still debating the idea when something rubbed against her thigh. Letting out a surprised scream, she tumbled over, glancing around to see what had sneaked up behind her.

"What was that?" called one of the men on the docks.
"A woman?"

"No, probably a rat that got caught by one of them dogs."

Rhea looked down at the pale green eyes staring up at her, a tearful smile of relief crossing her face as she extended a hesitant hand for the big orange tabby to sniff. Then, as the cold nose butted against her hand, she laughed softly, and scratched the top of his head.

"You on guard duty, cat? Anyone else on board?" she asked him in a conspiratorial whisper. But his only reply was a loud, demanding meow.

"Hungry? Not as hungry as I am, I'll wager," Rhea told him, glancing around the gangway to see the two men still sitting there, their pipe smoke rising slowly into the cold afternoon air.

"Well, I don't know about you, but I—" Rhea began, looking down to where her furry companion had been. But he had disappeared. With a sigh of disappointment, she settled herself down for a long wait, thinking that those men might sit down there for hours.

But the cat had not abandoned her, for a second later she heard the padding of his feet across the deck, then his low meow, this time slightly querulous as he moved up against her persuasively. Then he walked away from her again, halting at the head of the companionway. And there he stood with an expectant look on his face, his long tail twitching in irritation at her lack of understanding.

"So, you are as hungry as I am," Rhea said, giving in to his wishes as she crawled toward him on all fours. The cape hindered her slow progress across the deck, but when she felt the first big raindrop, she hurried the final few feet, making her way, with the help of the cat's guiding meows, along the companionway. She found him standing in obvious annoyance before a closed door.

He meowed impatiently, scratching against the door as she stood there indecisively. But she heard no movement coming from within, and finally with a show of confidence she didn't really feel, she opened the door. The cat rushed past her into the cabin as if he owned it.

. Rhea glanced around the shadowy cabin, noting the mahogany paneling and fine furnishings polished to a high gloss. Beyond the stern windows Rhea could see that the rain was falling in earnest now, and that the waters were growing choppy in response to the oncoming storm.

As Rhea stood there thinking about what she should do, she became aware of an incredible odor. Her nostrils flared as she glanced around, her eyes hypnotized by a blue-checkered cloth draped across something bulky on the table. Swallowing the saliva that was forming in her dry mouth, Rhea reached out a timid hand, then snatched the cover from the plates set on the table.

She stared in absorbed fascination at the turkey drumstick sitting squarely in the center of one of the china plates. She licked her lips; for a moment her sight was clouded by faintness. Then the persistent growling of her stomach swayed her toward an act of thievery, and with no further hesitation, she reached out and grabbed the drumstick with a shaking hand, her teeth tearing into the succulent meat. She could barely swallow fast enough to satisfy her appetite, as she devoured the first decent morsel of food she'd had in over two months.

A thick wedge of cheese beckoned to her from another plate, as well as several slices of ham, freshly baked bread and newly churned butter, and even a generous piece of apple pie. A feast, Rhea told herself with a grin, as she claimed all of the food on the table as her own.

But she had been mistaken, for while she stood there satisfying her hunger, she felt the cat pressing up against her, his meows becoming worried as he saw his coveted dinner disappearing.

"Here, boy," Rhea said. She pulled off a couple of pieces of meat and handed them down to the cat who was weaving around her legs, his purring growing louder as he understood her intentions. His approval of those intentions was obvious as he quickly dispatched his share of the booty.

Her initial hunger appeased, Rhea glanced around the cabin wondering if she might find something to drink, for the cheese and bread were sitting uncomfortably high in her throat. Looking inside a small cupboard, she discovered only rolled-up charts and navigational equipment. A sea chest sat in one corner, but she didn't think there would be anything to drink in there, so she ignored it and wandered instead to another cabinet. A triumphant smile lit her face when she saw a dozen or so bottles lined up against the back, a metal bar holding them secure. With little deliberation, she selected the dustiest-looking bottle, thinking it would be the least likely to be missed.

Carrying it back to the table like a prized possession, she made herself comfortable in the captain's chair and began to pry loose the cork. It took most of her strength, but after she struggled with it for a minute, it popped free.

Holding the glass up to the bottle, she began to pour; then her eyes widened with dismay as sand filled the glass instead of wine. Peering inside the narrow neck of the bottle, Rhea noticed something there, and with a slender forefinger, she reached inside and coaxed out a piece of rolled-up parchment. Curiously, she unrolled it and stared down at an elegantly sketched map.

The legend was written in a foreign tongue, which she guessed was Spanish, as she traced with her fingertip the beautifully executed, flowery script. Delicately drawn tropical birds, sea shells, and palms decorated the corners. One Gorgonesque face blew a gust of wind from a northeast direction, and another, which was equally ugly, blew from the southwest. A painted ship sailed the seas, which were filled with sea monsters lurking in the crested waves. An elaborately drawn X had been placed among some straggly-looking islands at the base of a larger land mass.

Rhea continued to stare with interest at the map; then, as she felt the continued dryness in her throat, she began to roll the map back into the bottle. But her hands were so stiff with cold that she couldn't seem to roll it tightly enough to fit inside the narrow mouth.

She paused, thinking she heard something on deck, but it was only the rain. Glaring at the unrolled parchment, she left it and went back for another bottle of the captain's wine, vowing she'd get that map back inside the bottle if it took her the rest of the afternoon. Selecting another bottle from the rack, she held it to the fading light to make sure that it did indeed have wine inside. Satisfied, she uncorked it and poured herself a liberal amount of dark red wine. She shuddered slightly as she swallowed half of it, her thirst making her greedy for its soothing wetness, but as a warming glow began to spread through her body, she began to sip it more slowly.

Then she walked over to the big, square stern windows and sank down on the narrow seat beneath them. From there, she stared out on the sullen waters of the bay, wiping at a tear clinging to her lashes and sniffing back any more that might have fallen. Needing comfort, she reached automatically for the locket hanging around her neck, the possession that was her only remaining link with her family. It had been a constant reminder during that long voyage that she was Rhea Claire Dominick, and that her home would always be Camareigh. She had kept the locket secret even from Alys. She knew she should have shared it with her, even though nothing could be seen in the darkness of the hold, but still, she had wanted to keep it to herself. For inside the locket were painted miniatures of the Duke and Duchess of Camareigh.

It was gone! Rhea's fingers felt about her neck, searching for the familiar feel of the gold metal, but it was not there. With a low moan, she realized that she must have lost it in the struggle with Daniel Lewis, or perhaps when she'd run along the docks.

With a sob of despair, Rhea curled up on the seat, her tears falling freely while she thought about all that she had lost, and wondered if she would ever return home to Camareigh. She wondered about Alys, the girl's cries for help still echoing in her ears. She had promised her she would take her back to Camareigh with her, but she had failed, just as Benjamin Haskell had failed to fulfill his promise. But in the end, Rhea thought, as a numbness spread through her body, he had given his life for her, and that was something that not many people would have done. But it had all gone for naught, for if Daniel Lewis were to be believed, then all of Charles Town would think that she had murdered the captain of the *London Lady*.

Crying silently, Rhea slumped over in defeat. She was so tired. All she wanted to do was go home. She was startled then by something touching her thigh, and opening her eyes, she stared down into the pale green eyes of the big tabby. When she picked him up, he kneaded her lap with his paws and purred comfortingly, and Rhea buried her face in the warmth of his soft fur.

Rhea rested her cheek on her drawn-up knees, the cat cradled in between. The wine and the gentle rocking of the ship began to lull her into a fitful doze, her dreams taking her back to the gently sloping countryside surrounding Camareigh . . .

Dante Leighton was late returning home that night. After having finished the complimentary drink of Sir Morgan Lloyd's, he and Alastair left the White Horses Tavern and called in at several others, testing their skill at cards and dice as the hours disappeared with the rising of a full moon. By the time Alastair and Dante left the last tavern, the moon was riding high in the clear night sky, the thunderstorm having moved inland toward the high country.

The air was cold and crisp, almost as heady as the rum punch they'd been drinking, Alastair thought as they walked through the quiet town. Their hired carriage had been dismissed long ago, and Alastair was enjoying stretching his legs, when Dante suddenly flagged down an empty carriage that happened to be passing. Once inside, the door had barely swung shut before Dante ordered the driver to get his team moving.

"What the devil, Captain?" Alastair demanded as he was flung back against the seat, his hat flying onto the floor.

But Dante was not listening. As he stared out the window, he saw his ever-present shadow start into a run, having realized Dante's move too late. As Dante sat back against the leather cushions, his low laugh filled the coach.

"I don't suppose he's had such a long night on the town in years. I wonder if Bertie will reimburse him for his expenditures?"

Alastair frowned. "Who exactly are we speaking about, Captain?"

"One of Bertie's hirelings. They've had me under surveillance for two months now, so I thought I'd have a little fun with them tonight," Dante explained.

"Lord, but it will be good to get out of Charles Town.

This waiting is worse than foundering at sea any day. I'm glad your ribs are well healed, and the *Sea Dragon* refitted, for I don't think I could stand another week of these townspeople. I've never had so many friends, or casual acquaintances, offering to buy me drinks, not to mention other things," Alastair said contemptuously, remembering the brazen woman of the day before who had openly propositioned him. And this woman was the wife of a well-known captain who had dined with them often. Alastair shook his head in bewilderment, thinking how some people would resort to any means to get what they wanted.

Dante smiled in understanding. "Pity you didn't accept," he said.

Alastair stared at his captain through the lantern-lit gloom. "Did you?" he asked bluntly.

Dante laughed. "I deserved that. But in answer to your question, no. Not out of any special courtesy to her husband, though, for I suspect he was behind her sudden generosity," Dante explained. "I just didn't happen to care for her looks. I'll get out here," he said, tapping on the roof.

Halfway out of the carriage, he added with a grin, "Cheer up, Alastair. If our luck holds, we'll have the *Sea Dragon*'s sails trimmed and filled by the morn, day after tomorrow."

"Aye, Captain," Alastair responded with a wide, pleased grin, his good spirits restored once again as he thought of sailing the *Sea Dragon* away from the confining atmosphere of Charles Town. Then, with a contented sigh, he settled down for the rest of the ride to his lodgings.

When Dante entered his silent house, only one candle still flickered in the wall sconces, its feeble light barely reaching the first step of the stairs as he made his way up them. He had untied his stock, the lacy-edged scarf dangling loosely in front of his leather waistcoat. Yawning widely, he entered his bedchamber, eyeing with appreciation the good-sized fire crackling in the hearth, thinking Houston Kirby was indeed a man to be treasured, for the little steward thought of everything.

Dante glanced over at his bed, ready to slip beneath the neatly folded-back covers. Then he stared in unblinking incredulity at the dark head on his pillow, and at the bare shoulders just visible over the covers of his bed.

A slow anger began to burn inside of him as he walked closer to the bed and gazed down on his uninvited guest. He breathed the pervasive fumes of liquor and stale perfume, saw the pile of discarded cards strewn across the coverlet and carpet, and the crumbs of food caught in the rumpled sheets. A look of distaste crossed his face as he realized his bedchamber resembled a bawdy house.

"Helene. Helene, get up. I have had enough of your games," Dante said harshly to the woman in his bed.

But Helene did not respond. With a sigh of impatience, Dante bent over her and started to shake her shoulder, but when he heard her light snores, he drew back, preferring to leave her undisturbed in the arms of Morpheus. He glanced over at the half-empty crystal goblet and the open bottle of Madeira on the table beside the bed. A tray carrying several plates of picked-over food was set aside on another table, while in a chair near the door was a disorderly pile of discarded clothing.

Dante glanced at the cozy fire, then at the naked woman sleeping soundly in his bed, then at the tray of cold food, and a smile of cruel amusement curved his lips as he speculated on Helene's attempt at seduction. The only problem was that the guest of honor had never arrived for her private midnight soirée. And in her boredom, she had consumed almost a whole bottle of Madeira and amused herself with his playing cards, before the wine and warmth of the fire had lulled her into a comfortable stupor.

With a half-muffled curse on his lips, Dante turned his back on the bed and Helene Jordane. A second later, the bedchamber door had closed softly but with restrained violence on his departing figure.

Dante made his way unhurriedly down the stairs he had climbed just moments before, but instead of going out the front door, he turned and made his way into the kitchen in the back of the house.

"I thought you might be around," Dante commented

to the little steward sitting at the big, well-scrubbed block table in the center of the kitchen. Kirby was holding a mug of steaming coffee cupped in his hands.

The steward glanced up at his captain, a look of approval evident on his weathered face. "Aye, I was hopin' ye'd be down right fast. Didn't want yer coffee to cool," he said matter-of-factly, as he got up and handed the captain his mug, which had already been filled to the brim with the hot brew.

"You are very certain of me, Kirby," Dante retorted dryly as he accepted the proffered mug, not certain he cared to be quite so predictable.

Kirby sniffed. "No, 'twas mostly wishful thinking on my part," he admitted. "Figured if I went ahead and poured it, well, ye might just show up. Reckon I've never had a contest 'tween my coffee and a shameless woman before."

"Speaking of which," Dante began, only to be silenced by Kirby's snort of derision.

"Reckon there's no stoppin' that woman now that's she caught scent of yer title. Worse than a coonhound, she is. Reckon we gotta get that garden gate fixed," he said, shaking his graying head.

"I gather that she did not stoke the fire, nor prepare her own meal?" Dante asked, as he finished off his coffee.

"Reckon not, although I was goin' to refuse if she'd asked me to unfasten her gown," Kirby declared. "A man's got some pride, he does. I figured," he added with a straightforward stare at his captain, " 'twas yer place to be settin' young madam on her beam-ends, not mine. Probably would've tried to box me ears anyway," he speculated. "Outweighs me, as well."

Dante grinned, watching his steward rinse out the mugs, then spread the cooling coals in the hearth.

"I'll sleep on board the *Sea Dragon* tonight, or, for what's left of the night," he amended.

"Aye, thought ye might be of that frame of mind. Reckon ye're not takin' any chances of bein' compromised by young madam, 'tho, I reckon she might have thought just her bonny eyes would be enough to ensnare ye again," Kirby stated, openly contemptuous of such a ploy.

"I suppose you will be following shortly?" Dante asked, turning at the door, his expression enigmatic.

Kirby's eyebrows rose startlingly. "As fast as me short legs'll carry me, m'lord. Ye won't find me stayin' alone in the same house with that she-wolf," he proclaimed vehemently. "No, sir, I'll be along as soon as I can gather up a few things. Reckon when young madam awakens to an empty bed and empty house in the mornin', she'll be fit to be tied," he predicted. "And I don't want to be anywhere hereabouts."

"As you wish. I'll see you on board the *Sea Dragon*, then," Dante said. Then he was gone just as quietly as he'd arrived, leaving the little steward to clean up his kitchen.

Dante walked swiftly along the now deserted streets, his steps bringing him closer to the docks with each passing moment. He breathed deeply of the moisture-laden air, its cold sharpness clearing his head. As he neared a narrow lane cutting between two buildings, he became aware of footsteps echoing his. Stepping into the dark shadow of the building, Dante waited. He smiled when he heard the footsteps quicken as his own were silenced. As they grew loud, he stepped out into the path of the man who'd been following him all evening.

The man had little chance to avoid a collision with the broad shoulders suddenly blocking his path, nor time to speculate about the intent of Dante Leighton, for the bunched fist of the captain of the *Sea Dragon* connected at once with his jaw. The painful impact sent the man flying backwards into the gutter, where he lay and watched dazedly as the tall figure disappeared into the darkness.

"Who goes there?" called out the sailor on graveyard watch as Dante Leighton climbed aboard. The sailor's voice was more threatening than questioning.

"Captain Leighton, Webber," Dante called out, pleased that the young man had been so alert, for he wanted no prowlers on board the *Sea Dragon*.

"Oh, Cap'n, sir," the young sailor sighed, partly in relief and partly in disappointment at not having the chance to challenge the trespasser, for the night had been boring and quiet thus far. "Didn't know ye was comin' back on board, Cap'n. Only me, and I think Jamaica, on board the *Sea Dragon*. Though I couldn't swear to him bein' on board. Haven't seen him in hours. Mr. Kirby'd said the cat was stayin' on board. Said to leave the ol' buzzard to his tom cattin'," Webber said with an approving grin.

"All quiet, then?" Dante asked.

"Aye, Cap'n, and before that too, from what Baker told me when I relieved him. Said there'd been a bit of a ruckus on the docks, and he'd gone to see what the trouble was. But it was just some broken hogsheads of molasses, as well as some rowdy sailors racin' about the docks."

"Very well, Webber. Kirby will be along shortly, so do not mistake him for a prowler, will you?" Dante warned the watch before going below.

His cabin was dark, and fumbling with his tinder box, he struck a spark and lit the lantern swinging from the deck beam over the table.

Dante stared in silence at the disarray on the table top. The treasure map that half of Charles Town was seeking had been carelessly unrolled across the table; there were crumbs scattered over it's prized surface, and it seemed to have no more importance than the half-eaten drumstick and hunk of cheese.

Dante heard a low sigh and glanced up, a look of disbelief spreading across his face when he saw his cat curled up in the lap of a caped figure asleep before the stern windows. Jamaica opened one eye and curiously watched the stealthy approach of his captain. Then, being a smart cat with an instinct for survival, he sensed his master's unfriendly intent and decided he would be safer elsewhere. With little hesitation, he abandoned his bedmate and bolted beneath the table.

Rhea was jolted awake by the sudden movement, and opening her sleepy eyes, she found a tall, lean stranger staring down at her with the coldest, palest gray eyes she had ever seen.

As Dante Leighton continued to stand there, he felt his simmering anger begin to rise. Was he never to know

281

another minute's peace from these jackals and grovelers? By now, extortion, chicanery, toadying, and seduction had been attempted in order to win that cursed treasure map and curry favor with him, but so far all of those ploys had met with failure.

So he certainly should not be surprised at yet another act of beguilement, although, of course, until now, none had been so bold, or so reckless, to confront him on board the *Sea Dragon.*

Dante continued to eye Rhea warily, as if she were some strange creature with unknown intentions who had climbed on board the *Sea Dragon.* Her fine show of cowering fright was part of the deception, and he was not fooled, for only the most audacious of opportunists would have dared to come this far.

" 'Tis a pity, but . . ." he murmured unregretfully, his patience with playing the dupe having worn too thin to humor this double-tongued chit.

"Who are you?" the cunning brat demanded, as if questioning his right to be on board the *Sea Dragon.*

"Who am I?" Dante repeated incredulously. "Who the blazes are you?" he inquired, his silky-toned words masking what had now become a towering rage. Then, before Rhea could fathom his intent, he had reached out and grabbed her roughly by her narrow shoulders and jerked her from the seat.

She was a thin little thing, Dante thought as he held her up easily before him, her feet kicking harmlessly in the air. She was far younger than he had thought at first, but that did not dampen his anger, nor soften his scornful opinion of her. Ragamuffins like this one learned to ply their trade at an early age, and these small hands were just as nimble-fingered in lifting a purse as more experienced ones.

The devil take the insolent whelp, Dante swore inwardly, as the toe of his captive's boot struck his inner thigh in a spot far too close for manly comfort.

When Rhea saw the fierce gleam enter the stranger's eye, she realized with a sinking of her heart that she had in some unaccountable way made an enemy out of this ill-tempered man. If only she could explain to him the desperateness of her situation. Surely she could convince him of the truthfulness of her claims, perhaps even elicit his help in extricating her from her plight. There was no reason why he should not believe her, she thought hopefully.

"Please, you must help me. I am in serious trouble," she began, only to be silenced by his harsh laughter.

"Yes, indeed you are," Dante responded not at all helpfully.

"I-I can explain, truly I can," Rhea tried again.

"Can you really? Forgive me, but I doubt that very much. Do please try, though. It could prove interesting. Well, I am waiting. Come now, I haven't got all night. I would have thought you'd have this carefully rehearsed by now. I am disappointed, for I was rather looking forward to our matching of wits, unequal though I suspect it would have been," Dante taunted her, his gray eyes narrowed thoughtfully, as if trying to guess her next move. Then he released her shoulders from his vise-like grip.

Rhea rubbed her aching arms as the blood rushed back into them. She was struck dumb, unable to find a sane reason for this man's unnatural hostility toward her. She expelled a shaky sigh as her eyes met his, and she saw in their contemptuous expression the futility of trying to change his opinion of her. Her shoulders slumped in weary defeat. If only she could sit down, rest for a moment while she thought about what she must do now. . . .

Then she heard his hateful voice again, "Still at a loss for words, my dear?" queried the hateful voice. "Well, why don't I refresh your memory?" he offered helpfully, while his smile was anything but friendly. "Actually, I can well understand why you might be confused, for there are several explanations for your presence on board the *Sea Dragon*. Although I imagine I know two reasons which figure more importantly in your scheme than a sudden penchant for the captain's charms. A humbling lesson I have learned only too well of late," Dante mused.

Captain, thought Rhea dully. Now she knew he would

never believe her story over the lies Daniel Lewis was spreading about her, especially when concerning the death of a fellow captain. Perhaps that was why he was so suspicious of her. He had already heard the allegations against her and perhaps intended to take her back to the *London Lady*. With growing panic, Rhea realized she would never have a chance then to tell the truth.

"Now," the captain's voice continued, "shall we consider your first explanation, since it is the simpler of the two? Most likely you heard, during your wanderings along the docks, that I had discovered a treasure map, which you thought you would like to have a look at yourself. Maybe you had even planned to sell it to the highest bidder?" he asked conversationally. "Thought you would make a tidy little fortune, did you? But you miscalculated, because I returned to the *Sea Dragon* unexpectedly. I hardly thought at the time that I would be thankful for the circumstances that sent me here, but now I am most grateful to a certain young woman."

Rhea stared at him as if he were out of his mind, for nothing he was saying made any sense to her. "I do not know what you are talking about," she told him nervously, thinking the man might be crazed. "Let me go, please. I will not trouble you any longer."

"Oh, no, we still have far too much to discuss, haven't we?" he asked in a dangerous tone, his eyes glowing with malice.

Rhea stared up at his chiseled face and shuddered, for he looked like the devil himself as he glared down at her with those pale gray eyes. "I-I haven't done anything wrong, despite the lies you may have heard about me. I do not know who you are, except that you say you are the captain of this ship, but that does not give you the right to accost me in this manner. I am trespassing, I admit it. So take me to the authorities. I demand it!" Rhea challenged him, deciding suddenly that she would far prefer to face their condemnation than this madman's.

"Yes, you would like that," Dante responded sarcastically. "Then your cohorts could waylay me while I was escorting you to gaol. I would most likely end up with a knife in my back for my efforts. Odds are you work with a gang of petty thieves, and the disturbance my man mentioned to me was merely a diversion to get you on board the *Sea Dragon* and give you a chance to find that treasure map."

Rhea frowned over these words and his constant talk of a treasure map. Then, as she involuntarily glanced at the table where the unrolled parchment lay, her eyes widened as she guiltily remembered the taste of that drumstick.

"I did not damage your map, if that is what has angered you so," she retorted, her own anger beginning to simmer. "I only took that bottle of wine because I was thirsty," she said, but was hardly prepared for his sudden burst of disbelieving laughter.

"You were thirsty?" he repeated incredulously. "God, but that is rich!" he exclaimed, laughing again, his pale gray eyes missing nothing about her shabby appearance. "You ought to spare a little more liquid to the outside of your body, my dear," he commented. Then, with a strange gleam in his eye, he reached for the thick braid hanging over her shoulder. When he grasped the greasy rope of hair, a disdainful look passed over his face.

Rhea jerked her hair free, her face burning with mortification as she stared at this grinning devil. "I do not know anything about your map! I was frightened, that is the only reason I came on board your ship. I am terribly sorry that I trespassed, please do forgive me." She spoke with haughty sarcasm, her voice trembling with anger and pride. "To me your ship looks like any other ship," she continued, oblivious to her unintentional insult.

"Does it indeed?" Dante Leighton demanded. "And what of its captain? Does he resemble every other man?" Now his voice sounded too courteous. "Which brings me to the merits of your second explanation, my dear. It's one that involves a bit of self-sacrifice on your part, doesn't it? No doubt you have heard about my title," he commented casually, but with a watchful quality in his eyes that belied his easy manner. "My, what a challenge I must present to the skirts of Charles Town, from well-bred ladies of untarnished reputation, to nameless whores. I have never been such a popular fellow," Dante said, his lips twisting with contempt, although Rhea could not be certain at whom it was directed.

"What an enticement I must be for a dirty little street beggar like yourself," he said callously, eyeing Rhea's pathetic figure. "Especially as titled gentlemen are none too plentiful this side of the Atlantic. In fact," Dante commented dryly, " 'tis a pity a flesh and blood man must accompany the title at all. However, should you fancy yourself a prospective mistress of mine, then I am afraid that you will have to suffer my presence. Or," he added, with an eyebrow arched quizzically, "do you actually enjoy a man's company—if the price is right?"

Rhea felt a burning tide of embarrassment spreading across her face, for never before in her sheltered life had she been subjected to such insulting remarks and blatant contempt.

"Of course," Dante continued, enjoying her obvious discomfiture, "I should warn you now, my dear, that most titled gentlemen of my acquaintance, including myself, are dirt poor. Ofttimes, due to these most unfortunate circumstances, they are forced into the same, demeaning trade that you yourself are in, that of selling oneself to the richest customer. It is truly a shame the extremes a man is forced into sometimes in order to keep clean linen on his back. And unless my course continues to run smoothly, I shall have to find myself a very wealthy heiress, perhaps even a duke's daughter. That would suit my ambitions nicely, although, as luck would have it, she would probably have a forbidding countenance. Too often, my dear, the wealthier and more influential the heiress, the more ill-favored. That is why they are forced into buying what they want and," Dante added with a derisive grin, "why there are people like you and me in the world."

There was a satisfied gleam in Dante's eye as he noted her paling cheeks, but he was not quite prepared for the caustic words which flew from her trembling lips.

"You flatter yourself, *my lord*," Rhea responded in a voice so insolent that the arrogantly confident captain of the *Sea Dragon* was momentarily stunned. "If indeed you are what you claim to be. A circumstance I would find particularly deplorable. Of course, titles can be bought, *if* the price is right," she said, mimicking his earlier insult. Meanwhile, her casual perusal of his person was so insultingly brief that her doubts about his laying claim to an aristocratic heritage were quite obvious.

"You, sir, are beneath contempt. You are not fit to wallow with swine." Rhea thought these words would be the *coup de grâce* for this insufferable man, but she did not know her enemy. Dante Leighton was not a man to be bested by some gutter-bred halfling.

"I am impressed," Dante complimented her. His eyes, though, showed antagonism instead of admiration, as he stared at this disdainful creature whose reactions were totally different from what he had expected. "I have seldom heard better mimicry in Drury Lane" he continued. "You present more of a puzzle than I had at first thought. I am curious where you learned to speak in so refined a manner. Were you, perhaps, a kitchen maid, or milady's personal maid?" he questioned softly, then moved with a suddenness that caught Rhea off guard.

He held her chin firmly while he stared down into her face with an intentness that made her uneasy. There was little she could do except try to brave that pale-eyed gaze that seemed to miss nothing.

Dante was, in fact, experiencing a strange sensation of *déjà vu*. A vague memory of another woman with eyes of a similar, extraordinary shade of violet was insinuating itself into his thoughts. He remembered now, with a sense of loss, how long ago that had been. He had been so incredibly young and naive that year in London. What an idealistic fool he had been to believe in anyone other than himself. How pungent still was the taste of bitterness in his mouth from that season of betrayal.

And now the memory of violet eyes was bringing back too vividly all the regrets from that time. It was ironic how the memory of that woman could lash into fury all of the old hatreds. He did not even know her name, nor had he then, for it had been just a casual glance, a meeting of eyes across a room, a shared moment, nothing more. But in that instant of suspended time, she had been the embodiment of a young man's dreams. The image of her had remained untarnished after all else had been defiled.

His nameless woman had entered and left his life in that one night; yet here he was wondering about her and what her life had been like in the years since. She had been young, too—only a year or so older than himself. That season she was being presented to London, with her proud parents, no doubt hopeful that a brilliant match would be made for their beautiful daughter.

But she had stood apart from the throng, aloof and almost contemptuous of her surroundings. Holding her slight frame stiffly erect, her head tilted at an imperious angle, she had seemed to be daring anyone to approach her. Her proud bearing reminded him oddly of this young creature standing before him now—and yet they were nothing alike. One was in rags, the other had worn silk. One was fair, the other had been dark. But despite the physical differences, the image of the other woman seemed stamped on this young girl. It went deeper even than the elusive quality of dignity that both possessed.

Dante shook his head, freeing himself from that clinging memory. It had been the romantic fancy of a callow youth, and his gilded paragon most likely had wed some wealthy, titled gentleman and grown into a well-fed matron, whose only concerns were her children, and whether to serve leg of mutton with caper sauce, or boiled beef and pudding.

A look of distaste settled over Dante's already grim face during his speculations on the all too probable and mundane fate of his ideal. Rhea misinterpreted this glowering look as one of growing disgust for her and was filled with an ill-advised, yet overpowering urge to escape from yet another tormentor. Without stopping to think about the consequences of such an action, she sidestepped the brooding captain of the *Sea Dragon* and grabbed the offending map before he could make a move to stop her.

As Dante Leighton watched unbelievingly, the girl held it precariously close to the lantern's flame, for fool that he was, he had, in his surprise at discovering a trespasser on board, forgotten to close the lantern after lighting it.

"It will become nothing more than cinders," Rhea warned him as he stepped toward her. The glint in his pale eyes made her more frightened of him than she had ever been of Daniel Lewis. "Let me go! Or I swear to you, Captain, that I will destroy this map that you seem to prize so highly."

Dante Leighton measured the distance between himself and the girl, wondering if he dared call her bluff, for he knew that the parchment would go up like a torch if it touched the flame.

"Don't, Captain," the girl cautioned, reading his intent in the unnatural stillness of his body. "You speak in riddles, Captain, but I shall be very frank. Allow me to leave your ship unmolested, and in return I shall restore your map to you, intact," she said. *"Otherwise . . ."* She allowed the sentence to trail off, but her meaning was in little doubt as she held the priceless treasure map closer to the heat of the flame, until its edges began to curl and blacken.

Fortunately for Dante Leighton and the crew of the *Sea Dragon,* as well as for Rhea Claire herself had she known it, there was at that moment a disturbance, for the cruelly abducted daughter of the Duke of Camareigh was desperate, and certainly not bluffing.

In that instant, when Rhea's attention was distracted by the sound of pots clanging together, Dante made his move. Rhea cried out in pain as her wrist was caught between punishing fingers, which tightened until she was forced to release the map. It floated slowly to the deck, and it lay there forgotten while they glared into each other's angry eyes.

"I give you fair warning now," Dante said softly, which made his words all the more menacing. "Never threaten me again."

"If you had been sensible enough to listen to my explanation instead of acting like a maddened animal," Rhea accused in a shaking voice, "then this unfortunate episode need never have occurred."

Dante's unamused laughter jarred in her ears, and

she tried to turn her flushed face away from the cruel sound. His fingers still grasped her face, though, and forced her eyes to remain locked with his.

"My God, but you are the brazen-faced chit, aren't you? Well, this fine show of being the wronged party will serve for naught. You are carrying too much sail, my dear, and the seas are just beginning to roughen for you," he predicted, a look of anticipatory pleasure on his face at the thought. "So you do not care for my attitude? You think me less than civilized, do you?" he asked, and Rhea could sense that he had been stung by her hastily spoken words.

Dante Leighton, captain of the *Sea Dragon*, Marquis of Jacqobi, and master of Merdraco, grinned. "What exactly *did* you expect to find on board the *Sea Dragon*, my intrepid little trespasser?" he demanded curiously. Then he answered his own question. "A titled gentleman? A marquis, perhaps?"

Dante shook his head in pity, and his grin widened. "What a disappointment you must have suffered to find me when you awakened from your sweet dreams of future riches. You were, no doubt, hoping for a perfumed exquisite, who would kiss your hand and discuss the merits of current fashion. Unfortunately, you have sadly miscalculated, for as you can plainly see, I am no pale-skinned dandy in silks.

"You have the captain of the *Sea Dragon* to deal with, not a pampered marquis, and, my dear, he is a very different sort of fellow indeed. And certainly no gentleman, although he does bathe regularly, which should be quite a breathtaking change from your usual admirers."

Rhea blinked in disbelief. "What an insufferable man you are. And whether you are, as you would have me believe, a marquis, or whether you are a tinker, I would still find you the rudest, most vulgar individual I have ever had the misfortune to encounter."

"Well done, my dear. I am impressed by this splendid show of ladylike disdain, feigned though it be, but well done nonetheless. But the light of truth has revealed you in my cabin. Now, how do you explain yourself out of that?"

Dante glanced down at the map, which was lying at his feet. "Since the map is still here, I must deduce that *that* was not your intended object in stealing on board the *Sea Dragon*. Rather, you wanted to make my acquaintance. Perhaps you imagined that a marquis makes love differently from other men you have known. I assure you, except for my own personal perferences, I am no different from any other man."

Dante eyed the girl up and down, noting with distaste her limp hair and dirty clothes, and thought she couldn't be more than fourteen or fifteen. Perhaps she was older, but she was so thin it was hard to be certain. But one thing was for certain, which was that she was old enough to be held accountable for her misdeeds. She needed to be taught a sobering lesson, one that she would not soon forget, Dante decided, for he was in no mood tonight to show leniency to anyone. Besides, odds were, if she'd had a pistol tucked away somewhere, he would be lying dead at her dainty, secondhand shoes right now.

"So, my dear, you wish to get to know me better," Dante commented now, a speculative look narrowing his gray eyes until they were little more than flashes of silver as he stared at her. "You have been rather inept at engaging anything more than my curiosity thus far. If your scheme is to succeed, then you will have to make a few concessions to me. You should have taken more care to learn my likes and dislikes, my dear, before you attempted to seduce me. I am a very particular fellow about whom I let into my bed. And right now, to be quite frank, little one, you haven't a ghost of a chance to fulfill that wish of yours." Dante was pleased to see an expression of concern passing across her grimy face.

"However, that can be remedied quite easily," he continued. "I've never been one to stand in the way of another's ambition, as long as it does not interfere with mine." He sounded almost friendly, but Rhea was not deceived, for his painful grip on her wrists had not lessened.

"Either you are hard of hearing or extremely obtuse," Rhea declared furiously. "I despise the very sight of you and would find the burning fires of hell preferable to sharing a bed with you. I do not care if you have an arm's length of titles to your wretched name, whatever that might be. All I desire is to get off this ship, and away from you."

"Ah, come now, no more protestations against sharing my bed, for we both know how hollow they are," Dante responded easily. His smile was forced, though, for this insolent chit had a way with words that cut deeply into a man's self-esteem, and his had already been inflicted with a few jabs of late.

Dante's gaze clashed with the violet eyes that were glowing with hatred of him, and he resented the fact that such beauty should belong to a dirty little street urchin, who would spit in his face if she thought she could get away with it unscathed. Her contempt for him was visible in every quivering ounce of her, and yet she was the one who had set out to entrap and deceive him. He was the one with the grievances, not her, although to look at her one would think she had been the victim of foul play.

Dante allowed his eyes to linger on the contours of her face for a moment longer, a moment which seemed endless to Rhea. Then he smiled, and it was a strangely beautiful smile in spite of its coldness. Abruptly, he released her wrists, picked up the map, and walked away from her.

"You just might be a beauty if we could scrub off some of that grime from the gutter," he said over his shoulder as he sauntered across the cabin to the door. Then he called down the corridor to someone, his broad shoulders blocking the door and any escape Rhea might have contemplated.

"Bring me a tub of hot water, Kirby, and plenty of soap. I've got to scour through years of living in the gutter," he ordered his little steward.

"Ye be wantin' a bath this time of the evening?" Kirby demanded in disbelief, his face mirroring dismay and concern lest his captain had become deranged since he'd seen him last.

"Just do it, Kirby," Dante enjoined him, closing the door firmly on the little man's next words.

"Well?" Dante demanded, turning back to his dumbfounded captive. "Do you want to be dumped into the tub wearing those rags? It will be far easier for both of us if you take them off yourself. And it will not do you any good to look like that, for you are going to have a bath if it is the last thing I ever do. It will give me a great deal of pleasure to wash one of you untamed guttersnipes clean. I have had my pockets picked too many times to be very charitable toward your kind," he told her, moving steadily closer as he removed his coat and tossed it into the chair, then unbuttoned his vest and dropped it on top.

Rhea watched in fascination as he slowly rolled up the sleeves of his shirt, baring powerful, tanned forearms. "Leave me alone," she whispered.

"Oh, no, you cannot change your tune in mid-song, my dear, for 'twas you who came on board the *Sea Dragon* uninvited," Dante reminded her. "You thought you would waltz aboard my ship and it would be mere child's play to cozen me. Did you think I would so easily fall prey to your brand of blackmail? My God, what a fool this town must think me, that a cinderwench feels emboldened enough to play a double game with me.

"Very well, I shall not disappoint you, my dear," he continued. "I am curious to see how strong-willed, or perchance gullible, I really am. So, let us have a look at you, and see how well you would have played the seductress.

"What? No glib retort?" he taunted her when she remained silent. "I said to take off your clothes, or am I going to have to peel them off of you?"

Rhea still said nothing, only because she could not believe what she was hearing. The man was mad. What an incredible irony it was, she thought, that she should manage to escape the clutches of Daniel Lewis, only to fall into the hands of the demented captain of the *Sea Dragon*.

Discarding all thoughts of caution, she knew she had to convince this man that she was not what he thought her to be. "If you lay a hand upon me, Captain, you will live to rue the day," she warned him, taking a step backward. But he continued toward her, undeterred by her warning.

"I told you never to threaten me, my dear," Dante reminded her.

"You never asked me my name, Captain!" Rhea yelled at him.

"Indeed? Please forgive me my momentary lack of good manners," Dante replied politely. "I am Dante Leighton, as if you did not know, and you—you are?"

Rhea took a deep breath, for in revealing her true identity to the man she might well be placing herself in far graver danger. Obviously, this man was an opportunist, an adventurer, and might use the information she gave him to further his own cause. But then, Rhea thought on a note of rising hope, if he was indeed a marquis, then surely his hostility toward her would lessen, and perhaps he would even feel some kinship.

"I am Lady Rhea Claire Dominick, eldest daughter of the Duke and Duchess of Camareigh. If you are indeed who you claim to be, then you will have heard of my father. And unless you are completely crazed, you will know that if you hurt me, you will have him as your sworn enemy. Think on that, my fine captain, before you accost me further."

A flicker of something flashed in Dante Leighton's pale gray eyes, then was gone. "I have been absent from England for many years, but I have heard of the Duke of Camareigh. Indeed, in my misspent youth I even had the misfortune to sit across a gaming table from him. And if my recollection serves me well, I lost a considerable sum of money to him, money that I could ill afford to lose at the time. But he was a very hard man to beat, rather notorious in fact. However, I did take the chance that I might just win." Dante shrugged. "I also remember that he was a bachelor, and not likely to give up his freedom, which makes your claim of being Lucien Dominick's daughter rather doubtful, my dear," he said pityingly, taking a step which brought him too close.

"I don't care if you believe me or not. I am Rhea Claire Dominick. I am!" Rhea cried to his disbelieving face. "Turn me over to the authorities. They will believe me."

"Looking as you do, I seriously doubt that, my dear. The mere fact that you are here in Charles Town, apparently unattended and dressed like a scullery maid, does little for your cause."

"I was kidnapped from my home. I was drugged, put on board a ship which very nearly sank; I was starved and threatened and—"

"A fine tale, indeed," Dante commented, and to Rhea's dismay she saw him silently laughing at her. He had not believed anything she said.

"Damn you!" she said in a choked voice as she tried to escape his hands. But he had reached out so suddenly and purposefully that she hadn't had time to take so much as a step in retreat.

"I warned you," Dante said quietly, as his not-to-be-denied hands quickly dispatched her jacket and waistcoat, then easily pulled off her loose-fitting skirt.

As he was struggling with her chemise, Kirby knocked. When he was given a curt order to enter, the steward trudged in with a tub and a bucket of water. As he glanced over at the captain, his eyes widened incredulously to see him wrestling with a girl he hadn't even known was on board. And from the look of things, he could tell she didn't want to be. The eyes of the two antagonists were locked as they struggled in what was fast becoming a battle of arrogantly stubborn wills. Neither spared a glance for the gaping, unusually silent little steward as he scurried from the cabin, only to return moments later with two more buckets of hot water, which he poured into the tub.

"Cap'n, I—" Kirby began awkwardly, as he stood watching the extraordinary actions of his captain. "Cap'n, what are you—" he tried again, but was silenced by the captain's violent curse as the girl bit him on the wrist, then kicked him viciously on the shin.

"Get out, Kirby," Dante said between gritted teeth as he swung the struggling, naked girl into his arms, then dropped her with little ceremony into the tub of warm water. Her squeal of surprised fright as she lost her footing gave him a great deal of satisfaction. Then he nursed the angry teeth marks imprinted in the back of his hand.

Kirby had not obeyed his captain, but not out of insolence, for he was so amazed by what was happening that all he could do was stand by the open doorway and watch as his captain grabbed hold of the girl's head and dunked it beneath the water. At that point, her muttered imprecations were cut off abruptly. Then he lathered a handful of soap and began to scrub her face and neck. At first, his rough treatment of her tender skin caused tears to fall freely from the girl's eyes, but as Dante felt the frail bones of her shoulders, he was suddenly stirred by pity and his hands became gentle, less inhuman, as he rubbed her skin clean of the grime and sickness of two months at sea spent in a filthy hold.

"Ah, the poor, wee thing," the little steward muttered. Something in the pathetic drooping of her head on her slender neck touched Houston Kirby near his heart—not that he would ever admit that to anyone, and hardly even to himself. He continued to hover uncertainly near the door, not quite knowing what to do, but if the captain got too rough with the wee thing, well . . . he just hoped he wouldn't.

Rhea was numb with shock, and she wondered if this nightmare would ever come to an end. She had thought he was going to drown her—and it was possible that the thought had crossed his mind once or twice when she had splashed soap in his eyes—but suddenly all violence had disappeared. Now his hands were soothing, and he was almost caressing her. She jerked slightly when she felt his hands on her head, but his fingers only threaded through the thick braid, freeing the strands of hair as he washed them clean. He rinsed her hair with water from a pail, pouring it over the top of her head, careful to keep the soap out of her eyes.

Rhea sucked in her breath, as she felt his palm slide over her breasts, then along her thighs, as he soaped her skin with a rough piece of cloth. He pulled her gently, yet firmly, to her feet as he poured another pail of warm, clear water over her shaking body. Then she was lifted from the tub and wrapped in the concealing warmth of a large towel.

As Rhea's teeth chattered uncontrollably, this strangely quiet man began to rub her dry, leaving her skin pink and tingling. Sitting down on the bunk, Dante pulled the compliant girl between his legs and started to squeeze the moisture out of her hair, his hands patient as he took several long strands at a time until he had wrung most of the water out.

Dante took her chin in his hands and stared thoughtfully into Rhea's face, worried about the vacant stare in her violet eyes. He glanced up in surprise as he heard Kirby moving about.

"Thought the little one could use something warm inside her. A mite thin, she is," Kirby said, his face flushing with embarrassment as he stepped forward with a bowl of steaming broth.

When he noticed that the damp towel kept slipping from her shoulders, Kirby glanced around for her clothes; however, upon spotting the offending pile, he took it upon himself to procure fresh linen for her. Setting down his tray, he hurried over to the captain's sea chest, and digging down inside, reappeared with one of the captain's shirts. He handed it to Dante, then turned away discreetly as the captain slipped it around the shivering girl and lifted her onto the bunk. Dante sat down beside her, accepted the broth from his steward, then slid his arm behind the girl's shoulders. Then, with renewed determination, she drew away from him, and Dante's lips tightened ominously as he ignored her instinctive movement. Instead, he held her against his chest as he brought the spoonful of hot broth close to her lips.

"Eat," he ordered harshly, relieved when she acquiesced without a fight and swallowed a mouthful of one of Kirby's finest concoctions. Dante glared down at the girl's pale face, for he was experiencing an unaccustomed feeling of compassion for this maltreated creature, and part of it was guilt for his own actions. When his hands had touched that frail body, he had realized the greatness of his own strength. It would have been too easy to crush the life out of her, and it bothered him that anyone should be so vulnerable, so much at the mercy of another.

This pitiful ragamuffin had humbled him, which was not something Dante Leighton was familiar with, nor likely to forget—or to forgive.

"She found the map," Dante said suddenly, shocking Kirby out of his perusal of the young girl.

"B—but how?" he stuttered, for once almost at a loss for words. His eyes widened as he glanced around and noticed for the first time the map on the table.

"She claims she was thirsty, and I am almost inclined to believe her, for it is just unlikely enough to have happened," Dante explained with a twisted grin.

"Who could she be, and why is she on board the *Sea Dragon* then?" Kirby wondered aloud. "So ye don't think she came lookin' fer the map?

Dante remained silent for a moment. "I am not sure, but as long as I have any doubts, she will not be allowed to leave the *Sea Dragon*. Too much is at stake to make a mistake in judgment this late in the game. She has denied any knowledge of it, even of my identity." Dante shook his head wearily. "But she is so full of lies that I cannot be certain, and I will not take the chance that I might be mistaken about her purpose in being on board. Whatever her reasons, she saw the map, and I will not risk her selling her information to the likes of Bertie Mackay."

"Ah, ye don't think she would be workin' fer him, d'ye now?" Kirby asked, refusing to believe a wee thing like her could have anything to do with such a fellow. "She don't look too well, Cap'n," Kirby commented, watching the captain feed her the last of the broth and noting her flushed cheeks with a professional eye. "Ye shouldn't have lost your temper with her, Cap'n. Thought ye was goin' to murder the wee one, I did." He shrugged off the glint of displeasure he saw in his captain's eye and continued with apparent unconcern. "Reckon ye might be partly responsible fer the shape she's in right now. So, what are we goin to do with her, then?" he demanded, taking the empty bowl from his captain's hand.

"Keep her," Dante said curtly. "She might not agree with that right now, but she will be far better off on board the *Sea Dragon* than walking the streets. Maybe in the morning I will be able to persuade a few truths out of her. Then we can decide what to do with her. But until then, she shall remain our guest on board the *Sea Dragon*." Dante stared down at the girl's delicately molded face, unconsciously admiring her golden hair, which had dried in thick, shining waves. Then he eased his back against the paneling of his bunk, trying not to disturb the restlessly sleeping girl.

"I'll be right down the corridor if ye should need me," Cap'n," Kirby told him as he shook out a blanket and spread it across the slight form in the captain's shirt. Then he went to the table and rolled up the treasure map, carefully replacing it in the bottle, then putting the bottle back into its proper place on the rack. Stacking the dishes and glasses on his tray, he let himself quietly out of the cabin.

Dante settled himself more comfortably in the bunk, the girl's body so light that he hardly felt her pressing against his chest and thighs. He sighed as he thought over the events of the evening, wondering what more could happen before dawn came to Charles Town and brought this long night to an end. Closing his eyes, he cradled the girl against his chest, resting his chin on top of her golden head. He opened a wary eye as he felt something land on his feet; then he watched curiously as Jamaica curled up against the girl's side, for all the world like an old friend.

For the first time since waking up in her own bed at Camareigh, Rhea awoke feeling warm. But suddenly she was too hot. Irritably, she tried to kick off some of the heavy blankets. But her legs felt leaden, and as she tried to sit up, the room began to spin alarmingly.

Rhea felt something hard slide around her waist, preventing her from falling sideways against the wall. She turned her head slightly and stared down with heavy-lidded eyes at the man lying next to her in the bunk. His pale gray eyes were watching her carefully, almost suspiciously.

She had only a vague memory of that first unfortunate meeting with the less-than-friendly captain of the *Sea Dragon,* and now, halfway between sleep and consciousness, her memory was fragmented and confused. For an instant, as she openly met his gaze, Rhea felt none of the antagonism she should have.

His long-lashed eyes were extraordinarily beautiful—

like quicksilver in a sun-bronzed face. They subtly reflected light and shadow; they were chiaroscuro eyes, reminding Rhea one moment of the clear streams that wended down from the hills around Camareigh, and in the next moment, assuming the muted softness of a gray-winged dove.

Rhea was captivated by the touch of his eyes, then by the touch of his mouth against hers, but she felt something was wrong as she fought off the feverish haze that was clouding her thoughts. For the exquisitely molded lips were hard and demanding, and the gray eyes were crystalline with malice as they stared into hers, not softened by love as they should have been.

"You!" Rhea gasped as the bronzed face with the silver eyes became the devilishly grinning face of the captain of the *Sea Dragon*. This man holding her against his bare chest was the madman who had humiliated her and subjected her to ridicule when she had been in desperate need of help.

"Yes, none other. After all, you are in my bed," Dante reminded her, "and wearing my shirt," he added, his eyes lingering on the rounded curve of her breasts.

Rhea glanced down in growing dismay, for until now some of the finer details of the previous night had escaped her. She glanced back up, only to encounter a muscular expanse of bronzed chest with dark curling hair spread across its rippling surface. She looked away in embarrassment and confusion, this time to encounter a pair of damp, wrinkled breeches and a shirt looking much like the one she had on. They had been left in a disorderly pile on the deck, as if little thought had been given to them at the time.

Dante, following Rhea's glance, raised a questioning eyebrow. "You hardly expected me to sleep in wet breeches, did you, my dear?" he asked with a look of feigned surprise. "I'd have caught my death of cold, and you wouldn't have wanted that, would you?"

"Yes! I would have rejoiced at the news," Rhea declared, her cheeks flushed with anger and fever.

"Ah, now that would not have done at all," Dante said with a grin, his hand straying to a long strand of golden hair clinging to the hair on his chest. "I am afraid that they would hold you solely responsible for my untimely death. After all, 'twas you who soaked me through to the skin last night when I was trying to bathe you. They would not think kindly about so cruel an end for an act of kindness." Dante's lips twitched with laughter while he waited for her response to his bait.

"Kindness!" Rhea's voice was choked with anger.

"Now, now, you really should be grateful to me," Dante interrupted in a soothing voice, ignoring her look of incredulity. "I have abetted you in your cause, my dear. For you are in my bed and in my arms, and," he said, pressing his mouth against her slightly parted lips before continuing, "you are very close to achieving your goal of seducing me."

And lest she be in any doubt about the truth of his words, Dante slid his arms around her warm body, easing her closer to him as his hands slid beneath the shirt and moved slowly upward along her thighs. The shirt moved upward too, baring her flesh to him; his hands easily cupped her small buttocks and he brought her hips gently against his.

Rhea Claire Dominick was in no doubt about his passion, nor the truth of his words, for a burning heat was growing harder against her, touching her intimately, insinuating itself closer to the vulnerable softness between her legs.

In shame Rhea closed her tear-filled eyes, for she couldn't seem to escape the hard hands that were molding her ever closer against that relentless pressure. She drew in her breath in surprise when she felt his mouth against her breasts and then the soft touch of his tongue; then, opening her eyes, she gazed down at the head of wavy, chestnut hair lying heavy against her. Every inch of the man's hot flesh was like a brand burning into her, marking her with his manly scent and feel.

As his mouth caressed the taut arch of throat, Dante Leighton tasted hot, salty tears, and, startled, he glanced up, caught off guard by her unexpected response to his lovemaking. He stared at her, confused not only by her reaction to him, but by his equally strange reaction to her. He glanced down at his trembling hand with co-temptuous disbelief. Then, with the back of his hand, he wiped away the beads of perspiration lining his upper lip. He felt disgusted with himself for wanting this girl so badly that he would forget all else in the taking of her.

The violet eyes were so close to his that he could see a primrose ring encircling the widening pupils. And the unpleasant fact that they were widening with fear and revulsion, not ardor, left him feeling strangely uncomfortable. But despite her obvious dislike of his touch, he found himself experiencing the same fascination he had felt as when he had awakened to find his trespasser snuggled into the curve of his chest, her soft backside riding against his hips so trustingly and innocently.

His senses had filled with the warm scent of her. The soap he had used on her the night before smelled both familiar and foreign as it wafted to him from her skin. He had noticed the incredible loveliness of her hair, and burying his face in the deep golden tresses, he had breathed the heady fragrance of the sea and sandalwood.

She had rolled over suddenly, pushing restlessly at the covers, and Dante had found himself staring into her face. Her expression was serene in her sleep, and her cheeks were stained a wild rose color that contrasted startlingly with the ashen cast of the skin of her body.

She had seemed so immaculate in her sleep that Dante had to force himself to remember her lies and actions of the night before. She was no more sinned against than she had sinned, he had told himself, hardening his heart against the appeal of her seraphic appearance.

But when she had opened those limpid violet eyes, and he had found himself staring into them, all of his fine reasoning had been banished by the abrupt tightening in his loins. All he could think to do was to press his mouth against hers and elicit a response from their softness. He had wanted to feel her lips seeking his, her hands caressing him, her hips moving rhythmically against his. But none of this had happened; instead, she had shrunk away from him, as if she could not endure his touch. For one brief moment, when she had gazed into his eyes, he had thought . . . but no, a look of loathing had replaced her expression of strangely ingenuous sensuality.

Dante was rudely jolted from his thoughts by the painful impact of the top of her head meeting the curve of his chin. That this was no accident but a carefully planned assault, he soon realized, as he struggled to free his shoulder from the teeth sinking into them, while at the same time avoiding the sharp nails trying to shred his skin. He managed to evade the knee that would have done considerable damage to his self-esteem had it connected with a very vulnerable spot, but the small fist speeding toward his nose could not be eluded entirely, and it smacked a glancing blow to his cheekbone.

Making quick use of his greater weight, Dante rolled the squirming little hellcat beneath him, pinning her flat against the bunk, rendering her swinging fists useless for the moment. Then he tried to catch his breath. With the taste of blood still warm in his mouth from the blow she had dealt him, Dante stared into her now very frightened face. They were both panting, and Dante could feel every breath she drew against his own chest and belly.

And it was upon this intimate scene that a furious Helene Jordane, eyes flashing with temper, Gallic blood on the boil, stumbled unannounced. There had been a heated argument outside the cabin door, but neither Dante or Rhea had heard the commotion.

"I told ye the Cap'n was otherwise occupied," Houston Kirby reminded her, standing firm against a look from Helene's eyes that should have put him six feet under. He hid well his own surprise, for he hadn't quite expected to be greeted by this scene, but then, Dante Leighton was not a predictable man. And that was probably why they were all alive today.

"Damn you, Dante Leighton! Damn you to hell!" Helene Jordane cried in mortification as she stared at Dante and the golden-haired girl in his bed. Her eyes were mesmerized by that ivory-skinned leg entwined with Dante's deeply tanned one; it was quite obvious to her, in her wrathful indignation, that they had been coupling. The girl's beautiful face was flushed from his kisses, and even she, from where she stood across the room, could hear the ragged breathing of the two lovers.

Dante Leighton had humiliated her and was no doubt laughing silently at this very moment, while his whore snuggled up to him beneath the covers. She would never forgive him for this affront. She had planned last night so carefully. If she could have gotten him into her bed, she knew she'd have been able to conceive. After all, she'd done it before. That would have assured her of the Marquis of Jacqobi's ring on her finger. And this time she would have made certain that nothing happened to the baby.

"Helene," Dante murmured and sat up, the coverlet wrapping around his hips as he propped himself against the pillows. He held Rhea in the circle of his arm as he stared mockingly at his one-time paramour. "This is most unexpected. I have never known you to go calling before noon. You must have had a quiet evening and retired early. 'Tis a pity." He spoke casually, as if there were nothing out of the ordinary about the predicament he now found himself in.

Rhea, however, was so flushed and trembling with embarrassment that she felt ill. And the woman confronting them was almost convulsed with rage, leaving Rhea in little doubt that she bore some grievance against the grinning captain of the *Sea Dragon*. A sudden disquieting thought came to Rhea. What if this woman were his wife? This stunningly beautiful woman would certainly have reason to be infuriated at the discovery of her husband compromising another woman, but even given those sordid circumstances, Rhea still could not believe the vituperative language that was spilling from the woman's sneering mouth. Never before had Rhea heard anyone, much less a gentle woman, speak with so befouled a tongue.

". . . and you could have been in my arms, but instead you choose to consort with some common whore off the docks. Well, the pox on both of you!" Helene spat, her narrowed gaze not missing the way Dante's hand strayed to a golden curl on the girl's temple. The unconscious gentleness of the gesture blackened her spirit even more.

Dante looked at her pityingly, and only Houston Kirby

saw the gleam enter the captain's eye. The little steward knew him well enough to take the precaution of settling his feet firmer to the deck, for they were in for some stormy seas now. But even Kirby found himself reeling at the captain's startling words.

"My dear Helene, you really do my betrothed an injustice, and I do believe you owe her an apology," he said silkily, remaining unmoved by the shocked expressions on the two women's faces.

"Betrothed?" Helene laughed harshly. "By God, but you are mad, Dante. I ought to call your bluff, my dear, and announce the glad tidings all over Charles Town. Let me see, how shall I introduce you?" she asked coyly. "May I introduce to you Dante Leighton, captain of the *Sea Dragon* and Marquis of Jacqobi, and this sweet thing is his wife, the former whore . . . oh, I am sorry, my dear," Helene apologized, her eyes sliding over the golden-haired girl with insulting thoroughness, "I did not quite catch your name. You do have one, do you not? Even a first name will suffice, and that is perhaps all you are known by?"

"Her name is *Lady* Rhea Claire Dominick," Dante informed her. "And you thought I would not remember your name, didn't you, my dear?" he whispered in Rhea's ear. "You do not mind if I make use of your subterfuge, do you?"

"Be my guest, please," Rhea responded, thinking that the more people who learned of her identity, the better her chances were of escaping this madman.

But to Helene Jordane's jealous eye, it seemed as if they were sharing secrets and exchanging words of love, especially when Dante pressed a light kiss against the girl's forehead.

"Lady?" she snorted in derision. "More likely M'lady Whore."

"My dear Helene, you are making yourself look the fool. For this is indeed Lady Rhea Claire Dominick, daughter of the Duke and Duchess of Camareigh, and my betrothed. Surely you must have heard of the family while you were visiting in London?" Dante asked, smiling as he saw the look of doubt spreading across her face.

And, indeed, Helene Jordane was having serious qualms as she stared at Dante Leighton and the girl. She was definitely uneasy, for the name he had spoken so casually was not unknown to her. While in London she had listened avidly to all of the gossip, and although not invited to many of the more important parties, she had remained inordinately interested in every facet of their privileged lives.

Yes, she had heard of Lady Rhea Claire Dominick, and had been filled with envy for the beautiful heiress who had taken London by storm. She had glimpsed the girl only once, when she'd been pointed out by a friend, but she'd been at the opposite side of the theatre and all she had been able to see was the exquisite style of the girl's dress. Now, as Helene gazed at the golden hair, she remembered that Lady Rhea had golden hair, and was reputed to be quite beautiful.

Helene bit her lip in vexation, uncertain of what to do, and feeling suddenly quite foolish, as Dante had predicted. But still she was doubtful. "I thought you were supposed to wed an earl?" she asked now, thinking to entrap this creature if she were an impostor.

"As you can see, my dear," Dante answered, thinking to smooth over a difficult situation, "she did not."

"Are you speaking of Wesley Lawton, Earl of Rendale?" Rhea asked politely, thinking this her chance to prove her identity. "Wesley and I are long-time friends. He has often stayed at Camareigh. Are you an acquaintance of his? I shall have to ask him. . . ." Rhea broke off abruptly, with the painful memory that Wesley was dead.

But Helene did not notice the odd silence, for the beautifully accented words left little doubt in her mind that this was the real Lady Rhea Claire Dominick, wealthy heiress, and, most likely, the betrothed of Dante Leighton.

Seeming to read her mind, Dante added, "Did I never mention Rhea to you? I have known her since she was just a little girl. But I thought that I had lost her when I left England. I had promised her that I would come back for her one day, but as you can plainly see," he laughed softly, pulling Rhea closer against his chest, startled momentarily by the heat of her body, "she became impatient for me and sought me out. I must admit that I was stunned to see her. She seemed almost a stranger to me, but not for long."

"I am surprised you even recognized her," Helene said tightly, wishing this ship and its captain on the bottom of the sea.

"I very nearly did not, but true love never dies, does it, my dear?" he murmured softly against Rhea's cheek. His eyes clashed with Helene's, though, and their message was only too clear to her.

"May I be the first to give you my congratulations," Helene said. Then, unable to resist the temptation to plant a seed of doubt in this young girl's mind, she added, "And to wish you luck. You will certainly need it, my dear, for Dante Leighton is a bastard, and you will live to regret the day you crossed his path again. You do know that he is only marrying you for your fortune. He is not capable of love, my dear. He will destroy you, just like everyone else he has ever touched." Then, with a swishing of her skirts, she hurried from the cabin, leaving an awkward silence in her wake.

Houston Kirby breathed a deep sigh of relief to have her off the *Sea Dragon*, for she was bad luck. "Lord love us, but she's a wicked woman," he said.

"Where did she go? I wanted her to help me escape. I've got to get away from this madman," Rhea muttered fretfully. "I want to go home. I feel so tired. I can't seem to think anymore." Then she wept, muffling her tears against the pillow as she curled up beneath the covers. Her aching body refused to stop shaking.

"That don't look good, Cap'n," Kirby said, rubbing his jaw thoughtfully as he walked over to the bunk. "Reckon ye might have done her some harm by bathing her. Got her cold, ye did. Funny, she reminds me a bit of Jamaica when you brought him on board ship in Port Royal. He was just a poor, wee kitten, half-starvin', and lookin' fer a home, he was. Reckon I'm a mite confused, Cap'n," Kirby added, looking curiously at the

Laurie McBain

stony-faced man cradling the girl. "Is she really this girl, Lady Rhea Claire Dominick?"

Dante shrugged. "It does not matter who she is. Her future has been decided. She is sailing to the Indies on the *Sea Dragon*."

"Well," the little steward said with no outward sign of surprise, "reckon ye be responsible fer her now. This cold weather ain't helpin' her any. Reckon the warm trades in the Indies would put her back on her feet right quick. That, and a few bowls of my special broth."

Dante smiled strangely. "Aye, Kirby, I was thinking that very same thing. She is my responsibility now."

Jamaica seemed to understand his captain's words and hopped back up on the bunk, finding his special spot at the feet of Rhea Claire Dominick, latest crew member on board the *Sea Dragon*.

Though this be madness, yet there is method in't.
Shakespeare

Chapter 6

"Hmmm, what do you say to this one, Teddie?" Kate asked thoughtfully. "'A ministering angel shall my sister be.' No," she sighed in disappointment, "'tis too obvious, I fear. Ah!" she cried out suddenly, "Now this one is priceless. 'Tis quite brilliant, indeed. I must admit, I do astound myself at times," she chuckled, dipping her quill pen into the crystal inkwell that was part of an elaborate silver inkstand.

Teddie Waltham sourly eyed her ladyship. The busy scratchings of her quill pen were beginning to get on his nerves, but at least it kept her occupied and out of mischief. Teddie was thankful for small favors.

Day after day, there she sat, poring over dusty books. Her sometimes unintelligible utterances varied between pleased cooings and half-muttered curses, as she searched for the proper lines of poetry to torture and perplex her enemy at Camareigh. For almost two months now she had been playing her sadistic game, savoring her revenge, and Teddie could well imagine the Duke's reaction when yet another of her ladyship's little missives arrived.

It had been fortunate that they had sent the kidnapped girl off to the colonies, for London, as well as every sea-coast town and country village, had been flooded with broadsides and handbills describing the missing girl and offering a small fortune for information resulting in her safe return. He had been relieved, and at first thankful, to learn that he wasn't a murderer, for the gent he'd shot —who was no less a personage than an earl—had staked a reward for information and/or apprehension of the persons unknown involved in the kidnapping of Lady Rhea Claire Dominick and the attempted murder of his own person.

It had caused him a bit of concern at first, as well as indignation, when he'd found himself described as "a seedy ruffian of middling size, coarse-featured, and wearing a nasty, red velvet coat." Now, that had hurt, for a man had his pride regardless of what he was, and he'd always done his best, considering his straitened circumstances. Not to mention that the red velvet coat, so contemptuously described, had been one of his favorites. It had saddened him grievously to have to toss it into the river. Now Teddie stared in disgust at his plain brown cloth coat, thinking it did little to enhance his appearance.

"Do you know, Teddie, I think it is about time I breathed some fresh country air again," Kate said, not noticing Teddie Waltham's start of surprise. "Find someone to send this note off, then I think we should start packing for our journey," she told him, still unaware of his reluctance.

"*Our* journey?" he questioned doubtfully. "I'm quite content right here before the fire, m'lady."

"I'm sure you are, but that is not the point. I think I have lulled Lucien into letting down his guard. He cannot live forever holed up at Camareigh. I could scarcely believe my eyes when we journeyed back there a fortnight ago and found the place armed like a fortress. But I do think now is the time to act, and I shall deliver my next message to Lucien personally," she vowed, her voice ringing with the anticipated pleasure of revenge. "God, but it will be worth it all just to have the pleasure of seeing Lucien's face when I confront him. If he didn't have the devil's own luck, Percy and I would have succeeded in ridding ourselves of him years ago.

Why, when I think of all of the bungled attempts we made on his life, well, it leaves me quite stunned, let me tell you."

"It doesn't me," Teddie Waltham muttered, having come to the belated conclusion that nothing was impossible to believe where m'lady was concerned. He had always had suspicions that these folk calling themselves "quality" were crack-brained. Did things in style, they did, but mad just the same. Thought of themselves as eccentric, but it all came down to having rats in the upper story, same as any other raver. Only these swells had the funds to keep themselves out of Bedlam.

"Teddie?"

Teddie Waltham cringed, for he had come to dread hearing his name spoken in that wheedling tone of voice. Teddie remained silent, hoping against hope that her ladyship would forget her summons.

"Teddie!" Kate spoke his name more sharply. "Now do listen. I should like to become acquainted with a few of your friends. Now that we are without the useful services of Rocco, we shall have to find several other large fellows to assist us if my plan is to succeed. I am quite sure that you must know some beef-witted men who would be glad for a little easy work. You know the type, Teddie. More brawn than brain," she told him casually, as if expecting him to instantly produce the fellows from his coat pocket.

"Well, *m'lady,*" Teddie replied sarcastically, "seein' how me activities have been curtailed a wee bit, I might find it hard gettin' about town."

"Hmmm, well, you'll just have to do your best then, won't you?" Kate replied unsympathetically. " 'Tis a pity that fool lived to describe you."

"Aye, 'twas indeed," Teddie agreed glumly. "But 'tis even worse havin' a price on yer head, fer I've found out who Teddie Waltham's friends are, and that fat tart Farquhar ain't one of them. Heard tell she was the one talkin' to them Bow Street Runners, puttin' them snoopy noses of theirs on *my* scent!" he exclaimed indignantly. "Reckon she thought the chance of pocketing that reward was worth more than Teddie Waltham's neck."

"Well, I did tell you the old biddy was suspicious of

our clandestine activities. That is why, if you will remember, I advised moving to another inn. And I must admit, I rather enjoy being so close to the river. The stench and damp reminds me much of Venice," Kate remarked, more concerned about her present comfort than the future condition of Teddie Waltham's scrawny neck. "I should imagine, Teddie," she continued, "considering your lack of popularity in certain quarters, that you would be more than pleased to get out of the close confines of London. You really should be thanking your lucky stars that there is someone like me around to take you in hand." Impatiently, she eyed his sullen figure. "Now come on, Teddie. It won't do at all to sit here sulking when we've work to do. This will be the culmination of all that I have planned. I have been waiting for this moment for nearly twenty years, and by God, I'll not be cheated out of it. Oh, if only Percy were here to share in our greatest moment!" she cried, clutching her thin, pale hands almost as if in prayer.

Teddie Waltham shook his head; then, propping his stubby chin in his hands, he stared into the fire, thankful that this Percy fellow she kept mentioning was *not* here to share in m'lady's greatest moment. Even one of these crazed blue bloods was too much for him to handle, he thought on a rising feeling of impending doom.

The Duchess of Camareigh moved with unusual slowness toward the bed with its pale blue and silver damask hangings. The only sound in the room was the rustling of her silk skirts. She carefully straightened one of the lacy-edged pillows. Then, as if satisfied with her work, she glanced around the deserted room, where not a speck of dust could have been found. It was just as Rhea had left it that morning.

The Duchess paused before the rosewood and gilt dressing table, where the mirror reflected her slight figure in dark blue silk, the Valenciennes lace gracing her sleeves in deep ruffles giving a touch of brightness to her otherwise somber appearance. The elaborately embroidered and trimmed white silk underskirt, which usually accompanied the gown and relieved its darkness, had been replaced with a plain, dark blue quilted one.

Her small hand moved amongst the undisturbed toiletries, lingering on the engraved silver brush, in which remained a few golden strands of hair. She held a small crystal bottle to her nose and breathed the sweet scent of jessamine her daughter had been fond of.

The Duchess's bottom lip trembled slightly as she walked to the tall windows and stared out across the gardens below. Although Rhea's rooms were situated in the south wing, the windows looked westward. The Duchess watched as the light began to fade; darkness came earlier now with the approach of winter.

Reaching into the pocket of her skirt, the Duchess withdrew a carefully folded piece of paper. She opened it wide, her eyes straining in the dim light to read the words. But this was unnecessary, as the words were ingrained in her memory. She recited aloud the latest lines of poetry received just that morning:

> *If they be two, they are two so*
> *As stiff twin compasses are two,*
> *Thy soul the fixt foot, makes no show*
> *To move, but doth, if the other do.*

The Duchess stared helplessly at the words. If only she could fathom the meaning. Were there clues in those lines to the identity of the madman behind the kidnapping? And a madman he was, for this was no mere blackmailer's game, nor extortionist's plot. At least with an honest blackguard they could have paid the ransom and gotten Rhea returned to them. But so far, no demand for ransom had been received.

Or did those enigmatic lines refer to Rhea's whereabouts? the Duchess wondered, thinking of the riddle they had received just a little over a week ago.

> *All day they hunted,*
> *And nothing did they find,*
> *But a ship a-sailing,*
> *A-sailing with the wind.*

The Duchess closed her eyes in silent prayer, hoping that her worst fears were wrong, and that Rhea Claire's kidnapping had not been the act of an evil, twisted mind. But deep down inside she knew that Rhea was just a pawn in this madman's game. And that was what horrified her the most, for a pawn has little value once its purpose has been fulfilled. And what was that purpose? If it were to cause them the deepest suffering and anguish a parent could endure, if it were to torment them with baffling riddles, then this madman had succeeded, for they were living the agonies of hell.

And that was why, God help them, she believed that revenge was the motive. But revenge for what? Was it for some imagined misdeed committed by either herself or Lucien? Or perhaps it had been a genuine misunderstanding, where no harm had been intended? But merely by living from day to day, one could make enemies, and both she and Lucien had led very full lives. And each of them had made enemies in their lives before they had met and married. Lucien had had his share of duels. Was some grieving relative now seeking retribution? Lucien had also been a gambler, and one who had won more often than lost. Perhaps a son or daughter was out to avenge the loss. But why now? she wondered. Nothing untoward had occurred in the past few years. They'd had the unpleasantness of having to fire a footman for pilfering, but he had been illiterate and hardly clever enough to plan such a diabolical scheme of revenge.

So the question remained—why now? What had happened to set this act of madness into motion? And why kidnap Rhea Claire? Why not Francis or Robin instead? The only reason she could think of was that within this year, Rhea had been seen by most of London society. She had been a stunning success, her grace and beauty eclipsing other young hopefuls, whose future fortunes depended on a successful season of parties and routs and on making a good impression on influential people.

Rhea Claire would have been noticed by many people. Perhaps she had been watched by an unfriendly, calculating eye. Perhaps her family name had awakened a slumbering beast. A deep enmity could have smoldered beneath the surface for years, waiting for that certain spark to ignite it into a raging fire of vengeful hatred.

The Duchess knew her assumptions to be partly correct, for one line of poetry they'd received had said: "Thus the whirligig of time brings in his revenges." That surely referred to the cycle of time turning over a period of years to mete out its justice.

"Oh, Your Grace! I had no idea you was in here," gasped one of the maids as she lighted the candles, which spread flickering light into the shadows, revealing the Duchess's dark figure. "I'll come back later, if ye like," she offered, not liking to disturb Her Grace nowadays.

" 'Tis all right, Betsie," the Duchess told her, moving away from the chill in front of the windows. "I suppose I've missed tea again?" she asked, glancing at the clock on the mantel. For the first time, she seemed aware of the lateness of the hour.

"Aye, Your Grace," Betsie replied half-apologetically, thinking privately that Her Grace was going to fade away if she missed one more tea time. "Of course," she added, "His Grace missed tea, too."

"Did he indeed?" the Duchess murmured thoughtfully. "Is he in his study?"

"No, Your Grace. Heard one of the footmen say His Grace was in the Long Gallery. Lookin' at pictures, he was, and never knew the room was dark," Betsie said.

"I see. Thank you, Betsie," the Duchess said, a slight frown settling on her brow. Then, with a last glance around the bedchamber, she was gone.

Betsie also glanced around the lovely room, thinking it would be a shame if Lady Rhea Claire never returned to see it again.

The Duchess of Camareigh moved briskly along the corridors, finally arriving at the Long Gallery. The narrow length of room was lighted every few feet by a candelabrum and various sofas and chairs scattered along the gallery's great length cast strange shadows across the floor. The Duchess made her way purposely toward the tall man standing lost in thought before one of the paintings.

"Lucien? Lucien, what is it?" the Duchess asked softly,

coming up beside him and staring up at the portrait which seemed to hold him spellbound.

"I think I know who our enemy is, Rina," Lucien said, his voice barely above a whisper. But there was such a note of dread in it that Sabrina felt whatever hope she had left die in that moment.

Her eyes moved across the portrait of the Dowager Duchess and her three young grandchildren, the blond heads glowing brightly in the candlelight. "Your cousins?" she breathed in disbelief, for although Lucien had spoken of them just after they had been married, he had never since brought their names into any conversation. It was almost as if he had willed himself to forget their very existence—at least until now. She herself had never met either of them.

"What makes you suspect them, Lucien?" Sabrina demanded. "We've heard naught of them for almost twenty years. I remember the Dowager Duchess heard from them infrequently, and it was usually a demand for funds. But that was long ago, and I know she had not heard from them for some time before her death. They were traveling on the Continent, I believe. I've never heard a word about them returning to London."

Lucien continued to stare in fascination at the faces so like his own. His cousins. Kate and Percy, the twins, who had hated him with a murderous vengeance for most of their lives.

"I have no conclusive proof, just a feeling, Rina," Lucien warned her.

"A feeling is sometimes all we have to depend upon," she replied, her hand resting on his arm to encourage his confidences.

"Remember the veiled woman Francis mentioned?"

"Yes, we thought—especially when Lord Rendale remembered the big man—that it might be my stepmama, the Contessa. Francis had sworn that they were speaking Italian. That made her the most logical suspect, although I never did quite see her in the role. She might be grasping and selfish, but she's no murderess."

"No, I didn't really think so either, but we had to make certain. And besides, Francis did think the woman was

English, despite her foreignness. But we sent a man to Venice to discover if she had left the city, or was still in residence. His report eliminated her as the mysterious veiled woman, for at the time of the kidnapping she was in Venice, and there are witnesses who can swear to that. We also are not even certain that the man Lord Rendale saw was the same man who had been with the veiled woman. If it was not the same man, then she was exactly what she said she was, a traveler passing through the valley, and nothing more."

Lucien's voice hardened perceptibly. "And then came that note. And in it the warning, 'Ye that are of good understanding, note the doctrine that is hidden under the veil of the strange verses!' A coincidence, perhaps, but suspicious nonetheless. And, after all, that is the purpose of the poems, to entice us into guessing about hidden meanings. So once again we became suspicious of the veiled woman. Then today, we received the poem mentioning twin compasses, and because of that earlier poem, we automatically assumed it referred to Rhea's whereabouts. But what if the focal word in the line is not *compasses,* but *twin.* Had you forgotten that Kate and Percy are twins? That one never made a move without the other one? They are practically one entity.

"Then there is the riddle we received just before this one about the scars of others teaching us caution, and we assumed it referred to the mental scars suffered by others, but Rina," Lucien paused and glanced significantly at the little girl in the portrait, "what if it was meant literally?"

"Kate was horribly scarred that day," Sabrina recalled. "And she would blame you for it, forgetting her own treachery."

"Yes, and perhaps the words have double meaning, in that they refer to my scar as well. It is giving fair warning that some action of mine will elicit a violent reaction."

Sabrina gazed into the eyes of the angelic-looking Kate and Percy, their cherubic faces, haloed with golden curls, imprisoned forever on the canvas, giving away no secrets.

Unconsciously, Lucien rubbed his scarred cheek as he thought back on his uneasy relationship with his cousins.

It had only worsened through the years, until finally they had tried to murder him in order to inherit Camareigh and its wealth. If they were behind the kidnapping of his daughter, Lucien thought, then he was more frightened than he had ever been in his life—for their hate knew no bounds. They would delight in hurting that which belonged to him. They would be pitiless—and especially to *his* daughter.

The pain he had suffered when Kate had scarred his cheek was nothing compared to the anguish he felt now, as he realized that his daughter might be in the hands of the twins.

Sabrina leaned her head against his shoulder, and he moved his arm slightly to draw her closer against his chest. He felt her shoulders shaking as she wept silently. Lucien closed his eyes and rested his scarred cheek against the top of Sabrina's head. He felt almost weak from the wave of helpless rage coursing through him. With a deep sigh of weariness, he opened his eyes and found himself staring into the painted blue ones of a very young Kate Rathbourne. When, he wondered, would he come face to face once again with his cousins in the flesh?

"Damn coachman! I swear he has gone out of his way since we left London to hit every bloody pothole in the road!" Kate swore in wrathful indignation. "And if you moan and cross yourself one more time, Sophia," she warned, "I'll toss you out of the coach!"

Teddie Waltham eyed her ladyship almost indulgently, so accustomed had he become to her tantrums. "Beggin' yer pardon, m'lady. But if you had bridled yer tongue for once, the coachman wouldn't be doin' his damnedest right now to be shakin' out what teeth I've got left."

"The man was surly," Kate replied arrogantly. "He needed a setdown. And I still say we would have done far better with that fellow you hired the first time." Her teeth snapped painfully as the coach entered another pothole.

"He wouldn't have nothin' to do with me, or you, m'lady, after that hair-raisin ride a couple of months ago," Teddie Waltham informed her. "Said there wasn't money enough to get him to race through the night again like a madman. This—" Teddie's words were cut off when his head came within a few inches of the ceiling as the coach was jolted again. *"This* is the best I could do under the circumstances."

"And how about these other hirelings of yours?" Kate asked in a doubtful tone. "I trust they know how to do their jobs better than this lout of a coachman. They do know *where* to meet us, and *when?"*

"Aye, m'lady," Teddie Waltham replied flatly, wishing the day after tomorrow were over, and he were already on his way back to London. But here he sat in a draughty coach, the wind whistling around his stiff ankles, his nose freezing into an icicle, while M'Lady March Hare ranted and raved about potholes and poems, and hummed that damned song beneath her breath.

The Duchess of Camareigh cradled her two-month-old niece in her arms. Richard and Sarah's daughter had been born at dawn and christened Dawn Ena Verrick on an autumn day of somber joy. Dawn Verrick was a healthy baby who, by the few red hairs curling on top of her small head, promised to carry on the redheaded tradition of her Scottish great-grandfather. Motherhood seemed to agree with Sarah, for she possessed a new-found confidence and pride in herself, which had been missing before the birth of her daughter.

" 'Tis good to see the sun shining again," Richard commented, as he watched with fatherly interest his daughter's little hands waving in the air.

"But have you stepped outside?" Francis asked his uncle. " 'Tis colder than a Highland stream in the dead of winter."

"And if I remember correctly," Richard responded with a chuckle, "you should know. I had warned you that the rocks were slippery."

"Ah, but Francis is like you, Richard," the Duchess contributed. "He must find out for himself, despite the risks."

"An obstinacy which I inherited from you," Richard retorted.

With an answering smile, the Duchess handed her bundled-up niece into her mother's welcoming arms, amazed again at how naturally motherhood came to Sarah. Mary had been the same way with her first-born. The Duchess, however, could remember how frightened she had been the first time she held Rhea Claire in her arms. Now she prayed to have that chance again, to feel her daughter's head pressed for comfort against her breast. If only . . .

"I received a letter from Mary," she said now, forcing her mind from dwelling on Rhea. "She asks, first of all, about Dawn, and wonders if her hair is still the same red as her own. And—"

"—And will most likely grow brighter as the years pass," Richard declared, grimacing comically as he tried to catch a glimpse of his own red locks.

"—And asks about you, Sarah," the Duchess continued with a laugh.

"How was their journey home? No incidents?" Francis asked.

"She says it was bumpy, but they made surprisingly good time considering the rain and condition of the roads. Terence will be leaving for London tomorrow. He will be meeting with several officers who have been searching for news of Rhea in France. Others are due from Ireland and Wales. But the man sent to the colonies is most likely still at sea," the Duchess informed them, privately thinking naught would come of it, although there was always a chance that someone might have seen or heard something about Rhea Claire.

Through both Lucien's influence and Terence's connections with the military, troops had scoured the countryside for Rhea Claire. But so far it had been futile, for Rhea Claire seemed to have vanished without a trace.

"There is a note included from Stuart for you, Robin," the Duchess said, but she received no acknowledgment from her son.

She stared down at his dark head, and a worried expression appeared on her face. Robin had changed. He had always adored his sister, and was perhaps closer to Rhea than to Francis. Her kidnapping had transformed a giggling, mischievous little imp into a slightly sullen and disinterested boy. He had bottled up his grief, and she was beginning to despair of finding a way to help him.

Andrew was toddling unsteadily around the salon. In his explorations, he found Robin's stockinged legs of particular interest and wobbled toward them, his giggling baby talk cut off abruptly when he stumbled and grabbed at Robin's knee with sticky fingers.

Robin frowned, his gaze drawn away from the flames that had held him absorbed, and with a brusqueness of manner unusual for him, he pushed his brother away. The little fellow lost his already precarious balance and tumbled to the floor, his bellow of rage and his red, tear-stained face drawing every eye in the room.

"Robin!" the Duchess said sharply. It was a tone of voice she had never used before with her son.

Robin's lip quivered as he glanced shamefaced at his mother. "I didn't mean to push him, Mama. I-I didn't mean to, honestly. I'm sorry, Andy," he apologized, helping his brother to his feet and trying to pat dry his tears. He made funny faces at him and tickled him beneath the chin, but Andrew's feelings were still hurt and he continued to wail.

"Tea, Your Grace," Mason announced in his haughtiest voice, his eyebrows rising slightly when he realized that young Lord Andrew's shrill cries had drowned him out. "Tea, Your Grace!" he repeated, his voice just short of a yell. But at that moment, Andrew, with the capriciousness of the young, decided that he had cried enough, and just as abruptly as he had begun, he now stopped, leaving the pompous butler's words filling the void.

Under the Duchess's surprised gaze, Mason, for the first time in his life, looked embarrassed. "My pardon, Your Grace," he said, mortified by his lack of good manners. He was chagrined to realize that he had actually raised his voice like some common lout in a tavern. Had he been in Her Grace's shoes, he thought, he would have fired him on the spot. "Tea is served," he repeated, his voice well modulated once again.

"Thank you, Mason," the Duchess said, ignoring his outburst and allowing Mason to keep his prized dignity.

Meanwhile, her eyes dared either Richard or Francis to laugh out loud.

"Why don't you go and find your father, Robin," the Duchess suggested.

"Yes, Mama," Robin answered quietly, leading Andrew by the hand to his mother's chair, where the toddler, who was now smiling, was within easy reach of the tea table.

The study door was slightly ajar when Robin approached, and overhearing voices from within, he paused politely just outside.

"Your Grace, another letter has arrived, and I thought I should bring it directly to you," the footman was saying. "Mr. Mason was serving tea, or I would have waited for him, Your Grace. But considering the importance of the last letters, I thought I should not delay."

"Thank you. You did quite right—ah, Soames, isn't it?" the Duke said, with obvious approval of the young footman's actions.

"Aaah, yes, Your Grace, I-I am Soames," the flustered footman replied, surprised that so great a man should know the name of one of his lesser footmen.

Taking the plain envelope from the silver salver, the Duke slit it open and began to read its contents. He raised his hand, halting the progress of the departing footman. For what seemed like an eternity to the patiently waiting footman, the Duke stared down at the letter in his hands, his expression so severe that the young footman experienced a second's doubt about his actions in bringing it to His Grace.

When the Duke of Camareigh finally glanced up, the footman's worst fears were realized. Never before had that young man seen such a cruel, inhuman look in a man's eyes, for the Duke's strange, sherry-colored eyes were glowing with an intentness of purpose that sent a cold shiver up his spine.

"No one must know of this letter you have just brought me. I expect your silence in this matter. I especially do not want Her Grace to learn of its arrival. As far as the rest of Camareigh is concerned, you delivered no letter to me. Do I make myself understood?" he asked coldly.

"Yes, Your Grace. You have my word on it," the nervous footman reassured his stern-faced employer.

For the first time, the Duke seemed to notice the footman's worried expression, and on a sudden impulse—something he was not given to—he relented. "You did well, Soames," he said simply.

At the Duke's words of praise, the young footman's despondency lifted and, with a wide grin spreading across his face, he left the study. Little did he realize that his conscientious actions may well have set into motion certain events that would ultimately cost the Duke his life.

In less than a quarter of an hour the Duke had changed his clothes and was walking with quickening strides across the stableyard.

"Saddle my horse," he ordered the nearest groom, who'd been standing idly by the doors sucking on a piece of straw. He nearly choked at the Duke's sudden appearance, for usually word was sent on ahead from the great house that His Grace wished to ride.

As the groom hurried off to do his master's bidding, Butterick, who seldom missed anything that occurred in his domicile, caught sight of the Duke cooling his heels in the entrance and sent another groom to assist the first.

"Your Grace," Butterick began, an apologetic note in his gruff voice, "I am sorry for the delay. The message must not have been delivered, for I couldn't look meself in the eye if I kept you waiting, Your Grace." With a scowl of impatience, Butterick glanced along the row of stalls from which the Duke's horse should be appearing.

"I did not send a message," the Duke said rather shortly, his mind contemplating his next meeting. For all the attention he was paying to Butterick, the Duke might as well have been in his own world, for his eyes were narrowed in contemplation of open space. In his plain frock coat, buckskin breeches, jack boots, and neatly folded linen stock, his appearance was as severe as his expression.

Butterick cleared his throat nervously, wondering what the hell was keeping that looby, for it was becoming a mite uncomfortable to be standing here with His Grace.

323

"Butterick?" the Duke said suddenly. "How well did the late Mr. Taber know my cousins Kate and Percy?"

Butterick's mouth dropped open at the question. "Lady Kate and Lord Percy, Your Grace?" he repeated dumbly, for no one at Camareigh, including the Duke, had mentioned those two in years. Aye, they'd been a poisonous pair, that Lady Kate and Lord Percy. 'Twas bad blood they had, and he had blessed the day they left Camareigh.

Butterick jutted out his lower lip as he gave his full attention to His Grace's question. "Well, reckon the old gent knew the Lady Kate and Lord Percy as well as any other person hereabouts. Never forgot no one, he didn't. In fact," Butterick continued, pleased that he had captured the Duke's attention, "I remember he used to have words with your grandfather, the old Duke, about the way Lady Kate mistreated that little mare of hers. Had a mean streak in her, yes, sir, beggin' your pardon, Your Grace, but 'tis the truth," Butterick said, refusing to soften his opinion of the Lady Kate, even if she was His Grace's cousin.

But the Duke seemed oblivious to the criticism. "So, if Mr. Taber had happened to see my cousins, he would most likely remember them?"

"Aye, reckon so. Especially because of that little mare, Dove. Remember her meself, I do. Sweet little thing, she was. 'Twas a pity the Lady Kate rode her so hard she broke her leg. Upset, the old man was, Mr. Taber, that is, when he come to talk to the Duke about Lady Kate. Aye, remember it well, I do," Butterick said, folding his big arms across his barrel-chest as he recalled with satisfaction how the Lady Kate was denied access to the stables and to his beloved horses.

Finally the Duke's horse was led out, and he climbed into the saddle, feeling his sword riding against his thigh in almost a caress. "My saddle holsters, Butterick," he ordered.

Butterick sent one of the staring grooms hotfooting it after the requested accouterments, and became aware for the first time of the pistols the Duke was drawing out of his frock coat. Butterick's eyes nearly disappeared beneath his heavy brows as he frowned thoughtfully, wondering what the Duke was up to.

The leather holsters were attached to the pommel by Butterick himself; then the Duke slid the pair of flintlock pistols into their snug housings. Then with a curt nod, the Duke sent his big stallion out of the stable yard and rode into the distance without a backward glance.

If the Duke of Camareigh had chanced to glance back, he might have been surprised to see Butterick standing in the doorway watching him, his big hands on his hips, his expression one of concerned puzzlement. But suddenly the big man slapped his knee, the resounding whack drawing the attention of a young stable boy crossing the yard, whose steps faltered when he heard Butterick exclaim:

"Why, blast my butt from here to there! 'Tweren't no damned pigeon," he swore, his face turning a vivid red with the violence of his feelings. " 'Twas a dove! I oughta be horsewhipped for sitting on my brains all of this time. The Lady Kate's horse was named Dove. And *that* was what the old gent was trying to tell us. In his last breath he named the thing he rememebered the most about his murderer. Old Mr. Taber was drawing a dove. Couldn't write, so drew us a picture, he did. Only I was too damned blind to see it!"

He glanced at the empty drive, his puzzled expression replaced by growing consternation, as he suddenly realized where the Duke's solitary ride would lead him—to a confrontation with the Lady Kate and that conniving brother of hers, Lord Percy.

Robin Dominick slipped past the heavy door that usually served to bar the uninvited from entering the private domain of the Duke of Camareigh. Robin knew, with a trepidation that was causing his heart to beat loudly in his ears, that he was risking his father's ire by entering the sanctity of his study. It was a place forbidden even to family members. Only his mother dared to enter uninvited, and even she took the precaution of knocking first.

Robin glanced nervously around the quiet room, knowing he hadn't much time to forage about. Just in time, he had ducked into a shadowy alcove in the hall when his father had abruptly left his study, his destination *not* the salon and a cup of tea with the family as had been expected. Robin had watched in amazement as his father vaulted up the Grand Staircase, taking the steps two at a time in his haste. As he watched, his father had shed his coat as he had hurried along the landing toward the entrance to the south wing and the ducal apartments.

Robin wanted to enter the study then, but a group of gossiping footmen, standing directly in front of the study door, had kept him biding his time in the alcove. But with the sudden appearance of Mason's stiff-backed figure the garrulous threesome had split up, clearing a passage for Robin in the confusion.

Now, with the door safely closed behind him, Robin glanced around the room, which had book-lined, paneled walls and velvet armchairs situated on either side of the hearth. It was a very masculine room, almost austere, yet there was no lack of warmth, for the rich patina of aged wood, mellowed and polished, glowed softly in the firelight. Heavy velvet drapes hung beside the tall windows, where pale sunlight was filtering in through the heraldic designs of stained glass.

On the wall near the door there were several crossed swords and ancient shields bearing the coat-of-arms of the Dukes of Camareigh. Usually, this display held the attention of the present Duke of Camareigh's young son, but now the object of his unblinking gaze was his father's hallowed great mahogany desk.

Mesmerized, Robin stared at the cluttered surface of the desk. Two silver candlesticks stood sentinel at each end of the massive desk, while a silver-framed miniature of his mother occupied a place of honor at the center. A quill pen lay forgotten in an opened ledger, a pool of black ink soaking into the page of neatly inscribed figures.

Robin saw several buff-colored envelopes, their wax seals broken open, but he knew the letter he was searching for was not among them. Breathlessly, he slid past his father's armchair with its carved, cabriole legs, stumbling slightly over a claw and ball foot. His lower lip shaking with fear and excitement, Robin pulled open the center drawer, the one into which he had seen his father, only minutes earlier, slip the mysterious letter. And there it was, he thought, reaching out for it with a barely concealed chuckle of triumph.

"What the devil are you doing?"

Robin squealed in guilty surprise, which sent him tumbling backward into the chair, the coveted letter floating from his grasp and settling beyond his reach in front of the desk.

"Francis!" he cried in relief, despite his elder brother's glowering look.

"You are in deep trouble now, Robin," Francis told him, feeling little pity for his brother and his act of trespass. "And this time I think you deserve whatever punishment Father metes out to you. My God, but you must be mad to be rifling through Father's desk."

"Francis!" Robin yelled, then lowered his voice to an almost conspiratorial whisper. "You don't understand. I—"

"Yes, I do understand, and only too well," Francis retorted as he bent down and rescued the letter that had fallen out of his brother's prying hands. "That insatiable curiosity of yours has led you astray this time, Robin. I can see no excuse for it, and quite frankly, I am ashamed of you."

"My-my curiosity, Francis," Robin replied huskily, a glint of anger and tears flashing in his eyes, "may have something to do with Rhea."

Francis was finally silenced. "What are you talking about?" he asked quietly, noticing his brother's squared-off shoulders as he came from behind the desk.

"That letter you are holding was just delivered to Camareigh. I was at the door to the study and overheard Father telling the footman *not* to let anyone else learn of its arrival."

Francis looked doubtfully between his brother's intent face and the letter. "So? Father has many business interests that are not any of our concern."

"Father especially did not wish Mother to know about this note," Robin interjected. "He never keeps secrets from her."

"It is Father's decision and we should not question it, nor his motives," Francis stated firmly, unwilling to admit the strangeness of his father's actions.

"He's not having tea, is he, Francis?" Robin continued, unwilling to be swayed from a course of action he wasn't even certain of yet. "You would not have come looking for us if he was."

"He is most likely there now and wondering where *we* are."

"No," Robin contradicted him. "He is most likely at the stables."

"How do you know that?" Francis demanded, his eyes straying to the letter in his hand.

"Because I saw him going upstairs and taking off his coat at the same time. He was in a hurry. Whatever is in that note upset him. I have never seen him looking so angry," Robin said, glancing nervously at the door, as if expecting to see the Duke standing there watching him.

"Read it, Francis," he urged his brother, tugging insistently on his arm. "Read it."

Francis continued to stare down at the suddenly ominous-looking, buff-colored letter; then, with doubts about the propriety and consequences of reading his father's personal correspondence uppermost in his mind, he carefully unfolded the letter.

The Duke of Camareigh was riding east, toward the great oak mentioned in the anonymous letter. His suspicions concerning the identity of the kidnappers had grown into a dread certainty, for few people would know of the ancient tree's existence, much less of the narrow path twisting through the vale and around the pond at the far end. There stood the centuries-old oak that had spread its boughs to the skies through much of the history of Camareigh.

It had not always grown in a peaceful vale, for the blood of Saxon insurgents had been shed by battle-honed Norman swords some seven hundred years earlier, on a day much like this one, when gray clouds ran before the wind and the mighty oak cast no shadow. Legend had it that a hundred serfs, loyal to their Saxon lord, had fought valiantly with scythe and rusty blade that day by the oak, only to fall beneath the shining swords of the conquerors. But with his last dying breath, their liege lord had avenged their martyrdom and called down a curse on his Norman murderers, and upon the seed of their seed.

It was a prophecy that had yet to come true, but it had been remembered by each generation of Dominicks. For the dying Saxon lord had prophesied that he would have his revenge against them one day, when Norman blood would be shed beneath the oak and mingle with the blood of slain Saxons.

Nearing the oak, Lucien Dominick worried little about this ancient curse as he folded back the leather covers of his saddle holsters. His eyes searched the vale for some sign of entrapment, since he felt certain that he was now riding into a cleverly designed trap. Some might call him mad, or foolhardy, for having ventured forth into what must surely be danger. Some might even suspect him of courting his own death, but in his own eyes he'd had no other choice—not if he wanted to see his daughter alive again.

The note had stated quite bluntly that unless he came alone, he would never see his daughter alive. Should other riders be following him, Rhea Claire Dominick would be killed at that instant. The note had coldly stated that her blood would be on his hands.

Coming ever closer to the oak, he knew that his actions had been predictable, for he would take no chances where Rhea's safety was involved. And so he was playing into his adversaries' hands, but there was nothing he could do about it. He would, as the note had suggested, trade his life for his daughter's.

But he was no fool, nor was he about to die in vain, and before he would forfeit his life, he would have to be assured that his daughter's was to be spared.

Unfortunately, the Duke of Camareigh never had the chance to face his true enemy, for a carefully aimed pistol felled him within a few feet of the wizened oak. The ball scored deep into the flesh of his upper arm, but the spurting blood made his wound look worse than it actually was.

To his three attackers, the Duke appeared to be at their mercy, and so they moved with little urgency toward his figure, which was slumped over his saddle bow. As far as they were concerned, they had met their enemy and vanquished him.

They really should have shown more care, or taken the time to know their enemy better, for the Duke of Camareigh was not finished with them yet, especially when he overheard their conversation.

"Waste of bloody good powder, I says. Should've killed the bloke with yer shot. The way I sees it, ye be either a spindthrift or a fool. Goin' to be killin' the gent sooner or later anyway, so what's the difference whether 'tis now or then?"

"The difference, ye witling, is in gittin' paid in full."

"You oughta listen to your brother more, Jackie. I've been associated with her ladyship long enough to know that she means what she says. She's a tight-fisted bitch and would enjoy denying you your money," Teddie Waltham advised his hirelings. "No, the best thing to do is exactly what her ladyship orders. Best way of stayin' alive where she's concerned. That woman's got a heart blacker than the devil himself—and mean!" Teddie Waltham snorted. "Saw her shoot down her trusted servant without a moment's hesitation, I did. Rue the day I ever saw her black-clad figure. Should've taken to my heels then, but her ladyship has a way of tightening the noose around your neck. Cold-blooded, she is, and the sooner we get done with this, the better off we'll all be. We'll take him to her, let her amuse herself with him, taunting him about his daughter most likely, then we'll kill him off proper-like—as ordered," Teddie Waltham declared, thinking it would be a relief to finish this job and see the last of M'Lady Madness.

"What's this about a daughter? Ain't no one in the carriage except that veiled woman and the old one that's always muttering."

"It needn't concern you, Jackie. It was just a means of gettin' this fellow to come and meet her. The only way he will be meetin' up with his daughter again will be beyond the grave," Teddie reassured them, and sending them a grin over his shoulder, missed the sudden movement of his intended victim's body.

"Come on, lads," he urged them. "'Let's finish this quickly, then we can get out of the cold and warm ourselves with a bottle of rum."

At a safe distance, with the slope of the hill hiding the carriage from view, Kate saw Lucien lying slumped over his horse's neck, senseless to his surroundings and the impending danger. She clapped her hands gleefully as she saw Teddie Waltham and his two assistants emerge from their hiding place behind the oak. She wished now that she'd had the foresight to move closer, for she would love to have seen the hopeless expression in Lucien's eyes when he'd discovered he had been duped. But soon, yes, soon, she would have the great pleasure of seeing them widen with fear as he finally realized exactly who his enemy was.

Since Francis and Robin had been close to twenty minutes behind the Duke in leaving Camareigh, they'd had to ride hard to catch up with him. However, because of a short cut they knew, they had managed to arrive at the entrance to the vale just minutes behind him.

But apparently that had not been soon enough, for as they rode along the narrow path, they spied on the far side of the lake their father's figure slumped in his saddle. He had been hurt, and even as they watched in horrified fascination, three men revealed themselves from behind the big oak that the note had mentioned.

Robin lightly touched his whip to the flank of his frisky little mare, as he tried to keep up with Francis, for at the sight of their father's attackers, Francis had sent El Cid flying along the path, despite its rocky, uneven surface. Robin wanted to cry out for him to wait, but he knew he couldn't; instead, he bit his lip in frustration and tightened his grip on the reins as his horse followed in El Cid's dust. Suddenly, however, Francis slowed his pace, allowing the smaller horse to close the distance between.

"Robin!" Francis called back over his shoulder. "You take this pistol. It's primed and cocked. I don't care if you hit the man in the brown coat or not, just distract him from Father," Francis ordered, managing to lean back across El Cid's rump and hand the pistol into Robin's outstretched hand.

As Francis straightened and glanced ahead, he saw the three men closing around his father's wounded figure. But, just as Francis thought all was lost, the Duke sat up in the saddle, a smoking pistol held in his hand, the discharged shot caught his attackers completely off guard; the foremost figure grabbed his chest, then crumpled to the ground, mortally wounded.

The expression of pained surprise on the unfortunate man's face was no more extreme a reaction than what showed on the faces of Teddie Waltham and the late Jackie Porter's brother, as they watched their previously submissive victim turn on them with a sudden vengeance.

But Teddie Waltham hadn't survived for well over a quarter of a century in the streets of London without having learned a trick or two about survival, and now he pulled his second pistol from his belt and aimed it at the Duke of Camareigh.

So occupied had Teddie Waltham been in dealing with this less-than-obliging duke, that he never even heard the sound of quickly approaching hoofs, nor could he have anticipated the toe of his boot being shot off. His yelp of pain and the jerking of his arm not only frightened the Duke's mount but caused his shot to discharge well above the Duke's head. However, the shot did cause the horse to rear up in fright, and the Duke, whose wounded arm hindered him from controlling his mount, was unseated.

With Robin's wild shot spent in the ground, Francis charged into the group, El Cid's muscular shoulders effectively separating the fallen Duke of Camareigh and his would-be murderers. The actions of his sons had given the Duke the precious time he needed to draw his sword, and he quickly took the offensive against his adversaries. But in the back of his mind, etched there forever, was the image of his son Robin standing with short legs planted firmly apart, both hands wrapped around the butt of a pistol half the length of his arm, and pointing it with murderous intent at his father's attacker.

The surviving Porter brother was the first to feel the cold fury of the Duke of Camareigh; as he struggled to draw his own sword, the ringing clash of metal already sounded a death knell in his ears. For Tom Porter had known, from that first, easy parrying of his thrust by the Duke's sword, that he would be no match for this deft swordsman, who not only had an unequaled skill on his side but seemed to possess an almost inhuman strength— for he never faltered, despite the blood seeping through his coat sleeve and dripping down onto the grip.

Teddie Waltham was not having an easy time of it, either. And the worst of it was that he was being beaten back by a cub half his age—and one who wielded his sword like an expert. No doubt he'd been taught by one of France's finest fencing masters, Teddie thought bitterly, feeling a grudging admiration for this snarling pup who must surely be the son of the Duke of Camareigh. The resemblance had been startling at first and had given Teddie Waltham the discomfiting feeling that he was seeing double and that his prodigious consumption of spirits had finally taken its toll—and at the most inopportune of times.

And things were not getting any better, he thought grimly as he heard a sudden cry, then saw Tom Porter stagger and fall, his sword dropping harmlessly to the ground. Teddie Waltham gritted his teeth, for here was a lad of not more than sixteen, fighting with all of the finesse of a well-seasoned duelist. Every parry and riposte, with intricate variations, which Teddie had tried, had been only too easily fended off by his youthful opponent. The young lord's footwork was flawless and his timing impeccable, but it was the deadly accuracy of his unrelenting sword point that finally captured Teddie Waltham's respect and convinced him that a hasty, if cowardly, retreat would be the only way to stay alive.

Having made this decision, Teddie was then somewhat surprised to feel the point of that young buck's sword penetrate deep into his shoulder. With a look of disbelief, which eclipsed the strange expression on Francis Dominick's boyish face as he drew another man's blood for the first time, Teddie Waltham sucked in his breath as the steel drove deeper into his flesh. He staggered back, expecting to feel the *coup de grâce,* but this boy, who fought with the expertise of a master, was not bloodthirsty and did not follow up his advantage. In fact, after effectively disabling his opponent, he seemed more concerned with the fate of his father than the pitiful plight of the wounded Teddie Waltham.

Teddie Waltham might have been outclassed by a mere youngster, but he was no fool and he knew a chance to escape when he saw it. Besides, the odds were growing uncomfortably high against him. He was no gentleman of honor who would stay and fight to the death —especially when he saw the Duke of Camareigh heading toward them with a murderous look in his eye boding ill for one Edward Matthew Waltham, unless he turned tail and ran.

Standing in the safe shelter of the trees on the hillside, Kate gave a guttural scream of rage when she saw the second hireling fall to his knees, then crumple into a senseless heap on the ground. How could it possibly be? What the devil had happened to her carefully laid-out plans? Boys! Boys had ruined the revenge she had already been savoring. She could scarcely believe her own eyes. That little squirt had actually shot Teddie Waltham in the foot, while the other young man, the one she recognized as Francis Dominick, had ridden into the middle of the scuffle on that beast of a horse and was now actually dueling with Teddie Waltham.

"Damn him! Damn his soul!" she cried as she saw the intrepid and stout-hearted Teddie Waltham parry one last time, then turn on his heels and stumble up the hill, his skulking progress hindered by his toeless left boot.

Pounding her fists against the tree trunk, Kate glared down at the travesty of her dreams. Lucien had escaped her again! Lucien should have been hers. But always, always he managed to squirm out of her grasp. He should have been on his hands and knees before her, begging for mercy, but instead he was free. And those fools had bungled everything. It was not fair!

Teddie Waltham was experiencing remarkably similar thoughts as he struggled up the hillside. His feet were slipping in the mud, which made him seem to lose more ground than he was gaining. And it certainly didn't help matters that he may well have lost his big toe, he thought, limping along, looking more disreputable than he ever had before in his life. His shoulder felt as if the fires of Hell were burning in it. Certain that the hounds of that nether region were on his heels, he glanced back but was temporarily relieved to see no one in hot pursuit.

Teddie Waltham made his way slowly up the hill, losing his footing time and time again, then falling, then crawling, until panting, he finally neared the top, only to find her ladyship standing there watching. He held out a hand, falling again, but she never moved. She just continued to stand there silently.

"You failed. You fool. You oaf. You dullard. Y-you imbecile. You *radoteur!*" Kate spoke softly, her anger barely held in check as she approached her bloodied mercenary and stared down at him dispassionately. "You have destroyed all that I had hoped for. With your milksop courage you have managed to make a mess of everything. I should have kicked you out on your ass the minute I laid eyes on you! If it were not for your amateurish bungling, I would have Lucien here before me now, begging on his hands and knees like a sniveling cur."

"You're stark staring mad, woman! That man would never have gone down on his hands and knees before you or no one. And I'm beginning to see why he got rid of you all of those years ago," Teddie Waltham yelled back at her, his patience with this madwoman having expired with his courage. Now, whatever fears he'd had of her were quickly draining out with his lifeblood.

"I dunno what happened between you and the Duke," he continued, "but it apparently kept you and that Percy fellow out of the country and out of the Duke's hair for a good many years. And I say," he added, pulling himself to his feet and weaving slightly from the strain, "more power to him. He obviously knew what he was doing when he sent the two of you packing. God, woman, you make the inmates of Newgate look like martyred saints. And as

335

for myself, not being of a saintly disposition," Teddie Waltham declared, relishing his next words, "I shall bid you *adieu*, m'lady."

"What do you mean? What the devil are you blathering about? Where are you going, you fool!" Kate screamed, watching in disbelief as Teddie Waltham turned his back on her.

Her silken skirts rustled as she hurried after him, and a rage born of frustration and hatred began to consume her, leaving her senseless and blind to calmer thought. But Kate had only taken a couple of steps in pursuit of her errant knight, when he turned suddenly and grabbed her wrists, wrestling the pistol from where she'd hidden it in the folds of her skirts.

"I told you I was leavin', m'lady, but not in the same manner in which our friend, the late Rocco, did. I'm a mite sharper than poor Rocco was, although he did teach me a valuable lesson concerning the extent of your loyalties, m'lady." Teddie Waltham's mouth twisted into a grimace as he stared down at the pistol. "Reckon another step and I would've had a hole in me back, eh, m'lady?"

"You swine. Have you forgotten, with this new-found courage of yours, that I know who you are? I'll have that dunghill name of yours spread all over London. The authorities will have a thing or two to say to you, but perhaps *after* they have already stretched that precious neck of yours."

"Go right ahead, m'lady. But it won't be givin' you any satisfaction, 'cause good ol' Teddie Waltham ain't a-gonna be around to reap his just desserts. No pryin' eyes will catch Teddie Waltham's face in London, nor maybe in all of England. A change of name, then a change of country just oughta about do it fer me. Aye, I'll wager that *I'll* be around long after you've departed to warmer parts, m'lady," Teddie said tauntingly.

Kate stood in stunned silence as she watched this common thief and murderer walk away from her. How dare he speak to her, Lady Katherine Anders, in such an insolent manner? How dare he abandon her just when she needed him the most? He owed it to her, for it was his fault that she had failed again. She wouldn't let that bloody swine get away with it, she vowed, hurrying after his limping form.

She knew a moment's panic as she rounded the hill, for his pitiful figure had dropped from sight. Then she saw him again, heading for the horses tied just beyond her carriage. Her insane rage riding high, she picked up her skirts and ran, quickly closing the distance between them.

Teddie Waltham thought at first, when he felt his skin being torn and ripped by sharp talons, that a vicious hawk had fallen from the skies onto his shoulders. But when he saw the clawlike fingers with nails filed into dangerous points, he knew only too well the name of his attacker.

He flinched when her ladyship's nails sliced into his unprotected cheek, causing blood to drip into the corner of his mouth. With a desperate effort superceding the burning pain from the wound in his shoulder, Teddie Waltham reached up and grabbed hold of Kate's arms. Then, swinging her around, he threw her from his back.

Kate rolled into an undignified position, her breath coming in short gasps as she tried to right herself. But before she could even crawl onto her knees, she felt a viselike grip on the back of her neck, which effectively held her prisoner.

"Since we are about to dissolve our uneasy partnership and go our own way, hopefully never to set eyes on one another again," Teddie Waltham said silkily, "I think 'tis only fair that I should see the face of my mysterious benefactress. After all, it looks as if I'm goin' to be only half-paid for all of me time and effort, not to mention the danger I've put meself in time and time again."

"No!" Kate cried out, struggling with the superhuman strength of a madwoman as she tried to prevent Teddie Waltham from tearing the veil from her face. But her fanatical determination to keep concealed that which lay hidden beneath was equally matched with his own determination to see those carefully protected secrets revealed.

What Teddie Waltham had been expecting to see and had speculated on for months was nothing compared to the reality. As he ripped the molded mask from Kate's face, her clawing hands were not quick enough to conceal her horribly scarred face from his gaze.

Teddie Waltham took an instinctive step backward, raising his hands as if to shield himself from so grotesque an image. His look of horror was almost too much for Kate to stand, but his whispered "My God" of pity just about finished her. Kate continued to crouch on her knees, her pride and soul laid bare by this fool's calloused hands. All that she had sought to hide from curious eyes was now revealed to the harsh, unkind light of day.

Teddie Waltham continued to stare in hypnotic repulsion at the scarred half of Kate's face, where the scar tissue was thick and puckered, creating a monstrous travesty of what must have been once a breathtakingly beautiful woman. Whatever had gouged through the tender flesh of her cheek had left the side of her mouth gaping open and the corner of her eye drawn down, the effect of which was a baleful stare.

"Good God, but you are in a living hell, aren't you, m'lady?" Teddie said thickly, feeling sick as he turned away from her weeping, black-clad figure. Hurrying to the tethered horses, he mounted; then, without a backward glance, he turned his horse's head northwestward, toward Bristol, where he knew he would be able to catch a ship bound for the colonies. He had heard that Boston was a growing town, perhaps just the place for an enterprising fellow like himself. Teddie Waltham knew he had to put as many leagues as possible between himself and his soon-to-be notorious past.

And wise he was to take such quick action, for within the hour, all of Camareigh and the village of Camare had been alerted to the presence of the thwarted assassins. Soon the surrounding countryside was crowded with avenging footmen, gardeners, and grooms, not to mention every able-bodied villager who wanted to see the kidnappers of the Lady Rhea Claire brought to justice—although that might have been unlikely had any of this bloodthirsty mob gotten their hands on Teddie Waltham or the Lady Kate.

In the great house of Camareigh, the Duke was impatiently enduring the careful ministrations of a clucking, concerned Rawley. Her capable hands had efficiently cleaned and bandaged his wound, and now she was muttering and grumbling as her patient refused to follow her sensibly prescribed orders.

"A gunshot wound is a gunshot wound, no matter how slight. Even though ye be lucky the ball didn't shatter your bone, still 'tis a deep wound and ye've lost a powerful lot of blood. Reckon we won't be needin' that old fool of a doctor in here recommending bleedin' His Grace." Rawley snorted in derision. "Never did hold to that belief, no sir. If it meets with your approval, Your Grace?" she added almost as an afterthought as she glanced over at the Duchess, who'd remained remarkably still and silent throughout the whole ordeal of dressing His Grace's arm.

"Of course, Rawley. Quite sensible of you," the Duchess said, her voice devoid of emotion. Only the Duke realized the full extent of her emotions; he knew she was white-hot with rage.

"Thank you, Rawley," the Duke said now in a tone of dismissal, which penetrated even into Rawley's thick skin. "I shall be quite all right with the Duchess watching over me."

"Hmmmm, well, s'pose so, Your Grace," Rawley said with a sniff, not happy about placing her patient into another's hands, even if they were the Duchess's.

As the door closed on Rawley's dragging steps, the Duke glanced at his wife's stiff-backed figure. He did not need to guess wildly to know what she was enraged about.

"Damn you, Lucien," she said, her voice hoarse with pent-up emotion.

She had not disappointed him. Lucien knew what would follow as he watched her move closer to where he sat on the edge of the great bed.

"How dare you keep this from me. How dare you ride off to almost certain death and never say a word to me. How do you think I feel?" Her violet eyes were wet with tears. "They would have killed you, those damned cousins of yours. You would be dead right now, except for the timely intervention of your two sons, with no thanks to you. Oh, Lucien," Sabrina whispered, "if you had left me,

I do not think I could have borne it, not after losing Rhea, too. How could you put me in such a position? To have to choose between the two of you, and then, perhaps, to have lost both of you. I do not know if I can ever forgive you for this, Lucien."

The Duke's lips tightened grimly as he faced her wrath born of worry and her sadness born of hopelessness. But he knew that he could not have made any other choice than the one he had. If Sabrina had known of his plans, she would have ridden beside him and wielded a sword as aggressively as her son. It was not her fight; Percy and Kate were his cousins, and he would not put Sabrina into such jeopardy.

"I had to handle it as I saw fit, Rina. I know Kate and Percy. I have dealt with them before," he reminded her. "They are of my blood, and I have to deal with them. There is no one else to do it."

"Rhea is my daughter. Had you forgotten that I gave birth to her? I had the right to face her kidnappers the same as you did."

"Whether my actions were right or wrong, 'tis past now. They never had any intention of releasing Rhea for me. And if they had disclosed her fate to me, then, my dear, I fear that I would have taken that information to my grave with me. And you are right," Lucien added, a different note entering his voice, "that if it had not been for my sons, we would not be standing here now arguing."

Sabrina's hand caressed Lucien's cheek, lingering for an endless moment against the rough scar. "I would die a little every day, and each breath I took would be an agony if you had left me alone, Lucien. I am ashamed because it is a purely selfish wish of mine to keep you beside me. I am angry because I am so vulnerable. I would not know what to do without you, my love," she admitted, a pathetic droop to the dark head which was usually held so proudly. "What are we going to do, Lucien? We know no more than we did before."

The Duke glanced to the tall windows overlooking the lands of Camareigh, knowing that Kate and Percy were out there somewhere. Sabrina was right—they knew little more than they had before. One thing he knew now, however, was the face of his enemy. Deep inside, he knew that Kate and Percy were responsible for Rhea's kidnapping, and although they had escaped this time, they could not stay hidden forever. And when their time ran out, he would be there waiting.

"Unfortunately, I fear that they have not finished with us just yet," the Duke commented as he pressed his lips against the Duchess's forehead. She allowed herself to lean lightly against his shoulder, and he pulled her close with his uninjured arm.

Staring into the heart of the fire, the Duke was speculating on the next and ultimate meeting between himself and his cousins. He also thought of what he'd heard said by one of his attackers. Had they meant that Rhea was already dead? Or that it was merely his death that would keep him from seeing his daughter alive again? Whatever it had meant, he would not trouble Sabrina with it.

"Father?" inquired a hesitant voice from the partially opened door. "I knocked, but I guess you did not hear me. W-we wanted to know how you were." Francis ran his words together in his nervousness, for he was not certain of the reception he would receive from his father.

"Come in, son," the Duke said, beckoning with his outstretched hand.

"Robin is here, too," Francis added.

"Both of you, come in," the Duke repeated, his hand still held out to his sons.

Robin shot past his older brother, catapulting into his mother and father's bodies and pressing close to them.

" 'Tis all right, Robin, my love," the Duchess reassured him. "Your father is proud of you. Of both of his fine sons. If it were not for you and Francis, well . . ." The Duchess did not finish her sentence.

"You are not going to die. Promise!" Robin cried, his voice muffled against his mother's breast.

"No, I am not, thanks to you and Francis," the Duke told him, his eyes meeting his oldest son's. "Considering the circumstances, as well as my own actions, I cannot in good conscience reprimand you and Robin for going through my desk." Then the Duke added, smiling slightly as he saw that Robin was about to correct him, "Ah, I am sorry. I understand that you take full blame for the deed, and that Francis had no hand in that part of the conspiracy."

"I do wish you had come to me, my dears," the Duchess said, her voice still bearing some of the hurt she had felt at not being informed of their activities.

"I am sorry, Mother, if we caused you any pain because of our actions. But I will not apologize for keeping you out of danger. Time was of the essence in following Father, and begging your pardon, ma'am, you would only have been in the way," Francis said, his eyes so full of concern for her well-being that it robbed his words of any insult. However, he certainly was not prepared for her laughter, nor for his father's, whose deep laugh soon joined hers.

"They were not exactly Will and John Taylor to the rescue," the Duke said, which only he and the Duchess seemed to understand, for they started to laugh all over again.

Robin raised his wet face, a puzzled expression in his eyes. But as he listened to his mother and father, a shy smile was forming on his lips. It seemed certain that his father was not going to die, for if he were, he would not be laughing.

"I was just talking with Butterick," Francis said, "and he's reported that several grooms found the wheel tracks of a carriage around the far side of the hill. They followed the tracks back onto the road. I took the liberty, sir, of having riders sent along the roads out of the valley. Perhaps a carriage will have been sighted leaving the valley. 'Twould be a fairly uncommon sight if the horses were being whipped into their fastest gait."

"You did well, Francis, thank you," the Duke complimented his son, but when his words of praise seemed to fall on deaf ears, he inquired curiously, "There is something else troubling you, Francis?"

Francis started to respond, then looked away in embarrassment, and the Duchess would have sworn she'd caught the brightness of tears in his eyes. But when he looked back, his blue eyes not only were dry but blazing with a confused anger.

"I just do not understand how our own flesh and blood could do this to us. How could your cousins Percy and Kate actually kidnap Rhea? I cannot believe that there are people monstrous enough to do such a thing. And why are they doing this to us? What have we ever done to them? They once lived here at Camareigh with you, didn't they, Father? They are a part of the Dominick family. We all have the same forebears, and yet they are trying to destroy us. Why? And why take Rhea of all people? She is gentle and kind, and she has never hurt anyone. I swear to you, Father," Francis said solemnly, resembling the Duke more than ever, "that if they have in any way hurt Rhea, that I will take pleasure in killing them both. And no one will be able to stop me," he warned, for he had tasted blood that afternoon, and knew instinctively that he would again.

Before either of his parents could respond to his challenge, Francis Dominick turned on his heel and left the room. Robin stared in open-mouthed wonder at the closed door, where a stranger, who had somehow taken his brother's place, had stood glaring at them only moments before.

"Damn them!" the Duchess swore softly. "They have succeeded, haven't they, and in a manner which I suspect they never even planned on. They have robbed Francis of his innocence. He has learned how to hate, Lucien, and that frightens me. For if they have managed to taint Francis with their evilness, without ever touching him, then what have they done to Rhea Claire? How have they tarnished the shining purity and beauty that is so much a part of Rhea? Oh, dear God, please forgive me," the Duchess cried, "but I almost pray that she is dead. For I would not see her suffer pain or defilement at their hands. Please, Lucien, tell me that I needn't be sinful in wishing such a thing, and that she will come back to us unharmed."

Lucien Dominick embraced his wife and son, for he

had no answer and could offer them no more comfort than the warmth and protection of his arms.

Camareigh was silent. The heavy velvet drapes in the Duke of Camareigh's study were drawn against the coldness of the night. As the Duke stared morosely into the flames in the hearth, the only sounds were the steady ticking of a clock on the mantel and the logs crackling into ashes.

Francis's deductions had been correct; a carriage traveling at a dangerous speed had been spotted rumbling through a small hamlet southeast of Camareigh. That had been several hours ago, and now it was well past midnight. The search for Percy and Kate would have to wait until the revealing light of dawn.

The Duke's elbow was propped on the padded arm of the easy chair, and he rested his forehead against the heel of his hand. He felt lost. Never before had he known such a helpless feeling. He had kept to himself his deepest, most anguished thoughts, for he would not share his hopelessness with Sabrina. He could not destroy that last desperate hope, which kept her from falling into the darkness of inconsolable despair. Sabrina still believed, with that optimistic spirit she could not deny for long, that her daughter was still alive, whereas he, with a cynicism borne of having dealt with Percy and Kate for much of his life, believed that Rhea Claire, whose misfortune it had been to be his daughter, was in fact dead.

The Duke sighed, opening his tired eyes at the sound of baying hounds. A small army of footmen, stable hands, and gamekeepers, under the command of Butterick, were patrolling the estate with the dogs. The Duke was doubtful, though, that they would flush anything from the underbrush except a few irate quail, for Kate and Percy would not be insane enough to make another attempt on his life. Besides, their carriage had been spotted hours ago, and since they'd been traveling at a madman's speed, they were probably halfway to London by now.

Lucien heard a step near the door and turned, thinking it was Sabrina. Although he had left her sleeping, it had been only a fitful doze.

As a half-consumed log settled deeper into the flames, the fire suddenly flared brighter; in this glowing light, a black figure moved slowly from the shadows.

"Kate," the Duke said, knowing instinctively that it could be none other.

"Dear cousin Lucien," Kate murmured, her voice raspy with pent-up emotion as she finally came face to face with her most hated enemy.

"How did you get in?" the Duke heard himself asking conversationally. He himself was surprised by the calmness of his voice.

It must have shaken Kate even more, for she spat back angrily, "Always so calmly in control of everything and everyone in your life, aren't you, Lucien? You think you hold your destiny in the palm of your hand. Think yourself fortune's chosen one, eh, my golden-haired cousin? Always Grandmama's little darling, weren't you, Lucien?" Kate demanded, her voice vibrating with loathing.

"Lucien . . . Lucien . . . Lucien . . ." Kate hissed, both savoring and despising the name of her cousin. "Standing in the path of all that Percy and I should have had as our right. Meddling in all that we had planned, obstructing us every way we turned. Conspiring against us with that old woman. How we have hated you, Lucien. But," Kate said, her voice suddenly falsely bright and almost teasing, "you asked how 'twas that I got in? Oh, poor Lucien, fool that you are," she said pityingly, "you have always underestimated Percy and me, haven't you? 'Tis a pity for you, that you have always thought yourself so much smarter than we. You see, even though you have so cruelly denied me my home for over a quarter of a century, do you really think I would have forgotten *any-thing* about Camareigh? I still remember that underground passage used by our ancestors fleeing from the Roundheads. I easily found the entrance near the stone balustrade in the terraces, so cunningly concealed in the rose arbor. The kitchens were quiet when I entered beneath the back stairs, but then I suppose you dined hours ago, didn't you?

"And do you know where I have been?" she continued. "I have been waiting outside in the cold. For hours I stood there gazing at the lighted windows. Can you at all imagine how it felt to be on the outside looking in? How that warm yellow glow beckoned to me? I could hear a whispering through the boughs above my head, telling me that I had come home at last. Home, Lucien. Home to Camareigh after so many endless years of suffering the tortures of the damned. Percy and I have finally come home to deal retributive justice to you, Lucien. And you will not deny me my prize. 'Tis *my* inheritance from Camareigh, and this time I wll not be cheated out of it. 'Tis only fair that I should have it, Lucien. Percy would want it this way. I know he would."

Lucien glanced around curiously. "And where is that pale shadow of yours, Kate?" Then Lucien raised his voice in a command. "Percy! It is safe now, you may come out from behind your sister's skirts. Come now, do not be shy. Show me that sniveling countenance of yours, Percy."

Kate's shrill laughter halted any further taunts he might have issued. "If he does indeed show his face, 'twill be Camareigh's first ghost."

"What do you mean, Kate?" Lucien asked softly. Her quivering voice had sent a shiver of warning up his spine.

"He is dead!" Kate groaned. "And you are his murderer. 'Tis all your fault, Lucien. My Percy is gone. My sweet Percy," she cried, her voice heavy with grief and confusion. "They found him floating in the canal, an assassin's knife embedded in his back. One day he was alive and the next day he was dead. Oh, my God, how he must have suffered. My Percy, my sweet Percy," she whimpered, sounding as if she'd been dealt a blow which still could not be comprehended. But just as quickly her voice hardened as she added, "And do you realize how *I* have suffered without Percy? I might as well be dead, too."

Lucien moistened his dry lips. He knew now what had triggered this horrifying chain of tragic events. Kate was seeking revenge for Percy's death. Lucien shook his head in disbelief. Percy was dead. He had not thought of his cousins in years; yet, knowing that Percy was dead gave him a strange feeling.

He stared hard at the veiled figure. "You kidnapped my daughter, Kate," he said softly, his words almost imperceptible to Kate. "She never did you any harm, Kate. I am your enemy, not my children."

"She was a Dominick. Flaunting her heritage in my face. So beautiful. So pure. So gullible, she was." Kate laughed harshly. "She was dear to your heart, was she not, dear cousin Lucien? There is your reason why. You have suffered each day she has been gone from Camareigh, haven't you? And puzzled, were you, by my little notes?" she asked hopefully. "I did think that was rather clever of me, Lucien."

But Lucien hadn't been listening; his heart had leapt painfully at one of her casually spoken words. " 'Was,' Kate?" he asked.

"Was what?" Kate demanded, not fully understanding what he was asking. Then suddenly she chuckled deeply. "Oh, I see. You want to know whether or not your daughter is dead or alive, is that it, Lucien? Well," she hesitated, baiting him, "I shan't tell you. No, maybe I shall. Either way, 'tis bad news for you, I fear," she told him remorselessly.

Then, beginning to enjoy herself, she continued, "Actually, to be quite honest, Lucien, I really am not certain if the chit is alive or not. But I certainly would not bet on her chances of still being with us," she advised in a kindly tone. "You see, dear cousin, I sent your daughter to the colonies." She laughed contemptuously when she heard his sharp intake of breath.

"I sold your precious daughter as an indentured servant. She is probably slaving away in some whorehouse in the Americas right now—if she survived the journey, which I seriously doubt. She was such a pale, pitiful-looking little thing. I must say, Lucien, from what I have seen of your children, you certainly did not sire any robust heirs. And I am afraid that I fear for the Dominick bloodline. Grandmama would be so disappointed, don't you think so?" Kate inquired with all of the concern of a doting aunt. "Well, anyway, back to that whey-faced daughter of yours. I may very well be wrong; she might possess far more spunk than I'd given her credit for. But

347

I, for one, would certainly not wish to be in her shoes when she arrives in the colonies. Savage place, so I've heard. Of course, this is mere speculation, and perhaps completely irrelevant, for she was unconscious the last time I saw her. We had to drug her, of course. I wonder if we gave her too much of the sedative. She was breathing rather heavily, now that I think about it," she said thoughtfully.

When Lucien moved toward her, she said, "No! Stay where you are, Lucien!" Then her pistol appeared quite magically from the folds of her cloak.

"I am surprised that you did not kill her, Kate. You never were a very patient person, and apparently you took Rhea all the way back to London. I imagine that *is* where you bought her passage for the colonies?" Lucien asked easily.

"Please, do not be thanking me. That would be more than I could possibly bear," Kate said with amusement. "Your gratitude for the brat's life would be sorely misplaced, for I would have dumped her from the carriage the first chance we'd had. 'Twas that fool of a footman of mine who stayed her execution. He took a strange fancy to her and kept her cradled in his arms for the whole bloody journey. And I tell you now, Lucien, that was a damned uncomfortable ride through the countryside, with Rocco slobbering over the girl and growling if I so much as looked her way." Kate still smarted from the experience. "But I took care of Rocco later. No one betrays me and gets away with it."

"What happened?"

"He wouldn't part with her even in London. And that was damned awkward, believe me. Especially where that busybody landlady of mine was concerned. But Teddie and I—he was the bungling fool who shot you—had made our plans, and I was not about to let Rocco stand in my way. So I shot him. Then this friend of Teddie's came and took her on board his ship. What happened to her after that, well, I haven't the faintest idea. I must admit, 'twas Teddie's idea to send her to the colonies. Teddie," Kate murmured, his name filling her with a loathing almost as great as that which she felt for Lucien. "When

I find him, I'll kill him. Damn him, the swine," she swore, raising her free hand in a protective gesture before her face.

"But I will deal with him later," she continued, turning her thoughts once again to Lucien Dominick, Duke of Camareigh. "You have brought me such misery, Lucien. Everything Percy and I wanted in life, you ruined—and just because you were alive. When I think of our life in Venice, then look at you sitting here, looking so disgustingly healthy, I could scream at the injustice of it all. That would have angered Percy so. I am sure he hoped that you would get fat and gouty, but no, not you," she told him resentfully.

Then, suddenly changing the subject, she said, "Do you know, Lucien, I do rather like Francis, even though he did ruin my plans this afternoon. He is much like Percy, I think. Yes, just like Percy. I have not seen the twins yet, but I hear they are golden-haired, just like Percy and me. Once, Percy and I were golden-haired and beautiful, were we not, Lucien? Once, long ago," she whispered in anguish, her voice trailing away. "But the years have changed that, haven't they? Do you want to see what I look like now, Lucien? You should be curious; after all, you are the one who destroyed me."

Slowly and deliberately, she raised the filmy veil that floated eerily around her shoulders; at the same time, the pistol held so steadily in her hand was still pointed dead center at Lucien's chest. With a curious lack of trepidation or shame resulting from that afternoon when Teddie Waltham had gazed in horror upon her scarred face, Kate now waited with a smoldering anticipation for a similar reaction from Lucien. She wanted to see the look of uncontrollable revulsion cross his face; then she would have the supreme pleasure of turning it into a death mask.

Her hand now trembling, Kate bared her face and stared boldly into Lucien's eyes. But much to her disappointment, he did not flinch or recoil from the macabre sight of her flawed beauty. He continued to stare at her with the same haughty and indifferent look he had always reserved for her. That cold, contemptuous expression still had the power to infuriate her, and Kate realized she would never be free of Lucien, for he haunted her even in her dreams. He seemed always to be sitting in judgment on her and Percy. He was always there ridiculing them, goading them and hounding them. From the very beginning he had connived to have them banished from Camareigh. It was Lucien's fault that misfortune had befallen them, that sweet Percy had died in Venice, bloated with drink, and that her own beauty had become a grotesque mask. It was all because of Lucien. Dear cousin Lucien, who stood before her now.

Lucien watched silently as the violent display of emotions stole across her face; he knew that all her grievances against him were being rekindled and fanned into flames by her insane hatred of him. He gazed into the pale eyes, which were glowing with an insatiable lust for revenge, and he waited, knowing that he would not escape death this time.

The Duchess awoke with a start. She gazed blindly around the dark bedchamber. The fire in the hearth had burned down to glowing coals, leaving the room at the mercy of cold draughts seeping in through ill-fitting doors. She stretched out her arm as she rolled over, instinctively seeking out Lucien's warmth beside her.

She sat up in surprise when she felt the cold, empty space. Lucien's wound, was her first thought. He might be feverish, she thought, her eyes searching the shadowy room, but there was nothing to be seen except the bulky shapes of furniture.

"Lucien? Lucien, are you here?" she called out softly. But the only response was a deafening silence.

The Duchess hesitated for only an instant before throwing back the covers, sliding from the bed and slipping her feet into her silken mules. In the darkness her fingers found her soft, finely woven wool shawl, where it lay folded across the back of the chaise longue at the foot of the bed.

Camareigh seemed unusually quiet, the Duchess thought as she hurried along the dark corridors. Before leaving the bedchamber, she had checked the dressing room, thinking that had Lucien been restless, he might have gone there in order not to disturb her sleep. But the small room had been empty. She had walked the distance of the Long Gallery, hoping to find him gazing at that picture again, but the room was possessed of an almost deathlike silence. The Duchess berated herself for her midnight fancies, when the room suddenly began to feel like a tomb, with the dead staring down at her, resenting her intrusion into their solitude.

The Duchess shivered, wishing Mary were here to explain away such strange feelings. Holding the hem of her dragging nightdress in one hand and a candlestick and the ends of her shawl in the other, the Duchess descended the Grand Staircase, headed for Lucien's study. It was the first place that she should have looked, she decided, shivering with cold and wishing she were back beneath the quilts in her bed.

Absorbed as she was in making her way carefully down the stairs, she heard nothing until she had taken several steps across the marble hall toward Lucien's study. She paused, pushing her unbound hair out of her eyes when she heard voices coming from the opened door of the room. At first she thought it was a servant; then she realized with growing alarm that no servant would be speaking to the Duke of Camareigh in that tone of voice.

". . . and 'tis time I felt your blood on my hands, dear cousin Lucien. You should have died years ago. 'Twas remiss of me not to have taken care of this matter sooner. You really never should have been left alive to sire heirs to Camareigh. To think that you, of all people, should have sired twins. Even Percy never had twins, but then that cow of a wife of his hadn't any hot blood in her. I'm surprised she managed to give birth to anything, or that Percy persisted in trying," Kate was saying.

A log fell with a shower of sparks in the hearth, startling Kate for an instant. But her aim never wavered as she continued to stare hungrily at Lucien's face, his scar still having the power to fascinate her.

"This will be the very last time, Lucien. I shall finally put an end to your cursed existence. Good-by, dear cousin Lucien, and may your soul rot in hell!" she spat in a final burst of venom.

Kate never saw the flashing blade, but Lucien did; yet he still could not believe it, even as it swung down in an arc from the doorway, guided by Sabrina's hands.

As the curved edge of the blade sliced deeply into Kate's exposed wrist, she screamed with surprise and pain, the pistol dropping from her throbbing hand. She turned incredulous eyes on the small, black-haired woman standing in the doorway, who still held the bloodied sword in her hands.

Involuntarily, Sabrina stepped backward, for never before had she seen such a malevolent, nightmarish face. The pale, glittering eyes were cursing her silently, while the distorted mouth snarled such obscenities that Sabrina could feel her blood running cold.

Kate's hoarse scream of frustrated rage filled the room like a demon's howl, momentarily stunning Sabrina as she stood pressed against the doorjamb. Lucien knew Kate well enough, however, not to make the fatal mistake of underestimating her, for despite her wound she was still dangerous. She was also crazed enough to attack the woman who had foiled her last chance to destroy him.

But Kate, with the instinct of a wounded, trapped animal, sensed his move to block her from her only means of escape. Her pale eyes, filled with a desperate cunning, darted around the room seeking a weapon, but the room was unfamiliar to her. She stared down at the pistol lying at her feet in a pool of her own blood. Her glance drew Lucien's as well, and in that brief second when he was off his guard, she reached out with her uninjured hand and wrapped her fingers around one of the cold silver candlesticks on the desk; then, with a guttural cry, she threw the heavy piece at Lucien's head.

He managed to step aside, and it crashed with a splintering of wood against the molded paneling of the fireplace. But it had given Kate enough time to escape, and in a trice she was upon Sabrina, her clawlike hand pushing the smaller woman into the path of the pursuing Duke.

Sabrina tripped on the hem of her gown and fell to her knees, as Lucien, trying to avoid her, stumbled against the door.

He straightened slowly, favoring his injured arm. "Are

you all right, Rina?" he demanded, hesitating before following his cousin into the dark hall.

"Yes, please. Go after her, Lucien," Sabrina pleaded as she struggled to her feet, using the bloodied sword like a cane.

But he was not gone longer than a few minutes before returning and closing his arms around the Duchess. "Oh, thank God, Lucien," she breathed. "What happened? Where is she?"

"I couldn't find a trace of her in the darkness. She's just disappeared. We will need half the household to find her. I doubt, however, that she will get far with that wound," Lucien predicted as he guided Sabrina to one of the armchairs before the fire and gently forced her to sit. He then walked over to his desk, opened the middle drawer, and pulled out a pisttol. He paused beside the bloodstain on the floor; then, with a look of distaste, he picked up Kate's pistol. The butt was sticky with congealing blood, but he grasped it firmly and walked to the windows. Pulling back the heavy velvet hangings, he opened the window and fired each pistol, the sound echoing through the silence of the night like the roar of a cannon.

"Lucien! What—" Sabrina began, as the explosions reverberated in the room.

"That should alert Butterick and his men. Camareigh will be alive with people and lights within minutes. Kate shall have a difficult time of it, for the dogs will sniff her out if she is mad enough to still be on the grounds. Kate's days are finally numbered," he pronounced coldly.

"I cannot seem to forget that horrible face and those wild eyes. I do not think I have ever felt such evilness," Sabrina said, her lips trembling as she tried to hold back tears. "And to think that she meant to murder you."

"But she did not, my love. If it had not been for you and that sword, then she might well have succeeded," Lucien reminded her, his eyes lingering on the empty space on the wall where the sword had been crossed with its mate. Now it had been used as a weapon once again.

"Now, come on, my love, dry your tears," Lucien ordered, watching while she dabbed ineffectively at her cheeks with the back of her sleeve. "The worst is over."

Sabrina sniffed; then, as her focus sharpened, she became aware of the subtle change in Lucien's expression. It would have gone unnoticed by anyone else, but Sabrina knew Lucien's moods too well not to sense the difference. It was as if he'd had a lightening of spirit.

"What is it, Lucien?" she asked hesitantly. Then, as she saw a slight smile curving his lips, she felt her own excitement rising. "Please, Lucien. Tell me what it is," she pleaded.

"They did not kill Rhea Claire. No, listen to what I have to say first, Rina," Lucien warned her as she scrambled to her feet, her eyes glowing with renewed hope.

Forgetting that Kate's blood was staining his hands, Lucien took Sabrina's hands between his and stared into her expectant face. "Kate admitted that she had not killed Rhea, although not for a lack of trying. She said they had drugged Rhea, then sold her as an indentured servant. She was put on board a ship bound for the colonies. Even Kate does not know what Rhea's ultimate fate was to be," he said bluntly, afraid she would get her hopes up too high, for the horrors of such a journey were not unknown to him. The fate of many a traveler crossing the seas was uncertain, but the hardships were even greater for those who could not afford to pay for proper food and accommodation. But even if they could afford it, it mattered little if the ship were sailing on violent seas.

"The colonies?" Sabrina whispered, thinking of that untamed wilderness so far away. "Oh, dear God, my poor Rhea," she cried, agonized by the realization of what her daughter must be suffering. "What shall we do? How will we find her? Oh, Lucien!" she cried, but this time with tears of joy wetting her cheeks. "Rhea *is* alive. I feel certain. At least we have a chance now of finding her alive. 'Tis far better than not knowing anything." She spoke almost challengingly, as if refusing to believe the worst.

"Rina? Lucien? What is this about Rhea being alive? I heard the shots and came running, although it took me several endless minutes, and a stubbed toe, to figure out where the two of you were," Richard said from the doorway, his bare feet sticking out from beneath the hem of his nightdress and loosely hanging robe. "Are you all right?" he asked with concern as he noticed Sabrina's tear-streaked face.

"I am fine, Richard," Sabrina reassured him. "We are going to get Rhea back!" she exclaimed, unable to contain her exuberance.

"Rina, I don't think you—" Lucien interrupted, his words of caution drowned out as several well-muscled young men, led by a blustering Butterick, stormed into the study.

"Your Graces! Are you injured? Who fired the pistol? Is anyone hurt? Where's the culprit?!" he demanded aggressively, his sharp eyes missing nothing in the room, including Lord Richard in his nightdress, his red hair standing on end. "Was it the cousins, Your Grace?"

"It was Lady Kate. She is alone but wounded, and therefore very dangerous, Butterick," the Duke warned him. "She sneaked in through the underground passage. I imagine that is the way she will escape."

"That she-devil. Always was the meaner of the two. And Lord Percy? Will he be waitin' for her, do you think, Your Grace?" Butterick asked, wanting to be prepared if he came face to face with the two of them.

"Eventually, I suspect," the Duke said strangely, then shook his head. "Percy is dead. We have only Kate to deal with."

"Aye, that's enough, I'll wager," Butterick muttered, thinking privately he'd rather be going up against a maddened bull. "I'll send a couple of fellows to the outside entrance of the passage to catch her as she's coming out. Then, me and a couple more of my boys will go in this end. We'll cut her off between us, we will," Butterick promised. "She won't be gettin' up to any more mischief after tonight!"

Kate stared down at the peacefully sleeping child. Oblivious to her wound and to the blood dripping onto the quilted coverlet, she reached out and lightly touched the silken blond head. Kate glared around the room, cursing the darkness, for she could barely make out the features of this boy child. The banked fire in the hearth gave off little light and deepened the shadows, making it more difficult for her to see her way across the room. She had already stumbled once into a rocking horse. The scraping noise had sounded loud enough to wake the dead, or so she had feared, but the nanny in the narrow bed in the corner continued to snore undisturbed.

With a sly smile, Kate glanced over her shoulder at the covered hump in the bed, then over at the other crib, where the girl child continued to sleep pleacefully. She imagined herself sleeping there so long ago, so innocent of what her future would hold. In the darkness, the nursery looked much the way it had when she and Percy had lived at Camareigh.

"Percy," she said softly, lovingly. "I have come for you. 'Tis time we left, Percy. Wake up, love," she urged him, staring down at Andrew Dominick's cherubic face. Then she carefully lifted the slumbering child from the warmth of the covers.

Cradling him against her breast, she hugged this small body, which still possessed the precious breath of life. "Sweet Percy," she crooned as she walked to the door. "Sweet, sweet Percy. Kate has come for you."

A low, rumbling snort and cough from the bed of the nanny halted Kate in her steps. She stood staring through the flickering darkness at the slowly stirring shape beneath the covers.

"If ye please, now. Who be ye there?" a slightly querulous voice demanded. "Yer Grace, is it?"

Kate bit her lip in vexation as she heard a fumbling at the bedside table; then a light was struck and she was caught in its glow.

"Agin, I'm askin', who be ye? I'm not knowin' ye, am I?" the quivering voice questioned worriedly; although the old woman's mind was still fogged with sleep, a sense of urgency seemed to be penetrating it, warning her something was not right. "What have ye got there, now? To be sure, I can't be seein' a thing without me specs," the nanny muttered irritably. "Now ye be waitin' a minute. Just what d'ye think' ye be doin' in here, young woman? What is that ye be holdin' now? Mercy! 'Tis young Lord

Andrew fer sure! What d'ye think ye be doin'—" The words halted abruptly, for Kate had turned her face fully to the candle's revealing light, deciding there was one sure way of silencing the old biddy.

The nanny's scream of horror followed Kate's exit from the room and echoed down the halls of Camareigh, but by the time it had drifted to the brother and sister walking arm in arm along the corridor near the nursery, it sounded hardly more than a moaning through the trees.

"I think I understand why Lucien would wish to be there when they catch up with Kate," Richard was saying, shaking with cold from the icy draughts swirling around his bare legs. "You would think, however, that he would hate the very sight of her. And yet, do you know, Rina," he said curiously, "I think he pities her, though God only knows why. I've never really thought of Lucien being an overly compassionate man. Please do not misunderstand me," he added quickly, "for Lucien is a good man, but he is just a trifle hard and unforgiving at times."

"You are right, Richard, but Kate is, after all, family," Sabrina said. She herself was slightly surprised at Lucien's actions.

"I suppose so, strange though it is. Do you know, Rina, that when our father died I should have felt nothing. After all, I had only spoken to the man once to my recollection, and then I was scared to death of him. But when you told me the news, well," Richard said awkwardly, as if embarrassed by what he was about to admit, "I was saddened. I felt a loss, and yet I am not certain why."

Sabrina smiled understandingly at her young brother; then, resting her cheek against the curve of his shoulder, she said, " 'Tis only natural that you would grieve for something that you had never known, and by all rights should have. You were not crying for James Verrick, a man you never knew, but for some idealized man who could have been a father to you," she tried to explain. Her voice had taken on the brittle quality it always did when she spoke of their late father.

"You did not cry nor grieve, did you, Rina?" Richard asked now, looking down at his sister's still beautiful face.

"No," she answered shortly. "He has been dead to me

for a long time. He abandoned us, Dickie, and from that day forward he ceased to exist for me, except as some despicable creature to be scorned." The bitterness and hurt she had known all of those years was still vivid in her mind.

"Actually," she added, bringing the conversation back to their immediate problem, "knowing Lucien as I do, I really suspect that he wants to make certain that nothing goes wrong where Kate is concerned. A mistake like that could cost you your life. And even though she is quite mad, the woman is still a cold-blooded murderess. I do not think she will be able to escape the gallows this time." Then Sabrina glanced up and saw their usually decorous nanny reeling along the corridor like a drunken sailor.

Richard must have had similar thoughts as he stared in disbelief at the diminutive woman who, despite her tottering steps, was approaching quickly. With an uneasy laugh, he exclaimed, "Good Lord, she is certainly muddled. Well, you were warned, Rina, about taking on an Irishwoman as nanny," Richard said with a wink. "I can remember Mason warning you against such a risky decision. He said, while begging your pardon at the same time—always proper Mason is—that you would rue the day you took her on."

Sabrina snorted rudely. "That was almost twenty years ago, and besides, as you well know, Mason is prejudiced. 'Tis ancient history, but his fiancée ran off with an Irish footman when they were all in service somewhere else. O'Casey has always been above reproach, much to Mason's disappointment." Sabrina always had staunchly supported her choice of a nanny, although now, as the woman fell to her knees before her, she was beginning to have her doubts, especially as she listened to her hysterical babbling.

"Oooh, Yer Grace! Yer Grace. Lord help us, 'tis demons, they are. And they be comin' fer me next! Oooh, may the saints be preservin' us!" she wailed, wringing her hands. " 'Tis the devil himself, 'tis. Come fer us from the fiery gates of Hell. Had his she-devil with him, he did, and never, God rest me soul, have I ever seen such a face. Like a fiend, 'twas," she croaked, her fingers tightening around Sabrina's arm. "Came fer him, her did, and all aglow, her was! Then in a pouf of smoke, her was gone," she sniffed, then began to cry convulsively.

"Lord help us, is right," Richard said, eyeing the old woman pityingly, for obviously she had become demented. "I am certainly thankful you insisted on looking in on the children, Rina. No telling what could have happened with O'Casey here talking about demons and—" Richard paused, becoming aware of his sister's unusual stillness. "I am sorry, Rina. I didn't mean to disturb you. I really did not mean that anything had happened to the twins," he apologized, thinking his casually spoken words had upset her.

"Kate," Sabrina said, a strange expression in her eyes as she stared up the corridor beyond the nanny.

"Kate?" Richard repeated. "But she's already left the house."

"Has she?" Sabrina demanded doubtfully as she bent down and struggled to free her nightdress from O'Casey's deathlike grip. " 'Tis Kate she is babbling about, Richard. I know it is. Don't you understand? Kate was the she-devil who frightened O'Casey half out of her wits. If you had wakened to see Kate's scarred face staring down at you, you would be half mad, too."

"Here, let me help you," Richard said, prying loose the whimpering nanny's grasp. "God, I wish Lucien were here, and not somewhere out on the grounds," he said worriedly, the pathetic image of the elder Mr. Taber suddenly coming to his mind.

"I want you to find him, Richard. Please," Sabrina begged when she saw him shake his head. "If Kate is indeed loose in the house, we will need all of the help we can find. You can run faster than me, Richard. Now go! Please!"

Richard hesitated only an instant before he rushed off as bidden, retracing the steps they'd taken just moments before. Sabrina watched his figure disappear into the darkness shrouding the corridor.

"You wait here, O'Casey," she told the cowering woman. "I will only be a few minutes. I am just going to tuck in the twins. Do you understand, O'Casey?" she said gently, picking up the branched candlestick that Richard had set on the floor before running for help.

"Oh, don't be leavin' me! Oh, please, Yer Grace, don't be a-goin'! Herself'll be comin' fer me. 'Tis the devil after me soul!" O'Casey cried, crouching against the wall and rocking back and forth.

"I must go, O'Casey," Sabrina told her, her voice sharpening. It seemed to have a strangely sobering effect on the nanny, for suddenly she came to her senses.

"B-but her took him, her did! Her stole young Lord Andrew! I saw it meself! Left a changeling in his bed, I'm sure. Oh, 'tis powerful evil, and now it has the sweet lad."

In disbelieving horror, Sabrina stared down at the sobbing woman. She wondered if this were more gibberish, or indeed the truth. Without stopping to think about what she might come face to face with, Sabrina ran the rest of the way to the nursery. Once she was there, her steps faltered; one of the candles had been snuffed out, but there was still enough light to see the empty crib where her son had lain. She stood beside it and numbly stretched out her hand to feel the sticky drop of blood staining Andrew's pillow. He was gone! And there was blood on his pillow—but whose blood was it?

On shaking legs, Sabrina hurried over to the adjacent crib, not knowing what to expect. She breathed a sigh of relief and feasted her eyes upon her peacefully sleeping daughter. Her slumber seemed undisturbed, but as Sabrina stared down at Arden's innocent face, a drop of melted wax spilled onto the pillow, drawing her attention to another dark red stain.

More blood.

But it was not her daughter's, she thought thankfully, as she gently examined the small, vulnerable head of blond curls. Arden mumbled something unintelligible in her sleep, then gave a contented sigh as she slipped deeper into her untroubled dreams. With clumsy fingers, Sabrina covered her daughter's small shoulders with the soft wool coverlet, but she couldn't help thinking that Kate had stood in this very spot only moments before. And yet her daughter had been left unharmed. But what of her son?

Sabrina spun around. Where had Kate gone? Why had she slowed herself down by kidnapping Andrew? Then her own question was answered as she imagined the maddened hatred in Kate's pale eyes. She easily could have been halfway across the valley by now; yet she had not run, had not chosen to leave Camareigh—at least not yet. She had come for Andrew first.

With a last reassuring glance at her daughter, Sabrina took her first steps toward what she hoped would be a final confrontation with Lucien's cousin Kate. And this time, when they met face to face, she would be less merciful with this madwoman who had stolen her son.

Hurrying from the room, Sabrina turned in the opposite direction from whence she had come, her swiftly moving feet carrying her deeper into the south wing, away from the troop of men who were regrouping in the hall to puzzle over the whereabouts of their elusive quarry.

Pausing indecisively at the intersection of two corridors, Sabrina noticed for the first time a trail of blood. How Kate had managed to get even this far, wounded as she was and carrying Andrew, Sabrina could only wonder about. As she took the darkened corridor to her right, a slow realization of her destination was growing within her, for her steps were carrying her to the seldom-used back stairs that opened into an inner courtyard. From there was access to one of the kitchen gardens, which had a gate opening into the grounds—the way to Kate's freedom.

The stairs once had been a little-known exit from Camareigh. The ancient wooden staircase was rickety, its steps half rotted away, and because of the danger it held for any unsuspecting person, Lucien had decreed them restricted. They had been boarded up for years now. And just last month it had finally been decided to have the decrepit stairs torn down and a safer staircase erected. But even the workmen had not been immune to accidents, and the chief carpenter had broken his leg as a result of his fall. They would resume working on the job at the end of the month, but until then, the old staircase still stood. And since the workers would be returning, and everyone at Camareigh knew of the danger of the south stairs, they had not bothered to board up the entrance again.

Only a stranger to Camareigh would be unaware of the dangerous condition of those stairs, and in the darkness, which would hide the workmen's scaffolding, that person would have no reason to hesitate—especially if he were in a desperate hurry.

Sabrina quickened her steps, a dreadful foreboding gathering at the back of her mind. The knuckles of her right hand gleamed white against the taut skin as she kept a tight grip on the heavy silver candelabrum, while protecting the vulnerable flame with her cupped left hand. The corridor was bitingly cold, and since this section of the wing was left unheated, the damp had penetrated deeply into it. Few people wandered this way, except for a maid armed with a feather duster, who cleared the passage of cobwebs once a fortnight.

Sabrina was halfway down the corridor toward the south stairs when she heard a terrified scream. She needed no soothsayer to tell her the portent of that haunting cry. For an instant later a low rumble vibrated through the hall, becoming a thundering roar and climaxing in a deafening crash. Her unfaltering steps carried her into the thick, choking dust that was settling over everything, like a dirty shroud.

There was only one thought in Sabrina's mind when Kate's horror-filled voice was abruptly silenced, which was her fear for her son. In her mind's eye she saw the steep flight of steps leading to the flagstone floor of the courtyard. This image now made her sickeningly weak as she reached the opened door to the stairwell.

An icy draught of air hit her, extinguishing her light and leaving her poised on the edge of the gaping hole. Sabrina stood motionless in the somber silence, her eyes seeking blindly for something familiar to grasp.

She bit back a start of surprise when she touched the door and felt a splinter of wood dig deep into her palm. Supporting herself against the door, she carefully placed the useless candelabrum on the floor beside her feet, then leaned farther out into the blackness.

"Andrew? Andy, love? Where are you, Andy? Answer Mama, please, Andy," she called softly, but the deathlike silence only deepened.

"Andy!" she screamed, forgetful of her precarious balance in the doorway. "Oh, Andy, where are you?" she cried. But the ominous gloom seemed to mock her as it echoed back her words.

With a sigh, Sabrina surrendered to the despondency that had been shadowing her ever since Rhea had been kidnapped. The euphoria she had experienced upon learning that Kate had not murdered Rhea now vanished, plummeting her into a desolation of spirit. As she contemplated the certain death of her son, she now knew a depth of sorrow that filled her mind with a paralyzing black void.

Rough hands reached out and grabbed her as she began sinking weakly to her knees, too tired to fight any longer against her grief.

"Rina!" Lucien spoke harshly, because his relief was still overshadowed by the fear he had felt as he'd helplessly watched his wife slipping away from him, the gaping doorway looming perilously close to her swaying body.

As he had neared the south stairs, her white-clad figure had seemed appallingly ghostlike in the eerie glow of the torches being carried by the group of men following him. They had been climbing the Grand Staircase in search of Kate when Richard had met them with his alarming news; then, upon leaving the nursery, they too had followed the trail of blood into the south wing. It was only as they'd neared the corridor leading to the south stairs that he'd realized Kate's ultimate destination—for that was now her only hope of escape.

Butterick had turned back with a contingent of men and was circling the grounds in the hope of cutting Kate off, but now, as Lucien saw Sabrina's ravaged face, he realized that they had all been too late to stop Kate. Unlike Sabrina, he had forgotten the dangerous condition of the ancient staircase, but now, with a smoking torch illuminating the debris-filled stairwell, he remembered only too well.

"Andrew," he whispered.

Richard leaned closer, holding his flickering torch lower as he strained to catch sight of any figure or movement below. But the shadows were too deep, and the area remained a silent well of death.

Lucien held Sabrina against him, keeping her face turned away from the destruction below, in which the body of their young son lay.

Richard continued to squat in the doorway, his nightshirt billowing around him. He refused to believe that this was the end, that his innocent little nephew was lying dead in that heap of rubbish. As he continued to stare unblinkingly, the light from the torches intensified, until the whole stairwell seemed alight with a thousand candles.

"Lucien," Richard said, glancing back at his brother-in-law. And this one grimly spoken word was enough to warn Lucien against what he was about to see. "It's Butterick. They're searching the ruins."

Lucien tried to prevent Sabrina from glancing down, but she moved too quickly. Richard's words had struck a note of response inside her, which cut through the blank numbness that had held her enthralled. Lucien could feel her trembling, as they stared down at the nightmarish scene now revealed in the dancing torchlight.

Kate was dead.

Violent though her death had been, there was, strangely enough, a restfulness about her broken body. In death, Kate had found the peace that had eluded her so maddeningly in life. Her torment had finally come to an end —abruptly, yes, but the fates had smiled belatedly upon her at last. What she had so desperately sought to hide in life remained hidden in death, for the scarred half of her face was pressed to the earth. Enshrouded in black, the unmarred beauty of her face was like a cameo carved of palest ivory; it was smooth and cold to the touch and gave no indication of the ugliness that lay on the other side.

It was therefore difficult for the subdued group of men standing around her fallen body to believe that this was the madwoman who had murdered the elder Mr. Taber, kidnapped Lady Rhea Claire, and come close to destroying the Dominick family. There was only one among them who felt no pity as he stared down at Kate, and that was Butterick, who had known the wickedness of the young Lady Kate Rathbourne. But a few of the younger men, who saw only the beauty in the lifeless face, knew a feeling of sadness at the apparent senselessness of this lovely woman's death.

Kate would have been amused to know this, and Butterick could have sworn he heard laughter as he stood there in the stone courtyard, chilled to the marrow by the icy gusts blowing out of the west country.

He glanced around at the collapsed scaffolding and smashed remains of the old staircase. Shaking his head, he looked up at the silent figures standing above him like stone effigies. "We're goin' to have to be doin' a powerful lot of diggin' to get Lord Andrew out from beneath all of this, Your Grace," he called through cupped hands. He kicked at a fallen piece of stonework, trying to forget the image of Her Grace's anguished face. But it would only be getting worse, he thought unhappily, for the little lord could never have survived the fall, much less the collapse of the staircase and scaffolding.

Sabrina pulled free from the warmth of Lucien's arms and staggered against the far wall, unable to watch any longer. She was weeping softly, when she suddenly heard a shuffling, scratching noise. Thinking it a mouse, or even worse, a rat, she instinctively stepped away.

But to her horror, she felt something reach out and grab hold of her bare ankle. Her scream caused Richard, who was about to retrace his steps to join the searchers below, to totter on the edge of the stairwell. He had not, however, planned his descent in quite so dramatic a manner and felt quite grateful for Lucien's steadying hand pulling him away from the edge.

As Richard turned, the light from his burning torch revealed his sister's figure. Richard halted a foot behind Lucien, who had come to a sudden standstill when he caught sight of his wife.

For neither Lucien nor Richard were prepared to see

Sabrina standing there cradling her son in her arms, half-crying, half-laughing, as she met their disbelieving eyes over Andrew's golden head.

"He was crawling along the hall. I felt something grab my ankle. I thought it was a rat, and that is why I screamed," Sabrina explained, her quivering words interspersed with Andrew's pleased chuckles as she pressed kiss after kiss on his grimy face.

Lucien said nothing.

"Andrew is alive!" Richard called out to the men who were digging down below. Then he turned away, but not before he had seen Sabrina and Andrew enfolded in Lucien's arms.

Richard grinned widely in response to the cheer that went up from below; then he looked back at his young nephew, wondering why he was not dead. By all rights he should be, for Kate must have been carrying him when she fell to her death on the stones below. What had happened then, to spare his life?

He glanced around the dusty corridor, trying to re-enact the sequence of events; to Richard, a puzzle was a puzzle until he had solved it, and solved it must be before he could rest easy.

He imagined Kate's hurrying figure. Still, though, she would have been slowed by the small boy she carried in her arms. She would have been searching frantically for the door to the south stairs. She would have stopped before it, then opened it to escape down the staircase that she remembered from more than a quarter of a century ago. She would not have hesitated to rush down it. And then she and Andrew would have been dead—but only Kate had died.

A quarter of a century, Richard speculated, eyeing with growing curiosity the door to the stairwell. This was most likely the original door that had been hung centuries ago, and if the stairs were in so decrepit a condition that they had collapsed, then the odds were that the door was in a similar condition. To prove his theory, Richard reached out and firmly closed the door, momentarily startling Lucien and Sabrina from their absorption in their son.

Their curious expressions became even more puzzled when Richard exclaimed, "Ah-ha!"

Then he nearly fell into them when the door finally gave in to his ungentle persuasion and swung back at him with unnecessary force. Richard turned a triumphant face to his perplexed audience. "It was stuck."

"That was obvious," Lucien remarked with a smile, well used to his young brother-in-law's eccentric ways.

"Whatever are you talking about, Richard?" Sabrina asked in bewilderment. "But whatever it is, I think it can wait until we are out of this draughty hall. You and Andrew are going to catch your death of cold standing here in bare feet," she said sensibly, but more than that, the gloom of the corridor was beginning to unnerve her.

"Well, to put it quite simply, Rina, the door is warped," Richard said, as if that explained everything.

"I am sorry, but I don't quite see what that has—"

"Don't you understand?" Richard interrupted patiently. "Kate would have had a devil of a time opening it. And she certainly could not have succeeded, wounded as she was, and burdened with Andrew. She would have needed both hands to open it. She had to put Andrew down while she struggled with the door. Her time was precious. She must have been frantic, for while she was wrestling with that stuck door, she could probably hear your footsteps, Rina, coming ever closer. Perhaps she even saw the flickering candlelight at the end of the corridor," Richard said, his speculations vividly recreating the tragic scene of moments before.

"Finally, she would have succeeded in opening the door, then she would have picked up Andrew and descended—and both would have died." Richard spoke softly, for he had realized before either Lucien and Sabrina how close Andrew had come to dying with Kate on the stone floor of the courtyard below.

"You see, while Kate was struggling with that warped door, Andrew, finding himself in unfamiliar surroundings, crawled off to explore. Kate had no light to find him by, nor did she have the time to search the length and breadth of the hall for him. She had to make a decision—whether to risk capture or to flee while she had the chance. We

367

know which decision she made," Richard stated, resisting the urge to glance down at Kate's black-clad figure. Instead, he reached out and gently tweaked his nephew's nose.

Sabrina shivered, her arms tightening around Andrew's soft body as she pressed him closer to her breast.

"Come," Lucien ordered abruptly. "Let us leave here, and we will not speak of this night again. Kate is dead, and she no longer has the power to hurt us." Then Lucien guided his wife and child away from the scene of the lurid climax of Kate's life.

A few hours later the glow of dawn was lightening the eastern horizon as Sabrina stared out at the distant hills. Now a bishop's purple against the gilded heavens, they would soon turn somber against ashen skies.

Sabrina sighed and turned away, the warmth of the fire drawing her to it. Sleep had been a stranger to her, and now as she waited for Lucien to return from making the arrangements for Kate's burial, she found her thoughts lingering on what he'd said about Kate no longer having the power to hurt them.

"But you are wrong, Lucien," Sabrina whispered as she opened her clenched hand showly and gazed down at the delicate, diamond and sapphire ring resting on her palm.

"Rhea," Sabrina breathed, "I swear that I will never give up the hope that you still live. But where are you? What is happening to you now?" she cried, her shoulders shaking with the grief that would be her constant companion until she found her daughter. And unless that moment came, Kate had won.

Thou art slave to fate, chance, kings, and desperate men.
John Donne

Chapter 7

CLOSE to a fortnight had passed since the *Sea Dragon* had cast off her mooring lines and set sail for Antigua. The brigantine was laden with a cargo of lumber, tar, fish, and livestock, and it had been business as usual for its captain and crew, or so it had seemed to any interested bystanders on the docks in Charles Town.

Only the *Sea Dragon*'s captain, her supercargo, and the steward had known that this was to be no ordinary run between the Indies and the Carolinas. None but these three knew that once the *Sea Dragon*'s cargo was discharged in St. John's Harbour, she would set out on a venture which could change forever the lives of her crew. Whether her quest ended in good fortune or misfortune was the hazard of the die, but it was one which they had been willing to chance ever since prying open that strongbox unearthed on Trinidad.

Soon, however, the true destination and purpose of the *Sea Dragon*'s voyage would be a secret no more, and then Longacres, the coxswain, would once again be dreaming of his tavern in St. Thomas; Cobbs, the bos'n, would be imagining himself the Norfolk country gentleman; Mac-Donald, the Scots sailmaker, would be designing his shopyard along the banks of the Chesapeake; Trevelawny, the dour carpenter, would be seeing the familiar, rocky shores of Cornwall; Clarke, the quartermaster and self-styled dandy, would be conjuring images of himself in the finest silk, sipping a goblet of claret; and Seumus Fitz-simmons, the first mate, would be outfitting his newly purchased schooner for service as a privateer.

Young Conny Brady, the cabin boy, had never stopped dreaming of sunken treasure and Spanish galleons haunted by drowned sailors. He had remained fired by his boyish dreams of fame and fortune, which a lifetime of adventure would surely reap.

Houston Kirby's gruff demeanor certainly would not alert the crew to the *Sea Dragon*'s secret. He'd had months to speculate calmly on the possible outcome of this voyage, and he had come to the rather uneasy con-clusion that if a fortune they found, then 'twould have been an ill-fated voyage for one Dante Leighton.

Nor would the crew of the *Sea Dragon* have gleaned anything out of the ordinary from the behavior of their captain. His grim-visaged expression seldom varied, ex-cept when he gazed upon the girl; then it became strangely brooding, as if he were puzzled by her.

Dante Leighton was gazing at her now, an unamused glint in his narrowed gray eyes. She was whispering into young Conny Brady's ear, whose giggling laugh was draw-ing indulgent smiles from the men who always seemed to find some small task to keep them nearby whenever she came on deck. It seemed, at least to Dante Leighton's cynical eye, as if she had bewitched the crew of the *Sea Dragon*. Every man jack of them had been disarmed by a pair of gentle violet eyes, and what once had been a crew to be reckoned with was now little more than a pack of grinning fools.

Dante Leighton's scowling gaze settled on his men who were gathered around the companion ladder on the quarterdeck, where Conny Brady and the girl were sitting, their bare feet dangling short of the deck. Dante eyed with growing displeasure the beaming expressions on both Cobb's and Fitzsimmons's faces as they listened to the girl's quiet voice. She even had that old seadog Longacres hanging on her every word. MacDonald, who was sitting nearby on a crate of clucking chickens, was apparently not immune to witchery either, for his blonde mustache was twitching in response as he mended a length of canvas with sail needle and thimble. Dante's eyes widened perceptibly when he heard a strange laugh; turning his head slightly, he was startled to see even the Cornishman grinning over the girl's story.

His patience already had worn thin when he caught a whiff of something nauseatingly sweet. Looking around he saw Barnaby Clarke who, in fresh silk stockings and stock, would have been more at home in a salon than on the quarterdeck of a fighting brig. But it was when Dante saw Alastair Marlowe present the girl with a carefully peeled orange, the supercargo's hand lingering against hers for just a moment too long, that Dante's simmering temper boiled over.

"Trim and make sail!" the captain of the *Sea Dragon* ordered in a voice harsher than it needed to be since the ship had been running smoothly by the lee with the northeast trades filling her sails.

"Your coffee, m'lord." Standing beside his captain, Houston Kirby had spoken softly but won an irate look for his trouble. The captain knew well where Houston Kirby's sympathies lay.

Even Jamaica seemed smitten with the girl and was forever rubbing himself against her legs, his feline pride gone by the board for a pat on the head, Dante thought disgustedly. He had just spotted the big orange tomcat amongst the men palpitating over the girl.

Dante Leighton stared hard at Rhea Claire Dominick and wondered if this could possibly be the same girl who had sneaked aboard the *Sea Dragon* little over a fortnight ago. Although still dressed in the same tattered green velvet she had been wearing then, she bore little resemblance to that wild-eyed, spitting creature he had discovered in his cabin that night.

For under the conscientious, if at times exasperating, ministrations of Houston Kirby, the girl had begun gradually to regain her strength. Part of his cure had included countless bowls of chicken broth, tankards of warm milk laced liberally with brandy, and, when he had thought she was up to it, his special stew, which the crew swore stuck to your ribs for days afterwards.

Night after night, Dante Leighton had swung from a hammock stretched between two deck beams in his cabin, watching with half-closed eyes the feverish girl sleeping fitfully in his bunk. And not for the first time had he found himself wondering about her, for this girl calling herself Rhea Claire Dominick remained an enigma to him.

However, to the rest of the crew of the *Sea Dragon*, including Houston Kirby and Alastair Marlowe, both of whom should have known better, she was the tragic victim of foul play. To his men she was exactly what she claimed to be, and when her wide, innocent-seeming, violet eyes gazed into theirs, they never thought to question her or doubt her words.

On the other hand, he had been caught up in a deception of his own making, for how could he possibly tell his men of his suspicions concerning this girl whom he'd caught rifling his cabin? They would surely ask themselves why he should be so concerned that she had seen the treasure map that *they* all thought to be worthless.

And, to make matters worse, his men thought him a saintly fellow indeed to have rescued the girl, when both he and the girl knew that the reality was quite different.

She was no fool, however, this ragamuffin with the fine airs of lady, and since she knew only too well his skepticism concerning her true identity, she had made a valiant effort to befriend his crew. But in order not to lose the sympathies she had so easily culled from them, she'd had to take heed of his warning.

Their rather strained heart-to-heart talk had taken place shortly after she had recovered enough to ask to be allowed on deck. Dante still remembered now her almost pathetic attempt to maintain her dignity while standing before him in his shirt. It had been quite a remarkable feat. And despite the distraction of the hardening nipples of her small breasts against the soft silk of his shirt, he had refused to be swayed from his course of action. Too much was at stake to make a mistake now.

"If you value that pale-skinned derriére of yours, then I'd not speak a word about that map you so fortuitously discovered," he had warned her, smiling inwardly at that look of innocent surprise that had crossed her delicate-featured face. "If you intend to keep in my men's good graces, then I'd say naught of it, my dear. You see," he had explained, "your presence on board the *Sea Dragon* has been impossible to keep a secret, and quite naturally, my men have been curious about my guest. And thanks to the good offices of one Houston Kirby, your sad little tale has been regaled to the crew, until I daresay there has not been a dry eye on deck. Of course, sailors do love a good yarn. So, for your own protection, my dear," he'd advised, "I would continue to pretend to be the innocent they think you are."

"I could not care less about this treasure map you insist upon speaking of," she had reiterated. "I do not know who you think I am pretending to be, but I shall tell you who I really am, for you seem to have a very short memory. I am Lady Rhea Claire Dominick. I am the daughter of the Duke and Duchess of Camareigh, and I was kidnapped from my home. All I am concerned with, Captain," she had informed him almost contemptuously, although tears were not far off, "is finding my way back home. That is all I desire."

"Well put, my dear, but it has little to do with the rather delicate situation you now find yourself in on board the *Sea Dragon*. However, your actions on board my ship may well determine whether or not you ever see your home again," he had hinted, his voice intentionally threatening.

Then, when he saw the fearful consternation gathering in her eyes, he had elaborated further. "Whomever, or whatever you might be, you will only harm yourself by speaking of matters which do not concern you. You might very well find yourself marooned on some desert isle, and then, my dear, you would never find your way home."

He remembered feeling a slight twinge of guilt at the terrified expression that had settled over her face at his words, but still he had continued relentlessly.

"Some people say, and perhaps with good reason, that there is little difference between privateering and piracy. In fact, on the high seas, His Majesty's Navy too often refuses to recognize any difference between privateer and pirate. You've not met Longacres yet; he is the *Sea Dragon*'s coxswain and a reformed pirate, if that is indeed possible. You really must have a word with him, for although he seems quite civilized at times, he is certainly not a man that I would care to double-cross, for he remembers only too well the feel of a cutlass in his hand." With these words, Dante had driven home his point, for the girl's face had blanched alarmingly. "Think of this conversation as a friendly warning, my dear, for I truly do have your best interests at heart."

"I do not wish to cause trouble for anyone. All I want is to go home," she had whispered tearfully, her violet eyes downcast, her narrow shoulders slumped in defeat. A less determined man would surely have been touched by her obvious distress, Dante had thought, turning his back on her thin figure.

That had been over a week ago. And now as Dante's eyes strayed upward toward the sun-bleached sails billowing in the freshening breeze, he wondered if the *Sea Dragon* would continue to make good speed toward the Indies. Her yards were braced up and her sheets had been eased out to meet the thrust of a quartering wind blowing well abaft the beam. If all went well, then they should be sighting land by eventide on the morrow.

As Dante Leighton's gray-eyed gaze fell on the girl, he wondered how she would react when she heard that stirring cry from aloft that land had been sighted off to starboard, then heard the gull's cry mocking her as it soared high above the swaying masts, its outspread wings a flash of gray as it glided closer with the downdraft, only to fly away free at last.

What her thoughts were at this moment, he could not know, for her golden head was bent as she attempted to tie a complicated spritsail sheet knot with the help of young Conny. She was unpredictable, this woman-child, for one moment she would be laughing and playing riddle games in childish abandon with the boy; then, in the very next breath, she would be smiling with a captivating seductiveness into Alastair Marlowe's boyish face, or meeting the dark eyes of Seumus Fitzsimmons, who was acting to the hilt the charming Irish rogue.

There was one thing, however, of which Dante Leighton was certain, and that was that she would try to escape him once they had docked in Antigua. It would be her only chance to gain her freedom, and she knew it. She also knew that he had no intention of allowing her to succeed. For it mattered not whether she was a hireling of Bertie Mackay's, or a conniving wench off the streets who merely wished to better her station by becoming the mistress of a marquis, she would not be leaving the *Sea Dragon* when she docked in St. John's Harbour. Whatever her purpose for being on board ship, she would never have the opportunity to divulge what she had intentionally or inadvertently seen while on board the *Sea Dragon* or at least not until it was too late to cause harm.

Of course, it would be a far more dangerous situation all around if she were indeed the daughter of Lucien Dominick, Duke of Camareigh. He could well imagine her angry recitation of the experiences she'd had while on board his ship. She would not spare the *Sea Dragon*'s captain when telling her tale to sympathetic listeners. It would complicate matters no end to have His Majesty's Navy in hot pursuit with a warrant for his arrest, and the firepower to back it up should he be reluctant to comply with their wishes. Nor would it help matters to have a vengeful father, who also happened to be an all-powerful duke, out for his blood. He wanted no enemy of that ilk shadowing his every step.

That possibility seemed unlikely, though, for only a madman would have dared to kidnap a duke's daughter, and especially that particular duke's daughter. A sudden thought struck Dante and a slight smile curved his mouth as his eyes lingered on the girl's fair head. He noticed how her long braid gleamed like a shiny golden sovereign.

When Dante Leighton laughed softly, Houston Kirby caught his captain's expression and drew a deep sigh of relief, for he'd been having restless nights of late spent worrying about his master. Only once before had he seen the captain in so dangerous a mood, and then it had nearly ended in tragedy. And now, what with worrying

Laurie McBain

over the captain and what he might end up doing, as well
as being concerned over the intricate stratagems for the
salvaging of that Spanish galleon—not to mention his
fears about the prospect of returning to Merdraco—he
felt at times as if his short legs were carrying the weight of
the world.

But ultimately, 'twould be the worsening situation with
the girl that buckled his legs and brought Houston Kirby to
his knees, he fretted, for the uneasy relationship between
his captain and the young lady was growing into something he didn't like the look of at all. And it had him
grievously worried, that it did. So he was pleasantly
surprised to find the captain smiling as he watched the
girl.

"Aye, she is a fine young thing, that she is," Kirby commented with an almost paternal glint in his eyes. After all,
hadn't his cures and constant attention set her back on
her feet and put that rosy glow in her cheeks? "Ah, but
she is a true beauty, Cap'n. And so gentle, she is, with
never a sharp word for any of the crew," Kirby said,
ignoring his captain's snort of derision, for he knew only
too well the strained silence that often existed between the
captain and the girl. "Raised proper, she was. Reckon her
folks, the Duke and Duchess, be mighty grieved to have
her missing. Broken-hearted they must be wondering what
has happened to their daughter," Kirby continued sadly,
then sniffed for good measure as he eyed the captain.

"My sentiments exactly, Kirby," Dante remarked
agreeably. But the little steward was not deceived, and
the mocking glint in the pale gray eyes was causing him
considerable concern.

"I have just been speculating on what her worth might
be to the Duke of Camareigh," Dante said, "for if she is
indeed who she claims so vehemently to be, then he would
most likely pay quite handsomely to have his daughter
returned. If our search for sunken Spanish gold comes to
naught," Dante said, his eyes never leaving the girl, "we
just might be able to make up the difference by ransom-
ing our golden-haired prize back to the Duke."

"M'lord!" squeaked Kirby with horrified dismay, his
shocked disapproval leaving him almost but not quite

376

speechless. "To even be thinkin' such a thing, well . . . well, I'm ashamed fer the first time in me life to be associated with the name of Leighton, that I am," Kirby concluded.

Dante glanced down at the little steward. He recognized that woebegone expression too well to be completely taken in by it, but still he found himself saying, " 'Twas just idle speculation. Besides, I intend to return to England, which might be difficult if there were a price on my head. However, I think it unlikely that the temptation to ransom her off will ever arise. After all, who the devil would pay a fortune for this impudent pullet? The only title she has ever come close to is on the binding of a book, and since I doubt whether she can read or write, I'm sure that's as far as she got." Dante Leighton's eyes narrowed into slits as he watched Alastair's sun-streaked curls come close to touching the girl's golden head as he leaned closer, his hands guiding hers as she tied the strands of rope into a secure knot.

"Ah, Cap'n. Saddens me, it does, to hear ye speakin' so of the young lady. Reckon 'twon't be a day too soon when we reach Antigua and turn Lady Rhea Claire over to the authorities in St. John's. Almost regret now us ever bringin' her down to the Indies. Of course, we didn't have much choice. Figure she would've been dead by now if we hadn't taken her with us. Knew at the time, I did, that I didn't care a'tall fer the looks of them two who stopped me on the docks that day. Seumus Fitzsimmons knew well the name of that dog Daniel Lewis. Crossing paths with him usually means a brawl, and most likely a knife in the back. Aye, Mr. Fitzsimmons says ye best steer clear of that cullion. And that cap'n of his weren't much better. The name of Cap'n Benjamin Haskell seems to be more well known in taverns than anywhere else. He was a mean 'un when he was drinkin' hard, which was about all he'd do once he dropped anchor. Poor wee thing, Lady Rhea Claire, gettin' caught up between the two of them scoundrels. Aye, hate to even think about what might have happened to her if she hadn't been forced into climbing aboard the *Sea Dragon*. 'Twas one of them chance things," he said, awed by the fateful encounters that seemed to govern people's lives.

"I never knew you were so gullible, Kirby. I'm quite surprised you have managed to keep a step ahead of some enterprising female's ensnarement for so many years," Dante remarked. "Did it never occur to you that the whole affair might be planned? Perhaps you were singled out for your soft-hearted nature to personally escort the girl on board the *Sea Dragon*. And while you were seeing to her needs, preparing some of that famous broth of yours, she would be rifling my cabin. But, unbeknownst to Bertie Mackay, you were busy getting in stores for the *Sea Dragon*'s voyage, which was to be the following day, and not at the end of the week, as most of Charles Town assumed. But that having failed, they staged a commotion on the docks, conveniently close to where the *Sea Dragon*'s watch was standing duty. And while he was distracted, our little innocent slipped aboard and found the map," Dante Leighton concluded grimly. Whether or not this was idle speculation, or a theory he truly believed, only he knew for certain.

Houston Kirby, however, was not so easily swayed toward believing the worst of Rhea Claire Dominick. "Don't figure, Cap'n. Seems to me Bertie Mackay was takin' a mighty big chance that the girl could find the map and get off the ship without bein' caught. Reckon to me she would've stumbled across the captain of the *Sea Dragon* himself, seein' how he'd been aboard most of the day. The girl might as well have been on board an East Indiaman laden with silk and ivory off Madagascar fer all the good it would've done Bertie Mackay."

"There was little chance involved, Kirby," Dante responded, unimpressed by his steward's thoughts on the matter. "Have you forgotten that Bertie Mackay has had me followed for months? He knew exactly when I left the *Sea Dragon*, and where I ate my dinner, and when I retired for the evening. He even may have seen Helene entering my home earlier in the evening and mistakenly thought I would be kept occupied until late the following morning. He had not calculated on my lack of interest in the lady's charms, nor that I would knock out his man who'd been following me. As far as Bertie Mackay was concerned, there was little risk in the venture."

Houston Kirby sighed with exasperation at his captain's hard-headedness. "Then why not send this Daniel Lewis and his friend on board then?"

"Because I cannot quite see this Daniel Lewis engaging the sympathies of the crew, should he have been caught by someone. The girl, on the other hand, would have succeeded quite admirably, I am sure. After all, my crew is certainly proof of that," Dante said with a contemptuous glance at the grinning men gathered around the girl. "Who knows what information she could have wheedled out of them with those tearful violet eyes?"

The little steward looked heavenward and thoughtfully rubbed his bristly chin. "Could swear I remember ye sayin' ye just might believe the girl's story about not knowin' about the map. Reckon nobody in his right mind would be thinkin' the girl anything but a gentle-born lady," Kirby said with irritating logic.

Dante shrugged, seemingly unconvinced. "We may very well have on board one of this century's finest actresses."

"Ah, Cap'n," Kirby repeated, sighing in disappointment this time. "If only ye would believe the girl, 'twould make life so much easier fer all of us, and not while just on this voyage. If I hadn't become acquainted with the young lady, then just maybe I might have been inclined to believe your story about her workin' fer Bertie Mackay," Houston Kirby allowed. But in his next breath he quickly disabused his captain of the possibility that they were in agreement about her motives for being on board the *Sea Dragon*. "However, seein' how I have come to know the Lady Rhea Claire, I happen to believe every word she's spoken. How could ye not believe such a sweet young thing? Of course," the little steward added with a considering look at his captain, "if a man was tryin' hard enough he could be gettin' himself to believe anything, no matter how crazy 'twas!"

"Ah, Kirby," Dante mocked. "You are becoming soft in your old age. I never thought to see the day when a frilly petticoat would blind you to the truth. But whatever

Laurie McBain

it might be, *Lady* Rhea Claire Dominick does not disembark in Antigua. She will continue to sail with us," the captain of the *Sea Dragon* said, his tone brooking no argument.

Apparently, Houston Kirby was deaf to the implied warning. "Truth, is it, we be speakin' of now?" he questioned with an exaggerated look of incredulity on his face. " 'Tis yourself who's bein' hoodwinked, and by your own unsatisfied lusts. Aye, and ye can be knockin' me to the deck fer sayin' it, but I'm goin' to anyway," said the bow-legged little steward, standing his ground despite the blackening expression on his captain's face.

"Don't think I haven't seen the way ye look at the girl. I'm not blind to that, I'm not. Ye can't take your eyes from her. Ye're like some rutting stag sniffing at her skirts. And don't think I haven't seen the way ye glare at young Mr. Marlowe when ye think he's been trespassin' on what ye consider to be your property.

"Well, she ain't yours, Cap'n," Kirby continued, "to be doin' with as ye please. She be an innocent young girl, m'lord. She isn't like young madam in Charles Town, nor like any of t'other women ye've known and taken to mistress over the years. 'Twouldn't be right to be seducin' young Lady Rhea Claire, m'lord. No, sir, 'twouldn't be right a'tall, and ye'd be seein' that yourself if ye was thinkin' with your brain instead of that hardening bulge in your breeches," Houston Kirby said bluntly.

The cold gleam in Dante Leighton's gray eyes would have caused consternation among even the bravest of men, but Houston Kirby squared his shoulders and expanded his chest as he drew breath for further argument.

"My, my," Dante Leighton murmured softly, "I had no idea that you were my conscience as well as my steward. I see I shall have to start paying you double wages."

Kirby snorted. "Aye, mock me, Cap'n, but I've been doin' a powerful lot of thinkin' about this, and I reckon havin' me standin' here speakin' the truth, and aye, actin' yer conscience, makes ye a mite uncomfortable. Well, 'tis about time someone stood up t'ye, and I reckon 'tis gotta be me. Ye might have fooled t'others, but not me,

380

m'lord, not me. I'm well aware of the blackness that has been creepin' into your heart. Ye've lived by your own rules fer far too long. Ye don't answer to no man alive, only yourself. But if ye go through with what ye been plannin' and broodin' on, then ye'll have to be facin' that man ye've become, and I don't think ye'll be likin' what ye see," Kirby predicted, his lower jaw stuck out pugnaciously as he met his captain's eyes. Still, he was reminded too much for comfort of the old Marquis, who'd been famous in his day for his towering rages.

"Now, I'm not completely blamin' ye, m'lord, fer most of what's happened. Ye had little choice in what your future held all them years ago. Things could be worse than they are, I admit that, and ye've never brought shame to the name of Leighton. The old Marquis would've been proud of ye. But the sad truth of the matter is that ye're not the same Dante Leighton who was the young master of Merdraco. Ye've been changed, m'lord, by the course your destiny's taken over the years. Ye be an entirely different sort of man than that boy was and would have been, if he'd been left in peace to grow into manhood at Merdraco, surrounded by his loved ones and all that was rightfully his.

"That is why I'm sayin', m'lord, that ye can't be havin' Lady Rhea Claire Dominick. She is a part of the world ye left, Cap'n. If circumstances had been different, then perhaps ye would have met in London, courted, married, and raised fine young sons to inherit Merdraco," Houston Kirby told him, his eyes full of sadness for all that had been lost because of one man's infamy. "But 'twasn't meant to be."

"Damn you, Kirby," Dante Leighton swore softly at his steward. For Houston Kirby's words, in their revealing truthfulness, had the power to wound him. He stared past the figurehead of the grinning dragon, its lolling tongue feeding greedily on the frothy waves as the ship's bow dipped into the verdigris sea. There was a rawness to the sky above the *Sea Dragon*'s stand of sail. It was blood red, savage, like a gaping wound slashing through the indigo belly of the heavens. In the western skies the sun was sullen and copper-colored, as it was drawn irresistibly from its lofty perch.

The pagan beauty of the West Indian sunset was reflected in Dante Leighton's pale gray eyes, and he knew with a sinking of his own heart that Kirby was right. As he stood there on deck, the warm trades embracing him, he realized that he was more master of the *Sea Dragon* than master of Merdraco, and the Marquis of Jacqobi seemed but a pale shadow in his memory.

"Damn you," he whispered, his eyes meeting the steady gaze of the little man who, if he were asked, would have gladly given his life for the man he served.

"Aye, damn me then, fer I ken your feelings, m'lord. But what of young Lady Rhea Claire, m'lord? Does she understand what manner of man ye be? If ye succeed in seducin' her, makin' her love ye, then ye'll be destroyin' the girl. If ye make her a woman against her will, then she'll be damnin' the name of Dante Leighton," Kirby warned, his weathered face wreathed in a frown of concern.

"I have never raped a woman," Dante said quietly.

"There be other ways, less forceful but nonetheless brutal, of gettin' a woman in your bed. Ye've a way about ye, m'lord, and ye always have. Ye could be charmin' the devil himself out of a bit of fire, if ye put your mind to it. Aye, I've seen the way the ladies quiver when ye get that rakish look in your eye, and then they can't be denyin' ye nothin'. And ye haven't the right, just because ye be lustin' after the girl, to be denyin' her the life she was meant to have."

"Life is never certain, Kirby, haven't you learned that by now?" Dante said, his expression unreadable. "It doesn't always work out as it was meant to be. You, of all people should know that. Whatever the truth of her origin is, I am not responsible for her ending up on the docks in Charles Town. Her destiny had been changed before I ever crossed her path."

"Aye, but ye can be makin' things right fer her," Kirby suggested hopefully.

"I wonder . . ." Dante said thoughtfully. "Perhaps it is already too late to change what has occurred. The die has been cast, Kirby," Dante said, a strange smile curving his lips at some private thought.

" 'Tisn't too late, Cap'n. Ye could be letting her go free in Antigua," Kirby said hurriedly, worried by that expression on the captain's face. "She'll say naught about the map, if that is what is worryin' ye. She'll be so happy to be goin' home that she'll not give us or the *Sea Dragon* another thought. Let her go free, Cap'n. Ye'll never regret it," he said entreatingly.

"But what if I am right about her motives, Kirby? What if she is working for Bertie Mackay? What if she is an adventuress and sells what she has learned to the highest bidder? Will you take the responsibility for having the crew of the *Sea Dragon* denied their chance to make their fortune? Would you, without reservations, risk their lives on the word of that girl? Well?" Dante challenged him. "You say you trust her implicitly. Are you willing to take the chance that you might be wrong, that you may have misjudged her, been deceived by her wide violet eyes?" Dante asked him, forcing the little steward either to stand by his words or denounce Rhea Claire Dominick.

"Aye! Aye, Cap'n. I believe the girl," Kirby said finally, his voice husky.

"I see. Well, I am the captain of the *Sea Dragon* and I hold the lives of the crew in my hands, and I will not take that chance. Too much is at stake, Kirby. Our future depends on the outcome of this journey, and I will not jeopardize everything that I have struggled for over these long years just for the sake of a girl I know little of nor care much about. If there is a fortune in that sunken galleon, then I intend to retrieve it at all costs; nothing and nobody shall stand in my way. Then I will return to Merdraco, and no force on earth will be able to stop me from exacting my revenge."

"Aye, Cap'n, ye're most likely right about that," Kirby agreed grimly. "And then, after ye've savored your revenge, there will be nothin' to stop ye swingin' from the gallows-tree, either."

"That is a chance that I *will* take," the captain of the *Sea Dragon* declared challengingly, his pale eyes glowing with anticipation of that long-awaited confrontation with the man whom he had hated with a cold, controlled fury for close to fifteen years. Soon, very soon, dusk would fall on the day of reckoning for Sir Miles Sandbourne; and only then, his most despised enemy fallen at his feet, would the son of the tenth Marquis and Marchioness of Jacqobi know peace.

Dante Leighton, present owner of the ancient title and only surviving child of John and Elayne Leighton— and perhaps the last of a once-great dynasty—would risk everything, including his life, to settle the score. He would not rest until the day dawned when he could stand before their sepulcher and meet the stony stare from their effigies.

And so he stood on the quarterdeck of the *Sea Dragon*, stone-still and silent with his thoughts, and Houston Kirby, watching with a worried eye, felt the warm, gentle tradewinds turning bitterly cold—like a breath of devil wind off the bleak Devon moors.

"And what of Lady Rhea Claire, m'lord, when ye return to Merdraco hell-bent on seeking revenge? Is she, too, to become a victim of this self-destruction ye be planning? Because I'm tellin' ye now, m'lord, that if ye take her, then I'm thinkin' there will be plenty of angry folk seekin' revenge against ye fer the wrong ye done her. Ye might be the captain of the *Sea Dragon* now, and master of all ye survey, but if ye insist 'pon returnin' to Merdraco, then ye become Lord Dante Jacqobi again, and ye be honor-bound to do right by the girl. Then ye be wrongin' both of ye, 'cause ye don't care about her. Ye said so yourself. And ye won't be able to fool her fer long into believin' otherwise. What kind of life d'ye think ye'll be havin' at Merdraco, if ye survive your confrontation with yon bastard, that is? 'Twill be a hell fer both ye and the girl. She's become a challenge fer ye, m'lord, just like findin' this sunken treasure and outwittin' Bertie Mackay has. Ye live fer the danger of it all, takin' chances a sane man wouldn't even think of."

" 'Chance not, win not,' Kirby," Dante Leighton said suddenly, his eyes squinting against the blinding light off the gilded sea while he surveyed the proudly drawing sails of the *Sea Dragon*. "That has been the Leighton family creed for centuries, and it has always stood us in good stead. I shall heed it well, my doubting friend, and then we shall see who is right," Dante told his long-time companion. And because Kirby knew him so well, he could tell it was no idle statement, but the captain's next words gave him even more cause for concern.

"Actually, I am quite grateful to you, Kirby. Your well-intentioned words of wisdom have indeed given me cause for thought." Dante spoke with a look in his eye that Kirby did not care for at all. "No," he added with a mocking grin, "you needn't worry that I would be mad enough to try to ransom her back to Lucien Dominick. Even I am not that foolhardy. No, I thought it might be wiser, and far safer a venture, to present myself to the duke as a member of the family. The beloved husband, perhaps, of a beloved daughter? There would certainly be little risk in that, and indeed much to gain, for any daughter of the Duke of Camareigh is certain to be an heiress. And really, Kirby," Dante complained, his grin widening at the bemused expression on the little steward's face, "I am disappointed in your lack of faith in my abilities to convince the girl that I love her. I just might accept your challenge and prove you wrong."

Houston Kirby sniffed loudly, just to make certain the captain was in no doubt about his opinion on that claim. "More than likely 'twill be the girl herself who's provin' ye wrong, m'lord."

"Wouldn't care to lay a wager on the outcome, would you? No, I thought not," Dante laughed, "but then I s'pose it wouldn't be fair for me to win both the girl and your money. So we shall just have to wait and see, shan't we, Kirby?"

"Aye, Cap'n, that we will," muttered the little steward of the *Sea Dragon*. "If we got time," he added to himself as he looked astern and wondered just what might be following in their wake. His squinting eyes drifted westward, tracing the path of the descending sun, and he wondered anew what might be waiting ahead for the *Sea Dragon*, and whether he need even worry about the future. After all, he and the captain might never again see the rising sun's first light piercing the battlements of the gray-stoned towers of Merdraco.

There might be a fair wind filling the *Sea Dragon*'s sails now, but Kirby knew better than to be lulled into assuming that their voyage would continue on so smooth a course once she turned her bowsprit on a northwesterly heading. Capriciousness was not the sole possession of fortune, for a prevailing wind could just as easily become a high wind blowing into a squall, and one set of strange sails spied against the horizon could just as easily become two, then three, and then Dante Leighton and the crew of the *Sea Dragon* would have a real challenge on their hands.

Rhea Claire Dominick, however, was oblivious to this clash of opinions concerning her future, nor did she feel any of Houston Kirby's anxieties when she gazed up at the colorful western sky. At that moment her thoughts were occupied with the tangle of rough rope, which she was struggling valiantly, albeit unsuccessfully, to master.

"I give up," she conceded with an encompassing smile for the men who were watching her frustrated efforts. "I shall never again think myself clever for having sewn a straight stitch."

"Ach, well, it takes a wee bit of practicin', lass," Mac-Donald allowed generously. At least the bairn had tried.

"Why, it took Mr. MacDonald here close to a quarter of a century to learn how to tie an overhand knot, and ol' Longacres nearly twice as long to untie it," Seumus Fitzsimmons chuckled.

"Aye, laugh it up, codling, but if I had some of me old mates on board, we'd soon be teachin' a certain Paddy how to tie a proper knot. Aye, 'twould be quite a sight to see Seumus Fitzsimmons himself hobbling around the quarterdeck, them long legs of his tied into a shamrock knot," Longacres replied with a gape-toothed leer. But Rhea Claire, remembering Dante Leighton's words of warning about the one-time pirate, was less amused by the remark than the others.

Noticing her unease as she glanced at the grizzled cox-swain, Alastair took the liberty of patting her hand reassuringly, although it hardly looked as innocent as that to the man watching them from the deck above.

"Don't be concerned, Lady Rhea. Those two jack puddings are the best of mates. They're just making merry with each other," Alastair explained with an indulgent look at the two who were still trading quips.

"And was he truly a pirate?" Rhea asked softly.

"Aye, but that was long ago, and his bark is worse than his bite nowadays," Alastair said with a grin, for Longacre's two missing front teeth were only too obvious.

"Oooh, but the stories he tells, Lady Rhea!" exclaimed Conny Brady's young voice. "I reckon he's seen it all. He was in Charles Town when Stede Bonnet was hanged from the gallows."

"Must have been all of two at the time," Alastair commented disbelievingly.

"Mr. Longacres has a powerful memory, sir," Conny Brady said in support of his hero, for he believed every word the reformed pirate said.

"Next you'll be telling me that he served on board Blackbeard's sloop *Adventure*," Alastair said with a wink at Rhea Claire, whose eyes had begun to grow wide as she listened to the small boy's words.

"Oh, no, sir. If he had, he probably would've been dead, but he did see Blackbeard's chopped-off head swingin' from the bowsprit of H.M.S. *Pearl*. They say he was still grinnin' and his long black beard still glowin' with fire. Like a mad dog outta Hell, he was," Conny Brady breathed, sounding like Longacres himself when caught up in one of his pirate tales.

"Master Brady!" Alastair reprimanded him, his voice unusually sharp as he saw the color fading from Rhea Claire's face. "You shouldn't speak so disrespectfully in front of a lady."

Conny Brady looked chagrined, for he hadn't been around ladies of quality very often and Lady Rhea Claire wasn't one for putting on airs. Not that she couldn't have, Conny Brady thought in adoration, for she was more beautiful than any princess he had ever heard of. He wanted to put out his hand and touch her, just to make certain she was real, but when he looked down at his grubby, calloused hand, he snatched it back, for she was too fine to be touched by the likes of him. "I am sorry, Lady Rhea Claire," he apologized, his face burning a bright, painful red. "I didn't mean to offend ye, honest I didn't."

Unthinkingly yet quite naturally, Rhea put her arm around young Conny Brady's thin, boyish shoulders. He stiffened in surprise, then suddenly he relaxed against her shoulder, his cheek pressed against the thick, golden rope of hair. Such small shoulders, Rhea thought, yet they were shoulders that carried most of a man's full weight of responsibility. But in that instant, with that sheepish look on his face, Conny Brady had reminded her of her brother Robin, and she'd been overwhelmed by an intense longing for Camareigh and her freedom.

She glanced up and met Alastair's understanding gaze. He was no stranger to the gnawing pangs of homesickness, although not experienced under so traumatic a set of circumstances as Lady Rhea Claire's. He had, after all, left England of his own free will. But how different it would have been, he thought, if that press gang had succeeded in kidnapping him from the streets of Portsmouth, and he'd found himself on board a King's ship bound for the high seas, all hope of escape fading as quickly as the distant shores of England.

He had known of less fortunate men who had not escaped the greedy, indiscriminate grasp of the feared press gang. Many of those commandeered were mild-mannered clerks, shopkeepers, farmers, and even young boys, none of whom were suited for the rigorous and ofttimes dangerous life aboard one of the King's fighting ships. And far too often they ended with body and spirit broken by the unforgiving nature of both men and the sea. It was a hard life, the sailor's lot, especially for an unwilling man, and chances were he would never see again the familiar shores of England. If a slip of the foot high up in the rigging didn't take his life, and if he managed to survive grapeshot and cannon fire, then there was always the hungry sea licking at the bows of the ship, just waiting to claim him.

And yet here, on board the *Sea Dragon,* was a gently

bred girl who had suffered through a harrowing ordeal. She had known terror and death while crossing the Atlantic, only to fall prey to an assassin when finally reaching a safe port. But she had survived, her spirit unbroken. Alastair felt a growing admiration for the girl, which was openly revealed in his eyes.

She was probably thinking that this nightmare would never come to an end, when she found herself each day still further from her family and home. If only he could set her mind at rest, Alastair thought and vowed that as long as he drew breath he would see that she was safe and eventually returned to her family. He stood firm by that promise even when his eyes drifted in puzzlement to the solitary figure standing near the top of the companion ladder.

He did not often question his captain's actions, but he was suffering a great deal of uncertainty about them now, and he knew Houston Kirby was of a smiliar mind. The captain was a hard man to figure at times, but Alastair had always trusted his judgment in the past. Many thought, and rightly so, that the captain of the *Sea Dragon* was a harsh man, who gave no quarter and asked for none. He spared no man, but that included himself—even more so than others. He was his own unrelenting taskmaster, driving himself harder than ever as he came closer to vanquishing the enemy he had fought against for so long.

Dante Leighton was obsessed and because of his obsession he would, if challenged, ruthlessly dispose of any opponent who threatened him in his quest for revenge. And now, in the mind of the captain of the *Sea Dragon*, Lady Rhea Claire Dominick posed a threat to the successful culmination of all that he had planned for so carefully.

Alastair could well understand the captain's fears that word of the *Sea Dragon*'s destination would reach unfriendly ears. He was wrong, however, that the news would come from the lips of Lady Rhea Claire, but he'd not easily get the captain to believe that. Alastair sensed instinctively that Dante Leighton's hostile attitude went beyond an initial mistrust of her presence on board the

Sea Dragon. There was something indefinable that seemed to pass between them whenever gray eye met violet.

Whatever that elusive emotion was, neither was willing to admit or succumb to it; always, after a brief staring match, in which they seemed to be testing each other's strengths and weaknesses, their eyes would drift apart and the barrier between them would be more insurmountable than ever.

Alastair Marlowe's straightforward gaze rested in thoughtful consideration of his captain's aloof profile, then moved to linger on Lady Rhea Claire's young face. Her eyes were shadowed by memories that seemed to haunt her. It was a pity that both had suffered misfortunes which had left them suspicious and wary of each other's motives, Alastair reflected with deep regret. His own life, on the other hand, with the exception of that unfortunate confrontation with the press gang, had been devoid of personal complications and disappointments, and he was still a fairly optimistic fellow. And perhaps that helped him to perceive people and things a bit more clearly than either the captain or Lady Rhea Claire could.

Alastair caught Cobb's eye, then tapped his own pocket meaningfully. A moment later the lilting notes of a flute filled the air. " 'Tis a sweet sound, a soothing sound," Alastair murmured.

> *The king sits in Dunfermline town,*
> *Drinking the blue-red wine.*
> *"O where will I get guid sailor,*
> *To sail this ship of mine?"*

Rhea Claire listened to the beautiful baritone of the Scotsman MacDonald accompanying the music. She glanced up at the tall masts swaying over her head, the square white sails billowing as they filled with the trades. Sighing, she experienced a strange melancholy, for she was feeling both a sadness and a happiness of mind and spirit as she sailed into the West Indies on board the *Sea Dragon.*

"Make haste, make haste, my merry men all,
    Our guid ship sails the morne."
O say no sir, my master dear,
    For I fear a deadly storm.

A deadly storm, mused Rhea. How different this voyage was from that other one. She shuddered uncontrollably as she suddenly remembered the freezing cold that had penetrated to the bone marrow, and the black terror of that hold when she had thought to feel the ocean's might come roaring in on her with the foundering of the ship. She felt at times as if she had come out of the darkness into light. And even though she still did not have her freedom, and Camareigh might be on the far side of the world, she at least had a feeling that she was going to survive. A strange way to feel, considering she was being held captive by a smuggler and his crew.

Rhea felt something butting determinedly against her leg and glanced down to see her first friend on board the *Sea Dragon*. Jamaica seemed to sense her intent, for he jumped up into her lap before she had time to pat it invitingly. Rhea scratched his chin, eliciting a rumbling response of smug pleasure from the big tomcat.

I saw the new moon late yestreen
    Wi' the auld moon in her arm;
And if we gang to sea, master,
    I fear we'll come to harm.

Rhea Claire Dominick breathed deeply of the warm, salt-scented air of the quickly approaching Caribbean twilight. There was a subtle seductiveness in this balmy breeze that felt like silk against her skin, and she had to guard against being lulled into passivity. But that was hard to do when she was surrounded by people she was beginning to think of as friends.

How could she despise the funny little man who took such extra care in preparing his special broths and stews for her? And she certainly couldn't dislike a small boy named Conny Brady, who reminded her almost painfully of Robin as he tried to think up games to amuse her. And what of Alastair Marlowe? How could anyone think him other than a gentleman? He reminded her a little of Francis, and yet her brother, even at his much younger age, had assumed a certain sophistication of manner that Alastair would never succeed in acquiring. In fact, he reminded her more of her cousin Ewan. Yes, Ewan. Dear, sweet, practical Ewan, who always felt awkward when left to amuse her by himself. He was consumed by a sudden loss of words, he had once confided to her during one of those uncomfortable silences, and she suspected that Alastair suffered from a similar malady.

> *Half howre, half howre to Aberdour,*
> *'Tis fifty fathoms deep;*
> *And there lies gude Sir Patrick Spens,*
> *With the Scots lords at his feet!*

And then there was Alec MacDonald the Scotsman, who had fought beside her own great-grandfather at Culloden, and after surviving the slaughter on the battlefield had made a new life for himself in the colonies. How could she possibly feel threatened by a man who sang with such depth of feeling that his mates were left sitting in silence? When he had discovered that she was the great-granddaughter of Ruaiseart MacDanavel of Timeredaloch, his eyes, as blue as a highland loch, had filled with tears. And even though she was the daughter of an English duke, she was, in the Scotsman's eyes, a daughter of the highlands, and he had begun to treat her as though she were one of his kin.

Her deepest sadness came when she remembered Camareigh and found herself wondering what her family was doing at that exact moment. Was Robin out riding on Shoopiltee perhaps, or had her brother been up to mischief and confined to his rooms in punishment? Was Francis still taking fencing lessons from that temperamental dandy from France, or had he outmastered the master? Francis had become quite a swordsman, and Rhea was proud of her brother's skills, yet she hoped he would never have to prove them in a duel to the death with a bloodthirsty opponent. Perhaps Aunt Mary and

Uncle Terence were at Camareigh and the family was planning a picnic on the lawns, or . . . No, Rhea laughed silently, for it was still winter in England, and there might even be snow on the ground. There would be no picnics at Camareigh until spring—and by spring she would be home again.

Alys. The young girl's frightened face drifted into her memory. Alys was never far from her thoughts and she wondered what had been the fate of her friend from the *London Lady*. When she reached Camareigh, Rhea vowed, she would tell her father about Alys, and he would see that she was found, and if she wished, brought back to Camareigh.

"I will not forget you, Alys. I promise you, I will not forget about you," Rhea whispered, the memory of Alys's terrified screams as she was dragged from the ship still echoing in her ears.

"Lady Rhea Claire." A harsh, imperative voice cut through her thoughts and startled her from her troubled reflections. As if sensing that he now had her attention, Dante Leighton's voice became softer, almost silky. "Lady Rhea Claire, if you please? I should like to have a word with you."

Rhea instinctively met Alastair's sympathetic gaze, for the captain's words were a command, not a request. With a small shrug, Rhea stood up, still holding Jamaica firmly in her arms. With a look of genuine regret on her face, she said to the disappointed cabin boy, "You shall have to teach me that again. Although I suspect that I shan't be any more competent at it tomorrow, Conny."

"You learned the other knot, Lady Rhea. You can learn this one, too," Conny told her confidently, certain she could do anything.

"Aye, lass, ye've nimble fingers," MacDonald agreed, blowing a cloud of blue smoke over their heads. "We'll be makin' a sailor out of ye yet, and then yon popinjay just might be findin' himself out of a job," MacDonald commented, eyeing Barnaby Clarke, who had assumed his position at the wheel, but seemed more interested in the activities around the companion ladder. "Of course, there is one thing to be thankful fer, and that's that we're not downwind of him."

"Ye don't 'spose a sweet honeysuckle vine was entwinin' itself around the wheel during the wee hours, d'ye?" Seumus Fitzsimmons asked with a look of such concern on his handsome face that Conny Brady swung around to take a peek, just in case the wheel had sprouted honeysuckle.

"Gentlemen? I believe you all have duties to perform if we are to reach Antigua safely," the captain of the *Sea Dragon* reminded his crew, a slight look of annoyance on his face at being kept waiting for Rhea Claire to join him on the poop deck.

Holding Jamaica securely and steadying herself on the railing, Rhea slowly climbed the steps. Neither the ship's slight heeling, nor the captain's waiting figure at the top of the steps helped her move any faster. When she stumbled over the hem of her skirt for the second time, she felt hard hands that she remembered only too well grasping her around the upper arms and lifting her onto the firm planking of the deck.

"Thank you," Rhea said stiffly, avoiding the gleam in the pale gray eyes, which were staring at her with a strange expression. "You wished to have a word with me, Captain Leighton?" Rhea inquired with an almost little-girl politeness of manner. At this, the uninvited vision of the way she must have been at ten years of age suddenly intruded into Dante's thoughts, which was something that did not sit well in a man's mind, for she did not seem much different from that girl now.

Dante's lips tightened at this uncomfortable reminder of her youthful innocence. But then, perhaps that was the intent of those wide violet eyes, so guileless and clear of guilt. "I feel I have been remiss in my duties as your host while you have been aboard my ship. I hope you will forgive me my abruptness of manner, but I have had many worries on my mind of late," Dante Leighton explained, smiling in a way that had seldom failed to gain him favor in a woman's eyes.

But this time it failed, for there was no responding smile, nor any bashful fluttering of lashes over Lady Rhea

Claire Dominick's eyes. There was only a look of wary disbelief at this surprising admission and apology from the captain of the *Sea Dragon*. Then, as their eyes met and held, that other expression entered her eyes, the one he had seen too often not to recognize. Only then did she glance away from him, a rosy blush staining her cheeks.

He knew, without her ever having said a word, why she was so distant with him, why she was different with him than with any other member of the crew. After all, no other man on board the *Sea Dragon* had lain with her. No other man's hands had caressed that pale flesh; no other man had buried his face in that sweet-scented golden hair. Dante Leighton sensed, by the manner in which her eyes sometimes rested on his lips, that she remembered well the feel of his manhood pressed against her body. And once he had caught her lightly touching her lips before her eyes had strayed to his, and he had known that she was remembering the taste of his mouth against hers.

"I have been well looked after, Captain," Rhea replied coolly, while she rubbed her cheek against the top of Jamaica's head. By lavishing her attention on the pleased tomcat, she seemed to dismiss Dante Leighton's presence as unimportant.

"Yes, I am well aware of that fact, Lady Rhea Claire," the captain agreed as he saw Conny Brady approaching with a tray bearing a small silver mug, evidence of the fact that Houston Kirby hadn't wasted any time after going below. "You seem to have a way with animals and children, not to mention foolish old men."

"Mr. Kirby thought ye'd like a sip of his special lemonade, Lady Rhea. It tastes mighty good for somethin' that's supposed to keep sickness away," Conny Brady informed her, proudly presenting the tray and effectively halting anything she might have said in response to the captain's mocking words.

"Thank you, Conny," Rhea responded with the smile that Dante Leighton had been trying without success to coax only moments before.

Jamaica sniffed curiously at the mug, but not caring for the contents, he jumped from Rhea's arms and disappeared down the ladder, his destination most likely the galley and the little steward, who might be finagled into contributing a tasty scrap from his dinner preparations.

"I was just about to call Lady Rhea Claire's attention to the dolphins swimming off the starboard bow," said the captain of the *Sea Dragon* to the cabin boy, who was beaming his approval as Rhea drank the lemonade with obvious enjoyment.

"Dolphins? I've never seen any. I have only read about them in ancient Greek legend," Rhea said, her interest captured.

"You can read?" Dante asked curiously, his earlier doubts about that achievement still evident in his tone.

"Yes, Captain, I can. And I am quite accomplished at my letters, so should you require assistance in transcribing your log book, I shall be more than happy to oblige," Rhea offered generously, her smile full of understanding should he be less than skilled in the art.

Dante Leighton remained silent for a moment, and even Conny Brady could feel the tension mounting between the two people he idolized more than any others in his wide acquaintance. But then, when he heard the captain's deep laugh, he sighed in relief as he accepted the empty mug from Lady Rhea.

"My, my, you are quite the accomplished young woman," Dante murmured thoughtfully as he eyed her up and down. "I shall remember your kind offer, m'lady, and should I find myself in dire need of your services I shall not hesitate to call upon them. I should like to know, however," he added with the devilish glint in his eye that Rhea was coming to know too well for her peace of mind, "if this means that you will be available to me at any hour, say noontime, perhaps, or even in the midnight hour? And what is to be the extent of these services you have so charmingly offered me?" He had spoken so softly that Rhea had a hard time catching his words, but his expression left little doubt in her mind about what he might be referring to.

It passed over Conny Brady's head, however, like so much spindrift on the wind. "Mr. Marlowe's been teachin' me how to read, Lady Rhea. Been learnin' how to write me letters real good, too. Someday I'll be havin' me own ship to sail and me own log book to fill in from noon to noon," Conny Brady confided, his sea-blue eyes filling with the tall image of the captain of the *Sea Dragon*.

"I believe you shall, young Conny," Dante commented. When he saw the cabin boy's delight, Dante relented toward the girl whom he was beginning to feel was his other young charge. He gestured to the railing. "Would you care to view the dophins, Lady Rhea?" he asked with no visible sign of mockery.

"Yes, please . . . thank you," Rhea said hesitantly, not fully understanding the sudden change in his mood. Then, with a determined set to her chin that would have been recognized by her family, she promised herself that she would try to remain civil with this unpredictable man who held her freedom in his grasp. "Conny?" she inquired as the cabin boy started back toward the ladder leading to the quarterdeck.

"With your permission, Cap'n, may I go below? Mr. Kirby said to look lively or he'd have me peelin' potatoes until the sun came back o'er the foreyard," Conny explained, gazing yearningly at that place beside Lady Rhea at the railing.

"Very well, Mr. Brady. You've had your orders, see that they're followed, for we certainly do not wish an irate cook or we shall never dine," the captain remarked, thinking of his steward's grumpiness of late. "What is he so diligently preparing?" he asked a concerned Conny.

"Apple and orange puddin', Cap'n, sir!" Conny Brady cried back as he disappeared down the ladder.

"And no doubt he shall be licking the bowl clear," Dante murmured with a grin as he met Rhea's smile. For once neither of them harbored any pretense as they shared this moment in a strangely companionable silence.

" 'Tis considered a good omen to have the dolphin lending escort to your ship. Some feel it is a sure sign of a safe voyage for your ship and crew," Dante explained as they watched the frolicking dolphins swimming alongside the prow of the *Sea Dragon,* their strange cries and shrill whistles drifting up with the salt spray to blend with the creaking of the masts and thundering of the sails.

"And do you believe that is true, Captain Leighton?" Rhea asked, turning her gaze reluctantly from the shining gray shapes gliding just beneath the surface. But that had been a mistake, for he had leaned in closer to her in order to catch her words, and now their faces came close to touching, and Rhea found her eyes drawn almost irresistibly to the finely cut outline of his lips.

"Naturally I believe it is so. I might mock many things, Lady Rhea, but never the sea, nor her creatures. I would be a short-lived fool to do that. The sea is much like a woman, I suspect," Dante continued, his eyes holding Rhea's. "She can be unforgiving. Make a mistake, only one, and it might very well be your last one," he predicted. Then, so casually that Rhea was caught unaware, Dante Leighton had captured the long, golden rope of hair that so fascinated Conny Brady and was wrapping it around his fist. "Are you unforgiving, little one?" he asked strangely, his gray eyes looking deeply into hers, as if searching for something that had thus far eluded him.

Then he was laughing harshly, for he could read her damning answer in the aloof profile she seemed determined to present to him despite the increasing tension on her hair. "I suppose it is too much to ask of you. You are so damned young."

"Not too young to know right from wrong, Captain. I do not condemn you for your actions in Charles Town, however brutish they might have been," Rhea declared, willing to let bygones be bygones if it might help gain her freedom. "You found me trespassing on board the *Sea Dragon*, and being a smuggler and well accustomed to double-dealings you naturally assumed the worst of my motives. And I admit that the evidence did seem damning at the time, but I have explained about that wine bottle and the map. You seem to think that I have designs upon it and, more unlikely yet, upon your title. But I assure you, Captain Leighton, I have no interest in either one of your prized possessions," Rhea told him, her expression so honest that only a blind man could have doubted her.

The captain of the *Sea Dragon*, however, only smiled

in amusement, for this spirited discourse was most intriguing. Not only had m'lady fair forgiven him, but insulted him as well—and in the very same breath.

"Thank you, my dear, for setting my mind at rest. I have been having the devil of a time sleeping of late, thinking you about to crawl into my bunk. I s'pose I need not have worried after all about locking my door. Lud, but I was safe all the while."

"Mock me, Captain, but it is the truth. I realize you have only my word on that, and since you are reluctant to believe anything I say, I fear I am wasting my breath. But my word is the word of a Dominick, and that is a name I will never disgrace. Nor will my father take kindly to having his daughter humiliated and held against her will," Rhea informed him with a haughty look that masked well her inner trembling.

"That sounds like a warning, or perhaps even a threat?" Dante asked.

"A warning, Captain, for you may be dealing with me now, but sooner or later you shall have to answer to my father, and he is not a man many would care to anger. If, as you say, you do remember him, then you know I do not exaggerate. That is why, Captain Leighton, I am willing to make you a proposition," Rhea said boldy, turning her back on caution in her fight for her freedom.

"Indeed?" Dante remarked with a fine show of interest. "I was certain this conversation would become promising sooner or later, and I am a very patient man. Now, just what kind of proposition are you about to offer me? You are hardly in a bargaining position, my dear. And I doubt whether you are about to offer me that soft, yet unwilling ivory body of yours, are you, my dear?" Dante asked, his breath coming warm against her cheek. Then he wrapped the rope of living gold around his hand more tightly, until his knuckles were resting lightly against her jaw.

"My freedom for your life, Captain. I think that a fair trade," Rhea said softly, biting down on her lower lip to keep it from trembling. She was so frightened she could feel her limbs quivering, for never had she come up against a man quite like the captain of the *Sea Dragon.* He seemed at times to be a law unto himself, and almost beyond reasoning with. But as long as there was a chance, she would take it.

"A fair trade?" Dante repeated, a doubtful note in his voice. "I fear we perceive our present situations rather differently, for I had no idea that my life was in danger. Thank you for warning me. Should I be expecting a knife between my shoulder blades, or a blow to my head some evening when I've turned my back on you, my dear?" Dante demanded, smiling grimly now.

"You need fear nothing but my words, Captain," Rhea told him quietly. "I can be friend or foe, 'twill be up to you to decide. I am no fool, and were you a wealthy man you would hardly be resorting to smuggling. And this title of yours, which I shall presume is legitimate, apparently brings with it little more than a coat-of-arms. You, Captain, are in need of a fortune, and I, Captain, can provide it."

"Can you indeed?" Dante replied. "If you will forgive me, my dear, one would hardly think so to look at you."

Lady Rhea Claire Dominick, dressed in little better than rags, raised her chin proudly. "You are most perceptive, my lord, but hardly politic in reminding me of my straitened circumstances. You would do well, Captain Leighton, to take heed of something my mother is fond of saying, which is never to judge a person by his or her appearance," Rhea warned him. And thinking of her mother and the possibility of seeing her again gave her the courage to continue.

"My apologies, m'lady," Dante murmured, but his gray eyes were alight with mockery. "I should like to meet this wise mother of yours."

"My father, the Duke of Camareigh, should he be hearing exemplary things about you from me, would be more than generous in his gratitude. His generosity, in addition to the reward I am certain has been offered for my safe return, could add up to quite a fortune for the right man. You can be that man, Captain, and collect that fortune if you give me my freedom. All I wish is to return home. Is that too much to ask of you?" Rhea asked him, her eyes meeting his steadily, almost pleadingly.

But her pride was still riding high, and she would not grovel at his feet.

Her face was so close that Dante could see the silken sheen in the fine curve of her eyebrows. He had not been this close to her since they had lain together that first night, and now he noticed for the first time how the sun had planted its pale golden seeds across the bridge of her nose and the smooth expanse of cheek. Since she had been coming up on deck during the day, her skin had acquired a warm glow and her golden hair seemed burnished by sunlight. She was so breathtakingly lovely, so unlike anyone he had ever held in his arms. She was like a dream remembered, and one that was beginning to feel just as maddeningly elusive, for it was humiliatingly obvious that she found him loathsome and would resort to almost anything to escape him. And yet here she was just within his grasp, so why should he deny himself the satisfaction of possessing her?

"Maybe I shall not demand a fortune of your father, Lady Rhea Claire." Dante spoke so low that his words were hardly more than a whisper on the wind. "Perhaps only you, Rhea, can provide the means to your freedom. What is it worth to you personally, my dear, to gain that freedom? Is there a price that would be too high?" he asked, his unrelenting grip on her hair holding her lips just inches from his and making it difficult for her to escape his penetrating gaze.

Rhea Claire Dominick thought of the honey-hued walls of Camareigh, and of the bluebells scattered across the rolling meadowlands in springtime. She could see Robin on Shoopiltee as they galloped along the edge of the serene lake upon which white and black swans drifted. Her mother and Aunt Mary were sitting beneath the spreading arms of the old chestnut, the twins tottering about on their short legs as they explored their new-found world. Francis and her cousins were playing croquet on the lawns, while in the distance she could see her father's familiar figure as he strode across his land.

"There is no price too high, if it means I shall see my family and Camareigh again," Rhea said finally.

Dante Leighton continued to stare into her proud face.

Her violet eyes were dark with suffering, but he knew she would shed no tear while he stood before her. Only in the privacy of her small cabin would she give in to the struggling emotions which must be tearing her apart. For one so young she had a strength of will which was amazing. She begged not for pity or mercy, but stood seemingly inviolable before him, asking nothing. It damned him in his own eyes, and as the ship pitched into the trough of a wave, throwing her against his chest, he could feel her aversion to him in the rigid stiffness of her unyielding body. This revulsion, which she refused to hide, angered him, and he wanted to strike back and hurt her.

"I shall remember your bravely spoken words, *my* lady," Dante said against her ear, "when I ask for payment very soon. I look forward to the transaction, for you are a woman of your word, are you not, my dear? You have proudly proclaimed that a Dominick's word is never broken, so I foresee no difficulties involved," Dante said softly, his warm lips touching her cheek just briefly, as in promise.

"Hrrrmph!"

Dante glanced away from Rhea's flushed face and encountered Houston Kirby's woeful countenance. The little steward was standing at the head of the ladder, a cup of steaming coffee in his hand.

"Reckon I should've brought some more of that lemonade, Captain Leighton," Kirby said with a disapproving sniff, his formal address of his captain causing a curious expression to cross Dante Leighton's face. "Figure ye could be usin' a bit o' coolin' off, Captain, sir," he continued, stepping onto the poop deck and marching over to where Dante and Rhea were standing in an awkward silence.

He held out the cup, slopping some of the dark liquid onto the deck and just missing the captain's thigh. "Your coffee, *m'lord,*" the little steward said, with heavy emphasis on his title, as if to remind the captain of his past heritage and his gentleman ancestors who had, in Houston Kirby's mind, never sullied the good name of Leighton.

Dante rather reluctantly allowed his hand to slip free of the golden braid of hair and graciously accepted the proffered coffee, or at least it would have seemed so from the view aloft. The little steward knew better, however, as he met his captain's eye.

"I'll escort ye below, if ye be ready, m'lady," Kirby offered with a beaming smile as he held out his bended arm. "I was kinda hopin' ye might like to sample some of me special gingerbread. Put some in your cabin, m'lady." It was a bribe, proudly offered, and with her small hand tucked inside his elbow, he led her to the ladder, watching carefully as she descended, although with all of the interested eyes watching her from below, there would have been little chance of her falling. Then, with a last reproachful glance over his shoulder at his captain, Houston Kirby's grizzled head disappeared below.

"We goin' to be gettin' any of that special gingerbread, Mr. Kirby?" Cobbs asked with a hungry glint in his eye as they passed the still gossiping sailors. "Reckon we oughta have a lady on board more often. Makes fer much finer fare from the galley, that's fer sure. Gettin' pritty tired of pease puddin' all the time," he said with a wide grin at the look of outrage on the little steward's face.

"Reckon ye'll be gettin' something different all right, Mr. Cobbs," Seumus Fitzsimmons called to him. "Like maybe some saltpeter in your lobscouse tonight. Pity that, what with us bein' in port soon."

The raucous laughter of the crew followed the grinning steward as he led Rhea toward the entrance to the companionway, hurrying her past a vigilant Barnaby Clarke, who would have liked to detain her for a moment of polite conversation. To his disappointment, though, he received only a slight nod of recognition before she had disappeared below.

"Lobscouse!" Houston Kirby snorted in derision. "As if I'd be servin' lobscouse in a fine sea like this. D'ye know what lobscouse is, m'lady?"

"No," Rhea replied with little interest. Her thoughts were elsewhere as she paused at the entrance to the small cubicle vacated by Alastair Marlowe for her use while she was on board. After she had recovered from her fever, he had been most insistent about it and was backed up by the little steward, who said she ought to make use of the cabin, since it would allow her at least a modicum of privacy, something in short supply on board a ship. Her move from the captain's cabin into one of her own was something expected by the crew, who would have been surprised had she not, for they did believe her to be a lady of quality. If the captain had had objections he had kept them to himself. Alastair Marlowe was bunking with Seumus Fitzsimmons in a cabin across the companionway that was hardly bigger than a cabinet. And at the end of the short companionway was the door to the captain's cabin, a room she entered only to lunch and dine in.

"Well, m'lady, lobscouse can be fixed in different ways. Reckon with whatever ye got on hand, but 'tis mostly made with salt beef, onions, and potatoes mixed with ship's biscuit. Ain't much to speak about compared to one of me own concoctions, but 'tis good and fillin' when ye've a squall brewin'," Houston Kirby explained. "Now, ye just rest up here a bit. Dinner'll be ready in an hour or so, and I've roasted a nice breast of chicken fer ye. 'Tis one of me specialties, what with me own special sauce on it. And me Creole mutton's not to be bested anywhere in the Indies, if I do say so meself. Oh, but once we get to Antigua, m'lady, I can get me hands on some fresh pineapple. Select me own right off the bush, I do. Know just the kind that's the sweetest, and once ye've tasted me pineapple cake, well, 'tis nothin' quite like it. Would love to have that young brother of yours taste it. And 'tis the Cap'n's favorite, 'tis, and—" Houston Kirby stopped when he saw her expression, which seemed to say he'd said more than enough, unless . . .

"M'lady, the cap'n can be a difficult man at times, I'm not denyin' it. I've served his family fer nigh on half a century, and I wouldn't be with the cap'n now if I didn't believe he was a good man, but 'tis just that he has the devil's own temper, and when he's been riled there's just no reachin' him. He don't mean half of what he says, m'lady, so ye shouldn't be worryin' about it. Ye've got friends on board the *Sea Dragon*, and we'll let no harm befall ye, m'lady," Houston Kirby told her earnestly, hoping to set her mind at ease.

"Then please help me to escape him when we reach Antigua, Mr. Kirby," Rhea whispered in desperation, her nervous glance in the direction of the quarterdeck telling Houston Kirby only too clearly of her fear of the captain of the *Sea Dragon.*

"Ah, m'lady, it grieves me it does, to see ye so upset, but there's naught I can be doin' about it. I'm loyal to the cap'n, and although I'm not always agreein' with his ways, I'd die first before I'd betray him," the little steward told her simply, and Rhea knew he meant it.

"I am not asking you to betray your captain, Mr. Kirby." Rhea spoke softly, but there was an underlying intensity to her voice that worried Kirby, for when a person was thinking desperate, they often acted rashly.

"All I wish for is my freedom. I'll not say anything about how I arrived in Antigua. I will not implicate anyone on board the *Sea Dragon*," Rhea promised. "You have my word, Mr. Kirby. You, as well as many others on board have been kind to me, and I would do nothing to cause any of you harm."

"Ah, m'lady, it saddens me, it does, to have this happenin' t'ye. Ye be such a fine young thing, but . . ." Kirby's words trailed off into the tense silence.

". . . but there is nothing you can do for me." As Rhea completed his unfinished sentence for him, her lips trembled with growing frustration; then, with a muffled cry, she turned her back on the unhappy-looking little steward, never seeing the gingerbread placed carefully on the small table.

Houston Kirby stared at her shaking shoulders and her small back, which she held so rigid and straight as she tried to bear up under the ever-growing weight of her circumstances. She looked so young and defenseless, so alone, standing there in that green velvet that had seen better days. Houston Kirby felt his tender heart swell with pity for this young thing and he stretched out his hand to pat her shoulder comfortingly. But halfway there he hesitated, and with a sigh he turned and left her, for he knew there was really nothing he could say that would make her feel any less like crying.

Rhea heard the door closing softly after the little stew-

ard and allowed her tears to fall freely. As the gingerbread grew cold on the table, she sank down onto the
bunk and buried her face in her shaking hands.

"What am I going to do?" she asked the silent cabin,
her voice husky with a tear-fed hopelessness.

She had to break free. She had to escape the captain
of the *Sea Dragon*, before all was lost.

"They cannot understand," she cried softly as she
thought of the good intentions of the crew. "How can
they possibly understand when they are blind to what is
happening beneath their very noses?" Rhea laughed
harshly, and could the Duke and Duchess of Camareigh
have seen and heard their daughter now, they would
have been horrified to see the cynicism in the once-gentle
violet eyes and to hear the tinge of bitterness in the once-
soft voice.

"How can any of them possibly protect me from myself?" Rhea whispered, daring to voice for the first time
the self-doubts she had been experiencing since that first,
fateful meeting with Dante Leighton. Only she seemed to
realize fully the true danger which existed in her continuing to stay on board the *Sea Dragon*.

Rhea pounded her fists against her lap in impotent rage
as she tried to banish the vision of Dante Leighton from
her mind, but those pale gray eyes continued to stare into
hers; they mocked her, tantalized her, and seduced her,
until she felt as if a stranger were inhabiting her body.

She could not fully comprehend what had happened
to her while on board the *Sea Dragon*. She felt at times
as if Dante Leighton had cast some kind of cruel spell
over her, and although she walked and talked, she was
no longer the Rhea Claire Dominick she once had been.
She no longer knew herself—or trusted herself.

How far she had fallen from the Lady Rhea Claire
Dominick who had been so proud, so naively confident of
what she had wanted out of life. Never had she thought
that her life might not turn out as she had always imagined it would. Never had she foreseen such a tempestuous
awakening of her womanly desires, which now had left
her shaken and frightened. She hadn't wanted it to hap-

pen this way, and certainly not with a man such as Dante Leighton.

If only he had been an insufferable braggadocio or a corrupt bully who brutalized his crew, this captain of the *Sea Dragon*. How easy it would have been to despise him then. And if he had violated her, she would have sought her salvation in the sea, and that would have been the end of it. But Dante Leighton was not that manner of man.

And yet he was far more dangerous with his handsome bronzed face and clear gray eyes; his gentlemanly manner deceived a person into believing he was not the cunning opportunist he would have to have been in order to have survived this long in the perilous profession he had chosen.

Rhea rolled flat on her bunk, her folded arms cushioning her head as she stared up at the low beamed ceiling and pondered the ill-fated fascination she felt for Dante Leighton. She had met many handsome men last year during her season in London, and yet there'd been no chance meeting of eyes with any of those gentlemen that had caused the quickening in her blood she felt when her eyes were captured by the gray-eyed, mocking stare of the captain of the *Sea Dragon*.

There must be something else, something indefinable about Dante Leighton that had the power to hold her so entranced, despite her own instincts warning her against him. It had to be something other than the classical perfection of his features, for Wesley Lawton, Earl of Rendale, had been an extraordinarily handsome man, too. Yet, she had never felt that fire spreading through her when his hand accidentally touched hers, and perhaps that was part of the reason. The Earl of Rendale, ever conscious of his reputation and high standing in society, would never have dared to act improperly with a lady, especially a duke's daughter, and so any touching between them would certainly have been accidental. Genteel almost to a fault, Wesley Lawton had been court-bred and had allowed his life to be ruled by convention. Always *comme il faut*, that had been the late Earl of Rendale, Rhea thought sadly, remembering how he had looked the last time she had seen him, just before he had been felled by that assassin's bullet.

The captain of the *Sea Dragon,* on the other hand, apparently delighted in flouting convention. There was a damn-your-eyes attitude about him that mocked the very proprieties that Wesley Lawton had held so dear. If the Earl of Rendale could have seen Dante Leighton, a supposed gentleman, who claimed a title superior even to his own, climbing the rigging of the *Sea Dragon* in the company of common sailors—individuals whose existence Wesley Lawton would never have permitted himself to admit—he might have been shocked into uttering an indiscreet remark. Rhea remembered standing on the quarterdeck, the winds buffeting her as she looked up the seemingly endless, swaying length of mast to where the captain was clinging precariously to the main topgallant shrouds, his bare feet balanced on the ratlines as he fitted a strap around the masthead. He had been clad only in a pair of leather breeches; his broad back had gleamed like copper and his muscles had been rippling and shiny with sweat as he worked.

She had thought him a madman to go aloft when there were others who could just as easily have done the job, but as she continued to watch him, she had come to the startling realization that Dante Leighton was thoroughly enjoying himself as he fought to keep his footing in the unsteady shrouds while he climbed down toward the crosstree. As he descended into the tangle of rope of the lower shrouds, Rhea could see the simmering excitement still lighting his eyes. He had met the challenge and beaten it, but still he seemed to be restless, searching for a further, more dangerous test of his courage and skills.

Dante Leighton was a man who dared the fates, who stared insolently at the odds, then risked them to achieve some personal goal he had set for himself. He seemed to be defying the heavens when he went aloft, looking for all the world like Neptune, god of the sea, as he surveyed his kingdom while the hungry waters lapped at his feet. It was as if the captain of the *Sea Dragon* were tempting fortune into a reckoning with him.

Rhea closed her eyes, allowing her thoughts to drift

with the lulling motion of the ship while she caught at that elusive impression that had been puzzling her, bothering her. The more she had watched Dante Leighton, the stronger her impression had become that there was something familiar about him. She had the strange sensation that she had known his face for most of her life, and as she lay there, relaxed, it suddenly struck her why Dante Leighton, captain of the *Sea Dragon,* held so powerful a fascination for her.

How many times had she stood in the Long Gallery at Camareigh, staring dreamily up at that portrait of her ancestor who had been the adventurer-privateer during the reign of Elizabeth I. The similarity between the two men was not in an identical cast of features, for her ancestor was a much darker man, who sported the neatly trimmed beard fashionable during the sixteenth century. And where Dante Leighton's eyes were pale and crystalline with light, her ancestor's were like ebony. But that mattered not, for it was the expression in their eyes that made them brethren. They possessed a kindred spirit. And even though two centuries separated their existences, they could have stepped into each other's lives with little difficulty.

They were enterprising men of derring-do, who thrived in defiance of danger, crying to fortune and foe alike, "Come if you dare!" The bold stroke was their forte, and they would venture undaunted into the fires of hell if challenged to do so.

Rhea smiled in sudden relief, for she now felt at long last that she understood herself. She had been mesmerized for years by a portrait. She had fallen in love with a painted man, and now she had transferred that infatuation —yes, *infatuation*—to this flesh and blood man who so resembled in spirit the portrait that had held her spellbound. She was not in love with Dante Leighton, Rhea told herself, but with the memory of a man from another century, who seemed now to be walking the quarterdeck of the *Sea Dragon.*

Rhea sniffed back her tears and wiped their unwanted wetness from her cheeks. She chuckled softly, feeling as if the weight of the world had been lifted from her shoulders now that she had freed herself from the bedevilment of Dante Leighton.

Rhea felt something soft touching her cheek and sat up startled, her less than charitable thoughts concerning the captain of the *Sea Dragon* causing her to blush guiltily should the man himself have been standing there watching her.

"Jamaica," Rhea breathed in relief, then glanced in surprise at the door, which was now open. Even though Jamaica was capable of swiping a piece of fish from the galley, or a slice of beef from your plate when you were not looking, Rhea seriously doubted whether he was proficient at opening doors.

Then Conny Brady appeared in the doorway, staring with concern at her red-rimmed eyes and tear-stained cheeks.

"Ye've been crying, m'lady?" he questioned, sounding almost reproachful. "Why?" he asked, as if he couldn't possibly understand how anyone could be unhappy who was lucky enough to be on board the *Sea Dragon* and serving under Captain Dante Leighton.

"I was just feeling homesick," Rhea explained. "Don't you ever get homesick, Conny?"

"No," he answered honestly, his eyes wide with surprise at such a question.

"I would think you would miss your family. I am certain your mother and father must worry about you when you are at sea," Rhea said curiously, wondering how it was that Conny Brady became the cabin boy on board the *Sea Dragon*.

"Me mum died when I was five and me pa was a sailor. He went to sea and never came back. Reckon 'tis in me blood."

"Where are you from, Conny?" Rhea asked, thinking how different Conny Brady's life had been from Robin's.

"Bristol. Though me pa was a Paddy."

"A Paddy?"

"An Irishman, m'lady. He come into port and met me mum, begot me, then shipped out. Never heard of him again, we didn't."

"How long have you been at sea, Conny?" Rhea couldn't understand the boy's complacence.

"Oh, nigh on five years now, I reckon. Signed aboard me first ship when I was six—'twas a bit after me mum died. Reckoned bein' at sea was better'n bein' in some workhouse or asylum fer orphans. That's where the magistrate wanted to put me since I had no family, so I ran away one night. Never been back, I haven't, though . . ." Conny stopped and turned a bright red when he noticed Rhea's interested stare.

"Though what?" Rhea asked. "Is there someplace you'd like to go or see? You have probably seen much more than I ever shall. Come on, don't be bashful now. I can keep a secret, truly I can. I've all of my brothers' naughty deeds locked up tight in my head. Aren't you going to tell me?" Rhea asked. Her soft voice was at its most persuasive, and young Conny Brady never had a chance to deny her.

"Well," Conny said finally, his color still heightened, "I would kinda like to see Camareigh. The way ye've talked about it, well . . ."

"You shall see it, Conny," Rhea told him, touched by his confession. "I give you an invitation now to visit Camareigh whenever you so wish."

Conny Brady stood in silent disbelief. "Ye're not gullin' me, are ye, m'lady? This be truth, then? I've an invitation to come to see ye at Camareigh?"

"My word of honor you do," Rhea reassured the young fellow. "*If* I ever return to Camareigh," she added, more to herself then to Conny Brady, but he caught her words and grinned wide.

"Ah, Lady Rhea, the cap'n'll be lettin' ye off in Antigua. Then ye can be leavin' fer Camareigh, and in maybe a year or so, whenever the *Sea Dragon*'s back in English waters, well . . . maybe I'll be travelin' by and . . ."

"And you will come and stay for a month if you wish," Rhea insisted, her eyes twinkling as she realized he had already planned his future visit.

"Ye think maybe this brother of yours might be lettin' me ride his pony?" Conny Brady asked diffidently.

" 'Tisn't up to Robin," Rhea replied. Then she added quickly, when she saw the disappointment spreading across Conny Brady's young face, " 'Tis up to Shoopiltee whether or not you ride him, but he is a fairly well-behaved animal for a pony." Then Rhea noticed for the first time the bundle in his arms, and she nodded at it curiously. "What have you there, Conny?"

Conny's face turned an even brighter hue of red. "Oh, m'lady, Mr. Kirby'll have me hide fer takin' so long. What he must be thinkin'—coooee! Reckon he's waitin' now, along with the others to hear how ye like them. I knocked, I did, but when ye didn't answer I just came in. Besides," he added with a knowing look at the tomcat who was stretched out on the bunk cleaning himself, *"he* wanted in, and he's not very patient, he isn't."

"I am sorry I didn't hear you," Rhea said, a frown of puzzlement on her brow as she stared at the strange bundle held so protectively in Conny Brady's arms.

"I guess not, seein' how ye was cryin'," Conny agreed, not very tactfully.

" 'Tis our secret, eh, Conny?" Rhea requested.

"Aye, m'lady, 'tis our secret, but I reckon this'll cheer ye up some," he predicted, shyly holding out the carefully folded bundle of cloth.

"What is it?"

"Open it, m'lady!" Conny enjoined her, his eyes glowing with excitement. "Mr. Kirby would've liked to have been here, I bet, but he said 'tweren't proper like, so he sends me with it, and with the compliments of the whole crew, just about. We all contributed sonethin', those of us who had something, that is, Lady Rhea." Then he watched proudly as she slowly shook out the skirt and separate bodice which Houston Kirby, with an occasional word of unwanted advice from the others, had sewn for her.

Rhea's eyes filled with tears as she touched the soft leather patches, so diligently stitched together to make what could almost be called a proper skirt. The hem was of varying lengths, conforming to the individual pieces of leather. Altogether, the skirt hardly would have been considered proper attire except at a masquerade ball.

"Don't ye like it, m'lady?" Conny asked worriedly, looking crestfallen when he saw the tears glistening in her eyes. "That patch right there, and that one there," he said, pointing to a couple of fawn-colored pieces of chamois, "are from a pair of my breeches!" His young voice was full of nervous anticipation as he tried to gauge her reaction to this unexpected gift from the crew of the *Sea Dragon*. "Ye not goin' to cry, are ye?" he demanded in confusion, wondering what he had done to upset her.

"Oh, Conny," Rhea said as she reached out and hugged him. Then, to his intense surprise and pleasure, she kissed him on the cheek. " 'Tis the most beautiful and thoughtful gift I have ever received."

Conny Brady's grin spread practically from ear to ear at her words of praise. "There be somethin' else there, too, m'lady," he told her, unable to contain his excitement any longer.

"But Conny, how can the men afford to lose parts of their breeches?" Rhea asked. "This will cost them dearly."

Conny Brady seemed to find her wording funny and started to giggle uncontrollably. "Well to be sure, m'lady, us men of the *Sea Dragon* figured 'twould be an honor to donate our breeches to help make ye somethin' decent to wear, beggin' your pardon," he tacked on, realizing rather belatedly that he had just insulted her. "Besides, Mr. Kirby said 'twould be the cap'n's pleasure to reimburse us all for the loss of our best breeches, seein' how the most of us only had the one pair."

"Mr. Kirby seems not only a fine seamstress, but also quite accomplished at embroidering a bit on the truth," Rhea remarked, thinking of the captain's displeasure when he found out he would have to foot the bill, for she doubted very seriously if he had knowledge of his crew's generosity. "Did the captain contribute to my skirt, Conny?" she asked now, running her hand with obvious pleasure over the odd-shaped squares of buckskin and soft leathers fitted together in a careful, harmonious blending of shades of tawny, russet, and nut brown.

"Aye, m'lady, I remember Mr. Kirby sayin' 'twould be a perfect fit and color for someplace on the skirt, but don't remember exactly where," he told her. "But just about everybody knows where his patch of breeches is. Now, Mr. MacDonald made those for ye," Conny added, noticing that Rhea was examining in puzzlement the two sections of hard leather that had been cut and stitched into the shape of soles, with long lengths of rawhide woven through holes on each side. " 'Tis complicated lookin', m'lady, but Mr. MacDonald says to crisscross the straps over your foot, then wind them up your calves and tie them. 'Twill help hold your stockings up. Reckon your old boots be a mite uncomfortable without the heel."

Then Rhea brought from the cloth bundle a fine linen bodice that had been beautifully fashioned for her, the edging of lace around the décolletage and sleeves as delicately wrought as any she'd ever seen. " 'Tis beautiful," she murmured, then gave a gasp of surprise as she encountered the bunch of colorful silk ribbons that were wrapped up with the bodice. The ribbons were of jewel-bright hues of scarlet, emerald, saffron, plum, and sapphire. "Oh, Conny," she said, "where did you find these precious ribbons?"

"They be from Mr. Fitzsimmons," Conny Brady replied honestly, his wide blue eyes entranced by the sight of Rhea holding the colorful ribbons against her hair as she smiled playfully at him. "Cobbs says they were supposed to be for some coquette in St. Eustatius that Mr. Fitzsimmons has been after for the longest time."

"Oh, dear," Rhea said, a smile tugging at the corner of her lips. "I hope Mr. Fitzsimmons was not reluctant to part with these ribbons he bought especially for his lady friend."

"Coooee, no, m'lady!" Conny Brady said, whistling through his teeth. "For one thing, she ain't no lady, Longacres says, and for another, Mr. Fitzsimmons says he's just about spent the last shilling he intends to on the little whore—" Conny Brady, the cabin boy who innocently repeated much of what he overheard, stopped abruptly as he remembered with whom he was speaking. Then, with a face burning with mortification, he concluded rather lamely, "—and she probably has a trunk full of ribbons anyway, Mr. Fitzsimmons says."

"Well, you thank Mr. Fitzsimmons for his sacrifice," Rhea told him, pretending she hadn't understood what Conny had said.

414

"Aye, I will, m'lady," Conny replied eagerly, pleased that he had not offended Lady Rhea. "I better get back to Mr. Kirby or he'll be in a stew, and besides, I don't want anyone to lick the bowl. Mr. Kirby promised it to me, but ye can't trust nobody when it comes to Mr. Kirby's apple and orange puddin'," Conny told her, a look of concern spreading across his face as he realized how long he'd been absent from the galley and an unprotected bowl of pudding.

"Off you go then, and Conny," Rhea said and paused, her violet eyes seeming to swallow him up, "thank you. You are very special to me."

Conny Brady hunched his shoulders in pleased embarrassment, his eyes shining with an emotion he'd never known before, for no one had ever said that he was anybody special. " 'Twas our pleasure, m'lady," he mumbled as he quickly turned and left the small cabin, his feet hardly touching the deck.

"Oh, Jamaica, look at all of this." Rhea sighed in pleasure as her hands strayed once again to the soft leathers of the skirt. She took a length of green ribbon and tied it around the big tom's neck, the bow looking incongruous with the tom's lordly expression. "Sorry, sweeting," Rhea apologized with a grin, as she freed Jamaica's neck from its fashionable collar.

In growing excitement and anticipation, Rhea stared at her gifts from the crew of the *Sea Dragon,* hoping that the clothes would fit her, for she'd never been aware of Houston Kirby taking any measurements, and she wasn't certain who would have been more upset—herself or the crew—if she did not appear above deck in her new clothes. And so with little regret, Rhea ridded herself of the green velvet skirt and jacket that she had worn since that day, months ago, when she had been kidnapped from Camareigh. Her fingers were shaking slightly as she unfastened her quilted petticoat, letting it drop to the decking, for it had become cumbersome and unnecessary in the tropics. She had finally given up on her half-boots just the day before, for with one heel missing and the leather beginning to mildew, she had grown reluctant to slip her feet inside of them. Her stockings had been rinsed out and folded away.

Standing in her thin chemise and corset of soft faille, she carefully picked up the skirt and examined it, then stepped inside it and pulled it up over her hips. It fit snugly around the waist, with the two edges of the waistband overlapping slightly and secured by two small strips of narrow leather, which she tied in a small bow. The cut was far less full than what she was accustomed to wearing, and the lightness and softness of the fabric gave her a freedom of movement she had seldom known; indeed, she felt almost as if she were clad in the breeches from which her skirt had been patched together. The hem of the skirt was far more uneven than she had first thought, for it hung almost to her heels in back, yet curved upward to mid-calf in front, and she supposed that Houston Kirby must have run out of suitable breeches.

Rhea ran her hands lightly across the fine linen of the bodice, then, with a nervous sigh, slipped it over her head, pulling it down and over her breasts as she slid her arms into the slightly puffed sleeves with their deep edging of lace, which once must have adorned the cuffs of the original sleeves. Adjusting the bodice, she stared in dismay at its low décolletage and the soft rounding of breast revealed above the trimming of lace that cascaded along the deep curve. Canfield would have been horrified; perhaps she would even have fainted could she have seen her now. Rhea recalled well the lady's maid's insistence upon propriety at all times.

The little steward certainly had a good eye, for the bodice fit her well, while around the waist was a belt of plaited ribbons, which matched those for her hair. When it was pulled tight and tied, the loose material around her was gathered close to give a neatly fitted look.

Rhea spun around in pleasure, feeling like a different person already. As when she stopped, her long braid twisted around her, and she decided that new clothes demanded a new hairstyle. With a serious look on her face, she retrieved the small hand mirror that Alastair Marlowe had thoughtfully left behind for her use. A look of comical dismay spread across Rhea's face as she stared at her reflection and realized that Canfield never would have recovered could she have seen the golden tint to her highly prized, pale complexion. Canfield had always threatened to use cucumber water and lemon juice on her whenever she happened to catch her out of doors without a proper hat and gloves. But Rhea wished now that she had Canfield to assist her; she would even gladly suffer that woman's never-ending chatter.

Rhea freed her hair from the thick single braid, and taking another one of her borrowed items, a brush Houston Kirby had miraculously produced, she began to brush her hair free of tangles. She stared at herself in critical silence for a long moment as she tried to think what Canfield would have done with the unmanageable mane of hair. Then, with a look of determination, which Canfield would have responded to with a nervous clasping of her thin hands, Rhea began to divide her hair into sections, then patiently plaited the long strands into six braids, each interwoven with a different color ribbon. She then doubled the three braids on each side and tied them together above each ear with matching lengths of violet ribbon, leaving her hair to dangle in twisted golden loops that swung gently against her bare shoulders.

Pleased with the effect, bizarre though it might have seemed to fashionable London and to Canfield, Rhea shook her head, enjoying the feel of the swinging braids. She was slipping her feet into the sandals and winding the straps around her silk-stockinged calves when she heard the ship's bell announcing the change of the watch, the chime coinciding with the dinner hour in the captain's cabin.

Rhea took a deep breath and stepped from the safety of her cabin, feeling a nervous excitement about being seen for the first time in her new clothes, a strange sensation for one who was well accustomed to changing her gown several times a day to suit the occasion. Never before had she been overly conscious of her appearance, but now she almost dreaded the moment when those pale gray eyes would settle on her with embarrassing thoroughness.

417

But armed with what she thought was a fuller understanding of her feelings for the captain of the *Sea Dragon*, Rhea felt she could face anything or anyone. Her heart, however, was not paying heed to her mind's arrogant assumption that Dante Leighton's sensuality could be so easily dismissed; indeed, it fluttered wildly as she neared the door to the captain's cabin and heard the sounds of tinkling glass and low laughter. Swallowing her trepidation, Rhea knocked softly on the door, almost hoping that no one would hear it. After an endless second, though, she heard feet approaching, then the door was opened, and she found herself staring into the stunned face of Alastair Marlowe.

"Lady Rhea?" he spoke, finally finding his tongue, but he felt at a loss for words as he stared at the breath-taking transformation of the girl whom he'd seen on deck hardly two hours earlier.

"Mr. Marlowe?" Rhea responded, her head tilted to one side as she stared up at him with growing amusement and feminine satisfaction at the obvious response she was eliciting. "May I come in and join you, sir?"

Alastair Marlowe turned a dull mottled red as he quickly stepped aside to allow this stunning creature access to the captain's cabin. Then he hurriedly closed the door behind her extraordinary figure and turned around to catch the captain's reaction to his guest.

Dressed in a dove-colored cloth suit with gold buttons, a gold brocaded waistcoat, and a pair of gray silk stockings and round-toed shoes with golden buckles, the captain looked like any slightly bored, aristocratic gentleman engaged in casual conversation before sitting down to dine. His chestnut curls, usually windblown, had been brushed off his wide forehead and tied with a black velvet ribbon in a neat queue. As he took a sip of wine from a silver goblet, the delicate lace of his shirt sleeve fell in deep folds around a finely shaped hand that seemed to belie its great strength. Rhea, glancing down instinctively at the lace edging on her bodice, realized rather belatedly the origin of part of her clothing, and wondered if the captain had yet missed one of his shirts of finest holland.

Dante Leighton became aware of Seumus Fitzsimmons's sudden lack of attention to their conversation, and noting that gallant's widening eyes and slow grin of appreciation, he turned, fully expecting to see the *Sea Dragon*'s female passenger. But her captain was not prepared for what met his gaze.

"Ah," Seumus Fitzsimmons breathed, his eyes lifted heavenward and his hands folded as if in prayer, " 'tis true, then. I was knowin' if I kept me faith, I'd be havin' me prayers answered one day."

"What is true?" Alastair Marlowe asked curiously, watching with interest the different emotions playing across certain faces in the highly charged atmosphere of the captain's cabin.

"Why, that there be Nereids, after all. To be sure, I've always been fond of the story about sea nymphs, but until now I was havin' no idea of the deadly enchantment of such a creature, for me heart is close to breakin' at the very sight of ye, m'lady," Seumus Fitzsimmons proclaimed, his hand pressed above his heart as he stepped across the cabin and came to a halt before her, bowing most elegantly before bringing her hand to his lips in a most gentlemanly manner.

As he straightened, he caught sight of the colorful ribbons adorning her golden braids, and he sighed audibly. "Ah, ye be a grand lady indeed to be takin' pity on a poor Irishman's gift. If I could only be tellin ye, m'lady, what it does to a man to see ye wearin' his ribbons, well, 'tis—"

"—'tis certain ye'll be makin' an attempt to be tellin' her, Seumus Fitzsimmons," Alastair remarked in fair imitation of the glib Irishman. His purpose, however, was to interrupt the flow of words before they completely embarrassed Lady Rhea, who was blushing slightly, or managed to irritate the captain, whose gaze was narrowed in a manner which usually boded ill for someone.

"—'tis a sight that warms me heart, it does," Seumus Fitzsimmons continued as if never interrupted, his black eyes twinkling with pleasure. There was another emotion, too, when his roving glance spied a particular patch of leather riding against Rhea's thigh. "Ah, 'tis almost too

419

much fer me Irish soul to be seein'. To know a piece of me own dear breeches is touching so fair and soft a skin as yours, m'lady, well 'tis enough to—"

"It might be wise, Mr. Fitzsimmons, if you went on deck and got a breath of fresh air," Dante Leighton remarked lazily as he came forward, his pale gray eyes never leaving Rhea's face. "You seem to be suffering the effects of too much wine and it has gone to your head."

"Ah, Cap'n, 'tis a hard man ye be, for 'tis the warming of me Celtic blood by unsurpassed beauty, and a fair bit of dreamin', that has me actin' the fool," the irrepressible Irishman responded, gazing almost with regret at that soft patch of buff-colored leather. "And, I might be addin'," he said with an unrepentant grin for what he was about to say, "that as I'm recognizin' that fine piece of lace flutterin' ever so softly at m'lady's breast, I'm wonderin' if ye might not be doin' a fair bit of manly speculation yerself, Cap'n, sir?"

"I think a glass of Madeira might be in order for Lady Rhea." Alastair's friendly voice intruded into a silence which had grown suddenly tense. The Irishman's ill-advised words seemed to be hanging like an axe over his own head, which was unfortunate, Alastair thought, for there was not a man on board more loyal to Dante Leighton than Seumus Fitzsimmons. But this time the Irishman may have gone too far with his biting wit, which in the past had spared no man, including himself. Usually his stinging witticisms had met with equally devastating rejoinders; it was all done with good humor, though, for everyone understood the Irishman's brand of repartee.

Seumus Fitzsimmons may have felt a similar sense of impending doom, for he prudently withdrew to pour the requested Madeira for Lady Rhea, a wry look on his handsome face as he eyed his captain, for it was common knowledge on board the *Sea Dragon* that the captain was having a devil of a time with the young lady. Houston Kirby wasn't the only one who suspected there might be more between the two than met the eye, and speculation was rife amongst the crew on exactly how long it would take their captain to bed the wench.

And, aye, that was the problem, and not only for the captain and the Lady Rhea Claire, but for the crew as well, for angry words had been exchanged, as well as threatened fisticuffs, when it came to the young lady's reputation and protection thereof. After all, it wasn't as if the young lady were a courtesan of questionable virtue off the docks in Charles Town. Seumus Fitzsimmons liked to think that the crew of the *Sea Dragon* was made up of decent blokes and that their morals weren't completely piratical; thus, he, as well as many others, had found himself strangely affected by Lady Rhea Claire's misadventures.

MacDonald showed another fine example of the enraptured state which seemed to be possessing the crew, for the Scotsman was seldom ever disturbed by anything. He'd certainly been a stranger to anger for as long as Seumus Fitzsimmons had known him. Seumus remembered wondering how these clannish Highlanders had come to have such a fierce reputation, and if there really was anything to all these stories of blood feuds between the clans. Well, no longer would he doubt the truth of those stories, for to hear MacDonald speak, one would have thought he himself was about to be violated, or at least a daughter of his, but certainly not a young woman he'd only met close to a fortnight ago.

Seumus Fitzsimmons smiled in self-disgust, for he himself had made an attempt to bridle his own tongue, lest he hear the deadly whisper of a claymore over his glib Irish head. Aye, that was where the trouble lay, for MacDonald would swing that claymore on behalf of the captain as well, for he was loyal to the master of the *Sea Dragon* and would sooner betray his own clan than Dante Leighton.

'Twas a difficult situation, for the crew would have liked to see a match between their captain and the lady, but 'twas the circumstances under which such a coupling would be consummated that concerned them. For in the crew's estimation, the captain couldn't have found a finer young woman to take as wife, nor could the young lady have found a finer gentleman. Aye, 'twould have been nice to have attended the nuptials, but with Antigua just off the starboard bow, and Lady Rhea Claire anxious to return home to England, and the captain acting like a caged tiger, it just didn't look as if 'twould come to anything. Time was running out on the captain if he intended to make the lady his own, which, upon seeing the captain's expression as he gazed at the girl, was exactly what he had in his mind. Thinking this, the Irishman sighed with a mixture of envy and concern.

"Actually, Mr. Fitzsimmons, I was thinking that m'lady has very fine taste in lace." Dante Leighton startled the Irishman with these softly spoken words, causing Seumus Fitzsimmons a moment's discomfort as he imagined the captain reading his mind.

"Aye, to be sure, she does, Cap'n," he replied with a wide grin as he handed Rhea her Madeira. He was pleased to find that the captain hadn't taken undue offense to his earlier indiscretion.

"I wish to thank you, Mr. Fitzsimmons, for the ribbons. Conny told me you had wanted me to have them. They're quite beautiful," Rhea told him, as sincere as if he'd given her a precious jewel. "I do not know quite what to say to you, and to the rest of the crew for these clothes. It was a great kindness by all of you, and from what I have learned from Conny, quite a sacrifice. I will not forget your generosity," she said as she ran her hand over the soft leather patches of her skirt, glancing between Seumus Fitzsimmons and Alastair Marlowe, both of whom wore very pleased expressions.

"Young Conny talks too much," Alastair said with an indulgent grin for the cabin boy's loquaciousness.

"I, on the other hand, would have said he had talked not enough," the captain murmured, his narrowed gaze missing nothing of Rhea's appearance, including a certain finely tanned cinnamon patch of leather curving around her slight hip, "for I seem to be the only person on board my ship who knew nothing of this enterprise, which is quite extraordinary, considering I seem to have contributed more than my fair share to m'lady's garments."

"Ah, now 'tis the cap'n's privilege, that, and we all be green with envy, sir." Seumus Fitzsimmons spoke with a twinkle in his black Irish eyes as he watched the captain reach out and touch the heavy lace on Rhea's bodice, his hand just grazing her breast.

"No doubt Houston Kirby played a major role in this affair?" Dante asked, although he needed no answer. He knew his steward too well to think anything could occur on board the *Sea Dragon* without the little man's personal knowledge.

And as if he had been standing just beyond the door, listening for his cue to enter, Houston Kirby suddenly came bustling in, a heavy tray balanced before him, while Conny Brady followed in his footsteps, his eyes glued to the lighter tray he was so carefully carrying. Thus, he didn't see the little steward come to an abrupt halt at the sight of Rhea, or the way in which his face split wide with a grin of satisfaction at his creation. Conny walked right smack into Houston Kirby's back, almost causing a tureen of soup to upend against the little steward. But Dante's hands grasped hold of the deep dish and steadied it before it could crash to the deck.

Houston Kirby was busy steadying his own tray of food as several boiled potatoes escaped from a dish and rolled onto the floor, but it didn't hinder his tongue as he glared over his shoulder at a scarlet-faced Conny Brady. "Master Brady! What the devil d'ye think ye be doin'? Haven't ye got eyes to be seein' where ye be walkin'?"

"I suspect, Kirby, that 'twas *your* eyes that went astray," Dante commented as he set the tureen in a safe spot on the table. "No harm done, Conny," Dante told him, for the little boy looked close to tears.

"Aye, s'pose ye be right about that, Cap'n," Kirby admitted with a sniff and a wink at Conny, for he wasn't one to blame a person unjustly. His eyes strayed once again to Rhea, his expression almost cherubic as he examined the stunning results of his efforts.

"You might as well look your fill," Dante told him, taking the shifting tray from the steward's hands, "since you seem to be responsible for our guest's transformation."

"Thank you, Kirby," Rhea said, the golden braids swinging around her shoulders as she gave the beaming little steward a hug that left him as scarlet as Conny. "You really shouldn't have gone to all of this trouble."

" 'Twasn't any trouble a'tall, m'lady," Houston Kirby said, forgetting the late nights spent sewing by a flickering light and the hours on deck at dawn working with needle and thread.

"It fits perfectly," Rhea was saying as she turned around for him, allowing him to fully admire his work. "But how on earth did you do it without proper measurements?" she demanded curiously.

"Yes, please do enlighten us, Kirby," Dante said, his eyes lingering on the soft curve of breast revealed by the décolletage.

"Nothin' to it, m'lord," Kirby replied, refusing to be baited by the captain, for he wasn't quite certain of his master's mood. "I just took me measurements when I was groomin' Lady Rhea's clothes. Simple as that, although I had to hurry a bit in order to finish them before we reached Antigua. Wanted to see ye in them before ye left the *Sea Dragon*," Houston Kirby said, his eyes meeting the captain's eyes meaningfully.

"Aye, 'twas worth the loss of a fine pair of breeches to have had the pleasure of servin' ye, m'lady," Seumus Fitzsimmons said, lifting his drink in toast to her. "To your safe return home to England, Lady Rhea Claire. Although," he added with a mournful look at her, "we shall miss your beauty on board the *Sea Dragon* when we depart Antigua."

Alastair Marlowe lifted his drink in agreement, although on his part it may well have been wishful thinking, for he thought he knew his captain's mind on that score. And indeed, the captain was slow to respond to the toast.

"To a safe journey home, Lady Rhea," Dante Leighton finally murmured before emptying his goblet of its contents.

As Rhea lifted her glass to her lips, her eyes met his over the rim, and she realized that she was the only one aware that he had not proposed a time for that safe journey home. Rhea sipped her Madeira, and although she did not care for the slightly burnt taste of it, it sent a fire through her blood that warmed her spirit and made her recklessly courageous as she met that pale-eyed stare of the captain of the *Sea Dragon*. Feeling full of unreasonable confidence in her ability to resist him, Rhea allowed a small, enticing smile to curve her lips as she continued to stare boldly across at him, her chin set in almost a challenging tilt. Meanwhile, the expression in her eyes was one he had not seen before, and it intrigued him.

Dante lifted his refilled goblet in a silent, private toast, as if in acceptance of her challenge. And whatever that challenge might be, he felt certain he would soon find out.

Kirby, noticing the locked glances, hurriedly sent a bemused Conny Brady—whose eyes had never left Rhea's figure—back to the galley for another course of the meal, thinking it far wiser to occupy Dante and Rhea with something else for the next few hours, and if there was anything that would serve for that, it was his cooking. Of course, he supposed he was worrying unnecessarily, for what could possibly happen over the dinner table, especially with Alastair Marlowe and Seumus Fitzsimmons present? Fortunately for the little steward's peace of mind he had little inkling of the dangerous mood that Rhea was in, and he would have been struck dumb had he had the least suspicion of what she was about. Even a person of only slight acquaintance with the captain would know better than to bait the man, or try to make him look the fool, for Dante Leighton was not a man to play games with.

As it was, Alastair Marlowe and Seumus Fitzsimmons soon realized that they were unwitting participants in a game in which they knew not the rules. In uneasy silence, Alastair watched Rhea flirt with Seumus, feeling like a helpless spectator to a blood sport, for he could feel the tension rising at the table like a tangible presence. Dante Leighton, however, seemed to know exactly what the rules of the game were, and was even creating a few new ones of his own. Alastair watched with growing alarm as the captain poured more wine into Lady Rhea's already brimming goblet, something he had taken care to do since they had sat down for their first course.

Alastair wasn't even certain that Lady Rhea was aware

of the captain's ploy, so interested did she seem in hearing out Seumus Fitzsimmons's story about the leprechaun he had once encountered. The Irishman's audience was not uninformed about legends, however, and Lady Rhea Claire demanded to know if the little old man had led Seumus to his cache of treasure.

"Ah, to be sure he has, *mo mhurnin*," Seumus declared grandly, the Gaelic endearment slipping out naturally as he gazed amorously into her violet eyes, "for here am I sittin' with the fairest treasure in all o' the land, includin' Erin itself, and them golden braids of yours couldn't be any less golden than a treasure chest full o' golden doubloons," he said softly. One of the beribboned braids touched his cheek as Rhea tipped her head sideways to catch his words, but her eyes were on Dante Leighton's gray-clad figure setting so quietly across the table.

Dante Leighton seemed unconcerned as he watched them. A slight smile curved his lips and his gray eyes seldom strayed from the golden-haired beauty sitting across from him, but Alastair was not surprised to see the tightening of the captain's knuckles around the fragile stem of his crystal goblet when those primrose ropes of hair swung teasingly against the Irishman's tanned cheek.

"Ummm, 'a treasure chest full o' golden doubloons,'" Rhea quoted Seumus as she propped her elbow on the table and rested her chin in her cupped hand. "Now that sounds exciting, don't you think so, Alastair?" Then she turned her wide violet eyes onto him, which was what he had been dreading, for the captain's jealous eye was sure to follow, and, as it was, his dinner was already sitting like a swivel block in his stomach.

"Well, yes, it certainly does, although one must find the treasure first," Alastair answered with irritating practicality. "And that would be a rare find indeed," he said, pleased with his easy reply to so touchy a subject, although he wondered what sort of sport this was that Lady Rhea was playing at.

"I beg to differ, Alastair," Rhea returned sweetly, her expression one of total innocence, "for I have an ancestor who captured a Spanish galleon and looted it of its stolen gold. And," she paused, drawing breath to continue, a sparkle in her eyes as she glanced around the table, "I have personal knowledge of another treasure map, and have even seen with my very own eyes the X marked in gold. The adventurous will be guided to a hidden treasure chest full of gold, jewels—"

"Good Lord!" Alastair exclaimed as his hand accidentally came in contact with his goblet of wine, sending the dark red liquid spreading across the tablecloth and sending everyone to their feet in a rush. "I am sorry, how clumsy of me," Alastair apologized nicely, his eyes briefly meeting the captain's as he dabbed ineffectually at the wine dripping over the edge of the table. "I trust I did not spill any on you, Lady Rhea?" he asked concernedly as he stepped aside for a muttering Houston Kirby, who had been standing in the opened doorway like a still life as he had listened to Lady Rhea's soft voice revealing secrets.

"No, none at all," Rhea replied with a smile, unaware of what really had happened.

"The crew would most likely have hung me from the yardarm if I'd stained your skirt before they'd even had the chance to admire it," Alastair said jokingly, feeling the danger past. Then, with a feeling of horror, he suddenly heard young Conny Brady's piping voice.

"We had a treasure map, Lady Rhea," he told her with pride. "The cap'n won it in a card game in St. Eustatius and we went lookin' fer the treasure, only 'twas a sunken Dutch merchantman we found instead."

"Aye, for a couple of Paddies, we came mighty close to makin' our fortunes, eh, young Conny?" Seumus said with a bitter smile, for he was still feeling deeply the disappointment of that voyage that had come to naught, along with all of his hopes of becoming master of a schooner of his own.

"Cap'n, sir, what happened to that map?" Conny now asked, turning his wide blue eyes on his captain. "I wish we could show Lady Rhea the treasure map. Aye, fair 'twas to look at, even if it wasn't worth nothin'. It had birds and sea shells and a ship with—"

—"with painted sails billowing eastward as it sailed in a sea full of dragons," Rhea finished for him, somewhat startled herself at how vivid her memory of the map was. She shook her head, feeling slightly hazy, for she seemed to be seeing two maps instead of one. But the one she had been remembering earlier was not this one Conny was describing. Her map had to do with her great-grandfather, Ruaiseart MacDanavel, and her mother and Uncle Richard, but that map hadn't been in a bottle like this one had, she thought in growing confusion. Then she drew in her breath sharply as she remembered she was not supposed to mention that other map. Rhea swallowed painfully as she met the captain's gray eyes, and she knew he must think she had been deliberately defying him. But that was not so, she thought in desperation, for it was the unaccustomed amount of wine she had consumed during dinner that was making rational thoughts very difficult, indeed, near impossible. And now, as she stared at Dante Leighton, all she could think about was the feel of his hard mouth against hers and the unrelenting strength of those bronzed arms around her waist. It was madness, Rhea thought in growing panic, as she stared around the captain's cabin at the rich mahogany paneling, the broad stern windows slanting into the blackness of sea and night, the big sea chest in the corner, the cabinet where the rolled-up charts were stacked so neatly, the other cabinet containing the bottles of wine, the desk where he penned his log, and, finally, the bunk, where she had lain with the captain of the *Sea Dragon*.

Ever since then, upon entering his cabin for her meals, she had studiously avoided looking at that corner of the cabin. She had known he was well aware of her reluctance to be reminded of that evening, and she also had known that the memory of that evening afforded him considerable amusement. Often, she had caught that strange smile on his lips as he'd purposely glanced at his bunk, as if he enjoyed certain memories that it held for him. But until this evening, when her defenses had been weakened by wine and by her own arrogance in dismissing her feelings for him, her disturbing memories of the cabin had been kept in abeyance. But now she found them rushing back on a rising tide of ungovernable emotions that left her trembling.

This was not the way she had planned the evening at all, Rhea thought in dismay. Now her cheeks were growing fiery with embarrassment as she remembered too vividly the feel of his hands touching her bare flesh and the heaviness of his head against her breast as his mouth had caressed her hot skin. She could recall the feeling of surprised pleasure when she had opened her eyes and stared into his pale gray eyes, and how her first thought, before remembering who he was and how cruel he'd been the night before, had been of what a beautiful man he was.

Tonight she had wanted to prove to him that he had no power over her, that she was not affected by his almost overwhelming virility, that she could find Alastair Marlowe and Seumus Fitzsimmons to be just as fascinating as he was. And so it had come as a shock to find him unresponsive to her wiles. Dante Leighton, despite her every effort to draw him into the conversation, had silently watched, listened, and waited, but for what she was not certain. Rhea knew she had acted the wanton tonight, but thinking herself safe from scorching, she had willfully played with fire, despite the deep instinct warning her against such a dangerous act. She had taunted Dante Leighton, baited him, teased him, ridiculed him, and even tried to seduce him with alluring glances from her heavy-lidded violet eyes. And Rhea would have been alarmed had she realized how successful she had been, for the sweet witchery of her eyes and lips had captivated him, strengthening his resolve to make her his own.

She had not fooled him, and it was just as well that Rhea Claire Dominick had no idea that there never had been any contest between them. She was no match for Dante Leighton, captain of the *Sea Dragon,* nor would she ever be, for despite her brief attempt at seduction, she was too gentle-blooded a creature to ever be other than herself. And despite all that she had been through since being kidnapped from Camareigh, she would continue to be the entrancingly lovely Rhea Claire who knew a generosity and kindness of heart and spirit. That was the essence of her being, and that innate gentleness would be the guiding force in her life. Rhea Claire was like the gold of her hair, malleable, but with an inner strength that would allow her to adapt or yield to a stronger force, yet remain faithful to what she believed in.

And perhaps that quality was what would save Rhea's life, for Dante Leighton had lived too long giving no quarter. He had relied too often upon a measuring of swords to settle differences, and it was too late for him to change now, even had he so wished.

But as Rhea Claire Dominick, still secure in her belief that she could ultimately control her destiny, drowsily met the gaze of Dante Leighton, captain of the *Sea Dragon* and believer in fate, she was blessedly unaware that her future was already being decided by the circumstances of chance.

"Coooee! How the devil did ye know what the treasure map looked like, Lady Rhea?" Conny's incredulous voice was demanding to know.

"Because that is the way all treasure maps are supposed to look," Alastair explained smoothly, his lopsided grin twitching nervously as he noted the bemused expression on Lady Rhea's flushed face.

"Actually," Dante remarked, helping him out, "I think I still have that map around here somewhere, and I may have shown it to Lady Rhea, but," he paused, noticing her drooping lids as she tried to hide a wide yawn behind a casually raised hand, "as Lady Rhea seems to have grown fatigued, I suggest we postpone this conversation till the morrow. Lady Rhea?" Dante questioned softly, then was suddenly by her side and holding out his arm, leaving her little choice but to accept his assistance. "I shall escort you to your cabin, for the hour grows late, m'lady," he added in an undertone filled with a menace of which only she was aware.

"My apologies, gentleman, but I truly cannot seem to keep my eyes open. The evening has been a pleasure and the dinner was superbly prepared, Mr. Kirby," Rhea complimented the little steward. "Mrs. Peacham could not have done better. Gentleman, I shall bid you a good night then," Rhea said, hesitantly placing her hand in the crook of Dante Leighton's arm. But even so lightly touching him, she could still feel the hard muscles beneath her fingertips, especially when he placed his hand over hers, holding it trapped against him.

The door of the captain's cabin closed with a note of finality on the friendly replies from Alastair Marlowe and Seumus Fitzsimmons, who were pouring themselves brandies as they settled down to await their captain's return. Conny and Houston Kirby had already disappeared toward the galley with the last of the dinner dishes, and so the short corridor to Rhea's cabin suddenly seemed endless to her, and too quiet. The pressure against her hand became harder as they neared the door.

"Good night, Captain Leighton," Rhea murmured softly as she risked a glance into those pale gray eyes. But she was not prepared for the glint in them as they caught hold of hers.

"Good night?" he questioned. "The night could just be beginning for you and me, my dear," he said as he leaned past her shoulder and opened the narrow door, his movement forcing Rhea to step inside or be crushed against his broad chest.

She paused just inside, thinking to halt his progress, but he merely lifted her aside as he stepped in and closed the door; then he leaned his wide shoulders against it, his arms folded casually across his chest while he stared down at her with amusement.

"The game has not yet been won, Rhea Claire," Dante said, his tongue seeming to caress her name.

"What game?" Rhea asked, feigning bewilderment, reluctant to admit her complicity in such a venture, especially when her wits had been dulled too much by wine for her to be engaging in clever talk with him. "I have not the slightest idea of what you are speaking about," she told him with an attempt at haughtiness that ended up sounding defensive.

"I am speaking about the game you have been playing all evening long, my dear little liar. Seumus Fitzsimmons enjoyed it, unsure though he was to its purpose, but I am afraid you had poor Alastair a nervous wreck wondering what you were going to do next. He is far too honest a fellow for this sort of trick, my dear, but I don't suppose you gave him much thought, did you, so intent were you on inveigling me with your charms," Dante said, his gray-eyed stare encompassing her from the top of her head, with its coronet of golden braids, to her small feet encased in leather sandals. He noticed how the silk of her stockings contrasted oddly with the rawhide straps crossing over her instep and around her ankles.

His eyes lingered on her trembling lips, remembering the taste of them. Then he was looking deeply into her violet eyes, seeing the hidden depths of passion as yet unexplored by any man. On this he would have sworn. She was half woman, half child, half tamed and half wild, for the mystery of a man's body made her suspicious and wary of his touch, and he knew that he would have to curb his own impatient desire if he were to lure the passionate response from her that he wanted and that he knew she was capable of giving.

"I fear you are deluding yourself, Captain," Rhea said, her voice shaking slightly with the onrush of confusing emotions she was experiencing, for he was standing so close that she could feel the rising heat of his body and see the pulse beating so strongly in his throat.

"No, my dear, you are deluding yourself if you think that you have won this game, which you so foolishly started. You issued me a challenge, and now I am here to collect my winnings," he murmured as he slid his arms around her small waist.

"Let me go, Captain!" Rhea warned, but her words came breathlessly.

"Oh, no, my sweet Rhea," Dante told her as he pressed her shaking body against his, molding her pliant flesh to his muscular hardness. "You said earlier today that you would give anything to buy your freedom. Well, now is the chance to prove that your word, the word of a Dominick, is good. Is it?" he demanded, grasping her chin and raising her head so he could stare into her face.

Dante felt a tightening in his loins as he stared down at her exquisite face. She reminded him of an English garden, something he had missed during his travels, for she had the color of the damask rose in her cheeks and the deep purple of sweet violets in her eyes. Unconsciously, Dante raised his hand and lightly touched one of the golden braids that had an emerald ribbon entwined through its length. "Little daffadilly," he murmured, the expression in his eyes suddenly gentle with remembrance.

Rhea noticed the softening in his hard face and seized her chance. "Let me go, Captain, please," she pleaded. She thought she'd won a reprieve when his hand released her braid, but was startled from that thought as his arms pulled her roughly to him, curving her body even closer to his, as if he hungered for the constant contact of their flesh.

"No," he said simply, a brooding look on his face. "You played the game well tonight, for I want you, and I intend to have you," he told her, his softly spoken words promising her that he would have what he wanted. And although her eyes were filled with fear, he only smiled cruelly. "Ah, my sweet Rhea, I believe those violet eyes of yours could tear a man's heart from his body, but I am blind to their enticement," he told her, refusing to be moved by the soft pleading in their darkening depths.

"Do you know how you have tormented me this evening?" he demanded, and there was still a thread of anger vibrating in his deep voice, turning it harsh. "You played the harlot for Seumus Fitzsimmons while treating me like some fat eunuch, harmless in his emasculation as he sat nearby, watching. It was cruel how you leaned toward the Irishman with your gaping bodice revealing the ivory softness of your breasts, your golden braids teasing his cheek while you smiled so enticingly, for you both knew that it would come to naught, that he was not the man to awaken your desires. He gazed into your eyes and wanted you for himself. He looked at your soft lips and ached to claim them as his own, but you are mine, Rhea, and I shall be the one to take what you have so enchantingly offered. And you have offered it to me, my sweet Rhea," Dante reminded her, his breath warm against the top of her head as his lips traced a wandering path through her braids.

Dante felt her shiver in his arms and try to arch away from the branding contact of their bodies. "No!" she cried softly, straining away from his seeking lips.

"It does no good to fight it, Rhea. Sweet, sweet Rhea,

Laurie McBain

you want me to kiss your lips, part them and taste them.
You want me to caress your silken body. Your hungry
eyes have been telling me that all night long. You want
me to make love to you, Rhea. Perhaps not as much as I
want you, but that is only because you do not know of
the pleasures awaiting you. But when you do, you will
seek out the touch of my hands, the feel of my lips, for
only I will be able to satisfy the fire that will be burning
so deep inside of you," he promised, but somehow his
words sounded more like a curse upon her head than any
gift of love's pleasures.

"No," Rhea said, but even as her lips formed the word,
she knew it was a lie, and so did he, for his next words
were roughly spoken against her fiery cheek.

"Do not lie to me," Dante told her before his mouth
closed over hers, parting her lips as he had promised,
making her want to taste him as his tongue searched for
hers, not allowing her to avoid intimate contact. But nor
did she want to as she felt an almost suffocating feeling of
languor spreading through her, leaving her limbs weak
and trembling.

His lips lifted slowly, reluctantly, from her mouth and
Rhea drew a ragged breath, the cabin spinning around
her, but before she could seem to breathe again, she found
her throbbing lips covered by his once more. His kisses
were growing deeper, more demanding of a response from
her, and one of his hands slid down over her hips, holding
her to him, while his other hand cupped the nape of
her head immobile while his mouth plundered her soft
lips. Rhea was desperate to escape that smoldering contact, but he was too insistent, refusing to allow her to
break free and quench the consuming fire growing between them.

Dante's breath was coming raggedly as he kissed her
lips, unable to slake the thirst he felt for their sweet taste.
He liked the feel of the soft leather she wore, for without
the multitude of petticoats and a silk or satin overskirt,
he could feel the natural curving of her small buttocks
and slender thighs. She was so slight, yet so womanly to
the touch, and Dante's heightened senses filled with the
scent of her, his desires kindling anew as he remembered

another time when he had lain with her and breathed the heady blend of the sea and sandalwood.

Rhea felt his hands on her body, leaving no part of her untouched as he fondled her, learned the feel of her. His hands seemed to be everywhere, and then Rhea gasped in surprise as her skirt fell to the decking between them and she felt the coolness of the cabin caressing her bare thighs. His hands lowered the décolletage of her bodice, pushing it from her shoulders and down around her waist. Then it fell past her hips to the floor, following the plaited belt that he had freed easily from her waist.

Dante stood back and stared down at her standing before him in her corset and chemise, her breasts temptingly revealed by the thin linen with its slight edging of delicate lace. And it barely reached to the top of her pale thighs, teasing him with what lay above.

Rhea heard his low groan as he lifted her into his arms, his bronzed face looking like a stranger's as he carried her to the bunk and laid her down gently, his hand straying to her bare thigh as if he needed to feel her warmth even as he stood beside the bunk gazing down at her.

Rhea's eyes were closed as she lay there, knowing he stared at her. Her breath was coming jerkily from her trembling lips and all she could seem to hear was the roaring in her ears.

"Look at me, Rhea," Dante said softly. "Rhea," he said again, more urgently this time when she refused to look at him or answer him. It seemed to Dante then that she was trying to escape his presence by retreating into her thoughts.

"Damn you, Rhea, look at me," he demanded as he sat down beside her, his hands hard and hurting on her frail shoulders.

Rhea opened her eyes to see him bending over her. He had removed his coat and vest, and his stock had been loosened around his broad neck.

"Rhea, let me love you," he said huskily as he buried his face in the warmth of her breasts, his mouth searching until he found the soft pink nipples. Then his tongue was licking at them, suckling, until with a start of surprise, Rhea felt them hardening against his lips.

"No," Rhea whispered tearfully, ineffectually, as she felt his hard hands on her bare buttocks, guiding her closer to him. Then, through the material of his breeches, she could feel his hardening manhood pressing against her.

"Sweet Rhea, kiss me. Kiss me like this," he murmured as his mouth opened against hers and began to steal the breath from her body. Meanwhile, his hands were drifting ever lower, moving slowly and sensuously in an ever-widening circle across her hips, until lingering against the softest and most sensitive place in her now quivering flesh. He knew he was introducing her to an eroticism that she never had known before, but her body was responding whether she wished it to or not; she would never be able to forget the sensual pleasure he was arousing within her, as indeed he had promised her he could. He knew he was taking unfair advantage of her innocence, that his expertise made it easy for him to give her that all-consuming pleasure and ultimate satisfaction that would change forever her perception of herself. It would also alter how she perceived him, for he would be her first lover, which would make him special in her eyes and give him a power and influence over her that no other man ever would have. Dante pushed these conscience-ridden thoughts to the back of his mind when he suddenly thrilled to the feel of her lips seeking his, of her tongue sliding inside his mouth. He knew then that he had succeeded in awakening her desires.

Rhea felt him shivering in response as she shyly moved her hands over his back, then curved them around his chest as she rubbed the thick mat of curling hair. Rhea, too, was experiencing, though for the first time, that knowledge of the power that a woman could exert over a man. That she could by the mere touch of her lips against his cause him to react so violently, gave her the strange feeling of being able to control him. And never before had she felt that sensation where Dante Leighton was concerned.

But Rhea had only a moment's enjoyment of this newly discovered power, for Dante's mouth once again was demanding of hers, as his hands caressed her body in arrogant assurance of their invitation to explore her.

Suddenly the hard pressure of his body jerked away from hers, and Rhea heard a muffled imprecation. She opened her eyes, and in the yellow gloom of the flickering light from the lantern swinging from the overhead beam, she saw Dante standing beside the bunk, his shirt parted halfway down the front and hanging free outside his breeches. She could see the moist film of sweat gleaming across his muscular chest as he stared around him, searching the empty room.

Rhea cried out in fright as something landed beside her in the bunk; then she found herself staring into two shiny emerald orbs.

"Jamaica," Dante muttered harshly beneath his breath as he glared down at the big tomcat who was now curling up next to Rhea's shoulder. The cat's purring grew louder as he sensed the attention he was receiving from his master and the soft-voiced one.

"Damn," Dante murmured, touching his shoulder where the cat's claws had caught him. When he held out his hand, there was blood staining his fingertips. "How the devil did he get in here?" he demanded angrily.

"I think he has been in here all the time," Rhea said huskily, her voice sounding strange to her own ears. "He was in here when I was dressing for dinner. I suppose I forgot about him." Her voice had begun to shake when she realized how timely Jamaica's interruption had been, for now, as she stared up at the tall man standing beside her, whose beautifully chiseled face was shadowed by the sallowness of the lantern's light, he looked a stranger to her—and one that frightened her. A small muffled cry escaped her lips as she remembered their lovemaking of only moments before. She nearly had given herself to the captain of the *Sea Dragon*, a cold-blooded adventurer who cared for no one and was only interested in satisfying his own lusts.

"Damn. You forgot about him?" Dante repeated, feeling an unbelievable frustration as he stared down at her half-naked form huddled in the bunk. She had curled up, almost protectively, around Jamaica; her slender thighs were closed tight, but her position afforded him a tantalizing view of the pale curve of her bare buttocks, which taunted him with their smooth expanse of soft virgin skin.

Dante started to reach out a hand, thinking to unseat his cat from his place of honor on the bunk beside the girl, but as his hand came close, Rhea drew back in fear, a look of sudden loathing in her eyes when she met his glance in the hazy light.

"Don't touch me!" she spat with such venom that Dante fully expected to feel the pain of her claws.

"Your passion is certainly fleeting," he remarked softly. But there was savagery in his pale eyes as they roamed freely over her slightly clad body. "Perhaps you are right, my sweet, and the time is past—at least for now," he added, a warning glint in his eyes as he picked up his coat and vest from the table. He flinched slightly as the drying blood on his shoulder stuck to his shirt.

At the door he turned and glanced back, a bitter smile lingering on his lips. "Good night, little daffadilly," he said, and then he was gone.

Alastair Marlowe finally gave up waiting for the captain to return to his cabin and decided to call it an evening. He had been sitting in silence for close to half an hour now, for Seumus Fitzsimmons had left almost an hour ago to join a card game he knew was in progress in the crew's quarters. He'd had an anticipatory gleam in his eye at the thought of coming away with quite a pile of winnings.

Alastair glanced around the captain's cabin, making certain nothing was amiss, then quietly opened the door and let himself out. He was making his way along the short corridor when he heard quiet crying coming from his old cabin, now Lady Rhea's. He paused in surprised concern, listening for a moment longer to the muffled weeping. He was about to knock when the crying stopped; then all was silent beyond the closed door. Alastair stood a moment longer, undecided about whether he should intrude. No, it might be wiser not to, especially if the captain were on the other side of that closed door. That type of interruption might prove highly embarrassing for all parties concerned, thought Alastair, for after tonight's disturbing undercurrents he was not at all certain that the captain might not have received an invitation to enter the privacy of Lady Rhea Claire's cabin. It was becoming more obvious to him with each day's passing, that if her ladyship remained on board the *Sea Dragon* much longer, the captain would sooner or later end up in that cabin—invited or not.

But as Alastair Marlowe walked across the quarterdeck, breathing deeply of the balmy West Indian air, he saw the captain's solitary figure standing near the taffrail, his coat thrown casually over his shoulders. With a sigh of relief, Alastair settled against the bulwark, allowing himself the pleasure of enjoying the star-filled black skies far above the raking masts and singing sails of the *Sea Dragon.* Little did he realize that he had been staring at a desperate man.

In the glimmering light of her cabin, Rhea buried her tear-streaked face in the coolness of her pillow, muffling her deep sobs as she tried to banish from her mind the memory of Dante Leighton's searching hands on her body. But it was hopeless. She could still feel how possessive they'd been against her burning flesh when he had touched her intimately, discovering the secrets of her body, of which she'd had so little knowledge until he had revealed them to her.

Rhea touched her swollen lips, moaning softly, for they were tender from the unrelenting pressure of his mouth on hers. She felt groggy, as if his kisses had drugged her, leaving the taste of him in her mouth. She raised her head, placing her flushed cheek against her folded arm, only to find her senses filled with the scent of Dante Leighton on her hot skin.

Rhea glared up at the low beamed ceiling, her lips trembling as she realized that she no longer felt as if she belonged to herself. The captain of the *Sea Dragon* had become a part of her in some strange, almost mystical way.

She struggled to her feet, unseating Jamaica, who gave a plaintive meow as he jumped onto the table. He sniffed at the dried-up piece of gingerbread, then turned an indifferent back to it as he began to clean his whiskers with self-absorbed intentness. Standing on unsteady legs, Rhea fought the laces of her corset; when she finally freed herself from it, she dropped it to the deck, where it lay in an untidy pile with her chemise. With stiff, unresponsive fingers, she unwound the rawhide straps wrapped around her calves, then rolled off her stockings.

She stood for a long moment in silence, then hesitantly felt her small, delicately rounded breasts; next, her hands strayed down the curved line to her waist, then spread across her hips as if feeling her body for the first time. She continued to stand there, benumbed by this awakening of her senses; then, with a tired sigh, she began to unplait her braids, mechanically freeing the long strands one at a time, until her hair flowed loosely down her back.

She pulled a blanket from the bunk and wrapped it around her shivering body; then she crawled back into bed, huddling against herself, overwhelmed by disturbing emotions that refused to subside.

Dante Leighton, demon captain of the *Sea Dragon*, had kindled a spark deep inside of her, just as he had so confidently promised he would. And he was indeed a devil, for he had teased her and taunted her, lighting a fire in her blood. But he had not ignited it into that all-consuming blaze, which she knew instictively would come only when that ultimate fulfillment was reached. And now, as she found herself aching for the touch of his lips and hands on her body, she knew only Dante Leighton could satisfy this fever burning through her.

Rhea gave a slight start of surprise as she felt something climbing over her shoulder; then she relaxed as Jamaica curled up beside her, his rumbling purrs comforting her as she rubbed her cheek against his soft fur.

"Oh, Jamaica. What has your master done to me? Why has he tried to destroy me? What have I ever done to hurt him?" she asked helplessly, not fully understanding this woman's body that had been aroused by a man's lust.

"I have got to escape him, Jamaica," Rhea cried despairingly as she hugged the cat to her. "There will be no hope for me unless I can free myself from him. If he touches me again, if he kisses me, then I will be lost, Jamaica. Lost to all that I have ever known. I will be his slave forever," Rhea whispered, terrified of losing herself to him, of needing his touch to survive.

Rhea Claire Dominick's hot tears ran unchecked down her cheeks as her heavy-lidded eyes closed. Then she allowed the gentle rolling motion of the *Sea Dragon* to rock her into a sleep, which was no more than a temporary release from self-torment and revelation.

> *Fortune, good night, smile once more;*
> *turn thy wheel!*
>
> Shakespeare

Chapter 8

THE hills of Antigua, covered with sugar cane, loomed to starboard, rising out of the dawn sea in verdant waves as the *Sea Dragon* made landfall for the first time since leaving Charles Town. She closed the land and glided under a gleaming spread of canvas into St. John's Harbour, her leadsman taking a sounding as the *Sea Dragon* entered shallower waters. Her salute to Fort James, standing sentinel on the tip of a finger of cattle-grazed pastureland stretching into the bay, had been duly acknowledged and now she was brought to, her anchor biting the bottom. The local pilot, who had guided the *Sea Dragon* through the rocks to her safe anchorage, had already returned to shore, and now other island boats were making their way toward the new arrival.

The rolling hillsides enclosing the harbor were dotted with palmetto-trimmed fields that tumbled into the lush darkness of tamarind and cedar-shaded valleys, and there on the gentle pastoral slopes were the stone manor houses of the great plantations. The hot West Indian sun shone down brightly on a wealth envied even by the affluent English landowners in the mother country. Cylindrical stone sugar mills nestled amongst the cane bore stark testimony to this Caribbean prosperity.

A restless bank of fluffy white clouds was gathering over the emerald hills of Antigua, while a stirring breeze whispered through the waving fronds of the palm trees on the beaches of fine white sand, which from the *Sea Dragon*'s quarterdeck looked like silken crescents of moon that had fallen from the sky.

To Rhea Claire Dominick, who had just come up on deck, having been confined to her quarters by the captain's order until the pilot had left the ship, the tropical splendor of St. John's Harbour with its azure skies above aquamarine hills and its turquoise bay seemed a vision of unreality. Never before had she gazed upon such a brightness and variety of color.

"Aye, 'tis quite a sight, that," Seumus Fitzsimmons commented. "Even puts to shame the green hills of me own homeland, though I'll not be repeatin' that within hearin' distance of another Irishman," he said with a broad smile, his black eyes twinkling at Rhea. But her usually warm smile seemed forced, and there were pale mauve shadows around her beautiful eyes, as if she'd had a restless night.

"Ah, lassie, 'tis a fine sight ye are," MacDonald commented as he climbed the ladder to the poop deck, his eyes resting with a paternal glint on her leather skirt, then as he noticed the bareness of her arms and shoulders, not to mention the view of slender ankles and calves, his heavy, sandy brows lowered ominously. "Reckon I'll be havin' a word with Mister Kirby before the day's finished," he grumbled, not missing the light in the Irishman's eye as he continued to glance at Rhea's flawless profile and a bit lower, too, which gentlemanly discretion should not allow.

" 'Twill be a fine sight for the men, eh, Alec?" Seumus Fitzsimmons remarked.

"Aye, Seumus, and that is what has me worried a wee bit," he responded laconically, his bushy brows lifting as he heard the pounding of feet on the companion ladder and glanced afore to see Longacres's toothless grin as he neared the top. Following close behind Longacres was Conny Brady. "Aye, 'tis as I feared 'twould be," he said, blowing a billowing cloud of smoke aloft.

"Told ye, didn't I, Mr. Longacres!" Conny's young voice was carried to them on the breeze.

"Aye, that ye did, lad, that ye did," he chuckled, his squinting gaze enveloping Rhea's figure. "Aye, reckon 'tis as fine a sight as is a sail on the horizon to a marooned sailor," he growled, rubbing his stubbly chin and almost dancing a jig as he came toward her.

Rhea forced herself to smile at the old pirate, trying for the moment to put aside her own troubled thoughts. "I hope Conny repeated my appreciation for these kind gifts from you and the crew, Mr. Longacres," Rhea said as she looked him unflinchingly in the eye.

"Oh, aye, that he did, m'lady," Longacres said, pleased even at his age to have the young lady's attention centered on him.

"I am indeed very grateful," she told him, warming slightly toward the man when she felt the genuine pleasure in his smile.

" 'Twas me own great pleasure, as well as the rest o' the crew's," he said. Then he added with a devilish grin, "O' course I would've buried them alive if they hadn't!" He laughed, and Rhea wondered if he ever had done such a thing.

"Did ye happen to be seein' who was anchored not far away, lads?" Seumus Fitzsimmons asked with a meaningful glance aport at a ship flying a tartan flag.

"Aye, that I did," MacDonald said noncommittally, but Longacres wasn't quite as close-lipped about it.

"Seems we been seein' too much o' that buzzard of late," he said, sending a stream of brown tobacco juice over the railing.

"Reckon he's got business hereabouts," MacDonald said, not overly concerned by the sight of that tartan flag.

"Aye, Bertie Mackay's always up to something," Seumus Fitzsimmons said sourly, remembering the sight of those very same sails off Cape San Antonio.

"Bertie Mackay?" As Rhea spoke the name, she felt there was something familiar about it. "I seem to have heard that name before."

"Aye, ye might be sayin' he's in the same business we are," Seumus said with a grin and a wink at Longacres, who was glaring across the bay at the ship lying aloof of them.

"Then he is an acquaintance of Captain Leighton's?" Rhea asked, thinking the captain might lower a boat and pay a visit to his friend. Then, with him away from the ship . . .

"Coooee! That'd be the day! Reckon they've crossed each other's bows too often to be takin' tea with each other, m'lady!" Longacres guffawed, nearly doubling up in laughter at the idea of the captain sitting down to tea with Bertie Mackay.

"Shall I be puttin' it another way, then?" Seumus Fitz-simmons suggested, a slight smirk on his lips. "With a friend like Bertie Mackay, a man's havin' no need of enemies."

As Rhea listened to their less than complimentary comments about the other captain, she gradually remembered where she had heard the name of Bertie Mackay before. With a feeling of dread, she realized that the captain would most likely, being the unreasonable man he was, eye her more suspiciously than ever, thinking her in cahoots with the rival smuggler.

"Aye, and there ain't many still *alive* who can claim to be Bertie Mackay's enemy," Longacres said, spitting another stream of tobacco juice over the railing, despite Seumus Fitzsimmons's look of disgust.

"Reckon the cap'n's been his enemy fer a fair piece of time," Conny said proudly. "Got the best of him in the straits, we did."

"Aye, did I ever tell ye about that time, m'lady?" Longacres asked, clearing his throat to better tell his tale. "Ol' Bertie Mackay thought to do us in, the good lads o' the *Sea Dragon*, but I reckon he sailed too close to the wind that time, the cur. Planted a spy on board, he did. Thought to find all o' our secret coves, then turn traitor on us with the King's man," Longacres said with a scowl, obviously still feeling wrathful indignation at such a trick. "But we showed him, and his man, eh, young Conny?"

"Aye, the cap'n made quick work o' that scoundrel," Conny recalled with satisfaction.

"What happened?" Rhea asked hesitantly, for the look

in Longacres's eye must surely be reminiscent of his pirate days.

"Caught the spy who was on board, we did, then set him adrift in the straits. Put a signal light on board too, just so Bertie Mackay wouldn't get lost," the coxswain wheezed, choking on his quid of tobacco and turning a purplish color until MacDonald whacked him hard on the back.

"What happened to the man?" Rhea asked faintly. She was finally beginning to see the wisdom of the captain's advice about not mentioning the incidents of that evening when she had come on board the *Sea Dragon,* for if he had believed she was associated with Bertie Mackay, what then might these men believe?

"Could still be out there in the straits, I reckon," Longacres said huskily—and a trifle hopefully.

"Well, if he is, then 'twas a ghost I was seein' in St. Eustatius the last time we was there," Seumus Fitzsimmons recalled, causing a look of almost comical disappointment to appear on Longacres's face.

"Bet he wished he were still adrift in that gig when Bertie Mackay overtook him and brought him aboard," Conny said, wondering what that confrontation had been like.

Rhea glanced across the shimmering stretch of water that was crowded with shipping, first spying a Union Jack fluttering at the jackstaff of one ship, then the red, blue, and white of the Union Flag in the canton of several flags flying at the main of ships anchored nearby. English ships, Rhea thought on a rising tide of hope, as well as a king's ship. And Antigua was a British colony; surely she would be able to find someone to assist her—if only she could get ashore.

"Reckon the lads will be lookin' forward to gettin' ashore," Longacres commented, leering at the crew members who were hanging over the bulwarks, looking toward the town of St. John's sitting snugly in the curving of the bay. The town's narrow lanes and rows of shops and taverns opened onto an expansive view of the harbor, and were positioned to take full advantage of the cooling trades. Part of the town, however, had recently suffered a fire, for there were still several blackened buildings standing in proof of the conflagration.

"Reckon ye be just as anxious yeself," Seumus remarked.

"Aye, s'pose so, but don't be knockin' me down this time, mate, as ye hurry there yeself," Longacres retorted, not a man to be bested, and especially not by this smooth-tongued Paddy.

"Soon enough fer that, mates," MacDonald commented. "Reckon the cap'n'll be goin' ashore soon to enter the ship at the customhouse. Figure ye got time to spruce yeself up a bit, Mr. Fitzsimmons," he added offhandedly, his lips twitching beneath his thick moustache.

For what must surely have been the first time in his life, Seumus Fitzsimmons felt uncomfortable. Rhea's violet eyes had turned on him in curiosity, and he knew she was thinking of those ribbons he had given to her, and that he now would be empty-handed when he visited his paramour.

Rhea sighed, wondering what her next move should be. Since the captain had not told his crew of his suspicions of her, and since they were obviously in sympathy with her predicament, perhaps she could convince one of them to take her ashore after the captain had left.

As Rhea stood there in thought, a sudden cheer went up from the sea-men grouped together in the waist of the ship. Their waving arms and whistles signaled the small boats that had gradually approached from the lee side and finally closed the distance from shore.

Feeling familiar soft fur against her legs, Rhea reached down, without even bothering to look, and picked up Jamaica. She held him cradled in her arms as she leaned closer to the taffrail to see what the commotion below was about.

She glanced curiously into the small boats floating close to the *Sea Dragon*'s hull. They were loaded down with fruits and vegetables, fish, shells, and even colorful bouquets of flowers. Several of the black boatmen kept their oars propped against the *Sea Dragon*'s planking in order to keep at a safe distance.

"Lady! Lady! You want some pritty flowers, yes! Pritty

447

flowers for pritty lady!" called out a woman who was sitting in the bow of one of the boats, after she'd caught sight of Rhea's golden head peering over the taffrail.

Surrounded by an incredible display of exotic blooms, clusters of lavender bougainvillea, dusty pink frangipani, and scarlet hibiscus, she held up an armful of yet more beautiful and fragrant blossoms. Rhea could breathe heavy perfume in the balmy air drifting around her.

"Jessamine," Rhea murmured sadly as she caught sight of the delicate, cream-colored flowers of her favorite scent. She had a crystal bottle of it on her dressing table at Camareigh.

Seumus Fitzsimmons saw the sadness in her eyes as she stared down at the flowers, and tossing a coin down to the woman in the boat, he caught the bouquet of jessamine that she sent floating to them through the air.

"M'lady," Seumus said, presenting it with a flourish to a pale Rhea. "Beautiful they are, but not half as lovely as ye be, m'lady," he said softly, and for once his black eyes were not full of malicious amusement.

Rhea buried her face in the mass of fragrant blooms, breathing so deeply of the perfumed petals that she felt almost faint. "Thank you, Seumus," she said, her violet eyes warm with friendship.

And Seumus Fitzsimmons knew that was all that would ever be in her eyes for him. It was, however, better than nothing, he thought with an almost casual acceptance of what fate had meted out for him, which was not to be a life with the fine Lady Rhea Claire Dominick by his side.

Jamaica, however, did not care overly much for the sweet scent of jessamine, preferring that tantalizing odor of freshly caught fish that was drifting his way, not to mention the pails of milk being offered for consumption.

Feeling his hind legs stiffening, Rhea released the orange tom, who knew exactly where to go to attract the attention of a soft-hearted, generous islander who might enjoy seeing a cat catching a piece of fish on a port sill.

With a shrug, Seumus nodded below at the group of seamen laughing and calling out friendly, though suggestive remarks at several young women in the boats.

"Reckon I oughta see what they be up to and keep an eye on them," he told her with a wicked grin. Then he handed her the flowers and hurried after Longacres down the companion ladder.

MacDonald was contentedly smoking his pipe and staring at the island, his thoughts elsewhere, which left Conny and Rhea standing together near the taffrail.

"How come those flowers Mr. Fitzsimmons bought fer ye are makin' ye sad, Lady Rhea?" Conny wanted to know, his wide blue eyes full of confusion, for either a person was happy or they weren't, but Lady Rhea seemed to be both—and at the strangest times. "You seemed so happy a minute ago when ye was smellin' them."

"I suppose they brought back memories to me of another time," Rhea whispered, walking to the starboard rail and staring out at the water that held her prisoner on board the *Sea Dragon*.

"At Camareigh?" Conny questioned, sensing his lady was lonely for her family. He didn't like to see her unhappy.

"Yes, I miss them so much, Conny. I want to go home. I have to go home!" she cried shakily. Her tears were not far off, for the memory of what nearly had happened last night made her feel more of a stranger to herself than ever before. She needed to return home, to become the Rhea Claire that she had once been.

"Hey! Lady! Want some more pritty flowers for your hair? Have many to choose from. Pritty colors, for pritty lady! How 'bout some sweet oranges? Got banana, real good too!" a voice called to her from below from a single boat floating close to the *Sea Dragon*.

Rhea stared down into the boat, wishing she were in it and being rowed to shore. Suddenly a thought struck her. It was so simple that she shook her head in disbelief. Turning away from the taffrail, she glanced over at MacDonald, who was still lost in his thoughts, oblivious to what was going on around him. And the rest of the crew, well, Rhea thought with growing confidence, they were fully occupied flirting and bartering with the boats on the larboard side of the ship. They had their backs to the starboard side, as well as to the ladder leading down to whatever might be alongside.

Rhea waved to the black man in the boat below, signaling him toward the entry port and side steps of the ship. Then she turned to a puzzled Conny Brady, her expression sad as she gazed into his wide, innocent eyes, feeling almost as if she were bidding farewell to Robin.

"Conny, I am going to get in that boat, and go ashore. I cannot wait any longer, Conny. You must try and understand what this chance means to me. If you care at all for me, then you'll not tell anyone. Please, Conny, can I trust you?" Rhea pleaded.

"But the cap'n, he would've taken ye ashore, m'lady," Conny protested.

"No, Conny. This is a far better way, believe me, it is. This will save the captain having to bother about me. Will you say good-by to everyone for me? Oh, and Conny," Rhea added, hesitating in embarrassment for what she was about to ask, "I haven't any money. Do you have anything you can spare? Just so I can pay the boatman for taking him away from his profit on board."

Conny nodded, reached down into his pocket, and withdrew a couple of coins. "Here."

"Thank you, Conny. I will never forget you. You will come and visit me at Camareigh, won't you, Conny?" she asked as she gave him a hard hug and pressed a soft kiss against his flushed cheek.

Conny Brady's eyes became blurred with tears, and when he cleared them, she was gone. She had disappeared, just as he'd always feared she would. Conny stood frozen to the spot. What was he to do? It didn't seem right not to tell anyone, especially the captain. He glanced over at Mr. MacDonald, but he was gazing far off to port. She should not have just gone off like that, without saying good-by to anyone. Nor did it seem right her going into St. John's unaccompanied. Where would she go? he wondered worriedly, having been in enough port towns to know they were no place for a proper lady by herself.

Conny bit his trembling lip and glanced below at the boatman, who was pulling away from the *Sea Dragon,* a wide grin on his face as he pocketed the money given to him by the lady sitting in the prow.

"Well, Captain? What are you planning on doing about Lady Rhea Claire?" Alastair Marlowe was facing Dante Leighton in the captain's quarters, a determined glint in his usually mild hazel eyes, since he'd decided to march up to the cannon's mouth.

The captain in question took his time slipping into his bluish gray frock coat, straightening the lace around his sleeves with irritating slowness. "What am I going to do about Lady Rhea Claire, Mr. Marlow?" Dante repeated. "I should think you'd be so occupied with seeing to the cargo that you'd not have much time to worry about matters which do not concern you," Dante told him silkily as he turned away from the desk, closing the log book he had been checking.

"I would not ordinarily question you, sir," Alastair began, swallowing nervously as those pale gray eyes turned on him curiously. He was beginning to feel some of the strain Rhea must have experienced when subjected to that steely stare. "But I feel it my duty to bring this subject up, not only because I am concerned on your behalf, Captain, but because I feel it is the only decent and gentlemanly thing to do where Lady Rhea Claire is concerned. I cannot believe that you still suspect her of working for Bertie Mackay, nor that you think her some strumpet off the docks in Charles Town. I think you believe she is exactly what she says she is," Alastair concluded, breathless after his brave effort on behalf of Rhea.

"My, my," Dante said with a smile that was not at all pleasant, "it seems Lady Rhea Claire has quite a champion in you, Alastair. I have always suspected that you had missed your calling. You really should have become a barrister, since you plead on her behalf most eloquently. Did she, perhaps, tutor you?"

Alastair's lips tightened, for the lashing of his captain's tongue was something he seldom experienced. But stand by his guns he would. "Captain," Alastair began haltingly, not certain of what he was going to say, but knowing he would say something. "This is not like you, to act this way. To the best of my knowledge, you have never taken unfair advantage of anyone, and yet, forgive me, but you seem hell-bent on treating Lady Rhea in this callous, this ... this ..."

"Ungentlemanly manner?" Dante supplied, his eyes glinting.

"Aye, Captain," Alastair agreed uneasily. "She is a fine, gentle-born lady, and she has been through hell enough without us adding to it."

"Us?"

Alastair cleared his throat. "This voyage we are about to set out upon could be dangerous. Is it fair to jeopardize her life because of some strange fascination she seems to hold for you? Aye," Alastair said more firmly, as the captain raised a slightly curved brow, "you cannot deny it, Captain, for I've seen the way you watch her. She's bewitched you, but that is not her fault, is it? She does not belong on board the *Sea Dragon*, nor with us." Alastair paused, as if what he had to say was painful to him, then continued, "We are not the proper people for her to be associating with. To see her, so gentle and re- fined, sitting in her bare feet, trying to tie knots with the help of an old pirate, a honey-tongued Irishman, and other assorted rough seamen, well, 'tisn't right," Alastair concluded lamely.

"What you are so tactfully trying to say," Dante said softly, "is that *I* am not the sort she should be associating with. You think the lady objects to keeping company with a smuggler and his band of cutthroats?" Dante demanded. But his thoughts returned to the night before and the pas- sionate response he had finally coaxed from Lady Rhea Claire Dominick. He remembered the soft sweetness of her lips, and the way she had teased him with their but- terfly touch before surrendering them to him. He was uneasy about the way he had left her last night and did not like that look of loathing that had been in her violet eyes, eyes which only moments before had been dark with passion for him. But he would not worry about it overmuch, for if he had got her to respond to him once, he could do it again, Dante vowed, turning toward the light streaming from the stern windows and beginning to count the coins he had picked up from his desk.

"You can be most persuasive, Captain, and Lady Rhea is, after all, just an innocent young girl, certainly no match for your mastery in the arts of seduction," Alastair said bluntly. He'd wanted to sound reasonable as well, but as soon as he had uttered those unfortunate words and seen the captain's narrowed gaze, he realized that he had said the very worst thing he could have.

As Dante stood staring out the stern windows, his back and broad shoulders suddenly seemed stiffer than ever to a worried, saddened Alastair; he had served with the captain for too many years now—respecting the man, calling him friend—to see that friendship destroyed because of a woman. But there seemed nothing else for it. Alastair would never be able to live with himself if Rhea Claire came to grief, either physically, or spiritually, nor could he have the same high regard for Dante Leighton that he'd had once if that happened at the captain's hands.

"It seems to me, at least I like to think so, that we have been of some invaluable service to Lady Rhea Claire. When she was in desperate need of help, we were there and lended a hand. But I fear, as fond as we are of her, that it is time that we went our separate ways. Fate put us in her path for this one act of human kindness, nothing more. She belongs back in England, with her family. We don't have the right to deny her that, Dante," Alastair said earnestly, trying to reach his friend. But it seemed to Alastair that Dante had not heard a word he had spoken.

But he was mistaken. Dante had heard every word, had listened thoughtfully, in fact. Alastair was right, of course. Leave it to Alastair to see clearly when another might stumble, blinded by . . . by what? The desire to possess something uncommonly lovely and pure? Was that so very damning of him? Why should some other man take what he, Dante Leighton, captain of the *Sea Dragon*, had nurtured and was beginning to cherish? Why should Rhea be allowed to give to another man the passion that she would ultimately give to him? Why should he be denied this happiness? Dante wondered.

"But have we any control over our feelings, Alastair?" Dante asked him suddenly. "Are we thinking with cold-blooded logic, Alastair, when we fall in love?"

"Love?" Alastair said, feeling numb at the captain's startling words, unsure if he should be ecstatic or alarmed at the prospect of Dante Leighton being in love with Lady Rhea Claire. Lord help us if it's true, he thought suddenly, seeing the situation in a completely new light. There might now be a whole round of different troubles for Dante Leighton, and for Rhea Claire.

"You sound surprised, my friend, that I should be so frail as to fall in love, and especially with one such as Rhea Claire, who is so different from me. We are like night and day, are we not? Devil and angel? Saint and sinner? We began on a note of mistrust, which still exists, but perhaps now it is because of our vulnerability to one another. I have been cruel to her, frightened her intentionally, played with her, seduced her." Then Dante added softly, "But the game has been well met, Alastair, for she has the power to hurt me far more than I have ever hurt her. I am in love with her." Dante was voicing now what so far he had only dared to think. Last night, though, with the taste of her on his lips, the fragrance of her lingering on his skin, he had known that nothing like this had ever happened to him before. The realization had left him shaken.

"And Lady Rhea?" Alastair asked, stunned by receiving revelations from a man who had always kept his thoughts and feelings to himself.

"Given time, perhaps she could come to love me. She feels something for me, I know, but she is frightened of these emotions and—" Dante's words halted as he stared out the stern windows at an island boat sliding past. The object of his speculations was sitting in the prow and waving to someone on deck while she was being rowed toward St. John's.

Alastair was startled by the captain's sudden, harsh laugh. "It would seem as if m'lady fair has decided against giving me any more time," Dante remarked tersely.

Alastair came toward him and followed his gaze out the

stern windows. His eyes caught sight of the boat, but it took him a second or two to realize what had captured Dante Leighton's attention.

"Good Lord," Alastair murmured as he saw Rhea's guinea-gold head and the deep fall of lace fluttering at her elbow as she waved back at the *Sea Dragon*. And for one horrible second, he actually thought she could see them standing there and was audaciously bidding them a fond farewell.

Alastair stood there a moment, feeling more uncomfortable than he ever had in his life. After all, here was the captain telling him of his love for a woman, who, at her first opportunity, had fled him.

Dante watched silently as the boat drifted out of sight of the stern windows, his gray eyes narrowed into little more than slits.

"What are you going to do?" Alastair asked diffidently, thinking perhaps the game had been won.

"What *we* are going to do, Mr. Marlowe, is to go into St. John's, as planned. You have a cargo to load and I have business with customs, and unless I am mistaken, Lady Rhea Claire is in for a difficult time in St. John's. She'll be quite shocked if she expects to be welcomed as some long-lost daughter," Dante said grimly.

"What do you mean, Captain?" Alastair asked in puzzlement.

"Dressed as she is, unattended by a female companion, and having just arrived on board the *Sea Dragon*, as its only female passenger . . ." Dante speculated darkly. "I doubt whether anyone will believe her story of being the kidnapped daughter of a duke."

Alastair frowned with consternation as he thought ahead to what might happen to Rhea Claire in St. John's. Looking the way she did, she was bound to attract attention—but of the wrong sort.

"Now," Dante said, turning from the stern windows and their expansive view of the bay, which was now empty of that islander's boat, "I should like to discover how Rhea managed to get aboard that boat without being stopped by someone and," he paused, a black scowl lowering his brows, "who that was she was waving to on the quarterdeck."

Conny Brady turned almost expectantly toward the companion ladder when he heard steps, although he knew even as he watched that he would not be seeing Lady Rhea's golden head appearing. Still, he was not quite prepared to see the captain's chestnut curls, nor the dangerous glint in his gray eyes as they settled on him.

"Mister Brady," Dante said shortly as he drew nearer the pale-skinned cabin boy, whose blue eyes seemed to be filling half his face. "I suppose you have no idea whatsoever of Lady Rhea's whereabouts?"

MacDonald, who was still standing near the port rail, turned in surprise, for he thought Lady Rhea was still with young Conny. "Ach, well, she was here just a wee moment ago," he said, glancing below. "I was just havin' a word with her myself. Did she go below, young Conny?" he asked, noticing the boy's ashen face and wondering if he were sick.

"Do answer Mr. MacDonald, Conny," Dante suggested smoothly. His voice was harsh, though, and caused a puzzled MacDonald and a guilty Conny Brady to sense that something was amiss.

Conny bit his trembling lip until a little spurt of blood appeared. "She's gone into St. John's, Cap'n," he said huskily, his eyes downcast.

"St. John's!" MacDonald exclaimed in disbelief. "Ach, Cap'n, the lad's gullin' ye. To St. John's?" he repeated incredulously. "And what was she doin', flyin' like a bird across the water?"

"She found herself a ride in one of the island boats that was alongside," Dante informed the stunned Scotsman, whose pipe was growing cold in the palm of his calloused hand. "Do not despair, she did not say good-by to me, either, nor apparently to anyone else," he commented. Then he realized how Rhea could slip off the ship without drawing any notice to herself, for his crew were still grouped along the larboard bulwarks, their attention centered on the island boats plying their trade.

MacDonald ran his big hand through his silver hair as he glanced between the captain, Conny Brady, and

Alastair. "But why did the wee lass leave like that? I don't understand it," he mumbled, hurt that she'd leave without saying good-by. Then another thought struck him and he eyed the captain suspiciously. " 'Twasn't something ye did, was it, Cap'n? Been watchin' the two of ye together, and reckoned there be problems between ye."

"Aye, MacDonald, there are, but nothing that cannot be solved once we have the chance to talk together," Dante responded, not caring to have to answer for his actions to this Scotsman.

" 'Twasn't talkin' that has me worried."

"I needn't explain my actions to you, MacDonald, but if it will set your mind at ease, my intentions are honorable where Lady Rhea Claire is concerned," Dante told the Scotsman, meeting the Highlander's gaze steadily.

"Aye, reckon that answers any questions I might have had," MacDonald said, puffing on his pipe again as he tried to draw the flame back into it. "Wouldn't be on board if I could nae believe your word, Cap'n."

"She just said she was homesick, Cap'n. She didn't want to bother you, said 'twould be best if no one knew she was leavin'," Conny told his captain almost beseechingly, his eyes pleading for understanding and forgiveness, although he realized now that he had in some way betrayed Dante Leighton.

"You should have come to me, Mister Brady," Dante said, showing no pity for the chagrined cabin boy. "You are a crew member on board the *Sea Dragon,* and your loyalty lies with those men who sail her, and with her captain. By this lack of discretion on your part, you may well have endangered Lady Rhea Claire," Dante told the small boy, remaining unmoved by the look of dismay spreading across his face.

"I would never hurt Lady Rhea Claire," he said, tears now hanging heavy in his eyes.

"You have allowed her to go into St John's unescorted, with no money and no idea of where she should go for help."

"I gave her some money to pay the boatman," Conny admitted, his eyes avoiding his captain's.

"I see," Dante said, turning away from the unhappy

457

cabin boy. As Conny Brady stared at his captain's unyielding back, he felt his world crashing down around him, for he was responsible for putting Lady Rhea in danger, and now his captain was having nothing to do with him.

"If you can pull Longacres away from the railing, tell him to lower the boat. We are going ashore," Dante told Alastair, who was filled with pity for Conny Brady.

"Aye, Captain," Alastair replied, making his way back down the companion ladder.

"Cap'n, sir." Conny Brady was taking the risk of drawing his captain's wrathful eye.

Dante Leighton turned and looked down at the boy impersonally. Conny would have to learn his lesson, which was that he had to be loyal to his captain if he were to continue to serve on board the *Sea Dragon*. No other way was possible at sea, if you wanted to survive.

"I want to go into St. John's with ye, with ye permission, sir," Conny said in a rush. "I can help find Lady Rhea. Please, sir," he said huskily, his tears crowding close in his throat.

"Very well, Mister Brady. Since you are responsible for her leaving the ship, you might as well bear some of the responsibility for finding her. I only hope we will be in time." Dante spoke sharply, but if Conny Brady had chanced to glance up, he'd have seen that his captain's gray eyes seemed a little less frigid. But the boy was too embarrassed and ashamed to do anything but stare at his feet.

In St. John's, Rhea Claire was beginning to feel the frustrating truth of Dante's words, for she was a stranger, and a strange-looking one at that, dressed as she was in her beloved clothes from the *Sea Dragon*. Too late did she realize that she might have trouble soliciting help from these people, who most likely would find her incredible story hard to swallow.

Rhea had not lingered long near the wharves, for her solitary female figure had attracted remarks from the sailors milling around as they loaded cargo and from the fishermen mending nets. All this attention put a rosy blush in her cheeks and she hurried away. Her first polite inquiry had been met with a vulgar proposition from a man who had seemed perfectly respectable. He looked like a gentleman one might have seen on a London street, but this was not London, nor did she look like *Lady* Rhea Claire Dominick, the well-bred daughter of the highly respected Duke of Camareigh.

As Rhea progressed along the street, avoiding the partially domesticated pigs that ran wild through the town, she heard people calling to one another from opened windows on both sides of the narrow lane, and even though she seemed unable to gain assistance, the atmosphere of St. John's seemed friendly enough. She passed by an inn which fronted directly on the street, and thinking she might be able to gain some information, she started to step inside the shadowy hall, relieved to get out of the sun, which was beginning to get hot even at this early hour.

"Oh, no ye don't. Not in here, ye ain't!" a querulous voice charged her, stopping Rhea in her steps. "This be a respectable house, and not fer the likes of ye, missie. I'll not be havin' ye roll them big eyes of yours at me good-payin', decent customers. So git with ye, or I'll be callin' down the magistrate on ye!" To make certain that Rhea understood her meaning, this woman took the broom from a black woman who'd been sweeping the hall and came to the door swinging it in a threatening manner. When Rhea fled across the street, the woman's raucous laughter followed her.

Rhea jumped the last few steps to avoid being knocked down by a couple of prancing horses pulling a handsome open carriage. In the carriage was a beautifully dressed woman wearing pale green lustring, a wide, floppy hat of palest straw and a matching green veil covering her head to protect her from the sun. A mulatto maid sat opposite her, while a mulatto coachman handled the reins as well as anyone Rhea had ever seen at Camareigh.

The carriage disappeared up the street, leaving Rhea standing alone, uncertain what to do next, for she doubted whether she could gain entrance to any shop, inn, or house in St. John's. A well-dressed couple jostled her as she stood there thinking, and while she uttered her apology, she decided to try again.

"Excuse me, please. But if I might ask your help, I am La—"

"Really!" the middle-aged woman snorted in disgust, her gaze missing nothing of Rhea's bizarre attire. "The indecency one finds today in the common people, well, 'tis enough to make respectable persons keep to their homes. Do come along, John! Stop your gawking," she berated her husband, who had pushed his gold-rimmed eyeglasses up higher on the bridge of his thin nose in order to get a better view of Rhea's slender ankles.

With a sigh, Rhea watched them disappear down the street, which was crowded with people about their business, too busy to be bothered with a young girl standing alone. Her long gold braid brushed her hips enticingly as she continued her wanderings through town, uncertain of what she ought to do, and in some strange way, missing the gentle rocking of the *Sea Dragon*. As she thought of the ship, she wondered now what Houston Kirby was cooking, for when she'd passed a bakery, she had got a mouth-watering sniff of freshly baked pastry. Jamaica wouldn't be far away, she thought, nor young Conny. Unfortunately, to see either of them she would also have to see Dante Leighton, and that was somebody she hoped she never had to gaze upon again as long as . . .

Nearly tripping, Rhea stepped into the dark shadows of a doorway and came to a complete standstill. At the end of the street was a figure she knew only too well. She leaned against the cool stone of the building, her heart pounding as she gazed at the captain of the *Sea Dragon*, who was standing with legs planted firmly apart, as if he were still on the deck of his ship, still master of all he surveyed. Rhea was resentful that he looked so confident, so sure of himself, as he glanced up the street.

While Rhea crouched there in the cool shadows of the deeply recessed doorway, a door across the street opened, and a boisterous group of motley-looking seamen emerged. Several explicit oaths were being hurled after their departing figures by an authoritative voice, but it was a tavern wench standing in the doorway who came up with the most original descriptions about their persons.

Neatly sidestepping the buxom tavern wench who was blocking half the doorway, a portly man in velvet followed on the group's footsteps. There was a genial look on his flushed face as he pinched the girl's ample buttocks and immediately apologized for it, as though it had been an accident. The girl had squealed in surprise, apparently not suspecting such an act from so reputable a man.

As Rhea watched from the safety of her hiding place, the group made its way toward the end of the street, where Dante Leighton still stood. By now, he had been joined by Alastair Marlowe, MacDonald, Cobbs, Longacres, Barnaby Clarke, and several others from among the crew of the *Sea Dragon*, including Conny Brady. Rhea noticed that the boy was standing on the perimeter of the group, almost as if he were some kind of outcast.

She watched in fascination, moving slightly from the shadows to gain a better view, as the two groups converged on each other. Even from where she stood, Rhea could tell that it was hardly a friendly meeting of old mates, but something like a confrontation between hated rivals.

"Well, well, now, what have we here?" Bertie Mackay queried, as if uncertain about what he beheld.

"Hadn't heard any shellfish had been washed up on shore," one of his men cackled gleefully, jabbing one of his mates.

"That's because, mate, ye've been too busy tryin' to keep that bloater ye call a ship afloat," Longacres said, spitting his quid just short of the other seaman's toes.

" 'Ere, watch that, ye old buzzard," the man growled at Longacres. He did take a step backwards, though, as he saw the gleam in the old gent's eye, as well as a subtle move to his belt where his knife was kept.

"Well, well, what have we here?" Cobbs demanded, imitating Bertie Mackay's words. But his expression was even more disbelieving than Mackay's of what he was seeing before his eyes. "Can't actually be George Grimes, the driftin' man?" he asked, choking on his guffaw as he caught sight of the man they had set adrift in the straits.

"Wee Geordie?" MacDonald asked, his heavy mustache seeming to grow wider with his grin.

"Aye, and I reckon me mates and me might be havin' a few words with ye about that," Grimes said, feeling far braver now with his mates around him than he had the last time he had faced the murderous crew of the *Sea Dragon*. Now, if he could've gotten a clean aim, he wouldn't have hesitated to send the steely point of his knife into that wide chest of Dante Leighton.

"Now, now, fellows," Bertie Mackay said placatingly, not caring to make a scene when there were so many witnesses and fine, upstanding townspeople watching. After all, he had a reputation to protect. "This is hardly worth drawing the attention of the militia."

"Aye, Cap'n, reckon ye be right. Don't s'pose this fancy gent here would put up much of a fight anyways," commented one of Bertie Mackay's men; then he sniffed loudly and rudely at Barnaby Clarke.

"I'd soon enough teach you some manners, sir," responded the *Sea Dragon*'s quartermaster, reaching for his sword hanging at his hip.

"Why, sweet thing, I'd have ye sliced and quartered afore ye'd even git that sword off your hip," the other man warned, taking note of the flash of steel in the hand of the Scotsman.

"Planning on staying long in Antigua, Captain Leighton?" Bertie Mackay asked casually, easing the tension a bit by settling his great weight between his men and the crew of the *Sea Dragon*.

"As long as you, Captain Mackay, I should imagine," Dante replied vaguely, although both of them knew what he meant.

Bertie Mackay's laughter filled the street and drifted back to where Rhea stood waiting for the two groups to move so she could escape without being noticed.

"Ah, Captain Leighton, you always make me laugh, yes sir, always do," Bertie Mackay wheezed. "Still would like to be partners with you. Hadn't changed your mind about that, I s'pose?" he asked, his small eyes narrowed as he took in the surly-looking group surrounding the captain of the *Sea Dragon*. "Why don't you go back and get yourselves another couple o' rums, lads," he advised his men, and reaching into his purse, he pulled out several coins and tossed them into a couple of outstretched palms. "Off with ye, now."

Grumbling slightly, they turned and shuffled off, leaving a few choice remarks drifting behind. At the end of the street, they turned and disappeared, most likely to look for a different tavern this time.

"Now that the air has cleared a bit, I was wonderin', Captain," Bertie Mackay began, then glanced meaningfully at the men still grouped around Dante, and added softly, "if we might have a private word or two?"

Dante glanced around at his men, who were already impatiently looking up and down the street in hopes of spying a golden head of hair twisted into a long braid. "Very well," he said, nodding to Alastair and the others, who then drifted off in several directions.

"Now, what did you wish to say to me, Captain Mackay?" Dante inquired politely, though he was most anxious to be gone.

"Well, you might say, 'twas a continuation of a conversation we had a while back, Captain," Bertie Mackay said, smiling widely at a couple of local citizens walking past and removing his hat in polite deference to the lady.

"Indeed?" Dante remarked casually.

"Aye, Captain. I was thinkin' that you might be in need of a silent partner. Maybe a man like me could keep to me own business back in Charles Town, while you went about your own business here, if ye get my drift?" he said in a very confidential tone.

"Not quite. I fear I am slow to comprehend your intent," Dante murmured, his eye catching a flash of movement at the top of the street, which he could have sworn was Rhea Claire.

"I can make the others believe that you're just goin' about your business, and I can even make me own crew not suspicion a thing, Captain. Then there isn't quite so much to split up, should you just happen to find that treasure," Mackay offered with a beaming look.

Dante noticed Conny Brady hurrying up the street; the cabin boy hadn't moved off with the others and had been waiting for his captain in the shadow of the hotel. "As you said before, Captain Mackay," Dante said, "we have already had this most interesting but hardly profitable conversation once before. I see no need to continue it, since as you well know, the crew of the *Sea Dragon* found a wrecked Dutch merchantman, her holds full of rotting spices. I really would advise you to buy your clove and pepper in the local market. Good day to you, Captain Mackay," Dante bid him, stepping around a livid Bertie Mackay, whose expression and muttered oaths caused a genteel woman passing by to draw in her breath. Then, as her concerned maid fanned her faint-looking mistress, they scurried across the lane.

As the two groups split apart, Rhea remained, waiting for Dante to follow his men. Instead, he remained in conversation with the portly gentleman in velvet.

She was debating what to do when she suddenly caught sight of a blue uniform with gold lace and braid, and recognizing it as a King's naval officer, decided that now was her chance. She knew that with half the *Sea Dragon*'s crew, and her captain, searching St. John's for her, it was just a matter of time before they found her.

Rhea left the safety of her hiding place and dashed across the street, not even glancing toward Dante Leighton to see if he'd noticed her; thus, she did not see Conny Brady leave the shadows of the doorway he'd been standing in and start off in hot pursuit after her.

Rhea hurried through a crowd of people that suddenly seemed to be filling the narrow lane. Her strangely clad figure seemed to blend in more now as she wound along the street, careful not to bump against the black women dressed in white muslin jackets and petticoats, many of whom balanced white wicker baskets on heads wrapped in colorful turbans of gauze and silk. Since the men were clad in loose white drawers and waistcoats, the blue uniform of the British naval officer should have stood out vividly, but Rhea did not see him anywhere.

Glancing around, Rhea noticed her surroundings for

the first time and realized she had wandered into the marketplace, where hundreds of black people and mulattoes were crowded together to sell their produce of pigs, chickens, and all manner of fowl penned and displayed. As well, there were staggering piles of breadfruit, sweet potatoes, coconuts, papaya, avocado, and baskets of fragrant coffee beans.

Small children were running free, while dogs chased around in seemingly endless circles, snatching and barking at anything that crossed their paths. Rhea sighed in exasperation, wiping at the fine beads of perspiration beginning to form on her brow. There was no blue uniform in sight.

Giving up her search, she decided that her best plan of action would be to go back to some shop or inn. There, she would purposely cause an incident, which would force the proprietor, or proprietress, into sending for the authorities. Then she would be able to tell her story, and finally have someone listen to her.

Rhea was wending her way through the marketplace when she spied MacDonald wandering toward her, and she ducked behind a couple of stacked up crates holding some worriedly clucking chickens. As Rhea stood there and watched the Scotsman walk past her, so close that she could almost have reached out and touched him, she felt an almost unbearable loneliness for her friends on board the *Sea Dragon*, and for this Highlander who had known her great-grandfather. She watched silently, however, as he disappeared into the crowd; then, with one last look at his tall figure, she stepped from her hiding place and walked away in the opposite direction. She found a small, twisting lane leading out of the market square and followed it, the sounds of laughter and voices raised in barter drifting away behind her. She had just come to the realization that this was not one of the better sections of town, when a group of men suddenly erupted from a tavern almost abreast of her. Quickening her pace, she hurried past, anxious to go unobserved; alas, though, this was not to be, for one of the rum-soaked hearties spied her gently swaying hips and let out a hoot of delight.

Rhea glanced back in fright, startled to discover that this was the very same rowdy group of men who had been challenging the captain and crew of the *Sea Dragon* less than half an hour earlier. Now their mood was anything but harmonious and they were looking for trouble of one kind or another. And it seemed they did not care if it were a female or male who happened to cross their path. Whoever it might be, that unfortunate person would rue the day.

And Lady Rhea Claire Dominick seemed to be that unfortunate person, for as she started to run, the men broke into pursuit of her flying figure, following her golden braid like a beacon.

She sped along the uneven lane, stumbling once or twice. She was dismayed to find it all but abandoned; then, suddenly, the houses along it fell away and she was surrounded by lush, tropical undergrowth, so thick that further exploration was impossible. Rhea spun around in panic as she heard the group of men coming closer and wondered how she could feel such fear in broad daylight. Her eyes sought for some alternative escape route, but the thick, dark green leaves and branches seemed to be closing in around her. Then suddenly the silence was broken by the excited laughter and shouts of the drunken seamen, who now faced her across the desolate space of the forgotten lane.

"Mighty fine sight, eh, mates?" one of them asked.

"Why ye run from us, girlie?"

"Reckon we would've paid plenty, but seein' how ye put us to so much trouble, guess we've already done paid, eh, mates?" said the one known as George Grimes with a wide grin. His eyes were burning over Rhea's slight figure, noting with pleasure the rapid rise and fall of her small breasts.

"Oooohwe, but she's a beauty!"

"Aye, she's a fine sight, indeed."

"Reckon we oughta get to know her a little better, eh, mates?"

Rhea stared in mesmerized fascination at this group of evil-looking men; not since awakening in the dark on board the *London Lady* had she known such paralyzing fear.

"Hey, what be yer name, little one?"

"Come on, tell ol' Jacko, he sure wants to know."

"Lookie there at that hair. 'Tis like gold, 'tis. And them eyes, d'ye ever see such a color? Reckon I'm gonna take a closer look, mates!" he said with a leering grin as he moved a step closer, his eyes never leaving Rhea's face.

Rhea could feel her muscles trembling, and she knew if she tried to run she would probably fall, so weak did her legs feel. She watched the progress of the shaggy-haired man, whose dirty clothes lent proof to his state of mind, and cried out, "Don't come any closer!"

"Oh, but that be nice. She sounds like a real lady, her," he said, grinning, his step bolder as he gained support from his mates who had formed a half-circle around the clearine. "Come on, sweeting, say something else fer ol' Jacko. I likes the sound of yer voice, sure I do," he taunted her as he moved in closer.

"Don't ye touch her, ye son of a whoremonger!" cried out a high-pitched voice. Then a small form shot into the midst of the group, startling the seamen who had not heard his approach.

This small figure plowed into the back of the man called Jacko's legs, knocking him off his feet. The two rolled in the soft dirt, but it was no contest, for the figure that had come to Rhea's rescue was less than half the weight of the other man. Nor was he a murderer like this other man was, for the flash of the blade of a knife was in the air; then it was between the two rolling bodies. Then all was still, except for the man named Jacko, who staggered to his feet, a cornered look in his eye as he stared down at his victim.

Rhea stared down in horrified disbelief at Conny Brady's still form, the black curls tousled above his pale face. The wide blue eyes were now closed and the childish voice had been silenced.

"God, but he was just a kid," one of the men complained.

Then Rhea's screams of terror and grief ripped through

the air, making the hairs rise on the back of the men's necks.

"Shut her up, man. We could all go to the gallows fer this!" hissed one of them in warning.

The man called Jacko grabbed Rhea as she knelt beside the fallen Conny Brady, but he barely had time to grab hold of her hair before he was surprised by a stinging pain shooting through his shoulder. Glancing up, he cowered in fear as he faced the hard-bitten stare of one of the King's officers, whose pistol was still smoking. In his other hand, he held a carefully balanced sword, and its point was dallying too close to his chest for comfort.

"Unhand the lady, or face certain death," the officer said harshly, placing himself between the spot where the fallen child and the girl were, and where the group of men were standing. They were still feeling brave from their consumption of rum, and their faces still showed their ugly thoughts in such a way that the officer could easily read what was going through their minds. He was just one, and they were six, and even though he had a sword, they had their knives, and one of them could, if he had the skill, throw it from a safe distance with deadly accuracy.

"Be smart lads and return to your ship, although your mate here stays with me. He has a few questions to answer for the magistrate," the officer told them in a friendly tone of voice, while his eyes never left the group, alert to the slightest movement.

" 'Ere, ye'll not be leavin' me to take the blame," Jacko muttered thickly, his eyes sending a warning to those less brave among his comrades who had murmured thoughtfully to one another at the officer's suggestion.

"Think a moment, men," the officer continued, his voice smooth and reasonable, having the same calming effect on these men now as it did on his own men when they were under fire. "Would this brave hearty here, a man who would stab a child, stay and fight for any one of you? Think on that before you make that move that will put your necks in tightening nooses," he told them, his demeanor calm, and unhurried, giving them no reason to act rashly.

But Jacko had far more to lose, and as the officer's blue

back turned at an angle toward him, he reached inside his jacket and pulled out a knife, for he could throw it with equal skill with either hand. This he raised quickly, ready to throw, but never got the chance, for the loud report of another pistol sounded. In the next moment, he was staring down at his shattered hand, the blood dripping onto his already bloodied shirt front.

The officer glanced down at Jacko's harmless knife where it had fallen near his boots, then up toward the origin of that bullet. A slight smile curved his lips as he met the gray-eyed stare of Dante Leighton.

"Captain Lloyd," the captain of the *Sea Dragon* greeted him. Then, as he saw the crumpled form of Conny Brady and the weeping form of Rhea kneeling beside him, his eyes raked the group, and even those rum-soaked brains of Bertie Mackay's crew felt the murderous intent in their cold depths. If there was one man on earth they would not have wished to see standing there, it was Dante Leighton, captain of the *Sea Dragon,* for they knew he would show them no mercy. And so, to his bitter amusement, Sir Morgan Lloyd, captain of H.M.S. *Portcullis,* found five pairs of beseeching eyes trained on his King's officer's uniform—an article of clothing more often spat upon than not.

"Dante!" Rhea cried, when she saw his tall figure standing behind the group of men. She was kneeling beside Conny Brady, cradling his lolling head in her lap and trying to staunch the flow of blood from his shoulder. "He's been stabbed, and 'tis all my fault," she wept, her hot tears falling onto Conny's flushed face. But as she rocked him in her arms, his eyelids suddenly started to quiver, then opened slowly.

"Lady Rhea?" he mumbled. "I thought I'd never see ye again. I didn't want to see ye leave the *Sea Dragon,* but I didn't tell anyone. It made the captain mad, and he doesn't like me anymore," he whispered, his eyes glazed. "I saw you crossing the street and I followed you into the marketplace. Then I lost you for a few minutes, but when I found you again, these men were around you, and I had to help you, Lady Rhea," he told her, his eyelids drooping.

"Oh, you did, Conny. You saved me, truly you did," she told him, her tears falling faster.

Quietly Dante Leighton moved closer, his eyes taking in the group of nervous men, but when his eyes fell on the man who had tried to knife Sir Morgan, another look altogether entered them.

Sir Morgan Lloyd did not care for that look, for he had seen it many times on the faces of men in the heat of battle. It meant that blood lust was riding high in a man, and he knew that unless he did something soon, he would find himself in the position of having to bear witness against Dante Leighton, which was something he would rather not have to do.

"Dante!" Rhea spoke desperately, calling Dante's attention to her. "We have got to get Conny to a doctor. He's so pale and cold," she cried, giving Sir Morgan Lloyd the opening he needed.

"You know these two?" he asked.

"The boy's my cabin boy," Dante answered shortly, gazing down at Conny's quiet face.

"I would suggest then that you follow the lady's advice. The boy needs help. We have a very fine surgeon on board the *Portcullis*. If you wish, I will see that he comes aboard the *Sea Dragon* and has a look at the boy," Sir Morgan offered, thinking privately that the boy's chances did not look good.

"Thank you, but my steward is well practiced in doctoring; he will know what to do," Dante answered, his eyes straying to the group of very silent men. "And what are you going to do with this scum?"

"Well, I suspect it would be difficult to charge any of these men with anything other than being drunken, which is to be expected along the docks, so I would suggest we allow them to be on their way," Sir Morgan told Dante, who merely shrugged, his eyes straying to the wounded man.

"And him?"

"I shall personally escort our craven friend to the magistrate," Sir Morgan told him. "I will have to have statements from both of you. You will be in St. John's Harbour for a few days?" he inquired as he pulled a now sniveling Jacko to his feet.

"Another day or so. I plan to sail on Saturday," Dante told him, carefully lifting Conny Brady and holding out his hand to assist a wobbling Rhea to her feet.

"And the lady?" Sir Morgan asked, his glance politely curious, for the girl was dressed like some island woman; yet when she had spoken she'd sounded very cultured, and her features were certainly the most refined and delicate he had ever gazed upon. "Where shall I be able to reach her, should I need further testimony for the hearing?" Sir Morgan asked Dante Leighton.

But the captain of the *Sea Dragon* was not going to be very helpful, for he had decided in that split second that it was up to Rhea to answer. Now, if she chose, she could declare her identity and blurt out her story, condemning him and gaining her freedon in the process. Sir Morgan Lloyd was no fool and he would hear her out; then he'd make certain that she was well taken care of until her story could be verified. He might even send her back to England, reuniting her with her family, and then there would be no doubt of her true identity.

"Rhea?" Dante asked her quietly, his gray eyes locked with hers as he offered her this chance at freedom. Then he glanced away, leaving her free to answer as she wished.

Rhea glanced down at Conny Brady's feverish face and saw his lips moving almost soundlessly as he mumbled her name over and over again. "You may reach me on board the *Sea Dragon*, Captain," Rhea said softly, as she tenderly smoothed back a black curl from Conny Brady's brow.

"Rhea! Rhea! Lady Rhea! Don't be leavin' me, please. Don't be leavin'!"

"I am here, Conny. I shall not leave you," Rhea crooned to the feverish little boy, holding him pressed to her breast.

"Don't be mad at me, Cap'n, please don't. But she's so pretty. I only wanted to please her. She was crying. I saw her. Lady Rhea was crying. She was unhappy. She wanted to go home, Cap'n. She went home and left me,

Cap'n, just like ye'll do some day, too. Just like everybody does," he cried, his thin shoulders shaking.

"No, 'tis all right, Conny," Rhea reassured him, pressing a cooling compress against his feverish brow. "I am here with you. I shall not leave you, Conny. I promise you I shan't."

"And the word of a Dominick is never broken, is it, Rhea?" Dante asked softly, having entered his cabin without her hearing him.

"What will happen to that man who stabbed Conny?" she asked, rising wearily from her perch at the side of the bunk. For the past three days, this was the only place she could be found. As she rose, she pretended not to see the hand held out to assist her.

"I think the authorities were more than pleased to be able to find a gaol to house the man. He has been involved in trouble before in Antigua, so they knew him well. Also, it did not go in his favor that he tried to murder an officer of the crown, something frowned upon in most quarters. If Conny should die, then he will face the gallows," Dante said harshly. Then, when he heard Rhea's gasp of pain, he winced, for his words had been unthinkingly cruel, and he had not meant them so.

"Don't say that! He cannot die! Not Conny. It was all my fault, and if he dies, then I will be to blame," Rhea cried, her shoulders shaking with her pent-up grief and guilt.

She felt hard arms enclosing her, holding her, comforting her; she heard Dante murmuring soft words in her ear. She tried to draw away from his warmth, for she wanted no pity, no comfort; she deserved to suffer as long as poor Conny burned with fever in the bunk.

"No, do not draw away, Rhea," Dante entreated her. "You are not to blame."

"Yes, I am. I involved a young boy in my troubles. I made use of his adoration for me, turning him against you when I asked him not to tell you that I had left the *Sea Dragon*. I knew it was wrong, but I was so desperate to escape. I wanted to go home so badly. I was standing there breathing in the fragrance of jessamine, thinking of Camareigh, and I just could not bear it any longer. Then, the thought of facing you after that night when . . ." Rhea shuddered as her words were choked off by her tears.

"I know, and I do not blame you, Rhea," Dante told her with a grim tightness around his lips, thinking that her tears were for the memory of the revulsion she'd felt that night. He stared down at the top of her golden head, and she was so slight in his arms he felt as if he could crush her; yet all he wished to do was to hold her.

"The crew blames me; I can see it in their eyes when they look at me," Rhea said huskily.

"No, no, they don't. They are merely concerned for Conny's recovery. They were just as worried about you, my dear. They do not blame you," Dante said, trying to convince her, for it was true that they did not blame Rhea for Conny's accident. They were all proud of the boy's bravery against such great odds, and if there were blame to be placed, then it was on Bertie Mackay and his crew, or on himself.

"I will not let you savor your guilt alone, my dear. You may place the blame equally at my feet," Dante told her harshly, trying to awaken her from this apathy. "I spoke harshly to the boy, knowing full well how I was wounding him. I am the one who allowed him ashore to look for you. Then, carrying the memory of my words about you being in danger, he acted in a manner of which he thought I would approve. I am as much to blame, Rhea, as you are," Dante told her, his eyes worried as they lingered on the restlessly sleeping Conny Brady.

"I feel so helpless standing here, not being able to do anything for Conny," Rhea said, gazing up at Dante, engulfed by a feeling of helplessness. "I know Houston Kirby is doing as much as he can for Conny," she said, then hesitated, not wanting her words to sound like criticism of the little steward, for he had been tireless in his doctoring of the cabin boy, his careful ministrations seeming to soothe the boy's heated flesh time and time again. "But perhaps," she continued, "we should seek a doctor from St. John's."

"I am afraid that would be impossible," Dante answered shortly, and Rhea knew she must have offended him.

"I am sorry, I did not mean to cast doubt on Kirby's skills, but I am so worried about Conny," Rhea said lamely.

"I am afraid seeking another doctor from Antigua would be impossible because," Dante hesitated, his eyes straying to the wide stern windows, "we have set sail from Antigua. We are at sea, my dear," he added more gently as he realized that she had been unaware of the *Sea Dragon*'s weighing of anchor.

Rhea freed herself from Dante's arms and stared out on the wide expanse of empty sea now visible through the stern windows, her breath catching in her throat as she realized that any hope of fleeing the *Sea Dragon* and her captain was lost to her. And now she felt the gentle heeling of the ship, then, listening carefully, heard the low groaning of her timbers and the creaking of her masts as her sails filled with the trades. The *Sea Dragon* had turned her bowsprit toward her final quest.

Chapter 9

The *Sea Dragon*'s course had taken her into the Straits of Florida; there, the Gulf Stream and prevailing winds carried her swiftly through the treacherous channel, where sand banks might lie off the bow, unseen from the quarterdeck or aloft, or gales might blow up from any direction, sending the ill-fated mariner onto the sunken, saw-toothed coral reefs hedging the passage.

But fortune seemed to be sailing with the proud crew of the *Sea Dragon,* for she had safely rounded the straggling group of palmetto-and-pine-covered islets and sandy cays of the southernmost point off the mainland of Florida. They had sailed past stretches of white, virgin sand, where the water lapping against the beaches was a translucent blue that lightened to pale green in the sun-dappled and palm-shadowed shallows near shore. But just as frequently, they had sighted the low-lying marshlands clogging the bays and inlets, where the grotesque mangrove with its twisted webbing of roots rising out of the turbid swamp water reigned supreme, while man-of-war birds fought over roosting rights in its bright green crown of leafy branches.

If the crew of the good ship *Sea Dragon* had thought their captain slightly mad to be sailing his ship with her hold half-laden along the wild coast of Florida—an inhospitable place they'd sooner not have a closer look at—then they were soon given reason to believe him completely demented. Dante gave orders for the *Sea Dragon*'s anchor to be dropped in a sleepy cove, where the only visible inhabitants, a flock of pinkish orange flamingos, were leaving, their elongated necks pointing southeast toward the wide mouth of the cove.

With the exception of Houston Kirby, who everyone knew had half-addled wits, and Alastair Marlowe, who was too quiet to be quite normal, the crew of the *Sea Dragon* was prepared to forcibly restrain their captain when he pulled out that treasure map, in the eventuality of his turning violent, as was often the case when one went off his head. For every man jack of them knew that that treasure map was no good. And this wasn't even the right place, for the sunken galleon had been in a cove in the Bahamas, which had been clearly marked on the map they had all had a chance to get a good look at. The crew had muttered and nudged one another as they listened to their captain's crazed words. The only one of them who didn't, strangely enough, was Longacres, who'd just sat whittling away at a piece of wood, his gapetoothed grin widening and widening with the captain's words, as if he had been expecting all along that this strange incident would happen.

But soon they had all begun to get the captain's drift, and after their initial disappointment that the captain had not taken them into his confidence about the fake treasure map, a state of excitement had pervaded the *Sea Dragon*'s crew. Their dreams had been rekindled by the captain's words, and now, once again they knew a renewal of purpose, a newfound hope for something better than spending their lives at sea.

Rhea Claire Dominick shaded her narrowed eyes against the almost blinding glare off the rippling waters of the cove. To the southeast lay open sea, and against the horizon, Rhea could see bluish gray thunderheads accumulating and growing darker by the minute, a sure portent of a squall. It mattered not, however, for the *Sea Dragon* was lying snug and would safely weather the storm. The crew's search for treasure would surely be delayed, however, and Rhea did not know if the eager men could endure another day of disappointment—for they had yet to find their much-sought-after treasure.

Putting her hands behind her head as she lay on the warm sand, Rhea speculated on what had happened to her since she had first set foot on board the *Sea Dragon* that fateful day in Charles Town. She could understand now, or at least she understood better, why Dante Leighton had reacted in so brutal a manner. He had been protecting his future, as well as the futures of his men, the loyal crew of the *Sea Dragon*, who had served him well throughout the years. Now that she had time to consider the matter more carefully—as well as taking into consideration certain facts she had gleaned from a none-too-reticent Houston Kirby about a certain woman in Charles Town who had hurt the captain—she realized that Dante Leighton had been reacting to several sets of circumstances, and that she had been unfortunate enough to have crossed his path at exactly the wrong time, and in the wrong manner and place.

And because it was her nature, Rhea found herself forgiving him many things; he had, after all, given her a chance to gain her freedom. It had been her decision in St. John's to return to the *Sea Dragon*. No one had forced her, and so she could blame none but herself for what her future might hold.

Lazily contemplating a sky which was still azure over her head, she knew that if she had to do it all over again, that she would still be lying here on these warm sands, with the soft whispering of the palms like a lullaby in her ears and the hot tropical sun warming her skin.

Stretching sleepily, her hand struck a hard object and she opened a heavy-lidded eye to gaze at her treasure. Her hand settled on a cone-shaped shell with a smooth pink interior that rolled into a tiny point. Another had a bright orange color, its exterior rough to the touch, while several others were striped and speckled, some small, some tiny, others giant and curving. They were beautiful, and just as valuable to her, Rhea thought, rolling sideways and staring up the beach, as the treasure that was being sought by the crew of the *Sea Dragon*, for these had been a gift to her from a very special person.

Rhea lifted her arm in a casual wave as Conny Brady came bustling around the gentle curve of the cove, another shell held carefully in his hands.

"Lady Rhea! I've found another one! You can hear the ocean in it, too!" he called to her before dropping down beside her, his tanned cheeks flushed, his dark eyes bright with adventure. "Listen!"

Rhea tilted her head, holding the heavy shell against her ear, a surprised look crossing her face as she heard the roar of the ocean.

"Have they found anything yet?" Conny demanded, staring across the bay to where the *Sea Dragon* was riding anchor, her masts rising starkly against the skies. The deck looked deserted, and if there had not been an occasional splashing of water near the *Sea Dragon*'s starboard bow, one might have thought the ship abandoned.

"Do you think there really is a treasure?" Conny asked, disappointment riding high in his voice as he gazed longingly toward the spot where those seamen who could swim, the captain and Alastair chief among them, were diving amongst the coral reefs and curious fish in search of the remains of the sunken Spanish galleon. The sailors who preferred to stay on dry land were combing the beach on the far side of the bay from the place where Rhea and Conny were idling away the hours. They were hoping to find some pieces of eight, spars, figurehead, or debris of any kind that might have been washed ashore and would lead them to their fortunes.

Thunder sounded in the distance; then lightning streaked through the blackening clouds closing on the mouth of the cove. The rippling surface of the water was rising, growing choppy, and it was apparent that the skies were about to split wide in torrents of rain.

"Come, Conny," Rhea said regretfully as she got to her feet, dusting the clinging sand from her skirt and bodice. "I see Longacres rowing this way. I don't want you to get chilled," she told him, still worrying about his health, for even though he had recovered almost completely, there were shadows every so often in his blue eyes, and she often wondered if he still felt twinges of pain from his healed knife wound.

She helped him gather his booty of shells. Then they stood patiently while Longacres rowed close, then hopped out, and pushed the gig up on shore.

"Reckon that's it fer today," he said, glaring up at the sullen skies.

"No luck?" Rhea asked, feeling sorry for the old pirate, who had never found any sunken treasure for all his stories of pirates and sailing with brigands.

"Ain't givin' up, I'm not, eh, young Conny?" he grinned as he helped Rhea climb into the boat. Then he settled her in the prow and shoved off as Conny hopped aboard. "None o' us is givin' up!" he muttered.

He easily rowed the light craft across the small cove and alongside the *Sea Dragon*, which was beginning to swarm with life now that the day's search had been abandoned. But, as Longacres had said, it was not forgotten, for there was nothing *but* treasure spoken of by everyone on board the *Sea Dragon*.

Even she could feel the excitement of searching for sunken treasure stirring in her blood, Rhea thought later, while dressing for dinner. Never before had she given much thought to the grandeur of her surroundings, nor to the wealth that she had come to think of as her right. But ever since falling on hard times, she had come to a rude awakening about the lives that others less fortunate than she had to suffer through just trying to survive, and now she understood what it meant to have a chance to gain a fortune.

Remembering her wardrobes at Camareigh, which had burgeoned with gowns that she could scarcely recall, each a different color, material, and style, and all created especially for her by one of the finest French seamstresses in all of London, she knew it might seem strange to some that she should feel such fondness for her present wardrobe of clothes. But then, when you had only two dresses to choose between, and each one held some special meaning or significance in your life, you might find yourself placing an almost priceless value on them.

And that was how she felt about her leather skirt and

bodice, her gifts from the crew of the *Sea Dragon*. It was also much the way she felt about the gown she was dressing in for dinner. It was as fashionable as any that one would see in London, and had been a gift from the captain of the *Sea Dragon*. He must have bribed the St. John's seamstress with a small fortune in order to get her to turn over so beautiful a gown. Rhea thought it must have been part of some young woman's trousseau, or an expensive request for a very special occasion, for she had never seen such delicate material or fine workmanship. Of white muslin that was as light as a feather, it had treble flounces of lace falling from the tight, elbow-length sleeves, and a petticoat that was row after row of lacy ruffles.

It was exquisite—and it had been a complete surprise to her when she'd found it placed on her bunk shortly after they had set sail from Antigua. Delicate silk shoes and silk stockings had accompanied it, as well as a marquetry box filled with sundry items: a silver brush and mirror, a delicate, carved crystal bottle of perfume, fragrant soap and pins for her hair, as well as countless little gewgaws.

Rhea stared at her reflection in the mirror, liking the way her golden skin glowed against the paleness of her bodice. Her hair was braided in a coronet that curved over the top of her head; it was far more sophisticated than the braided loops of gold, which could swing so enticingly against a man's shoulder.

The first night she wore the dress, she had startled the men gathered for dinner in the captain's cabin as much as she had the night she had worn her leather skirt. This time, though, the gift was from Dante Leighton, and her eyes had held his shyly as she waited expectantly for his reaction. He had not disappointed her. He had carried her hand to his lips in a gentlemanly fashion, complimenting her with words that any woman would like to have heard. Meanwhile, his pale gray eyes gazing deeply into hers had spoken far more eloquently, leaving a rosy blush staining her cheeks as she turned away from him. Her memories of another night similar to this one still had the power to leave her trembling, and she suspected he knew that.

Why he had gone to the trouble to buy her this gown she did not know, for when she had expressed her gratitude, he had shrugged, looking almost embarrassed. But Rhea was sure he had been pleased that she was wearing his gifts.

Rhea adjusted the wide, square décolletage of her gown, which had a deep flouncing of lace that did little to cover the rounded curves of her breasts. In fact, it seemed to do just the opposite by drawing the eye, which was perhaps what had been intended. With the light scent of lavender clinging to her throat and wrists and to the warm cleavage so enchantingly revealed, Rhea entered the captain's cabin, steadying herself against Alastair Marlowe's arm as the deck slanted alee.

" 'Tis a howler," he commented with a wry grin, his hazel eyes rolling heavenward, as if he were questioning what had he done to deserve this.

"Ah, but here is our bright spot in the storm," Seumus Fitzsimmons responded, glib and grinning as always, his dark eyes feasting on her décolletage.

"Lady Rhea, I trust this storm will not overly disturb you," Barnaby Clarke greeted her, always politely solicitous of her health and well being. He was not, however, above taking an occasional sly glance at her bare shoulders, and Rhea decided that she far preferred Seumus Fitzsimmons's open admiration.

The captain of the *Sea Dragon* was standing before the rain-raked stern windows, his cinnamon velvet coat adding a touch of misleading warmth to his figure, for there was now a brooding look on his bronzed face, and his gray eyes seemed to be glowing with some inner fire, or perhaps, conflict. His chestnut curls had been ruthlessly brushed back and tied, as if little thought had been given to it.

"Ah, m'lady fair," Dante murmured, a slight edge to his voice, which drew the eyes of the others, for they'd not heard that sarcastic note in their captain's voice for many a week. Rhea certainly was not the only one to wonder what was amiss.

Houston Kirby came hurrying in, his tray loaded with pewter plates, for he was taking no chances of having his

481

finest china crashing to the deck. Jamaica was not far behind, nor was Conny, who had returned to his cabin boy duties with a renewed vigor, despite the captain's order not to tire himself. Indeed, there seemed always to be a helping hand with chores nowadays, making his days a little less long and giving him time for more of a boy's daydreaming.

The enticing aroma of lobster, freshly caught in the cove that afternoon, filled the captain's cabin. Taking their places at the table, they prepared to enjoy another of the little steward's finely prepared meals, which, though served on board a ship in a desolate cove in the wilderness, would have been fit fare for a king's table.

Throughout their meal the lantern overhead swung to and fro, casting strange shadows across the faces gathered beneath. Meanwhile, the storm increased in rage. It seemed to Rhea, as she grabbed for her goblet of wine, that the storm was venting all of its fury on the *Sea Dragon,* for the ship was straining against her anchor, and the sounds of the wind howling through the rigging and the rain slashing against the deck were almost deafening.

"Glad we're in a safe harbor," Alastair commented idly as he sipped his brandy, a look of contentment spreading across his face as he stared at his empty plate. "Lord, what a feast that was," he declared, lifting his glass in a toast to a smugly pleased Houston Kirby. "That coconut cake goes without comparison."

"Aye, 'twas tasty, that. I'm thinkin' we're goin' to be findin' that treasure, for with food like this, one has to be a king," Seumus Fitzsimmons mused.

"I trust you are right, Mr. Fitzsimmons," Barnaby Clarke said longingly, "for I've already selected the land I want to buy on Nevis, and 'twould be nice to think I'll not be too old to do more than sit in the garden."

"And to be sure," Seumus Fitzsimmons contributed, winking at Rhea who was smiling thoughtfully, "I'd like to be findin' meself a sweetheart with golden hair and eyes as fair as flowers. But I'll have to have me fortune in order to support her in a style she be accustomed to, and at the rate I'm goin', she'll be silver-haired and wizened by the time I can be askin' for her hand."

The captain of the *Sea Dragon* rose abruptly from the table. "Gentlemen, the hour grows late, and if we intend to do more than just talk of treasure, then I would suggest we get our rest. Tomorrow, if this storm clears, will be a full day's work for even an able-bodied man, much less one with only half his wits," he charged harshly, then turned his pale-eyed stare onto Rhea. "M'lady, I will escort you to your cabin, for it seems that the storm is not the only disturbance this evening."

Rhea accepted his hand as she rose from the table, smiling uneasily at the silent men who had quickly risen to their feet and were exchanging curious glances with one another.

At the door to her cabin, Dante paused, his eyes shadowed by thoughts that only he seemed to understand. He gazed down in fascination at the delicate rise and fall of Rhea's breasts, the lace fluttering enticingly against her pale golden skin.

"Captain," Rhea said, anxious to break that tense silence that developed between them whenever they were alone, "I have thought much on this today, and this evening, as I heard your crew talk of the treasure and listened to Mr. Clarke and Seumus speak of their hopes." Rhea paused nervously, not certain how to bring this subject up. "I'd like to ask, what if there is no treasure to be found?"

"That is a chance that we all knew existed," Dante remarked offhandedly, as if it were of no great concern to him.

"There still can be some sort of fortune for each man, though certainly not as much as his share would have been from a sunken treasure," Rhea said, her voice quickening with her thoughts. "There still will be a reward for my return, and it will be you and the crew of the *Sea Dragon* who have rescued me. I shall see that my father pays each man well," she said confidently. Then, when she saw the anger glittering in Dante Leighton's gray eyes, she could not imagine how she had offended him, since she was only trying to help. "And your share, Captain, would be considerable. It would—" But Rhea proceeded no further, for Dante had grasped her shoulders and pulled her to him while he stared down into her startled eyes.

"Do not ever offer me money, Rhea. I will return you to your father, but not for money. I am not that desperate a man," he said softly, his hand lingering against her throat where he could feel the pulse beating wildly. "Do I frighten you, my dear? Let that be a lesson to you that you should well remember. I may now believe that you are *Lady* Rhea Claire Dominick, daughter of the Duke of Camareigh, but I am still the same captain of the *Sea Dragon*, and we are anchored far from the shores of England, my dear. And I have not changed," he warned her just before his mouth closed down on her lips. Then he savored their softness, something he had thought of often.

As she trembled in his arms, he braced himself against the door while pressing her warm body to his, his lips exploring the scented softness of the curve of her breast before returning to her lips, which were parted, waiting for his in surrender. He knew then a surge of relief that she had not repulsed him, that she wanted him, that this strange spark that seemed to ignite between them could still flame into a passion, which if ever unleashed, would consume them, and change both of them forever. With that thought came a painful cooling of his ardor, and with an abruptness that left Rhea stunned, pushed her into her cabin and closed the door firmly between them.

Rhea stood for a moment in silence, disbelieving of what had just happened, for she could still feel the warmth of his lips against her skin. Then she sat down on her bunk, her violet eyes filling with tears.

Dante Leighton, breathing raggedly, leaned his arm against her closed door. If Rhea had had any idea of how much it had cost him to release her, she might have felt comforted. Dante smote the door with his fist, but it impacted in silence, the roar of the storm drowning out all other sounds. Dante stared around him at the familiar bulkheads of the *Sea Dragon*, his beloved ship, and with a feeling of growing frustration—a kind he had not known before, even when he had left Merdraco—

he realized that this would not be enough. Alastair Marlowe's words came back to haunt him, for he knew that Rhea Claire Dominick deserved better than a sea captain lover. The retrieval of this treasure meant more to him now than ever before, and his seeking of vengeance was paling beside his desire to possess Rhea. But with her being the daughter of Lucien Dominick, he knew he would have to be more than an ex-privateer and smuggler to become the husband of that particular duke's daughter. He needed that fortune to keep Rhea in the manner in which she deserved and to which she was accustomed.

He could take her now, make her cry out for him, love him, but it would not be fair, and because he did love her, he would not do that to her. He would lose her before subjecting her to the uncertainties and danger which fate held for a man who was little better than an adventurer. Nor would he crawl on his hands and knees to her father for support. None would ever be able to say that he had married Rhea Claire Dominick for her money.

As Dante stood there in the dimly lighted corridor, he knew a bitter, angry frustration, almost a helplessness, as he stared at that closed door, behind which was the woman who should be his but was just out of reach. With a bleakness of mind and spirit that he had not known in years, Dante Leighton went on deck, preferring to face the full wrath of the storm rather than his own restless, discouraging thoughts.

Dawn came with a brightness that seemed to instill new spirit into the crew of the *Sea Dragon*, as they set about once again on their search of the cove for their long-sought-after treasure. Rhea and Conny were preparing to cross the cove to their special beach, which had changed dramatically during the night due to the wind and tide. They could see that trees had been pulled from their moorings and that sand bars had created tide pools to explore. But suddenly, as they stood in conversation with Houston Kirby, who had been waiting with them for Longacres to return from depositing the anxious treasure hunters, a shout the likes of which Rhea had never before heard, nor would again, cut through the serenity of the peaceful little cove and sent the wild birds shrieking into the clear morning skies.

"What the devil?" Houston Kirby exclaimed, his eyes squinting into slits as he tried to see the shore.

"They've found something, Mr. Kirby!" Conny cried, jumping up and down, for his eyesight was far keener than the older man's, and he had seen the waving, dancing figures running along the sands of the narrow stretch of beach. " 'Tis the treasure! 'Tis the treasure!" Conny screamed, his shrill voice startling Jamaica, who struggled free of Rhea's arms.

"Ye just keep comin', ye old pirate!" Houston Kirby yelled to Longacres, whose hesitancy suggested he was going to turn back to shore without picking up his passengers. "Get yeself over here! If 'tis a treasure they be yellin' about, then 'twill still be there even after collecting us! 'Tisn't goin' anywhere after all o' this time," the little steward berated him from the quarterdeck. "Now row! Row!" he urged the panting Longacres as he sped across the stretch between ship and shore, never having rowed so fast, nor thought a piece of water so endless.

Rhea stared toward shore. She could make out the individual figures of some of the men as they ran toward the northernmost end of the beach, the point hidden by a promontory of land that jutted out and left just a narrow passage of sand around the headland.

"Well, come on, don't just stand there a-gawkin'!" Longacres called up to them as the gig bumped against the hull of the *Sea Dragon*.

They clambered aboard, rocking the boat dangerously as they settled down for the short row across the cove. As they neared the lee shore, their straining eyes were full of anticipation. Alastair was standing there waiting for them, and waded into the shallows to help Longacres and Kirby drag the gig ashore.

"Is it the treasure, Mr. Marlowe, sir? Is it?" Conny cried out as his feet touched the beach. But he waited not for an answer as he sped along the sand and sent it flying up into the faces of Longacres and Houston Kirby, who were hurrying along behind him, the little steward's short legs eating up the distance as he kept pace with the other two.

Rhea met Alastair's glowing eyes and did not need to ask the question. With her own eyes shining, she stood on tiptoe and flung her arms around him, pressing a kiss against his cheek.

"Oh, Alastair, I am so happy for you!" she told him, forgetting her own unhappiness of the night before as she was caught up in the exuberance of the crew of the *Sea Dragon*. At least she forgot about it until she heard that mocking voice.

"And what of me, Lady Rhea?" Dante asked, having walked unobserved along the beach, only to find Rhea kissing his supercargo. "Am I not deserving of congratulations, too?" he demanded. But there was no anger or sarcasm in his voice now, and his pale gray eyes were still alight with the exhilaration of the incredible discovery the crew of the *Sea Dragon* had made.

Alastair grinned, freeing himself from Rhea's lingering hand on his sleeve. Then, with a jaunty step, he hurried back up the beach, impatient to gaze again on the glorious sight.

"Congratulations, Captain," Rhea responded warily, not certain how to react to this new Dante Leighton, for the look in his eye was completely different than the one that had shadowed its depths last evening.

"Dante. That is my name, Rhea," he told her, coming a step closer. He was wearing only his breeches, his tanned chest bare to the sun's warmth and his sinewy arms glistening with sweat.

"Congratulations, Dante," Rhea said obligingly, feeling that devastating weakness spreading through her as she met his eyes. But she also felt something else, something far more dangerous creeping through her—it was a growing feeling of affection for this devilish captain of the *Sea Dragon*. It was an emotion totally different from the sensuous attraction he held for her, yet it was just as effective a form of seduction as those physical desires were.

He was standing right in front of her, and she could see the individual hairs curling across his chest. Her violet eyes met his eyes questioningly, her heart beating uncomfortably as she saw the warm tenderness in them.

"Do I not get a kiss? Since the *Sea Dragon*'s supercargo did, I should think her captain would be deserving of so sweet a token," he said, sounding almost humble.

Rhea stood on tiptoe again, her palms pressed flat against that muscular bare chest, and touched her lips softly to his hard cheek. But as she would have lowered her heels to the sand again, she felt his arms sliding around her waist, tipping her against his hips as he turned his cheek, his mouth meeting hers in a gentle, exploring kiss, in which neither of them demanded of the other, content just to be touching ever so softly.

Dante stared down at her, his smile gently mocking, enchanting her with its feeling of a shared gentle humor —and perhaps holding the promise of future shared moments.

"Come," he said, taking her by the hand. "Let me show you what the crew of the *Sea Dragon* has found."

It was incredible, as if another world had split wide and spilled forth a piece of time, for there against the far end of the beach rose a stark reminder of a once glorious past: the rotting mainmast of one of Spain's proud gold ships.

It rose bare of sail and rigging, standing at an angle above the skeletal remains of the galleon's decks. A gaping hole bit into the galleon's starboard side amidships, and in there Rhea saw rusty, worm-eaten chests scattered across the ship's hold.

"Our Spanish foretopman didn't even have to get his breeches wet to retrieve his booty," Dante commented as he eyed the wreck a trifle sadly, disliking to see any shipwreck. "The hurricane that caught the convoy must have blown this galleon into our cove here, crushing her against the rocks."

"Why didn't you find it sooner?" Rhea asked.

"We have the storm of last night to thank for this discovery, for we most likely would never have found it otherwise," Dante explained, gesturing at the newly formed sand banks and stretch of beach.

"It has been years since the Spaniard died, and during

that time I imagine there have been several hurricanes and great storms which have changed the appearance of this cove, just like what happened last night. The ship was buried under the shifting shoals. I think we have fortune to thank for being here during such a storm. Now, if we can salvage all of these chests before another storm comes along and buries the ship under another twenty feet of sand, then I shall think fortune is truly smiling on the crew of the *Sea Dragon*," Dante said with a laugh, a challenging glint in his eye as he stared up at the blue skies above his head.

"Come, let me show you our treasure," he invited Rhea, and guided her over to a chest that had been dragged free of the wreck, its warped wood having given way to the blade of an ax, which had freed its contents of gold and silver coins that now lay scattered in the sand.

" 'Tis a fortune, m'lady!" Seumus Fitzsimmons chuckled, rubbing his hands together as he eyed the chest of coins that would change his future. "Ah, m'lady, I'm thinkin' them violet eyes of yours have brought us good fortune!"

"We have already found several gold ingots, and there are more chests full of these newly minted coins," Dante said, his gaze narrowed as he watched his crew scrambling over the wreck. "As soon as their excitement levels off, we shall have to go about this in a bit more orderly fashion," Dante told Alastair, who had approached with an armful of artifacts.

"Found these in the stern. Must be from some rich passenger's cabin, or maybe the captain's," he told them, holding out a corroded pistol, its barrel eaten away by the sea. "Here's some silverware and a golden cross. 'Tis incredible to think that these once belonged to some Spanish captain, or grandee, perhaps," Alastair said with a shake of his head, obviously awed by the wreck and the memories buried with it.

Conny came running up, his hands full of golden coins. "Lady Rhea! We're rich! We've found the treasure!" he cried, his face full of excitement and adventure as he raced off again to explore further treasures.

Rhea stood for a while watching the salvaging, which Dante had finally managed to make orderly. All of the chests were being disgorged from the ship's hold and placed in neat rows along the beach, while Alastair started to compile a list of the contents—anything that was tossed to shore. Later, there would be an equal division of the treasure from the sunken Spanish galleon.

As the day passed, noontime coming and going, early afternoon drifting into lengthening shadows, Rhea made herself useful by aiding Houston Kirby in his preparations for supper; then she helped Alastair in the detailing of items, rinsing off crystal goblets and decanters that had somehow survived the destruction of the galleon in the hurricane. But most of her day was spent commenting on the different items brought to her for her inspection by each crew member, and listening to each man's dream of what he would do with his share of the recovered treasure.

Rhea saw little of Dante, for he supervised and worked alongside his men the whole day. Then, finally, when Houston Kirby was returning to the *Sea Dragon* to pack a hamper to carry back to shore, Rhea returned with him. The crew would be celebrating on the shore tonight, cooking their food over open fires as they talked, laughed, sang, and danced in a night-long celebration of their success as treasure hunters.

"Kirby," Rhea said suddenly, glancing at her grubby hands as she pushed a straggling curl off her cheek.

"Yes, m'lady?" the little steward replied as he rowed toward the *Sea Dragon*, which was looming out of the water before them.

"I feel so grimy I can scarcely stand to touch myself. If we are going to have a proper celebration tonight, then I want to feel clean. Will you let me fetch my soap, then row me across the cove where I can bathe in privacy?" she asked.

"Aye, m'lady, 'twill be me pleasure, only wish some of them others were so inclined," he said with a grin. "You wait here, and I'll get ye things fer ye, then ye'll be able to have a minute to yourself. Ye've worked like one o' the crew today, m'lady," he said, having seen that day

that she'd never lazed around, and had always been willing to lend a helping hand to someone.

After collecting her toiletries for her and rowing her
across the cove, Kirby beached the gig and told her, "I'll
be back fer ye in about an hour, all right? 'Twill take me
that long to get my preparations for the feast."

"That will be perfect," Rhea said. Then, as she turned
away, she heard the gentle stroke of the oars splashing into
the water as he made his way back to the *Sea Dragon*.

Rhea sighed in pleasure at having the beach to herself.
The sun was still well above the horizon as she walked
along the hot sands. The low-lying scrub and palms
shielded her from the distant shore at the other end of
the cove as she wandered around the gentle bend that
formed a secluded little bathing lagoon, which had a
sandy bottom that was visible through the still, crystal
waters.

Rhea quickly slipped out of her clothes, leaving them in
a neat pile on the sand; then she waded into the warm
waters of the lagoon, her bar of soap grasped firmly in her
fingers. Soon, she was floating dreamily under the blue
skies, her bare legs paddling her through the shallows.

She closed her eyes and drifted, thinking of nothing, not
even time, as she let the gently lapping waters soothe
away all of her cares. She opened her eyes with a start
when she felt a chill in the water, and glancing at the sky,
was surprised to find it a dark golden color that became
bronze at the horizon, where the sun, a molten ball of
fire, was fast sinking. Rhea splashed in the shadowed waters, rubbing the soap into a lather as she cleansed her
skin free of any remaining traces of grime. She dipped
beneath the surface and wet all of her hair, then began
the tedious operation of sudsing its long, heavy length.
She would have to hurry, she thought, dunking beneath
the surface, or the little steward might grow worried and
come searching for her.

Dante Leighton followed the single trail of footprints
around the bend in the beach. There was a concerned
expression on his face as he traced Rhea's path, for he
had been waiting at the gig for well over fifteen minutes,

491

and finally, when there had been no answer to his calls, he had decided to search for her.

Finally, he came upon the neat pile of clothes stacked along the water's edge. His hand lingered against the corset and chemise as he moved the pile to a safer distance from the rising tide, his eyes narrowed against the glare from the water as he searched for her in the stillness of the lagoon.

Suddenly he saw a splash, then a flash of pale gold against the surface, and he automatically stepped back beneath some palms that stood guard over the pool. He didn't have long to wait, for Rhea soon came walking out of the sea as if she had been born in it. Her slender body was glistening and she seemed an ethereal creature of gold and ivory; yet, at the same time, with the golden red sunset behind her, she seemed a natural part of this wild, primitive shore.

She was beautiful, Dante thought, gazing at her small, fully developed breasts. Their pink aureoles surrounded erect nipples that were like the hearts of flowers, and her waist was so tiny that he knew his hands could easily encompass it. Her hips were narrow, framing a flat, taut belly, and his eyes caressed the small area nestling between thigh and hip. Her thighs were slender, with smooth, tapering lines.

Like an amber cloak, her hair hung damply over one shoulder, the long strands curling down around her hips. He had not wanted to frighten her and had scarcely dared to breathe for fear of drawing her attention or causing her instinctively to cover herself when she caught him gazing at her naked body. Now, that same instinct warned her that she was not alone, for suddenly she halted, looking around warily. Her eyes widened in fear as he stepped from the shadows, but instead of the angry, embarrassed reaction he had been expecting, she continued to stand there in the sand, the tide lapping around her bare feet.

He felt stunned, for rather than covering herself up, she faced him boldly, her face flushed rosily and a shyness in her violet eyes. But there was no shame, no coyness, as her gaze began to mirror the yet-to-be-satisfied passions smoldering in his gray eyes.

She remained still while he took his first few steps toward her. Then he was standing before her, his gaze roaming freely over her gold-tinted body. His heart was pounding so loudly that it sounded like the ocean's roar racing through his veins.

Tentatively, he stretched out his hand, giving her time to reject him if she so wished, but still she continued to stand there, unmoving, waiting.

Dante's hand touched her breast, his thumb rubbing against the taut nipple, teasing it into an even higher peak, while his other hand slid around her waist, fitting easily to its curve as he pulled her with gentle persuasion against his chest, folding her closer until their bodies met at hip and thigh.

Rhea sighed in relief as Dante's mouth closed over hers. She parted her lips, meeting his kiss completely as his tongue touched hers, felt it, tasted it.

"Rhea, sweet, sweet Rhea," Dante murmured, his voice husky and thick with passion, as his hands caressed her soft, scented body, bared for him.

With a groan he picked her up in his arms and carried her out of the water, touching her feet to the sand that was still warm from the sun's kiss. And there, before her eyes, he undressed, baring himself to her, standing tall and muscularly lean. His wide chest, with its soft covering of wiry, light brown hairs, tapered to flat hips and a manhood bold with the passion that had yet to be met by her woman's body.

He spread his shirt over the sand, then took her in his arms, holding her against him, drowning in the feel of their flesh touching, warming with the contact, until he seemed to burn where his skin met hers. Cradling her in his arms, Dante knelt on his outspread shirt, laying her flat against the cushioned sand before he lay down beside her.

His lips covered her delicate-boned face in feathery kisses, leaving no area untouched, for he wanted to possess her completely, with no secrets between them. His lips finally contented themselves with hers, licking at them, nibbling, seeking the response from her that was slowly burning deep inside of her.

493

His mouth sought the lovely arching of her throat, while his hands fondled her boldly yet gently, as they discovered anew the woman who had been haunting his dreams since first he'd met her.

Now he felt her hands moving in a shy exploration of his body; encouraging her, he took her hand and guided it to him, letting her feel what power she had over him. He groaned with pleasure as he felt her touching him so intimately, and unable to bear it any longer he rolled her beneath him, his lips fastening on her breast as his tongue caressed the rising softness into hardness. Meanwhile, his hands moving over her body continued to fire her blood, for she was rubbing herself against him, kissing him hungrily, her small hands caressing him, until finally he pressed her into the sand with his hips hard against hers. Then her slender thighs had parted beneath the persistent pressure of his, and then he was becoming a part of her flesh, feeling her close around him as he thrust deeply inside her. He felt her initial start of surprise, then the quiver of pain as he drove deeper, and slowing his passion, he waited, kissing her, fondling her, until he felt a throbbing desire against him, and her hips began to move of their own volition, no longer needing the guidance of his hands beneath her soft buttocks.

Rhea cried out softly, feeling her senses turning into flame as Dante's body moved against hers, his hips joining her to his heated flesh, as he continued to carry her with him to unbelievable heights of sensual pleasure. The world exploded inside her head as she felt him move inside her, driving her wild with his hard touch as he planted his seed deep within a nurturing place and ignited an undying flame of desire and love for him that would guide the rest of her life.

The *Sea Dragon*'s sails had been loosed to catch the breeze and her anchor had been hoisted as her crew was sent aloft to trim the sails. There was, as well, a lookout keeping an ever-vigilant watch for a strange sail on the horizon. The ship had caught the Gulf Stream off the coast of Florida and had let that strong current carry her ever northward. They had dropped anchor only once, in

New Providence, and that had been a brief overnight stay, allowing them to take on fresh water and provisions before continuing on their journey. This time it was to be a far longer journey, for they were London-bound.

The crew of the *Sea Dragon* would stay with their captain until docking for that last time in the Thames; then each would go his own separate way, his share of the treasure carefully banked, or invested, or spent.

Once, a set of sails had been sighted on the horizon, and MacDonald had sworn that her mainmast was flying a tartan flag, but the *Sea Dragon* was not to be outsailed by Bertie Mackay's *Annie Jeanne* and her crew of cutthroats, and soon the genial smuggler's brig had fallen well astern.

Rhea Claire was standing beside Dante on the quarterdeck when they heard what they had dreaded—a cry aloft.

"Sail on the larboard bow!"

Longacres was climbing like a monkey into the shrouds, a spyglass tucked like a cutlass in his wide belt. Positioning himself, he trained the glass on the horizon and tried to identify the ship beating to windward as she bore down on them. Her intention was clear as she maneuvered toward them.

" 'Tis a king's ship flying English colors! A sloop by the looks o' her."

"Can you make her, MacDonald?" Dante said to the Scotsman and handed him another glass.

Endless minutes passed as the two vessels drew ever closer. "Aye, 'tis a king's ship right enough. Looks like . . ." MacDonald's words came slowly, ". . . aye, 'tis H.M.S. *Portcullis,* and she's signaling us."

The captain of the *Sea Dragon* narrowed his gaze as he speculated on why the captain of H.M.S. *Portcullis* should wish to come alongside. Had it been any other ship, under the command of any other captain, Dante would have sheered off and there would have been no crossing of bows. But he knew Sir Morgan Lloyd, and that was enough for him to give the order to bring-to the *Sea Dragon* and prepare for the captain of H.M.S. *Portcullis* to come aboard.

Captain Sir Morgan Lloyd boarded the *Sea Dragon,* feeling very much as if he had just walked into an enemy camp, for the eyes of the crew were trained on him as he made his way toward the companion steps, where Dante Leighton, captain of the *Sea Dragon,* was awaiting him.

"Captain?" Dante queried with unusual politeness, a wariness in his pale gray eyes as he stared at this fellow Englishman, who could very well turn out to be an enemy.

"Captain Leighton," Sir Morgan responded, not quite certain of what he should say next, for this was a most awkward situation, especially for a man more accustomed to facing his enemy while under fire. And, as of yet, he was not certain whether the captain of the *Sea Dragon* was to be friend or foe. But the next few minutes of conversation would surely decide.

"What can I do for you, Captain?" Dante asked, descending the steps, his eyes glancing across the width of sea between the two ships, which were so close that they were almost yardarm and yardarm. He could see the worried expressions on the small complement of redcoated marines standing at the ready on the quarterdeck of H.M.S. *Portcullis.* Their concern for her captain's welfare was evident in the nervous way they fingered their muskets.

"I believe you've quite a valuable treasure on board, Captain Leighton," Sir Morgan said casually.

Dante lifted a curious brow. ."Indeed, Captain?" he commented thoughtfully, his glance casual as he measured the distance between the two ships should he have to train his cannon on her decks or rigging. "I've but a hold half-laden with casks of rum. Hardly a treasure to interest the captain of H.M.S *Portcullis.*"

"'Tis not what, but whom, that I am concerned with, Captain," Sir Morgan retorted with a grim smile, his words eliciting a start of surprise from the now slightly bemused captain of the *Sea Dragon.*

"And which member of my crew is illustrious enough to command such an interest from a king's ship?" he inquired softly.

"Lady Rhea Claire Dominick." Sir Morgan spoke the

name, but it sounded more like a shout in Dante's ears. "I also have a warrant for your arrest in kidnapping the lady from Charles Town," he said and held out the document with its official seal.

"I fear that this voyage of yours has been a waste of time, Sir Morgan," Dante replied, not overly worried by the warrant

"That may well be, Captain, but if I might have a word with the lady, then I shall be able to ascertain that for myself. Not that I doubt your word, but orders are, after all, orders, and must be obeyed," he said quietly as he saw the anger kindling in Dante's eyes. "Of course, I am assuming that the lady is on board, but since I do remember quite vividly meeting her in Antigua and hearing her say that she could be found on board the *Sea Dragon,* naturally I supposed she was still sailing with you," Sir Morgan said reasonably. But Dante received the distinct impression that the man would be most unreasonable about leaving the *Sea Dragon*'s quarterdeck until he had spoken with the lady in question.

"By all means, Captain, speak with the lady," Dante invited him, a slight smile curving his lips.

Sir Morgan Lloyd had forgotten how incredibly beautiful Lady Rhea Claire Dominick was. Of course, their last meeting had hardly been under the best of circumstances, but now as he faced her in the captain's cabin on board the *Sea Dragon,* he felt his breath catching in his throat.

Dressed in her white muslin trimmed in lace, her hair caught up in thick waves and glinting like newly minted gold, she gazed at him with curious violet eyes. The orange cat curled up on her lap, however, ignored the king's officer with feline disdain. Rhea had hurried below when she had heard of Sir Morgan's desire to come aboard, and had changed from her leather skirt into a more respectable garment in case she had reason to meet this English captain for the second time in her life.

But she had not been prepared to hear that he had come looking for her intentionally. Having accepted the captain of the *Sea Dragon*'s offer of a brandy, he had settled down like an old friend to tell his tale, but there was a watchful quality in his eyes as he glanced between his curious listeners.

"My lady, you have become quite famous in the colonies. Every town and settlement has been flooded with handbills inquiring for information concerning your whereabouts, and carrying a description of you which, I might add, does not do you full justice," Sir Morgan complimented her. "After what you must have been through, m'lady, being so brutally kidnapped from your home, I am very pleased to see you looking so well. I must say I was quite surprised, upon my return to Charles Town, to discover the unfortunate circumstances of your arrival. The experience must have been terrifying."

"Yes, Captain," Rhea said softly, her eyes still shadowed with the memory of that voyage, "it was a nightmare that I shall not soon forget. It was fortunate for you, Captain, that you met me in St. John's and discovered that I was on board the *Sea Dragon*. That has saved you quite a search. Otherwise, a suspected murderess might be hiding anywhere in the colonies," Rhea told him bluntly as she remembered the murder of Captain Benjamin Haskell.

"Rhea," Dante said, his hand capturing hers as he shook his head to warn her against saying anything further.

"You need have no fear, Captain, that I shall arrest Lady Rhea," Sir Morgan reassured him. "She should be more concerned about the warrant I have for yours."

"Warrant?" Rhea said in confusion, glancing between the two men with growing alarm. "Whatever for?"

"For kidnapping, m'lady."

Rhea swallowed something painful in her throat, for at one time that would indeed have been the truth. "I am here of my own free will, Captain."

"Yes, I have come to believe that is the truth. But you see, that is not what the authorities in Charles Town were led to believe. You were wrong on both of your suppositions; for your presence on board the *Sea Dragon* in St. John's only confirmed what had already been learned concerning your whereabouts," Sir Morgan said, looking at Dante with a slightly mocking smile.

"Helene Jordane?" As Dante supplied the name, he realized that she would have liked nothing better than to cause mischief for him by informing the authorities of Rhea's presence on board his ship, thus branding him a kidnapper.

"Yes, her rather vivid testimony was part of the reason for the warrant for your arrest. Only it seems that Mistress Jordane was under the impression that the two of you were eloping. She seemed quite disbelieving, contemptuous even, of this kidnapping story, and content just to blacken your good names," Sir Morgan told them, a smile lurking around his mouth. Then he added, "But, alas, she was made to look rather the fool when certain *other* testimonies came to light."

"What other testimonies?" Dante and Rhea demanded almost simultaneously.

"The testimony of a certain young woman by the name of Alys, I believe?" Sir Morgan said softly, watching Rhea's expression with interest.

"Alys?" Rhea whispered in disbelief. She had feared that even after she'd returned to England and got her father to help in the search, they would still be unable to find her friend from the *London Lady*. "You have seen Alys? She is well? What happened to her?" Rhea asked excitedly, her restlessness disturbing Jamaica, who opened a curious, slightly irritated green eye to stare at Sir Morgan, the apparent cause of this interruption of his nap.

"She came forward, frightened half to death of this Daniel Lewis and the retribution he'd promised should she have said anything. I suspect that the authorities were reluctant to believe her at first, but she had one, very important item which lent credence to her story." Sir Morgan had spoken almost expectantly, but when Rhea remained blank-eyed, he said, "A locket."

"My locket!" Rhea exclaimed. "I lost it. I thought it had fallen somewhere along the docks." Then Rhea began to think back to when Alys had thrown herself at Rhea, but had been pulled roughly away. Alys had been grabbing at her neck, frantic to remain with her friend.

"Yes, and that locket was described in the handbills as a piece of jewelry that you had been wearing. She apparently told a very touching story, m'lady, and also corroborated part of a sworn statement from someone else, which had exonerated you, although not by name, of the murder of Captain Benjamin Haskell," Sir Morgan informed a spellbound Rhea.

"Whose statement could that possibly be?" Rhea asked, thinking that Daniel Lewis would hardly have admitted his guilt.

"The victim's."

"A dead man exonerated Rhea from the murder of this captain?" Dante asked disbelievingly. He took a sip of his brandy, thinking privately that Sir Morgan must have had his share before leaving his ship.

" 'Twas a deathbed statement," Sir Morgan explained, as if reading the captain's doubting mind. "Unfortunately for one Daniel Lewis, the captain did not die immediately. He lingered for several days; then, before he died, he named his murderer. Daniel Lewis denied it all, saying the captain was trying to protect the girl by blaming him, when actually it had been a lover's spat. Few believed him, though," Sir Morgan said quickly, as he saw the denial trembling on Rhea's lips. "The man had a most unsavory reputation, so few were taken in by his story. And now, with this Alys's testimony, he will not be long on this earth."

Rhea drew a shuddering breath as she remembered that horrible man too vividly for comfort. Dante's hand relinquished hers and moved to stroke her cheek lightly, a gesture of affection that Sir Morgan was not likely to miss.

"What has happened to Alys?" Rhea asked, shaking off the paralyzing memories of that voyage, Daniel Lewis, and the murder of his captain. "I promised her I would buy her indenture papers and free her. I wished her to see Camareigh. I owe her my life, for without her by my side I would not have survived the voyage from England."

Sir Morgan smiled with genuine pleasure. "I should think she is enjoying Camareigh right now, for the agent sent to the colonies to search for you returned to Charles

Town from Savannah, where he had been looking for you, and decided that the best way of serving the Duke was to take this girl back to your home. He realized, after hearing her story, that you had become friends. Also, I am quite certain that the Duke and Duchess will have wished to have expressed their gratitude to her in person."

Rhea sat silent for a moment, a great happiness enveloping her as she thought of her friend Alys, who had dreamed of seeing Camareigh one day, who had kept her alive by asking questions about life at Camareigh, and now, because of a brave act, would have her dream come true.

"However," Sir Morgan was continuing, his face hardening with his words, "what I have to say next may not be so pleasing for you to hear. I am under orders to return you to London," he said, sounding now like the dutiful captain of H.M.S. *Portcullis*.

The gray eyes of the captain of the *Sea Dragon* met Sir Morgan Lloyd's, the message clear in their pale depths. "I am afraid, Sir Morgan, that you shall be disappointed in the carrying out of that order," Dante informed the tense naval officer. "Rhea Claire is my wife," he said softly as he stood up and moved behind his wife's chair, resting his hands on her shoulders. "We were wed in New Providence, in church, and although we did not have the consent of her parents, the marriage is indissoluble."

Sir Morgan stared up at Dante Leighton, noting the tender way his hand played with one of Lady Rhea's golden curls. He had been well aware of the lovers' glances they'd exchanged during this conversation, and now as he watched in almost embarrassed fascination, Lady Rhea pressed her lips to the back of Dante's hand, then rested her cheek against it, as if gaining comfort from his touch.

"I see, well," Sir Morgan commented, hesitating for a moment, "since my orders are to return Lady Rhea Claire Dominick to England, should I find her, as well as to apprehend one Dante Leighton, captain of the *Sea Dragon* and Marquis of Jacqobi, I see no reason why H.M.S. *Portcullis* cannot lend escort to you on your voyage home. Since you are no longer Lady Rhea Claire Dominick, I think my orders must be adapted to suit the circumstances."

"Thank you, Sir Morgan," the captain of the *Sea Dragon* told his one-time adversary, a smile of genuine warmth lighting his eyes as he met the relaxed, slightly relieved gaze of the captain of H.M.S. *Portcullis*. "My wife and I would consider it an honor if you would dine aboard the *Sea Dragon* as our guest this evening. My steward is really not to be bested by anyone on land or sea."

"Please, Sir Morgan," Rhea urged, "we would indeed be honored. We never thanked you properly for your timely assistance in St. John's, a debt of gratitude not easily repaid, and now you bring me good news about my friend Alys. I am indeed in your debt, sir," Rhea told him, her violet eyes wide with entreaty, making Sir Morgan feel that he'd be churlish to refuse so warm a request.

Sir Morgan smiled, the expression softening what was usually a stern-visaged face. "Thank you, m'lady, 'twill be my pleasure," he responded, taking a sip of his brandy now that his business was safely concluded and he'd not had to draw his sword. He glanced around the warmly lit cabin and believed he was truly looking forward to this evening, and to the prospect of returning to England.

" 'Twas quite fortunate, you falling in with us," Dante remarked casually as he refilled Sir Morgan's glass.

" 'Twas no chance sighting, Captain," Sir Morgan replied, a spark of curiosity in his eye. "I calculated that once you completed certain business, you would be steering a course this way. I suspected the general direction and have been circling the area for over a week now, hoping I would cross your bow. Of course, I did have a bit of assistance," he added with a grin reminiscent of one of Dante's own devilish grins.

"Oh, and what was that?" Dante asked, enjoying himself.

"I did fall foul of Bertie Mackay off the coast. He was returning to Charles Town, apparently believing that you were, too. He was only too happy to inform me of his last sighting of the *Sea Dragon*, especially when I just happened to mention the warrant for your arrest."

Dante raised his glass in a silent toast.

"I am curious, Captain. Was your business successful?" Sir Morgan asked.

"Oh, yes, indeed," Dante grinned, his hand tightening on Rhea's shoulder while his gaze lingered on her golden head. "I found my treasure."

A full moon was climbing above the yardarm of the *Sea Dragon* as her bowsprit swung toward English shores, the grinning red dragon eating up the distance as she entered familiar waters.

Standing on the quarterdeck of his ship, his arms wrapped possessively around Rhea, Dante stared toward the stars guiding the way north.

"We shall have many questions to answer when we arrive in England. And I must confess that I am ill at ease at the prospect of facing the Duke. I will meet any man, but I have never had to look a father-in-law in the eye and explain why he was not invited to the nuptials."

"My father is wonderful, Dante. He will understand," Rhea reassured him. There was no doubt in her own mind on that score. She sighed with contentment, for soon she would be seeing her family again. She had missed them so, and now she wanted Dante to meet them—and for them to meet her husband.

"Fathers are not very understanding where their daughters are concerned. And since you are now mine, I know what a loss he will feel. You are a treasure, my dearest love, and he may well resent me," Dante mused, vowing that no one, including this family of hers, would take her away from him. He at times felt a jealousy when she spoke of them, for the love between these Dominicks was deep and lasting, and was something he had never experienced. He was the last of his family, and now he wanted Rhea to become part of it. Her own family still held a great influence over her, though, and knew a part of her that he never would.

"We are together, my love," Rhea said quietly. "That is

all that matters." And her words sounded like a renewal of her wedding vows.

Dante pressed his lips to her forehead, rubbing his cheek against a golden curl. "You know very little about me, Rhea. I fear I shall frighten you one day and lose that love you have so unselfishly given to me. When you could have walked away from me that day in St. John's, I very nearly died. You could have gained your freedom by calling out to Sir Morgan, but you stayed because of a small boy you scarcely knew, but who needed your help. I knew I loved you then, but it frightened me more than anything else I have ever had to face. I realized I needed you more than my life, little daffadilly," Dante said huskily, his lips finding hers for a long, treasured moment.

"Never fear that loss, Dante," Rhea told him. "Whatever we may have to face in England, we shall be together. I shall be by your side. I am your wife, and no one can take me away from you," she promised him, her head heavy against his heart.

Dante closed his eyes, his hard body warmed by her soft, gentle strength. He felt as if he had come home, and although they had not yet reached the shores of England, he knew that with her standing beside him, he could meet any challenge that the future might hold for them at Merdraco.

Houston Kirby smiled to himself as he sat in the shadows of the companion ladder. He gave a nervous start of surprise as something pounced on his lap; then, with a shrug, he let the big orange tom settle down. This was apparently what Jamaica had every intention of doing as he stomped around in a circle before curling up on the little steward's lap.

"Aye, 'tis a fine night, Jamaica," Houston Kirby remarked softly, staring up at the billowing sails of the *Sea Dragon*. His grin widened and he snorted as he looked to larboard and saw across the distance the sails of H.M.S. *Portcullis*, their personal escort to England, which would assure them a safe arrival in their home port.

Away beyond the horizon where the stars met the sea, on the rocky north coast of Devon, in the west country, lay Merdraco. Houston Kirby glanced back at the two figures standing so close, as if they were one, on the quarterdeck beneath the proud sails of the *Sea Dragon*.

"Aye, reckon 'twas destined all along, the captain and his lady," Houston Kirby told the purring tomcat. "Always figured I'd be bunkin' with ye one day, ye ol' scoundrel," the little steward muttered as he scratched the top of Jamaica's head, thinking it a mighty fine night indeed.

The rousing, unforgettable saga of
beautiful young Lady Elysia Demarice
and Lord Alex Trevegne—and the
impetuous, searing passion which
blazed in their hearts!

Laurie McBain
Devil's Desire

Out of the turbulence of these two lovers' clashing wills
comes one of the greatest love stories ever written . . .
a rapturous, monumental tale of love lost and won,
for the millions of readers who thrilled to
SWEET SAVAGE LOVE and
THE FLAME AND THE FLOWER.

48165/$2.50